Praise for K

"A word to the wise: if you bite your nails, you'd better wear mitts when reading *Kronos Rising*. It will drag you down to the depths of fear and take you back for a breath of air as fast as you can turn the pages. Readers beware: a new master of marine terror is in your bookstore, and his name is Max Hawthorne!"

> –Stan Pottinger, NY Times Bestselling author of THE BOSS

"Max Hawthorne explores the sinister side of the dark abyssal world with a new kind of beast, one that makes white sharks and giant squid as threatening as guppies and tadpoles."

> –Doug Olander, Editor-in-Chief, Sport Fishing Magazine

"Until today, the deepest, darkest depths of the ocean remained an impossible mystery. But no more – a violent earthquake has finally unleashed a wonderfully horrific secret waiting to eat you alive. From the opening scene of black market shark hunters invading forbidden waters, *Kronos Rising* sweeps you onto a surprising, wildly inventive, thrill ride. A fabulous debut by Max Hawthorne. Simply put, it's got teeth. Big ones!"

> –Chris Parker, screenwriter (Vampire in Brooklyn,
> Mulan II, Battle of the Year, Heaven is for Real)

"What a ride! An adrenaline pumping, non-stop descent into terror, *Kronos Rising* will do for this generation what "JAWS" did for the last one. Forget going *into* the water; I'm not going *near* it!"

> –Mara Corday, sci-fi classic star of *Tarantula*,
> *The Black Scorpion*, and *The Giant Claw*

Praise for MEMOIRS OF A GYM RAT

"Max Hawthorne's raunchy, revealing memoir is certain to induce bouts of calorie-burning laughter, embarrassed grins, and reconsiderations of one's gym membership. A smutty and enjoyable exposé of life behind health club doors, *Memoirs of a Gym Rat* is both a scandalizing and edifying read."

> –Foreword Clarion Reviews

Also by Max Hawthorne

MEMOIRS OF A GYM RAT

"None is so fierce that dare stir him up. Round about his teeth is terror. His back is made of rows of shields, his scales cannot be sundered. In his neck abides strength, and terror dances before him...When he raiseth himself up, the mighty are afraid... He maketh the deep to boil like a pot. Upon earth is not his like, a creature without fear."
-- Job 41:12-34 --

ACKNOWLEDGMENTS

It is with great pride that I acknowledge the following individuals for their support and/or contributions.

First and foremost, I wish to express my heartfelt gratitude to my publishers at *Far From the Tree Press*. Thanks for believing in me and my book.

A special thanks to my assorted publicity and marketing contacts. Without their tireless toiling, many would never know this book exists. I'd also like to extend my sincere appreciation to Satish Kodavali and his team over at Eprosoft, for manufacturing such a superb web site for *Kronos Rising*.

I'd like to give a shout-out to my shark-fishing buddy, NFL great Anthony Corvino, and a big "Rock on!" to screenwriter Chris Parker, for taking the time to guide a neophyte author along the dimly-lit path to creativity. Also, all my best to *Family Guy* former executive producer David Goodman, who helped show me how to take a run-of-the-mill story and make it great.

I'd be remiss if I didn't mention the individuals who were kind enough to read and contribute to *Kronos Rising* during its infancy. This includes my father Joe, my brother Stephen, and my often-verbose colleague, Chris Molluso. Without their combined efforts, this book would not be what it is today.

I am forever indebted to my one-and-only "Maestra of Typos," Hollywood screen legend, Mara Corday. Thank you for giving me much-needed feedback, for fine-tuning my manuscript, and for being such a good friend. I look forward to your book.

Lest I forget, a sincere thank you to paleo-artist Joshua Ballze, who weathered all of my "constructive criticism" and still managed to come up with a superb piece of cover art. Thanks, Josh!

Last, but certainly not least, to my incredibly supportive family: my eternal devotion. And to all of my readers out there: Thank you for your support. I'm honored to serve you. You have my solemn promise to always do my best to keep you entertained.

Max Hawthorne

ONE

The predator hunted.
Poised atop pearl-black seas as flat as a field of asphalt, the *Oshima* drifted alone in the darkness, one hundred and sixty miles off the coast of Florida.

From his vantage point, high above the ship's helm, Haruto Nakamura watched as the slaughter continued across the deck below him. He breathed deeply, drawing in the scent of fresh blood blending with the warm sea air. Off to one side, a dark splash of movement in their searchlights caught his eye. He turned, nodding his approval. Despite a ferocious struggle, another catch was being hauled aboard by the ship's foremost starboard-side hoist, its streamlined form thrashing violently back and forth as it was wrenched from the depths.

It was a blue – a big one. The fish's thirteen-foot body came crashing to the deck with a thud reminiscent of a soaked bag of cement. Overhead, the hoist's arm hummed as it released its hold on the hissing creature. The sounds of the blue's impact and subsequent writhing were punctuated by the encouraging voices of nearby crewmen as two pole men moved in.

Haruto watched with interest as the men lunged forward. Avoiding the blade-like tail and snapping jaws, they used their crescent-tipped tools to pin the quarter-ton fish tightly against the nearest railing. Deprived of oxygen, its efforts quickly subsided. With the majority of the danger removed, the stony-faced cutters moved in and went to work. Soon, new rivulets sprayed like crimson spider webs across the once pristine deck.

Backlit by the ship's powerful searchlights, Haruto smiled.

He surveyed the forward portion of the ship once more, then pulled back his shoulders and puffed out his chest. Adjusting his captain's hat, he rested his hands atop the railing in front of him, his index finger caressing its freshly painted surface.

"She's turned out even better than expected. Yes, Captain?"

Haruto glanced over to see Sagato smiling as he climbed up the metal rung ladder leading from the helm to the observation tower. He nodded almost imperceptibly as his first mate moved to his side, then returned to his surveillance.

Sagato waited a moment before clearing his throat, then held out the clipboard he was carrying. "I have our current tallies, sir."

Haruto wordlessly accepted the clipboard. He scanned it, nodded, and then handed it back. His lips were a tight line. The numbers were excellent; no doubt the reason behind his young first mate's enthusiastic demeanor.

Suddenly, a small photograph slipped out of the stack of papers, catching the captain's eye as it fluttered leaf-like to the floor. He glanced down and raised an eyebrow.

Flushed with embarrassment, Sagato knelt to pick it up.

"Sorry, captain," he stammered, fumbling to put the picture inside his uniform shirt pocket. "I forgot it was in there."

"May I?" Haruto's question was accentuated by the flailing of a seven-foot dusky as it vaulted over the port side and hit the deck in a shower of blood and salt spray.

"Uh . . . yes, of course, captain." Sagato bowed and handed the photo to his superior with both hands.

Haruto accepted it politely. He held it close, using the whiteness of the searchlights to illuminate it. "Your wife and son?"

Sagato nodded.

Haruto noticed the tiny beads of perspiration forming on his first mate's forehead. He nodded. "An attractive woman and a strong young boy. You are fortunate to have such a family."

"Thank you, Haruto-san." Sagato took the photo back, beaming at the praise and bowing low. "But you should know that you and the *Oshima* are just as much my family."

"Really?" The captain gave him an appraising look. "Well, she is a good ship."

"Yes sir. You of all people should know."

"Indeed. Very well, Sagato. You may resume your duties. I will join you on the bridge shortly to discuss your figures."

"Yes, sir."

Haruto nodded again as his first mate bowed and turned to leave. He glanced back over his shoulder, watching as Sagato placed the photo in his shirt pocket and carefully buttoned it.

Haruto found himself smiling. He liked Sagato, which said a lot. Despite his relative youth, he was proving himself to be an intelligent and able-bodied officer, one with the unique ability to magically appear at his captain's side whenever he was needed. His energy and devotion were boundless – an impressive feat. Especially considering his newly assigned position kept him at sea for months on end, away from the wife and young son that, despite his words, meant the world to him.

A commotion below caused Haruto to look down just in time to see the dusky being tossed back over the rail. He nodded approvingly at the men responsible, then turned and headed for the ladder that led to the ship's helm.

———

As he made his way toward the bridge, Sagato Atsushi struggled to rein himself in. The excitement he was feeling was almost more than he could bear. The *Oshima* was successful beyond expectation. In fact, the shiny two-hundred-and-forty foot vessel with her twin 1,600 horsepower diesels was fast becoming the pride of her company's notorious lineup.

At the forefront of her elite crew's growing pride was their renowned captain. Ever since he'd worked the docks as a teenager, Sagato had heard tales about Captain Nakamura. They said he was the descendant of ancient samurai lineage, a shogun in fact, who could find fish by simply sniffing the breeze; fish-finders and other man-made instruments were for average men.

Sagato believed the stories. He'd seen the ancient swords the silver-haired Okinawan kept in his stateroom. And his carriage and demeanor certainly fit the bill. Samurai warlord or no, the captain of the *Oshima* was a living legend revered throughout the country's well known fishing community. He was a hard but fair man, one who valued discipline and dedication above all things. He'd trained many of the fleet's current fishing captains, men Sagato had personally served under. It was said that good fortune followed both the man and those who served under him. For that reason alone, Sagato fought hard to obtain his current position. The young first mate was brimming with ambition. With a successful run as the *Oshima's* first mate, it was just a matter of time before he was awarded a command of his own, and the measure of success that came with it.

So far, everything seemed to be falling in place. Their ship had been blessed with tranquil weather and bountiful seas since leaving port. He smiled, secure in the knowledge he would succeed. His wife and son would never suffer the poverty he had in his youth.

Suddenly, another prize hit the deck. Sagato grimaced as the crew pounced. Although he didn't approve of what they were doing, it was the reason they came. Unlike the regular fishing boats that spent long days in Japan's coastal waters pulling in tuna or flounder, the *Oshima* was a long-range huntress that preferred to stalk her prey in distant seas, and under cover of darkness. Her crew was after something far more dangerous and profitable than mere flounder.

They were after sharks. Not the whole shark – which took up too much valuable hold space. They wanted only the fins. It didn't matter if their victims were bulls, threshers, or even great whites. With bowls of shark fin soup going for a hundred dollars apiece back home, the profits were astronomical. The ship's gigantic freezers were filling up at record speed with assorted pectoral and dorsal fins.

He entered the bridge and nodded to the helmsman and radar/ sonar operator. They were grinning ear to ear. It was a good time for those onboard the *Oshima*. The crew was happy, the captain was pleased, and the investors were ecstatic. Business was booming, and the Yen was rolling in off the water.

Of course, no one cared that their entire operation was illegal.

———

The bridge crew sprang to their feet, snapping to attention as Haruto walked in.

"As you were," he commanded. Then, to the helmsman: "How's our drift?"

"Textbook perfect, captain," came the reply. "We're moving south-southeast with the tide. Drift speed is one point seven knots."

Haruto nodded as Sagato took position by his side. He glanced at their radar/sonar station. "Anything to report?"

The acoustics operator's eagle eyes never left his screens. "Nothing of any significance, sir. I have a large reading holding position a hundred meters off our bow. It's stationary sir, probably a mass of kelp or debris drifting along with us."

"I'm interested in ships, ensign. Not seaweed."

"Uh, yes sir," the tech swallowed. "I have . . . one large ship, heading away from our position and moving due east. She's traveling at fifteen knots."

"How large?"

"Very large, sir. Container ship size."

Haruto tensed, his brow furrowing up. He peered over the operator's shoulder, intently studying his radar screen. "Military?"

"No, sir. At least I don't think so. I've been monitoring their transmissions. It appears to be a luxury liner of some kind."

"Humph. Very well then, but keep an eye on that scope, ensign," Haruto said. "Economic Exclusive Zone or not, we're far enough from U.S. territorial waters that the Coast Guard shouldn't be a problem. That being said, the last thing I'd like is to have an unexpected run-in with their navy."

"Aye, sir!"

Haruto moved to the rear of the bridge, gesturing for Sagato to follow him. He glanced back at the remainder of the bridge crew, waiting for his second-in-command to draw closer.

"Captain, are you really that worried about the Americans?" Sagato's eyes were wider than normal.

Haruto waved off the question. "I don't want them taking us off guard and concocting a reason to board us. We could lose everything. Our cargo . . . even the ship. If we have to, we'll cut our cables and ditch our lines."

"I see, sir. Don't worry. I'll stay on top of them."

Haruto nodded. He looked back toward the helm, his brow lines tightening, then leaned in closer to his first mate. "On to another point, Sagato. I've been reviewing your projections. Based on the unprecedented tallies you've shown me, we are catching many species of shark that should not even be in these waters, and in record numbers." Haruto glanced speculatively at him. "What are your thoughts?"

"My thoughts, Haruto-san?"

"Yes, Sagato," Haruto said. "We seem to be experiencing a mass migration of sea life. The whalers and white-tips I expect. But we've brought in bull sharks and lemons – shallow water predators that should be circling the Bahamas or Cuba right now. What do you think is causing it?"

"I wouldn't dare speculate on such a thing, captain."

"But I insist, Sagato."

"Um, I honestly don't know. Maybe it's the current changes brought on by global warming. Or maybe–"

Sagato stopped in mid-sentence, his hand springing up to his earpiece.

"Sagato?"

"I'm sorry, captain. There's a call from the watch commander."

"Yes?"

"Your reputation for good fortune continues. Portside hoist number two just reported a huge shark on the line."

Haruto forced down the smile that threatened to crease the corners of his mouth. "Ah yes, my reputation . . . did they say what kind of shark it is?"

"They're not sure, sir . . . but they think it's a monster mako."

Haruto nodded. "Very well, that is good news. You go on down. I'll be there in a minute to join you."

"Yes, sir."

Watching as his first mate bounded out of the room, Haruto moved over to stand next to the helmsman. Suddenly, he turned toward their sonar operator.

"Anything on the scope?"

"I have a fairly strong signal coming from a fish being hauled in by one of our hoists, sir. The cruise ship has moved out of range. Other than that drifting mass of flotsam, I see nothing."

"Very well, ensign. Keep up the good work."

The operator turned towards Haruto. "Yes, captain."

As Haruto left the bridge, neither he nor his sonar tech noticed the flotsam had changed position.

As Haruto made quick strides past one of the starboard hoists, he slipped in a thick pool of shark's blood. He cursed and made a desperate grab for a nearby bulkhead to keep from falling. Ahead of him, several members of a nearby hoist's crew were pointing and laughing. He followed their line of sight. Two of their comrades were hard at work, prying loose the jaws of a six-foot hammerhead that clamped down on the top railing before they could heave it over the side. Suspended tail-down over the waters below, the lacerated fish clung like a pit bull, while the frustrated crewmen pried away at its jaws with their tools. From forty feet away, Haruto could hear the sounds of teeth cracking as they tore through the railing's paint and into the metal beneath. A sudden wrench and the hammerhead came loose, plummeting down toward the darkness that waited. The crewmen cheered.

Haruto looked down. To his surprise, he could see himself quite clearly in the crimson puddle at his feet. He studied his reflection, particularly the convoluted worry lines that creased his brow like old tire treads. He closed his eyes for a moment and found himself pondering the full impact of what they were doing.

Shark finning had been banned in most international waters for a decade or more. In his private thoughts, Haruto conceded that the waste they were responsible for was beyond abhorrent. The sharks they were slaughtering were highly sought-after food species whose flesh could feed untold thousands. But instead, they were simply dumped back into the ocean, spiraling straight to the bottom to drown.

Haruto's eyes snapped open and his expression hardened. He straightened up, waving a hand before him as if dismissing such unproductive thoughts. In the end, it was all about the money. When the numbers were tallied up, shark meat just didn't bring enough. The profits from finning operations were too great to resist. Back in Washington, they could pass any laws they wanted, but with the *Oshima* and her ilk drifting in international waters a hundred or more miles from land, the ban was impossible to enforce.

He continued on. As he approached the bow section, he watched as the foremost starboard hoist yanked a frantically struggling sea turtle clear of the water and deposited it on the deck. Within seconds, the winch's crew tore the hook free and hurled the traumatized chelonian back over the side. They had the oversized hook re-baited and ready to go before the baby loggerhead hit the water.

The captain nodded in silent acknowledgment of their practiced efficiency with the ship's revolutionary catch-and-cull technique. Traditional long liner methods involved using several miles of steel hooks and leaders, baited and set to drift beneath floats that indiscriminately caught anything the ocean had to offer. The *Oshima's* cunning design utilized a far more exacting approach.

As was tradition, the ship's crew put out a vast chum slick of ground-up fish parts, blood and oil measuring dozens of miles in length. But instead of using hooks and floats, they drifted back large chunks of bait, hooked to steel lines directly anchored to eight onboard winches. Each winch and its accompanying hoist had its own separate diesel engine and operator, and was backed by a thousand yards of 20,000 pound test steel cable. With a pulling capacity of five tons, the winches dragged in the biggest sharks with ease, depositing them in the hands of the waiting crew. They quickly maneuvered the big fish up over the side for dismemberment, mercilessly hacking and carving.

To Haruto, the winch technique was gloriously cutting edge, and not just because he designed it. It eliminated unwanted by-catch such as marlin, porpoises and seals, and brought many more sharks to the boat. It also replaced thousands of yards of expensive rigged line. Rigging that was hard to conceal, and would have to be abandoned if the authorities showed up.

Haruto's winches were the way of the future. They had transformed the *Oshima* into what she was: a floating, shark fin-culling factory that worked non-stop to haul in the ocean's top predators, strip them of their mobility, and then toss them back, spurting blood, into the surrounding seas.

They were also the reason why something far more dangerous had been shadowing the ship for hours.

Drawn to the big steel vessel by its infallible sense of smell, the creature lurked a hundred yards off the *Oshima's* bow. It remained just beneath the waves, its huge body hidden from view. Initially focused on procuring one or more of the warm-blooded bipeds that scurried atop the vessel's uppermost regions, it was wary of the painfully bright lights that continually scanned the water's black surface.

Hesitant to move any closer, it remained where it was, descending every so often to inhale one of the still-writhing prey items that periodically drifted in its direction. Famished from its long swim up the Straits of Florida, the offerings were a welcome source of protein for the giant predator. Unfortunately, the sharks it devoured were only beginning to quench the searing furnace that burned within its belly.

Then, something garnered its full attention.

Deep down, a much larger fish had also responded to the overpowering scent of blood in the water, and was slowly being hauled from the depths.

Peering stealthily above the surface of the water, the creature could see a group of the tiny mammals gathering together on the ship. Scanning the rapidly fading fish below as it continued to ascend, the behemoth sounded with a hiss.

Two

Haruto could see excitement brewing on the decks of the *Oshima*. The news of an exceptionally large shark on the line had spread like wildfire. Especially, since it was said the fish might be a mako, a sign of continuing good fortune. At least two dozen officers and sailors crowded around the hardworking winch crew in order to observe the action. They snapped alert as their captain appeared, parting like the Red Sea.

"Well, Sagato?" Haruto asked. He turned toward his first mate, who took up position at his left.

"Definitely a big mako, Captain," Sagato announced confidently. He spoke loudly enough for all to hear, then angled his head and lowered his voice. "Very unusual for these waters though, sir. Especially this time of year."

"Indeed."

A crewman's exuberant shout interrupted the two men. "I think I see it!"

Haruto and Sagato moved toward the railing to observe the final moments of the spectacle.

According to the crew's log, the powerful fish had waged its losing battle against the hoist's relentless strength for nearly three minutes. Astonishingly, several times it even managed to pull a few yards of line from the diesel-powered device's oversized drag system. Now, however, the winch's retrieval speed was becoming smooth and constant; a sign the big shark had exhausted itself and was being hauled in for butchering. Everyone present stared over the railing into the searchlight-illuminated depths, all striving to be the first to lay eyes upon the *Oshima's* latest prize.

His eyes straining against the glare of their lights, Haruto caught a vague glimpse of something deep down. It was a shimmering flash of white and silver that could barely be seen. *It's our shark*, he thought. Then, he noticed something moving rapidly toward it. Something bigger than the mako – much bigger.

As Haruto gaped, the partially obscured shape of the thrashing fish abruptly vanished from view. The winch cable shifted noisily and then started to shiver. Watching in disbelief, the nearby crewmen started chattering wildly amongst themselves, jumping up and down as they pointed and shouted about how something had just eaten their shark. Tales of snagged whales and sailor-devouring sea serpents began to circulate, with some of the more senior crewmembers scoffing at the ridiculous speculation.

That was, until the impossible occurred.

With a horrific groan, the entire ship lurched to one side, sending anyone and anything that wasn't anchored to the decks slipping and sliding toward the vessel's heavy-duty, four-foot-high railing. Caught with his arm extended over the top of the rail, Haruto slammed into the metal barrier. He saw a flash of white and felt a searing pain in his side. He cursed, realizing he cracked some ribs.

He collapsed to the deck, fighting the exquisite agony that shot through his side, and stared in astonishment at the thick steel cable behind him being wrenched from its spool. Its progress was slow at first, but then the cable's speed accelerated. The winch's complaining sound grew ever louder, until it seemed as if a nuclear submarine was attached to the other end.

Screaming to be heard over the racket, Haruto scrambled to his feet and ordered the winch thrown into maximum reverse power, in an attempt to stop the headlong flight of whatever was on the other end. The bug-eyed technician swallowed hard and nodded, then seized the resistance meter lever with sweaty hands and hauled back on it with his entire weight.

Nothing happened.

Haruto drew closer, pushing crewmen out of his way. His eyes went wide in disbelief. Another hundred yards of his indestructible cable screamed off the giant spool like fishing line. Barking orders, he watched as two crewmen hosed down the now-smoking hoist with the high pressure washes used to clean sharks' blood and skin particles off the metal decks.

Despite his decades of experience, Haruto found himself on the verge of panic. The winch spool was down to less than two hundred yards with no sign of slowing, and the overheated engine was straining to maintain resistance. If he didn't shut it down, the expensive diesel would burn out. And if he shut it down, the cable would continue to be stripped until its backing was gone.

Then anything was possible. The creature on the other end of the line might become exhausted, allowing them to retrieve their gear, and it as well. Or, the cable could snap, maiming or killing anyone standing close by. Haruto was betting on the latter. From what he had already seen, whatever they hooked into, be it an unfortunate whale or the *Kraken* itself, it appeared to be unstoppable.

Dismissing the notion of trying to cut the thick cable with a nearby fire axe, he took one final glance at the near-empty spool and made up his mind. He had no choice. He turned to order his men to clear the area and cut the power in order to save the engine.

Before he could utter his command, the cable ran out. There was an incredibly loud twanging noise, and the sound of straining steel was replaced by thunder, as the five-ton winch assembly and its housing was ripped off the *Oshima's* swaying decks. Too fast to follow, it slammed into the nearby railing, heading straight for the moonlit seas beyond. Its deafening impact on the reinforced rail drowned out the screams of those who, unable to dive from its path, were scattered like ten pins.

Wild-eyed and trembling, Haruto sucked in a breath and clutched his side as he made it to his feet. Beneath him, the deck continued to rise and fall. His captain's hat was gone, and his immaculate white officer's jacket was now stained with soot and oil. All around, dazed men tried to stand, a few slipping on the viscous layer of shark's blood that coated the deck. Several men lay where they were, unable to move, their agonized cries echoing across the surrounding waters.

Haruto fought down a powerful wave of nausea and dropped down next to the nearest, a pole-man who desperately cradled his left thigh with both hands.

"Are you alright?"

"I don't know . . . sir!" The man grimaced, his ashen face a mask of untold agony.

At Haruto's gesturing, the man hesitantly removed his hands. Instantly, a fountain of arterial blood sprayed from his leg, striking the captain directly in the face. A wicked looking hunk of steel from one of their tools protruded from the man's thigh. He gasped aloud, desperately trying to stem the flow.

"Good God!" Haruto wiped at the blood that ran down his cheek and chin. He reached over and placed his own hands atop the man's, increasing the pressure on the wound. He looked around and frowned. For the first time he could remember, his first mate was nowhere to be seen. "Sagato," he yelled, "get a medical team up here at once!"

There was no answer.

"Sagato!" Haruto gestured hurriedly for another crewman to take over for him as he hunted for his second. "Sagato, where the hell are you?"

"He's . . . over here, sir."

Haruto turned in the direction of a nearby deckhand. The man was standing next to what was left of the ruined hoist, his arms tightly clutching his ribcage, his back pressed against the ship's railing. He was trembling, his skin the color of cream.

"Where is he?" Haruto demanded, looking in every direction but seeing no one.

"There, sir," the man said. He pointed to the blown-out section of railing obscured by the hoist's wreckage.

Haruto stopped in his tracks.

Unable to fling himself clear in time, the *Oshima's* first mate had been caught in the winch's path as the pickup truck-sized assembly came crashing into the railing, burying itself in the heavy barrier and deforming it until five feet of twisted steel bulged out over the waters below. With no chance to escape, Sagato was entombed in the wreckage, his body crushed from the chest down. His death had been instantaneous.

Unable to move, Haruto stood there staring, his disbelieving eyes locked onto Sagato's glazed-over ones. Try as he might, he was unable to pull himself away from the ghastly visage. He could barely hear the sounds of the wounded or the cries of the ship's medical team as they fought to give aid to their injured comrades.

Finally, he shook it off and grabbed at the man nearest to him. "Get these wounded men down to the medical station at once! And I want all of this debris cleared up!"

"Yes, sir!"

Haruto gave Sagato a parting bow, then turned to face the watch commander approaching him. The man was moving in an s-shaped pattern as he drew closer, avoiding limping crewmen and stretcher crews as they arrived on the scene.

"Captain Nakamura, Watch Commander Iso Hayama, reporting for duty," he said, his body rigid and eyes straight ahead as he saluted.

Haruto reached for the clipboard Iso held under his arm. He scanned it and handed it back. "I need a casualty report from you in five minutes, commander. I want to know how many wounded and how many dead."

"Yes, sir."

"Before you provide me with that, I want you to go around to all the hoist crews and have them retract their lines. Tell them to prepare to get under way."

"Go around, sir? You mean, in person?"

"That's right, commander. I don't want any overhead announcements. I want you to inform the crews personally."

Iso looked bewildered, but nodded as he turned to go.

"Watch Commander?"

"Yes, sir?"

"Whatever did this is still out there," Haruto said. He gestured with a blood-spattered arm at the winch's wreckage, then out at the darkened seas behind him. "I don't plan on losing any more of my winches to it. We're moving, quickly and quietly. I don't want any more panic on our hands than we already have."

"Aye, sir." Iso hesitated, his gaze wandering back to the downed hoist.

"Is there something wrong, commander?"

"Oh, no, captain. It's just that I was wondering–"

"Wondering, what?"

"Well, I was wondering what we're going to do about . . ."

Haruto followed his eyes. "I see. Don't worry, commander. Mr. Sagato will be properly seen to."

"Aye, sir. Thank you, sir."

Haruto watched him go, before turning to the shaken deckhand who remained by the railing. He was young, sixteen at most. "Ensign, come here."

"Yes, captain?"

"What is your name?"

"Akira Hidari, captain." The teen's hand trembled as he struggled to pull off a salute.

"Ensign Hidari, I know we've all suffered a terrible shock, but I need you to pull yourself together," Haruto said. He fixed him with a stare. "The *Oshima* is wounded, and she and I need your help. Now, I need to know that we can count on you. Can we, sailor?"

"Yes, sir!" The boy puffed out his chest, trying hard to control his rapid breathing.

"Very well then, ensign. I have an assignment for you. I need you to get a crew of welders up here, as soon as the wounded have been cleared from the area."

"Welders, captain?"

"Yes, welders. I'm not about to leave our first mate to the gulls," Haruto said, nodding his head in the direction of the still-smoking hoist. "There's no other way to free him."

Ensign Hidari glanced fearfully at Sagato's still-bleeding remains. The look of agony on the dead man's face was enough to make anyone cringe. He swallowed hard and nodded to his captain. A quick salute, and he turned and vanished from view.

Haruto paused for a moment, taking in a few deep breaths while he mulled over his next course of action. He had a few minutes before the hoist crews finished. Walking over to the destroyed winch assembly, he willed himself to ignore Sagato's stare and peered out at the darkened seas beyond. To his surprise, the winch's cable was still attached to the spool. It was so close; if it wasn't for the wreckage, he could have reached out and touched it.

Suddenly, he spotted a pair of men he recognized from a nearby hoist. His eyebrows lowered. "You two, come here at once."

"Yes, sir?" the men said as one.

"Shift your hoist's arm in this direction. I want a splice made between your cable and this one."

"You want us to salvage the cable, sir?"

"No, gentlemen." Haruto shook his head at the confused looks on their faces. "I want to see if there's anything left on the other end of it."

A few minutes later, the crimped connection between the two hoists was successfully rigged. Satisfied the splice would hold, Haruto surveyed the nearly clear decks. The wounded had been evacuated and much of the debris around the ruined hoist removed. Nearby, a small group of men gathered once word spread of what the captain was planning. Normally a rowdy lot, all of those present were remarkably subdued.

Only Sagato was quieter.

"All right, men. Let's bring her in," Haruto said.

At his order, the sweating crew of the nearby hoist turned their motor on at a reduced power setting. Their diesel engine shuddered to life and soon was pulling in yard after yard, storing it in neat rows atop its own withdrawn cable. Like pallbearers at a funeral, Haruto and all the men present lined the railings, watching and waiting with baited breath to see what, if anything, remained at the cable's end.

"Doesn't seem to be much there, Captain. Almost no weight at all, sir," the winch commander said, as he looked up from his dials.

Haruto nodded. Several of the crew could be heard placing wages under their breath, betting amongst themselves whether the cable had snapped, the hook straightened out, or simply broke off. Two minutes later, their fish came bobbing to the surface. Or rather, what remained of it.

"Hold it!" Haruto exclaimed, raising one hand to signal the winch crew to stop.

"What the hell is that?" a crewman blurted out from one side. "That's no shark!"

Haruto ignored him. "Okay, bring it up."

Both captain and crew stepped back as the nearby hoist arm maneuvered its load up over the railing, then swung it around and deposited it on the deck with a thud. Moving closer, Haruto dropped down on one knee to examine what remained on the end of their industrial-size circle hook. As he did so, Iso Hayama appeared at his side.

"Good lord, captain," Iso asked. "What in the world is that? And where's the rest of it?"

His eyes wide, Haruto grimly studied the enormous silver and white mass of teeth and gills, highlighted by an amber-colored eye the size of a cantaloupe. He took in a deep breath and held it before letting it out. Then, holding his injured side tightly, he rose to his feet.

As he looked at the anticipating faces of his crew, Haruto shook his head in what he knew was an uncharacteristic display of wonder and disbelief. He paused to straighten what remained of his bedraggled uniform and waved off a barrage of questions. Iso dutifully followed him as he walked away. He stopped when he was certain their conversation could no longer be heard.

Iso could contain himself no longer. "Haruto-san, forgive me, but I must know. What *was* that thing?"

Haruto started to speak, but then said nothing. He turned away and walked over to the big ship's railing, where he stopped and stared out at the endless blackness lurking just beyond the range of their searchlights. A shiver ran down his spine and he stepped hurriedly back from the rail.

"I'm ready to hear your casualty report, commander," he said, loudly clearing his throat.

"Yes, captain. We um . . . have six wounded, two of whom are in critical condition, and one dead, sir." He paused, shuffling papers. "You should know that, according to the ship's physician, only one of the injured will be fit for duty before we make port, sir."

Haruto continued to stare out at the surrounding seas. He reached into his jacket pocket and produced a folded sheet of paper, handing it to Iso. "I want you to call this number. Tell the dispatcher who we are, give them our coordinates, and have them get a helicopter out here on the double. Tell them it's a delicate matter. They will understand."

"A helicopter? Is it for the wounded, sir?"

"No, commander," Haruto said. "Let me make this clear: Nobody leaves the ship. We treat our wounded here."

"Then, it's for Mr. Sagato?"

"No. Have Mr. Sagato's body and the remains of that thing on the deck prepped and placed in our forward freezer at once. Get a detail of men to assist you."

"We're putting him in the freezer with the fins, sir?"

Haruto turned and looked him in the eye. "That's correct, commander. Do you have a problem with that? Or better yet, would you prefer that we sail into Key West and deliver his body to the U.S. Coast Guard personally, and the *Oshima* right along with it?"

"No sir . . . I didn't mean that, I–"

"This ship is my responsibility, commander," Haruto said. He paused to bend down, peeling the bloodstained picture of his first mate's family off the deck at his feet. He glanced at it, then straightened and put it in his breast pocket. "As is the responsibility to write to Sagato's widow, and tell her of his unfortunate passing."

"Yes, sir. I'm sorry, sir." Iso bowed apologetically.

"So am I, commander." Haruto turned back to the water one last time. He frowned and reached for his wallet, removed a business card, and handed it to Iso. "Here. I want you to punch in this ship's transponder code and find her for me. Her name's on the back. I want to know her exact location, and before that chopper gets here."

"Yes, sir," Iso said, mustering as much enthusiasm as he could.

Haruto started to walk away. "I will be in my quarters filing my report. Call me when the bird arrives."

"Yes, sir. Um . . . sir?"

"Yes, commander?"

"What do you think caused all of this?"

Haruto turned and looked back at him, his face cast in concrete. "I have absolutely no idea, commander. But whatever it was, I feel a great amount of pity for anyone that finds themselves in its way."

"Yes, sir."

———

As his injured captain made his way below deck, Watch Commander Iso Hayama turned toward the throng of crewmen, still crowding around the bizarre mass of flesh that lay sprawled upon their deck. He drew closer and glanced down at it, then took in a deep breath and shook his head. He signaled for the nearest crewman to come close, whispering instructions in his ear. The deckhand nodded and took off running.

Iso paused for a moment, fumbling in his pocket for a handkerchief to wipe the thick layer of perspiration from his neck and brow. Then he reached for the business card his captain had given him. He held it up to the nearest light and read aloud the name of the ship written on it.

The Harbinger,

Jake Braddock could see the ship's name clearly as she sliced her way through the early morning swells, a half-mile from shore. From the look of things, she was headed toward Paradise Cove.

He studied her. Compared to their resident charter boats she was big, at least seventy yards long, probably seven or eight hundred tons. He lowered his binoculars, his eyes squinting as he took a second look. A frown creased his tanned features.

Jake glanced at his watch, then turned back to check the dirt road that led to the parking lot. The expensive optics hung loosely around his neck, the nylon strap irritating the skin of his nape as it seesawed back and forth. He shook his head as he started to reach for his cell phone, then changed his mind. With no other view available, he turned back to the unpleasant distraction to his left.

It was a six hundred yard wide swath of virgin sand. Shielded from hikers and joggers by warning signs and fences, the tiny beach basked in the glow of the Floridian sun. It was a government-sanctioned paradise of gently lapping waves and tall palm trees: pretty much the only completely secluded parcel of land remaining within thirty miles. It was also, undoubtedly, the reason why the mother leatherbacks flocked to it, year after year.

Jake studied up on them when he first moved back. Over eight feet in length and weighing up to a ton, the endangered sea turtles were the largest living chelonians in the world, the adults having few natural enemies. Like others of their ilk, the big reptiles came ashore to lay their eggs. Unlike the adults, as soon as they hatched, the baby turtles faced a deadly gauntlet of adversaries. Once they managed to dig themselves out of their sandy nurseries, they faced an interminable crawl down to the sheltering surf. Along the way, they were vulnerable to an assortment of predators, all eager to pounce on defenseless turtle hatchlings.

Hovering overhead like a malevolent cloud, the high-pitched screeching of gorging birds could be heard for a quarter-mile. Jake stuck his fingers in his ears, his eyes unblinking as he watched. With deadly precision, the foul creatures repeatedly dive-bombed the help-less hatchlings. Careening down, they smashed beak-first into their targets at lethal speeds. The little leatherbacks were being butchered. Out of the one hundred or more eggs laid in each nursery, three or four *might* make it to sea.

Grimacing, Jake turned his head away from the slaughter, resist-ing the urge to grab his shotgun and take in some feathery target prac-tice. The same thing happened every year during this time. Someone needed to inform Fish and Game that their efforts to protect the turtles' nesting sites weren't being particularly effective. Either that or they needed to start telling the baby leatherbacks to limit their sea-ward sprints until after dark.

With a final glance at his watch, Jake straightened up, stretched to relieve stiffened muscles, and walked back to his truck. He opened the dusty Tahoe's driver's side door, flipped the seat forward, then reached into the backseat and grabbed his bag and gun. Quickly checking the Beretta's magazine and safety, he holstered the nine mil-limeter and slammed the door closed.

Jake stood there for a moment, staring tiredly out past the nearby dock. He checked his badge and spare magazines and tucked the back of his uniform shirt in before feeling for his wallet. A painful groan escaped his lips. His driver's license might have said he was only twenty-eight, but the way his joints ached he felt eighty-eight. The wind started to kick up, and Jake took a moment to enjoy the feel of the cool sea breeze as it forced its way through his chestnut-colored hair. His face began to heat up and he shielded his eyes with his free hand, glaring back at the rising sun, bearing down against its fierce early-morning brilliance.

To a stranger passing by, the muscular, six-foot-two lawman would have appeared strong enough to have been hewn from solid rock. But he also had a worn-out look about him, as if he carried some interminable burden draped across his broad shoulders.

Exhaling heavily, Jake turned and was just shouldering his gear bag when he heard another car approaching. He frowned, recognizing the automobile through the cloud of road dust and grit that accompanied it. He turned, activating his car alarm just as his deputy pulled up.

"Hey, boss," Chris Meyers blurted out as he nearly fell from his dilapidated Dodge. Popping the vehicle's rusty trunk, he rushed to the rear of the car and rummaged through its litter-strewn contents. When he emerged he was wearing a salt-stained backpack and toting a beat-up cooler and a brown paper bag. His scraggly, sand-colored locks were tucked under an old baseball cap, and his unkempt uniform seemed to hang off his five-foot-ten, one hundred and fifty-pound frame.

Jake sighed. *At least he remembered his sidearm this time . . .*

"Wow, what's all that racket?" Chris said, looking over at the distant cloud of screaming seabirds.

"Never mind that." Jake gestured at the still-smoking car. "I thought you were going to get that tune-up and oil change done."

"Sorry Jake. I meant to, I just didn't have the time."

"You 'didn't have the time'? Listen, kid, I didn't give you that old car so you could run her into the ground. If you don't keep up on the maintenance, she's going to give out on you. And I *don't* have another one lying around."

"Sorry, boss. I'll try and find the time to do it today."

"Really?" Jake asked. He felt himself getting annoyed. "Gee, Chris. I'd have thought you had the time to get it done this morning. You know, during the *forty five minutes* you kept me waiting."

"Um . . . actually, I stopped to get you coffee." Chris grinned sheepishly. "And a ham, egg and cheese croissant." He held out the paper bag as if it were a peace offering.

"Oh, did you now . . ." Jake smirked. Unlike the majority of their resident seagulls, he hadn't had breakfast yet. "Ham, egg and cheese, you said?"

"Yeah, I know it's your favorite, boss," the youngster said, nervously holding the bag out again.

There was a moment of silence before Jake reached over and took it. He opened it and inspected the contents. He popped the lid off the coffee, took a sip and fought down a smirk. "French vanilla, eh? Not exactly my usual. But, I gotta give you credit, kid. When you kiss up, you really go all out."

"I try."

"All right, enough of this. Let's get going." Contentedly drinking his coffee, Jake started marching toward the dock, his deputy following behind. Without warning, he stopped. He turned back, handing Chris the weighty shoulder bag he was carrying. "Here. I'll be better able to enjoy my breakfast if you carry this."

"No problem, boss," the teenager said with a smile. "Are there any other penances you have in mind for me before we get started?"

"I'll be sure to let you know," Jake said, taking a bite out of what was admittedly a very tasty breakfast sandwich. The kid did make it hard to stay mad. "Just don't get too comfortable with this whole tardiness thing, Chris," he added through a mouthful of food. "Taking advantage of my addiction for good coffee is only going to get you so far."

"Yes, boss," the teenager said, following behind and struggling under the weight of his added burden. "It's not all my fault this time, just so you know." He grunted as he stumbled on a small stone. "It's my girlfriend, Amber. We've been having some problems. And if that wasn't enough, she kept me up all night modeling the lingerie and high-heeled shoes she made me buy her."

"Ah, scantily-clad women in stilettos . . . Such are the burdens of youth," Jake chuckled.

Stopping at the auxiliary dock, Jake peered out across the murky water, giving his patrol craft an appraising look. She was a sleek, twenty three-foot center console with a single outboard engine. The name *Infidel* was emblazoned across her hull in bold letters.

"I guess you need to lay down the law with your new girlfriend, my young lad. Either that," Jake said, fondly running rough hands over the edge of the Pro-Line Sport's gunnels, "or you're going to have to go out and find yourself someone who's a little less demanding and a lot more responsible."

"You're right, boss," Chris nodded. "Maybe I should sit her down and have a good long talk with her."

"Indeed," Jake said. He smirked inwardly as a thought popped into his head. "Or *maybe* you should just tell her you've been late five times in the last two weeks, and if it happens again you're going to get fired."

"Hey, that's a great idea! Do you think she'll believe me?"

"Oh, definitely," Jake said, springing agilely over the side of the boat and then reaching over to take the bags from Chris. He fixed him with the stare he used on the area's infrequent perps. "Because it's true."

"What? Are you serious?" Chris's face flushed, his hazel eyes wide with alarm as he struggled to climb aboard. "You're going to fire me, Jake?"

Jake kept his back turned and said nothing.

"Geez," Chris continued nervously. "I really need this job. I don't know if I can find another one. Plus, my mom's not working much."

It was true, Jake thought to himself. Chris's habitual tardiness, coupled with a string of tempestuous relationships, had gotten the poor kid fired from just about every restaurant and store in town. There probably wasn't anyone else who would give him a job.

"Relax," he said after a moment, waving off Chris's discomfiture, "I'm just kidding." He grinned, sitting back in his padded captain's chair and took a long draught of his remaining coffee. "After all, where else am I going to get quality caffeine like this so early in the morning?"

"That's right," Chris nodded. He collapsed into the copilot's seat next to Jake, breathing an audible sigh of relief. "You know, you really scared me for a minute."

"Don't sweat it kid," Jake said, inserting his key into the throttle, powering the *Infidel's* sputtering two hundred horsepower Yamaha outboard to life. "Now, let's look this girl over good before we get started."

"Yes, boss. So, how's she running?"

"Seems okay," Jake answered thoughtfully, revving up the motor's rpm's and checking her dials. "Outboard might need some servicing though; she gave me a few problems turning over earlier. Fortunately, I had plenty of time to play with her before you got here."

Chris fidgeted as he turned and stowed his gear. "Say, you sure you weren't serious about firing me?"

"Positive," Jake said. He cast off their mooring lines as he spoke and pushed the *Infidel* away from the dock with a shove. "As hard as it is for *me* to get a vacation, do you actually think I'm going to let you run off and lie on some beach somewhere while you collect unemployment for six months? No way. Remember the galley slave scene from that old Charlton Heston movie your mom had on? *We keep you alive to serve this ship. So row well, and live.*" Jake laughed aloud, gunning the engine again for effect.

"Very funny," Chris smirked as he sat back.

Jake glanced off the port side. The wind was kicking up a bit. Ahead of them, the choppy waters of the sound lay waiting.

Chris's face suddenly brightened up. "Hey, by the way boss, did you see the pictures of that squid they had on CNN last night?"

"No. What squid?"

"They caught some sort of new species of giant squid off the coast of Cuba. Attacked some swimmers or something. It was huge!"

"Really? How big?"

"As big as this boat, I think," Chris said. "Say boss, wouldn't it be great to run into a monster like that while we're out on patrol?"

"Oh, *brother*. Yeah, that'd be great, kid . . ."

Shaking his head, Jake maneuvered the *Infidel* out toward the waiting sea.

———

Already miles away from the wounded *Oshima,* the creature altered its course, displacing tens of thousands of gallons of seawater as it glided silently through submarine depths. It was traveling instinctive migratory routes stored deep within its brain, paths bequeathed to it by ancestors that ruled these exact same oceans, eons prior.

Suddenly, it sensed shallower waters far off in the distance – waters teeming with life. Alert now, the creature shifted its bulk in the water column once more. As soundless as the seas surrounding it, it began to move in that direction.

THREE

The approaching dawn was a ghostly glimmer on the horizon when Amara Takagi woke up. Her opal eyes opened slowly, taking in the steely familiarity of the riveted bulkheads that lined her captain's quarters, before focusing on the green glow of her nearby alarm clock. She resisted the urge to grumble as she reached over and disabled it.

Amara shifted position and swung her long legs over the side of her bunk, her feet easily reaching the cool metal floor of her stateroom. As her toes began their morning quest for her ratty slippers, a sharp spasm of pain shot through her hip. She winced despite herself, took in a deep breath, then let it out slow. Still bleary-eyed, she reached for her nightstand, her hand closing on a nearly empty bottle of Ibuprofen. She spilled a half-dozen pills into her waiting palm. When she realized the glass of water she left out the night before was empty, she tossed the caplets into her mouth and started crunching. They were beyond awful, their acrid taste an unwelcome jolt to the nervous system that no cup of coffee could provide.

Shuddering, Amara summoned as much saliva as she could and forced them down, reaching for her nearby com link as she waited for her six little saviors to come to her rescue. Her face was a grimace as she paged the bridge.

"Willie . . . how far out are we?" she croaked.

"We be making port in tirty minutes, boss," Willie replied amiably. "I have us docked within another half hour of dat."

Amara sighed. She loved him to death, but sometimes her first mate was so disgustingly chipper in the morning she couldn't stand it. She wondered if he ever needed sleep.

"Thanks, Willie. I'll be up in twenty."

Reaching over to shift some of her weight onto her nightstand, Amara tried and failed to make it to her feet. The pain was intense – worse than normal. She shook her head, taking in a few more breaths before struggling upright. Her bed sheet cascaded to the floor, leaving her covered by nothing but her sleep shirt and panties. It was chilly in her quarters and her skin registered the sudden drop in temperature, but she was more concerned with keeping her balance as she staggered drunkenly toward the bathroom. The normally comforting sway of the ship was now a serious impediment. At the start of the day, the stiffness of her injury made her feel like the Tin Woodman minus his oil can.

Amara made it to her tiny bathroom, grasping the doorjamb for support as she worked her way inside. She plopped down onto the toilet, grateful for the cool respite, her hands repeatedly massaging the jagged scar that decorated a good portion of her left hip as she tried to restore lost circulation. When finished, she washed up, brushed her teeth, and limped over to the tiny stove and sink that made up her kitchen.

The sound of tap water hitting the inside of the metal teapot drummed like raindrops on a tin roof in Amara's ears. She turned on her miniature propane stove, set the tea to boil, and turned on some relaxing jazz music in an effort to take her mind off what was coming.

As she rolled out her yoga mat for what must have been the three thousandth time, Amara wondered once again what it would be like to be normal, to wake up each day pain free and fully functional. To not have to groan and strain and chip away at the arthritic adhesions that clung to her hip like rust on a hinge. She sighed. *Maybe I'll have it easier in my next life*

As she eased herself down onto the thin mat and began forcing herself through her regular morning routine of ballistic and static stretches, Amara gritted her teeth. The grueling positions that enabled her to go through her day without looking and feeling like a cripple were always painful. She counted silently, forcing herself to relax as she bounced slowly up and down in a full straddle split. Her breathing began to grow labored, more from the pain shooting through her complaining leg than from the actual intensity of the exercises. Sweat began to flow down her brow and into her eyes as she glanced up, blinking repeatedly to clear her vision. She focused on the nearest wall, grunting aloud as she shifted position to work her weaker leg.

Amara looked at her calendar as she stretched. It was sent by one of the wildlife organizations they did business with. The current month featured a baby Harp seal peering forlornly into the camera, its fluffy white coat and large black eyes looking utterly adorable.

She found herself smiling involuntarily at the photo of the tiny pup. The icy crispness of the picture's wintry scenery looked so inviting, the animal so soft and cuddly, that it wasn't until the baby seal's high-pitched shriek resonated through her subconscious that she unexpectedly found herself pulled back in time.

Suddenly, it was twelve years ago, a few weeks after her eighteenth birthday. After months of cajoling, she'd finally convinced her father to take her along on one of his adventures. He was a fiery *Sea Crusade* activist with five years under his belt. His daring exploits, coupled with an unnerving willingness to place himself in harm's way, had made him a legend within the ranks of the well known animal rights organization.

Amara's exuberance at being able to join her father and *Sea Crusade* was beyond description. To top it off, her initial assignment involved something she'd supported for years: an expedition to protect Canada's baby Harp seals from being slaughtered by hunters during the annual pup roundup.

Hikaro Nakamura tried repeatedly to prepare his headstrong daughter for the harsh realities of the upcoming hunts. Amara chose to focus instead on the majestic natural scenery they would be witnessing. She naively romanticized the entire situation. She thought it would be more along the lines of what picketers experience when working a site in some major city; carrying signs and banners and chanting slogans. She half expected the seal hunters to be intimidated by potential media coverage and simply pack up and go away.

Their six hundred-ton mother ship, *Sea Green*, entered the Gulf of St. Lawrence via the Honguedo Strait, chugging stealthily along between the south shore of Anticosti Island and the Gaspe' Peninsula. Under cover of darkness, they acquired a near-shore anchorage, an advantageous position to launch their operations, with the plan being to intercept the approaching hunters at first light. It was day one of the legal hunting season, and they wanted to make a big impact.

To Amara, an aspiring photojournalist, the Gulf of Saint Lawrence turned out to be everything she expected and more. The world's largest estuary, the sprawling beauty of its limitless ice floes was wondrous to behold. Hundreds of the region's population of breeding Harp seals had already gathered on the nearby pack ice, the larger, darker mothers popping in and out of their air holes like oversized prairie dogs as they returned from feeding to nurse their constantly mewling offspring. The babies themselves, with their dark, supplicating eyes staring out from a background of soft, white fuzz, made Amara want to pick them up and hug them. As she took picture after picture of the hungry pups, she wondered to herself how anyone could bring themselves to hurt such helpless animals.

The first skirmish took place earlier than expected. Not on the ice floes, as expected, but rather, out on the surrounding waters. Amara's father got the radio call: one of the commercial sealer ships, annoyed with the *Sea Crusade* inflatable's attempt at fending them off, rammed one of the animal rights' scout ships, capsizing the eighteen-foot Zodiac and nearly drowning several members of her crew. By the time the sealer ship's longboats made landfall and the hunters hit the ice, Hikaro, Amara and nearly two dozen other angry activists were gathered and waiting for them.

As soon as the first hunters approached, Amara felt a cold quake of fear. The men were big, grim, and armed to the teeth with knives, rifles and clubs. From the tips of their gloved hands to the soles of their spiked boots, they were dressed to kill. Their cold weather gear was permanently stained a dull, rust color, the remnants of dried blood, forever embedded in the fabric from year after year of butchering countless animals. Their eyes were the dark, deep-set eyes of men who spent their formative years working in slaughterhouses: cold and hard and unmoved at witnessing death.

Infuriated with the activists' attempts to interfere with their livelihood, the seal hunters went on the attack the moment their landing craft's prow touched the pack ice. Uttering profanities, they hurled buckets of baby seal's blood and organs directly at the protesters, painting them a horrid blackish-scarlet and staining the surrounding ice for a dozen yards in every direction.

Amara, holding onto her father now, gagged uncontrollably as seal intestines struck her in the face. She lost her grip and her balance as she dropped to the ground, shaking and vomiting uncontrollably.

Enraged, Hikaro snarled and threw himself on the hunter responsible. Savagely wielding a broken sign handle, he began beating his daughter's attacker about the head and shoulders. Several of the man's comrades rushed to his aid, and in seconds it was a melee. Hunters not involved in the brawl took instant advantage of the situation. Outnumbering the protestors four to one, three score of them flooded the football field-sized ice floe, their heavy clubs raised as they charged the nearest group of seals.

At first, the growling mother Harp seals held their ground, their teeth bared as they shuffled awkwardly forward in an attempt to defend their helpless brood. A few well placed rifle shots quickly dispersed them, leaving two of their number lying dead and several more sliding into the water to bleed out and drown.

Still clutching her heaving stomach, Amara twisted her aching head to one side. She tried repeatedly to spit the fishy taste of seal guts and bile from her mouth, her blood-streaked hair soaking into the crimson ice beneath her. Unable to move, she watched in wide-eyed horror as the butchery began. She could hear the sounds of the hunters' boots crunching into the frost as they nimbly surrounded their quarry. The crackling noises their feet made were quickly overshadowed by yells and cheers.

The men methodically performed their task, herding the baby seals into tightly knit groups. Immobile and defenseless, the tiny, white pups could only utter high-pitched, bleating cries as, one by one they were clubbed and beaten to death. Most of the hunters, not wishing to risk ricochets off the ice, slung their rifles over their shoulders and used homemade clubs, baseball bats and hakapiks to do the job.

The hakapik would haunt Amara forever. A five-foot long wooden handle, topped with a flat-faced steel hammer head on one side and a viciously curved spike on the other, the seal killer's favorite weapon reminded her of a medieval war hammer, something knights once used to crush helmets and split skulls. Still on her hands and knees, she gasped in horror as she watched. One of the hunters lunged suddenly forward, grinning broadly as he brought his hakapik down on the nearest pup's face and skull region. The results were devastating, with the poor animal's whimpering cries immediately silenced by a sickening crunch. The hunter then leaned over the still-twitching seal and used his gloved hand to palpate what remained of its skull, checking to make sure it was dead before he dragged it off and moved on to the next one.

A few dozen yards away, a less experienced hunter partially missed his mark. He didn't bother to finish off the wounded seal pup. Grunting in frustration, he seized it with rough hands and unsheathed a wicked looking knife. As Amara gasped in horror, he bent down and began to flay the frantically struggling animal on the spot. Its piteous screams as it was skinned alive pierced the air, causing even the most jaded of his fellow hunters to grimace and turn away.

As she tried once more to make it to her feet, Amara scanned the devastation around her. She realized that the entire colony of baby seals was being wiped out. The formerly wintry-white landscape was now spattered with blood, bits of brain and bone as her fellow humans' murderous rampage continued. The pups were all going to die for money, and there was nothing she could do about it. She saw her father and his fellow conservationists a dozen yards away, yelling and cursing as they continued to battle back a sea of armed bodies. They were outnumbered, outmatched, and unable to do anything but curse and scream in rage and frustration.

Amara shuddered as she realized the majority of the seal pups were already dead. The few remaining began to squeal in utter terror. Their combined high-pitched distress calls, designed to summon their mothers through the ice, shrieked across the landscape and the surface of the frigid waters.

They went unanswered.

Amara blinked in surprise. Fifty feet to her left, she spotted a lone seal pup the hunters somehow missed. Cowering behind the still warm body of its dead mother, the shivering pup managed to remain unnoticed. As its cries blended with its suffering brood mates,' Amara knew it was just a matter of time before it was spotted and killed.

Sure enough, within seconds, one of the hunters turned in the baby seal's direction. At six-foot-four and built like a linebacker, he was a terrifying vision. With his hakapik held loosely in one hand, he stomped mercilessly toward his next victim. He was breathing hard in a heavy jacket encrusted with blood, deliberately rotating his free arm in small circles to prepare for the anticipated blow.

Teary-eyed and panicking, Amara realized she was the only one who could possibly help the pup. With a gurgled cry, she launched herself to her feet and lunged toward the distracted hunter. She was a dozen steps behind him and closing the distance rapidly. As he moved within striking distance, she gave a shriek that matched that of the wailing seals. Using pure adrenaline, she flung herself forward, her body soaring through the air. Sailing past the startled hunter, she landed hard, sliding across the blood slick ice and covering the baby seal with her body.

The seal hunter, already in mid-swing, was knocked off balance by her impact with his shin. His razor-sharp hakapik continued its deadly downward stroke and landed with a thud, its five inch metal spike ripping right through Amara's parka and bib pants, burying itself in her hip. Her agonizing scream overpowered the cries of both the protestors and the remaining Harp seals.

In shock, Amara lay gasping, paralyzed on her side, no longer able to cry out. To her amazement, the hunter yanked his weapon free to bash the hapless seal pup she'd tried so hard to defend. Using the hammer portion of his *hakapik*, he killed it instantly. The pup's crushed muzzle landed inches from her nose, its eyes boring into Amara's as life fled its tiny body. She saw the last of its frozen breath whisper from its bleeding nostrils and watched in detached horror as the hunter reached down with one gloved fingertip and gave the dead seal the 'blink test," his bloody digit touching one of its large, black eyes to make sure it was dead. Then, with that same gore-encrusted hand, he took hold of her chin, twisting her head to ascertain her condition.

Amara felt her heart pounding in her chest as she stared death in the face. She felt herself slip away as a wall of darkness closed in on her. Soon, she could see nothing: not the hunter, the dead seal's eyes, or even her father's distraught face as he relentlessly fought his way to her side. Everything had gone black, and the only thing she was aware of was the cries of the surviving Harp seal pups. Their shrieks seared into her brain like a steam whistle.

The whistle . . .

Frantic, Amara suddenly found herself back aboard the *Harbinger*. She was breathing like she just ran a marathon, her skin slick with sweat. She blinked rapidly, struggling to find something in the present to focus on. Her eyes finally latched onto the tea kettle that was furiously boiling away, its whistle rising in intensity and volume. Still shaking, she cursed and rose to her feet, grabbing it and removing it from the flame. She set it down angrily and turned off the stove, lowering her head and locking her shaking hands onto the countertop as she calmed herself.

Looking up, Amara caught a glimpse of herself in the appliance's stainless steel surface. She lowered her chin once more and continued to breathe, her chest rising slowly up and down. A minute later, she pushed herself fully erect, chin up and shoulders pulled back, and walked steadily into the shower.

The creature continued toward the island. Its movements were becoming slower and less fluid as it cruised at a depth of one hundred feet. The tiny parcel of land it had targeted was a non-descript patch of sand and palm trees, but it was acceptable for its purpose.

The last leg of its thousand mile journey was rapid, with it covering forty miles in the last hour. Uncharacteristically wary as it approached the islet, it traveled beneath the ocean's surface as much as possible. It was a master of sub-aqueous flight, and could remain submerged for longer than two hours if it chose to.

In need of air, the creature breached the surface with a blast of water vapor. To its left lay the Florida Keys, to its right, the inviting blackness of the Atlantic Ocean. It slowed its pace and scanned the temperate seas ahead with all of its senses. Eyes focused on its destination, it began to cruise quietly on the surface, feeling the tepid waters beneath its monstrous bulk shallow rapidly.

Pausing out of instinctive caution as its pale belly rubbed against the sandy bottom of the lagoon, the creature studied the moonlit shores of the island. Other than the high-pitched tone of a pair of night birds and the shrill squeaks of some bats scrounging for tropical insects, there was no sign of life.

Its eyes gradually narrowing, the creature remained where it was. It held its position, using the tips of its paddle-shaped flippers to dig into the soft bottom and stabilize itself against the heaving waves. Finally, it closed its eyes and rested.

Sunrise was hours away.

———

Jake Braddock handled the *Infidel* with practiced efficiency; cruising along at thirty knots, his sleek vessel skimmed across the surface. Overhead, the sun beamed down across the azure waters of the Atlantic, a sea of blue that seemed to go on forever. To his left, his tense-looking young deputy sat lost in thought, his youthful eyes squinting as he focused on the horizon.

Suddenly, something white and viscous plummeted toward them, splattering against the crown of Chris's head. The teenager recoiled in surprise, reaching up and running one hand through his hair. It came back covered with coagulated seagull excrement. He smelled it and made a face, cursing and shaking his fist angrily at the hovering flock of birds that pursued them. He leaned over the side, soaked a clean rag in seawater, and then settled down, a dejected look on his face as he scraped and scrubbed at his soiled locks.

Jake turned away, clamping his jaw tightly to keep from laughing. He blew out an exhale, trying to focus on anything but his deputy.

He thought about the time one of the local dockworkers asked him if Chris Meyers was his adopted son. He shook his head and grinned. In many ways, and despite all his faults, the kid did, indeed, remind him of himself, albeit ten years earlier. Except Jake wasn't a klutz with an annoying tendency of falling overboard, he was consistently punctual, and he didn't have the self-destructive habit of dating the most manipulative women imaginable.

Jake glanced good-naturedly back at Chris. He'd finished cleaning himself up and was leaning back, his wet hair pressed down against his head and his lips tightly pursed. He interlocked his hands; the sound of him cracking his knuckles was audible even over the roar of the outboard.

"You really need to stop doing that, Chris," Jake advised. "You're going to give yourself arthritis, long before your time."

"I know boss, you've told me a hundred times. But with all due respect – and please don't take this the wrong way – I'm not sure I should be taking medical advice from someone whose mitts look like yours."

His face an unreadable mask, Jake kept hold of the steering wheel with his right hand. He raised his left to the light and studied it. The skin was hard and quite calloused, particularly the knuckles, finger-tips, and the blade edge of the palm. "Hardcore MMA isn't for every-one, kid. But it keeps you in shape. And, sometimes it helps with the job."

"Either way, looks pretty scary to me," Chris said, turning back to gaze into the low-lying swells that rocketed towards them.

Jake's attention shifted from the palm of his hand to the scuffed-up white gold band he wore on his ring finger. He absentmindedly rubbed the ring with a circular motion using the tip of his thumb. Sighing, he reached over and raised the volume on their marine radio, tuning it to a local station.

. . .with tonight's low a balmy, eighty one degrees.

In international news, the official report from the Cuban government states that last week's unexpected volcanic eruption of Diablo Caldera, a thought-to-be-extinct volcano some nine miles off the coast of Cuba, was caused by an undersea earthquake that measured 6.8 on the Richter scale. The eight mile-wide caldera broke apart and crumbled into the sea, wiping out thousands of fish, birds and marine mammals. Fears of a deadly tsu-nami resulting from the geothermal event were, fortunately, unfounded. As devastating as the eruption was, local marine biologists have stated that, in the long run, the resultant debris and lava released from the col-lapse of the bowl-shaped formation would serve to form the core of new reef systems which would one day become the home for countless fish and other assorted marine life.

The report also stated that, due to the maze of deadly reefs sur-rounding the volcano, the island has been classified off limits by the Cuban Department of Science for decades. Other than a portion of the region's abundant sea lion population, there was no known loss of life . . .

Jake reached over and clicked off the radio.

"Okay, enough depressing news. Almost there, kid," he said, nodding toward the bow. "What do you say we–"

His words were drowned out by the rotors of a large helicopter as it sped directly overhead. Distracted for a moment, Jake pulled back on the throttle as they began to cruise into Paradise Cove.

Soon, the familiar vastness of Harcourt Marina began to spread out before them, its maze of docks splaying forth like the arms of a gigantic octopus. The marina consisted of hundreds of slips that housed almost every type of boat imaginable, from well known deep sea charters to the dreaded *Sea Tow.*

Renamed in recent years, the antique harbor had been the South's answer to Nantucket for decades, and was the economic hub of the tiny coastal town known as Paradise Cove. With Florida's east coast winters as mild as they were, the place saw action year round. It was mid-June now, and the summer's fishing and tourist season was in full swing.

Jake checked his watch. It was 9 a.m. and still fairly quiet. By noon, both the marina and the restaurants and shops that catered to it would be a veritable anthill of activity, crammed with the assorted whale watchers, charter fishermen, divers and weekend romantics whose tourist dollars were the lifeblood of the town. Despite its relatively small size, Paradise Cove was a goldmine.

"So, boss, what's on our agenda for today?" Chris opened up.

"Let's find out," Jake said, trying to sound more energetic than he felt. He flipped open a small notepad he kept in his left shirt pocket. "Let's see . . . we've got a complaint from Ben Stillman that someone's been raiding his lobster traps again. Steve Barter at the ski shop is claiming that kids have been sneaking into his slip after dark and taking his rental Jet Skis out for late night jaunts, and the captain of *Deep Trouble* has reported some of their scuba gear's been stolen . . ."

Jake frowned. "We'll stop in the marina first," he said, shaking his head. "You get us gassed up while I go talk to Steve Barter. Then we'll pull up next to *Deep Trouble* and see about their missing gear." He drew a deep breath, letting it out slow before he continued. "We can check out Ben Stillman's trap problem during our afternoon patrol sweep."

"Sounds like a plan, boss," Chris said with a thumbs up.

As he guided the *Infidel* into the main docking area, Jake studied the fleet of boats, lined up like soldiers at attention. He spotted a few newcomers here and there, noting their names as he went. Even when he was at his absolute worst, and he'd had some bad days over the last three years, he never got tired of reading the names of some of the vessels he watched over, or laughing at the ingenious language use their owners managed to come up with.

The boats of Harcourt Marina ranged in size from tiny pleasure crafts like the nineteen-foot *Bluegill King* and the *Angry Badger* – a Boston Whaler the owner named after his ex-wife – to huge fifty-five and sixty-foot deep sea fishing yachts like the *Conquers All* and the *Marlin Brando*, the latter's primary target species being apparent.

Jake's personal favorite was docked just off their port side. The *Grisly Bare,* a forty-foot Bertram, had an owner with a flagrantly antisocial sense of humor. A chubby stockbroker who bore a striking resemblance to a certain portly porno star, he never seemed to tire of treating other boaters to the sight of his furry self, lounging around on his boat nearly naked, clad only in a brightly colored thong. Today it was metallic fuchsia.

Averting his eyes and shuddering at the sight, the amused lawman chuckled as he piloted the *Infidel* up to the gas dock and tied her off.

"Hey boss, check it out!" Chris exclaimed suddenly, tapping Jake on the shoulder and pointing to a gray-colored ship docked just outside the inlet. "She's the *Harbinger,*" the excited deputy read aloud, peering through their binoculars. "Wow, for these parts, that thing is huge! Say, what kind of boat is that?"

"I'm not sure, Chris," Jake took the binoculars and studied the two-hundred foot craft with interest. "I saw her earlier, before we left the auxiliary dock. She looks like a whale killer, actually," he remarked dryly, as he focused on what appeared to be a harpoon cannon attached to the ship's menacing looking forecastle. "Which is next to impossible; whaling's been outlawed here for ages."

"Maybe she's Russian. I read online that they still hunt whales, and the Japanese do, too. Do you think she's after our blues?"

"I certainly hope not." Jake continued to eye the vessel. He turned to his deputy, reached for his wallet and handed him a debit card. "Here, Chris, why don't you stay here and get us fueled up? Have Sal look over the outboard, and see what's causing the problem. I'm going to go check out our mysterious visitor."

"Uh, sure thing, boss."

Jake stepped over the *Infidel's* gunwales and onto the wooden dock. He checked the snap on his holster and then turned to go.

"Hey, Jake?"

"Yeah?"

Chris glanced nervously at the imposing form of the *Harbinger*. "Be careful."

Jake gave him a reassuring grin, one thumb hooked in his gun belt, "Always am, kid."

———

"Hmm, quaint little town," Amara Takagi said, gathering her long hair and tying it back as she made her way gingerly down the *Harbinger's* wooden gangplank. She removed her sunglasses, placing them on her head as she took in the marina as a whole.

"Wow, this is a pretty serious pier they've got here," Amara said to Joe Calabrese. Turning her head from sea to shore, she took in the full length and breadth of the grayish concrete and steel construction they stood upon. It had a strong smell, a pungent mixture of sea salt and bird droppings, that invaded one's nostrils. "It looks very old." She gestured at the rusting wrought iron streetlamps that dotted its three hundred-foot length. "I wonder how far back it dates?"

"To the late-1800s, actually," a voice announced, causing the two of them to jump.

"Whoa, take it easy sneaking up on people, buddy," Joe said, his stocky frame wheeling in the direction of the newcomer.

"Sorry about that." A surprisingly pale, ferret-faced man with thinning hair walked over to them. He extended a cadaverous hand. "The pier was originally built to accommodate old steamers, back in the days when Paradise Cove was little more than a shanty town, and coal was worth more than crude oil is today. I'm Stanley Berkowitz. I manage the marina for Mr. Harcourt. I believe we spoke on the radio a little while ago. Ms. Takagi, isn't it?"

"Yes, we did . . ." Amara paused in mid-sentence as she noticed his eyes ogling her. Hers narrowed. "Ah, you're Mr. Harcourt's bill collector."

"If you would prefer to see it that way, Ms. Takagi," Stanley said, averting his gaze and shifting his weight nervously back and forth now.

"That's *Doctor* Takagi, actually," Amara remarked. She looked him up and down in turn. At five-foot-ten, she was taller than he was. "This is my chief engineer, Joe Calabrese." She turned her attention away from the man and back toward the nearby wharf and its assorted buildings.

"As you wish, Doctor Takagi," Stanley nodded. "At any rate, there is the matter of your extremely large vessel's daily docking charge. How long will you be remaining in port?"

"Only today, Mr. Berkowitz. So sorry to disappoint you."

"Now really, Ms . . . *Doctor* Takagi, I believe you will find our rates very reasonable."

Joe cleared his throat. "That's not what we've heard."

Amara frowned, holding up a hand. "Whatever. My first mate is still aboard. He will be handling the necessary details, Mr. Berkowitz. Just go to the top of the gangplank and ask to speak with Willie."

"Willie?" he echoed. "Should I–"

Amara had already turned and walked away. "Annoying little creep," she muttered, her long legs picking up the pace.

Smirking at the incensed look on Stanley's face, Joe rushed to keep up. "Yeah, but you do know the prick's going to try to overcharge us now," he said, walking faster and looking over his shoulder to make sure the agent actually knew what a gangplank was.

"Let him try. You're forgetting he's going to be dealing with Willie. And believe me, by the time they're done negotiating, that guy's going to have earned whatever he gets."

"We'll see," Joe said. The sun glinted off his salt and pepper hair as he huffed and puffed, his short legs struggling to keep pace.

The wharf front of Harcourt Marina opened up before them, revealing a dozen intriguing antique shops, art galleries and restaurants, along with a plethora of souvenir stands. The stone and stucco buildings with their slate tiled roofs had an alluring, vintage look about them, giving the wharf an old world charm that was furthered by the town's well-maintained cobblestone streets.

As they walked along, Amara noticed the marina was sparsely populated. It was still early. Many of those running around appeared related to the marina's well developed fishing and whale watching industries. Faces set, they went about their routines, smiling and waving to each other as they carried buckets of bait or pushed wheel barrels filled with gear, rods, ice and refreshments to their assorted boats.

Amara stopped and looked around. "I like this place, Joe," she said, stretching her arms and reveling in the breeze rolling in off the ocean. "It has a peaceful feel to it. And the people seem very nice."

Suddenly, a barrage of curses interrupted her ponderings.

"Yeah, they're real sweethearts," Joe snickered, pointing down toward the nearest dock. A blonde-haired teenager was engaged in an argument with the incensed pilot of an idling flats boat.

"Hey, fuck you, Paul," the well-tanned teen blurted out. He climbed off a black and yellow Jet Ski, beer in hand, and began to make his way up the dock, toward the landing where Amara and Joe stood waiting. Overhead, the sound of a passing helicopter temporarily drowned out the verbal dispute.

"–you gonna move that damn thing or not?" The boat owner repeated his request, his hands on his hips.

"Sure I am," the teen said. He stripped off his t-shirt and tucked the end of it in the back pocket of his shorts. Then he hauled back and threw the half full beer back at the boater, just missing him. "When I'm good and ready, asshole! You got a problem with that; you know where to send the complaint!"

"You son of a . . ."

The muscular adolescent had just hit the landing when he caught sight of Amara in her cutoff shorts and t-shirt and stopped short. "Well, well, well! And what do we have here? A hot little China mama, eh?" he said. He reached down to adjust the crotch of his shorts, leering as he stepped boldly in her direction.

Amara's blood started to boil. Her almond shaped eyes flashed angrily. "What did you just say?"

"C'mon baby, how about a little fucky-sucky? Me love you loooong time!"

Before she could respond, Joe was already in motion. With his big fists clenched, the retired ironworker took a quick step toward the drooling teen. "C'mere, you smart-ass prick. How's about I love *you* long time with my foot up that wise ass of yours?"

"Hey, whoa there, New York!" The teen belched, backing away with his hands palms-out in a placating gesture. Still smirking, his eyes traveled from Joe to Amara, then back again. "Sorry man, I didn't realize that was your piece. Nice work though!"

"Why you . . ."

"Stop it, Joe!" Amara grabbed at her companion's tattooed arm. "Look, we don't need a confrontation here. We've got work to do."

"If you say so," Joe said, still glaring after the rapidly retreating source of his ire. "Man, you should have let me kick his ass."

"A problem we don't need. Now come on, 'New York,' let's go find what passes for law in this town."

They'd traveled less than a dozen steps along the railing bordering the docks when Amara's belt radio squawked something unintelligible. "This is Amara, please repeat."

"Hey, it's Lane. I think you guys should come back to the ship."

"Why's that?" Amara asked into the unit. "Is there a problem with the docking?"

"No, but there's a delivery here for you."

"A delivery? That's strange. Is it the truck? Because it's not due for five or six hours."

There was a moment's pause. "It's not the flatbed. This delivery came via chopper."

Amara exchanged perplexed glances with Joe, both recalling the helicopter that passed overhead mere moments before. "Okay . . . So, what is it?"

"I'm not sure. It's a big wooden crate. It's got your name on it. Not sure what's in it, but it weighs a ton."

"Who delivered it?"

"Some Japanese guys."

Amara arched an eyebrow. "Japanese?"

"Yeah, at least I think so," Lane said. "They didn't say much. Just asked if this was the *Harbinger*, dropped it and took off."

Amara fretted for a moment, her lips a taut line. "Alright Lane, I'm going to send Joe back to take a look at this mysterious crate. I have no idea what it is, but we're not expecting anything. I'll be back in a bit."

"Okay, Lane out."

"You're not coming back to see what it is?" Joe asked.

"Not just yet," Amara said, inclining her head forward and peering over her shades at the man striding in their direction. She focused hard. He was wide-shouldered and athletic looking, a fact that was evident from twenty yards away, and wore a badge and a gun. "I think I just found the law. Go see what's in that crate while I talk to this policeman about our arrangements."

"You got it, boss," Joe said, grinning as he walked away. "I'll call you if I need you."

Amara watched as Joe disappeared into the crowd behind her. The officer had stopped and was speaking with one of the locals. She removed her hair clip and gave a quick headshake, her shimmering locks cascading down past well-toned shoulders. Fighting down her nervousness, she headed purposefully in the tall newcomer's direction.

———

Jake barely made it from the gas dock to the wharf landing before someone called out his name and came huffing and puffing in his direction. He sighed. *It's going to be a long day.*

"Hey sheriff, you got a minute?"

Jake turned to see who it was. Lenny Fitzpatrick, a local charter captain who took clients out for snook and tarpon. A nice enough guy if you didn't mind all the beer cans, but he was always complaining about something; if it wasn't about the fishing, it was the ever-increasing price of gasoline.

Jake nodded, staring past the out of breath fisherman, toward the foreboding hulk of the distant *Harbinger*. His curiosity concerning the mysterious whale killer anchored next to the old fishing pier was going to have to wait.

"Good morning, Lenny. What can I do for you today?"

"I tell you, sheriff, I've about had it with this shit. Did you see what just happened?"

Jake shook his head, following the man's gaze down toward his boat, which was tied off to a piling some twenty-five yards away.

Lenny was red-faced and angrier than he'd ever seen. *God, have they raised gas* that *much?*

"Sorry, Lenny. I'm afraid not. What's bothering–"

Jake paused in mid-sentence, his eyes shifting to his left. A young Asian woman with a determined expression on her face was fast approaching him. She was tall – taller than Lenny in fact – with angular cheekbones, long black hair, and wearing sunglasses. Clothing-wise, she was dressed plain-Jane style, with no jewelry or makeup to speak of, and wore simple khaki shorts and a tied off t-shirt. Even so, he couldn't help notice she was a real head-turner.

Momentarily oblivious to Lenny, Jake focused his attention on the woman as she walked purposefully up to him. She'd come from the direction of the *Harbinger.* As he stared at her, Chris's words came back to him in a rush. *'Maybe she's Russian . . . they still hunt whales and the Japanese do, too . . .'* He blinked at the sudden realization. *Hmm, maybe they* are *after one of our blues . . .*

Lenny Fitzpatrick interrupted Jake's thoughts, "Hey, are you listening to me?"

"Sorry, one second," Jake said. His gaze intense, he took a step forward. "Yes, miss, what can I do for you?"

"Excuse me, officer." She smiled at him, extending her hand. "I'm Doctor Amara Takagi."

Wow. Jake felt his jaw drop. Her smile was dazzling, like the sun peeking through on a cold, overcast day.

"Sheriff Jake Braddock," he managed, shaking hands with her and trying hard to cover up the deer-in-headlights-look he feared he was wearing. She had one helluva grip, he thought. "And this is . . . uh, Captain Lenny Fitzpatrick, one of our finest resident charter captains, in case you're looking for one."

Also taken by Amara, Lenny had forgotten about his griping. At least for the moment. He blushed at the compliment.

"Nice to meet you, doctor," he said.

"You too." Amara nodded. Her eyes shifted quickly back, boring into Jake's. "Sheriff Braddock, eh? Well then, sheriff, would you be able to tell me who's in charge around here?"

"You're looking at him, Doctor . . . Takagi, you said?"

"That's right," she said.

"You're Japanese?"

"As a matter of fact, I am. At least part." She tipped down her sunglasses and peered over them, scrutinizing Jake from head to toe before removing them altogether. "Is that a problem?"

She was definitely a bold one, Jake thought. He sucked in a quick breath as Amara cleared a few wisps of hair from her face and locked gazes with him. Her eyes were blue. Not a normal shade of blue, like his. They were light blue, like a wolf's or huskies' – almost scary. Her moistened lips were naturally red and pouty and stood invitingly out from a background of pale, silky smooth skin.

As the wind shifted in Jake's direction, her scent washed over him; her smell was perfume-free and clean, a distracting blend of flowers and honey that only nature could create.

"Not at all, doc," he managed on an exhale. "You're, um, from that whaler docked over by the channel?"

"You mean the *Harbinger*?"

"Yes. Are you their medical doctor?"

"Wrong on both accounts, sheriff." She smirked, flicking open her sunglasses and putting them on her head.

"Oh, really?" Jake arched one eyebrow. "How so?"

"Well, firstly," Amara said, "I'm not a medical doctor. I'm a cetaceanist, a marine biologist specializing in whales." She extracted an ID from her shorts' pocket. "I also hold a PhD in underwater robotics. And secondly, the *Harbinger*'s not a whaler. Not anymore, at least. My organization and I salvaged and refitted her. Nowadays, she's a floating science laboratory and research vessel." She pointed at the far off ship. "I'm sure you can see the harpoon cannon on her bow. It's non-operational, of course, but we purposely left it there as a reminder to all that board her of the horrors this ship once inflicted – that we're seekers of knowledge – not death."

"Research vessel, eh?" Jake handed back the ID. "And what exactly do you and your organization research?"

Amara's eyes lit up at the question. "Two kinds of whales, specifically: sperm whales and orcas. To be exacting, we monitor orca predation on sperm whales. Unfortunately, there's been a lot of that occurring around these parts lately," she added glumly. "Three pods of killers in particular appear to be responsible. They're unusually aggressive, even for transients. I'm determined to find out why."

"Interesting," Jake mused. "And what can I do for you?"

Lenny Fitzpatrick cleared his throat loudly, drawing Jake's eye. "Yes?"

"Sorry guys," Lenny said, looking from Amara to Jake and wiping the sweat off his brow with the back of one hand. "This is fascinating stuff, but I've got a real problem on my hands that can't wait any longer."

"I'm sorry, doc." Jake glanced back at Amara. "First thing's first. Yes, Lenny. What were you saying?"

"I've got a big problem, Sheriff."

"A problem with what?"

"Not what, who!"

Jake sighed, "Okay, Lenny. A problem with *who*?"

"Brad Harcourt."

Wonderful. "Okay, Lenny. What did he do this time?"

"The son of a bitch parked his goddamn Jet Ski in my slip," Lenny fumed, "and he won't move it." He turned away, spitting irritably on the ground. "Just because his old man owns the marina, the little bastard thinks he can leave his stupid water toy anywhere he damn well pleases, and the rest of us can go fuck ourselves. At the prices we pay? I don't think so. This is bullshit."

"Okay, Lenny. Calm down," Jake said. "And watch the language."

"Sorry, miss." Lenny cast a quick glimpse over at Amara, nodding apologetically. "Look, Jake, I've got a charter coming in a few hours and I need to get some rest. I need that little you-know-what's ski out of my slip. Now are you going to help me or not?"

Amara rested her hands on her hips. "You probably should do something, sheriff. I saw the whole thing, and Lenny's right. In fact, just a few minutes ago, my friend and I had a confrontation with the exact same individual. His oratory capabilities appear limited to perversity and profanity, and not much more."

Jake smirked. He could only imagine what came out of Brad's mouth. For some reason, Amara's deliberate avoidance at repeating his foul language made whatever he'd said seem even worse. "Interestingly put, doc. As for 'doing something,' I'll take care of it. This is my town, and I look after my people. I know how to handle this type of situation."

"Good," Lenny added, "because the 'situation' we're talking about is hanging out inside the ski shop, right over there."

"Lenny, I said I'll handle it," Jake said. He could see Brad Harcourt through the shop's main window, standing by the register. "Now, considering that this will probably get ugly, I think it would be better if you weren't up here when I speak with him."

"Uh . . . good point," Lenny said. He turned to go. "Thanks, Jake."

Amara watched him leave. "So, what's the story with this 'Brad Harcourt' kid?"

"The usual: spoiled rotten rich kid. His dad's a politician who owns the marina, as well as half the town, so Brad thinks that means everyone and everything in it, too. We've had run-ins with him before. Anyway, doc, what can I do for you?"

"Actually, it's Amara," she said, smiling sweetly. "I'm not into titles."

"So why introduce yourself as a doctor to people if you don't intend to use the title?"

"Good point." Amara pondered, "I'm interested in people's reactions to what I do. People make immediate assumptions about me based on my appearance," she said, tossing her hair back for emphasis. "And the rest get pretentious or intimidated when they hear my title."

"I see," Jake said. He was listening to her, but looking back toward the ski shop. "You still haven't told me what you need."

"I'm sorry," Amara said, holding up the clipboard she held in her left hand. "I've got a flatbed coming in with some heavy duty equipment later, and I wanted to show you our manifest so you know everything is in order."

"No problem." Jake took it and flipped through the papers.

A gruff voice suddenly emanated from Amara's radio. "Base to Amara. Come in, please."

"Yeah Joe, I read you."

"I think you should come back, right away," he said.

"Why? What's wrong?"

Joe could be heard clearing his throat. "It's about that crate that was delivered."

The faintest of frowns marred Amara's brow. "What's the problem?"

There were a few seconds of hesitation before Joe radioed back. "To be honest, boss, I don't think we should talk about this on the air. And frankly, I don't even think I could."

Amara's impatience began to show. "What are you talking about? What's going on?"

"You'll have to see for yourself," Joe said. "Come back to the ship as fast as you can."

Amara looked over at Jake. Her expression was blank as she took back the clipboard.

Jake gave her a contemplative look, gauging her expression and body language. "Something going on onboard your ship I should be concerned about, doc?"

She shrugged her shoulders. "I don't believe so, just some supply delivery snafu. Happens all the time. Anyway, I'm sorry, sheriff, but duty calls. I guess the paperwork will have to wait for a bit. Can I catch up with you later?"

"No problem. From what I've seen so far, everything looks to be in order," Jake said distractedly. He could see a certain troublemaking teenager near the exit door of the ski shop. Brad was still standing by the register, but his movements were growing animated.

"Okay, Joe. I'm on my way," Amara radioed. "And this *better* not be one of your practical jokes, mister."

"Believe me, it's not. Joe out."

Amara turned to leave. "I'll see you later, sheriff."

"It's Jake," he said, matter-of-factly, and then added, "I'm not into titles."

She chuckled. "It was nice meeting you, Jake Braddock."

"Same here. Oh, by the way," Jake called after her, "who's your helmsman, in case the harbormaster needs to speak to him?"

"You're looking at him."

"Okay . . ." he drawled. "And if I have any questions regarding either your shipment or your manifest, who's the man in charge of that heap?"

"*Still* looking at him!" Amara yelled back.

Grinning as he watched her walk away, Jake turned back just in time to see Brad Harcourt bursting out the door of the ski shop with the infuriated shop owner right behind him. Even from seventy-five feet away he could see and hear the fierce argument going back and forth between the two.

Jake was halfway there when he saw Brad turn his back and glance from left to right. He started fumbling with the front of his shorts and his shoulders took on an uncomfortably familiar hunch. A moment later, a dark stain streamed down the shop's nearby wall.

Jake's jaw dropped as he did a double-take.

Why, that little son of a bitch!

Teeth clenched, he moved in Brad's direction.

FOUR

Amara panted hard as she trudged up her vessel's worn gangplank. It was hot. So hot, even the air was starting to sweat. She wiped her brow and jutted out her chin, blowing a breath straight up to push her hair away from her eyes. "Okay, guys. I was wrapping things up when you interrupted me, so this better be good!"

"Oh, it is, boss," Joe Calabrese said.

"We'll see." Amara scanned the *Harbinger's* decks, impatient to see what all the mystery was about. "Well, where's the crate?"

"We used the portside crane to lower it into the hold."

"The crane? Just how big is this thing?"

"It's pretty big, maybe six by four feet. Weighs a ton," Joe said, clomping along behind her as she made her way expertly down a set of winding metal stairs. "I'm not risking my back."

Amara shook her head. "Okay, whatever. So, what's in it?"

"I'm not really sure."

Amara stopped short in the middle of a dimly lit corridor. She wheeled on him, pointing an accusatory finger. "What do you mean you're not sure? You mean you didn't even look inside? I warned you about joking–"

"Hey, it's no joke," Joe replied defensively. "I saw what's in there. It's a specimen of some kind. I just don't know what it is."

"And Adam doesn't know either?"

"Nope."

"That's curious. Adam knows everything. He's a living, breathing search engine."

"Maybe his servers are down?"

"Ha. Well, I'm telling you right now, it better not be another half-eaten oarfish." Shaking her head, Amara led them to the ship's hold. "Okay, where is it?" She gazed up at the sunlight streaming through the open hole above her, then at the surrounding archways that led in four different directions.

"We put it in the freezer," Joe said. "Adam said it was very important that whatever-it-is be kept frozen. He's standing guard, waiting for you outside."

"Standing guard, eh?" Amara snickered at the mental image of her diminutive videographer sporting military fatigues and combat boots. *Well, whatever it is, if Adam's taking things to such extremes, it has to be interesting.*

The two entered a cramped corridor that wound a dozen yards before opening into the main hallway. Up ahead, Amara could see Adam Spencer standing outside the freezer room. There was a cardboard box marked "dissection" at his feet, and a stack of thick coats piled on a metal bench to his right.

"Hey, boss," Adam called out.

He was stamping his feet up and down, his hands in his pockets. His eyes had an excited look, visible even through the coke bottle-thick glasses that were the astute little naturalist's stock and trade.

"What's with the cold weather gear?" Amara pointed at the bench.

"I figure we might be in there for a while." Adam reached down and grabbed two coats, handing them each one.

Amara nodded her approval of his foresight and accepted the bulky parka.

Joe chuckled as he donned his. "Arctic clothing in Florida, and in June no less! Who'd have thought?"

Amara grinned as she zipped up the front of her coat, "Say, where's Willie? Has he seen this mysterious thing yet?"

"Not yet," Adam said. "He's watching for the flatbed."

That's Willie, Amara thought. *Poor guy probably hasn't slept all night, checking and rechecking preparations in anticipation of our pending delivery.* "I see." She motioned for Joe, "Alright fellas, let's see what all the excitement is about."

Stepping to the freezer's oversized door, Joe removed the chained locking pin and gave its shiny steel handle a yank with both hands.

The door protested noisily, then flew open wide, releasing a wall of frozen air that enveloped them and spewed into the hallway.

Amara made a face, waving a hand to clear her view. Beside her, Adam frowned as he removed his glasses and wiped them on his parka's shearling collar.

As the frosty air cleared, the three made their way inside. The old freezer room was a fairly good size, measuring twelve feet square. Amara noticed that the usual food the room held – boxes of frozen fish, meats and vegetables – had all been pushed to the back and piled high, making way for the yard-high wooden crate. She moved into the room, squeezing between the crate and stacks of food. Its weighty lid was already freed and sitting loosely on top. "Joe, if you wouldn't mind?"

Joe nodded and stepped forward, grasping the lid's edge. "You got your little camcorder ready, Adam?"

"Absolutely," Adam said, extracting it from his coat pocket and pressing it to one eye.

"Okay then, here we go." Together, Joe and Amara removed the lid, lifting it to one side and resting it against a nearby wall.

For a moment, Amara stared confusedly at what was inside. She blinked rapidly, unsure at first of what she was looking at. A tingle swept through her, growing more and more intense, until she reached down on impulse and yanked away the clear plastic tarp that partially obscured the crate's contents.

"What the . . . hell?"

"Maybe that's where it came from," Adam said, grinning as his recorder focused on her bewildered face. "Might be, because I've never seen anything like this before."

"Oh . . . my . . . God!" Amara's hand trembled as it inched hesitantly forward. Before her, lay the head of some kind of fish. It was huge, at least four feet long and three feet high, with an immense, undershot jaw, lined with dagger-like teeth, six inches in length. The upward curve of the corners of its mouth gave it a malevolent smile, and its lidless eyes, each bigger than a grown man's palm, glared mockingly up at them.

"See, now you know why we called you," Joe said, grinning ear to ear.

Off to one side, Adam continued filming. "So, you're the marine biologist. Any ideas, Amara? At first I thought it was some kind of monster tarpon, based on the silver color of the scales and the general shape of its head, but with those teeth, I knew it was something entirely different."

"It's impossible, but I . . . I know *exactly* what this is," Amara said, her mind whirling with the realization. She felt herself trembling and took a moment to revel in the sensation. "Guys, this is the find of a lifetime. We're going to be all over the news."

"Really? Cool." Adam looked confused. "Uh . . . so what is it?" His camera panned from Amara's face to focus once more on the frozen mass of flesh before them.

"It's something that's supposed to have died out millions of years ago," Amara took a deep breath, then reached into Adam's dissection kit for a pair of latex gloves and a pair of long steel forceps. Leaning forward, she carefully poked around inside the fish's cavernous mouth, checking its teeth. Satisfied, she looked up. "This is the head of a *Xiphactinus audax*. Paleontologists call it the "bulldog fish." It was one of the top predators of the Cretaceous seas, competing for prey with mosasaurs and prehistoric sharks."

Joe gaped. "You're saying this thing is a dinosaur?"

"No." Amara shook her head in awe. She reached forward with a gloved hand and felt the shape of the fish's mandible, knocking on it with her knuckles. "But it lived during the time of the dinosaurs."

"Wow, it sure looks big enough," Joe said.

"It's absolutely amazing!" Amara looked over at Adam, who had stopped filming and was making adjustments on his camcorder. "Did you gather any data yet?"

"Just the basics. Besides general measurements, the piece we have weighs approximately three hundred and forty pounds. Since I'm not at all familiar with the species in question, I can't extrapolate further until I have additional data."

Amara nodded. "I can. Based on the fossil record and comparing it to modern species, the entire fish would have tipped the scales at anywhere from twenty five hundred to three thousand pounds. Length, I'm taking an educated guess at, but I would say somewhere between eighteen and twenty feet."

Joe whistled. "Holy shit, this thing was twenty feet long?"

Amara pursed her lips. "Or close to it."

Joe shook his head. "Man, that's one bad-ass fish."

Amara scrutinized the specimen a moment longer. Then her eyes narrowed. "Yes, but it looks like we've got something a lot *more* bad-ass swimming around out there."

"Why do you say that?" Joe asked.

"Look." Amara pointed to the severed end of the fish's head. "This fish was somebody's *dinner*. The rest of its body was taken off in one bite. You can see the gouged out tooth marks where something bit down on it, shearing right through flesh and bone."

"Like a shark?" Adam asked.

"No way. Bigger than that. Much bigger. Also, the teeth are conical in shape, not triangular." Ignoring the freezing temperatures, she removed her coat and leaned down, bending her arm at the elbow. With a quick glance at her two comrades, she inserted the meaty part of her forearm directly into one of the semi-circular tooth marks. It fit. Perfectly.

"Good lord," Amara muttered, raising her blood-streaked elbow and gawking at it. She could smell the fish's aroma on her arm, its odor pungent and alien. Her frozen breaths became rapid as she numbly accepted her coat back from Adam.

"Any ideas?" he asked. "A whale, maybe?"

She shook her head.

"So, what do you want to do?"

Amara shivered involuntarily, then shook it off and drew herself erect. "Okay, first thing's first, guys. This specimen needs to be protected at all costs. I want you to gather any data you can, then I want it sealed and kept frozen."

"You got it, boss," Adam said. "Joe, help me with the lid?"

Joe nodded, reaching down and raising the crate's cover. Handing one end to Adam, they lowered it back in place, sealing the mysterious fish's head inside its insulated coffin.

"What's next?" Joe asked.

Amara ground her teeth as she mulled things over. "We prepare material for a press release."

"What about our mission?"

"The mission goes ahead," she said as she folded her arms across her chest. "We have too much invested. We'll present our toothy friend to the world when we get back."

Adam said, "Hey, if you're right about this thing, we'll be famous."

"Oh, I'm right. But I do have important questions we need answered."

"Like what?"

"Like where this thing came from and how many more are out there. Who sent this to us?"

"I don't know," Adam said. "Joe, you have the packing slip?"

"Yeah, it's right here." Joe reached into his pocket and extracted a folded letter. "It was attached to the outside of the crate." He handed it to her.

Amara's eyes scanned the yellow piece of paper. Her eyebrows lowered and her jaw tightened up. "Well, that answers one question."

"Why, what's up?" Joe asked.

"Never mind," Amara said. She tossed the steel forceps to Adam. "You guys get this taken care of and keep it under wraps. I don't want any of our interns emailing their friends and letting the cat out of the bag." She turned to leave, muttering irritably under her breath.

Adam wore a concerned look as he stared after her, "What did you say?"

Amara looked back at him. "There's someone I need to talk to." Clutching the packing slip tightly in her hand, she made a beeline for her quarters.

———

Swimming silently just beneath the surface, the blue whale cow rose for a quick breath before continuing on her voyage. At one hundred and nineteen feet in length, the colossal *Balaenoptera musculus* and her kind were the largest creatures to inhabit the planet. The truest of titans, they dwarfed the biggest terrestrial dinosaurs that ever lived, and exceeded even the prehistoric fish *Leedsichthys* in both length and mass.

Like *Leedsichthys* before it, the huge whale was a harmless plankton feeder, gorging herself daily on five tons of krill filtered through baleen plates projecting from her upper jaw. This endless food supply, coupled with the water's life sustaining embrace, enabled the cetacean to achieve an astounding natural weight of one hundred and ninety tons. Currently, the female was even heavier, weighing closer to two hundred.

She was pregnant, and her calf was almost due. Soon, she would give birth, releasing her twenty-five foot offspring into the surrounding sea. A caring and experienced mother, the gigantic female would provide her rapidly growing infant with over one hundred gallons of fat-rich milk each day, and would continue to care for and protect the helpless calf for the next seven to eight months.

Submerging deeper, the whale moved ponderously along, scanning the surrounding seas with active sonar as she went. Every so often, she emitted a deep rumbling sound, a call so low in pitch it could be felt as well as heard. The reverberating bellow was a long distance call that traveled far underwater, enabling the gentle giant to communicate with others of her kind across distances measuring hundreds of miles.

As she rested some forty miles off the coast of Boca Grande, the colossal female picked up the resounding replies of several of her species, all many miles in the distance. One was from a big male, her current calves' sire, in fact. The two others were adolescent females, one of whom she gave birth to five years earlier. The cow sighed loudly, the mournful sound resonating through the water.

Once, there had been many of her kind. At one point, they had numbered four hundred thousand strong. That was before the humans and their noisy metal ships had taken their grisly toll. Each year, tens of thousands of the harmless cetaceans were mercilessly slaughtered, their bodies melted down and consumed. After a mere forty years, over ninety-nine percent of the great animals were eradicated. Now a protected species, their numbers were slowly rebounding, with a currently stable population of some ten thousand adults.

Emitting a series of quick clicks and pings, the blue whale's sonar echolocation brought the surrounding waters to life in vivid detail. Given the accuracy and efficiency of her sonar, eyesight was more a luxury than a necessity.

As her brain transformed sound waves into images, she sensed all that went on around her. She knew instantly that the cloud-like school of krill she followed would continue on for many miles, assuring her several more days of bountiful feeding before she migrated to the place she would birth her calf. A thousand yards to her left, she detected a pod of bluefin tuna, cruising by at high speed, scattering a school of frightened bluefish as they went. Behind them, a prowling eighteen-foot white shark provided the reason for their impetus.

Oblivious to the nearby predator, the enormous female continued on with a flick of her twenty-five foot flukes. Again, her rumbling vocalizations echoed underwater, informing the other, far-off titans of her impending approach.

The nearby white shark meant nothing. By size alone, the gigantic blue whale had no natural enemies. Not since the prehistoric shark *Carcharodon megalodon* died off had there been anything that swam the seven seas that would even consider challenging one of the sulfur-bottomed titans.

———

The creature picked up the sound of the whale's booming calls from thirty miles away. It ran silently, relying on its incredible sense of smell and the repeated vocalizations of its prey to guide it. Ravenous from the previous night's exertions, the predator accelerated to its top cruising speed, striving to close the distance between itself and its potential meal.

Closing to within five hundred yards, the creature peered into the gloom, studying the noisy life form. A ring of specialized bones encircling its eyes compressed inward to aid its sight. Unlike the enormous fish and squid it often hunted, it possessed binocular vision and could see superbly underwater, even over extreme distances. Focusing hard, it made out the outline of the unfamiliar animal looming in the distance.

As it moved in for a closer look, the creature became fascinated by the sheer size of the other. For the first time in decades something gave it pause. Not since it reached adulthood, some forty years prior, had it seen a living thing that exceeded it in size.

The creature hesitated. Its instincts for caution in the presence of a larger predator were honed by days spent hiding out from its own kind. Its appetite temporarily suppressed, it became content with running parallel to the whale, observing its movements and probing for weaknesses.

———

The blue whale was alarmed. She had sensed the unknown creature's presence as it attempted to approach her from the rear. Whatever was pursuing her now swam a hundred yards off her starboard side, following soundlessly along, matching her speed. Where she went, it went. When she changed direction, the newcomer did too.

A quick scan from the whale's sonar told her that her mysterious admirer was *not* another whale. In fact, it wasn't mammalian at all. It appeared to be some kind of gigantic reptile. Judging from its teeth, it was a predator, and from its half-opened jaws, a hungry one.

Snorting loudly in alarm, the blue whale cow's next course of action was instinctive and immediate. Fearing for the safety of her unborn calf, the giant female rose to the surface, spouting noisily while taking in a tremendous breath of air. Then she sounded, accelerating with all of her strength as she sought to flee the enormous carnivore that hounded her.

———

As he climbed back over the paint-chipped gunnels of *Deep Trouble*, Jake glanced at the antiquated vessel's well maintained racks of oxygen tanks and gear. He paused, shaking off a sudden chill that radiated through his powerful frame, and took a moment to center himself. He looked down, his expression regretful as he checked his day's paperwork. Nailing that cocky troublemaker Brad Harcourt with a pile of well deserved fines, as well as a court appearance, had certainly been a pick-me-up, but being onboard dive boats always brought Jake unpleasant memories. He checked the time. It was almost an hour past his shift's end. He frowned. There was no one waiting for him at home, and as the main source of law and order in Paradise Cove, he didn't think twice about pulling extra hours. But a sideways glance at Chris told him his youthful deputy was predictably anxious to be out and about his business.

"Thanks, Pete," he yelled to the boat's heavyset captain. "I've got everything I need for my report. I'll send you a copy for your insurance company. If I find out anything, I'll be sure to call."

"Thanks, Jake," Pete replied, good-naturedly. He nodded his bearded head and disappeared below deck.

"Let's get going, kid," Jake said, grabbing onto a side rail as he climbed deftly aboard. Thirsty from the day's heat, he reached down into a small cooler, grabbed an ice-cold can of diet cola, and cracked its tab. He savored a long draught from the perspiring can, then glanced over at Chris to see if he wanted one.

"No thanks, chief. I'm good."

"Suit yourself. Say, it's getting late and you must be tired. What do you say we call it a day?"

Chris smiled, eagerly cracking his knuckles. "Sounds good to me."

Nodding, Jake took another sip and inserted the *Infidel's* key to turn over the ignition. Instead of starting smoothly, the powerful Yamaha engine made the same screeching noise it had earlier. He cranked it repeatedly, making several attempts before he got the five-year-old outboard to come to life. He gave Chris an annoyed look. "I thought I asked you to have the motor looked over back at the dock?"

"I tried, chief," Chris explained, "but Sal said he was full up and couldn't give it a good once-over until tomorrow afternoon. He said to bring her back around three."

"Wonderful." *Story of my life*, Jake mused. *Another much-needed repair put on hold.* He reached down with his free hand, threw off their mooring lines, and started them moving gently away from the dock. Just then his radio squawked loudly, causing him to spill the remaining half of his soda on himself. He cursed as he grabbed his radio. "This is Sheriff Braddock."

"Jake, it's Molly," his dispatcher radioed back. "I got a very insistent call from Ben Stillman over at *Above the Claw*. He wants to know if you were able to look into his missing lobster traps yet. Over."

"Tell him that's a negative," Jake said, wiping irritably at his soaked uniform shirt. With an effort, he kept the exasperation out of his voice. "We weren't able to make it out that far today. Too many local issues, including some boat trouble. Tell him I'll be out there in the morning and I'll call him when we come in. Over."

"Thanks, Jake. Over and out."

Jake permitted himself a low growl of irritation. There weren't many people he felt that way about, but he couldn't stand Ben Stillman. It amazed him how Molly managed to stay so nice when forced to deal with idiots like that. Still annoyed, he removed his soggy shirt and reached into his steering console. He extracted an old Hawaiian shirt he had folded inside and put it on, tails out. Comfortable now, he clipped his badge to his belt, then turned toward Chris, who was already in the process of unloading and storing his sidearm. As Jake watched him, he chuckled. He knew from experience that the kid would have his gear stowed and be back in civilian clothes long before they reached shore.

"Strictly between you and me, Chris," Jake reached down and adjusted their trim, "I think Ben Stillman's either a lousy lobster fisherman or the fat bastard's eating all the profits himself."

Chris shook his head, laughing. He stopped suddenly, opened his mouth to speak, but then hesitated. His expression grew uncharacteristically serious. "Hey, chief . . . can I ask you something?"

"Sure, kid. What's up?"

As he watched, Chris's face contorted as if he tasted something bitter.

"It's about the girl I've been seeing . . ."

Jake nodded. "The new one you were talking about before?" A nightmarish thought popped into his head. *Oh God, please don't tell me she's pregnant.*

Chris took in a breath. "Yeah . . . I mean, we've only been going out a few months, and maybe it shouldn't be an issue yet, since we're not going steady yet and all . . . but–"

Jake raised a calming hand. "Take it easy, kid. What's the problem?"

"I think she's cheating on me."

"You think or you know?"

Chris folded his arms across his chest and stared crestfallen at the *Infidel's* deck. "Well, a few weeks ago, she asked me if I'd mind if some other guy started paying her bills."

"Paying her bills? *Sheesh.* Is this girl a pro?"

"Not that I know of . . ."

"I'm sorry, kid. Keep going."

"The other night, I saw a text come in on her cell phone while she was in the shower. It was pretty obvious . . ."

Jake slowed their pace to a crawl, the sleek patrol boat easing its way along. He studied his deputy's wounded expression and measured his next words with care.

"Listen . . ." He cleared his throat. "You can't blame yourself. It happens. I went through it once. Before I met Samantha I dated someone I was head over heels for. And she put me through hell."

Chris looked shocked. "Really?"

"Yes, really. Her name was Anita. She was a tall, Amazonian beauty from one of those war-torn eastern European countries. Hair like spun gold and built like a . . . well, never mind."

"Wow, she sounds like trouble."

"Oh, she certainly was," Jake grinned ruefully.

"So . . . what happened?"

Jake's eyes softened as he allowed himself the memory. "She went back home to renew her visa, came back knocked up with some rich guy's baby."

Chris's face changed color and he nearly choked. "Holy shit! Are you serious?"

"Yes."

"Oh, man, Jake. What did you do?"

"What any guy in my position should do, and what you're going to have to," he said, giving Chris a stern-but-supportive look. "I walked away. But I did it like a man, with my head held high."

Chris gnawed his lower lip raw. "Well, mine's gonna get hers, when I'm done telling her a thing or two . . ."

Jake reached over and rested a hand on his deputy's shoulder. "Forget it. She's not worth it. You've got a heart of gold, and you deserve better. Besides, people like that usually get what they deserve."

Chris took a deep breath, exhaled slowly and nodded.

They spent the next few minutes cruising in silence. As they circled the farthest point of the marina, Jake's eyes narrowed. He threw the *Infidel* into neutral, grabbed his binoculars, and scanned the channel, focusing his lenses on the *Harbinger*. He spotted a large flatbed tractor-trailer pulling up directly adjacent to the big whaler with a covered load, and several members of her crew coming down to meet it.

Jake turned to his deputy. "Hey, kid . . . I think I'm going to stick around for a while and check out a few things."

"Um, okay . . ."

"Don't worry. I know you're itching to get home," Jake nodded. "If I drop you off at the landing, do you think you can find a way back to your car and meet me here in the morning?"

"No problem, chief. I'll just call my soon-to-be-ex-girlfriend and have her pick me up. Probably cost me dinner or something." Chris paused thoughtfully. He cracked one knuckle hesitantly, then checked his pants pockets. "Um . . . hey, Jake, can you lend me another twenty bucks until payday? Please?"

"Oh, *brother*." Jake made a show of rolling his eyes as he reached for his wallet and turned the *Infidel* back toward shore.

Ten minutes later, Jake piloted the *Infidel* next to the *Harbinger's* deepwater mooring. Slowing to a crawl, he pulled up beside the enormous, barnacle-coated pilings that supported the ancient steel and cement dock. Ignoring the sun's oppressive rays, he grabbed hold of the closest piling and tied his bobbing craft to a pair of cleats. He donned his shades and checked his watch before climbing the nearest ladder.

Paradise Cove Pier, or, "the fishing pier," as it was known to the locals, who caught snapper and jacks all along its one hundred yard length, was an ambitious, early twentieth century construct. Situated right along the drop-off point that separated Paradise Cove from the sound, proper, the pier was immensely popular with tourists and anglers.

As a dock though, it saw little activity. Elevated fifteen feet above the high tide mark, the cove side of the pier was universally rejected by boat slip renters, who turned their noses up at the idea of climbing a slippery ladder every time they wanted to use their vessels. There were more convenient slips readily available. Actually, the only docking use the pier ever experienced occurred when a large ship such as the *Harbinger* arrived.

Jake grabbed the gull dropping-encrusted railing at the top of the ladder and vaulted onto the hard surface of the pier. He was surprised to find no one in sight, especially since there was a miniature submarine resting on the flatbed he'd spotted earlier.

Moving over to the big tractor-trailer, he scrutinized the vessel it carried. At seven feet in width and over twenty feet in length, the gleaming white submersible was something Jake had never seen before. Cylindrical in shape, the *William* rested on two metallic pontoons, assumedly used to control the vessel's ballast. There was a large prop and rudder assembly comprising the aft section, and a small conning tower to direct movement located centrally above the craft.

What Jake found to be the most interesting part of the tiny sub was its prow. Shielded by four intersecting tubular pieces of steel, the nose of the *William* consisted of a five-foot wide hemisphere of some lightly tinted material that formed an observation bubble. Shielded from the ocean's deadly effects, its occupants could view the surrounding sea with ease. Extending out from beneath this bubble was a pair of long metal arms equipped with pincers on their ends and an array of under-water cameras and lights.

Jake shielded his eyes with one hand in an attempt to block out the sun's glare. He pressed his forehead against the bubble and peered inside, trying to discern the helm's layout. The tinting made it difficult to see, but he could make out a pair of contoured chairs. There was a confusing array of equipment arranged toward the nose of the sub, and the equipment designs were like nothing he'd ever seen. Fascinated, Jake continued to study them, straining his eyes in an effort to make out details. Just then, vice-like fingers dug deep into his shoulder.

"What ya tink ya doin, mon?"

Caught off guard, Jake glimpsed a hulking male figure brandishing a heavy wrench. A lifetime of martial arts training took over. Spinning around, he tore his attacker's hand free with a circular motion and twisted it about, maneuvering the trapped limb into an agonizing wrist and elbow lock that brought the yelping man to his knees.

As he noticed the wrench was still in his attacker's hand, Jake dramatically increased pressure on the imprisoned arm. He heard a loud scream, accompanied by the satisfying clatter of metal as the heavy weapon dropped from nerveless fingers.

"Aargh! Gosh, mon, what da hell ya doin?" his opponent sputtered struggling ineffectually to rise.

"What am I doing? You see this?" Jake freed one hand and yanked his shirt tail up, exposing his badge. "In the future, you might want to take a good look at who you're dealing with before you start putting your hands on people."

An alarmed voice called out, "Jake? What the heck is going on?"

Looking up, Jake saw Amara Takagi walking nervously in his direc-tion with two men in tow. One he recognized as Stanley Berkowitz, the sniveling bill collector. The other, from his dress and mannerisms, had to be the flatbed driver.

"Afternoon, Dr. Takagi," Jake said through his teeth. He realized to his annoyance he'd left his handcuffs onboard, and tried to look as nonchalant as possible. "Sorry about the intrusion. I'm just having a little conversation with someone. Be out of your hair in a minute."

"A conversation?" Amara repeated. She moved surprisingly close to the two struggling men. "Well Jake, if you could finish having your 'discussion' with my first mate, I could really use his help getting this thing loaded." She gestured toward the mini-sub.

"First mate, huh?" Jake asked. "Well, if he's going to go around assaulting people, maybe you should keep him on the ship." He nodded at the fallen wrench for emphasis.

"Jake, I honestly don't think Willie was trying to attack you. He probably thought you were snooping around our very expensive DSOV. And *this*," she picked up the discarded tool, hefting it for effect, "is what we use to attach our winch assembly in order to bring her onboard. Now, can you let him go, please? We plan to sail in the morning, and we've got a lot of work to do."

The sincerity on Amara's face quickly convinced Jake of the truth. He relinquished his grip and reached down to help the disheveled man to his feet.

Obviously embarrassed, the *Harbinger's* first mate avoided making eye contact with Jake. Sullenly rubbing his wrist, he looked to Amara for support.

"Thanks, Jake," she explained. "I'm sorry I wasn't here to introduce you guys. Unfortunately, I was being forced to address Mr. Harcourt's outrageous docking bill." Behind her, Stanley Berkowitz fretted, his weasel-like appearance the same as always. "Do you have any idea how much this character is charging us for our brief stay?"

"I can only imagine." Jake glanced at Stanley and fought back a smirk. He turned toward the tall fellow in the Bahamian shirt and khakis and extended his hand. "Sheriff Jake Braddock. Sorry about all of this. I hope you'll be decent enough to accept my apology for the misunderstanding."

"No problem, mon," the big Jamaican replied. He hesitantly took Jake's hand. "I understand how tings looked."

"Jake, this is Willie Daniels," Amara said, beaming so brightly she lightened everyone's mood. "He's my second in command and co-designer of the twelve million dollars of unbridled excitement you see lying before you." She spread her arms wide, trying to take in the entire mini-sub with the gesture.

"A pleasure, Willie," Jake nodded. He followed Amara's stare back to the unusual craft. "So, what exactly is this thing? A DSOV, you called it?"

"Deep Submersible Observation Vehicle," Amara said. She leaned her head back, catching Jake off guard with her smile. "The *William* weighs just over six tons. She's got both battery and diesel power, can carry up to four passengers including pilot and manipulator, and has a top submerged speed of five knots. With over four hundred hours of total life support, she's going to be our eyes and ears for an exciting new age of cetacean studies."

Jake nodded, impressed with her pride in the gleaming white craft. "The *William*, you said?" he asked, looking at Willie. "Named after you?"

"Actually, da wee sub is named after da great bard himself," Willie said, bowing at the waist as he continued. "As am I honored ta be."

"The bard?"

"William Shakespeare, Jake," Amara said. "Mr. Daniels here is the world's biggest Shakespeare fan."

Jake pursed his lips and nodded. "Really?"

"Oh, really," Amara continued with a smirk. "In fact, I don't know how I'd survive some of those boring days at sea, sitting around and waiting for something to come within range of our cameras and acoustics, if I didn't have him quoting Hamlet all day."

"I see," Jake said. "And the design thing? I thought you said you studied whales? You design submarines too?"

Amara laughed, "No, Jake. I told you I have a degree in underwater robotics, which has nothing to do with submersible design. The main portion of our mini-sub is a standard construct made by an affiliated offshore manufacturer."

She ran her hands over the *William's* prow as she spoke. "*Our* big contribution," she said, pointing to Willie and herself, "was in the design for the manipulators."

"The arms?" Jake pointed at the six-foot long extensions.

"Exactly. We have a state-of-the-art, neurologically linked control system that lets the manipulator's operator control the mechanical arms as if they were his or her own. And with just as much control and dexterity, I might add. With a little practice . . ." She raised one eyebrow for effect. "You could pick up an egg with one of these things without breaking it."

"Remind me to never let you make me breakfast." Jake's face colored the moment the words left his lips. "I mean, not that you'd be interested in cooking me breakfast . . ."

Amara grinned. "Actually, if you experienced my culinary skills, I don't think you'd be interested." She winked at Willie. "Right?"

Her first mate leaned forward, palms on his thighs, and chortled like a braying sea lion. "It's true, mon. I taught her last omelette was hash browns!"

Jake chuckled. "Sounds yummy."

Amara looked up, gave the crewmembers staring down at them from the *Harbinger's* railing the thumbs-up sign. "I'm sorry, but if you don't mind excusing me, Jake, we've got to get the *William* loaded and secured before it gets dark."

"No problem, doc," Jake said. He looked up, his gaze following the cable that hung suspended over the waiting mini-sub. It was attached to the nearer of a pair of matching cranes lining the rear portion of the big ship. They were situated port and starboard, each just inside and above the gunnels. They seemed like miniature construction cranes, their jointed arms controlled by an operator who sat cocooned inside a tiny cockpit, swiveling the arms back and forth with a joystick. "Say, this may sound like a dumb question, but did those cranes come with the ship?"

"You are correct, Jake," Amara said. "Those cranes were originally used to manipulate the carcasses of slaughtered whales, to prevent them from drifting or sinking. Now, we put them to productive use, such as loading heavy crates of gear and supplies, bringing the *Sycophant* on deck for servicing, and of course, launching and retrieving our new submersible." She thumped the *William's* hull proudly for effect.

"The *Sycophant*?" Jake echoed, looking up at the *Harbinger's* sprawling decks.

"Our Zodiac." Amara pointed down at the waterline, near the big ship's aft section. A sixteen-foot, outboard-equipped inflatable bobbed gently up and down from where it was tied off to the ship's metal launching platform. "We use it to do reconnaissance while we're anchored, and to move gear and personnel to the scene of an Orca attack."

"I see," Jake said.

The portside crane operator swiveled the diesel-powered device and lowered its connector assembly toward the *William*. Jake was impressed. As soon as the cable came within range, Willie moved into position, using his wrench to make the necessary connections between the mini-sub and the winch hook.

"Just one more question, doc," Jake said.

Amara turned toward him. "Yes?"

"I notice you brought your ship in stern first. As the helmsman, knowing that the shallower portions of this cove could pose a serious risk to your props, wouldn't it have made more sense to pull in prow first and then back out later?"

Amara smiled sweetly. "Jake, from the moment I met you I could tell you have a remarkably firm grasp of the obvious," she said. "Actually, you are quite correct. However, our starboard side crane is on the fritz right now – some sort of hydraulic problem. And, since I doubt even a big, strong officer of the law like you is capable of picking up a six-ton submersible and carrying it onboard for us, I figured it made more sense to back the ship in carefully, and then use the portside crane."

"Serves me right for asking," Jake said. Shaking his head amusedly, he turned and walked away.

———

As Jake headed back toward his patrol boat, Amara watched him leave. Behind her, Willie looked up from his work and cleared his throat. She glanced over and noticed him intently following her gaze.

"Well, what ya tink?" he said with a conspiratorial grin. "Interesting fella, wouldn't ya say?"

Amara blinked and shook her head in disbelief. "Are you kidding me? He's a cop. Not exactly my type."

"Yeah, but we both know him got some *damn* strong hands, mon." Willie rubbed his arm and smirked. "Can't ya just imagine dem gently massaging dat bad hip of yours when ya wake up in da morning?"

"I'm trying not to. And in case you didn't notice, he's wearing a wedding ring."

"So . . . when he massages ya, he'll take it off!"

"Very funny. Seriously, though. Even if he wasn't married, we both know the only man in my life is my work."

Willie gave forth an exaggerated sigh, then turned to her and winked. "Oh well. I guess I'll keep looking, den. After all, I can't have ya ending up some crotchety old spinsta, ya know."

"As always, you're my guardian angel, Willie," Amara laughed. She looked up, arching her slim neck as she yelled up at her waiting crane operator and crew. "All right you lazybones, let's move with a porpoise!"

Both guffawing now, the two friends went about their business.

Far below, Jake Braddock was already back aboard the *Infidel* and motoring out to sea.

———

The creature advanced on the blue whale. The sight of potential prey fleeing had stimulated its hunting instincts and it surrendered to its primeval urges to stalk the larger animal. Closing to within fifty yards of its quarry, the creature scanned its target's colossal bulk. Its jaw muscles flexed in anticipation, yet caution kept it from blindly attacking.

Suddenly, its deep-set eyes blinked. The larger animal appeared to be struggling along, as if it were suffering from a wound or malady of some kind. An injured animal meant an easy kill.

Millions of years of engrained instincts and evolution took over. The creature's fear of becoming prey vanished and a voracious feeding response took over. Accelerating to maximum velocity with its enormous fangs bared, it slammed into the whale with the speed and power of a freight train. Crunching down, its arsenal of teeth sheared through thick layers of blubber, tearing deeply into the muscles of the whale's exposed flank.

The attack drew a fountain of blood that instantly stained the surrounding seas a bright crimson. Though unable to completely avoid the attack, the cow sensed the creature's strike as it was about to happen. Spiraling away in an effort to protect its exposed abdominal region, the whale drastically diminished the force of the blow.

The cetacean uttered a grunt of pain and fought back ferociously, slamming its twenty-five foot flukes down upon its attacker's exposed muzzle with a force sufficient to shatter a bull killer whale's spine. The blow was staggering, and left the creature stunned. Its thick skull ringing, it drifted lopsided toward the surface, slowly swiveling its monstrous head from side to side.

The blue whale wasted no time. Disregarding its injury, it accelerated to full speed, seeking to put as much distance between them as possible.

Drifting upward, the creature regained consciousness in a loud blast of air bubbles. It shook its head violently as it righted itself with its flippers and took in the situation. Its opponent was moving rapidly away, trailing blood but apparently unhampered by its injuries.

It considered breaking off the chase, but the smell of fresh blood wafting through the water column continued to call to it. It opened and closed its jaws as it hovered in place, tasting the shredded fragments of tissue that remained embedded in its teeth. The familiar flavor of mammalian blubber greeted its taste buds. It was similar to that of the elephant seals it had fed upon its entire adult life. The instant association linking the two tastes triggered a crave response in the creature's primitive brain, reinforcing its desire to make the larger animal prey.

With a water-muffled roar, it took off at top speed. Within moments it reached a velocity approaching fifty miles an hour. Closing the gap between itself and the whale, it moved in from the rear, readying itself for its next assault.

The whale sensed its enemy's approach and began to swim in an evasive pattern, its giant flukes working furiously to speed it along.

Only twenty yards back, the creature hesitated, its ruby-colored eyes fixed on the blue whale's barnacle-tipped tail. Its head still rang from the force of the thunderous blow it sustained, and it knew better than to make the same mistake twice.

Toothy jaws spread, the creature accelerated straight up behind the fleeing whale and lunged savagely forward.

This time it went for the whale's flukes.

FIVE

E arly the following morning, Jake loitered by the docks. He leaned against the wooden railing bordering the marina, shifting his weight and picking at an annoying splinter that dug into his forearm. His gaze lingered on a nearby throng of pleasure boats, anchored in their berths. An eerie morning mist wafted off the harbor's waters, the smell of fresh ocean air mixing with the distinct odors of diesel fuel and rotting fish.

Oblivious to the gradually awakening businesses springing to life behind him, Jake focused his attention past the sheltering docks, out toward the fog-enshrouded sea. Below, a pair of shrieking gulls fought over the putrid head of one of the largest barracuda he'd ever seen. Other seabirds began to gather, eager to join in the floating feast. He grimaced at the squabbling birds. His jaw muscles bunched up and a too familiar frown crept across his bronzed face.

He focused on the fog. Overnight, a pea soup-thick layer of the stuff had blanketed the sound like a snowdrift, whitewashing everything in sight and posing a hazard to boaters and jet skiers alike. The fog was incredibly dense, heavier than it had been in years. The last time he saw weather like this he'd been in a helicopter, flying toward the worst day of his life.

Jake flinched as the unwelcomed images jabbed into his brain. He sensed himself begin to stagger and made a frantic grab, his nails digging into the railing's rough wood. He gave a low gasp as he saw Sam's face, eyes wide and terror-stricken amidst the swirling blackness. She was flailing wildly, her limbs thrashing against the suffocating pressure, her mouth poised to scream . . .

Jake shuddered, and with effort freed himself from the awful image. He leaned heavily on the rail and gulped a deep breath, cursing as he glared back at the fog. He realized something wasn't right. He could feel it clawing cat-like in his gut, a dull ache in the pit of his stomach. He dismissed the possibility of a pending squall. South Florida's violent storm season was hardly in effect, and other than the usual sporadic showers, the forecast for the rest of the week looked remarkably good. It most likely wasn't trouble brewing in town, either. To the best of his knowledge, as of the previous evening no problems had presented themselves.

Frustrated, Jake finally shrugged it off. He turned away from the railing and began clomping back along the dock, the worn wooden deck boards creaking loudly beneath his heavy work boots. He checked his watch. It was 7:30 a.m., and still quiet at the marina. Only fishermen and their charters were up and about this early in the morning, and most of them had already left the harbor. With half an hour to go before Chris Meyers was due to show up – assuming he wasn't late again – Jake began to stroll toward the *Cove Hove* for breakfast. He was halfway up the gangplank when he heard a familiar voice.

"Why, Jake Braddock, how the hell are you, young fellow?"

Turning toward the voice, a rare smile flashed across Jake's rugged features. "Captain Phil! Hey, I haven't seen you all season. How are you?"

Jake walked over to the grizzled charter captain. The old man was dressed in shorts and a faded t-shirt and was seated in the fighting chair of a docked Bertram. Still smiling, Jake stepped over the vessel's gunnels and took his hand in a firm handshake.

"I'm hanging in there, Jake," the elderly fisherman said. "Some days are better than others. You know how it is."

"I do indeed, Captain Phil." Jake nodded, still smiling, and gestured at the big boat. "So, how's the *Sayonara* treating you these days?"

"This old rust bucket?" Phil chuckled, thumping the Bertram's teak flooring with one foot. "She's like me, a little worn out, but somehow still managing to keep afloat!"

As Jake settled back onto the transom of the vintage fishing boat, the old man's grin sent him spiraling back in time. He was fourteen years old again and waking up to what promised to be a gorgeous, sunny Saturday. It was day one of his highly anticipated summer vacation, and he wanted to enjoy every moment of it. He planned on fishing every minute, torturing the unwary residents of the canal behind his family's home with his newfound angling skills. He had a sweet rod and reel combo waiting for him that he purchased with the money he saved doing odd jobs. He also had a fancy, stake-in-the-ground rod holder, to keep it from being pulled in by some oversized bass or channel cat, a fully loaded tackle box, and an aerated bait bucket as well.

Jake smiled and rolled lazily onto his side. Everything was going to be great. He'd won every fencing meet he entered for the last twelve months, and his parents were thrilled. More importantly, they were getting along. Best of all, as long as he did his chores without being asked, his father acted surprisingly civilized – meaning he wasn't pushing him around.

The sudden thump of a car door caused Jake to open his eyes, interrupting his thoughts. He leaned groggily up on one elbow and glanced through the blinds next to his bed. He checked the sun's position and looked at his alarm clock. 7 a.m. It was still early, and the day was full of promise. He sat up and stretched, smelling the heady fragrance of a nearby grove of orange trees wafting through his open window.

Voices, punctuated by another slamming car door, caused Jake to peer outside. To his bemusement, his mother and father were lugging cardboard boxes and oversized suitcases to the family's well-worn Bronco, loading them into its spacious cargo area. When he saw his father carrying his golf clubs, Jake grew animated. He sprang out of bed, put on his slippers, and made his way downstairs on quick kitten's feet.

His mother was holding the door as his father carried two weighty cartons outside. She looked up as Jake approached, her smile a warm and welcoming one.

"Jake, you're up," she beamed, rushing over and hugging him.

The screen door banged shut as John Braddock disappeared outside.

"Mom, what's going on?" Jake asked sleepily. He rubbed his eyes, looking confusedly at their disheveled kitchen and pantry.

His father abruptly reappeared in the doorway. "Your mother and I are taking a trip," he announced with a grin.

"A trip?" Jake gazed alarmingly at the empty kitchen cabinets. Their doors were ajar, their shelves stripped. It looked more like the family was moving.

"Yes, sweetie," his mother said. "Your father got an unexpected invitation to spend some time with his relatives in South Carolina, hunting and fishing and discussing a possible business venture. He's taken a leave of absence from work."

"Am I going with you?"

"Sorry, kiddo," his father interjected. "It's adults only." His smile broadened. "Don't worry; we'll only be gone four weeks."

"Four *weeks*?" Jake echoed. His jaw dropped.

"Actually, it's only three and a half, sweetie," his mom said, noticing his flustered expression. "You're going to be fine." She pointed at the coffee table. "There's an envelope there with plenty of money for groceries, and a number where you can reach us if you need anything. I made you some sandwiches, too, so you'll have something to eat while you're fishing the canal."

"Um, thanks, Mom," Jake managed. His head shook involuntarily but he tried to appear calm, as if nothing out of the ordinary was happening. Inwardly, however, he was frightened and confused, his head spinning at the sudden change in events. A month by himself? He'd never been left alone longer than an overnight. How would he get to the store? Who would look after him? Who was going to clean the house?

John Braddock wrestled the last suitcase out and popped back inside. He turned to his wife. "Okay, darling. I think that's about it. Did we cover the entire checklist?"

His mom checked her notepad. "I think so . . ."

"Great. Why don't you go get yourself situated, dear? I'll go over our list of do's and don'ts with our deputy sheriff here."

"Sounds great," Jake's mother said. She gave him a huge hug and a kiss on the cheek, holding his face with both hands. Her smile was wide, but there was a hint of nervousness about her. "Don't be scared. You're gonna have a blast. And if you need anything, we're just a call away." She kissed him on the forehead and pulled reluctantly away. "I love you."

"I love you too, Mom," he mumbled. He stood there in a daze, watching her walk away. It felt like she was walking out of his life. He couldn't believe this was happening. And he didn't know what he was going to–

The moment his mother was gone his dad leaned over and snatched up the envelope of cash. He opened it, counting out three hundred dollars in twenties, and put it in his pocket.

Jake turned pale. His surprised inhalation was a fear-filled gasp. "W-what are you doing?"

His father looked over and gave him one of his trademark smirks. "What, you thought I was gonna leave you all this money so you could blow it on the arcade or more fishing tackle? Oh, no . . ."

Jake tried to speak but couldn't. Next, his father looked amusedly at the phone number his mother left.

"You won't need this, either," he said, his eyes cold and hard. He crumpled up the paper and put it in his pocket, too.

"But, what am I supposed to do?" Jake stammered. "How am I supposed to eat?"

"You'll find a way," John Braddock remarked. "Maybe you can eat all those fish you planned on catching all summer, goofing off."

Jake glanced wildly at the door, his breathing shallow and rapid.

"Don't even think about it," his father warned. He rested one hand on the teen's shoulder with frightening pressure. "Don't cause your mother any trouble before we leave."

His bloodshot eyes bored into his son's.

Jake's head wilted toward the floor. He swallowed hard and nodded.

"Good," his father said. He headed to the door. "Look at it this way . . . maybe the next few weeks will make a man out of you." He shook his head in disgust. "God knows following in your mother's footsteps with all that fencing crap sure hasn't."

John Braddock walked out without saying goodbye. Jake heard the truck's door open and close and the big V-8 start up. He stood statue-still as cold fear ran through him in uncontrollable shivers.

Suddenly, the Bronco's engine turned off. He heard his father's heavy footsteps draw near and his heart did handsprings in his chest. *Maybe this was all just a joke, or some sick test? Maybe his dad was giving him back the money, or maybe they were taking him with them, after all?*

John Braddock walked in, shaking his head. He ignored Jake and moved wordlessly to the refrigerator. He opened it and emerged with the plate of sandwiches his wife made. He looked at Jake and grinned.

"Something for the road," he chuckled. "You know how hungry I get during long drives . . . told your mother I gave you some extra cash to make up for it."

His father guffawed as he let the screen door slam hard behind him.

The boy stayed where he was, listening as the Bronco moved out of the driveway. The sound of its noisy engine gradually faded until there was nothing – nothing but the sound of the morning breeze rustling through the trees, bringing empty promises with it. He waited a full five minutes before he sat down and started to cry.

An hour later, Jake dusted himself off. He gathered his wits about him and decided to assess the situation. Things were far grimmer than he feared. He discovered his father had thoroughly ransacked the house in his quest for provisions. A thirty-minute search garnered the teen only a can of olives, two cans of beans, four eggs, some moldy flour and a half-stick of margarine. With his savings already spent on fishing tackle, he was penniless. He tore through the house like a whirlwind, searching under couch cushions and in drawers and cupboards, hoping to find some secret stash of money. He came up with only $11.23, most of it in nickels and dimes.

Jake decided to go on the offensive. He refused to just lie down and die, as his father undoubtedly expected. He would survive, but in order to do that he needed to do what grown-ups did. He needed a job. He cleaned himself up and got dressed. It was ninety-six degrees outside, and a six mile walk to town, but he didn't care. He bolstered his courage, filled a bottle with water from the tap, pulled on his sneakers, and started out.

Six hours later, Jake found himself sitting alone on the wharf of Paradise Cove's newly renovated marina, defeated and dejected. He kicked at a loose deck board in frustration, his face contorting as he painfully stubbed his toe. His attempt at finding gainful employment had been a complete waste of time. He'd tried them all: stores, shops, even souvenir stands. They all said the same thing – he was too young and no one could hire him. He was starting to feel like a Jehovah's Witness, with door after door being slammed in his face. He was exhausted and hungry and faced with a hellish walk home, on feet that were already blistered.

"Say, there, young fellow. Why so glum?"

Jake looked up to see an old man staring down at him. He was of medium height, probably sixty, though his weathered skin and features made him look ten years older. His leathered limbs looked frail, but his eyes were as sharp as knives. They were a shark's hide gray, but kind.

"I just had a bad day," he replied, not really wanting to talk.

"How so?"

Jake's mouth opened and closed like Pac Man's. He considered telling the stranger his problems just to let off steam, but his pride decided against it. "Just some bad luck, that's all."

The old man studied him intently. His gaze grew weary after a bit and he sighed and started to turn away. "That's fishing, kid. Get used to it."

Jake's ears pricked up. "You fish?"

The old man turned back, gunmetal eyes glinting. "Oh . . . you could say that." He grinned, pointing over his shoulder at a big canyon runner docked some fifty feet downwind.

Jake was on his feet in a millisecond. "Holy cow! Is that your boat?"

"Sure is," the old man chuckled. "Name's the *Sayonara*. Had her for ten years already."

"Wow. She's a beauty."

"You fish?"

Jake gave a small nod. "A little. Freshwater mostly. Just got my first new rod and reel, but it looks like I won't be able to do much now."

The old man frowned. "Why not? Beautiful day. Weather's perfect."

Jake looked downcast. He exhaled heavily. "I gotta find a job."

"Your parents told you that?"

"Sort of . . ."

"What's your name, kid?"

Jake looked him in the eye. "Jake Braddock."

The old man extended his hand. "I'm Captain Phil Starling. How old are you, Jake?"

Jake stood up straight and shook his hand. "Fourteen. I'm big for my age."

Phil looked at him, nodding approvingly. "You're an honest man, Jake. I like that. Wanna come work for me?"

"Are you serious?"

"Heck, yeah. These days the *Sayonara*'s too much for me to handle by myself. Been thinking of hiring myself a first mate. You'd be doing me a big favor by taking the job."

Jake's eyes began to widen, but he reined himself in. "Hmm, that sounds workable. What's the pay?"

Phil's eyes twinkled and he smiled. "Forty bucks a day, plus one half of whatever tip the charter gives."

"Sounds great!" Jake exclaimed. "When can we start?"

"Actually, I've got three guys going out tomorrow. They're regulars. Can you be here at 6 a.m.?"

Jake was grinning ear to ear as he shook hands with him again. "You bet, Captain Phil. I'll be here!"

Phil tousled his hair and turned to leave. "Sounds great. See you in the morning, kid. And don't be late. We'll see what kind of fisherman you turn out to be!"

Jake nodded and watched him go, before turning to start the arduous six-mile hike back. It took him two hours, but his feet didn't bother him one bit. Surprising, considering that he skipped along for half the distance. When he got home, only his face hurt. But that was from smiling so much.

He was still smiling and nodding as his thoughts wandered back to the present. Phil Starling had proved to be a good mentor and friend at a time in his life when he needed one most. He was a fair and generous employer as well. Those carefree summers were the best of Jake's life, and a small part of him still regretted not becoming a charter fisherman. When he left for college he'd missed Phil terribly. After losing Sam and returning to Paradise Cove, the old man was one of the first people he looked up. That was when he found out about his leukemia.

"Ah, you'll be fine," Jake said, managing a lie. "You know how the old saying goes: 'Time spent fishing is not deducted from one's allotted lifespan.' You should be around 'til judgment day!"

"We'll see, matey," Phil said, turning toward the open water.

An uncomfortable silence settled between the two friends.

"So, what are you going out for?" Jake pointed at the huge rod his former employer was holding.

"Giant bluefin," Phil said keenly. "I got word of some big schools moving through the sound last night. Monsters – six or seven hundred pounders, maybe more!" He smiled excitedly, winking at Jake. "We're talking some serious sushi dollars, if you know what I mean. Anyway, we're stocked up and ready to roll. I want to be out there when the tide shifts so we can have a good shot at one."

Jake grinned. One thing he knew about addicted-for-life fishermen, no matter how sick or exhausted they felt, the prospect of catching a marine monster the size of a Honda Accord always got a rise out of them. Of course, fighting a fish with that much size and power was a risky proposition even for the very young . . .

"You did say, *we*?" Jake looked anxiously about. "You do have someone going with you, I hope?"

"Oh, sure," the old man said, shifting uncomfortably in the hard chair. "Oh geez, I'm sorry, Jake. I forgot my manners. Hey, Stevie! Can you come up here for a minute?"

"Sure thing, Uncle Phil," a voice yelled back from below deck.

A moment later, a wiry teenager popped his head up through the Bertram's double doors, springing up onto the aft deck with youthful exuberance.

"Hi there," said the smiling youngster, extending his hand. "I'm Steve."

"Jake Braddock," Jake replied affably.

"Jake Brad . . . hey, you're that fencing champion, right?" Steve gushed. "Yeah, my uncle told me all about how you used to be his first mate a long time ago. Our whole family watched you on TV when you won the gold medal. I remember that cereal box with your picture on it. Wow, you were great!"

"Thanks, kid," Jake said, feeling confused and a little embarrassed. "Your . . . uncle?"

"That's right, matey." Phil grinned. "My brother's youngest, in fact. Stephanie and I were never able to have kids of our own. So, I'm training this young buck to take over the business for me, once I ride that big charter up to the sky." Phil winked at Jake, pointing a crusty thumb back at his nephew. "Say, Jake, does he remind you of anyone you know?"

Turning to watch the energetic teenager, who was already back hard at work checking rods and lures, stowing gear, and cleaning up at the same time, Jake had to admit he did indeed. "Maybe, Captain Phil," he smiled. "But can he set a hook on a fifty-pound Dorado, while netting another at the same time?"

"Oh, please," Phil scoffed. "As I recall, you backlashed the rod and dropped the net and the fifty-pounder into the drink. We had to use the gaff to bring it back onboard, fish and all!"

Steve Starling paused to look up from his appointed tasks, his eyes wide in mock astonishment. "I guess that's one fishing legend shot to hell."

The three men burst out laughing. Then, the uncomfortable silence started to return.

"Well, I'd better get going Phil," Jake said somberly. "I know you've got a tide to catch, along with a monster tuna, and I've gotta get some breakfast before my deputy drags his sorry butt down here."

Phil winced, and despite Jake's protestations, struggled from his chair. He extended his gnarled hand once more. "It's good to see you, kiddo," he said, smiling and shaking hands again with surprising vigor. "I'll be around for a few more weeks of the season before we take the *Sayonara* down to Key West. By the way," he half-whispered. "I heard you had another run-in with that bastard Harcourt's son the other day. Folks are saying you taught the little prick a lesson. Good for you! If you ever get tired of dealing with all the bullshit around here and you want your old job back, you just give me a call!"

"Thanks, Captain Phil," Jake said. "That's actually not a bad offer." As he turned to go, he hesitated for a moment, his eyes wandering back past the marina, out toward the fogbound sea. That same unshakable feeling of foreboding was still there. He looked back at his old friend. "Say . . . you be careful. It's been rough out there the last few days."

"Now, don't you go worrying about an old salty dog like me," Phil said as Jake hopped over the gunnels and onto the dock. "I've been doing this a long time. And a little bit of excitement comes with the territory."

As Jake walked away, Phil Starling yelled out "Hey, Jake! Don't forget the reason why we became fishermen. It's the limitless possibilities. Once you drop your bait into those briny depths, you never know *what* you're gonna get!"

Turning around and smiling sadly back at the old man, Jake nodded and waved once more as he walked toward the *Cove Hove*. Eventually, the sounds of the *Sayonara's* charter captain and mate faded in the distance.

Suddenly, the sheriff stopped in his tracks. A familiar looking limousine drove slowly through the marina, shadowed by an SUV with tinted windows. Jake's eyes narrowed. It occurred to him that Dean Harcourt might be the source of the anxiety that welled up within him. There was plenty of unfinished business between them. Whatever the case, he was not in the mood to deal with either the senator or his watchdogs this early in the morning. Especially not on an empty stomach.

Behind him, three pairs of watchful eyes tracked his every move.

———

"So, that's him, eh?" Darius Thayer leaned forward, tilting his wolfish head toward the limo's tinted windows.

"That's right," Senator Dean Harcourt said, lighting an expensive cigar. "Mr. Jake Braddock, the 'legendary' sheriff of Paradise Cove. Take a last look, Brad, because once I get my way, he won't be around any longer."

Brad Harcourt said nothing. He exhaled slowly and continued to stare out the window.

Thayer's gaze wandered from Brad back to his father. He studied the wealthy politician surreptitiously, all the while coveting the $5,000.00 Italian suit he was carelessly dripping ashes on. A heavily built man in his mid-fifties, Harcourt was the most infamous and feared resident in all of Paradise Cove, as well as Darius's employer. The head of an extremely powerful family that, among other things, owned the marina and most of the buildings that bordered it, he presided over Paradise Cove's town council. He had heavy connections with the FBI and the Coast Guard, and wielded tremendous clout within the Republican Party proper. His money, and the almost unlimited media that came with it, was the source of his power, and on the Hill they loved him.

The two men and teenager were seated in the back of Harcourt's armored limousine, its soundproof partition sealed tight. Behind them, the senator's security detail waited for instructions.

Thayer leaned back in his seat and exhaled through his nose. A lean man in his early forties, he had devious eyes he kept hidden behind a pair of Brooks Brother's glasses. He was Senator Harcourt's long-time friend, attorney, campaign manager, and a master of dirty tactics; he had an uncanny knack for finding career-destroying information. Behind closed doors it was said that, although the senator had the power, his political advisor wielded it.

"If you don't mind my saying, I honestly don't get it, Dean," Thayer commented, squinting as he removed his glasses to clean them. Outside, the object of their scrutiny disappeared into a nearby establishment. "Didn't you seek out and hire this guy in the first place? I remember you saying he was – what was the term – 'politically useful'?" Thayer replaced his glasses before continuing. "Now, all of a sudden, you want to destroy him?"

Harcourt drew fiercely on his cigar, blowing out a cloud of smoke that filled the car's interior. "Three years ago Jake Braddock was a valuable commodity. He was an Olympic caliber athlete, fresh off winning the nationals. Probably would've won metal at the Olympics if he didn't fall apart after his wife died. So, when I heard he quit competing, I snatched him up."

Thayer was already intimately familiar with everything Harcourt was saying, but for now was content to let him ramble.

"It seemed like a great move for us, Darius. Braddock was born and raised in Paradise Cove. After he lost everything and came crawling back, it was like the prodigal son returning home. He was a celebrity."

The senator paused momentarily.

"So, what went wrong?" Thayer prodded.

"Everything. The sympathy we were hoping to get from hiring him after his tragedy never materialized." The senator started to puff ferociously on his cigar, like a locomotive building up steam. "And his celebrity persona we were planning on capitalizing on, ended up being replaced by some goddamn blue-collar working-class hero etiquette I never expected. He refused to make personal appearances and wouldn't let us use his name for publicity." The senator removed his cigar and spat irritably. "And don't get me started on that interview he did . . ."

Annoyed, Harcourt stopped to tap the end of his cigar into a nearby ashtray. He reached up and scratched at a jagged scar that ran down the entire right side of his jaw.

"Still hurts?" Thayer asked.

"No, not much, but it itches a lot."

"Looks better than it did the last time I saw you."

"Oh, yeah, it's goddamn beautiful," Harcourt snorted. "In fact, I'm thinking of having a matching one done for the other side. Believe me, Darius. Not a day goes by that I don't wish that fucker lived long enough for me to give him a scar just like this."

Thayer remembered watching the scene on the evening news like it was yesterday. The media coverage of the botched assassination had been a gift from the gods. Hell, you couldn't *buy* that kind of publicity. "Listen Dean, you and I both know that scar helped win your re-election. A little sympathy goes a long way."

"Oh, yeah? Well, how about next time you take the assassin's bullet. And I'll give *you* some sympathy!"

Thayer started, but held his tongue.

His eyes fierce, Harcourt sucked in another puff.

"Anyway, to finish answering your question, rather than serving as an ambassador of goodwill, Jake's opposed me at every turn, like striving to block us regulating whale-watching, or raising public awareness against our increasing slip-rental fees. And the damn people love him for it."

Disgusted, Harcourt put out his Cuban, nearly crushing it.

"So, that's it?" Thayer said, probing deeper. "Are you sure there's nothing else? Nothing . . . *personal* in this whole thing?"

Harcourt's eyes were hard and glittering as he studied his longtime ally. He held up a fistful of orange summonses. "If you're referring to the incident with my son from the other day, of *course* there's something personal in it. I'm a firm believer in Machiavellian philosophy, Darius. An eye for an eye. But there's more to it than that." His gaze fell on his son, who avoided his father's stare by contemplating a nearby palm tree. "You see, Brad's minor indiscretions received a disproportionate response from Jake."

Suddenly a thick stream of saliva spurted from Harcourt's mouth, running down his chin and dripping onto his lap. He cursed, reaching into his breast pocket for a handkerchief to wipe it.

Thayer politely looked the other way. The senator's routinely grotesque and uncontrollable drooling was exacerbated by agitation or excitement. It was a parting gift from the religious fanatic that nearly ended his life a year ago.

Harcourt put away his handkerchief and leaned forward. His dark eyes bored into Thayer's. "Look, Darius. The bottom line is this – Braddock has outlived his usefulness. He can't be controlled, and he's become a liability. He's got to go."

"I see," Thayer said, leaning slowly back into his seat. "Look, don't get me wrong here, Dean. I'm just curious as to how you propose to eliminate him. If he's as popular as you say, he'll win re-election next year, even if he doesn't campaign."

For a moment, Harcourt didn't respond. He stared through the limo's tinted glass, focusing on the *Cove Hove* so intently it seemed he could see the object of his enmity through its stone walls.

"He's got to have an Achilles heel, Darius. Everyone does. I simply want *you* to find it."

"Actually, that might prove to be a little difficult," Thayer advised, looking down and shuffling some papers he carried. "After you called me, I took the liberty of running a background check on your 'protector of the people,' and he looks pretty clean." He skimmed the pages as he spoke, flipping them one by one with his finger. "His credit is good, he doesn't drink or gamble, and he hasn't been involved with anyone since his wife died. On top of all that, he's rescued three drowning victims over the last two years, including a little girl's Labrador retriever puppy, if you can believe that!"

"People believe what you tell them, Darius."

Thayer looked up, closing the folder dismissively as he did. He shook his head. "True. And what the *people* are telling each other is that crime in Paradise Cove is down sixty seven percent since Jake Braddock took office. He's a workaholic, but that's about it. Frankly, I don't think we're going to find much we can use."

Harcourt's ruddy lips curled back into a snarl, revealing his tobacco-stained teeth. His already intense face turned a deep red and the raised scar on his jaw began to pulse. His fists clenched as he moved forward in his seat. "Look, don't get me wrong here, Darius, but I don't give a *damn* about what your little pile of papers says. I want you to find me dirt on this man. *Real* dirt. Dirt I can use to destroy his reputation, cost him his job, and ruin his life! Do you hear me?"

Thayer froze as he saw the unpredictable look in Harcourt's eyes. The senator seemed dangerously unstable, like a man perched on the edge of a very deep precipice, ready to plunge off on a whim, or throw you off instead, and laugh uproariously as you fell.

"What, do you think I'm crazy, Darius?" Foamy saliva was starting to collect in the corners of Harcourt's mouth. "You think this is some kind of game? Well it's not. Now you go out there and find me that information I asked for. No matter how long it takes, or how much it costs. Do you comprehend what I'm telling you?" Harcourt raged on, his spittle spraying over Thayer's face. "If you can't find what I need, then create it! I will not be denied my vengeance!"

Speechless, Thayer sat there gaping, his eyes peeled wide behind his saliva-stained glasses. His mouth had gone dry, making him labor as he swallowed hard. "Uh, sure thing Dean," he said warily, pausing to clear his throat. "I . . . think we understand each other completely. I'll, um . . . get right on it."

"Excellent," the senator said. He smiled eerily, relaxing back into his seat as if their entire conversation might have been about nothing more than a passing cloud. Tapping a button on his padded armrest, he opened the intercom to his chauffeur. "Pull us closer to the dock so my son can get out, please. Then, if you don't mind, would you be so kind as to drive us back to Mr. Thayer's car?" Sitting back in his seat as the limo started to move, Harcourt didn't say another word. He merely stared out the window with a chilling smile playing across his bloated face.

Darius Thayer also sat there quietly, but his mind was working furiously. Despite maintaining a cool exterior, he was both frightened and disturbed. The senator's private war with the small town sheriff was exploding into full-blown obsession.

Based on what he just experienced, Thayer came to two inescapable conclusions: Brad Harcourt was completely and rightfully terrified of his father.

And Dean Harcourt was going insane.

———

From his table in the *Cove Hove*, Jake watched Brad Harcourt exit his father's limousine and make his way down toward his docked Jet Ski. A moment later, the big black car drove off, accompanied by its security detail. Shrugging off the deranged senator, Jake turned his attention back to the spinach and egg white omelet sitting on his plate. The place was eerily quiet, the only discernable sounds coming from the kitchen and an overhead television set. With the usual early morning rush of charter captains and their clientele already out at sea, the restaurant and bar were practically deserted.

The *Cove Hove* was a quaint place, one with a reputation for good food and great atmosphere. Its ornate windows overlooked the marina proper. Decorated to mimic the layout of a 19th century pirate ship, it had a huge captain's wheel as its centerpiece. Its steady stream of tourists and residential visitors made the popular establishment consistently profitable.

Jake glanced over at the nearby bar; its glasses suspended overhead like crystalline grapes, its inverted stools lined up atop its polished length. He thought back to the days following his return to Paradise Cove. He'd been a wreck following Sam's death, and nothing anyone said or did could buoy his spirits. His career was over, and his life hard on its heels. The money he made from endorsements was mostly gone, with just a little left to drink. Luckily, everyone in town was clamoring to buy him a brew. They all wanted to be able to brag that they shared a beer with a gold medal winner; they were lining up like soldiers.

Jake grimaced, remembering all the nights he'd staggered out of the *Cove Hove*, shit-faced and miserable. His plan to escape reality had backfired, and seclusion only made matters worse. The only thing he was accomplishing was boozing himself comatose night after night, and waking up in desiccated puddles of vomit. If he hadn't accepted the sheriff's job he'd still be sucking face with some bottle.

"More lemons for your tea, sheriff?" a voice called out. "How's your breakfast today?"

Jake looked up. The waitress, Mary, was a petite but buxom brunette, perpetually dressed in pink. A transplant from nearby Boca Raton, she fawned over the well-built lawman whenever he frequented her establishment. The moment she saw him she ran to the restroom and sprayed herself with jasmine-scented body splash.

"Everything's great, Mary. Thanks," he said with a half-smile. "But I've told you a hundred times, you can call me Jake."

The young girl beamed at him before wiggling off to attend to her remaining customers. Jake took a deep breath, exhaling slowly, then turned his attention to the overhead television.

The broadcast showed a group of reporters at Seattle-Tacoma International Airport. They were in pursuit of an obviously uncooperative figure with dark hair and a pronounced mustache, barraging him with questions. The sight of media made Jake lower his eyes.

. . . on the national scene, big game hunter Karl Von Freiling, well known for his capture of oversized snakes and crocodiles, came under fire after the failure of a top-secret expedition. The expedition ended in disaster when four team members were killed.

Von Freiling refused to elaborate on the deaths, except to say that the men all died in a tragic boating accident. Attorneys for the victims' families have called for a formal investigation . . .

. . . in international news, the huge squid that attacked surfer Manuel Diaz off the coast of Cuba last week has been confirmed to be an unknown species. Scientists who examined the remains of the twenty-five foot mollusk stated the squid is similar to the well-known giant squid, but does not possess its two elongated attack tentacles. They have concluded that this new species is most likely a shallow water predator that hunts by stalking and pouncing on its prey.

In this video footage released by the Cuban government, the specimen is being pulled off of twenty-two-year-old Manuel after being shot three times with a spear gun and immobilized with a bang stick. Manuel suffered massive tissue and blood loss and was airlifted to a nearby hospital. He is listed in critical condition.

Sightings of other such squid by boaters and surfers have led to speculation that the cephalopods may be responsible for a rash of disappearances that have taken place over the last week. At least seven people have vanished from boats and in the surf off of Cuba and the Bahamas. It was presumed they all drowned . . .

Jake stared blankly up at the television screen. His eyes widened as he felt the first wave of nausea flood over him, nearly toppling him from his chair. He dug his fingers into the hard edge of the table as if it was his only anchor to reality, his heart pounding like a jackhammer in his ears. The walls of the *Cove Hove* started to fall down on him like dominos, and he felt like he was going to suffocate. The rapid breathing, the clamminess, the tunnel vision – there was no fighting it. His doctors called it Post-traumatic Stress Disorder. Jake wouldn't call it anything. Stubborn to the point of pigheadedness, he steadfastly refused treatment for his condition, including the assorted medications they prescribed.

Sucked into the spiraling vortex of his mind, Jake could see the nightmare happening once again. It was always the same. He was flying over the water in his chartered helicopter, searching for the dive site. Even with their radar, the thick fog was making it difficult. As they made their approach, Jake glanced out the window. He could see the faces of Sam's teammates as they crowded around her. He spotted a medical chopper heading toward the group of dive boats, and felt a sickening cramp in the pit of his stomach as he realized something was terribly wrong.

Sam was down and she wasn't moving.

Too worked up to wait for the pilots to land, Jake hurled himself out of the chopper from ten feet above ground. He came crashing down onto the surrounding dock, hard enough to shatter two bones in his foot. Ignoring the pain, he limped through the onlookers, observing the growing dread on the faces of the EMS techs as they worked away on his wife's lifeless body using CPR, adrenaline, and the defibrillator. Again and again they failed to restore her breathing. He watched with sickening horror as their expressions of frustration gave way to resignation as they were forced to accept the worst.

Acceptance was replaced by shock and astonishment as Jake howled a scream of rage and denial. He rushed to Sam's side, knocking down several EMS workers. His face intense, he began performing CPR compressions on her chest. He could feel the cool clamminess of her skin as he pounded her chest with his calloused palms. He remembered the taste of her cold, blue lips as he pressed his warm mouth tightly against hers those last few times, desperately trying to breathe life into her waterlogged lungs. He watched in abject horror as her lifeless eyes remained focused on him.

Unable to handle her unblinking gaze, he toiled on. He felt the animalistic rage well up within his chest as Sam's teammates, exasperated with his unwillingness to accept the inevitable, tried to take her from him. He sensed himself snap. Two decades of martial arts skills forgotten, he went berserk with grief, using his sledgehammer fists to fracture jaws, flatten noses, and shatter ribs.

Still flailing away, he felt the sharp jab of a needle in his arm. Then, there was nothing but darkness, the kind no light could illuminate. He woke up in the hospital a few days later, blaming himself for Samantha's death.

It was my fault. If I'd been by her side for the diving competition, instead of posing for a fee, I'd have been there when she needed me. I could have saved her. I could have–

"My God, Jake," a voice called out faintly. "Isn't it horrible? Jake?"

He heard the distinctly female voice again. For a moment he thought . . . *Sam?* He heard the voice once more speaking his name.

"Jake? Can you hear me?"

As Amara Takagi's hand settled on his shoulder Jake's head snapped in her direction, his eyes mirroring his pain.

"Jake? Are you okay?" Amara asked. Her exotic features hosted a concerned expression.

"What?" Jake managed after a moment. He regained his composure. "Oh, yeah, I'm fine. Thanks." He cleared his throat. "Sorry doc, I must have drifted off. Rough night, you know?"

Amara smiled. "Gee, sheriff, must've been a lulu. From the way you were sweating there, I thought you just ran a marathon. Anyway, isn't it terrible?"

"What was that, doc?" Jake stalled, poking at his cold breakfast.

"On the news," Amara said. She pointed at the TV. "That poor whale!"

Following her gaze, Jake stared up at the current broadcast.

. . . as seen from the live feed of a Coast Guard chopper, the carcass of a giant blue whale has been spotted drifting forty miles offshore. The

rarest of the great whales, the blue whale is the largest known animal to ever inhabit the earth. The whale pictured here measured at least one hundred feet in length . . .

As he watched the broadcast, Jake could feel his trip-hammer pulse gradually returning to normal. "I'm sorry about the whale, doc," he offered. He reached over and pushed out a chair. "Join me?"

"Thank you," Amara said in a quiet voice. She plopped down into the chair, her eyes still on the screen.

"Can I get you anything?" Jake asked, gesturing for the waitress.

"No, no. I'm fine."

"C'mon, it's my treat. You can have anything on the menu." He leaned forward and winked. "As long as it's one of the breakfast specials . . ."

Amara blinked, stared, and then chuckled. Before she could reply, Mary came prancing over, her happy-go-lucky expression evaporating as she realized Jake was no longer alone.

"Yes, sheriff?" she asked, pretending quite convincingly that Amara didn't exist.

"Can I get another ice water, and–"

"Sure thing," Mary said, spinning on her heel.

"Whoa, hold up there," Jake said with a titter. "You forgot my friend."

"Oh, sure. Sorry." Mary whirled back, order pad in hand. "What can I get you?" she asked coolly, her green eyes scrolling across the top of her pad as she studied Amara in detail.

"I'll have an ice water too, please. With lemon," Amara replied.

The waitress walked off with wide strides.

"Are you *sure* you don't want anything?" Jake prodded. "I was joking about the specials, and the food is pretty good here."

"I think your girlfriend is pretty jealous here," Amara replied, hawking Mary's retreating form as she disappeared into the kitchen. "I'm nervous enough getting water from her. Lord knows what she'd do to my breakfast."

"Mary's not my girlfriend," Jake emphasized. "And she's really very nice."

"If you say so."

"I do," Jake said. He cocked his head. "See, here she comes already."

Mary strolled over, placed the two glasses on the table, and gave Amara a wide smile, before moving off again.

"Figures . . ." Amara muttered through taut lips.

"What?"

"The little brat forgot my lemon."

"That's okay," Jake replied. He smiled, put his tea down, and scooped up a slice from a saucer to his right. "I've got plenty."

"Thanks." Amara smiled.

He extended his hand over her glass and gave a smirk. "May I?"

Amara gave him an inscrutable look, then grinned. "Knock your-self out."

As Jake's thumb and index finger came together, the gleam in his eye vanished. A spritz of juice spurted across the table, striking Amara square in the face. The cetaceanist recoiled, her right eye clos-ing tight and blinking uncontrollably as the lemon's acidic juice went to work.

"Oh shit, I'm so sorry!" Jake sputtered. He fumbled for a napkin, leaning forward as he held it out to her. "Are you alright?"

"Oh, sure," Amara pretended. She dipped the napkin in her water, dabbing it gingerly around the edges of her spasming eye. "This is a real pick-me-up, first thing in the morning."

Jake felt his face grow hot and anxiously scanned the restaurant, focusing on the television. "I'm really sorry about that. Did they say how it died?"

"My eye?" Amara remarked. She sniffled loudly and rolled her eye around, trying hard to blink away the last of the pain.

"No, the whale . . ."

"Oh . . . the newsman says it bled to death from an enormous abdominal wound." She wiped away a tear and pointed with what remained of her napkin. "You can see it there."

"Wow," Jake said as he studied the screen.

"The Coast Guard believes it collided with an ocean liner and got its tail chopped up by the ship's propellers."

As she focused once more on the newscast, Jake studied Amara with interest. With her fingers intertwined like she was praying, and her pale eyes glued to the screen, the cetaceanist seemed more like a frightened child than the tough ship's captain he met the other day.

Amara let out the breath she'd been holding. "I wonder . . ."

"Wonder what?'

"What? Oh, nothing. I was just thinking."

"About what? About what killed the whale?"

"No, never mind. The collision killed the whale. After its flukes were damaged it must have been unable to maneuver and was sucked back into the propeller, eviscerating it."

Jake shook his head. "That's horrible. Do you think that's what really happened?"

"What do you mean?"

"What I mean is, do you think there's any chance your transient killer whales had anything to do with this?"

As the broadcast came to its conclusion, Amara turned back toward him. "I considered that, but I doubt it," she said. "I mean, it's possible. But unless they're desperate, killer whales tend to tackle far easier prey than a blue whale twenty times their weight. I've seen pods harassing calves when the mother was distracted, but I've never heard of them attacking a healthy adult." She closed her eyes and started rubbing her temples with her fingertips. She leaned forward, her high cheekbones and delicate chin giving her face a heart-shaped appearance. "Besides, the wound is far too large. I'm afraid the Coast Guard is right."

Nodding, Jake wiped his hands on a napkin. He reached into his shirt pocket, pulled out a small wad of money and left a couple of bills on the table. "So, do you think the whale just ended up blundering into the ship's path?" he asked. "I thought whales had sonar, not to mention common sense."

"Who knows?" Amara sighed. "Maybe she was sick or old. I just hate to see an endangered species like that die so needlessly."

"Me too," Jake said. He rose to his feet. "Listen doc, I'm about to start my day's adventures. I hate to say it, but you look like your best friend just died. Can I walk you anywhere? Sometimes it's nice to have a police escort."

Amara managed a feeble smile. "Thanks, Jake. Actually, we're about to cast off. I just came in to grab breakfast for my crew. We'll be out at sea for two weeks or more, and I can't have Willie cooking for those smelly bilge rats every day!"

To his surprise and confusion, Jake suddenly felt sad. He smiled to conceal it and reached for the bags. "Well spoken, matey. You sound like a regular Captain Bligh. Come on, doc. I'll walk you down to your pirate ship."

Behind them, the news re-aired the broadcast of the dead blue whale drifting on the surface, its giant mouth gaping and its stomach wide open, leaving a wound large enough to park a limo inside.

Six

Like a stealth submarine, the creature cruised undisturbed through the undersea canyons. It was headed toward the *Cutlass*, a towering, scimitar-shaped mountain peak jutting up from the ocean floor, some seventeen miles off the coast of Paradise Cove.

Since the moment it escaped, the giant carnivore generated fear in everything it approached. As it loomed in the distance, the ocean before it became a desert, its occupants fleeing in terror before the approaching leviathan. Sharks, marlin, even whales fled. The creature detected the mass exodus of sea life and reveled in the reality that nothing in the surrounding seas could challenge it.

Spiraling into an underwater roll that displaced tens of thousands of gallons, the beast's highly evolved sensory systems focused on the endless variety of life forms all around it. Giant schools of squid and shiny silver baitfish abounded, with shoals measuring as large as a football field. Undulating forests of green kelp added to the sights that piqued its primitive curiosity.

As it passed directly over the fifteen-hundred foot Cutlass, the creature's blazing eyes spotted an enormous grouper lurking just outside a large cave opening, near the very top of the underwater mountain. A top ambush predator, the Volkswagen-sized fish took one glance at the approaching nightmare blotting out the sun and immediately retreated for the safety of its lair. To the creature, neither the grouper below, nor the life forms fleeing ahead, mattered in the least. It wasn't hungry.

Its battle with the blue whale had been a ferocious one, but in the end it succeeded in dispatching its significantly larger opponent. As it moved in to feed, it was rewarded with the discovery of a fully developed fetus, writhing within the giant cetacean's still-warm womb. Its deadly jaws tore open the whale's stomach region. Mercilessly wrenching the still-living infant from the uterine cavity of its mother, it gorged itself upon it. The blubber-enriched meal was a delicacy, and sufficient to sustain the huge carnivore for several days.

Passing the Cutlass and picking up speed, the creature scanned the surrounding waters and the landmass of the continental slope. A water-muffled grumble issued from its toothy jaws. It detected nothing but an alien landscape. The creature was in a state of confusion. It had followed the serpentine coastline of eastern Florida for several days now, during which time it sought out the deepwater trenches and submerged landmarks it expected to find. But none of them were there. The shallow inland sea that covered a huge portion of North America during the time of its ancestors was long gone, as were the migratory routes they once used. Frustrated that its inherited sense of direction no longer served any useful purpose, the creature's brain eventually accepted the futility of the situation. Like a circuit breaker tripping, its highly evolved instincts redirected it to focus on exploring its newfound territory.

Noisily breaching the surface with a blast of water vapor and sucking in tremendous lungfuls of air, it closed its watertight nose flaps and dove beneath the surface. Trailing bubbles, it spiraled slowly down, its skin and eyes sensing the day's heat and light fading as it descended into the void. As it passed the four-hundred foot mark, the creature's infrared vision began to lose effectiveness. Soon, it could no longer detect either shape or movement. It arched its massive neck and a group of specialized muscles that lined its muzzle began to undergo tiny spasms.

It started emitting a prolonged series of loud ratcheting noises, similar to an enormous door creaking open on rusty hinges. The deep clicking sounds were produced by specialized organs housed within the creature's nasal passages, and traveled through the water as sonic waves at four-and-a-half times the air speed of sound. As they bounced off nearby objects and animals they returned with a series of echoes. The echoes brought with them translated images, absorbed by specialized bones in its gigantic mandibles, and sent directly to its brain. To enhance the effectiveness of this technique, the creature's tiny outer ears were acoustically isolated from its brain, enabling it to use the sound waves it emitted as a substitute for eyesight. It was able to "see" over incredibly long distances, even in complete darkness.

It was using echolocation – an ability the creature's kind had perfected millions of years before such well-known sonar specialists as whales and dolphins swam the seven seas.

As it hurtled past the one-thousand foot mark, the chilling temperature and water pressure began to exert their deadly effects. The creature's circulatory system sensed the dangerous drop in temperature and automatically diverted blood flow away from its heavily insulated skin, sending it toward its body's core. Like modern diving animals, it was able to create a significant temperature difference between its core temperature and that of the surrounding water, enabling it to function effectively for hours on end in freezing water.

As the deadly hydrostatic pressure continued to build, the creature's powerful ribcage and lungs became too compressed to function. The increased oxygen carrying capacity of its blood and surrounding tissues took over, compensating for the strain, and enabling it to function with efficiency during the most strenuous deep-water dives. It was a biological machine built to survive.

At fourteen hundred feet, the creature neared the ocean floor. It leveled off and cruised at a comfortable pace, exploring the bottom as it went. A few minutes later, it spotted the beginnings of a precipitous drop that gaped across the rocky seabed, its unplumbed depths draped in perpetual darkness. After passing over it and scanning it with its senses, the creature entered the giant chasm, accelerating swiftly as it descended.

Time stood still as it descended like a phantom through the watery void. At five thousand feet the rocky walls of the deep crevasse began to grow barren, and the only life forms it detected were the omnipresent foot-long squid, crustaceans and bioluminescent fish that made the stony slopes their home. As it prepared to head for the surface, something piqued its interest.

Six hundred feet below, suspended within the invisible trough of a deepwater current, was an enormous squid. It was similar to the ones the creature fed upon during its youth, but a third larger, measuring forty feet in length and weighing nearly twelve tons.

Ignorant of the larger animal's presence, the cephalopod remained motionless. Cloaked within the darkness of the blackish waters, it waited patiently for unsuspecting prey to come within reach.

High above, the creature studied the squid. Though not hungry, the sheer size of the prey item instilled a palpable inquisitiveness within the prehistoric titan. Such squid were dangerous and difficult to capture, requiring a stealthy approach and a last moment burst of speed, before the oversized mollusk could utilize its jet propulsion and obscuring ink cloud to escape.

With a shrug of its flippers, the creature drifted on. It was beginning to feel the need to surface and turned its scar-covered muzzle in the direction of the distant light.

Just then, the squid shuddered.

The marine reptile paused, watching with undisguised interest as it spasmed, rocking back and forth and lashing out with its arms in every possible direction. The convulsions worsened, and the squid began to drift in an unnatural manner. It appeared the mollusk's sense of equilibrium no longer functioned properly. Despite a full belly, the creature was beginning to become aroused.

Suddenly, a blast of sound waves swept through the watery void. The creature reflexively scanned the surrounding darkness for the source of the alien sonar. A thousand feet up, a fast-approaching life form emerged. It was warm-blooded and of similar size, akin to the sulfur-bottomed colossus the creature recently slew. Unlike the plankton-feeding blue whale however, the newcomer was a predator like itself, possessing huge jaws lined with teeth designed to impale large prey. The creature stole toward the intruder, scanning it repeatedly with its own sound waves.

Oblivious to the creature's approach, the intruder continued to home in on the squid. The creature moved closer as the other animal descended past it at a steep angle, still focusing on its prospective prey. The newcomer possessed the same sound emitting sight as the creature, but kept its underwater vision focused only on the struggling squid.

Despite the new predator's slothful attack speed of only twenty miles an hour, the squid did not flee. It continued to loll in a confused manner, its numerous arms darting and lashing violently at nothing.

A snarl-like grimace creased the creature's wrinkled muzzle, revealing scores of razor-sharp teeth. A red-hot rage flooded its mighty chest cavity, as the thought of a rival predator daring to challenge it for food sank into its primeval brain. The newcomer was a competitor, and evolution had taught it and its kind the best way to deal with competitors.

Destroy them.

With all four of its flippers working to accelerate to full speed, the creature charged through the void, hurtling directly toward the unsuspecting whale.

———

Jake stood atop one of Harcourt Marina's main docks, a few rows from his boat slip. In the distance, he could identify Amara Takagi by her long, dark hair as she climbed the boarding ramp leading to the *Harbinger's* main deck. From what he'd gleaned, she and her crew were slated to spend the next two weeks at sea, testing out their new submersible on nearby sperm and killer whale populations.

Jake cocked his head to one side as he watched Amara disappear from view. The lady whale doctor was definitely unlike any woman he'd ever met. Despite an air of fragility, she was athletic, intelligent, and quite beautiful. Strangely, she was either aloof to her own attractiveness or viewed her looks as a detriment, rather than the asset they definitely were. All that mattered to her was science and whales. He amusedly imagined she must've caused quite a few sleepless nights among the marine biology geeks back in grad school. His eyes crinkled up in amusement, picturing study hall jammed to capacity.

Smiling, Jake turned to make his way down to the *Infidel* to wait for Chris. It was nearly 8 a.m. and the marina was already infested with its omnipresent plague of seagulls, their cries for handouts a perpetual source of annoyance for local inhabitants.

Jake checked the time. *Ah well. Back to work.* As he made his way toward his patrol boat, he was surprised to find his deputy already on board, his gear stowed and feet propped up as he sat back and drank his coffee. Noticing his employer's surprised expression from fifty feet away, Chris raised his cup in mock salute. He held up a second coffee and smiled.

Jake grinned at the stunt, and at the irony. He couldn't begin to count how many times he'd done the same thing for Phil Starling ten years earlier, to make up for oversleeping or an occasional lapse in judgment. He might not be a charter captain, and the *Infidel* was certainly no fishing boat, but the poignant parallels between him and his young deputy were undeniable.

A hint of movement caught Jake's eye and he clocked the *Sayonara*. She was a hundred yards out, chugging through the no-wake zone that bordered the marina. He could see Captain Phil standing at the helm, pointing at something as they went and spouting instructions to his nephew. Knowing better than to waste time shouting, Jake tried in vain to get his former mentor's attention by waving his arms. Disappointed, he stood by and watched the big Bertram pick up speed, eventually disappearing from sight.

As the well-known charter boat faded in the distance, Jake felt apprehension wash over him yet again. He shook his head. Of all people, Phil Starling could certainly take care of himself.

As Jake arrived at the *Infidel* he reached over the gunnels, shook hands with his cocky deputy, and accepted the proffered coffee. "It's dark and strong this time. Very nice, kid," he said. He held the cup steady, slowly sipping the steaming beverage. "Wow, you're on time and I still get good coffee? Either you dumped your nasty girlfriend or you're bucking for a raise."

"Actually I did, and I wasn't, boss," Chris stated. "But, um . . . do you think I could get one?"

An ominous glance from Jake silenced him without further ado.

Chris glanced over Jake's shoulder at an approaching mountain of a man dressed in denim overalls. "Watch your back," he said.

Jake turned to see a heavy-breathing Ben Stillman plodding toward him with a purposeful expression on his face. "Oh brother," he muttered.

"Hey Sheriff . . . glad I . . . caught up to you," Ben huffed and puffed, leaning forward to rest his hands on his knees and catch his breath.

Jake stared down at him, reflexively recoiling as he was enveloped by a combination of bad body odor, even worse breath, and the stench of rotting bait.

One of the least popular inhabitants of Paradise Cove, at six-foot-five and three hundred and fifty pounds, Ben Stillman was about the biggest man around, with the strength to match his oversized frame. A one-time former heavyweight boxing contender, the fifty-year-old owner of *Above the Claw* now suffered from chronic back pain and was severely overweight. He also had a reputation for being a cantankerous barroom brawler and an abusive spouse.

Ben remained in his assumed crash position, his noisy exhalations sending malodorous waves of freshly caught lobster washing over Jake. The pungent smell clung to the lawman's nostrils, its familiar scent unleashing an unexpected wave of queasiness. It brought memories back with it – memories Jake would have loved to forget.

It was Christmas Eve, and he was five years old. His mother was in one of her legendary holiday cooking frenzies. He sat at the kitchen table and watched, mesmerized, while she stirred pots, added seasonings, and taste-tested sauces. She was wearing a brightly colored apron, new shoes, and a new dress. She moved with energy and grace, her smile bright and her figure tight and trim, despite motherhood and having retired from competition years earlier.

Jake gave a small giggle of delight as his mom lowered a wooden spoon to his mouth, allowing him to test one of her homemade creations. He nodded his eager approval, watching her whirling away through the worshipping eyes of an adoring child. To him, his mother's movements were wondrous to behold, a kind of magic that transformed the mundane into the mystical.

That magic ended with the slamming of a door. His father was home early. His complexion was red and his clothes reeked of booze. He stalked into the kitchen, his nostrils flaring and his expression vicious. Jake's eyes lowered as he shrank down in his seat. More often than not, his father ignored him; he hoped this would be one of those times.

"What's that smell?" John Braddock demanded. His eyes grew irritable as he roamed the kitchen, poking into every nook and cranny like some looter looking for a prize.

"You're home early, dear," Jake's mother said, her forced smile unwavering.

"They cut my hours at the warehouse again, the bastards."

"Oh. That's okay, John. We can–"

John stopped in front of the stove. He looked down, then whirled on her. "Don't try to sidetrack me, woman." He reached for a furiously steaming pot, his calloused hand closing on the metal lid's handle. Amanda Braddock was too late to stop him.

John yanked his hand back, cursing furiously. He flipped on the faucet and held his burned fingers under the cold water. He looked around angrily for a potholder, before snatching the pot's lid off to peek inside.

"Lobster?" he spat incredulously. "My salary just got cut by a third and you buy fucking lobster?"

"Its okay," Jake's mom placated. She took an involuntary step back, her smile faltering. "I finally got that endorsement check today, so all our problems are solved."

John wheeled on her, his fury obvious. "Solved? You mean *you* solved them for us? Gee, thanks, honey. I guess you forgot who the breadwinner is around here, didn't you!"

"Wait, John – what are you–"

Jake's mother cried out in alarm. She sprang back as his father seized the tall lobster pot and toppled it to the floor. The blood-colored crustaceans spilled everywhere, the permanent surprise in their dead bugs' eyes mirrored by their claws' open-mouthed gapes. The stove's smaller pots quickly followed suit. The clanging noises they made as they struck the tiled floor were punctuated by Jake's cries of fear.

"John, what the hell's gotten into you?" Amanda said, stepping closer to stop him. "You're scaring him!"

The backhand came out of nowhere, a powerhouse slap that sent her flying backward. She bounced off the kitchen cabinet and collapsed in a heap, laid out atop a congealed mass of lobsters, mashed potatoes, and string beans.

His eyes tiny globes of terror, Jake hid under the table, cringing in fear. His mother's sobs echoed in his ears. Above him, his father continued his rampage, ripping open cabinet doors and extracting dinner plates, smashing them one by one against the floor.

"Your nice, fat endorsement check, eh?" he snarled. "Great, you can use it to replace all this crap." He extended his gorilla arms, clearing the kitchen counters with huge sweeps, sending condiments and silverware violently clattering, merging with the mountainous mess he created. He stood upright and glared hatefully down at his wife. "Now clean this shit up! I want this place looking brand spanking new!"

Jake watched, paralyzed, as his mother dragged herself across shards of broken china. Blood trickled from her mouth, and her dress was heavily stained with sauce and crushed vegetables. His father gloated as he stood over her, reveling in his victory.

Jake slipped unnoticed under the table. Crawling on all fours, he tried to make it out of the kitchen. He got a full ten feet before he was grabbed by the nape and hauled forcefully back.

"Where the hell do you think *you're* going?" his father barked from two inches away.

Jake closed his eyes and whimpered; the smell of cheap beer combined with lobster was making him nauseous. He uttered a yelp of pain as he was slammed down hard into his chair.

"Now, sit your ass down and don't move."

Jake watched in terror as his father stepped over his mother. He reached for the utensil drawer, ripping it open so hard it came off its rollers and dropped to the floor, spilling its contents.

John Braddock poked through the scatterings, settling on a pair of stainless steel tongs. He made a quick grab and stood up. He held one of the lobsters up and shook it, its mashed potato-coated claws waving like the fungus-coated legs of a rotting spider. He headed straight for Jake, thrusting it under his nose and holding it there.

"Here you go, you little bastard," he said, smiling. "Your *mother* thinks we can afford to eat like royalty! Well, the only royal you may be is a royal pain in the ass, but at least you're going to *eat* like a king!"

"John, no!" Jake's mom shrieked. She struggled to her feet using the sink for support.

Jake's heart stopped as his father whirled menacingly on her.

"Stay out of this, woman!" he warned. "You wasted our money on this shit, so your little bastard is gonna eat it!"

Jake gasped as his father shoved the steaming lobster under his nose. His little jaw clamped tightly shut and he shook his head, more from fear than refusal.

His father slammed the lobster down hard on the table, its lifeless black eyes locking onto Jake's. He uttered a tiny bleat but was too afraid to move.

"I said *eat* it!" his father roared. "If your mother has her way, we'll be eating off the floor soon, so you might as well get used to it!"

When Jake failed to comply, John brought his fist down like a hammer, reducing the crustacean's hard shell to fragments, sending hot lumps of potatoes and lobster juice spraying into his son's face. Jake flinched and blinked repeatedly, but remained rigidly immobile.

His father leaned down, whispering frighteningly in his ear. "You've got three seconds to start eating, or I'm gonna make you! One . . ."

Jake opened his mouth to cry for help. His father stopped at two, seizing him by the back of the head with one big hand and forcing his face onto the crushed lobster.

Jake tried to struggle, but his cries only forced steaming-hot hunks of half-cooked shellfish into his mouth. He felt stabbing pains as his tongue and palate were pierced by sharp pieces of shell. His stomach heaved and his muffled cries were stifled as he vomited. He gazed piteously upward at his mother as she screamed at her husband, pleading with him to release their son. She beat futilely at him, her flailing hands like pigeon's wings flapping against a stone statue.

Jake closed his eyes and prayed for it to end. The last thing he remembered was the smell and taste of lobster.

"Take it easy," Jake said, suppressing a shudder as he shook off the haunting stimuli. He stared scornfully down at Ben Stillman, trying to breathe through his mouth. "We're not in any rush. What can I do for you?"

"Thanks," Ben said, straightening up and patting his stomach with his ham-sized hands. "Whew! Guess my wife is right. It's time to stop hitting the buffets and start hitting the gym!"

Jake would have preferred he just stopped hitting his wife.

"Sounds like the woman knows what she's talking about," he said.

"Maybe. Anyway, sheriff, I was wondering if you could check my traps later. Two are just plain missing, and the rest, well . . . someone's been pilfering lobsters out of them. The *Infidel* is much faster than my old tub." He pointed a thumb at his bulky lobster boat. "So if there's any chance of catching the culprits, I figure you've got the best shot."

"You know, Ben, I appreciate you taking the time to run over here, but my dispatcher already told you we were going to investigate your complaint later today."

"Well yeah, but–"

"We'll be covering over twenty miles of water up and down the sound, so we're bound to end up passing your traps during our rounds." Jake started to turn away as he spoke. "So, if there is someone out there robbing them, I'm sure we–"

"Actually that's not where I'm having the problem, sheriff," Ben said. "I have a few traps farther out. And those are the ones I think people keep mucking with because they normally produce big time."

"Farther out? Just how far out are we talking, Ben?"

"By the Cutlass," Stillman said. His voice was low and his eyes shifty.

"The Cutlass?" Jake looked back at him as he climbed over the *Infidel's* gunnels. "Are you frickin kidding me? Who the hell ever heard of anyone catching lobsters all the way out there? That's way out of our way, and also out of my jurisdiction."

"Yes it is, but–"

"Sorry Ben, but it's not happening."

"Oh, c'mon now, sheriff. Okay, it's true you can't arrest anyone out there. But, if someone's looking to obtain a dinner at my expense, and they happen to see your patrol boat out there, I'm sure they'll take off and think twice about coming back."

"I told you once already. The answer is no."

Ben leaned closer to Jake with a conspiratorial expression on his face. "Actually, sheriff, if you can keep a secret, the lobsters off that point are the biggest I've ever seen. They average eight pounds, and some weigh over fifteen." He paused, sizing Jake up. "I'll tell you what. Now, I don't want to be misconstrued as someone who'd try to bribe an officer of the law. But, if you should happen to be out there, and manage to check on three or four of those traps for me . . . well, let's just say I'd be more than happy for you to help yourself to half of what's in them. Hell, I'll even throw in a steak dinner."

Jake turned slowly back around until he was facing the huge fisherman. "Say, how's your wife, Ben? Everything okay at home? I haven't seen her in town for a good week or so."

Ben Stillman looked confused.

Jake leaned forward, resting his thick knuckles on the *Infidel's* white gunnels and stared the other man dead in the eye. "Thanks for the offer, Ben. But you're wasting your time. I don't care much for lobster. As for you buying me 'dinner,' well . . ." He raised himself to his full height and looped his thumb inside his gun belt. "We'll discuss that another time. Who knows? Maybe one of these days I'll get a call to come over to your place and we'll settle up on things then?" Jake folded his arms across his chest and smiled, his expression a predatory baring of teeth.

Ben Stillman turned noticeably pale. He stared at Jake for a long moment. "Uh, sure thing, sheriff," he said finally. "We'd . . . love to have you."

"Have a nice day, Ben." Jake turned his back on the bigger man, leaving him standing there with his mouth hanging open.

Flabbergasted, the frustrated fisherman remained immobile for a moment, his projecting brow furrowing up. Then, with a sigh and a shrug of futility, he turned and trudged away.

"What a jerk," Chris said, interrupting the silence. "Can you believe the prick offered you a bribe?"

"Technically he didn't," Jake remarked, "just some crustaceans."

The sound of a vessel's underway horn interrupted their conversation as it echoed across the marina. Looking up, the two men watched as the *Harbinger* chugged its way out from its deep-water mooring, adjusting its course as it headed out to sea. Jake contemplated the big whaler for a moment, then turned back to his deputy. "Forget about Stillman, kid. We'll deal with him when the opportunity presents itself. Like I said before, if there's one thing I've learned in life, it's that people like him usually end up getting what they deserve."

Chris nodded. "Say, boss, we're not going out to the Cutlass, are we?"

"Absolutely not," Jake said, looking up from the *Infidel's* console as he spoke. He tapped on the fuel gauge a few times. "We've got bigger fish to fry. Now, start her up, and let's get this show on the road." He patted Chris on the shoulder, then smirked, "Oh, and you're driving."

"Yes, boss," Chris said. He turned the ignition key. The big Yamaha sputtered loudly, tried to take, and then died.

Jake shot his deputy a pissed-off look as the teenager nervously turned the key again and again, causing the engine to make loud revving noises as it struggled to start. After the fifth attempt, the outboard finally caught and turned over, a cloud of acrid smoke billowing out as it did.

"Don't look at me like that, Jake," Chris protested. "I took her in, just like you said. Sal's partner had her there for *hours*. She's supposed to be fixed."

"Right," Jake drawled. He sat back in his chair and interlocked his hands behind his head. "You know what kid, one of these days I think you're going to be the death of me."

"That's not funny, boss."

"No, it's *not*."

SEVEN

Standing high atop the *Harbinger's* bow, with her hands gripping its railing, Amara surveyed the seas passing beneath her feet through half-closed eyes. She could feel the deck of the old whaler surge up and down as its prow cut through the waves, its rise and fall a hazardous lullaby to one in her line of work.

She'd snuck off to the ship's sun-drenched forecastle in an attempt to find some inner solace, and for some much needed brooding. Much had happened of late, from the butchered blue whale, whose drifting remains she saw on the news, to the fore end of the prehistoric titan she'd secreted in her vessel's freezer. Then there was Jake . . .

Amara felt a sudden pang of guilt as thoughts of Robert unexpectedly popped into her head. He'd been gone so long – nearly a decade now – yet at times the loss still felt like an open wound. She wondered what Robert's reaction would have been to the *Xiphactinus*. She smiled at the thought – he was never one to hold back when it came to voicing opinions. Her smile faded a bit. She could only imagine how he would have reacted to . . .

Damn. Jake again.

Amara sighed, shaking her head and lowering it in the hope of espying some dolphins or porpoises hitching a ride on the pressure wave created by the *Harbinger's* bow.

Oh, well. Sometimes it's good just to be alone.

Amara glanced to one side, her peripheral vision picking up the menacing form of her ship's decommissioned harpoon cannon. It was lurking behind her as always, its rusted sights locked on the horizon, its deadly projectile welded in place, never to claim another life.

The wind began to bluster. Before long, it was shrieking across the ship's bow, its shrill cry escalating as it ricocheted off the oversized gun. Amara's hair straightened out from the gusts' pull, her black locks flagging out behind her like the proud mane of an Andalusian stallion. The bobbing motion of the water, coupled with the whipping wind and the shadow of the metal monstrosity, brought on an unwelcome deluge of images. She clung tightly to the railing as she remembered.

She was twenty-one and seated in the foam-coated bow of a fast-moving inflatable, the frigid air burning her nostrils as she sped along the coast of Greenland. It had been three years since the accident with a seal hunter nearly claimed her life, and eighteen months since she regained full use of her leg. She shifted in her bouncing seat to improve circulation. The pain of the five operations she endured paled when compared to the regimen of physical therapy she put herself through.

In the end, she proved all the doctors wrong. Not only did she show them she could walk again without an aid, she proved she could fly. She completed her master's degree from the isolation of her hospital bed, and was moving on to her doctorate like there was no tomorrow.

Up ahead, she could see the whale killer *Nagata* as it closed in on its quarry, its mechanized bulk a foreboding sight as it cut through the frigid waters of the sound. Its target surfaced with a blast of compressed water vapor and carbon dioxide, two hundred yards off the ship's starboard side. It was a young bull sperm whale – a decent-sized male, measuring nearly sixty feet in length and weighing over sixty tons.

The *Sea Crusade* team got word a week earlier that the Japanese brought a whale killer into the area, with the intention of targeting the local sperm whale population. Incensed by the news, they rushed in immediately to defend the whales, and invited the press for publicity. Sperm whales were a threatened species, so the slaughter of a pod was controversy ripe for media coverage.

When they arrived, the activists expected to find an entire fleet of whale killers and support ships; but after calling on a news helicopter to do surveillance, it became apparent the Japanese weren't equipped to kill multiple animals. They brought only a single vessel, not the two or three they typically used. Nor was that vessel accompanied by one of their horrifying factory ships: floating furnaces that reduced the sea's greatest animals to steaming piles of gore, before packaging them for consumption.

After shadowing the whale killer for several days, the confused *Sea Crusade* team and accompanying news crew found what the Japanese were really after. They'd been hired for a hunt, like some oversized fishing charter, and they were targeting one specific animal. They were stalking a bull cachalot. His name was "Avalanche," and he was a rarity. Unlike all the other sperm whales in the world, Avalanche was pure white.

Since his surprise birth, two decades earlier, the press periodically followed the bull's travels. Heralded as a true life *Moby Dick*, the majestic, ivory-colored mammal was not simply a pigment-deprived albino. Avalanche was a naturally occurring, snow-colored mountain of teeth and muscle, well-suited to rule the ice-capped oceans he prowled. Despite an irascible disposition – one he'd displayed several times by charging whale watching boats – the public couldn't get enough of him. His pictures were featured in assorted natural history magazines, and his poster hung in grade school classrooms worldwide. He was considered an ambassador for cetacean preservation across the globe, loved by parents and children of all ages.

"Get us over there quick!" Amara shouted over the outboard. She blanched as she swallowed a mouthful of salt spray and glanced back to make sure the pilot heard. There were five of them, huddled together aboard the fast moving inflatable: Amara, two chatty British naturalists whose faces and names were so similar she could never tell who was who, Willie, a tall Jamaican fellow who never stopped smiling, and Francis, the stern-faced Korean woman with the military haircut, who was manning the helm.

Suddenly, Francis waved frantically to get Amara's attention. She pointed at the *Nagata* as it shifted course to close on Avalanche's position.

Amara gave a confused gasp. For some reason the white bull just bobbed on the surface instead of sounding to escape. Amara gnawed her lower lip and reached for her binoculars.

A quick glance through the optics confirmed her worst fear. There was a small, black square fixed high atop the big sperm's humped back. She squinted hard to make sure, then cursed aloud. It was a satellite tracking device.

Somehow, the whale killer's crew managed to attach a transmitter to Avalanche during their pursuit. For days it allowed them to track the wily whale's position, finding him over and over again, forcing him to keep moving until he wore himself out. The bull's frozen breaths were coming in gasps, his flanks shuddering as he desperately sucked in air. He was completely exhausted and easy to kill.

Amara immediately radioed their mother ship *Sea Green III* for assistance. Faster and more powerful than its predecessors, the pride of the *Sea Crusade* fleet was already closing rapidly from their starboard side, preparing to place its welded steel hull between the *Nagata's* weapon and Avalanche's vulnerable form. And her fiancé Robert was in command.

As she watched *Sea Green III* draw near, Amara's calculating eyes bounced repeatedly from the whale killer to its pending victim, then again to *Sea Green III*. Her lips drew back, revealing clenched teeth. The *Nagata* was too close.

"*Sea Scout* to command. It's no good, you're too far!" she shouted, realizing how tiny her voice sounded on the open sea.

Robert's reply was instantaneous. "Don't do anything foolish or risky, Amara. Just hold tight, we're on our way."

She shook her head, exchanging doubtful glances with her teammates. She exhaled heavily, her frozen breath fogging up her sunglasses. "Get us over there. We're going to buy Avalanche some time."

As the rest of her crew grabbed onto any available handholds, the helmswoman swallowed hard, nodded, then twisted the throttle open. Within seconds they were up on plane, skipping across the arctic whitecaps, their fleet vessel eating up the blue-white water between them and Avalanche. From her position in the bow, Amara could see the *Nagata's* gunner manning the ship's harpoon cannon. Within moments, his helmsman would have the sperm in perfect position, enabling him to discharge his explosive-tipped weapon directly into Avalanche's exposed side, blowing open his ventral cavity and killing him instantly.

"Not on my watch," Amara swore.

Ignoring Robert's impassioned pleas as they reverberated from her handset, Amara set her jaw and held on as they executed an organ-wrenching turn and decelerated, depositing themselves between the whalers and their intended victim. The *Nagata* was seventy yards ahead and Avalanche twenty yards behind, with *Sea Scout* smack in the middle.

"Keep us between them!" Amara exclaimed. She glanced back at Francis. "Don't let them get a shot!"

The helmswoman gritted her teeth and gunned her outboard in reverse, back-trolling hard as she fought the current and swells and did the Secret Service thing with an armed vessel a thousand times their size. She turned fearfully towards Amara as she watched the whaler's gunner repeatedly try to get a bead. Her face was the epitome of panic. "That thing's got a fucking grenade on it! If he fires, the explosion will kill us all!"

Amara shook her head defiantly. "They won't. Not with that chopper filming every–" Her words ended in a throttled gasp, her eyes widening as she scanned the surrounding skies. The network helicopter was gone.

"Dey must have gone in ta refuel," the big Jamaican announced. "Dat being said, dis may not be da best place ta be sittin . . ."

To punctuate his words, the *Nagata's* oversized diesels roared to life, their deep-throated growls drowning out the sounds of Amara's engine. A moment later, the huge ship surged straight toward their position.

"They're going to capsize us!" Amara shouted. She glared angrily up at the approaching helm, striving to meet her captain's gaze. "I can't believe it."

"I can," Francis replied grimly. "He's bound for hell, that one. I'm sorry, Amara."

Amara opened her mouth as if to speak, then said nothing; her eyes were locked on the rust-tinged wall of steel that was fast approaching.

———

Onboard the *Nagata*, Captain Haruto Nakamura lowered his binoculars. "Helmsman, prepare to change course," he said irritably.

"Belay that," a deep voice interjected.

Haruto saw his pilot hesitate. His face darkened as he whirled angrily on the speaker. "That is a member of my family out there."

"Well then, I guess she must be from the shallow end of the gene pool if she doesn't have the sense to get out of the way," his visitor answered smugly. He cricked his black-maned head to one side and rolled his shoulders back, powerful muscles bulging even through his winter gear. "Regardless, my backers are paying you what this tub is worth to nail that trophy, so unless you want to piss them off royally *and* jeopardize your career, *Captain-san*, I suggest you give the go ahead."

Haruto's eyes grew hard and dangerous. The whole "Captain-san" routine was just one more thing about his arrogant visitor that was sawing away at his nerves. As he sized up the figure next to him, he cursed himself for accepting their current charter.

The scar-covered European was nearly a head taller than most of his crew and half again their weight. Far scarier was the scent of death that radiated from him. It hung around like a lungful of dank and fetid air, seeping from the portals of a dilapidated mausoleum.

Haruto's jaw tensed and he exhaled hard through his nostrils. He was no stranger to killing. All the creatures of the sea were fair game to him and his crew –if the price was right. The man standing beside him, however, was no sea farmer. He was a murderer. People and animals had the same value to him. Haruto could see it in his anomalous eyes. What lay behind them was a terrifying glimpse into the torment that awaited them all.

"Helmsman, take us around the inflatable," he ordered, ignoring the sharp glance he received from his guest. "Tell our gunner to prepare to fire. We'll jog around them to give him a clear shot."

"Aye, aye, sir."

"They're forcing their way around us," Francis said.

Amara's eyes popped as she saw the *Nagata's* massive bow wedge itself between them and the still floundering Avalanche. Their captain was using the same technique she used on him – putting his hull between them and the hapless sperm whale to gain a clear field of fire.

Out of the blue, Avalanche righted himself and began to move. Still too weak to sound, the big bull's fourteen-foot flukes rose slowly up and down as they propelled him forward. It was the exhausted warrior's last ditch effort to escape his pursuers.

The *Nagata* charted the whale's path and rumbled past the *Sea Crusade* inflatable, its towering hull a rampart of blackened steel as it barreled along in pursuit. Amara calculated they would arrive at their slow-moving target in seconds. She needed a plan.

"Hard to port," she called to Francis.

The tenacious helmswoman gunned her outboard to the max and commenced an intestine-straightening maneuver toward the shrinking stern of the *Nagata*.

Amara felt herself stiffen as she gauged the distance.

Just then, *Sea Green III* made its move. As huge as the *Nagata,* the conservationist mother ship's diesels roared like a lion as it kept pace with the whale killer.

As her inflatable drew alongside the *Nagata*, Amara could see over its hull. She spotted her own vessel's bridge and her fiancé, personally gripping the wheel. His face taut and his dark blonde hair damp with sweat, Robert began to play a risky game of cat and mouse, forcing the opposing vessel off course by threatening to run into her. The distance between the two vessels was miniscule, only a dozen yards and closing. Angry shouts and profanities could be heard from the whaler as alarms began to resonate from both ships.

Seconds later, the *Nagata* faltered and began to give ground. *Sea Green III* kept up the pressure, herding the whaler to port like a cowboy rounding up a wayward steer.

"He's doing it!" Francis cried out.

"Oh God, look," Amara gasped. Avalanche had stopped moving. Drifting helplessly on one side, the magnificent bull was dead in the water. She realized why the *Nagata* had given ground so easily. Robert's attempts to push them off course were inadvertently guiding the whalers right to their quarry.

"Get us over there!" Amara demanded.

"What are you going to do?" Francis yelled as they sped along. They raced past the *Nagata*, into the open water between the dark-hulled whaler and Avalanche. The din of the two dueling ships continued to shake their tiny craft.

"We're getting between them and that whale if it kills us!"

The two Brits spoke as one. "Are you daft, woman? That's *exactly* what will happen!"

To her dismay, Amara felt the inflatable slow. She shot Francis a deadly look.

"Sorry, girl, but my life's worth more than some whale's," the helmswoman announced as she shifted into neutral.

With a cry of fury, Amara sprang the length of the inflatable's rigid floor. Her expression was pure rage. Easily overpowering her astonished helmswoman, she flung her to the floor and seized the outboard's tiller. The two Englishman moved determinedly toward her but Willie rose and barred their way, his jaw and expression set in stone. He glanced over his shoulder at her as he fought to keep his balance on the rough water.

"Do what ya got ta do, mon."

Amara nodded and kicked the inflatable into gear. Skimming the surface, she pulled ahead of the *Nagata*, causing the larger vessel's engines to pull back noisily from the sudden stop. She drew near to Avalanche, momentarily taken aback by the size of the big male. Her outboard sputtering, she turned toward the *Nagata,* her bow pointed defiantly at them. Up on their foredeck she saw the ship's gunner, his hands gripping the trigger controls of their harpoon cannon, its armor-piercing point aimed at her position. To their left, *Sea Green III* was also slowing; Robert was waiting for some signal before choosing his next course of action.

"You're crazy," Francis spat through bloodied lips. "They're going to kill us!"

Amara's eyes shimmered with anger, her jaw muscles knotting up. She lifted her chin to see the face of the *Nagata's* captain through their tinted windows, but couldn't. Still, she knew he was looking at her. All of a sudden, a disturbing chuckle emanated from the whaler's overhead speaker.

"That's quite a ballsy maneuver, young lady. I'm impressed. But it's game over now. You have thirty seconds to clear the area, at which point we will open fire."

Amara had no idea who the speaker was, but it wasn't Haruto Nakamura. The voice was much lower in tone and naturally menacing. She started to shake. "Go to hell!"

The ship's gunner cupped one hand to his ear and nodded. His expression shifted from uncertainty to deliberate focus as he pointed his harpoon cannon directly at Avalanche's defenseless form. Amara and everyone watching knew that she and her crew were still in the strike zone. She held her breath as the gunner's thumbs crept toward his weapon's twin triggers.

"Oh blimey, we're gonna die!" one of the Englishman cried out.

With a diesel roar, *Sea Green III* surged closer.

Amara closed her eyes in prayer as she waited for fate to make up its mind. As she did a horrific rumbling sound assailed her ears, startling her and jolting her eyelids back apart. She gaped in astonishment, powerless to act as things went from bad to out of control. The *Nagata's* bow suddenly spun wildly, crashing into the bow of *Sea Green III*.

The impact nearly toppled both ships. Men and machinery went crashing in every direction. The *Nagata's* gunner, clinging desperately to his weapon, gave a startled cry as it went off. The oversized harpoon launched with a hiss, slamming into the bridge of *Sea Green III*, detonating in a thunderclap of red and orange. Hunks of metal flew in every direction and the conservationist ship's bridge was engulfed in an inferno of smoke and flame.

Birthed by two thousand tons of steel, a wall of icy seawater engulfed Amara's vessel, capsizing it and depositing them all in the frozen Greenland Sea. Her screams of panic were quickly drowned. She tried fighting her way to the surface but her lungs filled with frigid seawater and she went numb. Her eyes felt like frozen marbles rolling around in her skull. She sensed herself being buffeted by the current, but was powerless to resist. Enveloped in cold, she felt her back and buttocks brace up against a cushion of warmth. She realized she'd collided with Avalanche. Still recovering from his ordeal, the white cachalot remained motionless as Amara's tiny form slid down his living room-sized head. Dreamlike, she clung to him, running her fingers over his surprisingly soft skin, marveling at the occasional rough lines: scars caused by battles with squid and rival males. She saw something round and realized through a fog of hypothermia it was his eye. Their gazes met and Avalanche gave a tremendous shiver. His lower jaw slowly opened and he uttered a mournful groan, a deep bellow that vibrated through Amara's frame, penetrating her very core. Her own body shook in response as she sensed the immeasurable despair he felt. She experienced remorse welling up inside her, as well as a fierce maternal protectiveness, but the burgeoning feelings deadened along with the rest of her body. She knew her brain was shutting down from hypothermia but she no longer cared. Her numbed body could no longer sense the ocean's frigidness as she drifted sleepily.

Suddenly, she was yanked back, her head snapping forward. She felt her eyes burning as she broke the surface. Someone was pulling her back, their strong arm holding her, their encouraging voice whispering into her ear. She opened her mouth to speak, but only seawater gurgled out. A dark cloud settled over her vision.

Then, Amara's world became black.

―――――――

As she opened her eyes to painfully bright white, Amara's relief at being alive abruptly vanished. A barrage of flashbacks from her previous hospitalization formed an alliance with her pounding headache. The pressure inside her head grew until the suture lines of her skull felt like they were beginning to split. She wheezed in a lungful of plasticized air as she recalled the moments before she blacked out. With time, her vision cleared and she felt relief with every drawn breath. Slowly, she took in the sterility of her room.

"Mon, it's a good ting ta see ya awake, finally."

Amara turned toward the familiar voice, her headache spiking so badly it made her want to scream. She blinked through the pain, focusing on the voice coming from a nearby armchair. She stared blankly.

"It's Willie," he said with a grin.

"Oh my God," Amara started. She fumbled to remove the oxygen mask that obstructed her nose and mouth. "Was it you that saved me?"

Willie nodded solemnly, his gaze dropping to the tiled floor at his feet. "I did what I could."

"What happened?"

"We was all in da freezing water. Wit all da smoke I couldn't see any ting." Willie's skin goose-bumped and a shiver ran through him. "I only found ya because I followed da sound of da whale, calling."

"And the rest of our crew?"

"Dem people on da runabout are all okay. When I dragged ya onto da upside down *Sea Scout*, dey was already clinging to it."

Amara nodded slowly in acknowledgment. "Avalanche?"

Willie gave her a hesitant smile. "He got away in all da confusion."

Amara breathed a small sigh of relief. Then she felt another surge of panic. She swallowed hard before asking the question she truly feared. "Robert?"

His eyes still down, Willie pursed his lips and shook his head. "Da *Nagata's* harpoon took out *Sea Green III's* entire bridge. Dere were no survivors. I'm sorry."

Amara's rib cage became a hollow steel prison, trapping her breath inside her chest. She began to shake. Her fiancé was gone. She sensed it when she saw the explosion, but still couldn't believe it. With her father gone this past year, Robert was the only person left that mattered to her. And they killed him. All the good he would do for the oceans and the world died with him.

Amara felt tears stream down her cheeks, her face flushing hot with grief. Then she felt a flame light within, the kind that came with fast growing fury. She blinked away her sorrow, her eyes becoming as cold and hard as sapphires. "What about my uncle? What's become of him?"

The big Jamaican looked confused. "Your–"

"Haruto Nakamura. He was the captain of the *Nagata*."

"The captain . . . ?"

Amara felt her lips draw back over her teeth. "Yes, Willie. My uncle was commanding the ship that killed Robert and our bridge crew. Is he dead? Is he in custody?"

Willie turned ashen, obviously dreading what he was about to say. "Da whaler broke off after da explosion and vanished before da authorities made it dere. I'm sorry. Dey got away."

Amara felt tears of rage and frustration replacing those of grief and loss. After a minute, she turned back to Willie, a tiny sniffle prefacing her speech.

"Thank you for saving my life."

"It was my privilege," Willie said. He leaned forward, his elbows on his knees and his long hands forming a steeple against his lips. "I gotta look after ya. No one else can keep up."

Just then, a tall, middle-aged nurse walked over to Amara, chart in hand.

"It's good to see you awake, young lady. You gave us quite a scare when they brought you in." She gave a motherly smile as she reached over and adjusted Amara's IV and pillow. She looked down at her clipboard, comparing her chart to her patient's monitors. "Well, Miss . . . Nakamura. You seem to be healing up quite well. I imagine the doctor will release you tomorrow, next day at the latest."

Amara nodded and gave her a determined smile. "Thank you, for your kindness. But there's been some kind of error. My last name is not Nakamura."

"Really?" The nurse wore a confused look. She double-checked Amara's chart and left abruptly.

Amara stared up at the ceiling, her chin jutting out. "The Nakamura's are despoilers of the sea. And now, they're murderers as well." She exhaled slowly, the sound like steam escaping from beneath the lid of a covered pot. "I'm going to take over Robert's work. I don't know how, but somehow I'll get my own command. My father's gone, and I have no desire to be associated with his brother or the rest of the Nakamura clan. Screw all their money. They're dead to me. I'll use my mother's name from this point forward. It's Amara Takagi now." Her eyes softened as she looked at Willie. "You can call me Amara."

Willie's inclined chin and lowered eyes were the equivalent of a courtier's bow. "It will be my pleasure, Amara. So, what ya gonna do now?

Before she could reply, the nurse returned.

"There's a gentleman calling for you. Due to your condition we've been holding calls, but he's quite insistent – says it's urgent. Something about your accident . . ."

Amara sighed. "Sure, I'll take it. Thanks." She accepted the handset from her, leaning wearily back as she hit the speakerphone. "Hello?"

"Ms. Nakamura?"

Amara felt a chill penetrate her like a pickaxe. It was the man who threatened her from the loudspeaker of the *Nagata*. She could never forget his voice. She swallowed hard, struggling to find her own. "Who is this? What do you want?"

"Don't be alarmed. I want to speak with you."

"Speak with me?" Amara's rage began to overpower her fear. "You've got a lot of nerve calling me, whoever you are."

"*Who* I am, is not important. *What* I am may be."

"What's that supposed to mean?"

The speaker's deep tones remained smooth and sure. "I'm what some might refer to as a procurer of . . . trophies. Been doing it for years, never paid it any mind. But yesterday's experience had a profound effect on me."

"I don't understand."

"It never occurred to me that someone might actually get hurt on one of my safaris. Now that it's happened, I–"

Amara felt herself snap. "*Now that it's happened*? Do you *know* what you've *done*?"

"I wasn't in command of the *Nagata*. Your uncle was, if I'm not mistaken. Have you spoken to him?"

"No, and if I have my way, I never will – unless it's when I testify against him in court."

The speaker stifled a chuckle. "That's fine. I sympathize with you. And I respect your desire for revenge." There was a long pause. "I'm . . . curious about you. Perhaps we can meet?"

Amara's eyebrows lowered, her nostrils flaring. "Oh, I'd *love* for us to meet. I'm curious too. I want to find out who you are, so I can have you arrested for being an accomplice in my fiancé's death!"

There was a momentary pause. "I wasn't in command, hence, I am not responsible. However, I've decided to turn over a new leaf and I want to help."

"What are you talking about?"

"I want to make amends for your loss. Call it a donation."

"A donation?" Amara repeated. "You mean a bribe?"

"Hardly, I'm prepared to offer you the advance I received from my backers – the foreign fucks who wanted that poor whale's head mounted in their corporate office."

Amara scoffed. "Oh, so, it's a 'poor whale' now, eh? Yesterday you wanted to kill him. Why the change of heart?"

"Because your bravery and passion made me realize how small a person I really am. I want to make up for the things I've done." The speaker cleared his throat. "Look, if you don't want to meet me I understand. But at least let me mail you a check. You can donate it to whichever organization you deem worthy."

"Look, I don't need your pathetic donation, I will–"

"It's seven hundred and fifty thousand dollars."

"Seven hundred and . . ." Amara's words ended in a strangled squeak.

"Yes, Ms. Nakamura. Where should I send the money?"

Amara exhaled through bowed lips. She glanced at Willie from beneath raised eyebrows. He wore a skeptical look, but nodded.

"It's Amara," she said finally. "Alright, I'll meet with you, mister . . ."

"Thank you for your compassion, Amara," the speaker said silkily. "My friends call me Pierce."

As she hung up, a splash of cold water struck Amara square in the face. She gasped and spat, tasted brine. She opened startled eyes to find Willie gone and her hospital room with him. She was back on the *Harbinger's* bow, her hands firmly locked onto its sturdy railing.

With an effort, she relinquished her grip. She stared bemusedly down at the swells that continued to reach for her. The headwind was howling, punishing her repeatedly with bone chilling whiplashes of salt spray. She felt a cold shiver run through her and hugged herself tightly. She shook her head and headed carefully back the way she came, toward the waiting shelter of her quarters. She yearned to climb back into bed, hit the lights, and cocoon herself for the rest of the day within her comforter's downy womb.

Some dry clothes and a hot cup of coffee would have to do.

———

Supremely confident in his species' unchallenged dominion over Earth's oceans, the bull sperm whale silently stalked his quarry. His enormous flukes moved effortlessly up and down, propelling him deeper into pitch-black hunting grounds. Measuring a full seventy feet from nose to tail and weighing over ninety tons, the male *Physeter macrocephalus* was a giant. His massive head made up nearly a third of his total length, and his enormous jaws were lined with conical teeth twelve inches long.

At thirty-five, the whale was the region's dominant bull for nearly a decade, emerging victorious in scores of battles with rival males.

The Equator's winter breeding season where the big bulls fought for the privilege to mate with harems of females was still months away. Until then, the great beast would travel to the Antarctic Ocean, searching for food as the hot summer months wore on. The journey was a long and arduous one, with peril at every corner. It would require tremendous amounts of energy to sustain itself.

Although a twelve-foot thresher shark already rested within the whale's sizable stomach, the cetacean was unsatisfied. Too impatient to scrounge for food on the surface, like the cows and younger males did, the bull dove deep to seek out his favorite prey. He hunted a rapacious killer, one few living things made contact with and survived: the giant squid.

Majestically, the monarch of the seas descended. He could hold his breath for an hour and a half, controlling his buoyancy by drawing in ice-cold seawater to cool the spermaceti wax stored within his head. Thick layers of blubber and a powerful musculature shielded him from the icy water and pressure.

As he approached his target area, the whale gave forth a series of noisy clicks and pings. The mile-long sonar cone he was emitting reverberated back, leading him directly to his prey, suspended a thousand feet below. It was fortunate to find food so quickly within the vastness of the abyss, but the detailed sound image the whale got back was disconcerting.

The prey item was huge.

Hovering within a deep-water current, the squid was a terrifying apparition. Known as a Colossal Squid, the female *Mesonychoteuthis hamiltoni* was itself a formidable predator. It measured at least forty feet from the tip of its caudal fin to the ends of its shorter tentacles, and weighed as much as a full-grown basking shark.

Besides its intimidating size, the squid's tentacles had twelve-inch suction cups equipped with swiveling black claws as large as the suckers themselves. These razor-sharp talons were capable of ripping a full-grown tiger shark to shreds. Only the largest and most dominant sperms dared to tackle such dangerous prey. A whale embroiled in battle with a mollusk of such proportion could run out of oxygen while locked within its opponent's embrace. Predator could easily become prey.

This alpha male, however, feared nothing. The scars crisscrossing his enormous head gave evidence to that. Of all the creatures that swam the seas, only pods of killer whales gave him pause. And even the deadly orcas usually preyed upon the smaller female sperms, which lacked the giant bull's strength and foul disposition.

Closing quickly on his prey, the whale channeled his sonar emissions into a tight beam, a ray of sound focused directly on the squid. This beam was nature's greatest innovation in the arms race between predator and prey. In a chase, the whale would be far slower, but his sonar beam was a long range weapon that enabled him to attack and disable the squid from afar. By stunning the *Mesonychoteuthis* with bursts of sound waves, he could reach it before it jetted away, clamping down on it before it had a chance to defend itself. The battle would be over before it began.

Blasting away with his sonar, the whale prepared to attack from a steep angle. The cetacean could see his sonic bursts taking effect. The cephalopod was drifting helplessly, its tentacles splaying out in every direction. Accelerating to maximum velocity with repeated sweeps of his eighteen-foot flukes, the sperm ceased his sonar attack at the last possible moment and spread his gigantic jaws.

He powered into the squid with devastating effect. Seizing it by the mantle, he crunched down, driving foot-long teeth deep into the rubbery tissue directly above the squid's glowing green eyes, seeking to crush its tiny brain.

Still reeling from the sonar attack that scrambled its primitive synapses, the squid began to rebound the instant the assault ended. Sensing the whale's approach by the pressure wave preceding it, it turned to fight just as its enemy descended upon it like a grey-colored rockslide. Though dazed, it was far from defeated. It lashed out with its two retractable tentacles and fastened them like grapnels to the whale's head and shoulders, ripping its fleshy exterior to shreds. Bloody scraps of skin and blubber obscured the already dark waters. Now in full attack mode, the mollusk utilized its eight shorter tentacles, wrapping them around the whale's lower jaw and probing for its eyes.

If it could tear into the whale's sensitive ocular region, the cetacean would have to spit it out to save its vision. If not, the squid would immobilize the whale's jaw, keeping it from inflicting further damage.

Its adversary would eventually tire and have to surface. Once that happened, the cephalopod would have the upper hand.

The deadly struggle continued. Locked in combat, the two underwater titans struggled silently back and forth in the dark, each seeking to destroy the other.

The whale, wearying of the stalemate, began to tear away at the squid with undisguised fury. Shaking the smaller predator from side to side as a terrier would a rat, the bull flung his cottage-sized head back and forth, trying to free himself of the clinging arms. The squid's toothy tentacles began to tear loose one by one, leaving trails of blood in their wake. The whale could sense his victory.

Out of nowhere, he felt a pressure wave. Disbelief flooded his immense brain. There was another predator down there with him, as huge and formidable as he. Focused on his food, the bull had neglected to scan the surrounding depths before attacking. Whatever else was down there in the darkness was closing in on him at incredible speed. And it *wasn't* another whale.

The sperm whale heaved back and forth, desperately struggling to free himself from the remaining tentacles that prevented him from defending himself. At the last possible moment, the cetacean's titanic strength came through and he flung the injured mollusk away into the darkness. Twisting in the pitch-black depths, the whale turned in the direction of his attacker, jaws open and ready to fight.

It was too late. The intruder slammed into the whale's flank with the speed and power of a locomotive. Toothy jaws sliced through thick layers of blubber and tore deep into the rock-hard muscles underneath. So powerful was the impact, the ninety-ton bull was pushed sideways a hundred feet from the force of the blow. His roar of pain echoed through the water, accompanied by most of his air supply.

Furiously snapping his jaws, the bull circled warily back, scanning his mysterious opponent with a barrage of sonar clicks. The intruder was something the whale had never encountered before – a monstrous crocodile with flippers instead of feet.

Short of oxygen, the wounded cachalot pointed his nose up and raced for the surface. His flukes flailing, he vanished into the darkness, streaming blood. Behind him, the whale heard the unmistakable sounds of feeding, as his attacker devoured the injured squid.

EIGHT

Cruising along at twenty knots, the thirty-six foot Bertram *Sayonara* made its way steadily offshore.

As he manned the wheel, Captain Phil Starling couldn't help but smile. Despite all the hardships he endured, he was having the time of his life. It was a very good day for him, and he'd learned to appreciate the good days now more than ever. The weather was beautiful, the seas were calm, and the nausea and discomfort he experienced after receiving his chemo was unusually mild. On top of that, he was out at sea and in command of his own ship, on a quest to land a fish the size of a minivan.

Phil tossed a quick glance at his enthusiastic first mate and smiled again. Young Stevie was a godsend, perpetually by his side, always attentive, and eager to help. The kid never ran out of energy or vigor, and never, ever complained. Even now, he was busy scanning the radar and horizon, alert for floating debris that might pose a danger to the old boat's hull.

"So, Stevie boy," Phil said, clapping the well-tanned teenager on the back. "Are you fired up to take a shot at a grander tuna?"

"You know it, Uncle Phil." His exuberant mate smiled back at him from behind his sunglasses. "But, we've caught bluefin before."

"True, but not like this," Phil shouted over the sounds of the engines. He changed course slightly as he followed his GPS. "These are mature adults, my boy. The big dogs! Not the hundred pound juveniles we were pulling in a month ago. No, sir!" Phil chuckled as he turned toward his nephew. "The smallest fish we'll hook today, Stevie – if we're lucky – will weigh six hundred pounds. And they get over twice that size!"

"Sounds good to me. I know we can handle whatever comes our way."

"You're a good kid," the old man affirmed. "And I hope you're right about that. I'm not as young and fit as I used to be."

"That's why you brought me along." Steve took a half-step back and gritted his teeth, clenching his fists and flexing his muscles as he attempted to strike a "most muscular" bodybuilding pose. "And any tuna that messes with you is going to have to answer to me first!"

Phil laughed amusedly. He turned back just in time to spot a vessel about to collide with them.

"Son of a . . ." Cursing, he threw it into neutral in a desperate attempt to slow their forward momentum. The sudden inertia tossed them both into the nearest bulkhead with bone-jarring force.

Just then, a roaring black and yellow Jet-Ski with a single rider leapt across their path. At forty miles an hour, it narrowly missed a deadly collision with the *Sayonara's* pearl-white bow.

"Goddamn stupid son of a bitch!" Phil raged. Staggering to his feet, he leapt toward the port side and reached for his binoculars. "Just wait until I find out who the hell . . ."

Phil peered through his electronic range finders, focusing on the Jet Ski and its rider. His eyes narrowed into slits behind the device's rubbery eyecups as he recognized the culprit.

"Who is it, Uncle Phil?" his nephew growled through clenched teeth. He wiped away a trickle of blood that ran from his nose.

"Brad Harcourt," Phil said. He lowered his binoculars, a disgusted look on his face.

"The little prick who's dad owns the marina? We should call this in!" Steve grabbed at the vessel's radio.

"No point, it won't do any good." Phil said solemnly. He watched as the Jet Ski loitered nearby. He reached down and pushed the throttle lever back to the forward position. "C'mon, let's get back on course."

Picking up speed, the big Bertram climbed back on plane, motoring toward the fishing grounds. As Phil looked back, his face darkened. It looked like Brad Harcourt was preparing to follow them.

Sure enough, the high speed craft began cruising up behind them, just off the starboard side. With his hair pressed down and a smile on his face, Brad ran parallel to them, matching their speed. Then, he pulled a ninety degree turn to port, running directly at the churning wall of water created by their passing.

Accelerating to full speed, Brad bounced his craft off and over the oncoming wake, rising ten feet into the air before crashing back down with a splash. With the Jet Ski spitting water, he sped noisily away from the *Sayonara*, only to return from the opposite direction. He aimed his prow once again at the larger vessel's wake, his speed increasing rapidly.

"He's wake-jumping us, that little bastard!" Phil shouted over the engines. Behind them, Brad repeated his previous maneuver, flying into the air only fifty feet back this time. "He's gonna get himself killed, damn him!"

Phil threw the *Sayonara* into neutral once more. Shaking his head, he went below. Behind him, his nephew stood like a statue, his lean arms folded across his chest as he glared at the black and yellow watercraft's owner.

From below decks, Phil peered through a salt-stained porthole. A hundred feet away, Brad sat quietly on his craft, waiting for the *Sayonara* to get under way again so he could continue the game. The seconds ticked by. Apparently irritated with the delay, the teenager revved his engine several times in an effort to communicate his growing impatience. Phil grabbed what he needed and headed back above. He heard Stevie start to say something.

"Uncle Phil, what should we–"

Stevie stopped talking. He glanced apprehensively down at his uncle's left hand.

Phil adjusted his grip on the shotgun. "I'll tell you what we should do," he said. He kept the formidable weapon held low and hidden from view. "What we should do is chase that cocky little son of a bitch down and blow his little water toy out from under him with ol' Charlotte, here." He patted the gun affectionately. "Then, we should haul his waterlogged ass back into port to turn him over to Jake Braddock."

"We should?" his nephew said. There was astonishment on his face.

"Yeah, we *should*." Phil smirked. "But then his daddy would undoubtedly end up owning this old girl here." He tapped the boat's teak flooring with his foot. "And you and I would probably end up in jail, instead of that little bastard out there." He gestured at the distant Jet Ski, which was starting to creep closer.

"So, what are we going to do?" Steve said. He stared nervously at the gun.

"I'll show you." Phil answered with a grin. "Hey, Harcourt!" He shouted loudly, his voice traveling across the water. "I think we're going to anchor up and start fishing right here, so you might as well go seek your entertainment elsewhere!"

"That's bullshit!" Brad's response echoed back at them. "I know for a fact that none of you charter yahoos do any of your fishing around here, so you might as well get back on course." Smiling ear to ear, their nemesis waited a moment before adding, "Don't worry. I'll try not to end up in your props!"

"If only he would . . ." Phil said to himself. "Hey Brad, maybe you're right! I hear it is pretty hard to draw fish around here." He hefted his weapon into view as he continued. "Maybe I should try a technique we used around Montauk in the old days, to draw prowling sharks in. They're attracted to the noise, you know."

Raising the heavy Mossberg to his shoulder, Phil pumped a shell into its chamber and fired a thunderous round high into the air.

Visibly recoiling in his seat, Brad Harcourt screamed back. "Are you out of your fucking mind, old man? You scared the shit out of me!"

Ignoring Brad, Phil moved around the *Sayonara's* white fighting chair to the rear of the boat, the smoking weapon resting on his shoulder. "Gee, it looks like that didn't do it," he said, shielding his eyes with his free hand and making a deliberate show of scanning the surface of the water. "I guess the fish in these parts need to actually *feel* the sound waves in order for them to get the point."

"What the hell are you–"

Brad didn't get to finish his sentence before Phil chambered another round and swung the scattergun smoothly to his shoulder. He fired it again, this time directly into the water less than twenty feet from where Brad was sitting. Like a cherry bomb, the heavy deer slug sent a miniature geyser of water splashing eight feet high and foam spraying in every direction.

"Jesus Christ, you crazy old bastard!" Brad shrieked at the top of his lungs. "You could have killed me! My dad's gonna have your head!"

Chambering yet another round, Phil moved forward until his thighs were pressed tightly against the *Sayonara's* transom. "Hmm, maybe my aim was off," he mused, his gray eyes narrowing portals of granite. "Third time's a charm?" Raising the shotgun to his shoulder one more time, Phil swung it around in the Jet-Ski's direction.

Brad Harcourt shrieked, ducked his head and threw his craft into high gear. Turning around, he cursed, flipped them the bird, and took off.

"Holy shit," Steve said as the watercraft and its rider faded into the distance. "For a second there, I actually thought you were going to shoot him."

"Nah." Phil grinned. "I was bluffing from the beginning. I only had two shells on board." He winked and laughed aloud at the surprised expression on Stevie's face. "C'mon kiddo, let's get moving. We've got a tide to catch, and hopefully, a bluefin or two. By the way, how are those butterfish holding up?"

The teenager moved over to the big boat's rear bait box, raising its fiberglass lid as he peered inside. The school of ten-inch long silvery baitfish swirled around nervously. "They're all looking good," Steve said, standing beside his captain.

The old man brought the twin diesels back to life. "You know Stevie-boy, if you ask me; best bait in the world for giant tuna is live butterfish. They love em." He turned and gave his nephew a smirk as they quickly picked up speed. "One thing I've learned, when you're fishing for big meat-eaters kiddo, you've got to give 'em something they like to sink their teeth into!"

Accelerating to top speed to make up for the unwanted interruption, the *Sayonara's* captain guided them on their way.

Twenty miles to the south, and a half mile from the underwater chasm known as *Ophion's Deep*, the *Harbinger* lowered her anchors. Under Amara's command, the twenty-four person crew of the seven hundred and forty ton vessel operated as a well-oiled machine.

Standing within the ship's museum-like bridge, Amara spoke smoothly into a handheld microphone. "Come in, Joe." She paused as she felt the vintage steel vessel shudder slightly under her. "How're the anchors holding?"

There was a static-laden delay before Joe Calabrese responded. "They're in there good, boss. No problems here. You can prep the mini-sub for launch whenever you're ready."

"Thanks." Amara turned to the two crewmembers standing behind her. Red-haired Lane Brodsky and his balding colleague Mike Helm were both on loan from the University of Miami's Marine Biology Department, and were trading their time and labor for room and board, as well as some invaluable thesis material. The two of them were already shaping up to be topnotch assistants, and Amara knew that either of them could pilot the *Harbinger's* sixteen-foot scout craft as well as she could. "Lane, I want you and Mike to get the *Sycophant* launched ASAP. I want you guys out circling the area. Give me a perimeter of a thousand yards to start, and I want sighting reports every five minutes."

"You got it, boss," Lane said.

As they turned to go, Amara added, "Oh, and bring the video equipment, guys. Just in case there's any action going on. Surface footage may not be as exciting as the *William's* underwater cameras, but it will still get you guys into the pages of National Geographic."

Grinning at their enthusiastic smiles, Amara walked over to her waiting first mate. Still bent over his charts punching fuel figures into a nearby calculator, Willie had been fussing over the preparations for the *William's* initial launch all night. Amara smiled and patted him on the shoulder. "Okay, big guy. Let's go down to the observation room and see what's going on before we send our baby off on her maiden voyage."

"Straight away," Willie said.

Originally an enormous storage room, the rectangular forty foot-long space had been converted into a high tech tracking and surveillance station that would have made the CIA proud. A score of LCD screens lined the walls and desks of the assorted stations, some with screens five feet wide. A dozen techs were busy manning their computers, photographing specimens, monitoring sonar and radar, tracking weather, and editing video footage. Scrutinizing the scene, Amara could see the place was a beehive of scientific documentation, a floating film studio with one purpose in mind: to record nature's most intimate wonders as they happened, and then share those finds with the world. It was what she lived for, and she loved it.

"Willie, do me a favor, get on the sonar, please?"

"Aye, boss."

Amara moved purposely to a nearby station, where Adam Spencer sat observing a monitor screen directly in front of him. "Well? Do we have anything yet?"

"We sure do," Adam replied, turning in his seat and peering over his thick lenses at her. "All six of our main hull cameras are active and fully functional." There was a clacking sound as he rolled laterally in his chair, pointing to several nearby monitors with a pencil for emphasis. "Our port viewers are focused on nothing right now, since the action is toward the starboard. I've set them for motion sensing with alternate-frame auto-record, in case they pick up anything."

Amara nodded her approval.

Adam turned toward the viewer directly in front of him. "The real action is being picked up by cameras two and three right now." He tapped the nearest screen with his pencil's eraser. "I've got a pod of fourteen female sperms with a half-dozen calves frolicking some three hundred yards to starboard. From the looks of it, I'd say the pod is one of our regulars for this time of year. Looks like L-22 and her group."

Studying the monitor, Amara watched the whales with fascination. Though the video feed was poor, she could still make out the streamlined shapes of the forty-foot females as they gently corralled their young. They undulated through the water, some moving slower than others as they suckled their calves.

"Can you do anything about the picture quality?" Amara was tempted to reach over and adjust the monitor's settings herself. However, considering Adam's temperament when it came to people messing with his equipment, she thought better of it.

"Sorry, boss. At three hundred yards out, even at maximum zoom, this is the best we're going to get. It's a matter of water clarity. We can try and move closer if you'd like, but then we risk spooking the pod."

"No, you're right," Amara said. "This is fine. We'll get some top-water footage from the *Sycophant*, once the action starts. If it looks like the females won't mind, we'll bring the *William* in right on top of them and get some never before seen shots."

Adam remained focused on his monitor, periodically making adjustments and glancing over at several other video screens before returning to the main one right in front of him.

Amara looked over at Willie, busy as always, watching his desk-mounted sonar screen and listening intently into a pair of oversized headphones. She reached over and touched him gently on the elbow. "Anything?"

Willie removed one earpiece and inclined his head in her direction. "Not a damn ting, woman," he replied. "I'm not pickin up any sign of even one of ya pods of killer whales. Dey must be many miles from here, if da hydrophone can't pick dem up."

"I kind of hope you're right," Amara said. She breathed in deep through her nostrils and exhaled slowly through her teeth. As much as her partners at the Worldwide Cetacean Society wanted this study on Orca/Sperm whale "interaction," she wasn't thrilled with the idea of having to sit there and wait for a marauding gang of transients to come in and rip one of her whales to pieces while she watched. Illuminated with a green glow on the black screen, the pod of sperms showed up as a single, convoluted sonar image, with the pod's depth readings ranging from the surface down to two or three hundred feet.

Willie studied her sorrowful expression. "Aye girl. For all ya know, dem killer whales ain't even in dis part of da world right now. Maybe dey won't even show up."

"No, Willie, they're out there somewhere," Amara said evenly. "Orca pods *alpha*, *beta* and *gamma* have all been recorded making kills in this region, during this exact time period, yearly, for the last decade. That's why we scheduled the next two weeks to do our studies in the first place."

The killer whales would come. It was inevitable. The three groups she mentioned had been slaughtering the region's sperm whales for the last four summers. They were the top predators in the area, and opportunistic feeders. With nothing able to stop them, there was no reason why they would give up an easy meal like a sperm whale calf, or even a cow if need be. They knew where and when the dinner banquet was going to be held, and they'd be hungry when they arrived.

Willie nodded his head and started to replace his earpiece.

"Say, Willie," Amara stopped him with a touch. "Are you sure you haven't heard *anything* out there?"

"Da only ting out of da ordinary was a muffled sound or two coming out of da abyss, Amara," Willie said. "I don't know for sure, but my nose tells me dat one of your whales is down dere, and had hisself a run in wit a giant piece of calamari." He winked at her, his strong white teeth forming an ear-splitting grin.

"You know, you're making me hungry, Willie." Amara chuckled. "Not that we've any shortage of seafood out here. Anyway, keep me posted if you hear anything."

"Don't I always?" Willie asked, grinning as she moved off.

With a half-smile brightening up her abnormally serious features, Amara trudged over to her desk and plopped down into her padded leather chair. Grateful for the fresh cup of coffee one of the interns offered her, she reached for the hand radio suspended at her belt.

"Lane, it's Amara. Are you reading me?"

"We read you loud and clear," Lane answered.

Judging from the amount of background noise, the two men were already navigating the inflatable dinghy that functioned as the high-speed scout in their operation.

"Well, what have we got?" Amara tried not to shout. She reached over and gave her blank monitor a gentle rap on one side. "We're not receiving your video feed."

Adam's head shake confirmed her statement.

"We're having some sort of transmission problem, boss," Lane explained. "We're going to have to go with the old-fashioned camcorder approach. No sign of your killer whales. Do you want us to shoot some footage of the mother sperms and their calves?"

"That's a negative. Unless you see something unusual, we've got plenty of stock footage of the females and their young. Just keep working the perimeter and call me if anything breaks."

"Will do, boss."

Sitting back, Amara sipped her coffee. Her monitor shimmered as Adam transferred the underwater feed of the whales back onto the screen. She tapped the nails of her free hand on the top of her glass-covered desk like tumbling dominoes, trying to force herself to relax. As much as she loved her job, she hated the endless monotony of being forced to sit back and wait for something to happen.

Or for something to get killed.

With a thunderous snort that was audible a quarter-mile away, the creature breached the water's surface, directly over the abyss. It peered about, taking deep breaths that quickly replenished its muscles with oxygen. Hissing loudly, it closed its nose flaps and submerged, its lifeboat-size flippers propelling its massive bulk through the water with deceptively gentle strokes.

As it swam, the creature's scarred snout wrinkled up. It yawned wide, expelling a fragment of tissue that remained lodged between two of its machete-sized fangs. Like a flower stalk caught in a stiff breeze, the six-foot fragment of one of the colossal squid's tentacles spiraled into the depths.

Having inflicted serious injury upon its mammalian rival, five thousand feet below, the creature opted to ignore its retreating opponent. Instead, it pounced upon the hapless prey that spurred its competitive instincts to life.

The squid had struggled desperately in its bid for freedom, viciously slashing the creature with its beak and tentacles while writhing to and fro. It was useless. Even its slippery skin couldn't save it. Evolution had enhanced the creature's jaws with rows of hooked rear dentition, assuring that prey partially within the confines of its cavernous mouth traveled one way only – into its stomach. Dispatching its thrashing victim with a quick snap that nearly severed the giant mollusk in two, the creature sheared away its bothersome tentacles and seized the remaining mantle portion in its mouth. Wary of the sharp fourteen-foot gladius bone that gave the cephalopod's body its rigidity, it crunched down on the squid repeatedly until it reduced both the mantle and gladius to a pulp. What was left was quickly shaken apart into manageable-sized portions and systematically swallowed.

Rising ghost-like out of the abyss, the creature extended its senses in all directions in an effort to detect its injured opponent. The currents that emerged from the abyss were strong, and neither its sound images nor its phenomenal sense of smell could pick up any trace of the wounded whale. With no discernible sign of its adversary, it descended once more, content to continue its exploration.

Leveling off at a depth of four hundred feet, the creature picked up speed. Less than a thousand yards away, something piqued its interest. It could sense a score of life forms gathered in a group. A quick scan confirmed that the animals were the same species as the one it just routed, though significantly smaller. Given the presence of their young and their body structure, they appeared to be females.

It was apparent to the giant predator that the sperm whale cows were alarmed by its presence. They began to form up in a tightly packed school with the young in the center. It cruised closer. It would be an easy matter to plow into the school, decimating their ranks and returning to pick off a victim at its leisure.

The creature ignored the whales and started to veer off to the south. Suddenly, its flippers stiffened and splayed straight out from its sides, creating a braking effect that slowed its body. As it did, its immense head shifted sharply, its nostrils working furiously. Its highly sensitive olfactory system had detected the faint scent of fish blood, wafting though the water. The smell was diluted, originating several miles from its current position. Cocking its crocodile-like skull to one side, it strained its tiny ears, listening to the heartbeat of the surrounding ocean.

There, mixed in with a symphony of sounds, was the alluring resonance of a dying animal. The thrashing sounds were unmistakable. Although its vast stomach was almost full, the creature found itself drawn. Easy meals were few and far between, and like a gorged bass that couldn't help but snap at an injured baitfish, its inherent response to the stimulus took over.

With a tremendous splash, it headed unswervingly toward the banquet. Its four flippers resumed their rhythmic thrusting, building up speed. Cruising directly beneath the huddled school of frightened sperm whales, the creature continued to accelerate. As it rose toward the surface, it moved in the direction of the huge metal object that lay directly in its path.

—

"Bloody hell, mon!" Willie's face held undisguised astonishment as he sprang to his feet. He clutched at his oversized headphones, pressing them tightly to his head. All heads turned in his direction as his coffee mug crashed loudly to the floor.

"Willie, what is it?" Amara asked.

"Ya not gonna believe it." Willie breathed excitedly. He dropped a DVD into a nearby recording device and started pushing buttons left and right. "Adam, can ya get me an audio recording of what I'm about to send ya, mon?"

"Believe what?" Annoyed at being ignored, Amara rose and moved to his station. "Willie, what the heck's going on?"

"One second please, boss." Willie held up a hand as he continued making quick adjustments on the electronics. His eyes intense, he glanced over at Adam, waited for his nod of approval, then threw both live audio feed transmission switches. Turning back toward Amara, Willie gestured at his scope. "We got us a *bloop*, mon!" he said, gushing with excitement.

"A bloop?" Amara echoed, her hands resting on his sonar table as she watched the screen. "Are you sure? I don't see anything."

"Aye," Willie said, nodding his head vigorously. "It's dere. I tell ya, mon, I neva seen or heard nuttin like dis in my whole life."

Adam Spencer raised his pencil and eyebrows. "Forgive me for asking, but what the hell is a bloop?"

Amara folded her arms across her chest. "It's an unexplained audio signature. The US navy first started picking them up in 1997, using Cold War technology designed to track Soviet submarines." Her eyes were like telescopes as they focused on the screen in front of her. "The sound supposedly matches the profile of a living creature, something from the extreme deep. Whatever it is, based on signal strength it's supposed to be huge, larger than any known creature, including a whale."

"Really?" Adam's eyes went wide behind his glasses. "Sounds intriguing. So, what does the navy think this 'bloop' is?"

"Unknown. Possibly some undiscovered species of gigantic octopus or squid, at least based on what they've seen. But that's only a theory, of course."

"Dere it is, mon!" Willie said, holding his headset tightly with one hand. He snapped his fingers. "Adam, put dis on da overhead speakers. Quick, if ya please!"

Adam reached over and flipped a switch. He leaned back in his seat and cocked his head, listening for the thump of the feed kicking in. Soon, all the scientists and interns in the room were hearing what Willie was listening to.

The sound echoed throughout the observation room. It was deep and loud, reminiscent of steel grating against stone. It had a repetitive, ratcheting quality to it as it rumbled from the ship's audio system, so base in pitch it reverberated in their bones as well as their ears. For a long moment, no one said anything. They all simply stood or sat where they were, transfixed by the alien noises.

Finally, Amara spoke up, breaking everyone out of their hypnotic state

"Okay, everybody, let's get focused and find out exactly what we're dealing with." She turned to Willie and placed one hand on his shoulder. "Willie, besides the audio file, do you have a verifiable sonar reading on this thing?"

"I did for a minute, when it first come out of da abyss, but den it–" He hesitated, adjusting his screen settings. "Wait, dere it is again! Look!" Willie's hand shook as he pointed at the screen. On the monitor before them was an enormous sonar signature. It was moving swiftly beneath the surface of the water, less than a thousand yards away.

"Definitely organic," Adam said.

"Jesus, you were right," Amara half-whispered as she scrutinized the wavering image. "I assume you're recording this?"

"Of course." Willie pointed to the lit-up DVD burner.

"My God, if I'm reading your scan correctly, that thing is huge!" Amara exclaimed. "How big do you think it is, and more importantly, *what* do you think it is?"

"I dunno what it is, but it's big all right. As big as any whale I've eva seen." An alarmed look slid across Willie's face. "Amara . . . I tink we have a problem."

"What's that?"

"Whateva dis ting is, it's headin in da direction of da sperm whales . . . and our inflatable."

Her eyes peeling wide, Amara grabbed her radio. "*Sycophant*, this is Amara, come in!"

There was no answer. Furiously checking the radio's settings and power readings, she tried again. "Attention Lane or Mike, this is Amara calling. Do you read me?"

"This is Lane. We read you loud and clear. Sorry boss, but we've got a bit of a situation brewing out here. What's up?"

"A situation? What's going on out there? Is everything okay?" Amara glanced over at Willie's sonar screen, watching as the huge sonar mark they were tracking moved relentlessly closer to the unsuspecting whale pod – and the *Sycophant*.

"Bloop speed is twenty five miles an hour, Amara," Willie advised. He pointed at the monitor. "And gettin faster."

"The whales are going crazy, boss." Lane's normally calm and controlled voice was laced with nervous excitement as it crackled through the radio. "They're extremely skittish and have formed up into a defensive Marguerite formation, with the adults in a circle and the calves on the inside. There must be killer whales around. I've never seen them like this before, I . . . holy shit!"

A faint hiss spewed out of the microphone.

Amara raised the radio to her lips. "Lane? Lane, come in . . ."

No answer.

Casting a glance over at Willie, who shrugged his shoulders and pointed to the still-moving radar image of the small dinghy, Amara repeated herself. "Lane, come in, Lane. This is Amara. Can you hear me?"

"Sorry, boss. You're not going to believe this, but one of the cows just charged the *Sycophant* and tried to take a bite out of us! We barely managed to get out of her way. Mike got some great footage of it!"

Shaking her head angrily at her employee's cackling, Amara yelled into the microphone. "Lane, get the hell out of there and head back to the *Harbinger*, immediately."

"Why?"

"There's something out there that's scaring the whales!"

"What kind of something?" Lane asked.

"Something big. *Real* big. And it's heading in your direction. Now move your ass, goddamn it!"

"Geez, it's probably just a whale shark or something, but okay. We're on our way."

As she lowered the radio, Amara looked up with alarm. Once again, the deep ratcheting noise thundered out of the overhead speakers, causing the room to vibrate. It sounded closer.

"Willie . . ." Amara's voice was a whisper. "Where is it?"

"Four hundred yards from us and closing, boss," Willie said. "Depth is five hundred feet and gettin shallower. Oh, mon. Speed is now . . . *forty*."

"Forty? And the *Sycophant's* top speed with the new outboard?"

"About tirty," Willie replied. He sucked in a breath, pointing at the screen. "Da bloop is comin into contact wit da whales right . . . *now*."

On the screen before them, the huge signal merged with the readings reflecting off the sperm whale pod. For a moment, the two appeared as one. Then, as Amara breathed an audible sigh of relief, the alien signal separated itself from that of the pod and continued on – heading straight toward the *Sycophant*.

"It's gaining on dem," Willie said. He jotted down some numbers. "Bloop is tree hundred yards to us, one hundred yards to da inflatable, and closin fast."

"You really think it's after Lane and Mike?" As Willie's quick nod added to her growing fears, Amara bellowed into her radio. "Lane, I need you to head for us at top speed! Do you hear me? Top speed straight to the *Harbinger*, and don't look back!"

"I don't see anything. What the hell's going on?" Lane asked.

"Never mind that. Just do it!"

"We're coming, we're . . . holy shit! There's something here! God, look at the water. It must be fucking huge!"

Amara turned back to Willie. "Distance?"

"Two hundred yards to us, fifty yards to da dinghy and closing *real* fast, boss. Bloop depth is two hundred feet. Speed is now *forty-five*." Willie blinked, checking his readings to make sure.

"That's it. Willie, come with me," Amara said, heading rapidly for the stairs. "We're going to see this thing for ourselves. And bring Adam's camcorder." As she exited the room, she yelled back over her shoulder. "Adam, make sure those starboard cameras are all set to full auto. I want live video footage of whatever the hell is out there! Let's *move* people, and look alive!"

The room behind her was a flurry of activity as Amara ran up the stairs. She took them two at a time, clenching her teeth at the pain in her hip, her radio gripped tightly in her hand, and Willie in tow. The rumbling call from the overheads shook the room once more.

Rushing quickly up on deck, the two reached the ship's railing where two interns stood, pointing and questioning aloud what all the excitement was over. In the distance, the *Sycophant* could be seen bouncing from wave to wave as it flew toward the big steel mother ship. As her pale eyes scanned the dark waters directly behind the inflatable, Amara raised her walkie-talkie. Simultaneously, Willie snapped opened the side monitor of his video camera and started filming.

"Adam, do you have those cameras up and running?" Amara asked.

"All of them."

"Do you see anything?" Amara's eyes remained focused on the surrounding ocean. Below them, Lane and Mike drew rapidly closer. They were running full out, and judging by the looks on their faces, it was as if the devil himself was chasing them.

"Dere it is, mon!" Willie shouted. He pointed toward the swirling waters below, while filming with his free hand.

Rising up directly behind the fleeing inflatable was a wave-like disturbance in the water that measured an astounding one hundred and fifty feet across. The ocean within the disturbance was swirling with such violent fury that it looked like a giant boiling pot.

As Amara gazed in awe, the *Sycophant* flew up parallel to the *Harbinger*, executing a spine-cracking turn at the last possible moment to avoid smashing full-force into the vessel's steel hull. The dinghy's outboard literally screamed from the piston-straining effort, creating a tremendous wake of foam and bubbles that slapped against the *Harbinger's* side before spreading across most of the larger vessel's starboard flank.

Sitting helplessly within their tiny vessel as the disturbance barreled beneath them, Lane and Mike screamed and held on for dear life. Their inflatable was tossed like a champagne cork bobbing in a hot tub. Above them, Amara gasped in astonishment as a giant shadowy form flew directly underneath her ship at unbelievable speed. It was still a hundred feet below the surface, but the sheer size of the object was mind-boggling. The entire two-hundred foot long, seven-hundred-plus ton ship she stood on rose several feet in the water, displaced by the force of its wake.

Then, it was gone.

Heaving slowly up and down in its aftermath, the *Harbinger's* lurching movements were accompanied by creepy groans emanating from the hull.

For a full minute, Amara did nothing but stand there, her trembling hands tightly gripping the railing of the still-swaying ship. Above her, a pair of noisy black-backed gulls circled.

Amara tried to speak, but managed only a high-pitched croak. She swallowed hard, cleared her throat. "Willie, you've been a sonar operator for ten years. What the hell *was* that?"

Willie said nothing. He just remained where he was, staring blankly down at the water that continued to slap against their rust-marred hull.

Amara shook her head. Even her stoic first mate was shaken by what just happened. She peered over the railing at the *Sycophant* and its shivering occupants. "Lane, are you guys alright?"

The tentative thumbs-up signal Amara got back from her two waterlogged interns was reassuring. At least her crew had survived the encounter with their giant mystery guest. Exhaling heavily and shaking her head a few times to clear the cobwebs, Amara called into her radio. "Adam, tell me you got that!"

There was a long pause.

"That's a negative, boss," Adam said. "Interference from the inflatable's engine disrupted the transmission on our cameras. I've got some far-off footage showing something, but it's so grainy you can't really make out much. Sorry."

"Damn it!" Amara cursed. She clamped her finger onto the radio's mute button, exhaling slowly as she struggled to remain calm. "It's okay, Adam . . . no problem. I know you did your best, as always. We'll be right down."

A quick glance over Willie's shoulder as he played back his footage showed the watery disturbance they witnessed in full detail. But it failed to shed any light on the identity of the culprit that panicked a pod of sperm whales and displaced enough seawater to cause their entire ship to sway.

Amara stared across the *Harbinger's* deck, out at the ocean's now calm surface. She shook her head. Lips taut, she turned to Willie and let out a heavy sigh. "Well, I guess we had enough excitement for one day." Her face glum, she headed toward the winding stairs that led below deck. "I don't know about you, but I'm feeling pretty drained right about now. You know what I mean?"

"Aye, Amara, dat I do," Willie's said. "But if ya tink about it, it could have been far worse."

"Really?" Amara paused in mid-stride. She turned and looked back at him, an inquisitive expression on her face. "How so?"

"Well . . ." A slow smile crept mischievously across Willie's face. "At least nobody got eaten!"

"The day's still young," Amara said. "C'mon, let's go check out whatever footage Adam has and see what we can make of it."

Below her, an exhausted and bedraggled Lane and Mike made their way slowly up the *Harbinger's* grated boarding steps and emerged topside. Their haunted countenances were grim indicators to everyone they encountered of just how close they'd come to the unknown terror that nearly claimed them.

NINE

P hil Starling hung on for dear life, leaning back into the *Sayonara's* sturdy fighting chair as the tuna made yet another blistering run. It was over two hours since the mammoth fish inhaled one of their butterfish, yet the monstrous bluefin was showing no signs of fatigue.

Phil, on the other hand, was nearing the point of exhaustion. His breathing was coming in ragged gasps, and his worn t-shirt was soaked with perspiration. Even so, he tenaciously hung on. Removing his aching hands from the rod's reinforced handle and shaking them out whenever his giant adversary ran, he paced himself with all the wisdom his decades at sea provided him.

It was the fight of his life. He'd gotten a good look at the gigantic tuna early on. The fish was one of the largest he'd ever seen, and weighed at least eleven hundred pounds. In sushi dollars, it was worth a small fortune to the avaricious Japanese brokers who would be waiting at the dock, once the call went out that the fish was being brought in for auction. Depending on fat content and fight time, the bluefin would net him as much as thirty thousand dollars and would make his season. It would allow him to not only catch up on his mortgage and medical bills, but also enable him to finish paying off the *Sayonara*. Owning the latter meant the world to the old man; with his wife gone these past two seasons, he desired nothing more than to leave his precious boat to his nephew, fully rigged and debt-free.

"Get ready," Phil said. "She's heading down deep again!"

Behind him, Steve Starling made quick adjustments to the boat's throttle with one hand, while manipulating the fighting chair with the other.

Stevie had proven himself a godsend as the fight wore on. An apt pupil who readily absorbed everything Phil threw at him during their first season together, the teenager quickly showed his worth. He calmly set the hook and handed the rod off as soon as the take took place, reeled in the other lines to avoid entanglements, and most importantly, maneuvered the big Bertram like a pro as his captain directed him. This included backing down on the fish when necessary, changing angles as needed, and putting her in neutral when he was told. Phil couldn't have asked for a better assistant.

Fifteen minutes later, after several more scorching runs that pulled close to two hundred yards of braided line off the big Penn International reel, the tide finally started to turn. The fish's runs were growing noticeably shorter, and the gigantean force being applied against the sturdy trolling rod was slowly diminishing. The bluefin was tiring at last.

Invigorated at the prospect of victory, Phil smiled as he began to exert more pressure on the giant fish, pulling steadily, forcing the tuna to exhaust itself even further so they could finally finish it off. It rankled him that he'd wasted his ammo earlier and couldn't kill it with a quick slug from his shotgun. The flying gaff would have to do. Once its huge barbed hook was embedded in the bluefin's flesh, it would be simple to put a tail rope on it and use their heavy-duty gin pole to hoist it clear of the water.

Phil reared back against the pull of one of the tuna's remaining runs and yelled over his shoulder, "Stevie, get the gaff ready!" He was gasping, sweat streaming down his face. "And make sure the line's attached to one of the main cleats. I don't want anything going wrong in case this mama's got any surprises up her sleeve when we stick her!"

"The gaff's already prepped, Uncle Phil," Steve said. "I'm ready whenever you say the word. How far out is she?"

His face intense, Phil leaned forward and cranked the reel handle like a maniac, then eased himself back in the fighting chair. He looked down at the hot spool before answering. "Not far," he said breathlessly. "Maybe fifty yards, if that! Get ready, kiddo. It won't be long now!"

Buoyed by a burst of adrenaline-fueled strength that surged through his chemotherapy-ravaged body, Phil smiled like a Cheshire cat. The giant bluefin was finished. He could tell by the vibrations running up the braided line as it made its way through the rod's roller guides. The fish was spent. As long as the hook stayed in, all he had to do was keep exerting slow, steady pressure.

Arching carefully back, Phil leaned forward once more, this time moving the reel's sealed drag system lever to its maximum setting. He took a deep breath and slowly cranked in another of the precious yards separating them from the beautiful bounty waiting on the other end. He smiled again, knowing they were going to win.

With a metallic screech reminiscent of a girder bending, the massive tuna rod suddenly bent nearly double. To the two men watching, it seemed the fish on the other end somehow quintupled in weight. There was a groan as the entire stern of the *Sayonara* dipped six inches from the force of the downward pull, then line started screaming off the reel like the other end was tied to a speeding Corvette. One hundred yards vanished in seconds, then two hundred.

"Jesus Christ!" Phil spat, his frail legs shaking as he strained to keep from being pulled out of his fighting chair and yanked overboard. "Stevie, grab hold of me!" he screamed as his knees started to buckle.

Already in action, the teenager sprang behind the *Sayonara's* fighting chair, wrapping his wiry arms around his uncle in a powerful bear hug, holding on for all he was worth. Even with their combined strength, all they could do was hold on and pray as the two hundred pound test line continued unchecked off their spool. The screeching sound was punctuated by several loud popping noises as, one by one, the tuna rod's heavy-duty steel roller guides broke off. Suddenly, the pulling ceased.

Caught off guard by the unexpected cessation of pressure, Phil yelped as he crashed back into the hard wooden chair with enough force to herniate discs. His nephew was sent flying head over heels, ending up in an embarrassing heap, piled against the nearest bulkhead. Crawling painfully to his feet and dusting himself off, Steve made his way over to his uncle to check on his condition.

For a long moment, neither of them spoke. Finally, it was Steve that broke the silence. "So, what do you think happened?" His right hand grasped the tuna rod where it still sat in the gimbal. He began examining the ruptured roller guides.

"What happened?" Phil cranked furiously on the smoking reel to retrieve whatever was left at the end of the now-slack line. "I'll tell you what happened. Some goddamn overgrown shark came along and made himself a meal out of our hard-earned tuna!"

"Wow, really?" Amazed, he scanned the surrounding waters. "But Uncle Phil, what kind of shark eats a thousand pound bluefin?"

Phil growled and continued reeling. Just then the tag end of the heavy-duty tuna rig came flying up over the side. Unhooking his bucket harness from the reel lugs and leaning forward, Phil caught the end of the line as it wafted in the breeze. He examined it in detail. "Just like I thought, Stevie. The leader's bitten clean through, only two feet below the barrel swivel. That was a four hundred pound test leader. Goddamn it!"

Flinging the loose end of the line away in disgust, Phil sat there fuming, his weathered chin resting uneasily on the back of one gnarled fist. "I'm sorry, Stevie boy," he said after a moment. "There's only one kind of shark in these waters that hunts giant tuna and can bite through a leader like that." He twisted his lips angrily as he continued. "A great white. And from that little tug, a damn big one."

"A . . . great white?" Steve repeated the words, a tinge of awe creeping into his voice. "Holy cow, should we try to catch it?"

"Against the law, kiddo," Phil replied, his face still resting on his hands as his tired eyes studied the swells beyond the *Sayonara's* transom. "Even if it wasn't, we don't have anything to use as bait except butterfish. And I don't know about you, but I've never heard of any shark that likes to smear butterfish on its food." Phil smiled sadly. He pulled the damaged tuna rod free from the gimbal and swiveled the fighting chair around using his feet. "Say, anything interesting showing up on the fish finder?"

Stevie took a quick look at the monitor. "Not a thing, Uncle Phil," he said, trying to hide the dejection they both felt. "Should we call it a day?"

Exhaling heavily, Phil checked his watch and the position of the sun overhead. "Nah, let's give it one more shot. Who knows, maybe the school will come back." He sighed and handed his nephew the broken rod. "Here, kiddo. Take this downstairs and bring me the backup rod, if you don't mind. And another tuna rig also, please."

"You got it, captain!" Steve replied with forced fervor. Spinning on his heels, the teenager disappeared below decks.

Phil rose painfully to his feet, limped over to the *Sayonara's* helm, and took one last look at the fish finder before turning off the Bertram's twin diesels. Still disgusted by how close they came to landing the fish of a lifetime, he made his way back to the boat's fighting chair and slumped slowly down into its uncomfortable frame. As he sat there, staring out at the unforgiving sea, his age weighed heavily on him, and he found himself feeling worn out and old.

Less than a hundred yards away, the creature's monstrous body remained suspended beneath the sparkling surface of the water, an occasional flutter from its powerful flippers keeping it silently in place. With a quick shift of its jaws, it finished swallowing the hapless fish it purloined, the skin of its throat stretching to accommodate its meal. It spouted twice and continued its explorations. As it descended, something drew its attention.

There was a boat nearby.

The creature avoided boats. The high frequency sounds they gave off were like fingernails on a chalkboard to its sensitive eardrums, and this one was no exception. Annoyed by the screeching racket, it snorted loudly and changed course.

As it started to move off, the noise suddenly stopped.

Curiosity, combined with the scent of blood still lingering in the water, began to tug at the monstrous reptile. Though nearly gorged, the possibility of purloining another meal was too powerful to resist. Caution gave way to gluttony, and the creature crept closer. Its superb vision focused past the water's shimmering surface, toward what waited above. Stopping only ten yards away, it studied the white vessel – and the small mammal seated in its chair.

Reclining in the *Sayonara's* fighting chair, Phil took a moment to relax. He closed his eyes and rested his weary head against the hard-but-comforting wood, reveling in the sensation of the sun beaming down upon his weatherworn skin, the sea breeze dispersing its heat, and the gentle rocking of the waves as they lapped against the hull. Though losing their prize fish still chafed him, Phil knew better than to dwell on bad luck or past failures. There would be other tuna. If not today, tomorrow. It didn't really matter all that much. It was all part of the bigger scheme of things. Opportunities would always present themselves for those that sought them, and life was long.

Well, maybe not for everyone, he mused silently.

Spinning the tuna chair around so that his back was to the transom, Phil closed his eyes once more, waiting for his nephew to return so they could prep for another drift, and another shot at improving their fortunes.

As he dozed off, the old fisherman was unaware of the darkness that slowly enveloped him – its enormous shape rising up out of the water and climbing high into the sky, until it towered over twenty feet above the *Sayonara's* glistening hull.

———

As he rifled through several of the *Sayonara's* tackle bins, Steve Starling fought off the sense of frustration that gnawed at him. Although he didn't know the exact details of his uncle's financial state, nor would he have asked, the teenager was both intelligent and observant. He knew the giant bluefin would have made a substantial difference in his uncle's fortunes. They'd come *so* close, only to be robbed at the last possible moment.

They fought the fish with textbook efficiency, using every appropriate tactic and technique to their advantage. And his uncle had shown amazing strength and endurance, considering his age and condition. How could they have known there was a prowling shark that size lurking in the area?

Steve shrugged off the feeling of exasperation and grabbed the backup rod with its heavy monofilament backing. He checked to make sure everything he carried was in order and turned to head above deck. Then, the ceiling came down and nailed him with a knockout punch.

Stevie opened his eyes and found himself lying on his back. He was covered with an assortment of deep-sea rods, lures, coolers, and boxes of tackle, all fallen from their usual places. Bewildered, he struggled to sit up. A wave of dizziness swept over him. He instinctively brought his hand up to his face, pushing away some of the items that blocked his vision. A wince of pain made him pull his hand away from his aching head.

It was bloody. Gingerly touching the nasty scalp wound, Steve struggled to his feet. As he did he felt another sharp spasm of pain, this time in his forearm. The hook from a fallen marlin lure was buried in the fleshy part of his left forearm, right below the elbow. Stifling a curse, Steve called out to his uncle for assistance. He was greeted with silence.

Still dazed, he leaned back against a nearby bulkhead and carefully grasped the tine of the hook, above the point where it pierced him. Grimacing, he reversed the hook, easing the point backwards to minimize any additional damage. The pain was excruciating. The injured youngster forgot about his aching forehead for the moment, despite the trickle of blood that started to seep into his left eye.

Finally, working the oversized hook free from his now lacerated arm, Steve breathed a sigh of relief. He checked his torn scalp once more while scanning the dimly lit room. He surveyed the devastation. To Steve, the inside of the boat's cabin looked like a tornado had torn away at it.

Still confused, he stared at the tangled pile that was once their well-organized tackle and gear. He dreaded what his uncle would have to say about the mess.

"Uncle Phil!" The teen forgot his own woes and leapt up the nearby steps, flying through the double doors that led below deck, back up to the *Sayonara's* cockpit.

The sight that greeted Steve stopped him dead in his tracks. The entire rear portion of the expensive charter boat had been ravaged beyond recognition. Jagged chunks of oil-stained wood and fiberglass lay scattered like leaves across the *Sayonara's* normally pristine deck. The stern portion of the vessel was also damaged: one third of the heavy wooden transom was missing, ripped away, leaving behind a jagged section of raw wood.

His eyes wide open, Steve staggered a few paces forward, struggling to take in the chaos all around him. Then, he realized the boat's tuna chair was completely gone. Other than a few scraps of wood, all that remained of the fighting chair was a jagged section of base where it was bolted into its heavy metal floor plate.

As he took another tentative step, Steve's right foot suddenly slipped out from under him, causing him to lose his footing. The burgundy-colored oil that stained the soles of his boat shoes was thick, viscous, and strangely coagulated.

Stumbling backwards as the horror dawned on him, Steve cried out in dismay. The entire rear of the *Sayonara* was splattered with reddish brown droplets of half-dried blood, putrefying in the midday sun. The boat looked and smelled like a slaughterhouse. And his uncle was nowhere to be seen.

"Uncle Phil!" Steve yelled out, cupping his hands around his mouth. His mind engaged in a desperate struggle to hide the awful truth from itself. As he took in a breath to call again, a wave of nausea wracked him and he staggered back. Slipping on another thickening puddle of his uncle's blood, Steve threw his head over the nearest gunnels and vomited uncontrollably.

After what seemed like hours, the painful retching sounds started to subside and the drained first mate slumped wearily down into a seated position, his back pressed against the *Sayonara's* thin fiberglass hull. He stared into space, wishing his nightmare would be over.

Shaking, Steve struggled to figure out what happened. Another boat couldn't possibly have caused the damage their cockpit sustained. A collision between two vessels would have completely ruptured the Bertram's hull, or at least the transom portion.

It had to be the shark. Great whites grew to immense size – up to twenty-five feet in length – and could weigh several tons. A fish that size could definitely rear up over the side of their boat and cause the damage they sustained.

Suddenly, the charter boat's radio squawked. Startled by the sound, Steve realized he forgot about the radio. It functioned even when the boat's powerful diesel engines were offline. He could call for help. In a heartbeat he was on his feet, grabbing the wired microphone.

"Calling the *Infidel*, this is the *Sayonara* calling. Repeat: *Sayonara* calling. Come in *Infidel*!" he shouted into the metal and plastic handset.

No answer.

Fighting the growing hysteria that threatened to overwhelm him, the distraught teen tried again. "*Infidel*, this is Steve Starling onboard the *Sayonara*. Repeat, Steve Starling onboard the *Sayonara*. This is an emergency! Do you read me?" On the verge of hyperventilating, Steve clenched the hand mike tightly in his fist, desperately willing Jake Braddock to answer.

"This is Sheriff Braddock, *Sayonara*. What's going on there?"

Steve wanted to cry for joy at the sound of the lawman's voice. Struggling to stay in control, he yelled into the radio, "Jake, this is Steve. I don't know what happened, but my uncle's gone! I think a shark got him! The boat's a complete wreck, and there's blood everywhere! I don't know what to do. You gotta help me!" By the time he finished his last sentence Steve was screaming.

"Gone? What do you mean gone?" Jake's fierce voice ripped out of the squawk box. "And what shark? Where are you? What happened?"

"I'm not sure of our exact location, Jake." Steve cradled his injured head in his hands, fighting back a moan. "We're about five miles west of the Cutlass, on an inshore drift, I think. How soon can you get here?"

There was a long silence. "All right, I know the area. We're on our way. We'll be there in about twenty minutes. Stevie, tell me what happened to Captain Phil. Where is he?"

An unexpected thump beneath the boat diverted Steve's attention. His jaw fell. The noise might be his uncle surfacing under the boat, perhaps even struggling to get back onboard. He nearly cracked the mike's talk button with his thumb. "Sorry, Jake, I gotta go."

"Go? Go where? Steve! Come in, goddamn it! Where is Phil?"

Steve dashed to the back of the boat. His eyes wide, he planted his palms on the shattered transom, leaning out over the water, struggling hard to peer into its murky depths. He stood there, breathing hard and praying for a sign that Phil Starling was still alive, that he was only injured and would miraculously return.

He caught a glimpse of a dark shape passing underneath. Then the entire stern portion of the thirteen-ton vessel launched itself six feet above the water, catapulting the off-guard teenager over the side. Suspended in the air for a moment, a muffled cry of alarm escaped Steve's lips as he plunged headfirst into the tepid waters of the Gulf

Stream. An expert swimmer, the athletic teen found himself flailing against an inexplicably strong undertow that sucked him under.

Gasping for air as he surfaced, he realized the powerful current had dragged him a hundred feet from the stern of the *Sayonara*. He rubbed his burning eyes with the backs of his hands and turned to make his way back to the boat. He started to sidestroke, trying to ignore the merciless hammering in his head and the stinging pain as seawater ate into his injured forearm. The riptide that pulled him under was now nowhere to be seen.

He was sixty feet away when he felt the pressure. It was the sea pushing against him, like the displacement waves he'd seen dolphins ride in front of cruise ships. Casting anxiously in every direction, Steve saw nothing. Still alarmed by the sensation, he turned back toward the boat and resumed his efforts. Then he heard an explosive sound, like an old-fashioned locomotive giving off excess steam.

Breaking the surface of the water not fifty yards away was the largest animal he ever saw. It was gigantic, like a dinosaur, but as huge as a whale. Its wrinkled head was bigger than a station wagon, and its feral eyes glowered at him like giant rubies with bottomless black centers. He could see its exposed arsenal of razor-sharp teeth, dozens of which protruded over its scaly lips like a bristling forest of ivory.

Steve began to shake uncontrollably. An overpowering adrenaline rush brought on by sheer terror spewed through his veins in gouts. He blinked rapidly, his eyes on the potential haven of the *Sayonara*, its white hull bobbing up and down atop the swells. The Bertram was barely fifty feet away, but it might as well have been a thousand.

As if on cue, the nightmarish apparition moved in his direction. Steve uttered a primal scream of terror, then turned and swam for his life. With his heart thumping so hard his chest hurt, he plowed through the water like an Olympic athlete, too horrified to think of looking back. He could feel the water pressure change as the monster drew closer, and he redoubled his efforts, flailing away like a mad-man. He could see the *Sayonara's* stern, dead ahead, and could just make out her name, boldly inscribed across the back of her battered transom, the tops of the letters missing where the wood was torn away.

She was close – only thirty feet. If he could just make it onboard, he could kick the charter boat's powerful diesels into high gear and make a run for it. He doubted very much it could catch the fleet canyon runner at its top end speed.

Only twenty feet to go. His limbs on fire, Steve refused to surrender. Even though he sensed the creature was right behind him, he wouldn't quit. He would make it. Just as that beacon of hope began to shine down upon him, the bright sun overhead vanished from view. A looming shadow enveloped him. Confused, he gazed wide-eyed as the daylight grew dim. Then, he realized the ultimate horror: the creature had overtaken him, its jaws opened wide.

He was in its mouth.

With only ten feet separating him from the *Sayonara's* beckoning stern, Steve Starling's youthful world ended in darkness. The monstrous jaws of the giant predator closed on him like a collapsing cave, its ceiling draped with ivory stalactites. As the crushing blackness stifled his muffled screams, the last thing Steve saw was the word *Sayonara*, scrawled across the battered transom of the old charter boat, just beyond reach of his outstretched hand.

———

The glass and steel exit doors of Atlanta International Airport sprang apart with a hiss, as Karl Von Freiling emerged. Terse and tired, he squinted as the bright sunlight stabbed at his eyes. He glanced back at himself in the door's reflective surface and scowled. He desperately needed a shave, and his hawk-like face looked absolutely haggard from lack of sleep. He donned his Maui Jims, grateful for still having them, and took a moment to stretch muscles that were cramped from being jammed into a coach seat for six hours. He adjusted the weighty shoulder bag he carried and made his way toward a waiting taxi. The driver he picked stood with his back to the terminal, one hand leaning on the roof of his brightly colored minivan.

"Hey there, chap. How goes it?" Von Freiling asked.

"It is good my friend, where-" The driver whirled around. He was Pakistani, judging from his accent, and his anticipatory gaze grew fearful as he sized up his prospective passenger.

Amused, Von Freiling smiled disarmingly from behind his shades. He was used to such reactions. His size and the scars that coated much of his skin often caught people off guard. Of course, the drops of dried blood splattered across what remained of his barely concealed undershirt didn't help any . . . "I need to get to Daytona Beach," he said, placing his luggage on the sidewalk and casually buttoning up his intact outer shirt.

"Daytona Beach? That is very far, my friend. It is at least a six hour drive." The driver eyed him nervously up and down. He glanced at the bag.

"Nearly seven, if we're obeying posted speed limits," Von Freiling winked. He reached into his back pocket and pulled out a wallet whose sides bulged like a gorged anaconda. He grinned, noticing his soon-to-be chauffeur had forgotten his previous nervousness. "How much?"

The driver hesitated as Von Freiling made a great show of peeling off one hundred dollar bills. "I am . . . not sure. I've never taken anyone so far. I will have to call dispatch."

"Hmm. How does six hundred sound?"

"Six hundred dollars? Um, it sounds very well, but there's also the cost—"

"I'll throw in another one-fifty for gas."

"That sounds excellent indeed, my friend. I think you have got yourself a deal." The driver gave him a thumbs-up sign and smiled amiably. He started to reach for his passenger's luggage.

"That's okay, I got it," Von Freiling said, hoisting it with one hand.

"Very good, my friend," the driver said, holding the passenger door for him. "By the way, I am Aziz."

"Gesundheit!" Von Freiling smirked. He tossed his bag in the back and removed his sunglasses, then turned and took Aziz's hand in a ligament-straining grip, looking him dead in the eye. "Just kidding. I'm Chuck. Nice to meet you."

The cabbie paled when he saw what lay behind the shades. "Um . . . nice to meet you too, Chuck," he managed.

With a smirk, Von Freiling stretched out across the backseat, his shoulder bag placed beneath his head, and his size thirteen shitkickers propped up. He pretended not to notice how Aziz's hand trembled as he struggled to insert his key into the ignition.

Still shaken by her vessel's encounter with the intruder, Amara returned to her cabin. She sat on her bed for a minute or two, shifting her hip when it started to ache. As small as it was, her stainless steel shower looked very inviting. The thought of shampooing all the sea air and salt out of her hair while hot water ran over her aching head and neck was tempting . . . Instead she shook her head, got up, and moved over to her computer desk.

She logged onto her PC, waiting impatiently for the wireless connection to take hold. It was her tenth attempt since they received the mysterious crate, and she was growing more and more frustrated. There was a direct connection between the prehistoric fish head they'd been sent and the enormous creature that nearly swamped them. There had to be. Their simultaneous appearance and the bite marks on the specimen were too much of a coincidence.

As her contact list popped up, Amara quickly scanned it from top to bottom. The bastard still wasn't there. Or, he was blocking her. *Damn.*

A second later, a loud twanging noise heralded a previously hidden icon revealing itself.

It was him. Tora50. Amara gasped, reaching for the keyboard.

Surprisingly, he wrote first:

Tora50 [10:43 A.M.]: *I've been expecting you.*

WhaleGirlsRule [10:43 A.M.]: *Oh, really?*

Tora50 [10:44 A.M.]: *Naturally. I have not been able to remain online for more than a few moments at a time. My duties prevent it. My apologies.*

Amara's eyes started to narrow.

WhaleGirlsRule [10:44 A.M.]: *Your 'duties'? That's a fine way to put it.*

Tora50 [10:45 A.M.]: *It has been a long time. I hope we can avoid arguments. Let us keep things as civil as possible.*

WhaleGirlsRule [10:45 A.M.]: *Cut the crap. And don't get all Japanese on me. You sent me something. Do you have any idea what it is?*

Tora50 [10:45 A.M.]: *No, but I knew you would.*

WhaleGirlsRule [10:46 A.M.]: *You're right. I suppose I should be grateful. So thank you.*

Tora50 [10:46 A.M.]: *You're welcome. I am curious though. What is it?*

Amara hesitated, her fingers suspended over the keys.

WhaleGirlsRule [10:47 A.M.]: *I won't discuss it over the web. Too risky. Tell me, where was it found, and how long ago?*

Now, it was Tora50 who hesitated.

Tora50 [10:49 A.M.]: *I cannot give you that information. It is, as you said, too risky.*

WhaleGirlsRule [10:49 A.M.]: *Too risky? To who?*

Tora50 [10:49 A.M.]: *To myself and my ship. I am sorry, Amara. But I know your dedication to your field, and to your beliefs. You are just like your father. Just as tenacious, and just as misguided.*

WhaleGirlsRule [10:50 A.M.]: *That's a riot. I'm misguided? You go around emptying the oceans so that you and your investors can line your pockets? You rape our planet for money! Which of us is misguided? And don't you DARE talk about my father!*

Tora50 [10:51 A.M.]: *I see now that it was a mistake to contact you. Forgive an old man for his sentimentality.*

WhaleGirlsRule [10:51 A.M.]: *Where are you? You must be close or you wouldn't be afraid to give me your location.*

Tora50 [10:52 A.M.]: *Not as close as some would wish. I am sure that your American Coast Guard would like to ascertain my location so they could impound my ship and imprison my crew. I am sorry, Amara, but I cannot risk you giving them my coordinates. I hope you can understand: duty is everything.*

WhaleGirlsRule [10:53 A.M.]: *Look, you sent me the scientific find of the century. If there are more of these fish out there, I need to know so they can be protected. I don't give a damn where you and your murder machine are right now. I've got bigger fish to fry! I need that location.*

Tora50 [10:54 A.M.]: *Such insolence. I see you are spending far too much time with Americans.*

WhaleGirlsRule [10:53 A.M.]: *I am an American. Didn't anyone tell you? Now, are you going to give me the location where you found this thing or not?*

Tora50 [10:54 A.M.]: *I already told you, I cannot. At least, not at this moment.*

WhaleGirlsRule [10:54 A.M.]: *You go to hell.*

Tora50 [10:55 A.M.]: *In time, Amara, in time.*

Amara's snarl of rage echoed throughout her cabin. She sprang to her feet, her hands grasping her monitor screen. For a moment she thought about smashing it against the nearest wall. She shook her head, released her grip, growled, and took in a few deep breaths. Her eyes intense, she sat down and grabbed her mouse, clicking a quick end to the infuriating conversation.

She continued to sit there, closing her eyes and focusing on calming herself with yoga breathing exercises. A few minutes later, she felt her calmness finally begin to return. She opened her eyes, stood up, and started to disrobe.

She needed that shower.

———

With its outboard smoking from thermal buildup, the *Infidel* skimmed across the sea like a hunting missile. Jake Braddock stood like a granite statue, his hands tightly gripping the center console's chromed steering wheel as he continued to push the sleek craft beyond its limits.

From his boss's demeanor, Chris could tell Jake was beyond worried about his former mentor. The sheriff's piercing eyes gave him away, sweeping back and forth like pendulums from the horizon to their radar screen and back up again. Several times his gaze fell on their boat's radio, but after a dozen failed attempts at reaching Steve Starling, Jake seemed disinclined to continue trying.

"Wow, forty-five knots, chief," Chris said over the roar of the outboard, trying for the fifth time in the last twenty minutes to initiate a conversation. "How long before we get there?"

He got no response. Chris opened his mouth once more, then closed it. Slumping back into his copilot's chair, he resumed scanning the horizon with binoculars in the hope of spotting the *Sayonara*. Suddenly, a tiny spot of color appeared in the distance. Chris focused. It was a Jet Ski, a single rider, cruising at high speed in the direction of the marina.

"There's a skimmer off the starboard bow, chief. Five hundred yards away." Not bothering to wait for a response that wasn't coming, he kept on talking. "Maybe the rider saw something. Let me zoom in and see who it is." Cranking the high powered optics from twenty to fifty, he took a closer look. "Hmm, it's Brad Harcourt. Wow, he's really hauling ass. I wonder where he's going in such a hurry?"

"To hell, one hopes," Jake said unexpectedly. "Keep on those binoculars, Chris. We're within a mile of the location Steve was talking about. I'll keep an eye on the radar and sonar."

"You got it, chief." Chris smiled, reached over and clapped Jake on the shoulder. "Good to have you back."

Jake said nothing. He just continued looking and driving.

Five miles from the *Infidel's* position, the creature floated motionless on the surface, the thick hide of its broad back drying in the afternoon sun. A groan escaped its thick-scaled lips and sent an approaching mako shark scurrying for its life.

It was completely gorged, its distended stomach stretched to the limit from over ten tons of flesh and debris. Nearly comatose from feeding so heavily, the predator drifted atop the swells, the sun's rays beating down upon its dark-colored skin.

Fearless in its supremacy, the basking monster fell into a deep slumber.

Jake rubbed his temples as he slowed the *Infidel* to just below cruising speed. The search was taking its toll, and aggravation and frustration were forcing their way through his normally stolid exterior. He exhaled through his teeth as he reached for the radio once more.

"This is the *Infidel* calling the *Sayonara*. Repeat, the *Infidel* calling the *Sayonara*. Do you read me, *Sayonara*?"

As he waited for a response, Jake studied his radar screen intently. There was no signal – and no answer. He repeated his broadcast two more times before hanging up the microphone in disgust. As he reached for the patrol boat's throttle lever, Chris tapped his shoulder excitedly.

"Hey Jake, I think I spotted her!" he exclaimed. "She's half a mile due south. Look!"

Quickly handing Jake the binoculars, Chris took the wheel.

"Get us over there," Jake ordered.

Chris slowly pushed the throttle back up to flank. With the *Infidel* back on plane, he pointed her prow at the distant charter boat.

Within a minute they were close enough to positively ID the old Bertram. A cursory glance revealed no sign of life.

From a hundred feet away, the damage to the fishing boat was readily apparent. The rear portion of the boat appeared to have suffered a collision, with much of the wood crushed or ripped away.

As they circled the *Sayonara* from fifty feet out, Jake reached for the radio, but then changed his mind. Drawing his pistol instead, he chambered a round and turned toward Chris. "Bring us in parallel, as quietly as possible. We're going to tie ourselves off to her starboard cleats."

"You're going aboard?" Chris asked. His eyes were huge as he brought them alongside and then cut the engine.

"Of course. Somebody's got to." Jake paused as he noticed his deputy's alarmed expression. "Look kid, I don't know what happened here. From the looks of things, I sure as hell don't think this was some shark attack. So keep your wits about you and your sidearm ready. If anything goes down, you're to cut the *Infidel* free, move to a safe distance, and call the Coast Guard for backup." As he readied himself, he turned back toward Chris and fixed him with an unwavering stare. "Is that understood?"

"Uh, yeah . . . sure thing, chief."

Waiting until the *Infidel* was about to bump hulls with the larger vessel, Jake placed the palm of his left hand on the *Sayonara's* gunnels and sprang silently aboard her. He stayed low and reached back with his free hand, steadying their center console until Chris was able to tie two dock lines to the older boat. From his crouched position, Jake looked warily around, exhaling slowly as he surveyed the devastation around him.

The *Sayonara* was a wreck.

There was broken wood and fiberglass scattered everywhere, and dried blood covered everything. What stood out most though was the absence of the big tuna chair Captain Phil spent years saving for.

Jake moved carefully around the boat, calling for Steve. With no answer, he went below and searched the beleaguered vessel for either Starling. He emerged minutes later, to the obvious relief of his deputy. Holstering his nine millimeter, he moved within conversation distance.

"Any sign of them?" Chris hazarded as he caught sight of Jake's expression.

"No." Jake shook his head in frustration. "I don't get it, Chris." He indicated the *Sayonara's* damage with a broad gesture. "What the hell happened here? The boat looks like someone took a swipe at it with a Paul Bunyan-sized axe." As he walked cautiously toward the back of the vessel, Jake fought to keep his exasperation under control. "And where's the fighting chair?" he asked, scratching his head. "It looks like it was ripped out by the roots!"

"I don't know, chief. Maybe it was some kind of shark, like Steve was yelling about on the radio?"

"No way. I don't buy that for a minute." Jake snorted. "Don't get me wrong – they might have encountered a big fish, but there's no shark in existence that could lunge onto a boat this size and devour two experienced fishermen. Not to mention an entire tuna chair."

"Maybe there is, Jake. Look at her transom. It looks like something really big bit into it. Maybe Steve was right. Maybe it was a huge shark, like one of those *Megalodons* people say they see sometimes?"

Exhaling sharply, Jake gritted his teeth and strode to the mangled transom to examine it. "Let's stay within the realm of reality, here. We're not dealing with a fish that's been extinct for millions of years. Now, I've caught big sharks before, *real* big ones, and their skin is like coarse sandpaper. If a shark came down on top of the *Sayonara's* stern, its rough skin would have stripped the wood bare, like a rasp. Now I don't know about you, but I don't see any marks that–"

His eyes growing wide, Jake dropped to one knee. "Hey, wait a minute . . ." He breathed excitedly and started picking away at something with his thumbnail. "Chris, open that tool kit we keep onboard, and hand me a flathead screwdriver."

Tool in hand, Jake began to pry at a circular white object embedded in the thick teak wood.

"What'd you find?" Chris asked, leaning over the *Infidel's* gunnels to get a better look.

"I'm not sure yet." Jake grunted as he continued to pry away. "But whatever it is . . . it's *really* in there!"

The embedded object finally came loose. Jake pulled it free in one smooth motion and held it close, looking it over. It was ivory in color and almost nine inches in length. It was conical and slightly curved, tapering in thickness from four to five inches at its thickest part, until it ended in a sharp point. Hefting it in his hand, Jake estimated it weighed several pounds. Though he could scarcely believe it, he knew right away what he was holding.

Chris teetered on his toes, "So, what is it? What did you find?"

"A tooth," Jake replied, holding it up. "And it's not from any shark, either."

"Holy shit!" Chris whistled loudly as he caught a glimpse. "What kind of animal has teeth that big? And what animal with teeth that big attacks boats and eats–"

Chris stopped, wincing as he saw the embittered expression on Jake's face. "Geez, I'm really sorry. For a second there I forgot about Captain Phil and Steve."

His face grim, Jake gripped the huge fang. "It's okay, kid. Don't worry about it. We're going to call the *Sea Tow* and have her bring the *Sayonara* in so a forensics team can look her over."

"No problem, chief," Chris said, reaching for the radio. "I'll get right on it."

"Before you do, I want you to do something else first." Jake climbed carefully back onboard the *Infidel*, the evidence held tightly in his hand. "I want you to get on the horn, and get me Doctor Amara Takagi of the *Harbinger*." He studied the hunk of ivory he held, rubbing its pointed tip with his thumb. "I need to inform her that one of her whales has developed a taste for human flesh." Jake fixed his wide-eyed deputy with a stare. "I think we have a serious problem on our hands, Chris."

TEN

Brad Harcourt was only five miles from the marina and *still* couldn't get a decent signal. Disgusted, he slapped his cell phone shut and shoved it back inside his personal flotation device. He checked to make sure his emergency shutoff lanyard was in place, turned on his GPS, and kicked the brand new Kawasaki back into gear.

It had taken a good ninety minutes for Brad's initial shock to wear off. Now, he was seething. He'd made several frustrating attempts to reach his father at his emergency number, each time failing to get through.

He thought it over and decided it didn't matter. It was better to speak to the old man in person. His dad always said, "When it comes to discussing delicate matters, never do it on a cell. When you're a high stakes player in the political arena, you never know who is listening."

Cruising steadily along, Brad cut a foam-flecked swathe as he closed the distance between himself and home. He fought to keep his temper under control, distracting himself by preparing a mental checklist of all the babes he'd invited to Friday night's pool party. He tried focusing on the ones most likely to put out, but it didn't help. No matter how many girls he dwelled on, he was unable to quell his anger at the *Sayonara*'s wrinkle-faced captain. He was indignant that the crusty old bastard dared to pull a shotgun on him. He swore to himself, that when his father was gone and *he* was in charge of Harcourt Enterprises, charter fishing yahoos like Phil Starling were going to behave far differently – or they would find somewhere else to dock their smelly boats. That was, assuming they could afford his new slip prices at that point.

Brad's anticipatory smile vanished when he checked his fuel gauge. There was only a third of a tank left. He shook his head; his expensive new four-stroke was turning out to be a real gas guzzler. *Oh well,* he mused. There was still enough to get back, and to have some fun along the way.

The teenager scanned the horizon through his designer sunglasses, hawking for fishing boats or pleasure craft. Disappointed that no one was around, he focused on ratting Phil Staling out to his father. As enjoyable as it was to torment the region's boat owners with his wake-jumping, the prospect of seeing Starling fry for gun charges was infinitely more desirable. And the fact that he was friends with Jake Braddock was a nice bonus.

Brad stopped to reach back and open a hatch containing a small cooler and extract a beer. The can popped with a loud spray of suds, and he guzzled two thirds of it. Shielding his eyes from the afternoon sun, he wiped his sweaty forehead with the cold brew, belched loudly, then pitched the aluminum can out as far as he could. He watched dispassionately as it filled with water and drowned.

Brad started his Jet-Ski again, ducking down against the onrushing wind. He tried once more to push Phil Starling out of his mind. There were much more pleasant things to think about, such as his upcoming date with that hot little waitress at the *Cove Hove*. He grinned as he visualized himself nailing the ditzy girl doggy-style. Just as he was getting to the good part, he came across an object floating on the surface of the water, directly ahead. Whatever it was, it was huge.

Brad slowed his fuel-injected mount to a stop and bobbed noiselessly up and down. As he shaded his eyes to see, a mischievous smile crept across his tanned face. There was a whale drifting on the surface, a hundred yards ahead.

He could see it plainly, its enormous hump visible atop the swells. He'd seen whales before, but never one this size or this close. The huge mammals usually sensed his approach from afar and submerged long before his arrival. Brad smirked. The peaceful giant was asleep.

Like a cat about to swallow a canary, he crept his Jet Ski closer to the slumbering cetacean, until he was only a hundred feet away. His forearms flexed as he revved his expensive toy. Adjusting his sunglasses, he readied himself. His eyes intense, he took a couple of deep breaths, then threw his skimmer into gear, its prow aimed directly at the whale's broad back.

As he careened forward at full speed, the unsuspecting behemoth failed to notice his noisy approach. Its monstrous bulk grew larger by the second. He held his breath and braced himself, throwing his weight back as he plowed into the whale.

Brad's speed, combined with the cetacean's curved back and the streamlined prow of his Jet Ski, propelled him twelve feet into the air. He sailed a full forty feet forward, clearing the whale's thick body and landing with a scream and a monstrous splash.

Whooping at the top of his lungs, Brad regained control of the sputtering Kawasaki and spun back around. He blinked in disbelief. The whale still lay there dozing, adrift on the water's surface without a care in the world. For a moment, the perplexed teen thought it was nothing more than a rotting carcass, but a gentle exhalation from its blowhole convinced him otherwise. It was definitely alive.

Two possibilities passed through Brad's mind. The first was that he was completely insignificant to the whale. Like a fly attempting to disturb an elephant, he was simply beneath notice. The other possibility was that the great beast was giving birth or ill, perhaps even dying, and thus incapable of movement.

Brad maliciously gunned his craft into high gear. It didn't matter to him why the whale failed to react. Its immobility meant he could jump it again. With a cry of expectation, he flung himself forward at breakneck speed, aiming once again for the cetacean's indigo-colored back. As his momentum increased, the two hundred feet between them started to vanish.

One fifty.

One hundred . . .

At the fifty-foot mark the whale woke, its head breaking the surface and swiveling groggily in his direction.

Stunned, Brad threw his craft into reverse to avoid crashing into it. Despite the obscuring spray, he caught sight of one of its deep-set eyes, glaring at him. It was dark red and oval, like a melon-sized garnet. Then, unexpectedly, the whale snapped at him. Its mouth was enormous, and unlike the feathery krill strainers he expected to see, it was filled with big, sharp teeth.

His eyes wide, Brad backed nervously away. The whale shook itself like a giant dog and surged to life. He blinked in disbelief as it reared its head out of the water. Its skull was long and wedge-shaped, like a gigantic crocodile's, and covered with overlapping scales. Its eyes glared at him as it opened its dripping jaws and let out a booming roar that pealed across the surrounding waters like a foghorn.

Brad closed his eyes and clamped his hands over his ears to shield them from the sound. A high-pitched shriek escaped his mouth as the monster wheeled in his direction. Its wrinkled lips snarled slowly back, revealing an arsenal of interlocking fangs as long as his forearm. It sucked in a huge breath, hissing as if it was the father of all serpents. Its foul exhalation washed over him in fetid waves, its stench the nauseating scent of putrefying flesh. Paralyzed with fear, he gagged repeatedly. A hot, wet sensation told him he'd urinated on himself, but he was too terrified to care.

The creature lunged at him. From forty feet away, its limo-sized jaws snapped shut with a sound like thunder, closing only a few yards away and showering him with drool and flotsam. With a scream of horror, he regained the ability to move and took off like a missile. Gunning the Jet Ski's engine, he rocketed across the surface of the water, his eyes the size of dinner plates.

It was coming after him.

Jake leaned wearily back against the *Infidel's* helm. It was nearly two hours since his radio call to Amara Takagi. He'd spent the time scanning the waves and studying his fish finder. His eyes grew tired and he drew his sidearm. Ejecting the magazine, he inspected the Beretta's action, reloaded it, and made sure its safety was off. He kept a watchful eye on the water the entire time. Images of Phil and Steve Starling screaming in terror as a sperm whale reared up over the stern of their vessel and seized them in its jaws kept popping into his head. The wind shifted, and even though the *Sayonara* had been towed in an hour earlier, he swore he could still smell their blood, splattered across the old Bertram like they'd been thrown into a mulcher. He shuddered in disgust and shoved the pistol back inside its holster, wondering how much the fine would be for emptying it into the cetacean responsible for their deaths.

He checked the sonar again. There was a ton of movement, but nothing big enough to be a whale. As he watched, the screen got so congested he wondered if the transducer was fouled. It cleared, only to fill up again a minute or two later. He frowned. It was peculiar, considering it was slack tide.

Suddenly, a fast moving blip on the radar caught Jake's eye. He scanned the surface with his binoculars and spotted a small runabout approaching. A closer inspection revealed it to be the *Sycophant*, the *Harbinger*'s inflatable scout craft. Amara stood at the helm, her first mate Willie by her side. Jake frowned as they drew near, their outboard engine idling noisily as they pulled alongside the *Infidel*. He hauled back and tossed them a bow line.

"How are you, Jake?" Amara asked as she tied her craft to his. Jake leaned over and reached out to help her aboard. She smiled and accepted his hand. "I was surprised to hear from you." Her smile faded as she caught the grim expression on Jake's face.

"Hello, doc," Jake nodded. He turned to Amara's second-in-command, who appeared content taking up position at the *Sycophant's* helm. "Willie, it's good to see you again."

"Good ta see ya too," Willie craned his neck and looked over Jake's patrol boat. "Dee *Infidel*?" He chuckled, pointing at the center console's name. "Well now, I guess dat's not exactly what I'd be callin politically correct deez days, now is it, mon?"

"Never gave it much thought. Lately, I've got more important things to worry about." Jake turned toward Amara, a befuddled expression on his face. "So, what's with the *Sycophant*? Why didn't you bring the *Harbinger* like I asked?"

Amara's eyes turned apologetic. "I'm sorry Jake, but I couldn't interrupt a million dollar scientific study for a possible boating accident." Noticing the dour expression he wore, she added. "Besides, you said it was urgent, and our inflatable is a hell of a lot faster than our mother ship."

"Fine," Jake exhaled. He couldn't argue with that. "I just figured you might have some advanced testing equipment on board to analyze what I found."

"Okay, Jake, I don't usually come off as pushy, but you radioed me a wild story about a whale attacking a fishing boat." She gestured about. "I don't see any whale or boat."

"The boat's already been towed back."

"I see," Amara pressed. "You also said you got your hands on one of the whale's teeth as evidence of the attack. Where is it?"

"What I *said,* doc, was that we received a distress call from a local charter boat. When we arrived we discovered the boat was badly damaged. There were bloodstains everywhere and the people were missing. I believe a sperm whale was responsible."

"Sperm whales don't usually attack boats. Not unless they're harassed or threatened." Amara moved a few steps from him and sat back on the gunnels, her legs crossed and hands resting on the hard fiberglass. "I've never heard of one deliberately devouring a human being."

Jake rested his hands on his hips. "Regardless, Dr. Takagi, I am absolutely convinced that one of your whales was responsible."

"One of *my* whales?" Amara and Willie exchanged looks. "Okay, Jake. And why are you so convinced that one of *my* whales was responsible?"

Jake turned and reached for the bundle he'd stashed in his forward console. "Because I pried *this* out of the *Sayonara.*" He unwrapped the tooth and held out his hand. "Now, I'm no whale expert, doctor, but I believe this came from a big bull sperm whale."

Amara walked over and nervously accepted the razor-tipped hunk of ivory. Her eyes flew open wide. "You said you . . . pried this out of the damaged vessel's hull?"

"That's right, doc," he said, feeling sufficiently vindicated. "It was buried in the transom. Or, what was left of it."

Amara was either confused or excited. Jake couldn't decide which. She handled the tooth as if it were made of expensive crystal, turning it repeatedly and examining it from different angles. She held it next to her forearm and then hoisted it for Willie to see. Her first mate's expression seemed to bolster her bewildered state.

"So, do we have a whale problem?" Jake interjected.

"To be honest, I have no idea what this is from, but it's not from a sperm whale." Amara blew out her breath and sat down on the *Infidel's* rear bench seat. She gestured for Jake to join her.

"First of all, you can see the tip is much too sharp. The teeth of a large cachalot are fairly blunt." She ran her thumb down the inside curve of the item. "You see this sharp ridge?"

Jake nodded.

"Sperm whales have teeth designed to pierce and impale things, like fish or squid. They swallow their prey whole." Amara looked up at him. "Whatever lost this piece of tooth was what we call a bolt-shake feeder. Its teeth are designed to bite through the flesh of large prey items. It then uses a powerful headshake motion to rip bite-sized pieces loose so they can be swallowed."

She held the tooth up for emphasis as she finished.

Jake gaped at her. "Whoa, did you say a piece of tooth?"

"Oh, yes." Amara pointed at the tooth's rough-edged cross section. "This broke off far above the gum line. It's completely solid. There are no root canals visible at all. I'm positive; the whole tooth was definitely larger."

"How much larger?"

Amara held the tooth at arm's length and closed one eye. "I'd say it measured another six or eight inches."

"Jesus."

Amara nodded.

Jake shook his head in frustration. "But you have no idea what kind of creature we're dealing with? If I've got a man-eater on my hands, it would help to know what kind I'm looking for!"

Willie chimed in unexpectedly. "Probably da same one dat spooked da whales before, mon. I tink a beast wit teeth like dose could scare almost any ting!"

"What's he talking about?" Jake stared at Amara.

The cetaceanist hesitated, shooting Willie an irritated look. "We had a . . . incident earlier. Something frightened one of our resident pods of sperms. Unfortunately, we didn't get a good look at it. But it was very big and very fast. And yes," she added as she saw the expression on his face, "it's possible that the tooth you found came from the same animal."

"I see . . ." Jake said. He reached over and took the fragment back. "Thanks for your help, doc. If you find out anything that will help identify this creature, I'd appreciate you letting me know."

Amara wore a pouty look. "But Jake, I . . . thought you wanted us to run some tests? If we're going to find out what animal we're dealing with, the equipment we have onboard the *Harbinger* will be our best shot."

"I'm sure, doc. But the forensics team that's documenting the *Sayonara* is going to look this over first." Jake hefted the huge fang. "Once they've photographed and logged it, I'll release it to you – temporarily, of course – so you can give it a good once over."

"Um, no problem, Jake. In the meantime, if it's alright with you, I'd like to examine the damage to the boat."

"That might be a little difficult," he announced. "What's left of it is back at the marina by now. And I doubt very much you want to go bouncing all the way there on your little runabout."

"I see."

Jake walked back over to the *Infidel's* gunnels and offered her his hand. "Sorry, doc."

Amara remained where she was. "How about if Willie takes the *Sycophant* back and I ride with *you*?"

Jake admired her tenacity. And despite everything, truth be told, the two of them spending time alone together on his boat wasn't the absolute worst idea he'd ever heard . . .

"I don't know. Seems like an awful lot of trouble."

"Not at all," Amara persisted. "That way, I can not only get a look at what happened to the vessel, I can compare the damage to the tooth you found. Just to make sure they're definitively linked. Then, after your guys are done doing their thing, you can give me a ride back to the *Harbinger* on your trusty steed, here." She smiled and gave the *Infidel's* gunnels a fond pat. "And, we can use my equipment to do a more formal analysis."

Jake felt himself beginning to cave. He nodded. "I guess that'll work. I do want a full report on this thing, to find out where it came from. Or rather, *what* it came from. Then I'll know how to find it, and how to deal with it."

Amara studied his expression. "I'll certainly do my best, Jake. But, I have to be honest with you. My interest is finding out if we're dealing with an undiscovered species. I'm not a policeman or some deranged big game hunter."

"Point taken, doc," Jake replied evenly. Knowing the cetaceanist's philosophy when it came to preserving marine life, he was hardly surprised. Unfortunately, her dedication might get in the way. He leaned toward her, his expression grave. "Now let *me* be just as honest with *you*."

Amara smiled nervously. "Okay . . ."

"This 'previously undiscovered species' you're referring to has killed two people, both of whom were friends of mine. That makes it a confirmed danger to the public. Like an enormous, rabid dog. And, you know what happens to *them*, don't you?"

He gave her a meaningful look.

Amara's smile disappeared. "I understand, and I'm very sorry for your loss, Jake. Believe me. But let's see what we're dealing with before we jump to conclusions. For all we know, some drug dealers may have kidnapped your friends and left the doctored-up tip of an elephant's tusk behind to throw you off the track."

"You don't actually believe that, do you?"

"Not really. But I'm trying to keep an open mind."

"Fine, let's go then." He turned to start the *Infidel's* outboard. The big Yamaha screeched loudly and failed to turn, requiring six or seven attempts before it shuddered to life amidst a white cloud of burning oil.

"Um, time for a tune up?" Amara suppressed a giggle.

"Tell me about it," Jake grumbled, tossing off the dock lines and grabbing the helm. He spun his steering wheel hard to starboard, maneuvering the center console away from the *Sycophant*, and then waved to Willie.

"Willie, I'll call you when we get to shore. Be careful!" Amara yelled out.

Her first mate nodded and waved back as they sped off.

Unknown to the two of them, five miles away and five hundred feet below the surface, a huge form moved steadily through the swirling blackness of the ocean's depths, scattering the surrounding sea life as it headed in their direction.

———

It was gaining on him.

Brad Harcourt couldn't believe what he was seeing. His horror-filled eyes glanced down at his speedometer. He blinked and swallowed hard. At fifty miles an hour he was nearing his craft's maximum speed, yet the beast was catching up to him.

Chancing a quick glance over his shoulder, he saw it barreling along just beneath the surface, its monstrous presence betrayed by the mountain of seawater it was displacing. It was barely fifty feet behind him and relentlessly closing the distance.

Brad was frantic. He couldn't believe anything so big could be so fast. The bizarre chase had worn on for five miles already, with the horrified adolescent weaving back and forth in a dogged effort to discourage his pursuer. He'd hoped to wear it down and exhaust it, yet if anything, it was becoming more determined.

Turning sharply to port, Brad resumed a westerly course. With only two miles separating him from the refuge of the marina, his mind focused on making it to that destination. He glanced down at his gas tank reading to see the needle approaching the red line. Soon, the Kawasaki's warning light would come on. Once it did, he'd have only a few minutes of fuel before his Jet Ski died.

He turned his head to the side, hocking out some of the accumulated salt-spray that kept working its way into his surprisingly dry mouth. As he did, he checked his right-side mirror. That momentary glance saved his life.

The creature reared its enormous head up and out of the water, lunging forward in a ferocious attempt to envelope Brad and his mechanized mount in a single bite. He screamed hysterically and twisted the Jet Ski to starboard. The maneuver nearly caused him to flip over, but it also caused his pursuer's monstrous jaws to close on nothing but seaweed. Relief swept through him and he tried to cheer, but nothing came out except a squeak. Looking over his shoulder again, he did a double-take.

It was gone.

Brad glanced around warily, looking in every direction. The monster was nowhere in sight. He slowed and started to zigzag, in case it was tailing him from beneath the surface. Although he prayed it had given up, he kept watch, expecting at any moment the telltale disturbance that heralded its arrival.

After five minutes, he felt his breathing gradually return to normal. He blew out the breath he'd been holding and took one final glance back, then reached for the Kawasaki's autopilot.

When he looked up, he was about to drive down the creature's throat.

Brad's blood ran cold as he spotted the fang-rimmed opening. The monster had taken advantage of his decreased speed. Calculating his path, it surged ahead of him, waiting just below the surface. At the last moment, it rose up, its streaming jaws spread wide enough to envelope a rhino.

Shrieking loudly, he threw the Jet Ski into reverse, twenty feet from its beckoning mouth. The creature, bereft of any momentum, was unable to lunge and was forced to close its jaws in frustration. It submerged with a hiss of annoyance and then surged powerfully forward, resuming the chase.

Hysterical, Brad abandoned his evasive maneuvering. He threw his expensive vehicle into gear, cranked it to full and made a beeline straight for home. He fought to stay in control, gazing repeatedly into his rearview mirrors as he jabbed a series of buttons that activated the Kawasaki's autopilot. He re-checked his lanyard, then hunched down to decrease air-resistance.

A moment too late, he saw the piece of wood.

Bobbing up and down in the water ten feet ahead was a piece of telephone pole, fifteen feet in length. With a cry, he slammed into it. Both rider and mount went flying. The watercraft landed first, careening down hard onto its side and rolling twice before slowly righting itself. Brad flew head over heels thirty feet before crashing headfirst into the water. He broke the surface with a frightened gurgle, spouting seawater and mucus as he looked around wildly. Once again, the creature had vanished.

Whimpering piteously, the athletic teen swam like a maniac. He reached his watercraft in seconds. Gripping the nearest handhold, he looked around, his heart pounding. It was close by. He knew its habits now, like he knew his father's. It would never stop.

He grabbed the cushioned handlebars of his Jet Ski and climbed aboard with a speed and strength born of pure terror. Inserting the safety lanyard's key and cranking the machine's engine back to life; he tightened his grip. Suddenly, the water's natural fluidity grew harsh and violent. The ocean beneath his bucking craft was churning across an area a hundred feet across.

It was right below him.

Spouting profanities, Brad gunned the Jet Ski into gear. It shuddered and sprang forward, spitting water in a high arc. A millisecond later, the creature surfaced like a runaway locomotive, just missing him. Its water-streaming body rose fifty feet into the air, its sword-like teeth coming together in a thunderous snap. It hung suspended and Brad gazed up at it with a mixture of fear and fascination. He could see its ruby eyes glaring down at him. Blanching beneath its serpentine gaze, he turned and sped off, increasing his speed to maximum.

Behind him, he heard a crashing sound as the breaching monster came down like a falling redwood. Its roar of frustration echoed across the water. He glanced back and saw it submerge, preparing to take off after him once more. He checked his GPS. A feeble smile spread across his cracked lips. The marina was less than a mile away, hidden behind the fog. If he could hold out just a few minutes more, he would make it home.

The shrilling buzzer that signified a near-empty tank was barely audible over the sound of his engine, but the flashing light next to it was unmistakable. Brad felt queasy as he stared at the blinking orb. All of a sudden, the marina was a hundred miles away and he was riding on fumes. His plan of action had been made. The thing was right on his ass and there wasn't any fuel left for fancy evasive tactics. He had enough gas for a straight-line run – if that. The next few seconds would determine whether he lived or died. He tightened his grip on the skimmer's handlebars, threw the four-stroke into high gear and locked it down. Setting his autopilot for the main dock, he dropped low and ducked his head. With his watercraft's impeller screaming like a banshee, he rocketed across the surface of the sound, topping out at nearly sixty miles an hour.

Too afraid to look into his mirrors, Brad's fingers fumbled for his cell phone. Ahead of him, he could make out the marina, its forest of docked boats pallid phantoms, peeking through the afternoon mist. It was *so* close.

He flipped open his phone with his right hand, held the button to his father's line and waited. It was a long shot. The phone's earpiece could hardly compete with the roar of his engine. Still, he had to try. Behind him, the barely-submerged head of the giant carnivore drew steadily closer, its speed a match for the big Jet Ski, even at full throttle.

The phone started ringing.

Just then, the monster made its move. Speeding up beneath the surface, it surged forward, its triangular-shaped head bursting through the green and white swells, ten feet to the right. Turning in the direction of the disturbance, Brad heard two distinctive sounds simultaneously. One was the deafening hiss issuing from the creature's spreading jaws. The other, the familiar sound of his father bellowing.

"Brad, what have I told you about using this number? This sure as hell better be an emergency!"

Brad stuttered in fear. "D-dad, it's . . ."

An ear-splitting roar drowned out his words as the monstrous reptile snapped in his direction. As the wall of teeth approached, Brad held on for dear life to the handlebar of his Jet Ski. Still grasping his phone, his right arm extended out in an attempt to stave off his pending doom.

There was no time to scream.

From behind his private sanctum's desk, Senator Dean Harcourt stared confusedly at the phone in his hand. His son's voice had been cut off by a sudden roaring noise, similar to a passing train. Now there was nothing. The politician's face crinkled up and his expression changed from puzzlement to genuine annoyance. He reached over and stabbed a button on his intercom.

"Gladys, if my son calls back take a message. I don't want to be disturbed again until dinner time."

"Yes, senator."

Leaning back into his padded chair, he unbuttoned his jacket and opened the day's paper. The cover story was sensationalistic as always – something about a squid attacking some surfers. Humming quietly to himself, he skipped the article and began skimming through the financial sections.

Eight miles from Harcourt Marina, the *Infidel* crossed the sound, with Jake manning the helm, and Amara at his side. The lawman remained stoically silent. If it weren't for him periodically checking the *Infidel's* instrument panel or the position of the afternoon sun, he wouldn't have moved either. Most of his time was spent focused on the seas before them, but every so often his gaze wandered down to his control console's storage bin, and the mysterious item wrapped in cloth and concealed behind the tinted Plexiglas.

The tooth continued to call to him.

Given his passenger's overprotective nature when it came to cetaceans, Jake was far from convinced that the oversized hunk of ivory came from something other than a whale. Even so, he resisted the urge to reexamine the razor-tipped fragment or initiate a conversation on the topic. In his mind's eye he saw Phil Starling's face, just as he left him that morning by the *Sayonara*. He cursed himself for not taking his earlier feelings more seriously. He'd sensed that something terrible was going to happen. And, once again, he'd found himself powerless to intervene.

Amara's shifting drew Jake's eye. He glanced over at her and saw her change position once more. He couldn't see her eyes behind her shades, but from her expression she looked like she was in pain.

"Hey, you okay?" he asked.

Amara glanced over at him. "Yes, fine. Why do you ask?"

"You seem uncomfortable. Forgive me, but do you need to use the head or something?"

"No, silly, I'm fine." She shook her head and grinned. "Believe me; I'm not shy about going to the bathroom on boats."

Jake nodded, then caught her pressing her hand lightly against her stomach. "Are you sure?"

Confused, Amara followed his line of sight. "Oh . . . no, I'm fine. I just haven't eaten all day and my stomach is starting to hurt."

"So, why didn't you say so?"

"Jake, you've been through a lot today. I'm certainly not going to bother you about food at a time like this."

"Doc, I appreciate your concern and good manners, but the last thing I need is you getting sick on my account." Before she could argue the point he added, "Look, I can't get it while driving, but if you want it, there's a cooler stashed in the starboard floor compartment. There's a turkey and Swiss hero in it. It's not much, but it's fresh. There's water, too."

"Um . . . are you sure?"

Jake gave her a friendly nod and slowed down. "I insist. You might as well be comfortable. I have a feeling we're going to be spending a lot of time together."

"Okay," Amara smiled. She held onto a nearby handrail and eased herself down to open the compartment, gritting her teeth as she reached for the cooler. She extracted the hero and a bottle of spring water, then pulled herself upright and made her way back to his side.

"Thanks for the sandwich, big guy," Amara said. "You want the other half?"

"No thanks, maybe later. Hey doc, can I ask you something?"

"Sure."

Jake hesitated, running his tongue over his teeth before he spoke. "Were you injured recently?"

Amara's head snapped in his direction. "What do you mean?"

"Well, I've noticed your gait is a little uneven, and I saw you wince just now when you stood up."

"I'm fine."

"Really . . ." Jake drawled. "Sorry, doc, but I'm not buying it. A minute ago, you weren't going to admit you were starving. So what do you say we skip all the mock swordplay and you tell me what's wrong?"

Amara studied him through her eyelashes. "Fine. I got attacked with a *hakapik* a few years ago, and spent three months learning to walk again."

"Holy shit!" Jake sputtered. "What the hell is a *hakapik*?"

"It's like a pickaxe, but with a hammer on one side. Seal hunters use them to crush the skulls of baby Harp seals."

Jake shook his head, his mind reeling. "I don't get it. Were you wearing a white fur coat and running around on all fours at the time?"

Amara shot him a withering look. "No . . . and I don't think they give the mentally disabled hunting licenses."

"Seriously, what the hell happened?"

She hesitated. "I was with *Sea Crusade*, on a mission with my . . . Look, it's really not all that interesting."

Jake pursed his lips and turned back toward the horizon. "Sorry, doc. I didn't mean to pry."

"It's not that. It's just that I normally don't . . ."

Jake turned to her and nodded. "You're a private person. I get it."

Amara cleared her throat, her eyes boring a hole through the deck. "Something like that."

"I can relate. If I had a nickel for all the things I didn't want to talk about, I'd be rich. There are some parts of my life I just don't like discussing."

Amara nibbled her lower lip and nodded. "Yeah . . . I guess. Sometimes it's good to talk, though."

Jake shrugged, gripping the steering wheel with both hands. "Only if you've got someone worth talking to."

"Are you worth talking to?"

"Depends on the day."

There was a long moment of silence that seemed to last forever. "Okay, Jake Braddock. You win. I'll give you the Cliffs Notes version of my accident. Maybe you'll understand why I do the things I do. But I'm telling you now, I don't want to be judged, and I sure as hell don't want any sympathy."

Jake glanced down at his worn wedding band and sighed. His eyes lifted, focusing once more on the sea before them. "Believe me, doc. Of all the people in this world, I'm the last person who should go around judging . . ."

———

Her eyes on the horizon, Amara's mind raced. It felt good to unburden herself to someone. Except for Willie, there was no one onboard the *Harbinger* she could really talk to. But she felt strangely unsettled as well. She didn't understand why she'd opened up to Jake, especially about her accident and what happened to Robert. It didn't seem . . . appropriate. Sure, the town sheriff was likable – and then some – but in truth, she hardly knew the man.

She felt a strange little chill run through her and distracted herself by focusing on the identity of their mystery predator. The scientist inside her was bursting with excitement. Although she had little to base her notions on, she was betting they'd unwittingly stumbled upon a new species. It was a fantastic discovery. True, there were several small baleen whale species discovered in recent years. But if tooth size was any indicator, Amara's find would replace the sperm whale as the largest living predator on the planet, perhaps of all time. It was mind-boggling to conceive of a breeding population of animals that size existing and never being seen, let alone documented.

Jake cleared his throat loudly. "By the way, any info you can give me on what happened will be very helpful, even theories. I'm going to have to speak with Captain Phil's family at some point, and they're going to have a lot of questions."

Amara felt her anticipation evaporate. "Of course. Listen, I know it doesn't help any, but I'm really sorry about your friends." She touched him tentatively on the shoulder.

He nodded. "Thanks. We were very close. And I'm privileged that you felt comfortable talking to me." He cleared his throat. "Back to the matter at hand, are you absolutely sure that tooth isn't from a whale?"

Amara stalled by taking a bite from her leftover sandwich. She stared at the floor as she chewed, then swallowed. "I don't think so, Jake. But we'll know more after I give *Archimedes* a chance to look at our discovery."

"Archimedes?" Jake repeated. "Who's that, one of your scientists?"

"Not exactly," Amara chuckled, brushing a few strands of hair from her eyes. She raised her voice to be heard over the *Infidel's* engine. "*Archimedes* is our analytical archive system. It's a multi-million dollar program containing bio-schematics on every documented life form on the planet: fish, birds, reptiles and mammals. All of them, past and present."

"And this system you're speaking of, it will identify the animal responsible from just one tooth?"

"Hopefully," Amara said.

"Interesting. But if this animal happens to be a completely unknown species, then your computer system won't have any data on it, anyway."

"True," Amara admitted as she leaned back in her seat. "If that's the case, we'll end up with an unknown listing. An anomaly, if you will."

She closed her eyes. An anomaly would be just fine by her. By process of elimination, she would know for certain whether they'd discovered a new species of whale or not. And if she was going to be credited with the discovery.

———

His lips pursed, Jake mulled over Amara's tale. He was very impressed by their earlier conversation, and what he'd gleaned from it. She possessed an appealing timidness, yet was by far the bravest and most outgoing woman he'd ever met. *Anyone who would take a blow from a pick-axe to protect a baby seal must have balls the size of honeydews.*

He realized he found the marine biologist admirable and adorable at the same time. Despite everything she'd been through, she was one hundred percent dedicated to the preservation of marine life, and whales in particular. She would do anything to protect them – even one that went rogue. Which meant, unfortunately, her reliability when it came to their current situation was dubious.

His ruminating was interrupted by a static-strewn message blaring out of his radio. He turned the volume up but still couldn't decipher the transmission. Annoyed, he killed the engine and picked up the hand mike.

"This is Sheriff Braddock onboard the *Infidel*. Repeat, Sheriff Braddock onboard the *Infidel*. Please repeat your broadcast."

Jake waited for a response. Beside him, Amara moved toward the fish finder, her long legs showing as she bent to study its liquid crystal screen.

"Jake, it's Chris!" His deputy's panicky voice blurted out of the speaker. "You better . . . back to the marina, ASAP, chief. Something's happened . . . Brad Harcourt!"

Jake held down the talk button. "What do you mean, 'something's happened' to him? What's going on, Chris?"

There were almost ten seconds of garbled sound before Chris's nervous response.

"Sorry, a lot going on here. I don't think we . . . talk about it on the radio, chief. I don't . . . who is listening. There are reporters crawling all over the place . . . for a story. It's getting ugly! How soon . . . you get here?"

I'm on my way, Chris," Jake said. "Be there in ten. Don't say anything to anyone. And I mean it. Braddock out."

Returning the microphone to its cradle, Jake was about to restart the *Infidel's* engine when Amara motioned excitedly to him.

"Jake, what do you make of this?" She removed her shades and pointed at the boat's sonar unit. On the bottom of the LCD, a large sonar echo was rising up from the ocean floor.

"I don't know, doc," Jake said, staring at it. "You're the marine biologist. Maybe it's one of your whales?"

"I'm not too familiar with your little gadget here, but that looks like a pretty big signal to me."

"So what?" Jake shook his head impatiently. "Whales are huge. Everybody knows that. Anyway, what's the big deal? It's just a sonar reading. It could be anything: a strand of kelp, some floating debris . . ."

"Well, your 'strand of kelp' is building up speed," Amara said. "And, it's heading straight for *us*."

Jake reached over and swiveled the sonar unit's screen around. He swore silently. She was right. The sonar reading was very large and moving very quickly. And it was coming right at them. "Hold on." He reached for the ignition. "I'm getting us the hell out of here."

Amara nodded and sank into her co-pilot's chair.

Jake twisted the starter key, his free hand on the vessel's throttle lever, ready to shift into gear. There was the same high-pitched shrieking sound as before, then nothing. The motor wouldn't start.

"Damn it!" Jake snarled, twisting the key again and again. Amara's head swiveled in his direction, her ice-colored eyes wide with alarm. On the screen below them, the enormous reading drew closer, moving from three hundred feet to two hundred and climbing rapidly.

"Uh . . . Jake?" Amara stared fearfully at the screen.

"I know, doc, I know," he said, turning the key repeatedly. "Well just think," he remarked, "you may get the chance to examine your 'new species' a lot sooner than you thought!"

"That's not funny, Jake!"

The signal was less than a hundred feet below them.

Amara was sweating. "Can't you do something?"

His eyes dangerous, Jake released his hold on the boat's ignition key. He glanced at the reading one last time, then drew his pistol and stepped to the portside gunnels. He chambered a round, then grabbed tight onto a nearby railing and pointed his weapon at the water.

"Hold on tight, doc," he said. "You might want to close your eyes. This may not be pretty."

The surface of the ocean around the *Infidel* began to bubble violently. Jake sucked in an anticipatory breath and held it. Whatever was coming had to be enormous to move so much water.

He saw a dark shadow directly beneath them. Then there was a tremendous crash, and the center console was lifted completely out of the water. Jake's cry of astonishment was cut short as he made a desperate grab for the sturdy side rail. Hanging over the side, he heard Amara screaming. He caught sight of a dark-hued shape as big as a tractor-trailer pushing violently up against them. He saw teeth as thick as his forearm everywhere he looked, prepared to shear through their fragile hull and crush them both to death.

He was looking at the creature that killed Phil and Stevie.

Jake's heart could barely handle the adrenaline-fueled rage that pumped through his bloodstream. He twisted wildly and managed to regain his footing on the slippery deck. Holding onto the railing, he leaned over the side of the boat and let out an animalistic roar of defiance. The deafening sound of gunfire echoed across the water as a stream of jacketed hollow points slammed into the monster. Then, there was an uncanny silence.

His ears ringing, Jake realized he'd emptied his weapon of all seventeen rounds. Behind him, Amara was still shrieking, her eyes shut and hands clamped over her ears. Shaking his head to clear it, Jake reloaded and waved his hand back and forth to clear the cloud of gunsmoke.

He could see the creature. It was immobile and stretched out like a blue-gray mountain. A cloud of seabirds began to circle overhead, their hopeful cries a reassuring din. Based on the amount of blood in the water, Jake figured the thing was dead. He holstered his sidearm, then reached down and took Amara by the arm, helping her to her feet. "It's okay, it's over. I killed it. Whatever it was."

Amara waited for her legs to stop shaking before she edged her way to the *Infidel's* portside. Gripping Jake's bicep for support, she peeked fearfully at the enormous carcass. Her jaw dropped in astonishment. "Oh my God, Jake . . ." she shuddered, slipped, and lost her footing.

Jake grunted as he caught her. "What is it?"

Amara shook her head in disbelief. "That's Elvis!"

"Elvis?" Jake stared at her, wondering if the strain took more of a toll than he thought on the girl's mind. "What are you talking about?"

"Elvis! He's one of our whales – one of *my* whales!"

"One of your–" Jake studied the dead animal more closely. He could see the rectangular shape of its head beneath the surface and its narrow lower jaw with its conical teeth . . . Amara was right.

"This is Elvis, Jake," Amara said, placing her hands on the gunnels and leaning over to get a closer look. "I know his markings. He's been the dominant bull in this region for a decade. He's the alpha male. And now he's dead!"

"I'm sorry," Jake said. He stared bleakly at the ragged bullet holes he'd inflicted on the giant mammal. "I didn't mean to kill it."

"Kill it? What are you talking about? This whale's been dead for a half a day, if not more. Its body's been traveling with the current. It must have risen to the surface from the build-up of internal gases." She shook her head from side to side. "You didn't kill anything. But something sure as hell did . . . look!"

Jake's nostrils twitched from the sickly sweet odor of rotting meat. He looked at the region of the whale Amara was pointing at.

"Holy Christ . . . "

"Amen to that."

There was a wound bitten clean through the whale's left flank. The fleshy crater was enormous – a gaping hole the size of a king-size mattress. Overhead, the seagulls multiplied, with several swooping down on floating scraps of skin and blubber.

Amara took a deep breath and let it out. "Okay . . ." she said. "Now, we need the *Harbinger*. I'm going to order her into the vicinity, to document the damage to this animal."

"Sounds good." Jake handed her his radio. "But, we can't wait for them. I've got to find out what all the commotion is about at the marina."

"You're right," Amara said. She stared in disbelief at the dead whale. "Because I have a feeling that things in the tranquil waters around Paradise Cove are about to become a lot less tranquil."

"Me too, doc. Me too."

His face grim, Jake eased the ignition key clockwise until the outboard caught, then shifted hard into reverse. After a few attempts, he began backing the *Infidel's* bow section off the whale's body, gunning it until they were floating freely. He spun the wheel hard and began to move away, keeping his velocity down until Amara finished her call.

Moments later, they were cruising for the marina. Behind them, the mutilated remains of one of history's greatest carnivores floated lifeless atop the swells, its broad back dotted with scavenging seagulls pecking furiously away, squabbling over loose scraps of flesh. As he glanced back, Jake felt sorry for the old bull. He began to ponder the identity of its killer, and what kind of creature could slay such an immense predator.

The concept was mind-boggling.

He considered the awful possibility that whatever killed the giant cachalot might be linked with Chris's desperate call about Brad Harcourt. If something had happened to Dean Harcourt's son, it would bring the mother of all shit storms down on Paradise Cove. And *he* would end up getting caught in the middle of it.

Shuddering at the thought, Jake continued in silence. Then a strange sensation came over him, and he chuckled at the realization he was wishing a spoiled-rotten punk like Brad Harcourt good health.

Now *that* concept was mind-boggling too.

ELEVEN

It was late afternoon as Jake maneuvered the *Infidel* into Harcourt Marina. From a hundred yards out, he studied the media storm that had settled over the normally calm waterfront. There were hundreds of people on the main landing, weaving to and fro like foraging leafcutter ants, with droves more on the narrow docks. Although the majority was curious townsfolk and local business owners, there was a fleet of news vans – some local, a few from the national networks – lined up like soldiers across the wharf. Every available parking space was taken, including those reserved for the handicapped. While camera crews and lackeys invaded the landing proper, reporters aggressively interviewed anyone who would speak with them.

As the *Infidel* drifted into the nearest slip, Jake's face grew grim. Fifty yards away, the battered hulk of the *Sayonara* loomed into view. Visibly listing to one side, the blood-spattered Bertram was the focal point of several reporters, who took pictures despite protests from the forensic team examining it.

Jake hated the media. Early in his career he'd learned to be wary of those vultures. Their tabloid-style articles were an incessant source of irritation. Far worse were the weeks following Samantha's death, when their fabricated stories proved an endless source of misery for the newly crowned saber champion. He'd loathed them ever since.

Discretely concealing the tooth fragment within a canvas shoulder bag, Jake placed one hand on the starboard gunwales of his boat and vaulted onto the dock. He turned to lend a hand to Amara.

"Hmm, pretty athletic, aren't we?" she said, observing the burly sheriff with newfound admiration. "I imagine you must work out a great deal."

"A practical necessity, doc," Jake said. He took in the scene. A fleet of ambulances, police cars, and a coroner's truck were drawn up, their flashing lights creating a strobe light display bound to give one a headache. "Wonderful. This should be pleasant."

"Looks like a real madhouse," Amara said. She moved closer to him. "What do you think happened?"

"One way to find out." Jake headed toward the main landing, where most of the action was. Pausing in mid-stride, he turned back to Amara. "Not a word of our discovery." He patted his bag for emphasis. "Not until we know what we're dealing with."

"Don't worry, I'm not saying anything to anyone."

Jake nodded and began to stride along the narrow dock, his boots thudding atop the weather-beaten boards as he passed one moored vessel after another.

Up ahead, he spotted Chris Meyers standing behind a line of police barricade tape. He was arguing with a particularly pushy news reporter, who continued to shove her microphone in his face. He turned toward Jake and his expression changed from anguish to relief. Moving away from the newswoman, he asked a pair of uniformed officers to protect the flimsy barricade and began jogging in Jake's direction.

"Thank God you're here!" Chris said frantically. He was breathing hard and drenched with sweat. "They're totally out of control! I can't handle these people!"

Jake rested one hand on his shoulder. "Take it easy, kid. From what I've seen, you're doing a great job. Now fill me in. Exactly what caused all of this?"

Chris gaped at Amara. "Are you sure? I mean . . . in front of her?"

"Oh, sorry," Jake said. "Chris Meyers, this is Dr. Amara Takagi from the *Harbinger*. She's assisting with our investigation."

Chris nodded. He looked about before he spoke. "It happened about an hour ago. The damn thing came out of nowhere. It was really moving, too!"

"What thing?"

Chris gestured at the taped-off section of landing. Behind the barrier, partially concealed by the two troopers, was a wrecked black and yellow Jet Ski. Its nose was embedded in the dock's frame, with splintered boards scattered in every direction.

"It just slammed into the dock?" Jake asked as they moved toward the crash scene. He paused in mid-step, eyes widening. "That's Brad Harcourt's toy. Is that what this is all about? Was he hurt in the accident?"

"You don't understand," Chris emphasized. "We don't know where he is. His Jet Ski came back riderless. It crashed into the dock all by itself. It's a miracle it didn't hit one of the docked boats and blow up!"

"You're right, Chris. I don't understand." Jake paused outside the taped area. The two uniformed officers recognized him and nodded as they made way for the popular town sheriff. "Why all this excitement, if all the little shit did was forget his emergency cord and let his watercraft run off without him? Why all the media for a simple search and rescue?"

"That's just it, chief," Chris said. He blanched as he pointed at the damaged Kawasaki. "He *was* using his shutoff lanyard. Look."

Following the frightened youngster's gaze, Jake saw something that gave him pause. He scrunched his eyes tight to make sure he wasn't seeing things. Chris was right. The safety-lanyard *was* still plugged in. In fact, it was wrapped around its owner's wrist. There was a hand gripping the rubberized handlebar, its safety strap cinched tightly in place.

The pallid body part had been amputated mid-forearm.

"Holy shit," Jake muttered.

He signaled the two troopers to keep the reporters at bay, then ducked under the barricade, gesturing for Amara. He froze in place, a sickly feeling making its way into the pit of his stomach. The severed limb was sporting a gore-covered watch. He breathed through his mouth, reached into his back pocket for a pair of latex gloves, and grasped the watch. Turning it around, he scratched away the dried blood that caked its diamond-studded face with his thumbnail. His face darkened.

Shaking his head, Jake dropped down on one knee, positioning himself so anyone behind him couldn't see. He shifted the shoulder bag he carried until it was hanging in front of him.

"Chris, help keep those vultures out of here," he said over his shoulder.

Continuing to use his deputy and the troopers as a blind, Jake extricated the cloth-wrapped tooth. He checked to make sure no one saw, then held it next to the sundered forearm.

"Well, what do you think?"

Amara drew shoulder to shoulder with him, her trained eyes focused. She took the tooth fragment and compared it to the limb. She gave a low whistle and nodded.

The curved body of the tooth fit the gouged out end of the forearm like a cookie fit its cutter. It was undeniable. Whatever creature assaulted the *Sayonara* and its crew was responsible for the attack on the Jet Ski – and its rider.

"Shhh . . ." Jake whispered. He wiped the tooth clean, rewrapped it, and stashed it inside his bag. Rising to his feet, he turned a deaf ear to the fusillade the reporters threw at him and walked over to the troopers.

"Gentlemen, I appreciate your assistance. If you wouldn't mind, I'd like you to stick around and make sure no one touches anything – other than forensics and our coroner, of course."

"No problem, Jake. Glad to be of assistance," the heavier of the two said. "Forensics has already been here. As for the coroner, I think that's him right now."

Jake spotted Saul Rigby approaching. A small, creepy-looking man in his fifties with thin lips and shifty eyes, the little mortician was the type of person people went out of their way to avoid. And not just for professional reasons.

"Saul," Jake said with forced pleasantry. He shook the smaller man's hand. "It's a pity we only run into each other during such unpleasant circumstances."

"Comes with the job, youngster," the older man quipped, his squinty eyes taking in the scene behind Jake. As he caught sight of Amara, his sour expression changed.

"And what have we here, Sheriff Braddock?" he asked, unabashedly eyeing the attractive scientist. "You haven't introduced me to your lovely friend."

Jake cast Amara a sympathetic look. "Saul Rigby, this is Dr. Takagi. Dr. Takagi, Mr. Rigby, our town coroner."

"A pleasure, missy." Saul grinned dementedly as he extended a gnarled hand. "My goodness, what a looker . . . and a doctor, too! You'll have to forgive the pun, Doctor Takagi, but as we say in the business, it's about time we got some fresh meat around here!"

Amara yanked her hand back as if she'd touched a live tarantula.

Accustomed to the reaction, Rigby shrugged and went about his work. "Well, I don't think we'll need a stretcher for this one." He cackled as he donned gloves and bent to examine the remains. "Actually, come to think of it, this should fit nicely in my cooler. Good thing I packed lunch today!"

Reveling in the look of loathing Amara was giving him, Rigby continued. "Say, Jake . . ." He grunted loudly as he wrenched the stiffened limb off the Jet Ski's handlebars. He held it up and waved it at them. "Can I give you a *hand* with anything else, or will this be it?"

"No, I think that'll be quite enough from you," Jake admonished. "Actually, come to think of it there *is* something. I'll be needing fingerprints off that hand ASAP."

"How soon?"

"Tonight, Saul."

"Tonight? What's the dang rush?"

"Well, Saul . . . the watercraft you're standing next to belonged to your favorite Paradise Cove resident – Brad Harcourt. And a certain individual is going to want to know if that hand you're so affectionately holding is his."

The undertaker's sudden inhalation was a frightened wheeze. He looked nervously around, then straightened up and made a great show of handling the piece of arm with a tenderness that bordered on reverence. Placing it gingerly in a plastic bag, he kept his head down and continued his business as quiet as a church mouse.

Jake grinned at the realization he'd finally found a use for Dean Harcourt, then started guiding Chris and Amara through the crowd. The reporters were waiting.

"Sheriff Braddock," the first one called out, "is it true that the son of Senator Dean Harcourt is missing and presumed dead?"

"Sheriff, there's word on the dock here that a local fishing boat was attacked by a rogue whale and that its crew is missing. Any comment on that?"

"Sheriff, it's been said that-"

Bristling at the barrage of questions, Jake held up a hand.

"Look, people. I'm sure you've heard this a hundred times from other people, but now you can hear it from me. We have no comment at this time, period. Thank you. Let's go," he said to Amara, forcing his way through the frustrated news people. He stopped to look back at

Chris. "Hey kid, I'd like you to stay with the troopers and help keep an eye on things." He indicated the accident scene. "Dr. Takagi and I are going to check out the *Sayonara*."

"Sure thing chief, I . . . oh shit!"

Jake's head swiveled in the direction of the quavering teenager's gaze. Dean Harcourt and another well-dressed man, as well as his omnipresent security detail, were bearing down on them. "Damn," he fumed as the stocky politician drew closer. "Just when you thought things couldn't get any worse . . ."

Catching sight of Brad's father and his entourage, the press corps converged on their position, dousing them with a blinding shower of flashbulbs.

"Good afternoon, sheriff," Harcourt said. He stopped a few paces away, gesturing for silence from the expectant throng.

"Senator."

"I believe you've already had the privilege of meeting my security detail."

Jake nodded. "Gentlemen."

"Braddock," one of them growled.

"This is my campaign advisor, Darius Thayer," Harcourt said, indicating the vindictive-looking man standing to his right. "Darius, I'd like you to meet Sheriff Jake Braddock."

Jake stepped forward and extended his arm, taking the attorney's hand and measure in turn. The reporters surrounding them interpreted the introduction as the signal to attack and began bombarding Harcourt with inquiries.

"Now, now, everyone," the scarred politician raised thick hands that commanded silence. "I will have a formal statement in a moment. In consideration for my son's disappearance, I would ask for your kind patience, so I can confer with our town constable about appropriate action."

Momentarily mollified, the salivating press snapped photo after photo as Harcourt separated himself from his people and walked over to Jake.

"Now, Jake," Harcourt wiped his chin with the back of one hand and whispered into his ear, "I need your help, so I'm going to bat for you. Even though you and I both know my boy is probably dead . . ." His jaw muscles quivered and his eyes gleamed from the flashbulbs. "I want your promise, though, that you will leave no stone unturned until you find the perpetrator responsible for this. Man or beast, I want your word you will bring my son's killer in."

"If your son's killer can be found, senator, I'll do just that," Jake vowed, his thoughts on avenging Phil Starling and his nephew. He locked eyes with him. "And *that* you have my word on."

Harcourt nodded and turned to the expectant crowd.

"My dear friends from the press . . ." He waited for the tumult to dissipate. "As much as it pains me to say, I fear my son Bradford may be lost to me. His Jet Ski crashed into the docks behind us a short time ago. Rumors of him being attacked by a whale or some other creature are, as far as I know, unfounded. I suspect he may have been the victim of a terrible boating accident, though Brad was always careful around boats." Harcourt sighed heavily. He bowed his head, placing one hand over his heart. "Despite the obvious direness of the situation, I refuse to give up." He looked up, ignoring a shouted question, and raised tear-filled eyes to the heavens. The artillery barrage of flashbulbs intensified. "I have the personal assurance of my good friend, Sheriff Jake Braddock, that every possible search and rescue vessel is being sent out, in the desperate hope that Brad may still be adrift somewhere, clinging to life."

The senator reached over and extended his arm around Jake's shoulders. "Jake Braddock is a true friend of the community and has my complete confidence and support. I will be waiting, hoping that I hear the news I am praying for, that my kind and gentle son will be returned to me."

Turning sideways to the flashing cameras, Harcourt seized Jake's hand, clasping it tightly. "God bless you, Jake," he managed in a shaky voice. "Bring Brad home to me."

Releasing his grip, the senator plunged into the crowd, followed by Darius Thayer. The latter turned back for a moment, his sights locking on Jake before he followed his employer.

Jake's expression hardened as the larger of Harcourt's oversized security guards approached him. It was Fields, the former pro wrestler from Texas.

"Here ya go, gunslinger," Fields said. He whipped out a business card. "We'll be waiting to hear from ya."

His eyes never leaving the big bodyguard, Jake slipped the card into his shirt pocket.

"Oh, you'll be hearing from me, alright. You can count on it."

———

Hands clasped behind him, Darius Thayer walked contemplatively beside Dean Harcourt. The two men headed toward the senator's waiting limousine. Like a play that just ended, the sounds of Harcourt Marina faded in the distance. A cryptic silence lay between them, disrupted only by the clicking of their shoes on the hard cobblestones and tarmac. It remained as they approached the limo, ending when their chauffeur closed the car's soundproof doors behind them.

"You know, Darius . . ." Harcourt grinned as he settled his thick frame into the leather seat. "Sometimes the Lord presents solutions to your problems without you having to look for them."

Thayer stared at him. "What do you mean? You think Brad is still alive?"

"Oh, no . . . Not at all, old friend. Brad was a great swimmer, but no one could stay alive for longer than a few minutes with an injury like that. No, I'm afraid I have to accept that my boy is dead."

"Well, I don't know how else to say this, but you seem to be handling the news well," Thayer said. He concealed how he felt by removing his glasses and cleaning them.

"That's because the Lord, in His infinite wisdom, has just handed me Jake Braddock's head on a silver platter."

Harcourt studied the nonplussed expression on his counsel's face. "I want you to look into his location for the last twelve hours."

Thayer put his glasses back on. "Why?"

"Because, it's just possible he may be the last person to see Brad alive."

Thayer's jaw dropped. "Are you saying you plan on framing Braddock for Brad's death?"

"Frame him?" Harcourt sneered. "Humph. After their recent confrontation, our town sheriff is as good a suspect as anyone."

"So, you want to use your own son's demise as a weapon?"

"Why not? Wasn't Abraham willing to sacrifice his son to prove his worthiness to the Lord? Should I do less?"

One of Harcourt's eyes narrowed and he grinned, obviously amused by the mixture of disbelief and astonishment playing hop-scotch across Thayer's face. "Look at it this way," he explained. "Besides helping turn the entire town against Braddock, we can use my loss as a sympathy card for the upcoming election. It's only a few months down the road. Didn't you say 'a little sympathy goes a long way'?"

Thayer mulled over the situation. He saw the merit in Harcourt's plan – assuming, of course, that the senator was cold-blooded enough to implement it.

"Okay, Dean." Thayer leaned back, his thumb and index finger stroking his chin. "It's workable. More than that, it's genius. Evil genius, but still genius."

"It is indeed, Darius," Harcourt said smugly. He opened his suit jacket and reached for a Cuban, lighting a match by rasping it across the rough-edged scar on his jaw. The fiery glow from the match shone in his eyes. "Kind of makes me wonder what I pay you for. Lately it seems I've done most of the thinking."

Thayer grinned, though inwardly he bristled. "I'll get things started. And don't worry about the details. My contacts will jump all over a story like this. Before the week is out, Jake Braddock will be finished."

Following Dean Harcourt's departure, the marina crowd began to dissipate. Jake remained where he was, his eyes focused on the path the senator had taken.

"Well, he seemed pretty nonchalant about the whole thing," Amara said. "I'm surprised he's taking it so well. You don't think he believes his son is still alive, do you?"

"Not a chance," Jake said. "He's up to something. I'd bet my life on it." He touched her lower back lightly. "C'mon, doc. Let's go take a look at the *Sayonara*."

They walked along the main landing, turning toward the spot where the old Bertram was tied off. Up close, the damage was even worse than he remembered. The omnipresent blood splatters were a dull brown now, but still layered everything.

"Jesus . . ." Amara faltered at the sight.

Jake spotted the Miami forensics team climbing wearily out of the boat. Their bags were piled up on the dock. One of them – a swarthy fellow with a well-trimmed goatee – recognized Jake as he and Amara approached and moved to greet him.

"Hey, Jake, good to see you again, brother," the man said, clasping palms with the young sheriff. "I got the call and made sure to come myself. I'm real sorry about Phil."

"Thanks, Paul," Jake replied somberly. He looked at what was left of the old vessel and sighed heavily. "He'll definitely be missed."

"Jake, this is my assistant, Greg," Paul introduced the young technician accompanying him. "Greg, this is Sheriff Jake Braddock, a good friend."

"It's nice to meet you. I've heard a lot about you." The junior forensics examiner extended his hand, wincing from the grip he received.

"Nice to meet you, too," Jake said. "Gentlemen, this is Dr. Amara Takagi from the Worldwide Cetacean Society. She's an expert on cetaceans, as well as the commander of the oceanic research vessel *Harbinger*. She has generously offered to assist our investigation."

Greg stared as he shook hands with the tall cetaceanist. "The WCS, eh? So, you think a rogue whale did this?"

"I don't have an opinion yet," Amara said. "I'm here to get a look at the damage to this boat and to compare my findings to yours. We'll see where we go from there."

Jake took a step toward the *Sayonara*. "So, did you guys find anything?"

"Not much," Paul said, following him. "You were definitely right about what you called in." He gestured at the ravaged stern portion. "From the looks of things, something very large, and organic, rose up out of the water and came down on top of the transom."

Moving closer to the damaged section, Paul dropped down on one knee. He gestured for Jake and Amara. "If you look at the crushed portion, you can see how the wood has been pressed down at a steep angle. Whatever did this placed a tremendous amount of weight on the stern of the boat. Enough to crack the hull, in fact," he added meaningfully. "It also dragged itself sideways across the stern, pulling wood and fiberglass as it went. You can see the drag marks here."

Amara knelt down next to him. "You said it was organic?"

"Yes. We extricated this from one of the broken beams." Paul reached into his shirt pocket and removed a fluid-filled test tube. Swirling around inside was a ragged strip of dark-colored tissue as thick as a man's thumb.

"Do you mind?" Amara asked, eagerly. She thanked him with a smile as he handed her the test tube. "Any idea what it's from?"

"I'm no marine biologist," Paul said. "But I think it's an epidermal fragment from some animal. Tough stuff, though. I had to pull it free with a pair of pliers."

Amara held the shimmering tube to the waning light, twisting it to and fro as she examined its contents. "Can I keep this? I'd like to run some tests."

"Uh, I'm . . . not sure," Paul said. He glanced at Jake. "It's up to you, brother. I can loan it to her, but you'll have to sign for it."

"No problem. Did you take blood samples?"

"Of course. That was another strange thing."

"Strange? What do you mean?" Jake asked as he scribbled his name on a form Greg held out for him.

The forensicologist moved over to the *Sayonara's* starboard. "There's an awful lot of blood here. Until the samples we extracted are evaluated I won't know for sure, but it's highly unlikely all of this came from one person."

Jake's imagination began weaving gory nightmares.

"I could be wrong about the pattern," Paul emphasized. "I mean, there's blood everywhere. But for all of this to have come from a single victim, well . . . not to sound gruesome, but whoever this was, they'd have to be thrown into a giant meat grinder to be sprayed all over like this."

His face impassive, Jake's eyes traveled out past the marina, beyond the docked sailboats and charters, toward the waiting sea.

"Thanks, Paul," he said. "I appreciate you coming down. You guys about done?"

"Looks that way, brother," he said, shaking Jake's hand again before grabbing his bags and gesturing for his assistant. "I'll call you with the results of the blood work. It was nice meeting you, Dr. Takagi!" he yelled over his shoulder. The two men moved up onto the landing and made their way to their vehicle.

"Well, they were very cooperative," Amara said. She held up the test tube as the two men drove off.

"We go way back," Jake replied.

"How come you didn't tell them about the tooth?"

Jake hesitated. He drummed his fingertips on the bag he carried, then turned toward the *Sayonara*. "I don't know. Maybe I think you'll do a better job. You seem to know your stuff. Anyway, we're running out of daylight. Let's get onboard and see what your spin is on what happened."

Stepping over the Bertram's gunnels, Jake extended his hand.

———

A thousand yards from the *Sayonara*, the creature studied Harcourt Marina with interest. Attracted to the lights that danced like fireflies in the growing darkness, it cruised into the shallows to observe the tiny mammals moving. Cautious, it remained where it was, its vast bulk concealed beneath the murky waters. Every half hour it rose to breathe, its glittering eyes and blowhole breaking the surface. It was wary of the spinning props attached to the ever-present boats and submerged whenever one approached. Adjusting its buoyancy with an exhalation, it drifted noiselessly to the bottom and remained there until all was calm. To the mammals on the surface, it was invisible.

The creature's pursuit of the bothersome black and yellow Jet Ski had awakened its vast appetite. Already, the first pangs of hunger were assailing its highly-evolved digestive system. The irrepressible urge to hunt and kill gnawed at it, yet the barrage of loud noises and lights kept it at bay. Soon, darkness would fall upon the surrounding waters. Then it would travel into the shallower portions of the nearby harbor. And feed.

TWELVE

Karl Von Freiling opened his eyes. He sat up in the back seat, cursing at having added a stiff neck to his collection of aches and pains. He checked his watch.

"Pull over at this rest area, Aziz," he said a moment later. "I gotta shake hands with the champ."

The Pakistani's reflection in the rearview mirror was one of befuddlement.

"The champ? You mean one of your celebrated boxing champions is here?"

"No, man. I gotta take a piss!"

"Oh, uh . . . you got it, boss."

As his driver merged right and guided the Dodge Caravan toward the exit ramp, Von Freiling reached into his bag for the cell phone he'd picked up in Seattle. He gave the device's instructions a cursory glance before ripping apart the packaging. After inserting the batteries and giving it a quick check, he slipped the phone into his shirt pocket.

"Here's fine," he said, gesturing at a nearby burger joint. As they rolled into an open spot, he popped open the door and stepped out. "You want anything?"

"Sure thing, boss," Aziz replied eagerly. "A classic triple combo with a coke would be great."

"You got it." Von Freiling closed the door, dismissing the notion of taking the mini-vans' keys. With no money in hand yet, and nearly four hours separating him from home, the odds of his driver reneging on their arrangement were slim. He grinned with satisfaction as he headed toward the men's room. Out of the corner of his eye he saw Aziz pull over to the nearest gas pump.

Von Freiling headed into the men's room. He emerged a moment later and loped around the corner, heading for a secluded hillock located directly behind the building. He extracted his phone and punched in a number. The recipient picked up on the first ring.

"Hello?" a gruff voice said.

"Hey, Stubbs. It's me," he muttered. He kept his voice low as he peeked around the corner.

"Me who?"

"Don't be funny, asshole. It's your fucking boss."

There was a deep chuckle. "Sorry, brother. Didn't recognize the number."

"It's a disposable. Anyway, you saw the newscast?"

"Hell yeah, everybody did. We're at the proving grounds. What the fuck happened?"

Von Freiling paused as two giggling co-eds, shoulder to shoulder, raced each other into the women's bathroom. He hoped for their sake it was cleaner than the men's.

"It was a set-up."

"What do you mean?"

"Our wealthy "benefactor" was full of shit. Giant octopus, my ass. He was looking to hire muscle to help him move a shipment of coke."

"No shit."

"Yeah. When we turned him down things got ugly. Next thing I knew, we ended up in a firefight with his crew, and his buyer's boys as well."

"Damn."

"Yep, it was like the Gulf all over again. Lost the entire team."

"The bodies?"

Von Freiling's eyes tightened, his face closing up like a fortress battening down. He hated the thought of leaving men behind. "I had to let them burn with the boat. Couldn't risk the cops linking us to that scumbag."

There was a moment of silence on the line.

"Man, that's some fucked-up shit."

Von Freiling nodded. "Fucking-A. Anyway, we've got problems way beyond the mission. Not only did we lose four guys, we never got paid. And, we lost everything we brought: the boat, underwater surveillance gear, night vision scopes, re-breathers, weapons, ammo

– you name it. We're looking at a loss of seven hundred easy. Plus, you know we're gonna get sued on top of it."

"By who, relatives?"

"Hell, yeah. Lincoln had no family, but the other guys all did. Smitty had three kids. You met that fat-ass wife of his. You know that bitch is gonna want something."

"You gonna settle with them?"

Von Freiling hesitated. "We'll see. By the way, how's my babies doing?"

"Sleek and sexy. We've got em fired up and ready to rock."

"Good. About time I got some good news. Besides nearly getting my ass shot off and having to swim five miles in pitch-black, shark infested seas, I had the fucking press all over me when I checked out of the motel, trying to link someone to the missing boats. I had to take the only flight I could find, and it was economy all the way."

"We've flown worse," Stubbs snickered.

"Drops are different," Von Freiling said. Two snickering potheads headed his way, looking for a place to light up. He lowered his voice. "Hey, I gotta go. I'll call you once I get settled in and we'll discuss meeting with some prospective clients."

"Works for me."

There was a sharp click as Stubbs abruptly hung up. Von Freiling smirked. Rude bastard never did say goodbye. He was halfway to the cab when he stopped dead in his tracks. He snapped his fingers and whirled back around.

Damn. Forgot the camel jockey's murder-burger . . .

⸻

Even in near darkness, Jake could see Amara's face looked ashen.

"That was a pretty horrifying scene back there," she said.

"Yeah, it certainly was."

The two made their way along the deserted landing. Here and there, the silence was broken by the noise of couples sneaking off to their boats, or frolicking patrons flowing in and out of the *Cove Hove*. It was a far cry from the chaos two hours earlier.

Jake watched an obviously inebriated couple staggering arm in arm out of the bar. They headed toward a nearby docked sailboat.

Suddenly, the giggling woman lost a shoe and her footing and dropped to the ground. Her smiling companion laughed aloud as he was dragged down with her. As he watched them trying to get up, only to fall all over each other, Jake had a momentary glimpse of himself two years prior. He shuddered, shutting out the memory to focus on the here and now.

"So, what do you think happened?" he probed.

He was careful not to press the marine biologist too hard, figuring the bloodbath onboard the *Sayonara* had to be rough on her.

"Well, Jake," Amara paused to watch the last sliver of the sun's shimmering orb disappear beyond the horizon. "I think your theory on the attack, and an attack it was, turned out to be fairly accurate." She hugged herself as a cool breeze from the harbor gave her goose bumps. "I think your poor friends had an encounter with an unknown marine carnivore, one big enough to reach onboard a fishing yacht and snatch up two grown men like they were nothing. And at least one of them was sitting in the *Sayonara's* fighting chair when it grabbed him. That suggests our mystery predator has a bite powerful enough to reduce a heavy wood and metal chair to kindling in a single crunch."

Jake cursed and shook his head. "But you have no idea what it is? Is there anything known to have teeth like this," he hefted the canvas bag he carried. "And capable of doing what we saw?"

"I'm afraid not, Jake. It must be a new species. If I could log onto *Archimedes* I could at least confirm that much."

"Do you have to be onboard your ship to access the system?"

"What did you have in mind?"

"We have a high speed connection back at my office. And a lost and found full of digital cameras. Will that work?"

"That might do the job." Amara said. She looked wearily around. "But, it's getting late and I'm tired. Can this wait until morning?"

Jake stopped walking, "Doc, this thing is *eating* people. We can't wait. We need to find out what it is *now*."

Amara flushed. "You're right, of course. In that case, get me the number for a hotel, because without the use of our servers *Archimedes* will take several hours to do a complete search. I doubt either of us is going to be in any shape to go bouncing back to the *Harbinger* in the middle of the night."

Jake smirked at her. "A hotel in this town, in June, without a reservation? You've got to be kidding me, doc." He led her to his SUV and held the door. Closing it, he walked around and clambered inside. "We're booked solid from now until the end of July."

"Wonderful. So, what am I supposed to do, crash in your truck?"

For the second time since he met her, Amara's eyes revealed a glimmer of apprehension.

"Let's see . . ." Jake grinned as he clicked his seatbelt. "There's a sofa in my office you're welcome to crash on. We've also got a well stocked refrigerator and a full-sized bathroom, one my fanatical secretary keeps absolutely spotless. It's not glamorous, but I spent quite a few nights on that sofa before I got my apartment, and let me tell you, it beats sleeping in the backseat."

Amara chuckled. "I guess that will have to do. By the time I get off your computer, it'll look like the Hilton!"

Jake slid his key into the truck's ignition and started her up. He sat there, his gaze steady and unwavering as he waited for the V-8 engine to warm up. Beside him, Amara shifted her weight as she leaned tiredly back in her seat.

"Hey, Jake?"

"Yes, doc?"

The cetaceanist's lips parted, but she hesitated. "The man who owned the *Sayonara*, I heard your friend say his name was Phil?"

He nodded. "Phil Starling. He was her captain. His nephew's name was Steve."

"You knew them well?"

"Steve, I just met. But Captain Phil, I've known since I was a kid. He was a great guy. When I was fourteen, I started working for him as his first mate."

Amara sat upright. "When you were fourteen?"

He nodded. "Yep. Every summer, all the way until high school graduation."

"That seems awfully young."

"There wasn't much choice. If Captain Phil hadn't hired me when he did, I probably would've starved." Jake's mind wandered for a moment. "I'm sure he always knew that. Of course, he was far too classy to ever say it."

"I don't understand. Where were your parents?"

Jake's lips grew taut. He realized it was his turn to hesitate. "They . . . went away unexpectedly. I was left with no money or food for nearly a month."

Amara was aghast. "My God, that's awful. Who would do such a thing?"

"My father. He took all the money and food my mother left. She didn't know, and I never told her. He had some warped idea that the experience would make a man out of me."

"Did it?"

Jake looked at her. "Oh, yes, but not the broken kind he was."

"Good for you. I'm amazed you survived."

"You've survived worse things, doc."

Amara's eyes closed for a second. "Yeah . . . Well, regardless, I'm sorry your dad was such an asshole."

He chuckled.

"What?" Amara's expression of confusion bordered on offense.

"Nothing. It's just, I've never heard you use foul language before." He smirked. "It's very . . . refreshing."

Amara's face colored and she shook her head. "Sorry, I must be more tired than I thought."

"No problem." Jake smiled and leaned in closer to her. "How about your dad – how was he?"

"He was great. Unfortunately, he wasn't around much when I was little. He was a *Sea Crusade* activist, so he traveled around a lot. My grandparents raised me, mostly."

"What about your mom?"

"I never knew her. When I was still a baby, she died suddenly."

Jake's expression softened. "I'm sorry to hear that. I don't think I would've survived without mine. She was my world."

"Thanks, but it's okay." Amara sighed. "My world is the sea these days. It's pretty much all I know."

"Not anymore."

"What do you mean?"

He winked at her. "Well, now you get to tell people you know *me*."

Amara smirked and shifted position once more. Her eyes began to close. "Oh, brother. And here I was hoping that was one skeleton I could keep hidden in my closet . . ."

Jake grinned as he shifted the big Tahoe into gear and pulled smoothly out of his parking spot, taking care not to jostle his tired passenger or the bag he'd deposited in the glove compartment. Beside him, Amara rested her head against the cool side window, her eyes staring wearily at the moonlit waters of the harbor as they vanished from view.

Neither of them noticed the strange object cruising through the marina, or the slow-moving wake trailing it – a wake strong enough to disturb several boats in their slips.

———

"Hey, Jake, do you have anything to weigh the tooth?" Amara asked from behind the monitor. A few minutes after arriving at the sheriff's station, she was already hard at work, prepping her impromptu research facility.

"One sec," Jake yelled from the front office. "I'm locking up."

As time passed, Amara got lost in her task. She was so focused on her research she jumped when Jake walked into the room.

"Geez, you scared me!"

Jake tried not to laugh. "Doc, you spend your days around ten-ton fish, and *I* scare you?"

Amara's eyes crinkled up as she peeked over her screen. "So, any luck?"

"Actually, yes." Jake placed the armful of items he carried on the desk next to her. "One tape measure, two digital cameras, each with more mega-pixels than you can shake a stick at, and a bottle of Tylenol Extra Strength, in case your hip is still bothering you."

Amara beamed at him. "My gosh, could you *be* any sweeter?" She reached for the bottle, popping it's lid with her thumbnail and pouring herself a small handful. She winked at him. "Of course, I'm really an Ibuprofen girl."

"Me too. Normally. What I mean is, uh, I'm an Ibuprofen *guy*, that is. You know, being an athlete and all that. But anyway, I'm fresh out."

Amara smirked and got up in the direction of the water cooler.

"No, no, I've got it." Jake made it there in three quick strides, dispensing her a tiny cupful of water. "Here you go . . ."

"My goodness, you're spoiling me."

Jake felt his face starting to get warm. "So . . . do you prefer caplets or gels?"

"What?"

"Your Ibuprofen."

Amara scanned the items before her and gave a tiny frown. "It doesn't really matter. They both get the job done."

"But, don't you think the gels work faster?"

She stared at him. "Jake, if the need arises, I chew caplets dry."

He made a face and stuck his tongue out. "Yuck! My God, woman, you must be made of stone. Remind me to never mess with you!"

"I will." She grinned, then pointed at her desk. "No scale?"

Jake disappeared for a moment, returning with a small box which he deposited proudly on the desk in front of her. "One genuine postage scale. It's limited to five pounds, so I hope it'll do."

"There's one way to find out," Amara replied. She wheeled her chair over and reached for the tooth. Standing up, she placed it gingerly on the scale. She pushed a few buttons, double-checked her readings, then removed the tooth and returned it to a stack of paper towels next to the test tube containing the creature's skin fragment. She entered the acquired information into the computer in front of her. "Four point three seven pounds." She whistled breathlessly. "Wow, that's some piece of dentition. According to my calculations, the whole tooth must have weighed almost eight pounds."

Jake moved closer, peering over her shoulder.

Amara breathed in through her nostrils and swallowed. *Is it my imagination, or does the big galoot still smell good, even this late in the day?* Berating herself for getting distracted, she gave a tiny snort and focused on the task at hand.

"So, how are you making out? Any luck?"

"I tried the *Harbinger* on my cell. They're too far offshore. I had to instant message Willie and have him reroute *Archimedes* for an off-site linkup."

"So, we're . . . I mean . . . you're in now?"

Jake loomed over her, fascinated by the display of natural history images making their way across the screen.

"Yes, I'm in," Amara replied with a restrained grin. She twisted in her chair to jot down some notes, then rose, dodging him in the process. She began tabulating the tooth's dimensions. Catching the curiosity in Jake's eyes, she lowered her tape measure. She threw a glance at the wall clock and frowned. "Listen, it's almost ten. I can see you're interested in what's going on here, but you staying up to watch is only going to slow me down and leave us both exhausted."

She regretted her words immediately. "It's not that I don't enjoy your company," she emphasized, "but with this computer's connection speed, the analysis process alone could take hours."

"Say no more," he said, extending his hand palm out. "I'll get out of the way." He strode out of the room, returning moments later with a bundle of soft goods he deposited on the couch. "Here's a pillow, blanket, and some fresh linens." He pointed to a nearby doorway. "The kitchen and bathroom are through there, and there are fresh towels on the shelf. My secretary comes in at eight. I'll wake you up at seven so you don't give her a heart attack."

Amara looked up and nodded.

Jake sucked noisily on his teeth. "Well . . . I guess I'll turn in."

"Turn in where?" Amara's pulse quickened as she peeked over the top of her LCD screen.

Jake laughed. "In my apartment."

"Oh. Is it close by?"

"I guess you could say that." He pointed at a flight of steps leading upstairs. "It reduces traveling time. Feel free to knock if you need anything."

Amara smiled and arched an eyebrow. "Like what? A late night snack?"

Jake gave her a wry grin as he started up the steps. "Well, I don't know if my cooking skills rival yours, but I do make the world's greatest scrambled eggs. And they *don't* resemble hash browns. I'm saving them for the morning, however. Depending, of course . . ."

"Depending on what?"

"On how successful you are with your investigation, deputy Takagi."

"Ah, so it's *deputy* now, eh? Does that mean I'm getting paid for this?"

"I already told you . . . depends on how successful you are."

"I think I want a raise."

Jake chuckled. "Fine, I'll throw in toast and a cup of coffee. But I'm warning you now, all I've got is dark roast."

Amara sighed. "I always knew my research would pay off. I'll be thinking of you snoring your brains out while I'm down here slaving away."

"What a coincidence. I'll be dreaming of you slaving away, too."

She smiled as he loped off, then continued her analysis. Her fingers were a blur as she typed in information. Thirty minutes later, she leaned back, raised her intertwined hands over her head, and shifted her arms from side to side to stretch her neck and shoulders. A tiny bit refreshed, she reached for the desk lamp, adjusting its position so its light shined directly on her specimen. She wiped the desk with glass cleaner and placed sheets of paper underneath the tooth.

Amara stepped back to photograph the tooth from a variety of angles. After her last photo she closed her eyes for a few seconds, just to entertain the idea of rest, then opened them and began scrolling through the images in her camera. Satisfied with what she had, she removed the camera's memory card and inserted it into the computer. After a few keystrokes, she'd downloaded the pictures.

She was ready.

To her surprise, she found herself sitting rigidly upright, her finger suspended over the button that activated *Archimedes'* sensory scan. The anticipation of a potential discovery and the adrenaline rush that accompanied it swept over her.

Exhaling sharply, she pressed the button.

Archimedes' response and subsequent analysis were breathtaking. Systematically breaking down the object's mass, dimensions and composition, the program began to scroll through the divisions of the animal kingdom at light speed. Like a colored strobe light, creatures of every shape and design – from the largest to the smallest – flashed across the flat-panel monitor at a rate of twenty a second.

Archimedes mercilessly perused its data banks for any possible link. Every so often the system highlighted a prospective match, flashing the corresponding data so quickly it was impossible to follow. It latched onto a particular body part of the species it was focusing on, enlarging it for comparison and breaking it down into bio-schematic text. The teeth of Nile and Saltwater crocodiles, the tusks of African and Asian elephants, and even Pacific walruses all briefly appeared. Various whales' teeth were highlighted, including the killer whale, false killer, and the sperm. Yet each time, a glowing red letter X flashed across the suspected life form, as *Archimedes* ruthlessly eliminated it and moved on. Minutes became hours, and Amara's eyes began to close from too many images and too little sleep.

Shaking it off, she went to the kitchen and poured herself a cup of coffee so bitter it made her grimace when she gulped it down. She went back to her computer. Bored, she minimized *Archimedes* and started surfing the web. On a whim, she punched in "whale sightings" to see what came up. It was the usual stuff: killer whales at sea, info on the dead blue whale . . . nothing of interest. Next, she tried "sea monster" and "sea serpent." She found numerous postings on a new species of squid. There were three confirmed attacks on surfers off the coast of Cuba. Tourists were up in arms, and her colleagues were insisting a nearby volcanic eruption was responsible. Despite protests, the Cuban government was refusing to allow researchers from the international community to investigate the site.

Amara snorted. *Typical.* She continued looking to see if there was anything on the monster fish she had in her freezer. Nothing. And no reports of any King Kong-sized predator either. Her eyes fought to stay open as she checked the time – nearly three o'clock in the morning.

Suddenly, there was a chime from the computer signaling the completion of the database analysis. Excited, she clicked back to the previous screen. The system's notification flashed repeatedly.

No match found. No match found. No match found . . .

Disappointment weighed on her as her eyelids became anvils. Her head drooped, sleep coming so fast it was like she was hit over the head. Comatose, she failed to see *Archimedes'* screen change.

No match found. Searching fossil record.

With its contemporary files exhausted, the program switched to its auxiliary banks and began running checks on extinct life forms. The monitor screen swarmed with images of prehistoric beasts. Beginning with the Pleistocene Epoch, *Archimedes* checked the tips of mammoth and mastodon tusks, the claws of giant ground sloths and the fangs of saber tooth cats.

Finding nothing of significance, it moved further back in time, encompassing the Jurassic and Cretaceous periods. It examined allosaur and tyrannosaur teeth and claws, as well as the conical canines of primeval crocodiles. A few of these momentarily gave the system pause before they, too, were summarily dismissed.

Its data banks shifting again, *Archimedes* expounded its search parameters. Images of extinct fish and marine reptiles filled the screen, including monstrous sharks with jaws big enough to swallow a cow, and sinister-looking mosasaur lizards with long tails and crocodile-like heads.

The system noticeably slowed, scrutinizing the dentition of each creature in detail and listing a probability percentage beside each one. Eventually, it focused on marine reptiles, specifically the plesiosaurs. Images of such strange creatures as *Brachauchenius, Pliosaurus* and *Liopleurodon* appeared on the screen. With each one, the percentages climbed. Finally, the system stopped, zeroing in on one particular animal: a powerfully built creature with flippers and razor-sharp teeth. An error message began to flash across the screen. Something was conflicting with the program's built-in logic center. Checking and rechecking its findings, *Archimedes* discontinued its analysis and began to flash an alert.

Anomaly: specimen identified, probability percentage: 83%
Anomaly: specimen identified, probability percentage 83%
Anomaly: specimen identified . . .

Amara lay unconscious, with her head resting on one arm. The other was extended across the desk, fingers clinging childlike to the creature's tooth.

A foot away, *Archimedes* continued to sound its alarm.

At 5 a.m. Jake woke up. He'd slept fitfully, but some rest was infinitely better than none. He reached over and killed the CD alarm clock before it went off. He had a mixed 70's disc in it, but kept forgetting to change the wake up track. He was a fan of Barry White, but he swore if he heard *"Can't Get Enough of Your Love, Babe"* one more time, he was going to throw the damn thing out the window.

He rolled out of bed and started stretching immediately, his naked frame resembling some hairless tiger. Like most athletes, he knew his muscles responded best to flexibility conditioning first thing in the morning, and although he no longer possessed the drive or desire to compete, old habits died hard.

Fifteen minutes later, with his stretching complete, Jake slipped into a t-shirt and lounge pants and made his way into the kitchen. He opened the fridge, poured himself a glass of filtered water, and chugged it down. He glanced out the window. It was still pitch-black outside and would be for another hour or so. He wondered how Amara made out with her research, and if she'd found anything that would help identify whatever was roaming around out there killing people.

He sat his glass down on the kitchen counter and decided to refill it. As he reached for the refrigerator door, he spotted an old photo of himself and Captain Phil. They'd taken it during one of Jake's early ventures as the first mate of the *Sayonara*, posing with their very pleased charter and the enormous bull Dorado the husband and wife team landed after a fifteen minute tussle. The picture was reminiscent of Phil Starling himself, a little crinkled around the edges and yellowed with age, but still colorful and vibrant. Jake ran his fingertip gently over the surface of the old snapshot, studying his own youthful expression. He grinned sadly. His fourteen-year-old smile looked as bright as the day it was taken.

But that was fourteen years ago. Captain Phil was gone, and his ravaged Bertram wasn't taking anyone fishing ever again. Jake didn't smile like that anymore, either. Everything he ever loved was dead and gone, and there was nothing around that could make him smile.

He paused thoughtfully for a moment, then opened the door to his apartment and peeked downstairs. The office lights were still on, but except for a faint humming noise it was dead quiet. The possibility Amara had worked sleepless through the night dawned on him, and he decided to go down and check on her.

As he tiptoed barefoot down the stairs, he discovered the cetaceanist exactly where he left her. She was behind his computer desk, out cold, with her face and forearm resting on the keyboard. Her other arm was draped awkwardly through the office chair's armrest. He shook his head. How she could sleep with one limb in such an uncomfortable position was beyond him.

As he crept closer to her, Jake's eyes widened in disbelief and he took an involuntary step back. He stifled a chuckle. The humming sound he heard at the top of the stairs was now ten times louder, its source instantly identifiable.

Amara Takagi snored. Like a chain saw.

He moved next to her, cocking his head and dropping down on one knee to make sure he wasn't imagining things. Unable to turn away, he watched in abject fascination. Her perfect ruby lips compressed gently inward as she inhaled, the sucking noise they created remarkably similar to that of a straining vacuum cleaner. The sound of her exhalation was even louder; a throaty roar more reminiscent of a hungry animal than a human being.

Jake shook his head in bafflement. Amara was one of the most stunning women he'd ever seen, but watching the marine biologist sleep while listening to her snore was like seeing a swan open its beak and snort like a pig.

Amused, he made his way to the nearby couch and unfolded some of the bedding. He spread a sheet over the couch's interior, smoothing it out and tucking it in carefully around the edges of the cushions. Then he propped a pillow at one end and unfurled a lightweight blanket, placing it at the other. Satisfied, he moved quietly to Amara. He hesitated. The idea of picking her up and carrying her to the couch to tuck her in was instinctive. Lifting the girl up was not a problem. She weighed one-thirty-five at most. But he was worried she might wake up unexpectedly and become alarmed; or worse, misinterpret his intentions.

With a heavy exhale, Jake crouched down. His eyes moved furtively about and his hands began weaving their way around Amara's unconscious form, trying to decide what to grab and where. He took a deep breath and held it. For some inexplicable reason his fingers remained six inches away from her body. It was as if the girl was protected by an invisible force field.

His face contorted in genuine annoyance and he took hold of her anyway. He rested one palm gently across her lower back and reached down with the other, curling it around the underside of her thighs. Just as he was about to lift her up her mouth opened and she emitted a sharp, grumbling snort – something you might hear from an angry water buffalo. Jake's courage evaporated and he recoiled. Breathing hard, he took two steps back and waited. He shook his head and stood there, watching her ribcage expand and contract, while listening to the *National Geographic* noises emanating from her face.

He went to the couch and stared at the pillow, retrieving the blanket instead. Spreading it out, he draped it over Amara's form, covering her as best he could, allowing the excess to collect along the floor. He took hold of her left forearm, and with nervous fingers, carefully extracted it from the armrest, laying it gently atop the desk. His task complete, he looked her over, wishing he had other ways to make her more comfortable.

He shrugged and straightened up, then flipped off the light switch at the base of the staircase and made his way back up to his apartment as soundlessly as he came.

THIRTEEN

With less than an hour to go before dawn, activity levels aboard the *Harbinger* approached fever pitch. After arriving shortly before dusk at the dead sperm whale's approximate location, Willie Daniels and the crew of the former whaler found themselves hampered by high seas and failing light.

Anchoring in the darkness, they sat back and waited for the wind to die down before attempting to use the ship's radar and sonar to track the giant cetacean. The task of investigating the myriad sound images they received, any of which might be the dead bull, fell squarely on the shoulders of Lane Brodsky and Mike Helm, manning the ship's runabout, the *Sycophant*.

It took them a good two hours of bouncing from signal to signal before they finally got lucky. The two interns located the rotting whale, tagged it with a radio transmitter, and radioed its location back to the mother ship. Within a half-hour, the *Harbinger* was anchored next to the carcass, waiting for Lane and Mike to secure a line to it.

Willie radioed them. "Lane, how's it goin?"

"We finally got a cable around Elvis's flukes," Lane shouted into his hand unit, trying to be heard over the inflatable's noisy outboard. "You can reel him in if you're feeling nostalgic, but the King is definitely dead. This tub of lard stinks to high heaven!"

Winking at his friend Mike as he tossed the remaining length of cable overboard, Lane grinned and gestured for silence as he waited for Willie's reply.

"Dat's OK, mon," Willie said. "I got enough problems wit da smelly crew we got on dis boat already. If ya don mind, I tink we'll leave dat dead whale where he be."

"That's a big ten-four, Willie," Lane chuckled. "We're heading back now."

———

Willie Daniels sat in the *Harbinger's* observation room, arms folded. He scratched his nose, checked his watch for the umpteenth time, then spun his seat toward Adam Spencer.

"Mon, it's seven o'clock and we got no call from Amara. Her radio's off and I can't reach her by cell."

"What do you want to do?" Adam asked from behind his lenses. "She told us to document the sperm before it's chewed up by scavengers. With the current water conditions, you know the mini-sub's the way to go. I hate to say it, but we can't wait for her. Besides, she wouldn't want us to."

Cracks of frustration crinkled Willie's brow and he stifled a curse. As much as he hated the decision he was now forced to make, there was no choice. He brushed his hands off on his jeans and rose. All eyes turned toward him.

"Okay, guys, we followin da captain's orders to check out dis dead whale. I need everyone to dere places. We be launching da *William* for da first time."

Willie picked up his radio and gave the order forward to prep the submersible.

"So, who's going down with her?" Adam asked. As he spoke, his hands weaved their spell across two keyboards simultaneously. "You need a two-man crew, right?"

"Dat's right, mon," Willie said. He checked his sonar screen. "I was goin ta go myself, but wit Amara not here, it looks like Lane and Mike get da nod once again."

He sat and studied his scope. After a few last minute adjustments, he inserted a pair of video discs into the overhead units. "Any ting showing up on camera, Adam?" he asked without looking. "Sonar's showin a lot of activity around da dead whale."

"It's hard to tell." Adam turned a dial. "The water's clouded up big time. I imagine every scavenger within five miles will show up for a buffet this size."

Willie looked up as a loud creaking sound, punctuated by a tremendous splashing, echoed through the ship's hull. He looked over Adam's shoulder and watched the *William* creep past their hull cameras.

"Wow, that's something you don't see every day," Adam said. He pointed with his pencil as the gleaming mini-sub filled the nearest screen.

"I sure hope ya recordin dis, mon," Willie advised. "Ya know Amara will have ya head if ya don't."

"Relax, old friend." Adam grinned as he jabbed a few buttons. "It's bad enough she's not here for her sub's maiden voyage. You don't think I'd let her miss the rerun?"

Willie rolled a chair over to Adam's station and plopped down beside him, his big hands clasped under his chin. Oblivious to the interns around them, the two technicians studied the *William*, watching as the unwieldy-looking vessel moved away from the *Harbinger's* protective hull. With its diesel engine powering its shielded prop, the twenty-two foot submersible glided beneath the swells, its metal pontoons spouting tiny air bubbles from its virgin ballast system.

The *William* moved in, its rudder shifting it in the direction of the current-driven carcass. As it did, the six-foot observation bubble that comprised its prow became visible, along with its manipulators, drawn up beneath it like the claws of a praying mantis.

"She's looking good," Adam said with a proud grin. "Do either of them know how to use the actuators?"

"No, dey don't." Willie reached for his radio. "Lane, it's Willie. How's it goin?"

"Read you loud and clear, *Harbinger*," Lane's voice sprang out of the speaker. "So far, so good. We're approaching the carcass now. Distance is fifty meters and closing."

"Sounds good, mon," Willie said. He looked nervously at the overhead monitors. "Turn on all cameras and start transmittin. And no mucking around wit da robot arms, if ya please."

"No problem," Lane chuckled. The sound of flipping switches carried over the mike. "How's this?"

The room's monitors shimmered, their images changing as the feed from the *William's* cameras took over.

Like some colossus emerging from the gloom, the bull sperm emerged into view. Its gigantic jaws hung open in a hideous grimace, its tattered body filling the screen.

Adam dropped his pencil. "Holy shit! Forget what I said before. Now *that's* something you don't see every day."

"Amen, mon," Willie agreed. "Lane, circle da carcass and focus on where some ting bit da whale."

"You got it," he replied. "Whoa, check it out! It's like a feeding frenzy down here!"

Dipping under the heavy tow cable that bound the undulating carcass to the *Harbinger*, the mini-sub circled the cetacean's body at a distance of fifty feet. Amara's concerns were well founded. The sperm whale was peppered with clinging scavengers, writhing over and under each other. Dozens of bull, blue and mako sharks were present, as well as fish of every conceivable shape and color, all partaking in the mobile mountain of flesh nature provided for them. As the scavenging sharks tore into the flanks of the dead cetacean, they shook their heads in primal fury, shearing away gobs of blubber the size of a human head. They clouded the surrounding sea with billows of blood and fragments of tissue, spewing from their gluttonous jaws.

"God, mon. What a mess," Willie said under his breath. "Okay Lane, I need ya to send dat info please."

"Processing now, *Harbinger*," he replied.

With a hum, the *William's* laser scanning beam swept out, moving eerily back and forth across the whale's body in synchronized sweeps. The submersible inched closer, focusing its laser on the dead bull's flank.

"Sweet Jesus," Adam said. "Look at the size of that bite! That's impossible!"

"Obviously not, mon," Willie remarked. He raised his radio: "Lane, what ya got for me?"

"System is coming up now, *Harbinger*. Total length is . . . twenty one point eight meters, estimated weight . . . ninety three point five tons. Minus the bite, that is."

"Wow, that's a big sperm whale." Adam whistled, tearing himself away from the screen as he jotted the stats on a piece of paper.

"What about da bite?" Willie peered intently at the screen as the *William's* prow cameras zoomed in on the enormous wound.

"Bite radius is about two meters in width by three meters in height. Holy crap, that's huge!" Lane exclaimed. "Hmm, now *this* is interesting..."

"What?" Willie asked.

"Based on the gouge marks visible at the top and bottom of the excised area, and despite the damn sharks nibbling on the edges, the computer says the wound pattern indicates something called caniniform anterior dentition. What the heck is that?"

Willie exchanged speculative glances with Adam, then handed the videographer his radio.

"Lane, this is Adam. Did you say caniniform?"

"That's affirmative."

Adam's eyebrows dropped low over his eyes. He took his finger off the talk button and turned to Willie.

"Caniniform anterior dentition means that whatever took a bite out of poor Elvis has enlarged fangs at the distal ends of its jaws, enabling it to bite chunks from its prey. I've been a naturalist for ten years, but I have no idea what did this."

"I hear dat, mon."

"Hey fellas, check this out," Lane said. His voice was laced with excitement.

Shifting the *William*, he skirted the frenzied jaws of a dozen sharks and moved to the sperm's mountainous head. His cameras zoomed in on it, revealing a series of jagged, white lines that crisscrossed the bull's head and shoulder region.

"From what I see, it looks like Elvis had a run in with a squid of some kind, and a damn big one from the looks of things. Some of these sucker marks are a foot across! These wounds are fresh, guys. Do you think a giant squid did this?"

"I doubt it, mon," Willie called into the mike. "Maybe a squid fed on da whale after it was already dead. Who knows?"

Suddenly, a fourteen-foot tiger shark appeared on the screen. There was a loud thump as it collided with one of the *William's* pontoons, pushing the bulky submersible off balance and jostling its passengers.

"Well, that was interesting," Lane laughed into the radio as he pulled them level. "I think Mike just pissed himself! We've got quite a rogue's gallery gathering, guys. All we need now is the squid this whale was battling and we'll make it complete!"

Adam grabbed a hand mike. "We can't promise you an *Architeuthis*, Lane, but if you look out your port window, you'll see a couple of nice Humboldts headed your way."

A school of six-foot squid began to move past the hovering *William.* Known in the Sea of Cortez as *Diablos Rojos,* the "red devils" fastened themselves to the whale's head region and began tearing away with parrot-like beaks. A fraction of the size of their giant cousins, the two hundred pound cephalopods were vicious predators in their own right, ones that wouldn't hesitate to attack humans or even sharks if hungry.

"God, what a gang of marauders," Mike Helm chimed in. "It's like every nightmare in the ocean converged on this one spot."

"Aye, hell is empty. All da devils are here, mon," Willie said.

"You and your Shakespeare." Adam smirked. "Macbeth?"

"Da Tempest." Willie smiled wide.

The two men were still grinning when something huge appeared in the background.

"Holy shit!" Lane yelled. "*Harbinger,* are you seeing this?"

As Willie watched, the sharks and squid stopped feeding and scattered. Gnashing their teeth and flailing their tentacles, the big predators fell back, making way for something far larger and fiercer. Soaring enigmatically into view, it approached.

At twenty-three feet and over six thousand pounds, the female *Carcharodon carcharias* was the most feared carnivorous fish in the world. A notorious man-eater that often mistook swimmers for seals, the great white was a giant, its powerful jaws lined with triangular teeth over three inches in length.

Intrigued by their similarity in size, the white shark circled the hovering submersible. Its soulless black eyes glared inside the craft's observation bubble, intently studying its wary occupants.

"No sudden moves, Lane," Willie whispered. "Dat's one big muddah of a shark!"

"Are you kidding me?" Lane said. On the monitor, streams of sweat trickled down his face, despite the chilly temperature inside the *William.* "The only movement I'm contemplating right now involves my bowels, thank you very much!"

The great white eventually dismissed the strange object as a non-threat and veered off in the direction of the dead sperm. Void of emotion, the killer shark swam to the wound area and began to feed. Opening its mouth wide enough to engulf a grown man, its wrinkled upper lip pulled back in a hideous grimace, revealing rows of serrated teeth. Propelled forward by powerful sweeps from its tail, the shark buried its head to the gills in the dead sperm's muscles. Shaking its three-ton body from side to side, it sheared away hundred pound chunks of putrescent flesh like a deli-slicer carving luncheon meat.

"Jesus, what a monster!" Lane spouted fearfully.

As the white continued to feed, the smaller sharks returned en masse, nearly bowling the *William* over in the process.

"Shit!" Lane cursed as he struggled to retain control of his vessel. "Listen guys, we've gotten the data Amara wanted, and enough bonus footage to win every documentary award known to man. That being the case," he added nervously, "it's starting to get hairy down here. Now, 'JAWS' over there notwithstanding, we're sure this tin can we're sitting in is well made, and we don't want to sound like a couple of Marys. But, if you don't mind, Mike and I would like to get the hell out of here and come back onboard!"

Shaking all over, Willie chortled into his handset. "Okay, ya big chickens. Make ya way to da portside crane and we'll rescue ya lily-white asses."

"Actually, I haven't seen Mike's, but mine's furry and freckled . . ."

His eyes wide, Willie exchanged horrified grimaces with Adam, then collapsed into his chair. He rested his chin on his knuckles, his mind wandering to the previous day, and the mysterious entity that came up from the nearby abyss. What baffled him wasn't how it tossed the *Harbinger* around as it passed beneath them. A really big blue whale could do that. It was the thing's velocity that gave him pause.

Blue whales were the fastest of the great whales, maxing out at over thirty miles an hour. Their mystery guest had moved at nearly *fifty*, and might be capable of even greater speed. If he hadn't seen it first hand, he wouldn't have believed it.

Initially, he suspected the navy's "bloop" findings were correct, and that they were dealing with some sort of giant octopus, the ones said to inhabit the deepest depths. With a tentacle span of two hundred feet, an *Octopus giganteus* would have the sheer body mass to create such a monstrous wave. It would also be capable of such speed when jetting backwards.

Having seen the bull sperm carcass and the wound that caused its death, however, Willie now decided he was dealing with an entirely different class of predator. It was very big and very fast, with interlocking, armor-piercing teeth that could shear a metric ton of flesh from a struggling whale in a single bite. If he was right, they would have to rewrite the definition of *nightmare* in the Oxford unabridged dictionary.

Looking up, he reached for the CD that contained the audio profile of their gigantean anomaly. He turned it repeatedly in his hand, gnawing his lower lip before putting it away. He'd spent several hours of the last twenty-four listening for it on the hydrophone. Once or twice he thought he detected something, but the signal was too brief and too far away to be tracked. Still, it was out there somewhere. If the Blake Plateau and Ophion's Deep were indeed its home, as he believed, sooner or later it would come to them.

Willie's eyes burst open and he did a double-take at his sonar screen. A thousand yards off and closing was a massive reading. He adjusted his settings, increasing gain and contrast. The reading was impossibly huge, yet seemed to possess no set shape. It was spreading out in multiple directions at the same time.

It *was* a giant octopus.

"Lordy, mon!" Willie sprang to his feet and grabbed his radio. "Lane, where are ya guys?"

Adam's eyes shifted in his direction. "What's going on?"

Willie said nothing. He pointed at the starboard video screen, focused on the dead sperm.

Adam's head snapped back on his spine. He checked his glasses and gaped at the monitor. The feeding frenzy was over and all the predators were gone. Only the whale carcass remained. Even the monstrous white shark had fled the area.

"*Harbinger*, it's Lane. We're approaching the starboard crane now. You should see us waving any second."

"What's taking you guys so long?" Willie asked, trying to conceal his panic.

"Sorry. We had a delay down here. Out of nowhere, all our beasties took off running. There were so many of them, they nearly rolled us over. Pretty weird, huh?"

"Yeah, mon." Willie stared apprehensively at the growing sonar signal. Whatever it was, from eight hundred yards away it had frightened off a collection of the fiercest marine carnivores he'd ever seen. "Listen, Lane, surface by da starboard crane. It'll be faster."

Lane's voice took on that whiney tone he used when extra work was unexpectedly thrown his way. "But, isn't that crane having winch problems? What's the rush?"

"Ya remember dat ting dat chased ya dee other day?"

"Yeah, what about it?"

"It's back, mon," Willie said. "And it's coming dis way."

"Shit! Starboard crane it is! Tell those slackers to be ready!"

Willie glanced at the sonar screen. The amorphous green symbol continued to pop up with each repeated sweep. It was only four hundred yards off and closing steadily. He could hear the metallic groaning noises and thrumming vibrations that indicated Joe Calabrese was lowering the cable to the *William*.

Willie cursed under his breath. It was too late. The mini-sub and her crew wouldn't be clear in time.

He reached for the bright red lever that activated the *Harbinger's* warning claxon. A moment later, sirens throughout the ship shrilled, warning the crew to rush to their emergency stations.

And to brace for collision.

———

Amara awoke with a start.

There was a pounding noise vibrating through the ceiling, dragging her out of her exhaustion-induced slumber.

It was gone. *No, wait . . . there it is again.*

Sitting up with a gasp, her eyes bounced around the sheriff's station. Panic welled up within her as she took in the unfamiliar surroundings. A stiff neck, combined with the pain of sleeping with her face on a keyboard, brought her back to reality and helped slow her rapidly beating heart.

She sat upright, then groaned and lowered her chin onto her forearms. Eyes closed, she rested. Another barrage of sound forced her to open one eye and she narrowed it on the wall clock. A curse slipped out of her mouth. It was half past six.

With a grimace, she placed her palms on top of the computer desk and seesawed to her feet. Her injured hip complained more than a desperate housewife, and she found herself doing a drunken high-wire routine, swaying back and forth as she struggled to regain her balance.

She kicked at a blanket that had somehow collected at her feet and shook her head in disgust. She needed Advil and the world's strongest cup of coffee. Not much of a morning person, her condition invariably left her terse and grumpy when she got up. Five hours of frustrating research didn't do much to improve her disposition.

Groaning again as she dragged her tired dogs to the rest room, Amara splashed cold water on her face and rubbed gently at the embarrassing marks on her cheeks. The right one looked like she used a waffle iron for a pillow. Disgusted, she gargled with some mouthwash, then closed the door to pee.

As she trudged past the hard-to-resist couch, she heard it again. It was the same beating sound that woke her. It was coming from Jake Braddock's apartment.

Using the bathroom's poorly lit mirror, she gave her hair a few quick brush strokes. As she passed the station's tiny kitchen she thought about making a cup of coffee, but decided to investigate the strange noise first.

The door to Jake's apartment was closed, but she could hear the sound resonating through the wood. It was like a baseball bat colliding with an old tree stump. Curiosity overpowered caution and Amara knocked on the door.

No answer.

Frustrated, she knocked louder. Eventually, impetuousness took over and she tried the doorknob. A look of bemusement crept across her face as she realized Jake left his door unlocked. Opening it to the halfway point, she could see a dimly-lit, loft style apartment with tall, rounded windows, mostly blocked by drapery. There was a living room to the right, centered on a large LCD television, and a bedroom set cordoned off by Shoji screens.

Jake was nowhere in sight. Clearing her throat, Amara called for him. The muffled noise was almost deafening now, and was accompanied by loud music. She frowned and shook her head. *It's no wonder the big oaf can't hear.*

Amara's partially opened eyes grew annoyed. Impatience, combined with sleep deprivation, began to chafe at her. Throwing caution to the wind, she flung the weighty door open and walked brazenly inside. A few feet in front of her, a large punching bag creaked back and forth on its chain.

She spotted Jake off to her left and immediately started blushing. He was shirtless and barefoot, wearing nothing but loose sweatpants, and was an astonishing physical specimen. He had rock music blasting, while performing some sort of martial arts routine. Soaked with perspiration, the lawman was engaged in combat with a bizarrely constructed wood statue. It was man-sized and cylindrical in shape, with several pieces of wood extending from it like arms and legs.

Weaving in and around this durable construct, Jake launched a blinding barrage of attacks. Some appeared defensive, as he slammed his forearms and elbows against the protruding limbs with circular movements. Others were definitely offensive, as his thick knuckles smashed again and again between the protective limbs and into the exposed body, striking with a force that made Amara wince.

Unnoticed, she watched Jake with fascination. It was like observing a panther stalking its prey. His movements were fast and powerful, and very hard to follow.

Stopping with his sweat-soaked back to her, he bent to pick up a towel and a remote control. He clicked off the CD and stood there, chest heaving and guzzling a bottle of spring water.

"You're up earlier than I expected, doc," he said, turning and looking her in the eye. He shifted position, tossing the empty bottle into a recycling receptacle, then winked as he wrapped the towel around his neck and shoulders. "Just as well. You've relieved me of the dubious task of waking you up."

"Um, right . . ." Amara's face was on fire and she looked in any direction she could, as long as it didn't involve locking eyes with the perspiring Adonis in front of her. *God . . . Home Depot must have banned him for setting off every stud-finder in the place.* She exhaled slowly. "Sorry to interrupt your exercise routine," she mumbled, "the noise woke me. I didn't know you were beating up on . . . whatever that thing is."

Jake cocked his head. "The wooden dummy? It's an old kung-fu training tool. Sorry, it makes a lot of noise. There's never anyone around this early in the morning."

"A wooden dummy, eh?" Amara grinned mischievously. "Sounds like a couple of ichthyologists I know."

Finally starting to relax, she peered around his place. The layout was Spartan, and nearly half the available space was dedicated to training. There was a speed bag, a double-end bag, and a self-standing punching bag, designed to resemble a human being from the waist up.

It was the bristling array of awards and weapons that caught her eye. Standing against the wall like soldiers at attention were a dozen trophies and several medals, hanging from ribbons in glass cases. Beneath these awards, a series of wooden shelves supported an impressive sword collection. She could see a brace of ornate katanas similar to her family's heirlooms, as well as an assortment of broadswords, cutlasses and sabers. Some were new, albeit dusty, while others were antiques dating back hundreds of years.

Weaved between the deadly weapons and trophies were photos of Jake and a striking blonde. There were pictures with famous sports figures and celebrities, and even a few politicians.

"Wow, is that you with the president?" she asked, gawking at an autographed photo that hung beneath a glass case on the wall.

"Yeah," Jake replied, not looking up as he dried himself off. "That was taken after the nationals, four years ago. The sword was a gift from the first lady. She was a fan of my mom's."

"Your mom?"

"Yeah, she was a silver medalist in the Olympics, thirty years ago. She was the reason I started in the first place."

"Wow, your mother won a medal at the Olympics? In what sport?"

Jake gave a sarcastic smirk, his eyes doing a quick jog around the room. "Gee, I wonder what it could be."

Amara frowned and gazed wide-eyed up at the swept hilt rapier that hung point down above the framed photo. She looked around and found herself at a loss for words.

"I'm confused," she announced. "So, you're some kind of fencing champion?"

"Used to be," Jake said. "I don't compete anymore."

Amara whistled. "That's too bad. It looks like you were really good at it. I'm embarrassed to say, but I've never heard of you. Then again," she added, "I'm away at sea for months on end, and marine biology geeks don't usually follow sports."

"That's okay, doc," he said, squeezing into a t-shirt. "Like I said, it's in the past. It doesn't matter."

Amara paused in front of one of the photos. Curiosity got the better of her.

"The woman in these pictures, is she your wife?"

There was a long silence. "She was."

"Was?" Amara asked. She leaned on the wall as she studied the photo. "But you guys look like you were so much in love. Why did you divorce?"

"No."

"No what?"

"No, we didn't divorce. She died, three years ago."

"Oh!" Amara gasped. One hand covered her mouth. "I'm so sorry."

"Thank you," Jake acknowledged, dropping into a nearby recliner. Exhaling heavily, he reached for an ornately framed photo resting on the table in front of him. He stared thoughtfully at it, then put it back in its assigned place. "We were your stereotypical athletic couple. Samantha was a competitive swimmer, and I was headed for a career on the professional fencing circuit." Jake sat back and stared up at the ceiling. "A few months after we got married she got the diving bug."

"The diving bug? You mean, like platform diving?"

"I wish. She fell in love with free diving. Personally, I never saw the draw of it, but she loved the thrill and excitement. She just couldn't get the idea out of her head, you know? She was great at it. In fact, she took second at the world championships."

Jake closed his eyes. "That was a few months before she died."

Amara observed the mournful expression encompassing the sheriff's features. She sat quietly on the couch, her hands clasped on her lap, afraid to ask more.

"I should've been there, doc," Jake said suddenly. His eyes opened with surprising fierceness. "When she needed me most, I wasn't there."

"What do you mean?"

"Sam had a big competition coming up. Not more than six miles from here. I was offered a photo shoot for some sneaker company that same day. I was going to pass on it, but Sam told me 'Just go and show up when you can.'" He stopped talking and stared into space. "It was her first meet without me . . ."

There was an interminable silence. He stared grimly at the ceiling, his fingers interlocked across his chest, his mind lost in the past.

Amara cleared her throat. "Listen, if you don't want to talk about it, it's fine. I feel like an ass for ask–"

"It's okay, doc," Jake interjected. "It doesn't matter, anyway."

Amara walked shakily to his chair. Ignoring the pain that shot down her leg, she eased herself onto the edge of the coffee table and took Jake's hand in hers. His fingers felt as hard as concrete, and she wondered how deep those calluses went.

"Look, I know we don't know each other, but if you want to talk about Sam it's fine. And if you don't, that's fine too."

"She drowned," he said, his voice so mechanical it was frightening. "I was out posing with my sword, surrounded by models and hamming it up, while she suffered a seizure a hundred feet underwater."

He looked squarely at Amara.

"I could've left an hour earlier, but I was hanging around the set signing autographs. My ego wouldn't let me leave. By the time I finally got there, she was gone."

Amara didn't say anything. She just held onto Jake's hand, squeezing it with a scaled-down version of the hug she knew he needed but wouldn't accept.

"Did they discover what caused the seizure?" she hazarded.

"Yes, they did."

"What was it?"

"She was pregnant."

Amara swallowed a gasp. "Oh God, that's awful."

"Yeah . . . the autopsy said she was eight weeks pregnant." Jake shook his head. "I don't think she even knew. The oxygen depletion, combined with the pressure, was just too much for her condition."

"I'm so sorry, Jake." She struggled to get the words out. "You gave up fencing after that, didn't you? You blame yourself for her death."

It was a statement of fact.

"Free-diving is a dangerous sport," Jake said. "She was my wife. I should have been there. Instead, I was playing musketeer, while Sam and my unborn child were drowning. So to answer your question: yes. I'm done. I have no desire to touch a sword again."

"I see. If you don't mind my asking, how does your mother feel about your decision? Does she support it?"

Jake's eyes hardened. "My mom doesn't feel anything, doc. She was killed by a drunk driver, a month before nationals."

"Oh. I'm sorry." Amara's eyes dropped and she exhaled, long and slow. She looked up. "Hey . . . come to think of it, I remember seeing your wife's death on the news. They said the doctors tried everything to save her and couldn't. Forgive me, but even if you were there, a hundred feet of cold sea separated you. You wouldn't have even known what was happening, let alone been able to reach her."

He exhaled through his nostrils. "I would have found a way."

She released his hand and drew herself up. "Jake, you have to stop beating yourself up about it. I've seen you in action, and there's nobody I'd rather have by my side, but there was *nothing* you could have done for her."

Amara stood where she was, her tanned arms folded across her chest as she waited for Jake's response. When the big lawman sat there brooding, she turned to go.

"So . . . what happened with your research?"

Amara hesitated, stopping in mid-stride to turn toward him. She tried to see Jake's eyes as he rose to his feet but he avoided her gaze.

"The system couldn't find anything," Amara said with a shrug. "I nodded off around three. We ended up with an unknown quantity, as I feared. Anyway, I've got to log off before we get out of here," she said as she walked away. "I'll double-check the system's findings, but I don't expect anything of significance."

As she opened the door to Jake's apartment, Amara looked back at him with a perplexed expression.

"You know, I'm confused by what *Archimedes* found. Or rather, by what it *didn't*. Evolution is a laborious process. It takes tens of thousands of years to perfect a design. Yet, our mystery predator appears to have just sprung into existence from thin air. Or water, if you will."

"So, what are you saying?"

"Hmm? Oh, I don't know, it just seems very strange . . ."

———

Jake watched Amara close the door before he hopped in the shower. He turned on both faucets and disrobed while waiting for the water to heat up. As he stared at the miniature whirlpool vanishing into the bathtub's blackened drain, a cloud of nausea blindsided him. A curse escaped his lips as he felt his knees and equilibrium both take a vacation. He reached for the doorjamb, his hands clawing ineffectually at the wood. A moment later, he felt the floor's cold, ceramic embrace.

He was powerless. Clamping his eyes shut, he held on tight, his sweat-soaked body shivering in waves as he waited for the episode to run its course.

An eternity later, he relaxed his grip, opened his eyes and climbed wearily back to his feet. Relieved that Amara wasn't witness to what he considered an embarrassing display of weakness, he climbed into the shower, praying for the rushing water to wash away his regrets.

—

Downstairs, Amara collected her belongings. She was agitated over the morning's developments. Her conversation with Jake was revealing, but unsettling as well. The lawman carried so much sadness inside him. He reminded her of a lonely, battle-scarred old whale, left to wander the seas in solitude after watching its mate get slaughtered by hunters. He was a lost cause.

Of course, lost causes are *my specialty . . .*

She stared at the computer desk, still upset she spent a good portion of the night there. The mysterious tooth and skin fragment stared mockingly at her from their resting places. She frowned as she leaned over to initiate *Archimedes'* complex shutdown sequence.

She was so engrossed in thought, it took a few moments for her to realize it had found a match after all. It stared at her from the screen – a full-color illustration of a large aquatic creature. A cursory examination indicated it was not a whale, as she expected. It was a marine reptile: a predator with four powerful flippers, a short neck, and an enlarged skull filled with sharp teeth.

Amara gaped at the image. She eased herself down into her seat, her gaze latched onto the monitor screen. She blinked, straining her eyes as she moved closer to the image. She scanned the text and did a double-take as she spotted the animal's time period. The creature *Archimedes* had identified was from the Cretaceous period. It died out with the dinosaurs sixty-five million years earlier. She laughed until she read its scientific name.

A wave of lightheadedness swept over her and she realized she wasn't breathing. Consciously sucking in air, she continued to stare at the computer generated image of the extinct colossus. Her mind waged war over the incredulous nature of the find. The report was ridiculous and impossible. There must be a script error or undetected flaw in the system's interpretation program.

Archimedes had made a mistake.

Unless . . .

Suddenly, Amara's heart pounded in her chest. She looked fearfully at the giant tooth, sitting upright on the desk. She studied its ribbed edge, designed for ripping through flesh, and its armor piercing point. She blinked rapidly as a parade of gruesome images flashed through her mind in rapid-fire succession.

The disemboweled blue whale she saw on the news.

The blood-spattered wreck of the Sayonara.

The giant sperm whale, with its gaping wound.

The decapitated Xiphactinus, whose head she had on ice.

The monstrous shape as it passed under her ship . . .

"Omigod!"

A second later, she was kangarooing up the stairs to Jake's apartment and pounding on his door like a maniac.

FOURTEEN

The signal was almost on top of them.

Willie's exhalation was an icy chill escaping his chest. He cursed and snatched up his radio, spitting into the hand piece. "Lane, what da hell's takin so long? Where are ya, mon?"

"We're in position, *Harbinger*," Lane replied. "Joe just lowered the winch."

Willie's eyes met Adam Spencer's and he shook his head. "Dey's not gonna make it! I'm goin topside."

His boots rang as he bolted out of the observation room. He sprinted up the starboard stairwell, nearly bowling over two chatting interns. He emerged seconds later on deck, radio in hand.

The daylight was unbearable. Used to the confines of the dimly lit research vessel, the morning sun was blinding. Willie squinted against the glare, shielding his eyes as he waited for them to adjust. He moved to the nearby crane and rapped on its window.

"Hey, Joe!" he yelled, struggling to be heard over the crane's sputtering diesel engine.

The salt-stained partition slid open.

"Yo, Willie, what's up?" Joe Calabrese stuck his head out, pulling a pair of levers to lock the crane's cab in place.

"Can't ya get dem up any faster?"

"Seas are pretty rough," Joe said. "I can't just eyeball it like usual. I got the cherry down there trying to lock her in place."

His eyes wide, Willie rushed to the railing. He saw their newest intern, Christian Ho, with a snorkel, surfacing for air as he wrestled with the connector between the *Harbinger* and the submersible.

Willie rubbed his temples. Christian was an expert swimmer, but the idea of even their steel-hulled mini-sub being in the water right now, let alone a defenseless human being, was more than he could handle. The *Harbinger* was expecting some very unpleasant company.

"Adam, what ya got?" Willie's eyes scanned the sea for the approaching behemoth. He lowered his handset and peered over the side as Christian signaled that the link was finally secured.

"Whatever it is, it's almost within camera range," Adam said. "It's one hundred and fifty yards off our starboard and closing." His voice trailed off. "Hey Willie, come take a look at this. The reading is getting all weird!"

"Weird?"

"It looks like the signal is breaking up. I'm not a sonar guy, but if I didn't know better, I'd say we've got multiple readings!"

"Son of a bitch! Do ya have a visual yet?"

"Nope, the water's cleared up since the sharks took off, but whatever's doing this is still too far off."

The first mate watched Christian clamber exhaustedly onto the nearby launch platform and collapse. Lying on his back with his legs in the water, the exhausted teenager's chest rose and fell as he fought to catch his breath.

Willie shifted a few feet to clear the crane's boom and tapped his radio button. "Adam, turn on da hydrophone, please. Tell me what ya hear."

"You got it."

Willie looked apprehensively at the water. Large displacement bubbles were rising up around both the *Harbinger* and the sperm's bird-covered corpse. His eyes widened as he glanced over at Joe and leapt onto the crane's brightly colored cab.

"Ya gotta get dem outta dere!" He pounded on the cab's wall. "Whateva is down dere is comin up!"

Joe ignored him and gripped the ascension lever that put the winch into gear. He hesitated. "She still ain't at full power." He gestured at the dials in front of him. "The hydraulics ain't got enough pressure yet. We need more time, man! I dunno if I can get 'em clear to the deck!"

"Well, ya have ta try," Willie yelled as the water around them boiled over. "Punch it, mon!"

A frown creased Joe's bearded face. He mouthed a silent prayer, tightened his grip, and prepared to pull back.

Just then, Adam shouted over the radio. "Hey Willie, you can relax! Everything's alright!"

Willie wore a skeptical look as he placed a staying hand on Joe's shoulder. "What do ya mean every ting's alright? What's up?"

"It's just a pod of transients!" Adam whooped. "One of our study groups. I've got them on the viewers. They're all over the place!"

On cue, the whitecaps around the *Harbinger* erupted. The pod of orcas exploded into view, their squeaky cries echoing as they rose by twos and threes until two dozen were gathered around the *William*.

Willie released a pent up sigh and climbed down from the crane. He walked to the railing. Resting one hand on the smooth metal, he watched the group of killer whales milling about. Some cruised around the dead whale, scattering gulls and terns as they bumped it with their noses. Others hovered over their calves, staying away from the carcass and close to the *Harbinger*.

Willie whooped into his hand unit. "Tank God! I was worried da Leviathan hisself was comin after us. It's only transients. Ya recognize dem?"

"I sure do," Adam replied happily. "It's B-11 and her pod. I spotted her double-notched fin. And that *has* to be Omega-Baby towards our bow."

Willie turned in the direction Adam pointed to. He was right. They'd graphed the bull's measurements last year. At a solid thirty-two feet in length and weighing just over ten tons, OB-1, or Omega-Baby, as the crew of the *Harbinger* called him, was the biggest killer whale in the region. He was ten feet longer than the average-sized female, and the biggest mama's boy Willie had ever seen. A killing machine capable of destroying a great white shark in a single charge, the huge male spent most of his time following his mother around like some enormous black and white puppy, even attempting to suckle at times.

The *Harbinger*'s research confirmed early on that, despite older, erroneous reports that male killers were herd bulls that collected cows into kept harems, pods of *Orcinus orca* were actually tightly-knit matriarchal animals. The smaller cows ran the show under the leadership of an experienced alpha female, or matriarch. She chose their migration routes, planned their hunts, and led the pack. The huge bulls made use of their size and strength by acting as protectors against predators like sharks and squid, and served as heavy hitters when it came time to deliver the coup de grâce on large prey.

Oblivious to the cries of the killers as they circled the area, Willie continued to smile.

"Hey, Christian," he yelled down. "Just hang tight for a second. I want ta make sure da connector bolts hold!"

Christian gave a wave, then began playfully kicking seawater at the orcas, laughing whenever one of the toothy mega-dolphins came within range.

Willie turned to Joe. "Okay, I guess now's as good a time as any ta bring dose two chickens back onboard!" Chuckling at his long-time colleague, he turned back toward the railing.

As he watched, one of the orca cows spun the *William's* nose around by bumping noisily against one its aluminum pontoons. Willie's grin wavered. The impact was relatively gentle – undoubtedly an accident – though the sound still sounded like a muffled gong.

Willie's growing concern quickly turned to horror. Two of the twenty-plus-foot females quickly followed their pod-mate's lead, rising up in the water at high speed and ramming the now off-balance mini-sub with what sounded like thunderclaps.

The orcas were attacking.

"Holy shit! What the hell's going on?" Lane yelled, his panicked voice wavering beneath the impact of the cows' assault.

"Jesus Christ!" Willie swore.

Below him, he could see Christian still sitting there, frozen in place as chaos unfolded all around him. Suddenly, a battle-scarred killer whale propelled itself up and out of the water, showering the young intern with salt spray. Its massive head and forequarters towered over the landing platform, landing hard and depositing the weight of a full-sized SUV on the rust-coated deck. Willie's stomach cramped as he clocked the whale's ragged dorsal fin.

It was the matriarch.

The giant cow blinked as she stared menacingly down. Her eyes met Christian's, and she uttered a loud hissing warning that blended with the sound of straining steel. She snapped her jaws loudly together, then heaved her fourteen thousand pound body back into the water. To Willie's relief, not to mention Christian's, she left the frozen youngster untouched.

"Joe, get dem da hell outta dere!" he bellowed at the gaping crane operator, then shouted down, "Christian, get your ass up here! Now, mon!"

He watched as the shaken intern struggled to his feet and staggered up the stairs, muttering Cantonese curses.

Surprisingly calm, Joe worked fast, swiveling the crane's boom assembly toward the ship's bow to compensate for the current. His eyes tightened as he threw the diesel-powered retractor into gear and held on. The winch shuddered, issuing a metallic whining noise. It turned, struggling under the *William*'s twelve thousand pound load. Inch by inch, the pearl-white submersible was drawn up from the churning swells and away from the infuriated whales.

Undeterred, the agile female orcas continued to rain attack runs down upon the besieged sub. Leaping clear of the water two and three at a time, they brought their combined weight crashing downward, bludgeoning the swaying craft. Inside the *William*, Lane and Mike were screaming so loud their cries could be heard without the mini-sub's com system.

"Jesus Christ!" Lane cried. "What the hell's gotten into the whales? Joe, get us out of here!"

Willie stared fearfully at the crane's shivering cable. There was a sudden groan. Then the winch slipped. The *William* dropped like a stone, crashing into the frothing seas below. The orcas circled the downed submersible at high speed, their sleek forms a lethal ivory and obsidian whirlpool.

Willie barked into his handset. "Adam, I taught killer whales didn't attack people? What da fuck is goin on?"

"I don't know, Willie!" Adam's voice was quavering. "That's what I've always read. I don't think they're after Lane and Mike. They're very agitated and calling out repeatedly with their high-pitched acoustic cries. It's like they're trying to reach other pods."

There was momentary static.

"Willie, I think they've picked up on whatever killed Elvis! I think they're sensing a rival predator!"

"Well, that's goddamn great!" Lane yelled. "So they've decided our twelve million dollar submarine is that predator? That's fucking wonderful!"

Mike's words were drowned out by a shuddering impact as the matriarch made a pass at the mini-sub. The ferocity of the attack knocked the submersible's rudder assembly entirely out of place, jamming it into a twisted mass of rubber and steel. Stunned by the force of the collision, the big female drifted off balance. She twitched a few times, then righted herself and swam off.

Willie cursed as he saw how severely the mini-sub was damaged. Even if they managed to free the *William* from the *Harbinger's* restrictive cable, Lane and Mike had lost the ability to maneuver. Suddenly, the orcas ceased their attack and backed away.

Willie's rapidly beating heart sank into his bowels.

Omega-Baby was preparing to attack.

The frustrated matriarch had called for one of the bulls to move in and finish the battle. Hovering close to his mother, a suddenly no longer playful Omega-Baby responded to the whistling summons.

Willie roared at the top of his lungs. "Joe, ya got ta get dem movin! *Now*, damn it!"

His useless radio clattered to the deck. The *William* was still half-submerged and the giant male was racing back to gather momentum for a charge.

Willie felt like vomiting. His big hands grasped the hot steel railing so tightly it hurt. With the *William* pinned motionless against the *Harbinger's* hull, the orca's twenty thousand pounds of muscle would plow into it with the power of a bulldozer. He knew the submersible's design specs. When the orca struck, the *William* would be crushed like an aluminum can under someone's work boot.

Lane and Mike were going to die.

He started losing it. He rushed to the crane's open window. "Get dem up out of dere!" he bellowed, reaching inside and tearing at Joe's arm. "We gonna lose dose men! Do some ting!"

Joe's face contorted as he lashed out. "Don't you think I'm trying?" He pulled his arm roughly away. "Jesus! Just give me a fucking second! I'm giving the pressure time to build. If I don't, they got no chance at all!"

"Dere's no time, mon!" Willie screamed, staring bug-eyed as Omega-Baby started his attack run.

Joe reared up out of his seat and peered over his instrument panel. He caught sight of the mammoth bull as it surged forward, its steely body propelled by powerful strokes of its eight-foot flukes. The look on his face only confirmed Willie's words.

There *was* no more time.

Joe stared wide-eyed at his pressure gauges. He grabbed the retractor lever and pulled slowly back, praying the winch wouldn't slip again, leaving the *William* and her crew dead in the water.

Willie watched the dials, his lips trembling as he crunched numbers in his head. They only had sixty percent power. Based on the mini-sub's weight it might be enough, but he wasn't betting on it.

He held his breath. The battered *William* inched its way up as streams of seawater ran down its dented flanks. Joe closed his eyes and threw the retractor lever into full. The *William* lurched its way higher, its damaged pontoons free of the waves that yearned to drag it down. Willie wanted to cheer. It looked like they were going to make it.

Sensing his target attempting to clamber up the side of the ship, the giant orca submerged thirty yards out, curling his body into a tight underwater roll. He dove deep, then wheeled upwards, accelerating. With a roar, he exploded out of the water, directly beneath the hard-shelled object he sought to destroy. With his huge jaws spread wide, he lunged for the *William* with all his terrible power.

Inside, all Lane and Mike could do was scream.

"A dinosaur? C'mon doc, gimme a break." Caffeine in hand, Jake gave an irritable snort and sank back into his sofa.

Her hands on her hips, Amara stood irately. Exasperated, she turned and stalked back to her computer, where *Archimedes'* find still emanated from its screen.

"Jake, we've been going over this for half an hour," she said. "I've told you three times that the animal that lost this tooth is *not* a dinosaur. It's a marine reptile known as a pliosaur."

Amara held the huge canine point up as she spoke.

"A pliosaur." Jake shook his head in disbelief. She was trying to convince him that Phil Starling was killed by a reptile that died out sixty-five million years ago. He downed the remainder of his coffee and stood up. "Riiiiight . . ."

Amara rolled her eyes and started tapping away on the keyboard. "Look, I know how unbelievable it sounds. Like something out of a Spielberg movie. But the evidence is sitting right in front of us."

Arms folded, Jake drew closer, bending at the waist as he peered over her shoulder. "And what did you say the scientific name of this creature is?"

"*Kronosaurus queenslandicus*. It means 'God of Time Reptile.' It was named after Kronos, the ruler of the Titans in Greek mythology. He was the one who devoured his own children." She twisted in her seat, her chest rising as she gestured at the image she'd enlarged. "There's your mystery monster," she announced, "or something very similar to it."

Jake froze, realizing all he saw was Amara's cleavage.

She cleared her throat and continued. "These creatures were the dominant predators of the prehistoric seas. They were tremendously powerful, highly maneuverable eating machines with huge flippers that propelled them through the water. They tore their prey to pieces with massive jaws bristling with conical-shaped teeth. Sound familiar?"

Jake moved closer, resting his calloused knuckles on the desk beside her. His fierce gaze shifted from the tangible piece of dentition in front of him to the computer-generated image above it. "Well, if you're so sure about your findings," he said. "Why does it say it's only an eighty percent probable match?"

Amara shrugged. "I'm not sure. Either it's some sub-species of the same animal, or this tooth and the animal that owned it have changed over time." She swiveled around, her eyes widening. "Think about it, Jake. Sixty-five million years is an incredibly long time. It's inevitable that this creature adapted in response to its environment."

Jake sneered. "I'm not buying it, doc. There would have to be a large breeding population of these things running around in order for them to be alive today. Yet no one's ever seen one. How is that possible?"

Amara paused thoughtfully. "I don't know. Maybe the animals are normally reclusive and this one is some kind of rogue. Or maybe, there's a secluded population out there that we just don't–"

Jake held up a hand. "Hold on."

Outside the computer room, a door opened and closed. Jake walked over and opened the door leading to the station's reception area, revealing a plump, middle-aged woman dressed in a white blouse and khakis. She was in the middle of placing her purse and other personal belongings on the desk outside.

"Good morning, Molly," Jake said with a smile. He gestured for her to come inside. "I'd like you to meet Doctor Amara Takagi. Doc, this is Molly Simmons, the best receptionist and dispatcher I've ever had the privilege to work with."

"Oh, he's such a sweetie. Of course . . . I'm the *only* receptionist he's ever worked with." Molly smiled and took Amara's hand. "Wow, that's some handshake you've got there, Doctor Takagi. Oh . . . is this a house call? Is something wrong with my Jake?" Concern etched her face as she reached over, touching the back of her hand lightly to his forehead.

Amara replied with a straight face. "Nothing serious. Just a moderate case of jock itch. I prescribed some ointment and warned him to stop scratching, especially in public. Otherwise," she grinned evilly. "He knows it will only get worse."

Jake nearly choked. "Doc–"

"Oh," Amara cut in. "If you can, Molly, would you make sure he changes his underwear more often? At least every other day. And some baby powder might help, too. For the areas he's already chafed raw."

Molly nodded. "Of course, Doctor Takagi. I–"

Flushed with embarrassment, Jake shook his head. He smiled patiently. "I'm fine, Molly, really. *Doctor* Takagi is just kidding. She's not a medical doctor, she's a marine biologist, and she's here to help us with an investigation."

"Oh. Well then, in that case, thank goodness!"

"Yes, thank goodness . . ." Jake rolled his eyes. "Anyway, we'll do our best to stay out of your way and head out momentarily."

"Okay, you're the boss." As she left, the receptionist turned back. She cast a covert glance at Jake's crotch region, then looked Amara up and down, studying her face and figure, before giving her an approving smile.

"Very funny, doc." Jake whispered after she closed the door, "You should be careful. Molly is like my adopted mother. She likes to play matchmaker, and has a bad habit of trying to push every attractive woman she meets on me."

"Oh . . . so, you think I'm *attractive*, eh?" Amara teased as she moved back to the computer. "And by the way, how did I end up covered with a blanket last night?"

Jake's eyes widened. "Uh . . . what?"

"You heard me."

"Look, you'd been up all night working, and it was chilly. I couldn't just let you lie there all night on a hard desk and do nothing."

"Hmm . . ." Amara studied him intently, her aquamarine eyes flashing merrily. She gave him a coy smile. "Where were we?"

"We, um . . . were discussing your 'findings'," Jake redirected. "Look, we know we've got some mystery animal on our hands – *that* much I'll go along with." He grabbed a nearby chair, wheeling it next to her. He dropped into it wearing an exasperated look. "But if we start yelling there's a prehistoric monster on the loose, people will think we're insane. There's no precedent for this kind of thing, and other than this unidentified tooth fragment and that hunk of skin, we've got no evidence."

"Actually, we've got more than you think," Amara replied. She turned back to her keyboard. "We've got a growing string of attacks, topped off by a dead whale that looks like it was mauled by Godzilla."

She paused for a moment, moving her mouse and clicking on several items. "Here, remember when you said no one's ever seen one? Look at this."

Jake leaned in and listened.

"In July of 1734, a Norwegian missionary on a voyage to Gothaab, off the western coast of Greenland, reported that his ship encountered what he referred to as "a very terrible sea-animal which raised itself so high above the water that its head reached above our maintop. It had a long sharp snout and blew like a whale, had broad large flippers, and the body was, as it were, covered with hard skin, and it was very wrinkled and uneven on its skin."

Clicking her mouse again and again, Amara continued.

"During World War I, the German submarine U28, under the command of Captain Georg von Forstner, torpedoed the British steamer Iberian in the North Atlantic. His report read: "On July 30, 1915, our U28 torpedoed the British steamer Iberian carrying a rich cargo in the

North Atlantic. The steamer sank quickly, the bow sticking almost verti-cally into the air. When it had gone for about twenty-five seconds there was a violent explosion. A little later pieces of wreckage, and among them a gigantic sea animal (writhing and struggling wildly), was shot out of the water to a height of 60 to 100 feet. At that moment I had with me in the conning tower my officers of the watch, the chief engineer, the navigator, and the helmsman. Simultaneously we all drew one another's attention to this wonder of the seas . . . we were unable to identify it. We did not have time to take a photograph, for the animal sank out of sight after ten or fifteen seconds. It was about 60 feet long, was like a crocodile in shape, and had four limbs with powerful webbed feet . . ."

Amara turned around to face him. "So you see, this animal's exis-tence is not as inconceivable as you think. Perhaps they've survived all along in isolated populations. That would explain why they're not seen very often."

"But why now? Why would it show up here and now? Where's it been all this time?"

"I can't answer that. But, there is circumstantial evidence to sup-port it being here." She printed a two-page document, snatching it off the printer. "I got this off the wire." She held the pages up and began reading aloud. "A new species of monster squid has appeared off the coasts of Cuba and the Bahamas."

Jake smirked and shook his head. "I know. My demented deputy told me. He's hoping we run into one. Hey, come to think of it, maybe you two should hang out sometime."

"What? Why?"

"When it comes to sea monsters, he's much easier to convince than I am."

Amara's eyebrows lowered and her pearly teeth began to show. "Omi*god*, Jake Braddock. Sometimes you can be *so* infuriating."

"It's part of my charm."

"Oh, yeah?" She stood up and took a mock step toward him, her fists balled and eyes igniting. "Let me tell you something. Your mus-cles don't scare me, mister. How'd you like it if I come over there and kick your so-called charming butt?"

"Oh, goodness gracious, no." Jake smiled disarmingly, his hands extended palms outward. "Listen, girl. You can't threaten me with a good time."

"So, you're telling me you like pain? Because that's what I'm about to give you."

"It depends. Is it like *marriage* pain?"

Amara rolled her eyes and uttered a growl of frustration.

"Take it easy, doc," he chuckled. "I'm joking. Seriously though, the squid's appearance means nothing. I watch a lot of cable. They find new species like that all the time."

Amara took a slow, calming breath. "That's not the point. The report says the squid is similar to today's giant squid, except it doesn't have the two long tentacles that *Architeuthis* possesses. Its tentacle structure is reminiscent of a species of squid that died out tens of millions of years ago."

"So, you've got a previously undocumented species of squid." Jake said. "And yes, wonder of wonders, it's a survivor from eons ago, just like the *Coelacanth* is. Sorry doc, I don't see your point."

Amara's eyes began hardening again. "Here, mister sarcasm. Why don't you read it yourself?"

Jake perused the article. "Okay, so some scientists think this new squid is linked to a recent volcanic eruption. Maybe it was driven up from the depths because of it. I could see that being possible. But what makes it related to our dinosaur?"

"Marine reptile," she emphasized. "And the thing's gotta eat, right? So, maybe these squid, and other species that have popped up, are from the same place and are part of its staple diet?"

Jake looked at her. "What other species?"

Amara blinked. "Uh, never mind."

Hands resting on his lap, Jake sank back in his chair, contemplating her outlandish theory. He stared at the tooth, his thoughts drifting back to Phil Starling and his nephew. Certainly that hunk of ivory hadn't materialized out of thin air. It came from something. Maybe she was right . . .

"All right," he said flatly. "I'm not saying you've convinced me. But assuming you have, how dangerous would a creature like this be?"

"Incredibly," Amara said without hesitation. "It's undoubtedly used to being the greatest predator around. It fears nothing except others of its own kind, and as we've already seen, it's an opportunistic feeder. Anything that comes within range will be considered prey, from whales to people and everything in between."

"Wonderful. And the best way to kill it?"

"From a safe distance." Amara swiveled in her chair. "I looked at the skin fragment your friend retrieved from the *Sayonara*. It's only a partial layer, but it's still over an inch thick and tougher than a truck tire tread. Small arms would be useless against it. You'd need something bigger, probably military ordnance."

"I see. And speaking of bigger, how big do you think this thing is?" Jake's eyes intensified as he leaned forward.

"Well, keeping in mind the extremely limited amount of fossil material available on the larger marine reptiles . . ." Amara turned and began tapping furiously. "And that whatever fragments unearthed represent only the most microscopic cross-section of any given genus or species . . ."

"Get to the point please, doc."

"Sorry," she said. "A few years ago, Norwegian scientists exploring the archipelago of Svalbard discovered the remains of a previously unknown sub-species of *Pliosaurus*. One specimen was fifty feet long, with a skull ten feet in length and teeth the size of bowie knives."

Jake nodded. "I remember the documentary . . . I think they called it 'Predator X.' Very impressive. But even a creature *that* size doesn't seem big enough to kill a healthy sperm whale as big as the one we saw yesterday."

"You're right. But we're not dealing with a fifty-foot animal," Amara said. She pointed at some data. "I've compared our tooth's mandible placement to a similar one in the forty-foot specimen of *Kronosaurus* displayed in the Harvard Museum. Assuming they're from the same species, ours is substantially larger."

"How much larger?"

"Double the size."

"Holy shit."

Amara chuckled. "Precisely." Clicking her mouse on the screen in front of her, she enlarged a series of photos. "A few years back, scientists in Mexico found a skeleton of a pliosaur believed to be *Liopleurodon*, the ancestor of our animal." She pointed to some of the photos. "That specimen measured sixty feet in length and was estimated to have weighed at least fifty tons when it was alive."

"Now, *that's* a pretty big lizard."

Amara grinned. "Yes, but what was more interesting was that, based on bone structure and damage, this particular 'lizard' was a confirmed juvenile that was killed by a skull bite from an even bigger pliosaur. Based on the bite marks, researchers extrapolated that the larger animal may have measured eighty feet."

"Jesus Christ!" Jake sputtered. "Is our pliosaur that big?"

She pursed her lips. "Based on our tooth's mass and curvature, it could be."

"I don't know. That seems hard to believe."

"Why? In the water an animal's weight is fully supported, allowing it to grow far larger than gravity-prone, terrestrial creatures. Look at the blue whale, the largest animal that ever lived. And don't forget, reptiles grow their entire lives. There have been recent findings of pliosaur teeth nearly twice the size of *Liopleurodon*. And, they've found vertebrae at least forty percent larger than those of the largest *Kronosaurus* specimen."

"Sounds pretty scary."

"The prehistoric seas were a scary place, filled with terrifying creatures, most of which we've never even heard of, and probably never will."

Jake looked up at the ceiling and sniggered. "Okay, back to the here and now. So, basically, we're dealing with a man-eating reptile with teeth the size of my forearm, which measures at least sixty feet in length. Is that correct?"

"That's what it looks like." Amara's hair cascaded down as she leaned her head back to look at him.

"Wow." Jake exhaled. He stared at the papers in his hand. "How much would something like that weigh?"

"Depends on girth. On a guess, fifty to seventy-five tons."

His exhale was a whistle as he resumed reading. "Hmm . . . *Kronosaurus queenslandicus,* eh? I'm assuming from the 'queen' part that this animal is female?"

"No, Jake," Amara said amusedly. "The *queenslandicus* part refers to Queensland, where the first fossils were found. In terms of gender, I couldn't say. Based on its attack on Elvis though, which I interpret as a territorially-motivated one, I'd say it's probably an adult male. That's assuming, of course, that pliosaurs function like crocodiles, with the males fighting over territory, especially when there's a limited amount of it."

"So, we've got an aggressive bull on our hands, eh?"

"Probably, but we won't know for sure until we examine it."

"Come again?" Jake gaped at her. "You plan on getting close to this thing?"

"Not if it's dangerous. As much as I like a unique opportunity, I'm not stupid."

"Good. The last thing I need is to be filling out a missing doctor's report." He looked up for a moment. "Wow, seventy-five tons . . . well, at least it'll be easy to track. At that weight, it must be a slow swimmer."

Amara shook her head. "It's not. When it passed underneath my ship it was doing forty-five knots and accelerating."

"Jesus. Okay . . . just to make sure I have all of this in perspective . . ."

He took a deep breath. "We're facing a prehistoric, armor-plated, super-predator the size of a whale. One that's as fast as a speed boat and tears to pieces any living thing it encounters. Does that about sum it up?"

"Almost." Amara hesitated. "Since we may have to go after this creature, there's something else you should know."

Jake braced himself. "And what's that?"

"I believe this creature possesses advanced echolocation abilities. It was emitting active sonar when we detected it. That's how it found Elvis. If we hunt it, it's going to know we're coming."

Jake rubbed his temples. Before he could formulate his next course of action, there was a faint knock.

"Come in."

Molly walked in. Her face was ashen.

"I'm sorry to interrupt," she said. "But I've got bad news."

"What is it?" Jake looked up, his mind still reeling from the enormity of their problem.

"The coroner called." She wrung her hands. "He said to tell you the remains he collected have been positively identified as Brad Harcourt's."

"Okay. Thanks."

"He also said that Brad's death wasn't from a Jet-Ski related accident. The wound was consistent with some kind of large animal bite.

There's some kind of bacteria present along the wound edges. He hasn't been able to identify it yet, but it'll be detailed in his report."

"Thank you, Molly."

As she turned to go, Jake sprang to his feet. "Wait a second, please." He reached into his shirt pocket. "This is Senator Harcourt's private number. Do me a favor and inform him of the coroner's findings and express our condolences for his loss."

"I'll take care of it." Molly nodded solemnly, taking the business card and gently closing the door.

In the wake of her departure, Jake and Amara said nothing. They sat where they were, lost in thought and staring at the giant tooth. Around them, the sheriff's station remained as silent as the inside of a tomb.

"Hey, doc?"

Amara swallowed to clear her throat. "Yes?"

"I have one last question . . ."

"What is it?"

"I've watched documentaries on the Cretaceous extinction, including several on the Yucatan impact. There were global wildfires, tidal waves, a nuclear winter – basically hell on earth. How could these things survive *that*, let alone make it all the way to the present?"

Amara gave him an amused look as she tucked her hair back behind her ears. "Well, my little Discovery Channel nerd, I've got a theory on that."

CRETACEOUS OCEAN
65 MILLION YEARS AGO

The predator rested.

Well fed and content, the plesiosaur male floated tranquilly atop the swells, its pale belly bulging from the fish and squid that were its prey. Its name was *Cryptoclidus eurymerus*, and from the four flippers that propelled it through the depths, to its long neck culminating in jaws bristling with sharp teeth, the twelve-foot marine reptile was a superbly designed hunter.

The plesiosaur yawned ivory needles. Its glittering eyes closed and it drifted along the water's surface, allowing the sun's rays to warm its smooth hide. A true reptile, the solar radiation it absorbed helped speed its digestion, as did the small stones it ingested days earlier, now stored in its gizzard. Lulled into a relaxed state by the clear skies and the motion of the waves, the carnivore dozed, oblivious to its surroundings.

A moment later, the *Cryptoclidus's* peaceful isolation was disrupted. The ocean all around it began to boil over an area a hundred feet across. Its green orbs snapped wide in alarm as it realized the gravity of its situation. The pressure wave it felt was unmistakable. Something was hurtling up from the depths, displacing thousands of gallons of seawater.

Something huge.

Millions of years of instinct took over. The startled plesiosaur uttered a frightful hiss and sounded in a splash of foam, its wedge-shaped flippers propelling it forward and downward in a spiraling roll. It was a perfectly executed maneuver, used innumerable times to out-speed and outmaneuver larger and more dangerous predators.

And it was a split-second too late.

With a geyser-like explosion that sent a wall of seawater and flotsam flying in every direction, the pliosaur breached the surface. Like a volcano, its mottled sixty-foot body rose toward the heavens. It moved in slow motion, its thick hide streaming torrents of water as it settled back down, until only its scar-covered muzzle remained above the swells. Writhing within its toothy maw was the ruined body of the hapless *Cryptoclidus*. Rivers of saltwater mixed with blood ran down the larger monster's jaws, staining the surrounding seas a bright crimson. High overhead, a flock of shrieking pterosaurs gathered in anticipation of an easy meal.

Shifting its kill with a shake of its head, the pliosaur let out a deafening roar before crunching down on its victim. Conical teeth a foot in length pulverized the plesiosaur's flesh and bones and sent fresh gouts of blood and bits of tissue spraying. Repeatedly jerking its head back in crocodile-like fashion, the sea monster adjusted the position of the *Cryptoclidus* until it was satisfied. With a titanic gulp, it swallowed the smaller carnivore whole.

Oblivious to the winged scavengers that swooped down to gather up floating scraps of skin and flesh, the giant snorted loudly, then plunged headfirst back into the depths and vanished.

———

Its hunger satiated, the monster cruised soundlessly through the tropical seas it called home. Tiny bubbles danced along its scaly flanks as it descended. When it reached the two-hundred foot mark it leveled off. At sixty-two feet in length and weighing over fifty tons, the bull pliosaur and his ilk were the top marine predators, having ruled the planet's oceans for a hundred million years. A sub-group of plesiosaurs, they were characterized by short necks and long, powerful jaws lined with sharp-ribbed teeth. In the case of the big male, these jaws measured twelve feet in length and were armed with row after row of replaceable fangs.

The marine reptile glided through the depths, powered by barnacle-studded flippers as long as his cavernous jaws. The teeming oceans before him emptied of life. Other sea reptiles, giant proto-squid, and primeval sharks fled as the lord of the deep drew near. Only schools of small fish – too insignificant to make a meal – were undisturbed by the titan's presence. Nothing dared to challenge him. In his deadly, prehistoric world, the pliosaur was wary only of his own kind.

As he cruised along the continental shelf off the coast of what would one day be known as South America, the pliosaur's advanced olfactory system once again picked up the scent. Like his ancestor *Liopleurodon,* he possessed a stereoscopic sense of smell. Scoop-shaped openings inside the roof of his mouth funneled seawater through specially designed channels that linked to his olfactory receptors. Each worked separately, tasting and testing the water for stimuli. When something of interest was detected the nostrils acted like direction finders, infallibly guiding him to his target.

It was another pliosaur, a sexually mature female. Drawing even more water into his nostril receptacles, the male tasted the scent once more. The female was nearby – and in estrus.

From 500 yards out, he spotted his potential mate. The bull immediately slowed his approach, assuming a non-aggressive posture. The apex predators of their world, pliosaurs were territorial animals that rarely tolerated each other's presence. Chance encounters between adults usually ended in violence, often resulting in the death of one or both combatants. The only exception was during the brief mating season, when the impulse to breed took precedent over territorial disputes.

As the male drew closer, the need for caution on his part became more apparent. Pliosaurs mated in the water like sea turtles. And, like sea turtles, they exhibited sexual dimorphism. Because the female supported the weight of both the male and herself during mating, she tended to be substantially bigger. If the male was considered large for his kind, then the female was *enormous*.

Majestically, she emerged from the gloom. A fourth again his length and twice his weight, the cow was a colossus even by prehistoric standards. Her jaws were lined with broad-based fangs twice the size of a T-Rex's. Her skull measured over sixteen feet in length, her mass equivalent to a modern day whale.

As the female drew closer, the bull circled, giving her a wide berth. Diving deeper, he spotted an entire ecosystem hovering beneath the cow's armored belly. So large was the female that entire schools of foot-long fish had taken up permanent shelter underneath her, seeking refuge from both the heat of the sun and larger predators like plesiosaurs and sharks.

Continuing his sweeping arc, the male spotted a potential threat lurking several hundred yards northwest. Gnashing his teeth, he veered off to investigate. The intruders were a hunting pack of *Tylosaurus proriger*. A species of giant mosasaur, the fifty-five foot marine lizards were direct competitors. With six-foot skulls lined with crocodile-like teeth, the mosasaurs were similar in length to the bull, but due to their serpentine build, far lighter in weight.

The newcomers were, like the other hunters, simply hoping for an easy meal. Even a trio of them was probably not a match for a healthy male pliosaur. Still, for a dominant male coming into the rut, their presence was an annoying distraction.

Speeding directly at the mosasaurs, the bull opened his jaws wide and exposed a frightful armament of armor-piercing teeth. He turned sideways and gave the lead *Tylosaurus* a malevolent glare. Its own jaws half-open, the mosasaur immediately swerved off, followed by its brethren. Propelled by powerful strokes of their shark-like tails, the three invaders vanished into the deep.

Disregarding them, the bull wheeled back in the direction of the female. He could just make out her shadowy form, far off in the distance. He blinked rapidly as the female's hormonal scent washed over him, his refrigerator-sized heart beating rapidly in response, pumping adrenaline and oxygen-rich blood throughout his body. Sexual excitement began to build in him and he picked up speed.

FIFTEEN

Ten miles off the coast of Paradise Cove, the great white shark hunted in earnest. Normally the top of the food chain, the frustrated *Carcharodon carcharias* had been forced to accept that it was no match for the larger, more powerful orcas. It sensed their approach by the telltale sonar clicks that preceded them and fled the area, abandoning the whale carcass it traveled so far to find.

Disappointed and hungry, it sped away, its gray dorsal fin scything through the waves as it searched for another meal. Ahead, hundreds of marine animals fled, including the blubber-rich sea lions and dolphins that were its preferred prey.

As its hunger reached intolerable levels, the great white turned toward shore. Its six-foot tail beat rapidly as it accelerated. Ahead in the shallows, it sensed the presence of life – something to assuage the burning hunger that writhed within its empty stomach. Its toothy maw widening in anticipation, the shark sped hungrily on.

———

Karl Von Freiling had to fight to keep from laughing. As rusty as his Punjab was, there was no mistaking the conversation between his driver Aziz and the cabbie's dispatcher. The two of them were actually trying to hatch some hair-brained scheme to shake him down.

Ballsy.

"I am terribly sorry, Mister Chuck," the cabbie apologized as he hung up the microphone. He glanced at the spacious homes and gardens that dominated the upscale neighborhood, trying to avoid his passenger's unwavering gaze. "But my dispatcher has instructed me that the rate you and I agreed upon is insufficient for the distance and destination."

"Oh, really?" Von Freiling drawled through a Cheshire cat's grin. He'd waited until they traveled a block past his residence before instructing the driver to pull over. "And how much does he think I should be paying?"

Aziz hesitated. "Another . . . two hundred and fifty dollars."

Von Freiling stifled a snicker. He removed his sunglasses and studied his driver's reflection in the mirror. Although he was trying to appear calm, Aziz had sweat forming on his forehead and a nervous tic doing the tango on his right cheek.

"Hmm . . . let me give it some thought." Von Freiling smiled mirthlessly. "I'm thinking . . . *no*. You see, Aziz, a deal's a deal. As a gentleman, I *always* keep my word. Frankly, if you thought the money was going to be an issue, you shouldn't have agreed."

"But, my boss said I would be fired–"

Von Freiling waved him off and counted out eight hundred dollar bills. He passed them though the shoebox-sized opening in the minivan's Plexiglas partition. "Forget it, Aziz," he said. "Now, I *was* going to give you a fifty dollar tip. But not after hearing your conversation. And yes, I understood every word. Now, pass me my change, please."

The cabbie's face was a blend of astonishment and consternation. His fingers fumbled as he counted the money. "But Chuck, I need at least another two hundred dollars."

Von Freiling leaned forward in his seat, his glittering eyes frightening. "Listen, moron. I'm not giving you a fucking penny more. You're starting to piss me off. So I suggest you give me my fifty dollars, before things inside this vehicle get *very* unpleasant."

"Come on now, Mister Chuck, it is only fair . . ."

Von Freiling's neck muscles rippled as he gave the thin partition a calculating stare, pinpointing its weak points. A mental image of him grabbing Aziz by the nape and pulling him forcibly through it began to coalesce in his mind, and he smiled an awful smile. He felt an adrenaline rush begin to build and locked his gaze on the flustered cabbie. "I really don't think you appreciate the *gravity* of your situation . . ."

The cabbie turned in his seat. His jaw dropped and he swallowed hard. He turned away, only to turn back a second later to toss the Ulysses S. Grant through the partition.

Von Freiling snatched it out of the air. He grabbed his bag and climbed out, before sticking his head back inside. His smile returned.

"Have a nice drive back."

He left the minivan's door open and walked away.

———

"So, Jake, what should we do?" Amara asked as she finished shutting down the computer. She was bone tired, but at least she'd convinced the headstrong lawman to consider the possibility she was right.

"I'm not sure yet," he replied, glancing over from a nearby window. His arms folded, he stared out onto the street. The glass was streaked with rain from a passing shower. He traced the meanderings of one of the drops with a hardened fingertip. "But I'll tell you what we're *not* going to do. We're *not* going to broadcast this. Not until we have some more substantial evidence."

She took a step toward him. "But, you've *seen* all the evidence . . ."

Jake raised an eyebrow. "Yes. But it's circumstantial. The media will certainly say it is."

"Oh, give me a break," Amara fumed as she snatched some additional sheets off the printer. She was sick of the ongoing argument. "Look at these geothermal reports. Both of the previous incidents had substantial activity in close proximity to each sighting – in fact, only a few days prior to each occurrence. And *now*, less than a week after there was an eruption off the coast of Cuba, we have *this*!" She picked up the tooth and held it high.

Jake's shoulders tightened, then gradually relaxed. "Fine. You know, you're lucky you're cute when you get all 'outraged womanhood.' " He grinned at the indignant expression on her face. "You don't mind if we use your ship, do you?"

Amara stared at him. "My ship? For what?"

"For our very own monster quest. We've got to find this thing before it kills again."

She hesitated. "Look, I'm not in favor of going out and killing this animal. We're dealing with a unique species. It should be observed, not blown up." The cetaceanist paused when she saw the surprisingly harsh look on Jake's face. "But then again," she added hastily, "people have been killed, so we definitely have to do something."

Jake shook his head. "I need more proof, doc. I'm not going to put my head on the chopping block without it."

"I understand." She walked back to her desk and started tossing the remainder of her belongings into her purse. "I just wish our tooth and tissue samples, combined with *Archimedes'* analysis printouts, turned out to be enough. But you're right. We need something more substantial. Something people will regard as irrefutable proof."

"We need film footage." Jake began rewrapping the tooth. "We're going to have to go out, find this thing, and videotape it. Once we do, we'll be gold."

"It's too bad we didn't get it the other day." Amara sighed ruefully. "What do you mean?"

"Remember I told you the creature passed under my ship?"

Jake nodded.

"We tried to record it with our underwater cameras. They're integrated into the hull of the ship."

"And what happened?"

"Well, we thought the creature was chasing our runabout . . ." Amara's eyes widened with the memory. "We had them gun it all the way back to the *Harbinger*. Unfortunately, the wake they kicked up ruined all of our footage. We couldn't see anything."

"You only have these cameras on one side of the ship?"

"No, they're on both sides, silly," Amara said with a half-smile. "We were just turned in that direction and had the portside cameras set to . . . *Omigod*!"

Jumping out of her chair as if she'd been electrocuted, she started digging in her bag like a maniac.

"What's going on?" Jake asked bemusedly.

"I'll tell you in a second," she said, nearly beside herself with excitement. Snatching her radio out of her bag, she twisted the squelch button into position with trembling fingers. "Thank God I charged this last night." She raised the unit to her mouth. "Attention

Harbinger, this is Amara calling. Repeat, Amara calling. Do you read me?"

There was a long moment of static-laden interference before Adam Spencer's voice crackled out of the walkie-talkie.

"Amara, my God, we've been trying to get you on the horn for an hour!"

"Why, what's wrong?"

"We nearly lost the *William*! First the sharks ran her over. Then the whales beat the hell out of her. We barely got her back on board! You had to see it to believe it. If Joe hadn't thrown the winch into high gear, they'd have dragged her and her crew straight to Davie Jones's locker!"

"Jesus," Amara said, eyes wide. She fretted for a moment and pushed the talk button again. "Which whales, Adam? And is the crew all right?"

"It was one of our study pods of killer whales – alpha, to be precise. I've never seen anything like it. They just went berserk! Lane and Mike are a little banged up, but they're okay."

Amara bit her lower lip as she looked at Jake.

"Adam, from the evidence we've gathered, it appears we have a new species of predator around, something *very* dangerous. Ground everyone immediately. No one is to leave the ship. Do you read me?"

"Sure thing. You won't be getting any argument from Lane or Mike. Or from me, for that matter."

"Fair enough," Amara said. "Now, I need to know . . . wait, hold on a second." She saw Jake stiffen and she took her finger off the talk button. "Yes?"

"Find out about the sharks."

She nodded in agreement. "Adam, Sheriff Braddock wants to know what happened with the sharks, and so do I."

"We had tons of them feeding on Elvis's carcass, including a real monster of a great white. But they all got out of Dodge when the killer whales showed up. Why does he want to know about the sharks?"

Jake pushed a button on his intercom system.

"Molly, call Chris Meyers on his cell phone, please. Tell him to stop by Joe's Quarry & Mining Company and pick up a small dynamite kit, and to *carefully* bring it to the dock."

"No problem," Molly buzzed back.

Grim-faced, Jake turned to Amara. "With the prevailing currents, I can't risk that dead whale drifting too close to shore." He shook his head. "One of those sharks could cruise into the marina and mistake one of our well-fed tourists for a tasty-looking piece of whale blubber. Sorry doc, but I've got to sink what's left before it makes its way here."

Amara nodded and raised her radio to her lips. "Adam, I need you to keep Elvis tied to the *Harbinger*. Do *not* cut him loose. We're going to have to dynamite the carcass."

"No problem, boss. Gee, I guess the king really is dead, huh?"

She smiled sadly. Suddenly, her eyes popped. "Holy cow, I almost forgot! Adam, I need to know something of the *utmost* importance."

"Okay . . ."

"I need to know if you erased the hull camera's footage from the other day – in particular, the footage you took when that thing ran under the ship's hull."

"Not yet. But I told you before, the cameras came back with nothing but blotchy images. It was useless."

"Yes, but those were the *starboard* cameras, Adam." Amara held her breath for a moment. "I want to know about the *portside* cameras. Remember, you told me you had set them for motion sensing only?"

"The port cameras . . . no, I didn't erase any of it. I never even thought to – holy crap! Yeah, that footage is completely intact! Do you want me to–"

"I don't want you to do anything, Adam. Just guard that disc with your life. Sheriff Braddock and I are en route. We'll be there before you know it, Amara out."

"Aye, aye, captain."

As she shoved the radio back inside her purse, Amara couldn't help but notice the lawman strap on his weighty pistol belt. She moved to the door. "Jake my friend, I think I've got proof of our mystery monster waiting for us on the *Harbinger*. So, let's move it!"

His eyes bright, Jake grabbed his gear bag and followed her outside, closing the door of his office behind them.

Forgotten in the shadow of the computer monitor, the test tube containing the *Sayonara's* tissue sample stood guard. Beneath its crystal exterior, the ragged hunk of epidermis spiraled, writhing within the confines of its fluid-filled prison like a thing alive.

———

The creature was growing aggravated. Frustrated that the previous night's hunt failed to produce enough protein for its needs, it lingered near the docks, waiting to see if any additional opportunities presented themselves. It gnashed its teeth as it lurked beneath the surface, watching and waiting. Behind it, the sun scaled the horizon, its gilded rays warming the surrounding waters.

Finally, the creature lost patience and surfaced with a gurgling hiss. Using its binocular vision, it scanned the landing and surrounding area repeatedly. There was nothing edible to be seen nor had.

A low grumble of discomfort escaped its scaly lips. It was hungry. Unable to keep the searing effects of its digestive juices at bay any longer, it filled its gigantic lungs and closed its watertight nostril flaps. Submerging slowly, it began to move off.

Due to the cooler temperatures, the creature's movements were sluggish at first. Eventually, the heat generated by its exertions warmed it as much as the midday sun would have and it moved faster through the water column. Soon, its enormous body flew through the depths, propelled by perpetual sweeps of its powerful flippers.

Accelerating to its normal cruising speed, the creature headed toward deeper water. Its jaws were closed tight to reduce drag, its sonar scanning the surrounding seas for miles ahead. It continued to descend, leveling off at the three-hundred foot mark. Changing direction, it arced toward the abyss, hoping to find a meal substantial enough to satiate its irrepressible need to destroy and devour.

———

Amara grimaced as her stomach lurched and her hair flew up, landing in front of her face like a matted spider web. She uttered a groan and held on, pursing her lips and blowing fiercely in an attempt to clear her vision.

The road they were barreling along on was brutal. Calling it a "road" was generous. Its deep washes and twisting turns looked like the dried up remains of an old riverbed. Swirling clouds of dust and grit made it impossible to see, and unless you were an off-road enthusiast looking for a thrill, it was completely unsuitable for driving on.

She swallowed a curse as a sudden dip caused her to bite her tongue, then barked at Jake from the passenger seat.

"Say, this is some 'shortcut' you've got here, sheriff." She grabbed onto a handle suspended from the Tahoe's roof. "If I'd known the road was going to be like this, I'd have worn my sports bra!"

"Listen, it's three miles the regular way, or one this way." The corners of Jake's mouth twitched as he tried and failed to suppress a smirk. "You want it long, or you want it hard? Which one's it going to be?"

"Pig." Amara grinned amusedly. Then, for some inexplicable reason, she found herself blushing. She turned away, looking past the trees to their right. She could see the ocean through the leaves. "How much farther is it?"

"We're just about there," Jake reached for his cell phone and pressed a preset with his thumbnail. Driving with one hand, he pressed it to his ear. "Hey kid–" he grunted as the powerful SUV leapt over a small hillock. "Did you get what we need?"

There was a moment of silence as Jake held the phone tight to his head.

"Really? And nobody knows what happened?" Jake glanced at Amara, then turned back to his conversation. "Okay kid, we're almost there. I'll see you in a minute." He closed the tiny Motorola, clipping it back on his belt.

"What's going on?" Amara asked. She winced as Jake braked and swerved to avoid a large depression.

"I'm not sure," Jake said, veering back. "Something else has happened at the marina. We'll find out in a second."

———

The picturesque hamlet known as Paradise Cove emerged from the morning mist. Jake glanced at his watch. It was nearly eight 8 a.m. and the town's palm-lined, cobblestoned streets were fairly deserted. They jumped off the dirt road and landed on a paved side street. He maneuvered his truck around the outskirts of the municipality, ending up by the water. A few seconds later, he pulled the dust-caked vehicle into a reserved spot and threw it into park.

He spotted the ambulance. Its flashing red lights were visible even through the grime-obscured windows of the big Chevy. Jake turned on his wipers. The emergency response vehicle was encircled by onlookers. A pair of emergency medical technicians were struggling to load an oversized patient into the rear.

Make that a corpse.

Whoever it was, their face was covered.

His face grim, Jake headed toward the ambulance. He noticed his deputy, standing awkwardly off to one side with a few local business owners. He called out to Chris as he and Amara drew closer.

"Hey, kid. What's going on?"

"Hey, chief," Chris said. His expression changed markedly, and he made an effort to tuck in his uniform shirt. "Um, hi Doctor Takagi."

"Hello, Chris." Amara smiled, extending her hand.

"C'mon, kid." Jake strode toward the ambulance with both of them scurrying to keep up. He nodded a greeting to the EMS personnel, then took a chart off the ambulance door and peeked inside. "That's Ben Stillman, isn't it?"

"Was," the nearest medic said.

"What happened?"

"Heart attack. He must've been lying there all night, poor bastard." The medic pointed to a nearby section of dock, a few vessels away from the lobsterman's boat slip.

Jake scanned the chart, "Who found him?"

"Some teenagers. Said he was still alive, though barely. Kept babbling hysterically and pointing at the water."

"Did he say anything to you?" Jake asked as he put the clipboard back.

The EMT shook his head. "He was cold before we got here. We're taking the body to Harcourt Memorial. If you know his wife, you might want to notify her. Here's my card."

Jake accepted it with a nod and helped close the ambulance doors. They swung shut with a thud, sealing Ben inside. "I'll take care of it," he said.

The driver climbed in and closed his door. "Thanks, sheriff. I appreciate it. I hate giving bad news."

"I hear you."

Jake stepped back, guiding Chris out of the ambulance's path as the EMT turned on his sirens and made his way out of the parking lot. The breeze changed direction and Jake blinked rapidly as a refreshing fragrance invited its way into his nostrils. Amara stood next to him.

"That's terrible about that poor man," she said. "I feel sorry for his wife."

Jake's brows rose and he shook his head. "I don't. It's the best thing that could have happened to her."

Amara gasped. "Where did *that* come from?"

"Doc, this is my town," Jake stated, "and I know my people. That swaggering bully was a former heavyweight prospect. Yet the only thing he ever hit was his wife. I've seen plenty of that in my day. Now, I don't know about you, but I've got no tolerance for bullshit like that." He sucked in a deep breath and snorted it out. "Believe me. Stillman's wife getting his life insurance policy, as well as the chance to sell off that rat-infested tub of his, is small compensation for what she's put up with, but at least it's a start." He shook his head and began stomping toward the docks.

Stunned, Amara turned to follow him with Chris tactfully bringing up the rear. "Well, in that case, I guess his death does seem a little less tragic."

"Yes, it does." Jake stopped so suddenly she plowed into him.

Amara inhaled sharply. "Sorry. So, uh, are we heading to the *Harbinger* now?"

"In a minute." Still aggravated, Jake looked around the docks, seeking out Stillman's boat. "I want to check something first . . ."

He walked along the maze of planking, making his way to *Above the Claw* and the spot where Ben had been discovered. He stopped short, blinking at the dilapidated vessel.

She was heavily damaged. Her gunnels were crushed, in some places almost to her decking, and chunks of debris were scattered all over the ship. Still held to the docks by strong ropes, the forty-foot vessel was taking on water through a series of cracks in her hull. She was already listing to port, and Jake knew it was a matter of hours before the well-known lobster boat sank straight to the bottom.

"Wow, exactly like the *Sayonara*," Amara said, peering over his shoulder.

"Pretty much, except this time the damaged area is only to the port side. Which makes sense, if what landed on her came up out of the water . . ."

"You mean it's in the marina?" She took a step back and stared apprehensively at the oil-stained surface of the harbor.

"Could be," he said as he moved closer to the boat. He loosened his Beretta in its holster and rested one hand on the intact starboard gunwales. "Probably snuck in last night under cover of darkness. That would certainly explain what frightened Ben."

"Hey, chief, look at this!" Chris called out excitedly. Partially concealed by one of the dock's hose stations, was the butt stock of a pump action shotgun.

"That's Ben's, don't touch it," Jake said. He walked over and picked up the gun, carefully checking its magazine and chamber. "Empty," he announced. He gestured for Amara to join him. "It's been fired."

"How can you tell?"

"The smell . . . and those." Jake nodded toward a half-dozen discarded shell casings that littered the dock.

Carefully replacing the weapon exactly where he found it, he clambered to his feet and began to follow the trail of spent rounds, sprinkled like lethal breadcrumbs between *Above the Claw* and a large sailboat. Tracing and retracing his steps back and forth between the big sloop and the damaged lobster boat, he mouthed a curse.

"What's wrong, chief?" Chris said.

"This doesn't make sense." Jake dropped down and examined the trail of shotgun shells from ground level. "Assuming he was the shooter, from the position of these rounds it appears Ben started firing his weapon from over there." He pointed to the prow of the sailboat, some thirty feet away. "Then he must have retreated back toward his own boat." He turned back toward *Above the Claw*. "He dropped his gun once he realized it was empty and tried to run, at which point his heart gave out, causing him to collapse over here . . ."

He stopped at the spot where the fallen fisherman was found and picked out a spent shell wedged tightly between two deck boards.

"I don't understand the conundrum," Amara said. "That makes perfect sense to me."

Jake looked back and forth between the two points. "Ben Stillman was an idiot, but he wasn't a big enough idiot to go running around the marina firing a twelve gauge for no reason."

"Okay." Amara folded her arms across her chest. "You'd know better than me. So, in police terms, what does that mean?"

"It means that Ben must have seen something that scared him enough to run for his gun. He got his weapon, went back over by that boat and started firing . . ."

An unpleasant possibility dawned on Jake. His eyes narrowing, he rose and moved in the direction of the sailboat, a forty-five foot sloop with the name *Aquaholic* emblazoned on bow and stern.

His expression changed to one of wariness as he drew closer. He held up a hand that stopped Amara and his deputy in their tracks. "You guys stay where you are." A cool breeze began to blow, and he felt the hairs on the back of his neck prick up.

At first glance, the *Aquaholic* appeared normal and undamaged. As he moved past her bow he got the feeling something about the sailboat wasn't quite right. He caught a hint of movement by the stern and moved in to investigate.

There was a bird standing on the aft deck – a large brown and white seabird that reminded Jake of an albatross. Unfazed by the human's proximity, it remained where it was, shifting its weight from foot to foot, extending its wings as a warning to other gulls. As he approached the bird, his vision was obscured by the sloop's captain's wheel. He moved a few steps to his left to get a better view of what it was standing on.

"Oh shit!"

"What is it? What did you find?" Amara called out, charging forward with Chris Meyers hot on her heels.

"Stay back! Don't come over here!" Jake yelled. His right hand was extended palm out, the other cupping his nose and mouth.

Amara hesitated. "What's going on?"

"Chris, take her back to the landing," Jake said. He turned away and sucked in a couple of deep breaths before straightening up. Behind him, he could hear Amara's fierce protestations as his youthful deputy attempted to carry out his order. He cleared his mind and turned toward the scene that awaited him.

He stepped over the sailboat's thin rope railing, waving his arms and yelling to frighten off the infuriated gull. Reluctantly, it took wing, scolding him as it gave up its prize.

It was a body. Or rather, half of one.

The mutilated remains of a man lay draped across the rear deck of the sloop, his hands locked onto the bottom of the captain's wheel in a death grip. His pallid face was fused into a nightmarish death mask that personified agony and horror.

He'd been bitten in half at the waistline.

Grimacing, Jake shrugged off the chill tiptoeing up and down his spine and forced himself to remain focused. He examined the death scene for clues. A moment later, he yelled for Chris to join him. Amara remained where she was, her arms folded tightly across her chest in protest.

"Hey, chief, what do you . . . holy shit!" Chris stammered as he came running up. "Jesus, who the heck is that?"

"Angelo Melito, a wealthy real estate developer from New York." He knelt down and examined the wounds on the body. "Nice guy, too. He was vacationing here with that gorgeous new Filipino wife of his, poor bastard."

"My God, he's got no legs! What happened to him?"

"Well, he's wearing no wristwatch and no shirt. And everything from the waist down is gone. I'd have to say he was probably out for a late night swim."

"Yeah, but what *happened* to him?"

"Something ate him, or rather half of him, kid. From the look of things, he was in the water trying to climb back aboard when he was attacked. The spot where he's been bitten lines up with the edge of the hull, where those gouge marks have been made in the fiberglass."

Chris looked at the indicated area. As he did, he caught sight of the corpse's exposed spinal column and abdominal cavity, emptied of its entire intestinal tract.

"Ugh, I think I'm gonna be sick . . ." He blanched, gagging as he held onto a nearby rope for support.

"Okay kid, you can go back to the landing." Jake sprang back onto the dock and started to offer the shaken adolescent a hand. He paused thoughtfully, his lips a rigid line. "Actually, hold on. I hate to do this, but I'm going to need you to stay here and stand guard."

"What for?" Chris whined.

"Because Doctor Takagi and I have to take the *Infidel* out to her ship to find out what did this. I need you to mark off the crime scene and call back the forensics team. Most importantly, I need you to help keep a lid on this."

"A lid on what?" Chris stared back at the bloodless corpse. "For God's sake, what did this? What the hell's going on?"

"I can't talk about it now. I'm sorry, kid," Jake said. "I'll be back in a few hours, hopefully with some answers. In the meantime, if anyone asks what happened, just tell them you don't know. They'll think it was a shark attack, which is fine."

"It's fine?" Eyes wide, Chris shook his head. "Since when is a shark attack fine?"

"For now," Jake said. "Get some warning tape and a barricade from my truck. Then call Molly and see if anyone's seen Angelo's wife. I've got a bad feeling she was with him. If so, I doubt we'll be seeing her again, but we've got to check."

"All right, chief. I'll get to work."

"Thanks, kid."

Jake glanced toward a pacing Amara. "I'll fill the doc in on the way. Just take care of business."

"Will do, chief," Chris replied with a confidence he didn't feel.

"Hey, kid?"

"Yeah?"

"I'm counting on you. Because I know I can."

"Thanks, chief," Chris responded with a forced smile. "I'll do my best."

Jake watched him gallop off. A flurry of movement caught his eye and he clocked a small crowd of curious onlookers making their way down the landing. He took a deep breath and prepared himself.

They were in for one hell of a surprise.

SIXTEEN

The hearty smell of sea air mixed with oxidized iron filled Jake's nostrils as he worked his way up along the *Harbinger*'s riveted flanks. Overhead, a quartet of arguing seabirds circled, their stream-lined wings flapping hard to compensate for the updraft. He could see the ship's sturdy decks, dotted with hardworking crewmen, mop-ping and performing maintenance. He followed Amara Takagi in rela-tive silence, surreptitiously admiring her silhouette as she made her way up the rust-marred stairs. Below, the *Infidel* was tied off directly behind the *Sycophant*, the two vessels swaying in unison with the cur-rent generated by the *Harbinger*.

"So, this old tub really used to be a whaler, eh?" Jake opened, try-ing to change the mood after the morning's awful events.

Amara nodded. "Yes, it was." She paused at the top of the stairs and turned to him. "Jake, thanks for trying to spare me from seeing that mess back at the marina. I was upset because I felt you were treating me like a child, but after catching a glimpse of that poor man's body, I realized you were trying to protect me."

"You're welcome."

She nodded and gestured for him to follow her up onto the main deck, then headed toward the ship's starboard crane. Dangling from its boom like some gigantic fish, the mini-sub *William* hung suspended.

"C'mon," Amara glanced back with mock enthusiasm. "I want to see what horrors have been inflicted upon my expensive toy before we go below."

Before he could respond, a now-familiar voice called out from the stern.

"Amara, tank God ya come back, ya crazy woman!" Willie smiled as he rushed over and bear-hugged the cetaceanist so hard he made her wince. "I been goin nuts tryin ta run tings here all by ma-self."

"I missed you too," she said as he put her down. She grinned and rubbed her ribs. "I brought Jake with me. There's been a lot of unbelievable stuff going on and he's here to help."

"Welcome, mon."

Willie took Jake's hand in both of his own, vigorously pumping it up and down.

"Thanks, Willie," he replied.

"Okay," Amara said. "So, what exactly did you guys do to my mini-sub?"

"Not us," Willie emphasized as they walked to the swaying craft. "It was da whales. Dey all went bananas – some sort of defensive response. Dey was bouncing da *William* around like a big beach ball. I taught for sure we was goin to lose both da crew and da sub!"

Amara gasped. She stopped dead in her tracks as she took in the submersible's damaged portions.

"Wow, it's . . . a lot worse than I thought."

Jake moved beside her. "How bad?"

"Oh, it's pretty bad." She shook her head. The tree trunk-sized pontoons that formed the core of the *William*'s ballast system were dented in a dozen places. In some spots it looked like a battering ram had been used, and the entire rudder assembly was crushed beyond recognition. "We can fix her, but it's going to take weeks and cost a bundle."

Willie cleared his throat. "We can't do it here. We gonna have ta bring her in. I spoke ta Joe. He said we need ta do some serious cuttin and weldin we can't do on da ship."

"He's right," Amara nodded. "Well, it could have been worse. At least the observation bubble was spared."

Jake followed Amara to the submarine's prow. "Is it that expensive to repair?"

"Not repair . . . *replace*. But that's not the main worry. Yes, the acrylic hemisphere would cost a fortune to change, but the real danger would be if it had ruptured. If the observation bubble is compromised during a deep dive, the entire vessel will implode from the pressure. If that happens, you can kiss the sub and everyone aboard goodbye."

"Sounds comforting." Jake shrugged off the unpleasant image. "Remind me to stay on the ship."

"Yeah," Amara nodded. "Anyway, let's get down to business. Willie, I need you to find Joe and get him to Jake's boat. There's a case of dynamite, complete with blasting caps, on board. I need him to rig up enough to send Elvis' remains to the bottom."

Willie made a show of pumping his fist in the air. "Tank God. When da wind shifts back dis way ya'll know exactly what I mean!"

"Whatever you say." Amara grinned as her first mate loped off. "C'mon, Jake. Let me give you the fifty cent tour."

"Lead the way, doc."

As he peered over the *Harbinger*'s railing, Jake scrutinized the bloated body of the dead sperm whale. A victim of scavengers and decay, the once mighty cetacean was now unrecognizable. Even so, its ravaged carcass was a sobering reminder of the dire reason for their trip. If Amara was right about the hull recorders, in a few minutes they'd have proof of the creature that killed not only the giant cachalot, but also a growing collection of human beings.

He followed his host around the gently rolling ship. As they disappeared into a darkened doorway, he could hear Willie's voice behind them, along with a gruffer one, discussing the unenviable task Amara assigned.

"The ship was originally manufactured in Russia," she yelled back over her shoulder as she led the way through a noisy series of narrow metal hallways. They emerged inside the vessel's sunlit helm area. "You can probably tell by the old signage. She was launched in 1965. At seventy meters in length, a twelve meter beam, and weighing over seven hundred tons, she was the pride of the Soviet Union's whaling fleet for nearly two decades. God knows how many whales were slaughtered by this thing's grenade-tipped harpoons, before they decommissioned her in favor of more lethal whale killers."

Amara stopped in the center of the ship's antiquated steering room. "Next to our fancy control room, this is my favorite part of the ship." Leaning back and placing her hand on the huge metal captain's wheel, she grinned at him and gave it a playful quarter spin. "I love the view from here. When we're under way, I can see for twenty miles on a clear day. I guess that came in handy back when they were hunting the poor right whales and humpbacks to the brink of extinction."

Jake nodded, moving to the huge windows lined up across the room. The bridge's elevated position, so high above the decks, gave them an unparalleled view of the sparkling waters of the Atlantic.

"What's all this stuff?" Jake indicated a collection of weapons and antiques affixed to the bulkheads directly above the windows.

"They came with the ship," Amara said. "I keep that old harpoon up there for the same reasons we left the harpoon cannon on our bow – as a reminder of the horrors this ship once inflicted on innocent animals, and of our responsibility to protect them now. As for the other things, well, it seemed a shame to break up her old captain's collection."

"May I?" Jake gestured toward the harpoon.

"Sure, go ahead."

Jake reached up and carefully removed the aged weapon from its resting place. He brushed away some of the dust coating it and hefted it in his hands, examining its point.

"It's heavy," he said, shifting the harpoon around and feeling its barbs. "Pretty unpleasant – even against a whale. I wouldn't want to get stabbed with it."

Jake reached up and placed the menacing-looking lance back on the wall. He turned sideways, noticing a room that connected to the bridge. "What's in here?" He walked through the open doorway.

"That's the original communications station," Amara said, following him inside the dimly lit twenty-foot square space. "You can see the old radar and sonar equipment underneath all those dusty crates. We replaced it with new stuff as soon as we got the ship. It was outdated and useless anyway. This ship may be old, Jake, but our observation room downstairs is state-of-the-art."

"So, who exactly owns the *Harbinger*?" Jake asked, walking back onto the bridge.

"Thirty percent of her is mine," Amara declared proudly. Her head held high, she turned out one of the bridge's side doors and gestured for Jake to follow her. "I've invested everything in her. The majority shareholders are the founding members of the Worldwide Cetacean Society."

"So, hypothetically speaking, if we're going to use this ship to pursue our 'pliosaur,' we need their approval and authorization?"

"Not necessarily," Amara said over her shoulder. She shot him a smirk, then sidestepped down a narrow corridor, passing through a tight archway. Sunlight glimmered from a small porthole in the distance. As she reached the exit door leading to the ship's bow she stopped suddenly. The door was locked. She exhaled irritably and tried to reverse direction. Her face contorted. Jake's size, combined with the narrow corridor, prevented her from moving past him. Her expression turned contemplative and she took a step toward him, pointing upwards at a series of dials and levers directly behind him. "I'm sorry, I just need to . . ."

"Uh, no problem . . ." Unable to back up and realizing she needed to activate something on the nearby bulkhead, Jake nodded and shoved his upper back tightly against the wall, compressing his abs inward as best he could in order to give her space.

Amara smiled apologetically as she squirmed her way through. The space he was able to create was woefully inadequate, and she had no choice but to writhe against him as she strained to reach the door's release mechanism.

Jake gave an involuntary gasp as their bodies pressed together. They'd never been this close before. He could smell Amara's sweat and feel the heat radiating off her. He grunted, swallowing hard, and turned his head sideways in a pointless attempt at being polite. He felt the unmistakable sensation of her breasts rubbing against him. His pulse began to quicken and he experienced a familiar stirring. He tried to distract himself, thinking hard about all the groceries he needed to buy, and the huge pile of laundry he had waiting back home.

"There it is . . . got it." Amara smiled happily as she caught hold of the metal lever. She pulled down smoothly on it, causing the portal's internal locks to roll and click open.

Jake nodded agreeably. The cetaceanist grinned shyly and then reversed direction, squirming past him once more. Her scent filled his nostrils and he felt perspiration trickle down his neck and back. He exhaled hard, as much to relieve tension as to discharge the breath he was holding.

Oblivious to his discomfiture, Amara flung open the door. Sunlight and a strong breeze instantly filled the cramped corridor. With wispy white clouds framing her windswept hair, she stepped out onto the ship's upper deck and turned to face Jake. She smiled at him, then took a step backwards and straddled a ladder that led down to the forward deck. Sliding smoothly down it, she landed with a thump, her face tightening into a small grimace. She straightened up and waited for Jake before leading him toward the *Harbinger's* prow.

"The I.C.S. pretty much lets me do what I want," she continued breathlessly, stepping over the ship's exposed anchor chains as she walked toward the bow. "I've always delivered for them in the past, and as a partner, well . . . let's just say I have a pretty long leash."

Jake snickered. "So, your investors will have no problem with us going on a wild goose chase after a sea monster that may not even exist?"

"Very funny." She rolled her eyes, stopping next to the ship's ominous-looking harpoon cannon. "This is the weapon they used to murder so many whales." She hugged herself and shuddered. "It gives me the creeps every time I'm up here, but I thought you should see it. It's totally non-functional. It was decommissioned before we got the ship."

Jake ran his hands over the gnarled surface of the antique metal monster. "That's too bad. It might have come in handy against that creature of yours, assuming of course, we can find it."

Amara frowned. She turned around, heading back the way they came. "Well, I guess we'll just have to come up with another way to deal with it. Not every confrontation has to end in death, you know. It's just like that poor guy the creature scared to death, back at the docks. Sure, he was a real bastard, but that doesn't mean he deserved to die."

"Maybe not, doc. But whatever is out there is *eating* people."

"Yeah . . ." Amara's expression intensified. She looked troubled. "Jake, do you remember when you said you had plenty of experience dealing with domestic violence?"

Jake's head recoiled on his neck as he looked at her. "I remember. Why?"

"Well, I was–"

"Let me stop you before you go any further, doc. My father was a drunken Irishman who couldn't stand his wife being more successful than he was. He used to beat the hell out of my mom and me whenever the mood struck him. Case closed."

Amara lowered her head. "I'm sorry."

"We were discussing your partners' reaction to our mission."

She straightened up. "Yes, thank you. Once we see the footage I'm going to let them know that the *Harbinger* is setting sail to pursue an aggressive new species. One we have firm scientific evidence of, and wish to be the first to document."

"Works for me," he said. "Speaking of which, shouldn't we be looking at that footage?"

She gave Jake a contemplative look. "We should. But first, there's something I want to show you."

"What kind of something?"

"A . . . guest of ours we've been keeping onboard. I want to show him to you before we look at the video."

Jake's head angled slightly. "He sounds mysterious. But why am I seeing this 'guest' first?"

"Call it an insurance policy." Amara's lips curved up. "In case the video footage turns out to be a bust. If it does, what I'm about to show you should still convince you."

"Okay, doc. And when do we get to see your guest?"

"We're heading there now," Amara said. She headed through an open door and down a short flight of steps that led into the ship's darkened interior.

A minute later, Jake realized she was leading him to the *Harbinger's* freezer.

———

When they emerged fifteen moments later inside the ship's bustling observation room, Jake's thought processes were racing so fast he hardly noticed the array of equipment.

Amara led him to a hard-at-work individual, seated in the center of the room behind a trio of video monitors. "Jake Braddock, I would like the privilege of introducing the best videographer in the industry: my good friend, Adam Spencer."

"A pleasure, Adam," Jake said, shaking hands. "Quite a setup you've got here."

"Thanks, Jake," Adam replied with a forced smile, taking his hand back and shaking it to restore lost blood flow. "Say . . . you wouldn't be the same Jake Braddock I saw on TV a few years back, the one who swept the fencing championships in LA?"

"Guilty as charged."

"Why is it everybody in the world knows about that except me?" Amara commented.

"Are you kidding? This guy's a god!" Adam twisted in his seat. He turned back, a smile on his face, and a pencil in hand. "Say, can I get your autograph, and maybe a quick picture?"

"Later, Adam," Amara said. "Right now we've got work to do. I need you to pull up the files I radioed you about. I'm assuming you kept them under wraps like I asked?"

"Boss lady, *I* haven't even seen them. How's that for keeping things battened down?"

Amara smiled. "Nicely done. Okay guys, gather round and cross everything you've got two of. If the footage we're about to see is what I think it is, we're going to turn the entire scientific community on their collective ears."

"Amen to that," Jake said under his breath. "Although, you may have enough evidence to do that already."

Adam turned to Amara. "What's he mean?"

"I showed him our shrink-wrapped guest."

Adam raised an eyebrow. "Ah . . . how dramatic. But, I thought we were keeping a lid on that?"

Amara's nostrils flared. "It was necessary. Anyway, hit it as soon as you're ready."

Adam nodded and dimmed the overhead lights. He made a series of quick adjustments on his keyboard, whistling as he keyed up the sequence he wanted. Finally, he turned to the pair seated behind him, his finger suspended over a red button.

"Okay, kids, hold on to your shorts," he said as he pushed it. "The first thing we're looking at is the original sequence from the starboard cameras." He reached for a large round dial and sped up the video to the part he was looking for. "Like I said before, the interference caused by the *Sycophant* completely obscured the footage, so all you see is this dark, amorphous shape. Kind of looks like a giant manta ray from the front."

"Did you try to enhance it?" Amara leaned forward in her seat, squinting at the screen.

"This *is* enhanced," Adam said. He moved his mouse and pushed a few buttons. "Now, let's check out the portside footage. There isn't much – only a second or so, since the cameras were set for low resolution, alternate-frame motion-sensing only. Let's see what we've got."

As he hit the enter button, Jake held his breath. The film clip was short indeed: a fraction of a second. It showed a dark-colored object barreling past the camera with so much velocity it was little more than a blur. Then, it was gone, leaving behind swirling bubbles.

"Did you see that?" Amara leapt out of her seat. "That's it! We've got it!"

Jake held up his hands. "Whoa, hold on . . . I saw *something*," he said skeptically. "What it was, I couldn't say. It could have been a piece of wood. Let's not overreact."

"Okay, you're right." Amara took a deep breath, visibly reining herself in. "Let's allow my astute little friend to do his thing."

The cetaceanist winked at Adam and sat back, waiting while he scrolled the fleeting image back and forth. A tense few minutes passed, with the little videographer entering keyed codes and adjusting settings. Finally, he leaned back in his seat, exhaling heavily.

"Alright guys. I've enhanced the images to maximum and utilized our graphics program to compensate for the missing frames." He pushed another button. "Let's run her at one-tenth speed and see what we can see."

Emerging frame by frame, the primordial colossus soared gracefully past the *Harbinger's* central hull camera. The images were as plain as day. Its four flippers and enormous jaws, lined front to back with interlocking teeth, were clearly visible. Then it traveled beyond the range of the ship's fixed position viewers and was gone.

For a long moment, Jake and his comrades sat there, their glazed-over eyes fixated on the static that replaced the startling images.

It was the sheriff of Paradise Cove that finally spoke up. "Unbelievable. Doc, I'm no paleontologist, but that sure looks like the creature you showed me."

"Yeah, it does," Amara concurred. She licked her lips. "Based on the shape of its skull, I'm not sure it's the exact same species. But if it isn't, it's damn close. And, it's definitely what fed on our frozen fish." She cleared her throat. "I don't know about you guys, but I could use a stiff drink right about now."

"Sounds good to me," Adam said. His voice was hoarse from the dryness in his throat. "You buying?"

"I sure am." Amara stood unsteadily. "I've got a bottle of twelve-year-old scotch sitting in my desk drawer I was saving for a special occasion. I think this qualifies."

She moved to her glass-covered desk, retrieving the bottle and a pair of tumblers, then made her way back to her seat.

"I've only got two glasses," she mentioned. "Anyone care to drink out of the bottle?"

"Don't worry about it," Jake said. "I don't drink anymore."

"That figures." Amara grinned. "But, you never know. Before this thing is over, you might end up starting again."

His only reply was a partial nod. Lost in thought, he watched the two friends clink their glasses together in celebratory toasts.

"Watcha thinking about, big Jake?" Amara said after a moment.

"What? Oh, sorry, my mind was wandering."

"That's alright," Adam chortled as he emptied his glass. "You seem pretty down though, for someone who helped discover a living marine monster from the time of the dinosaurs!"

Amara leaned over and spoke into Adam's ear. "I forgot to tell you, Jake lost some close friends to our animal. And, there have been several other deaths attributed to it over the last few days."

"Oh Jesus, I'm sorry, man," Adam stammered. "I had no idea."

"How could you?" Jake replied, suddenly serious. "I'm just trying to figure out the best way to go about it, that's all."

"The best way to go about what?" Amara said through a scotch-inspired grin. "To spend all the money you're going to make from being interviewed about our discovery?"

"No, the best way to *kill* our discovery."

"What?"

"You heard me." His eyes as hard as agates, Jake reached for the radio at his belt. "Dispatch, this is Jake. Come in."

There was nothing but garbled static.

He made two more ineffectual attempts. Glowering, he wiped his hands on his pants and rose to his feet. "I'm going up on deck to get a transmission through to my dispatcher. I'm scheduling a news conference in regard to our scaly friend."

Jake pointed his walkie-talkie at the video monitor.

"A . . . news conference? Amara stared thunderstruck. "Don't you think that's a little sensationalistic at this point? You could start a panic."

"When that 'animal,' as you choose to call it, returns to Paradise Cove and starts ripping apart people and boats in broad daylight, *then* you'll have a panic." Jake cracked his knuckles one by one. "To prevent that, I have to shut down boating both in and out of the marina. People are going to want to know why. And I'm going to tell them."

Amara and Adam exchanged glances.

"You know, Jake, it really is just an animal," she said. "I'm truly sorry about your friends, but that doesn't make the thing evil. It's just doing what any other animal does to survive."

"It's a confirmed man-eater, doc," he responded evenly. "And it's got to be stopped."

"Yes, it does." Amara moved closer to him. "But that doesn't mean we have to kill it. If you can give me a little time, I think we might be able to capture it."

"Capture it?" Jake nearly choked. "Are you kidding me? You saw the size of that thing. Capture it with what, an aircraft carrier?"

Amara's voice began to rise. "I don't know yet. It's something we have to work on."

"What would be the point?" Jake asked. "And even if you could confine it, what would you feed it? Your precious whales?"

"Look, *sheriff*, we're talking about a unique, possible one-of-a-kind life form. It may be the last of its kind. As a research specimen alone it could be invaluable."

Jake scoffed. He knew she was getting angry, but he didn't care. "Whatever. I'm going up to make my call and then I'm heading back." He pointed a finger at Adam. "I'm going to need a copy of that footage, ASAP. It's evidence."

"Uh . . . no problem, big guy."

"Thanks, I'll be back in a few minutes."

Jake felt the intensity of Amara's stare as he walked toward the nearby stairwell. Suddenly, her glass clattered to the floor, fragmenting as she sprang out of her chair.

"Hey, Jake," she called to him, breathing scotch as she caught up to him.

"Yes, doc?" Jake paused to check his radio settings.

"It might be better if we bring the *Harbinger* back to Paradise Cove, and tow your boat along with us."

"What for?"

"It's quite possible our pliosaur had decided Harcourt Marina is part of its hunting territory. If it has, a ship this size is immune to an attack – at least, much more so than your little center console. Also, you might need me for your press conference. Last but not least, if we're going after this animal, we'll need my submersible repaired and running, something that is going to require more resources than we have here onboard."

Jake gave her an analytical look. "You're very persuasive, doc. Fine. I'll make my call and you start prepping things on your end. How much time will it take before we can get under way?"

"I'd say fifteen or twenty minutes. I'll radio Joe and Willie to see if they've finished rigging the explosives. Once they have, we'll weigh anchor."

"Sounds good," Jake said. "I'll be topside if you need me. Let me know when you're ready."

"No problem." She smiled cooperatively.

———

Amara remained immobile while Jake made his way back above decks. She waited patiently, her eyes alert and ears pricked. Finally satisfied, she jogged back to Adam's station and grabbed him by one shoulder.

"I need you to go online for me, quickly."

"What for?"

"I want the contact info for Fish and Wildlife, in the Department of the Interior, and the National Oceanic and Atmospheric Administration Fisheries, in the Department of Commerce, both in regard to the ESA. And as quickly as you can, please."

"The ESA?" Adam hung a confused sign on his face.

"The Endangered Species Act," Amara said. "Now hurry!"

Turning to keep watch as he typed furiously, Amara reached for her radio.

"Hey, Willie, it's Amara. How's it going?"

"We just about done," Willie radioed back. Amara could hear the whistling sea air in the background. "Da fuses are ready and we about ta cut da whale loose. Dis ting stinks like da devil, mon!"

"Good work. Cut the carcass loose and let's get moving. Tell Joe to weigh anchor. I want us under way in ten minutes or less."

"Okay . . . where we goin?"

"Back to the marina." Amara took a two-page printout from Adam, scanned it and smiled. "It looks like we've got a press conference to attend, old friend. And after that, a date with a monster."

"Oh, Lordy. Now don't dat sound wonderful."

The pliosaur drifted motionless, basking in the midday sun. Its considerable presence was betrayed by the flock of seabirds hovering above it, waiting to obtain scraps from one of its messy kills.

It had lain comatose for several hours, submerging only once, when it detected an approaching ocean liner. It sounded as the metallic monster passed overhead, remaining immobile beneath the surface until the noisy ship faded far into the distance.

Resurfacing later in an explosive blast of water vapor, the creature remained at the surface like the tiny island it was, its broad back bereft of vegetation. Oblivious to the wheeling gulls and the schools of baitfish that explored its vast bulk, it waited for something to draw its attention.

Moments later, it was unceremoniously yanked from its slumber. The cause was a reverberation of prodigious proportion that struck it to its core. The shockwave resonated throughout the surrounding waters, scattering birds and fish alike. Its origin was many miles away, and completely alien in nature. Still, to an opportunistic predator, it might be indicative of an unexpected source of food such as an underwater earthquake or landslide.

With its hunger and curiosity both stimulated, the pliosaur sprang to life. It filled its massive lungs and submerged. Powering its body along with rapid strokes of its boat-sized flippers, it cruised in the direction of the stimulating echo. At thirty miles an hour, it would arrive there in minutes.

SEVENTEEN

Two miles off the coast of Paradise Cove, the great white shark continued its relentless quest, scenting its way along the region's thermocline as it searched for prey. Bereft of a swim bladder, the six thousand pound predator was unable to remain suspended while at rest, and forced to swim endlessly through life.

At twenty-three feet in length, the giant *Carcharodon carcharias* female was at the peak of her power, a genetically perfect eating machine that feared virtually nothing except pods of killer whales.

Having been forced to give up the drifting sperm whale carcass to the encroaching orcas, the great fish now hunted in desperation. Her tremendous appetite had only been fueled further by the brief mouthfuls of fetid flesh she'd wrenched from the giant cetacean's remains. Now unbearably voracious, she was becoming more aggressive by the minute.

Suddenly, she twisted her giant body to and fro, jaws opening and closing, then turned in a more easterly direction. Her incredible sense of smell had detected something. Working feverishly, her olfactory system broke down and analyzed the scent. It was blood – mammalian. The odor was heavily diffused, miniscule in quantity, perhaps just a few ounces per several million gallons of seawater.

Increasing her speed with powerful thrusts of her man-sized tail, the huge fish cruised toward the source of the blood trail. It was coming from the nearby shoreline. The seas beneath her became shallower, and the female became more and more aroused.

The scent grew stronger. She could sense the food source somewhere up ahead. Soon, she would find it. And this time *nothing* would force her from her kill.

As he leaned over the *Harbinger's* railing, Jake couldn't help likening the crowd of reporters to a pack of bloodthirsty hyenas. Just last week, he'd watched a documentary on the spotted variety, cackling hysterically as they tore a zebra mare and her foal into bloody pieces. His jaw muscles slowly tightened. He had a feeling his impromptu press conference would end up being just as messy.

Amara moved next to him, touching him gently on the shoulder. "Are you sure about this?" she asked, as she studied the frenzied group directly below them. Ignoring the array of inquiries they yelled up, she shielded her eyes against the relentless barrage of flashbulbs.

"I'm used to dealing with the press, doc," he said coolly. "I've dealt with far worse than this."

"Yes. Listen, just so you know, I'm with you on this, one hundred percent. I would, however, like to know what you're going to tell them."

"The truth." He reached for his carry bag and turned toward Willie. To his amusement, the *Harbinger's* first mate seemed even more apprehensive than his captain as he took in the sea of reporters.

Jake grinned. "Don't worry, Willie. This is Paradise Cove, not Salem. They're not going to burn us at the stake."

"Maybe not, mon. But den again, ya never know."

Jake caught Amara's eye. "You ready?"

"You go on and get yourself situated," she replied, exhaling long and low. "I'll be down in a second."

Jake nodded. He moved easily, descending the research vessel's creaking gangplank. At the bottom, a group of uniformed officers were waiting to escort him to the podium Paradise Cove's town council had put together.

Amara remained motionless as Jake vanished into the crowd. Her lips were pursed, her brow furrowing up. She noticed Willie staring at her with an amused expression on his face.

"What?" she started. "Why are you looking at me like that?"

"Oh, no ting, boss," he said. He gave her an appraising look. "I was just tinking. Dat's all."

"Thinking about what?"

"Dat mon. I tink ya really be likin' 'im."

"Like Jake? Gee, I really hadn't thought about it but . . . yes, I guess, I do." Her wistful expression hardened. "Not that it matters."

Willie studied her intently. "Why, cause 'im married?"

"No, his wife died tragically a few years ago. But he blames himself for her death."

"Was it his fault?"

"Of course not."

Rising on her toes with her arms folded across her chest, Amara stared petulantly into the crowd, struggling to make out Jake's location amid the bickering paparazzi. She glimpsed him for a fleeting moment. Then he was gone.

"I'm worried he'll never get over it." She started to sulk, realizing she was battling her own emotions. "It's been three years, Willie. Don't you think that's enough time to mourn?"

"Everyone can master a grief but he dat has it. Ya know dat."

"Romeo and Juliet?"

"Nah, *Much Ado about Nutting.*" Willie grinned reassuringly at her. He reached over and put one arm around her shoulders, giving her a comforting hug. "Well, ya better get goin. I keep an eye out for any email from da ESA."

"Thanks, but it'll be a good thirty-six hours before even a preliminary verdict," she said, forcing herself to smile. As she moved toward the gangplank, she looked back. "I just realized something. The pliosaur killed one of Jake's closest friends. It doesn't matter if he does get over his wife, he'll end up hating me for protecting it."

Willie shook his head. "I tink ya assumin too much. But time will tell."

Nodding her head, Amara brooded her way down to the concrete dock that ran parallel to Paradise Cove's deepwater drop-off. Accompanied by police, she wound her way toward Jake.

Despite the circumstances, the big lawman appeared quite at ease with his surroundings, hobnobbing with a group of well-dressed business types. As she mentally separated herself from the mob scene, she unexpectedly found herself staring at the length and breadth of the huge pier.

Suddenly, she could no longer hear the crowd. The bits and pieces of an idea started to coalesce inside her head. It was an exciting notion, albeit challenging in both implication and application. She puffed out her cheeks, blew out a hiss of a breath. It would take a miracle to make her idea work. But then again, the way things were going, she was due for one.

———

As its massive body executed repeated figure-eights a hundred yards outside the marina, the ravenous great white shark grew frantic. The irrepressible need to consume flesh was beginning to overpower its innate cautiousness, pushing it to the brink of madness.

The source of the great fish's distress was an unprecedented sensory overload, caused by the cacophony of stimuli emanating from the wooden pilings directly in front of her. The sounds of splashing bodies and flailing limbs, along with the delightful scent and taste of discarded fish parts and blood, lured her into the area. With these enticing sensations was a painful barrage of noises being emitted by an assortment of fast-moving forms that swept over her with frightening regularity.

On edge and starving, the female reached her boiling point. An experienced hunter, she knew that the slow-moving bipeds by the docks were not her usual prey, but her finely tuned senses were overwhelmed. Slowly but surely, her brain began to misinterpret the stimuli they gave off as that emitted by the area's resident sea lion population.

Finally, the female's senses betrayed her completely. She shook her head and flew into a feeding frenzy, unable to differentiate between edible and non-edible objects. Swimming in tighter and tighter circles, she entered the marina proper. Her enormous mouth, filled with serrated teeth bigger than a man's palm, snapped reflexively at anything within range.

Up ahead, in less than twenty feet of water, she detected a small group of clumsily swimming pinnipeds. Twisting her three-ton body in their direction, she built up speed. Oblivious to all else, the huge predator began to stalk them.

His strong features well anchored, Jake looked down from his podium at the crowd.

Seated on the stage to his left was a group of local business owners. This included members of the town council, the harbormaster, and Amara Takagi. On the landing below was a colorful field of photographers, reporters and journalists. There was a smattering of local shop employees and patrons, as well as uniformed personnel.

Jake paused for a moment to wipe a trace of sawdust off the podium with his fingertips. He tapped hard on the microphone head before he continued.

"Good afternoon, everyone. I want to thank you all for coming." His voice emanated loudly from the overhead speakers. "Before I go into details, please be aware, that effective immediately and until further notice, my office is shutting down all boating activity in and out of Paradise Cove."

A harsh wave of inhalation traveled through the astonished audience, followed by an increasingly turbulent sea of finger-pointing, questions and comments. Jake waited for the inevitable tumult to die down, then pointed at a wiry reporter in the front row.

"Yeah, hi, sheriff . . . Mike Hodges from the Tampa Bay Herald," the bald man said. "We were told you uncovered the identity of Brad Harcourt's killer. What new information do you have?"

"You'll find out in a minute, Mike," Jake advised. He ignored the sea of raised hands and continued speaking. "I have a statement to make, after which all your questions will be answered as quickly as possible."

Oblivious to the crowd's response, Jake reached for the bag he'd tucked inside the podium, and placed it in plain sight.

"For those of you who are not aware, over the last few days there have been a number of deaths in and around the waters of Paradise Cove. I doubt you knew Phil Starling or Angelo Melito, but I imagine many of you did know, or at least came into contact with, Bradford Harcourt."

He gauged the crowd's reaction to the unpopular teen.

"All of these individuals had one thing in common." Jake said as he unzipped the bag in front of him. "They were all killed by the same animal. And until this creature can be tracked down and dealt with, I am closing the harbor."

Jake stoically waited for the shouting to subside. He gave Amara a sideways glance, drew a deep breath, then extracted the pliosaur's tooth. He held it up, shielding his eyes as flashbulbs went off by the score.

"This is a piece of tooth that was extracted from the transom of a boat the creature attacked," Jake said. He held it at arm's length, moving it from side to side. "I say a *piece* because, as big as it is, it is an incomplete specimen. Even so, it is still as large as the tooth of an adult sperm whale."

"Are you telling us some whale ate those people?" Mike Hodges yelled.

"No," Jake said. He placed the tooth on the podium in front of him, its needle-sharp tip pointing straight up. "Our research indicates the creature that lost this tooth is larger than most of the whales around here, and that it feeds on them as well."

"You keep calling this thing a creature," Mike managed over the increasingly raucous crowd. "Exactly what kind of animal is it?"

"I'm going to let someone else answer that question," Jake said. He gestured for Amara. "This is Doctor Amara Takagi from the Worldwide Cetacean Society. She's an expert on marine life, and the commander of the research vessel *Harbinger*, anchored alongside us."

Her eyes pensive, Amara stood up and walked stiffly to the podium. She paused alongside Jake, whispering as he stepped back. "Nice work, sheriff." She covered the microphone with her hand. "Tell me something. Do you always throw your friends to the wolves?"

Jake suppressed a smirk. "Listen, you're our resident marine expert. If you want to make a case for this creature's preservation, this is the best opportunity you're going to get. He winked at her. "So quit complaining and go for it."

Her eyes narrowed, Amara took possession of the microphone. She looked down, fidgeting her way through the disorganized stack of papers she carried. She started to speak, recoiling when her first words blared out, startling her.

"Sorry about that," she said, adjusting her distance from the mike. A breeze kicked up, blowing strands of hair in front of her face. She shook her head to clear her vision. "The uh, creature in question is a unique specimen. It is a leftover from the lower Cretaceous – a hitherto thought to be extinct species of pliosaur."

"English, please!" someone yelled out.

"Right . . ." Amara hesitated. She shot Jake a hateful look. Exhaling heavily, she lowered her eyes. "It's a . . . marine reptile from the time of the dinosaurs."

For a moment . . . silence. Then, derisive laughter ensued.

If Jake thought the journalists and paparazzi were ill-mannered before, their reaction to Amara's statement made their previous behavior look downright polite. The verbal abuse was unrelenting, complete with heckling catcalls, and continued until Jake grabbed the mike.

"That's enough. This is a news conference, not a free-for-all."

"Yeah, right, Sheriff Braddock. Manny Silver from the Miami Inquirer, here." A pot-bellied reporter with bushy eyebrows raised his hand. "Are you and your girlfriend trying to tell us there's a dinosaur running around eating people? Cause if you are, I gotta say you guys got a lot of balls, *and* a hell of an imagination!"

"It's not a dinosaur, it's a marine reptile," Amara said, leaning toward the microphone in an effort to be heard.

Jake calmed her with a raised hand.

"The creature we're talking about lives in the water," he said. He found himself wondering if Manny had any outstanding parking tickets, and fought down the urge to call him what he really wanted to. "It swims, it doesn't run."

"Oh, give us a break," the journalist shot back, smirking at his colleagues. "I want to make sure we're hearing you right. You're actually trying to get us to believe you have some sort of dinosaur on the loose in the waters around Paradise Cove!"

Jake glowered at him. "Obviously, you weren't here earlier when the medics wheeled one of its victims out of here. Or rather, half of him."

"That was a boating accident."

"Manny, you can spin this any way you want. We have definitive proof this creature exists. The problem is not convincing a posturing skeptic like you, it's how we're going to deal with it."

"Definitive proof, eh? Well, I hope it's more convincing than that tooth you've got sitting there."

Jake reached into his shirt pocket, extracting the DVD Adam Spencer made for him, and held it up.

"This disc contains footage of the animal in question. It was filmed a few days ago, after the creature attacked a large sperm whale. The whale's carcass and the damage to it were documented by the scientists of the *Harbinger*." Jake turned a deaf ear to the reporter's next comment and continued. "After this news conference, my office will be emailing the footage to the national networks, at which time your collective doubts should all be erased. If they're not, however . . . you two gentlemen are welcome to come back this evening and do some snorkeling in our quaint little marina." Jake smiled humorlessly at them and pointed at a distant section of the docks. "I'll arrange for you to use the exact same spot where this 'dinosaur' of ours made a meal out of the husband and wife that owned that bloodstained sailboat over there. Sound good?"

Before either reporter could respond to his "invitation," they were all distracted by the sound of screaming.

Moving to the edge of the stage, Jake shielded his eyes with the back of one hand and sought to pinpoint the source. His eyes picked up the panicky movements of a dark-haired teenager wearing brightly colored swim trunks. He was running full out across the sand and heading right for the press corps. Plunging into the crowd with no regard for personal safety, the teen bolted toward the stage. He made straight for the podium, hysterically crying all the while.

Jake wasted no time and sprang off the stage. His foot became entangled in the microphone cord and he pitched forward. He landed hard, dispersing the reporters closest to him. Regaining his footing, he charged through the crowd, intercepting the gasping fifteen-year-old at the halfway point.

"Whoa, hold on now, kiddo! What's going on? What's wrong?" Jake dropped to one knee, holding the frightened teen by the shoulders in an effort to reassure him and keep him from collapsing.

"M-my . . . sister . . . she . . ."

The boy was struggling to stand, his breath coming in ragged gasps.

"What about your sister?" Jake pressed, looking anxiously in every direction. A growing series of cries drew his gaze away from the terrified youngster, up towards the nearby beach. Paradise Cove's private beach was a picturesque swathe of white sand that formed a secluded swimming and tanning area. Typically crammed with beachcombers and sunbathers, it was nestled between the marina's maze of boat docks and the vintage concrete pier.

Jake released his grip on the youth and rose to his full height. He espied a flurry of movement near the water's edge. Groups of people were rushing toward the surf and pointing at something.

"A shark . . . a shark got my sister!"

Jake stared at the distraught boy, blinking rapidly. He craned his neck and peered over the nearest group of reporters, staring past the rumbling waves, out toward the froth-coated waters of Paradise Cove.

Less than a hundred feet from shore, in water thirty feet deep, was a girl not much older than the near-faint adolescent at his feet. She was open-mouthed and terror-stricken, flailing away with hands and feet in a desperate attempt to stay afloat.

Jake focused hard and his blood ran cold.

The water all around her was a bright crimson.

With a quick yell to Amara, he barreled through the crowd. Bowling over anyone unfortunate enough to be caught in his path, he stripped off his uniform shirt, boots, and gun belt and hobbled toward the shoreline. Like spawning lemmings, the reporters followed him.

Oblivious to all the flashbulbs, Jake sprinted to the water's edge and dove in. Powering his way through the stinging surf, he swam with a speed that would have made Samantha proud. Yard by yard, he closed the distance, his teeth clenched, his energy focused on fighting the tide. He could hear the girl's screams even underwater, and willed himself to swim faster. With the powerful undertow, he had only moments to reach her. Once she went under, she'd be lost.

Jake raised his head, gauging the distance between them. *Only forty feet to go.* He sucked in a breath and dove beneath an incoming swell. His confidence began to grow. In a few seconds he'd have her.

Then he saw the shark.

Jake's cry of astonishment cost him his air. He made a desperate lunge for the surface, spitting seawater and rubbing his palms against his eyes. It was the biggest fish he ever saw – the size of Dean Harcourt's stretch limo. Its dark grey dorsal fin measured over three feet in height and sliced through the water like an enormous scythe. Supremely confident in its power, the great white circled slowly, its lifeless black eyes locked onto its prey. Jake took a deep breath. Ignoring his searing lungs and the prowling shark, he made a break for the girl.

He'd watched numerous documentaries on white sharks over the years. Predictably, the girl's attacker had used the chomp-and-spit attack they usually relied upon when hunting sea lions. After inflicting a single, devastating bite, they circled nearby, waiting for their victim to expire from hemorrhage and shock.

Jake also knew that when a *Carcharodon carcharias* erroneously attacked a human being, it typically ignored people attempting a rescue. That was why so many shark attack victims survived their ordeals.

As he reached the stricken teen, Jake passed directly over the swirling vortex created by the shark. The traumatized girl was too weak to struggle and collapsed into his arms. She was pale and had suffered a horrific bite to her right hip. All of the skin and much of the surrounding muscle was stripped away, with blood seeping from a dozen gaping puncture wounds that traveled all the way to the bone.

Jake turned sideways and cradled the girl with one arm. Summoning all of his remaining strength, he made for the nearby dock. He hesitated, his breaths becoming shallow and rapid.

The great white was in his way.

———◆———

Creeping silently closer, the predator prepared to strike. It had successfully stalked its distracted prey while it remained at the surface. Now only fifty yards away, it spread its jaws and began to accelerate. In seconds, the distance between them would be nothing. The prey was small and weak. Despite the presence of other life forms, it could not escape.

It increased velocity to close the distance and attacked.

———◆———

They were facing the worst possible death; Jake could feel it in his bones. The shark wasn't behaving at all like the great whites he'd seen on cable. It was tenacious, relentless, and it simply would not give up its victim.

At first, Jake thought the giant fish was playing the waiting game, circling patiently as he struggled toward the dock. He soon realized its movements were deliberately and systematically cutting off their only escape route. It was consciously stalking the wounded child – and now him.

Its first approach was an exploratory one, with the fish deliberately brushing Jake with one of its huge pectoral fins. Like a giant rasp, the saw-toothed skin covering its flipper ripped a jagged gash across his ribs. He grunted a curse. With saltwater eating into it, the cut was painful and bled profusely. Worse, the impact pushed them twenty feet further from the dock, leaving them bobbing helplessly.

The ghostly apparition continued to circle, moving closer and closer. He could see its huge, gray head, just beneath the surface. With its jaws opening and closing, the shark seemed completely unfishlike. It reminded him more of a hungry Rottweiler, its tooth-lined mouth awash in anticipation.

Suddenly, the shark pulled a hard one-eighty and raced toward them. It accelerated, its submerged maw gaping wide, its dorsal fin and tail sawing through the surface. It was less than a hundred feet away and closing fast.

Jake's heart stopped.

Its mouth was big enough to take them both.

Furious at having left his gun belt on the beach, he looked for anything he could use to fend off the shark. There was nothing.

The nearest accessible dock was still twenty-five feet away and jammed with reporters, none of whom budged. Their lenses were all focused on the life and death spectacle.

"Hold on, chief. I'm coming!"

Jake's jaw dropped so low he nearly choked on saltwater. Chris Meyers was charging in to save them. With a determined gleam in his eye and a float ring worn bandoleer-style, the teen forced his way through the crowd. Jake spat out a nasty mouthful of brine and grinned at the irony.

Of all the people watching, only my off-duty, chronically irresponsible deputy has the balls to help.

If Jake wasn't fighting for his life he would have laughed.

"Out of the way, you guys!" Chris yelled. Moving at a full clip, he reached the end of the dock and crouched down to dive. As he sprang frontward, his sneaker caught on the strap of a reporter's camera bag and he tripped. He staggered forward, his eyes widening with horror. There was an appalling thump as his temple struck a bordering piling and he collapsed, tumbling forward headfirst into the water.

A groan escaped Jake's lips as he watched Chris sink like a stone. A moment later, the donut-shaped life preserver did its job and his inert form came bobbing to the surface. Eyes closed and arms hanging limply, he lay there, shifting with the waves with blood trickling from the side of his head.

Jake shook his head and uttered a sigh. Out of the corner of his eye, he watched Chris float by. He was relieved to see he was still breathing – which might be more than he could say for himself in a few minutes.

Realizing that the end was upon him, Jake gazed once more at the dock. His eyebrows crimped down over his eyes. He noticed Albert Mulling, a former marine-turned fisherman he knew for years. Petrified with fear, the bearded charter captain stood like so many others: staring wide-eyed and clinging to an exposed piling.

Jake yelled hoarsely, "Albert, when it comes for me, you dive in and get the girl! Then get Chris. Do it, and don't screw up!"

Despite the shivering panic that overwhelmed him, Albert swallowed hard and nodded.

Jake turned to face his demise. He started treading water with his feet only. Grasping the unconscious girl by the shoulders, he held her close. His plan was simple. At the last possible moment, he would toss her as far from himself as possible, aiming for the dock. If successful, he would deprive the shark of at least *one* of its victims.

He felt around hurriedly, retrieving the heavy pocketknife nestled in his pants pocket. He made himself a promise; however horrific his own death might be, he would make sure the fish paid a dear price for its meal.

The shark was almost on top of them. Swirling helplessly in its wake, Chris bobbed past its dorsal fin like a rubber ducky. It ignored his limp form, focusing entirely on the bleeding teen. Its yard-wide mouth broke the surface of the water. Jake exhaled heavily as he saw its jaws. For him, there would be no escaping its power. Clenching the knife in his teeth, he kicked hard and hoisted the girl out of the water, preparing to throw her clear. His eyes narrowed into navy-colored slits. It was twenty feet away ... then ten. Jake took a deep breath and hauled back, but before he could execute his throw, the shark stopped dead in its tracks.

With its guillotine jaws an arm's length away, the great white abruptly ceased moving. Its eerie black eyes rolled wildly in their sockets, a strand of seaweed sliding down its sandpaper-coated snout. It looked like it ran into an invisible wall.

His own eyes bulging in disbelief, Jake clutched the wounded adolescent protectively before him. He lowered her gently into the water, staring confused at the giant shark. It remained where it was, its head thrashing back and forth. For a moment, he thought it was playing possum – studying its food before striking. Then the shark twitched spasmodically, its mighty jaws opening and closing like a giant bear trap. It raised the darker, dorsal portion of its fore end above the surface of the water, its teeth gnashing together repeatedly.

As Jake watched, the white continued its bizarre elevation. Soon, its pale belly and pectoral fins were fully visible, its entire upper third rising above the swells. The waters of the marina began to convulse.

Mystified by the shark's gravity-defying behavior, Jake recoiled suddenly. The water pressure around him had changed, and a huge, submerged shadow began to grow beneath the great white. He gave a throaty gasp, realizing with dreadful certainty that something had stopped the shark.

Something bigger ... *much* bigger.

A collective gasp of astonishment swept over the marina. Like a cobalt blue mountaintop, the pliosaur broke the surface, the great white pinioned within its vice-like jaws. Jake desperately sidestroked away as it rose up. Seawater ran in rivers down its muzzle as it hoisted its prey out of the water and held it suspended in the air.

Jake glanced back and mouthed a curse. Unconscious, Chris was drifting right to the creature. Blissfully bobbing up and down, he was completely oblivious that he was floating next to the father of all man-eaters. In fact, the kid wore a ridiculously sublime expression – one more fitted to a resting infant. Grinning, he gave a half-spin as he curtsied past the pliosaur's giant fangs, even brushing up against its thick-scaled skin.

A deep, vibrating rumble echoed from the creature. Increasing in volume, its roar boomed like a thunderhead, drowning out the cries of those who watched, mesmerized. Reveling in its kill, it heaved the quivering shark high into the air. The blackish centers of its blood-red eyes glanced downward, dispassionately surveying the terrorized life forms below.

The pliosaur let out an indescribable hiss, then whipped its crocodile-shaped head down in a sweeping arc, slamming the great white against the surface of the water. Duplicating and reduplicating its attack, it savagely shook the paralyzed shark, smashing it with indescribable power. The impacts sent waves taller than a man surging up and over the docks, washing people and coolers into the water, and sending several nearby boats careening noisily into each other.

Jake spotted Chris, still comatose, traveling past the beast and toward the dock, moving three feet at a time with each wave created by the pliosaur's assault. Turning toward shore, the sheriff cradled the unconscious girl against his chest and paddled as fast as he could. He looked back, his disbelieving eyes fixated on the impossible.

The pliosaur, satisfied that the shark's back was broken, set about swallowing its dying prey. The horrified crowd looked on as the world's largest known carnivorous fish disappeared down the prehistoric predator's throat. It was a laborious process, but soon, only the shark's six-foot crescent-shaped tail remained. Then, after a colossal gulp, even that was gone.

The creature emitted a rumble of satisfaction. Like an engorged python, it lowered its head onto the water and began to float contently, its huge body drifting steadily toward shore, moved along by the incoming swells.

A short while later, bright flashes of light assailed its vision. Grumbling irritably, the pliosaur closed its eyes and sank beneath the surface, seeking to escape the painful onslaught of flashbulbs. It sensed the shifting of the tide and twisted its armored body, its belly scraping the bottom, ripping up the surrounding coral reefs as it began to force its way toward the deep.

Eager for the freedom of the open sea, the creature increased its speed, its monstrous body displacing hundreds of tons of seawater. Suddenly, it stopped, its deep-set eyes blinking repeatedly. Distracted by a full belly, it had unwittingly drifted into the very heart of the marina. It was trapped within a maze of wood pilings sprouting up from the seafloor, a bristling forest of submerged timber. The imprisoned reptile uttered a water-muffled roar of defiance and lashed out. Jaws spread, it launched itself against the support columns, smashing into them with unbelievable force. Above it, scores of terrified journalists screamed and fled for their lives.

So powerful was the predator's initial charge, that the central regions of the aged docks tore loose from their foundations, the thick columns splintering from the force of its blows. Roaring repeatedly, the pliosaur continued to fling itself to and fro, forcing its gigantic body through the unnatural barrier. Unable to withstand its furious bid for freedom, the docks collapsed in on themselves. Accompanying them were a dozen astonished reporters who stood their ground, brazenly snapping pictures even as they were drawn into the violent waters.

———

Back on shore, Jake Braddock staggered from the surf, the unconscious girl cradled in his arms. His breath came in harsh gasps as he stumbled across the debris-strewn sand. He looked around, spotting Chris Meyers being carried from the docks by Albert Mulling and a second man.

"Doc, call an ambulance, on the double!" He bellowed at Amara as he lowered the girl onto a beach towel.

Ignoring the stream of blood that seeped from his own side, Jake watched Amara struggling through the crowd, trying to keep her balance as she made the call. Half the town was gathered near the water's edge, their eyes focused on the prehistoric monster cruising just outside their shattered marina.

"Here, put pressure on these spots and hold tight!" He barked at a pair of local kids. He looked up, just in time to watch the pliosaur vanish from view. "Make sure you keep her wounds closed, or she'll bleed to death."

He glanced over at the bystanders gathered around Chris. Albert was bent over his limp form, his weathered face clouded with concern.

Jake jogged over and checked his deputy's pulse and breathing. There was a nasty gash on the kid's temple. He needed medical attention.

Chris gave a painful moan and slowly opened his eyes. "J-Jake?"

Jake leaned close to him, resting his palm on the kid's chest to keep him from moving or trying to rise. "Take it easy. You took a hard knock, but you'll be okay."

Chris' eyes rolled in their sockets like a Hail Mary-tossed pair of craps. "Geez, chief . . . I really made a . . . ass out of myself, huh?"

Jake shook his head emphatically. "No way, you were the bravest one out there. If you didn't distract the shark when you did, she would have had me for sure. You saved my ass, kid. You're a hero."

"Really?" Chris swallowed hard, trying to bring his eyes into focus. "Wow. Hey, what's all that . . . screaming?"

Jake glanced toward the dock, shaking his head. "It's nothing, kid. Just close your eyes and rest. I'll check in on you at the hospital later."

"Okay . . . thanks, chief."

Jake watched as Chris' eyes closed and he faded out. He gave Albert a quick nod of thanks and jogged off through the crowd. He looked left and right, searching impatiently for Amara. "Damn it, doc, where the hell is that ambulance?"

"It's on its way!" she yelled back from forty feet away. She had her radio pressed tightly to her ear to hear over the crowd.

Jake spotted a pair of state troopers moving toward him. He closed the distance between them with a few quick strides. "Guys, clear all the people off the docks and get everyone off the beach. Once backup arrives, we'll take my patrol boat out." He pointed toward the collapsed section of the docks. "We have to start circling the outside of the marina. A bunch of people ended up in the water. It looks like most made it to shore, but we need to make sure. The creature's moved off. But it may come back."

He turned and loped over to Amara. The cetaceanist was wide-eyed and trembling.

"Are you okay?" he asked, fighting down the urge to give her a hug.

Her eyes went wide and she gave an involuntary headshake. "Me? What are you *talking* about? You almost got eaten *twice* and you're asking about me?"

Jake gave a morose chuckle and shook his head. "I'm fine, doc. I learned at a very young age that I'm pretty tough to kill."

Amara frowned, bending at the waist and gently touching his injured side. "Yeah? Well, I think you're going to need stitches for that." She handed him his gear and boots.

"I'll be fine. I just need some butterflies." Jake's chest still heaved, and he winced as he donned his shirt and gun belt. He breathed a sigh of relief as a fleet of squad cars and ambulances pulled up. He walked over, waiting until he could speak to the medics taking care of Chris and the badly wounded girl, then guided Amara toward the deserted stage area. As he did, the pliosaur's distant roar shook the dunes beneath their feet.

"Oh my God, Jake, it's unbelievable! He's even bigger than I thought!" Amara exclaimed. She twisted against him, her gaze turning back to the docks.

"I'd go along with that." Jake gazed through haunted eyes at the damaged harbor. "Well, there's one thing we can say for certain . . ."

"And what's that?"

"We don't have to worry about anyone doubting our findings anymore." He wore a resolute expression. "The whole world now knows what we've got swimming around out here. Now we have to figure out what we're going to do about it."

Jake raised a hand to redirect the lens of a shoulder-mounted news camera that was pointed in his face, forcing his way past the irate reporter and his cameraman. He continued leading Amara away from the docks, toward the *Harbinger*.

Behind them, the pandemonium on the beach continued.

Dean Harcourt clicked off the enormous television mounted on his office wall. Disgusted, he sent the expensive device's remote control spiraling across his ornate Louis XIV desk and onto the floor. He drummed his fingers irritably on the wood before heaving himself back into his well-padded chair.

Sprawled on the desk before him lay a dusty mountain of memorabilia: newspapers, photo albums, and scrap books. He thumbed through one, smiling sadly at pictures of himself and Brad out hiking and fly fishing together. His smile flatlined and he closed the book.

The senator sighed heavily. He was surprised to find Brad standing by his side in almost every photo. His brow furrowed into deep crevasses. He began to blink rapidly and slumped down into his chair. His intercom buzzed, giving him a start.

"Senator, I have Mr. Thayer on line three," his secretary said.

Without so much as a "thank you," the stocky politician stretched out his arm and jabbed the phone line's button.

"Hello, Darius."

"Take me off speakerphone."

"Relax, we're alone. You can speak freely."

"Fine. We have a serious problem with the Braddock thing," Thayer said in his idiosyncratic voice. "I think we're going to have to shut down."

The senator took his cigar from its solid jade ashtray. He puffed fiercely on it, staring with hypnotic eyes at its fiercely burning tip before he replied.

"If you're referring to the situation I watched on the television, Darius, I am aware, as is the rest of the world."

"It's amazing, isn't it? I wouldn't believe it if I didn't see the footage myself. Like something out of 'Jurassic Park!' "

"Yes . . . amazing." The senator crushed out his cigar. He wiped his mouth, opened his desk drawer, and extracted a whiskey glass and a bottle of Johnnie. Unscrewing its top, he poured three fingers worth and began to sip.

"I've already called off our spin team," Thayer said. "Damn waste of money. But given what's happened in town, there's no doubt now what killed Brad."

"Indeed."

"So, what's our next move?"

"Our next move . . ." Harcourt held the chunk of crystal to his lips, savoring his drink. As he finished sipping he held the whiskey glass up to the light, peering through the amber-colored liquid. His mind began to wander, and he stared through the half-filled glass as if it were a window to another place or time. "I want you to use those gumshoes you've got in place to find out everything there is to know about the Asian woman that spoke at that press conference. I believe she's some sort of marine biologist. I want to know about her, and her ship."

"Okay . . ." Thayer's voice resonated back. "And we're doing this because . . ."

Harcourt cleared his throat. "Because, as you said, the whole world now knows the identity of my son's killer. And that includes me." His voice was soft at first. Then it hardened. "But more importantly, because I *said* so."

Thayer thought long and hard. "Look, Dean, I sympathize with your loss as much as anyone. But I'm not in the mood for cloak and dagger games right now." An unusually irate tone was beginning to emanate out of the speakerphone. "Why don't you tell me what you're up to? Call it 'professional courtesy,' if you will."

"I'm not up to anything." Harcourt downed the remainder of his drink in a single gulp. Holding the empty tumbler once more to the light, he resumed peering through its translucent surface. "I'm just keeping myself apprised of all the pieces on my chessboard. Because it's just possible one of those pieces may provide me with something I need."

"How so?" Thayer replied instantly.

"And thine eye shall not pity; but life shall go for life, eye for eye, tooth for tooth, hand for hand, and foot for foot."

"Cute, but this isn't Sunday school. Now what the hell are you planning?"

"Just get me the information I asked for, Darius."

There was a long sigh. "Okay, Dean. It's your dime."

There was a sharp click as the lawyer hung up.

Still holding his glass, Harcourt ignored the dial tone and subsequent screeching sound. His countenance began to change; like a shadow creeping catlike across the floor, it transformed from near-catatonia to pure malevolence. An animalistic sneer crinkled his heavy features and his fingers curled shut on his empty tumbler.

There was a sharp, cracking sound and shards of glass spilled out from between his fingers, along with a steady stream of blood. He stared at the shiny droplets. Opening his hand, he studied the ragged lacerations that decorated his thick-skinned palm. He watched the blood continue to trickle onto his desk, running like ruby-colored quicksilver along the plastic-coated sleeve of an opened photo album.

It collected at the bottom of one page, forming a viscous puddle that trembled as it continued to be fed.

"Life shall go for life," he muttered. His eyes gleamed as he ran bloodied digits across a yellowed newspaper article featuring a high school graduation portrait of Brad. His fingertips traced the dead teenager's face, leaving a dull crimson trail. He reached over, grabbing the paper and crushing it into an unrecognizable ball of wood pulp and plasma.

"Oh, yes . . . life shall go for life."

EIGHTEEN

From the shelter of the *Harbinger*, Jake and Amara stared in stunned silence. Below them lay the smoke-obscured desolation that was once Harcourt Marina. Paradise Cove had been gutted before their eyes, the pliosaur's reemergence and second attack so abrupt and overwhelming, there was nothing anyone could do.

The docks were gone, their fragmented deck boards dotting the surface like waterlogged Popsicle sticks. Only the sections closest to shore remained intact. Here and there, strings of shattered pilings jutted up, breaching the water like the vertebrae of some fallen giant. Impaled upon them or settled onto the sandy bottom was the pride of Paradise Cove's fishing fleet, their shattered hulls belching thick clouds of black smoke that smudged the normally pristine skies.

The marina was obliterated. What the creature failed to annihilate during its assault burned in the fires of its aftermath. Harcourt Marina's high-capacity gasoline pumps – their casings fractured by a nineteen-foot speedboat the beast flung into the air like a boomerang – had exploded, immolating everything within a hundred yards.

The destruction was astonishingly complete.

The impetus behind the creature's second attack occurred thirty minutes earlier, less than a mile from shore. Word had spread like wildfire of its appearance and initial assault. A group of camera-wielding fisherman, eager to see the thing for themselves, motored directly over the slow-swimming leviathan as it lounged beneath the surface. Fearfully gunning their engine when it rose up beneath them, they inadvertently tore a jagged groove in the creature's dorsal region with their stainless steel prop.

The pliosaur breached the surface and retaliated. Rearing back, it released a deafening roar and pounced on their boat. The astonished sportsmen screamed in collective terror as their twenty-foot Boston Whaler was hoisted out of the water and bitten in two.

With fiberglass spewing from its jaws, the creature directed its attention to the three survivors flailing in the water. Surging forward with jaws wide open, it crushed them all in one monstrous bite. Seconds later, it emitted a bloodcurdling bellow and began thrashing its head back and forth, frothing the surface of the water and gnashing its reddened teeth loudly together. It whipped its huge head around, focusing its eyes on the dozen fishing and pleasure boats still shadowing it. It uttered a dampened roar, and attacked.

The rubbernecking charter captains and their crews spotted the infuriated behemoth's approach and scattered in every possible direction. The creature somehow sensed their plan and utilized its superior speed to cut off their escape. Herding them like sheep, it accelerated and picked them off one by one. Within minutes, the surface of the harbor was strewn with broken vessels. For those entrapped within the cove, escape was impossible.

Some tried.

The *Travelin' Man*, a forty-foot Albemarle fishing yacht running full out, made for the safety of the sound. At fifty miles an hour, the pliosaur rose up beneath it like a vengeful shadow. Crashing into the big charter boat from below, it fractured it amidships, causing it to flounder and break apart.

A forty-five foot cigarette boat named the *Later Gator* nearly escaped amidst the chaos. At a blinding seventy miles an hour, its velocity was more than a match for the fast moving predator. Unfortunately, the boat's frightened captain was so focused on the prehistoric horror chasing them, he ran full-bore into a passing schooner. There was a tremendous thump as both ships erupted into a huge fireball. The shrieking survivors leapt desperately overboard to escape being burned alive, only to be greeted with an equally gruesome end in the water.

The attack continued for over thirty minutes. Horrified witnesses the world over remained glued to their television screens, watching in utter fascination as the live feed from hovering news choppers documented the disaster. Finally, the giant carnivore swerved back in the direction of the marina. A half-dozen craft still cowered within, hoping to escape its wrath by hiding within the battered waterfront. Its rage unabated, the pliosaur cruised undeterred into water barely deep enough to maneuver. Hissing repeatedly, it pierced the heart of the marina, searching for something to vent its wrath upon.

The state police were assembled and waiting – a tiny island of gray uniforms, clustered together like tin soldiers on one of the few remaining sections of dock. The pliosaur spotted the group and cruised deliberately toward them. As it drew closer, it slowed. Its torn dorsal scales became visible above the waves, and its armored belly started to drag along the bottom. It hesitated, its ruby eyes narrowing. Then it gave a great shudder, its monstrous body swelling with pent up rage. It uttered a terrifying growl and lunged violently forward, casting up huge showers of silt and sand as it determinedly squirmed its way through the shallows, trying to use its flippers like legs.

The troopers exchanged nervous glances but stood their ground, bracing themselves as it loomed closer. The wheezing creature's misshapen head broke the surface and it reared menacingly back, its eyes glaring downward as it prepared to strike. Faces taut, the troopers raised their weapons and waited. Not until its slavering maw was ten feet away, with its foul breath washing over them in noxious billows, was the command finally given.

They fired simultaneously, the thunder of their combined firepower competing with the creature's bellows. It reeled back in pain and confusion as the barrage of bullets and buckshot tore into it, then attacked. Its giant jaws descended with rattlesnake speed, pulverizing the section of docks upon which the troopers stood and engulfing three of them in the process. The survivors shrieked in terror, leaping headlong into the water in an effort to save themselves.

Infuriated, the pliosaur made for the huddled boats, smashing its way past any remaining pilings with violent twists of its gigantic body. Like oversized log cutters, its foaming jaws snapped from side to side, seizing anything that appeared to move, tearing it to pieces. The screams of its victims could be heard a half mile away. All around it, the remaining portions of the docks were engulfed in smoke and flame.

Jake grimaced and closed his eyes. The centerpiece of the town he'd protected for the last three years was being systematically destroyed. Helpless before the creature's primordial power, all he and the surviving residents of Paradise Cove could do was stand by and watch as the financial hub of their quiet coastal community was torn down around them.

———

Haruto Nakamura sat rigidly upright, alone in the austerity of his quarters. His aching ribs unerringly relayed the *Oshima's* sway to him, spasming left and right as the ship lolled lazily back and forth. He could tell from the sensations shimmying through her decks she was running heavy. Her draught was increasing as her freezer holds steadily filled. He nodded his approval. Fortune continued to shine on them. His gaze shifted, becoming intense and unblinking as his hands hovered above his laptop.

He was studying the news footage he found on the web a few minutes earlier. The current reel was pure pandemonium: live footage of an attack on a small town on the Floridian coast. The media was identifying the culprit as some sort of prehistoric reptile that once hunted dinosaurs.

Haruto winced as he watched the creature bulldoze its way through a section of the town's boat docks, its massive back snapping deck boards like matchsticks. People caught in its path were catapulted into the air, their fragile bodies slamming like rag dolls against nearby boats and pilings.

Out of nowhere, Sagato's shade materialized unbidden before him, his mangled remains a frightful specter as he took up position once more at his captain's side. Haruto shuddered and averted his eyes. He'd visited his dead first mate in the forward hold an hour earlier to pay his respects. His frozen corpse was propped up in one corner, encased in a shrink-wrapped shroud. His lifeless eyes peered through the translucent plastic, his mouth open, railing against his unjust fate.

Haruto ignored Sagato's presence and focused on the footage. There was a particular segment that interested him – an exhausted man emerging from the surf after surviving a face to face encounter with the beast. His side was bloodied and he was carrying a badly injured girl. Haruto absentmindedly touched the layers of tape that protected his own injured ribs. He watched as the man laid the girl down, quickly and expertly administered first aid, then attempted to restore order to the disaster unfolding all around him.

Haruto zoomed in on the man, scrolling forward frame by frame as he studied him. His face and physique were strong, his gaze intense. He was bold and fearless, someone born to lead men into battle. Haruto nodded in silent deference to what the man was – the quintessential warrior.

The warrior forced his way through the crowd, grabbing the arm of a nearby woman and guiding her to safety. She sported a dazed look as she turned toward the camera.

There was a knock. Haruto frowned and clicked the pause button. He looked up. "Come in."

Watch Commander Iso Hayama entered, bowing hurriedly. He had a clipboard tucked under one wiry arm and his eyes were bursting.

"Please excuse the interruption, captain-san," he said, moving to stand in front of the captain's desk. "I have our final tallies."

A wave of surprise filtered the pungent smell of shark's blood accompanying Iso, and Haruto arched one eyebrow. "Did you say our *final* tallies, commander?"

"Yes, sir. We've done it. We're filled to capacity and beyond. It's a new record, sir!"

Haruto remained seated. He pursed his lips as he accepted Iso's clipboard, thumbing methodically through the compiled papers. "This is . . . unprecedented, commander."

"Aye, sir. We've brought in more fins than any ship in the history of the company, sir. And in half the time."

"Eleven hundred and four tigers, six hundred and fifty-three makos, and one hundred and seventy-nine great whites? Are these numbers accurate?"

"Absolutely, sir."

"And this last heading, a . . . whale shark? Is this some kind of joke?"

"Um . . . no sir."

Haruto pegged him with a hard stare. "Whale sharks are plankton feeders. How could we possibly hook one?"

"Well sir, we . . ."

"Out with it, commander."

Iso's chin jutted out, his spine straightening like a two-by-four. "Well sir, the spotters noted a very large whale shark swimming past our starboard, less than ten meters from the hull." He hesitated, swallowing hard. "One of the winch crews–"

"Which winch crew, commander?"

"Um, crew number one, sir."

"Go on . . ." Haruto drawled.

"Yes, sir." Iso blinked as droplets of perspiration began to trickle into his eyes. "The crew was about to re-bait when one of them, as a lark of course, flung a bare hook at the fish . . ."

Haruto studied his subordinate. "You mean to tell me he snagged a whale shark with a lobbed hook?"

"Yes, sir. First cast."

"That's amazing," Haruto nodded. "And the hoist was able to handle the fish?"

"Not exactly, sir."

Haruto's eyes narrowed. "Did you damage another one of my winches, commander?"

"No, sir! It took a while, because the fish was so huge, but it eventually tired and we brought it alongside. That's when we realized it was too heavy to bring up . . . so we–"

Haruto could see Iso was beginning to get flustered and raised a calming hand. "Slow down, commander."

Iso took a deep breath. "Yes, sir. We managed to lock a second winch onto the fish, but even conjoined it still kept slipping. It was just too big."

"How big?"

"Over fifty feet. I'd say forty tons."

"So, what did you do?"

Iso swallowed again. "Um . . . two of the men climbed down the cables and cut the shark's fins off alongside the ship, sir."

Haruto gave him an appraising look. "I see. How big are the fins?"

"They're the biggest I've ever seen, sir!" Iso's hands waved wildly. "The pectorals alone are twelve feet long. They each weigh a ton, if not more. It's a bonanza!"

"Easy, commander," Haruto said. "That's very impressive. So, no equipment was damaged?"

"No, sir."

"And no one was hurt?"

"No, sir."

"Then, you've done a good job."

Iso smiled and assumed an "at ease" pose. "Thank you, sir."

"You're welcome. When we return to port, I'm going to recommend you for the position of first mate. In the interim, you're to take over as acting first mate, effective immediately."

Iso's eyes popped and he saluted sharply. "Yes, sir! Thank you, captain-san!"

Haruto began to examine the tallies in detail. "That'll be all."

"Yes, sir." Iso's weight shifted from foot to foot, hesitation plying his face.

Haruto glanced up. "Is there something else?"

Iso's lower lip disappeared for a moment. "Well, sir . . . some of the men have been talking and . . ."

"And what?"

"Well, sir. We've heard the reports about a creature attacking that town off the coast of Florida, and–"

"And?"

"Is it true it's the same animal that killed Mr. Sagato and damaged our ship?"

Haruto felt his jaw tighten. He nodded slowly. "I believe so."

Iso measured his words. "Well, sir, the men are saying, since we brought in that whale shark, maybe we could–"

Haruto's brows strategically fell over his eyes. "That we could what, commander? Try to capture it?"

"Well . . . yes, sir. Its fins would be worth a fortune. We could–"

Haruto sprang to his feet, his eyes brimming with fury. Above his head, the ornate, black lacquered stand that held his family's ancestral swords formed a menacing halo. "We could *what*, commander? Have it rip more winches off our decks? Have it tear this ship out from under us and send our entire complement and cargo straight to the bottom? Is *that* what we could do?"

Iso shrank back fearfully. "N-no, sir! What I meant was–"

Haruto slammed the clipboard down on his desk, his close-cropped hair glinting wildly. "What you meant was you were willing to risk my ship on a fool's venture? Let me tell you something, *commander*, whatever that thing is, it's no cow of a whale shark! You can forget about that promotion. Now get out of my sight and go about your business."

"Y-yes, sir."

Haruto watched as Iso scurried out of the room, bowing repeatedly before closing the door.

He shook his head irritably and sat back down, his knees cracking painfully. *The man's a complete idiot*, he thought. *Where's Sagato when I need him?* He picked up the clipboard, glancing at it, then snorted and sent it clattering across his desk. He tapped his laptop's keyboard, reopening the window containing the Florida attack footage. The scene with the warrior and his woman still remained, their pixels frozen in time.

Haruto gave a cursory glance, his finger lingering over the play button. His eyes widened in disbelief as he studied the woman's face. He zoomed in on her to be absolutely sure, his sudden inhalation a strangled wheeze.

———

Jake's eyes ached as he surveyed the devastation all around him. His shoulders bunched as his hands gripped the *Harbinger's* railing. It was an hour since the creature's last attack. What was once a sprawling maze of boat slips and docked vessels was now a drifting mass of burning debris: a floating graveyard of dead people and broken boats.

Jake exhaled sharply, his nostrils flaring. The acrid smell of burning diesel, wood, and human flesh continued to travel in with the wind. It was a noxious cornucopia that left the nasal passages singed and aching.

Except for the sounds of scavenging gulls, the ruined harbor was without sound. Besides himself, Amara, and the *Harbinger's* skeleton crew, the place was deserted. Surviving state police had cordoned off the area to shield Paradise Cove's inhabitants from harm, setting up road blocks and establishing a two mile-long perimeter. Jake shook his head. He was all too familiar with rescue efforts that came too late.

He turned outward and recoiled. It was the incoming tide, and with it, rising through a veil of whitish smoke, came sobering reminders of how costly the pliosaur's second attack had been. Interspersed with or draped over hunks of debris, its victims were returning home. Torn apart like dismembered dolls, their bodies drifted piecemeal. Those that still had faces stared blankly. Most were unrecognizable to those encountering them as they washed ashore, which was just as well.

Jake released a mournful shudder. He latched onto the frame of the ship's harpoon cannon with one arm, leaning on it to draw strength from the metal. Over the course of the pliosaur's rampage he'd wished repeatedly that the murderous weapon still functioned. He could've ended things then and there.

Something drew his eye downward. Floating face down beneath him was an intact body. Much of the flesh on its back and shoulders was burned away – an agonizing way to die.

Jake's trained eyes instinctively picked out details. The deceased was a Hispanic male . . . early teens . . . brightly colored trunks. Suddenly a swell flung the bobbing corpse against the *Harbinger's* prow with a gong-like thump. Its blackened limbs flopped as it turned right side up.

He spotted its face and gasped.

It was the boy from the beach, the one whose sister he'd saved.

The boy's remaining eye locked onto his, his lifeless expression grim. Jake released his grip on the harpoon cannon and staggered back, ill-equipped to withstand the child's accusatory stare. He backed away, retreating along the *Harbinger's* railing.

There was a loud, snorting sound, and Jake's head snapped back on his spine. He couldn't see it, but the noise was unmistakable. It was close by. His feet started moving and he charged toward the ship's boarding ramp, nearly running over Amara in the process.

His radio in one hand and pistol in the other, Jake exploded onto the fishing pier. He could hear Amara's rapid footsteps behind him as he made his way to the edge of the concrete structure. His eyes strove to pierce all the smoke and debris.

"Jake, what are you going to do?" Amara gasped, shifting her weight and rubbing her bad hip as she caught up to him.

"What the hell do you think?" Jake barked, his Beretta pointed at the water's surface as he prayed for a glimpse of their adversary. "I'm going to get close enough to put a dozen hollow-points into that thing's head!"

"Jake, that gun of yours isn't going to do anything. It'd be like throwing your shoes at an elephant." Amara kept back from the edge of the pier. "We've got to come up with a better idea!"

Before he could respond, Jake's attention was drawn upward. A pair of news helicopters arrived and began to circle the smoldering marina. Filming from a hundred and fifty feet up, the two competing network aircraft gathered footage of the chaos below.

Reluctantly holstering his sidearm, Jake turned his back to the water. He paused as he caught the horrified look on Amara's face. "What is it?" He felt the hairs on the back of his neck prick up, and was afraid to turn and see what she was looking at.

"Isn't that your boat?" Amara asked. She swallowed hard, pointing at a stretch of water a few hundred feet past the docks.

Jake shielded his eyes with one hand and squinted. He cursed. Amara was right. It was the *Infidel*. Alone on the water, the twenty-three foot center console cruised in wide circles. There were three men aboard. Jake shook his head in disbelief. It was the state troopers from the beach.

"FHP, this is Sheriff Braddock, what the hell are you doing?" he inquired into his radio.

The reply was immediate and indignant. "What do you mean? We're checking for survivors, just like you asked. Over."

"Survivors?" Jake echoed. "Have you lost your mind? That was before the marina was destroyed! That thing is still out there! Now turn that boat around and get your asses back here!"

"Omigod, Jake. Look!" Amara stared over his shoulder, her trembling hands covering her mouth.

Jake felt his heart sink into his stomach. The creature had surfaced, less than a hundred feet from the *Infidel's* stern.

"Guys, listen very carefully." The mammoth carnivore began to inch closer. "The creature is right behind you. Spin your wheel hard and gun it for the beach. Just so we're clear, I'm telling you to *ground* her. Do you understand me?"

There was a moment of silence. Jake sucked in a deep breath, praying his plan would work. The *Infidel's* fiberglass hull would take quite a beating from such a maneuver, but it was the surest way to get the men out of harm's way. All they had to do was remain calm, follow his lead, and they'd be fine.

Then the shooting started.

The sound of gunfire pounded through Jake's body. Focusing hard, he could make out two of the uniformed officers positioned by the boat's stern, weapons drawn and blazing away.

He thundered at them. "What the hell are you guys doing? Put the hammer down and get out of there!"

Fueled by the bullets ricocheting off its hide, the pliosaur attacked. Sweeping forward with surprising speed, it lunged for the *Infidel's* transom. The rookie trooper at the helm spotted its approach and gunned his engine, attempting to outdistance it. His shriek of alarm echoed across the water as the creature's room-sized jaws crashed down on the boat's stern.

"Jesus Christ!"

Amara covered her face with her hands.

Jake watched in horror as his sturdy patrol boat was shaken like a bath toy in the monster's clutches. There was a sharp, cracking noise as its hull began to give way. Seconds later, the *Infidel* was no more, smashed into pieces against the surface of the water.

Caught within the beast's cavernous jaws as it enveloped the boat's transom, two of the troopers were instantly crushed to a pulp, along with the center console's outboard and stern. The rookie driver was thrown high into the air, pin-wheeling as the enraged behemoth flung the *Infidel* to and fro. He landed hard in the water, the wind knocked out of him. Dazed and struggling to get his bearings, he shook his head and began to dog paddle toward the nearby pier.

From a hundred feet away, Jake could see the cop's terrified face. The deadly reptile cruised lazily behind him like some impossibly large crocodile. It was forty feet away and closing the distance.

"He's not going to make it! We have to help him!"

Before Amara's words registered in Jake's ears she was already in motion, pushing past him and moving to the pier's edge with surprising speed. She dug in her heels and screeched to a halt, teetering next to an opening in the pier's railing. She looked around wildly, her eyes leapfrogging from a woefully inadequate piece of rope to a nearby ladder leading to the debris-strewn water below.

Jake felt a cold spike of fear as he realized she was going to jump. He stifled a curse and made a desperate lunge, grabbing her from behind in a bear hug. He absorbed her forward momentum with a grunt and pulled back hard, hoisting her body off the ground and holding her suspended.

"Jake, what the hell are you doing? Let me go!"

Amara cursed and flailed, struggling frantically to free herself. Suddenly, her kicking and thrashing ceased and her body stiffened. She froze, horrorstricken, as the pliosaur picked up speed. Its flippers flicked hard, propelling it forward. Its monstrous maw yawned wide, revealing deadly rows of flesh-rending fangs. It overtook its slow moving victim with surprising silence, swallowing the screaming rookie whole.

"No!"

With Amara's cries echoing in his ears, Jake lowered her to the pier's gritty surface and wrenched his sidearm free in one motion. His teeth clenched, he charged along the pier's edge in a scarlet haze, firing round after round at the distant monster. His finger burned and he became cognizant of the clicking sound signaling his weapon was empty. He ceased pulling the trigger and sprang for the far end of the dock, closing the distance between the creature and himself while reloading.

Ignoring the hail of bullets that struck its armored skull, the pliosaur emitted a tremendous grunt and submerged.

Jake stood in the shadow of the *Harbinger*, his smoking Beretta pointed impotently at the open water. Silence settled over the area like a shroud, interrupted only by Amara's sobs.

He lowered his weapon. His shoulders slumped as his fierce gaze rested on the spot where the young cop had flailed about moments before. He uttered a heavy sigh before he forced himself erect, holstered his sidearm, and walked back to Amara.

"Jake, I could have done something! Why did you stop me?" She grabbed him by his shirt, shaking him. On impulse, he pulled her close, hugging her numbly, his brain somehow still aware of how warm she felt pressed against him.

Amara wrapped her arms around him and held on, her tearstained cheek burrowing into his shoulder. Her anguish gradually faded until she became quiet.

Suddenly, she pulled sharply back from him. "What the hell is wrong with you? I could have saved him. Why did you do that?"

Jake's face darkened. He stared at the ground and shook his head. "I . . . you'd have died too."

Amara's lips parted, but before she could reply, one of the helicopters hovered directly overhead. A look of animalistic fury erupted from Jake's face. He yanked his radio off his belt and mashed the talk button down.

"This is Sheriff Braddock calling news chopper 621. Come in."

No response.

Jake looked up at the helicopter. The cameraman had recorded the *Infidel's* destruction in its entirety. Now he was focusing his lens on Amara, feeding off the attractive scientist's hysterical state.

"I repeat: this is Sheriff Jake Braddock to news chopper 621, come in!"

Jake changed frequencies and repeated his message.

Bastards.

He shook his head in exasperation, then walked over to Amara and put an arm around her quivering shoulders. A sudden roaring noise caused him to look up. His fury was rekindled. The second chopper had rejoined the first and was now hovering over them. A minute later, the two birds moved off, heading out over the water. They stopped a few hundred yards out, hovering low, their noisy rotors whipping the seas below into a frothy white maelstrom.

"Now, what are those assholes doing?" Jake remarked. He drew away from Amara and stalked to the edge of the pier. He reached for his radio once more. "Molly, this is Jake. Come in."

"Oh, Jake, thank God you called! I saw some of the footage on the TV. I was worried sick! Are you guys okay?"

"No, Molly, we're definitely *not* okay," Jake said. "The marina's destroyed, dozens killed, and Chris is in the hospital."

"Oh my God!" Molly was crying.

Jake took his hand off the talk button, closing his eyes. He took a deep breath. "Listen, I need your help getting this situation under control. I need you to put in a call to the governor's office right away."

"Um . . . sure, Jake," she stifled a sob. "What do you . . . want me to tell them?"

"Tell them the situation here is beyond our control. I need the National Guard, and an official announcement that boating traffic is prohibited from Paradise Cove to the twelve mile limit." His eyes slits, he gazed up at the distant helicopters. "Then contact the local news networks and get me in touch with the choppers they've got circling around out here. I want those vultures off our backs."

"I'll do my best, Jake," Molly said shakily.

Replacing his radio, Jake stared up at the two helicopters, his soot and bloodstained arms folded across his chest. He was so infuriated at the two pilots he barely noticed Amara move next to him.

"What are they doing?" she whispered, wiping the half-dried tears from her face with the back of one hand.

"They're trying to get additional footage of your pliosaur. It's worth a fortune right now."

"Is it out there?"

"Probably."

Jake's radio squawked loudly as Molly's voice blared out of it.

"Jake, I called the stations," she said. "One chopper is not responding, but the other's radio is set to channel 11, if that helps."

"Thanks," Jake replied. He switched frequencies and raised the Motorola to his lips.

"Attention news helicopter 415, this is Sheriff Jake Braddock. Come in please."

There was a frustrating moment of silence before the pilot radioed back. "Sheriff Braddock, this is chopper 415, read you loud and clear."

"This area is dangerously off limits. I need you to clear out."

"With all due respect," the pilot explained, "your authority extends to the ground and the surrounding waters. You can't order us out. Sorry, sheriff."

Jake emitted a low growl of frustration. "Fair enough," he replied. "Just remember, it's your ass. Any sign of the creature?"

"Are you kidding?" the pilot radioed back excitedly. "The damn thing's right below us, hanging out just below the surface. Man, you gotta see the size of this thing! He's as big as a battleship!"

Jake scanned the water directly below the two circling craft. He could make out a shadowy form, suspended beneath the swells.

"It's out there alright," he said to Amara, then radioed the pilot. "Listen fella, you're flying kind of low. You don't want to get too close to that thing. What's your altitude?"

"Now, don't go worrying about us, sheriff. We're a hundred feet up. I'm sure we're fine. I . . . damn, it disappeared."

Jake cast an alarmed glance at Amara and pressed his talk button again. "Hey, fella. Maybe you ought to call it a day?"

"Are you out of your frickin' mind?" The pilot laughed. "This is the opportunity of a lifetime. My kids are gonna go nuts when they see this stuff, not to mention . . . holy shit!"

The pliosaur exploded up from the depths like a ballistic missile, its monstrous body nearly clearing the water. The startled pilot – staring straight down its throat – panicked and heaved back on his joystick, trying to distance himself.

Careening wildly out of control, the sleek red and white chopper went into a dizzy tailspin, plowing sideways into its rival agency's aircraft. The whirling propellers of both helicopters intersected at a forty-five degree angle, their silver rotors shattering into scores of smaller pieces. The lethal shards scythed through the air, slicing through the fragile aluminum walls of both fuselages like a hot knife through cheese.

Mesmerized by the spectacle, Jake stared powerlessly as the two stricken helicopters began to drop, their twisted metal frames molded into one another.

Frustrated at having missed, the pliosaur settled back down. As it gazed hungrily upward, the two aircraft plummeted toward it, their crumpled hulks poised to crash into the heaving swells below. A moment before impact, their fuel tanks exploded.

Wincing at the resultant fireball, Jake said a silent prayer for the pilots and their families. There was no surviving such a conflagration.

"Molly, this is Jake." The lawman shook his head in disgust. "Come in, please."

"I'm here, Jake," Molly called back. "I'm on with the Coast Guard right now."

"Good," Jake said. "I need you to get on the phone with the FAA, too. We just lost both news helicopters. We're going to need a no-fly zone established. I don't want any more accidents involving this thing."

"Oh God . . . will do."

Jake turned and stalked back toward the *Harbinger*. Behind him, Amara stared at the fallen fireball in horrified fascination. The burning wreckage of the two choppers lay smoldering atop turbulent seas, spewing dense clouds of smoke and steam until they sank from sight.

The pliosaur was nowhere to be seen.

Visibly shaken, the raven-haired cetaceanist shivered and pulled herself away. Her head bowed, she turned and followed Paradise Cove's beleaguered town sheriff back toward the shelter of her vessel.

———

A mile away from the devastation, the creature sounded, angrily scattering its accompanying flock of seabirds. Its attempt to crush the noisy insects hovering above its head had resulted in its scaly snout getting singed by scorching flames.

Infuriated by its burns, the prehistoric titan dove steadily deeper. Soon, the numbing effects of the icy sub-thermocline took hold, the frigid temperatures serving as a cooling salve to ease its discomfort. The searing sensations that afflicted its armored skin quickly subsided. As the pain vanished, the creature's savage temperament stabilized.

Now calm, it made its way to the surface to bask in the warmth of the soon-to-be-setting sun. Its belly full, it floated tranquilly upon the surface. Imperious, it closed its gleaming eyes and drifted off into a state of self-induced slumber.

———

With his six-foot-two frame draped across a leather recliner like some two-hundred-and-thirty pound mountain lion, Karl Von Freiling seemed more a part of his collection than a man. He shifted position, remote in hand, and extended one arm to raise the volume on the wide-screen LCD TV.

Above him, the mahogany-lined walls of his trophy room were saturated with past conquests. There were African lions, Bengal tigers, polar bears, elephants, and an endangered white rhinoceros. All wore expressions of primal ferocity, their frozen grimaces silent testimony to their violent deaths at the hands of a skilled hunter.

With his powerful physique and hawk-like features, Von Freiling had the look and mannerisms of a true predator. The assorted scars that decorated his tanned limbs were further accentuated by his shockingly colored eyes, and added to his thoroughly unnerving appearance.

He nodded almost imperceptibly as a buxom brunette tiptoed into the room and handed him a fresh bottle of ale. He gave the scantily-clad girl a quick smile, followed by a playful smack on the rump as she bent down to grab his empty. He watched her leave, then took a swig of the ice-cold brew, savoring it. Though he appeared unfazed and relaxed, the big game hunter was paying rapt attention to the astonishing broadcast that had enthralled not only him, but the entire world.

"... *And, as impossible as it may seem, the marine dinosaur that attacked the coastal town of Paradise Cove, Florida today, once again made its prehistoric presence felt. Seen from a passing helicopter, the huge animal leapt clear of the water, destroying both the helicopter filming it and another nearby. Both pilots and crew were lost ...*

In a related story, the governor extended his support to the besieged coastal community, dispatching hundreds of troops from the National Guard. It is believed the giant reptile that attacked Harcourt Marina this afternoon is the same animal that killed Senator Dean Harcourt's son yesterday. The governor's office conveyed its heartfelt sympathies to the senator. Any and all aid has been pledged ..."

Muting the oversized set, Von Freiling reached for the antique-styled telephone, resting on a stand next to his recliner.

"Hello ... operator?" He spoke smoothly into the receiver, a malicious grin appearing on his raptor's face. "Yes, I need the phone number for Florida Senator Dean Harcourt's office, please ..."

CRETACEOUS OCEAN
65 MILLION YEARS AGO

The pliosaur queen surfaced for air, her mighty lungs swelling before she continued to glide through her undersea domain. She moved with carefree grace, imbued with the supreme confidence that came from being the world's greatest predator. When she was smaller, she viewed others of her kind – in particular the dominant bulls – as a threat. Now, in the prime of her life, she feared nothing. No male could challenge her.

Ironically, she now sought their attention. The powerful phero-mones she exuded into the surrounding sea sang forth an irresistible siren song. This, coupled with her species' innate olfactory capabili-ties, gave her the power to attract every sexually mature male within a hundred square miles.

And that was exactly what had happened.

———

Something akin to rage filled the male pliosaur. He had competition. Approaching from the southeast, he spotted four other mature males. The rival jacks were all following the giant female at a respectable distance.

Wheeling in for a closer look, he sized up his competitors. The males ranged in size from an ambitious adolescent, barely forty-five feet in length – who wisely kept to the rear – to the frontrunner, a battle-scarred, one-eyed giant at least one hundred years old, who was even larger than the big bull.

He cruised closer, falling in with the other jacks. The rival males bristled at his approach, uttering thunderous grunts that vibrated through the water; their arched body postures and half-opened jaws mirrored their displeasure. The big male wasn't intimidated, and pulled up parallel to the one-eyed veteran. The older bull snapped his giant jaws together as a warning and immediately shifted position, keeping his good eye fixed on the powerful newcomer.

Despite all the vocalizations and attempts at intimidation, all of the bulls made it a point to remain a substantial distance behind the object of their affections. Although the female was in estrus, she had shown no indication she was ready to mate with any of her prospective suitors. A bull foolhardy enough to attempt a premature coupling risked receiving a vicious bite from the female's gigantic jaws. Such a bite could cripple, and a disabled animal of *any* kind in the violent Cretaceous seas, even a pliosaur, was as good as dead.

———

Out in the blackness of space, the asteroid hurtled along its predestined course. For eons the great rock had traveled the galaxy. Over the countless millennia, thousands of smaller meteoroids and other pieces of debris bounced off and pocked its ragged surface. Bereft of atmosphere or inhabitants, it annihilated everything it encountered. Soon, it would reach its final resting place: an inconspicuous little blue and green marble nestled in the cold, black void, only ten thousand miles away.

At over seven miles in width and weighing trillions of tons, the enormous hunk of space rock, iron, and iridium was the size of a city. It was a planet killer, the destructive energy it harnessed beyond reckoning. As it drew closer, the sunlight struck its jagged black surface at an oblong angle, giving it, fittingly enough, the glowing red and orange appearance of hellfire. Blazing through space at fifty thousand miles an hour, it would reach its target in minutes. As silent as death, the meteor continued on.

Eternity beckoned.

———

The female announced her readiness to mate.

Raising her giant jaws out of the water, she emitted a mournful bellow that scattered the omnipresent pterosaurs and pealed across the water like a foghorn. Miles away, her roar echoed off the slopes of a volcanic island. The five jacks, waiting a hundred yards off, raised their heads eagerly out of the water and began blinking rapidly.

The moment was about to arrive. Then, without warning, the pliosaur queen plunged into the depths. Her flippers pushing in unison, she took off at breakneck speed, abandoning her would-be-lovers. The mating chase was on.

Despite undeniable urges to procreate, the female would not simply submit to any willing suitor. Evolution didn't create a perfect killing machine without ensuring it was designed to withstand the test of time: the males would have to prove their worthiness to mate. Only the strongest and most powerful would win the queen, ensuring the most ideal genetic combination possible, and the ultimate furthering of the species.

Of the five male pliosaurs, three quickly assumed the lead. The big bull and the old one-eyed male led the pack neck and neck, sixty yards behind the female's enticing tail. A third male – a fifty-nine foot powerhouse with a huge bite scar on his muzzle – was right behind them and gaining steadily. The female, powering along at forty miles an hour, gave no indication of slowing or tiring. Though capable of greater speed, her chase was a test of strength, ferocity, and most importantly endurance. She would continue on until only the most dominant male was left. He would be her king.

Suddenly, the muzzle-scarred male made his move. With a quick burst of speed he rose in the water column, coming down directly between the two frontrunners with the intention of scattering them. It was a bold move, but a miscalculated one. The experienced big bull and the crafty one-eyed oldster simultaneously turned on their disfigured rival, smashing their heads into his cavernous chest and ribs from opposite directions.

Though not as damaging as their deadly bite, pliosaurs often used their armored skulls as battering rams. The technique was particularly effective during the mating chase, and helped to keep fatalities to a minimum. As it was, the sandwiching attack by the two larger males had devastating results. The muzzle-scarred bull had two shattered ribs on one side, and three cracked on the other. With a water-muffled roar of pain and rage, the injured male dropped out of the race and made his way agonizingly toward the surface.

As the big bull and the one-eyed male were launching their attack, the youngest of the pliosaur pack saw his opportunity and took it. At only forty-five feet and twenty tons, the adolescent bull was by far the smallest of the group. But he was also the fastest.

Accelerating to a blinding sixty miles an hour, the agile male looped effortlessly over his distracted rivals and came down exactly where he wanted to be, square on the giant female's back. Lunging forward, he clamped his powerful nine-foot jaws with their eight-inch teeth directly onto the female's exposed neck.

The male's bite was hardly injurious to the cow. Evolution had insured that the thick scales and skin on her nape and throat were better armored than the rest of her titanic body, solely to withstand such attentions. However, the smaller male was not her first choice, nor was the race over.

With an eardrum-shattering bellow, the female twisted her gargantuan body into a high-speed underwater roll, shrugging the young bull off. Dislodged and disoriented, the adolescent found himself in the path of the onrushing big bull and his one-eyed rival. Annoyed by his antics, the two came at him with vengeful fury, their jaws agape and eyes ablaze. The young bull opened his mouth to defend himself, just as the older, battle-scarred bull plowed into him with the force of an avalanche, knocking the air out of him. The big bull attacked from the opposite direction, slashing the smaller male's right fore-flipper with his jaws, and leaving the vulnerable appendage in tatters. Trailing blood, the young bull paddled limply away to nurse his wounds.

———

The meteor entered the planet's atmosphere and began its final descent. With its entire surface a blazing red inferno of molten rock and metal, it truly resembled the hell it was about to create. Below it lay an unsuspecting primordial world, lush and green and filled with wondrous creatures the universe had never before seen.

Blazing across the skies at a steep angle, the gigantic fireball continued on. Its target was dead ahead, at what would one day be known as the Yucatan Peninsula.

Relentlessly, it came on. It had no feelings. It had no remorse.

Its name was Armageddon, and nothing could stop it.

NINETEEN

Jake woke with a start. His t-shirt was soaked through, his heart pounding from the nightmare he'd been jolted out of. He gazed wide-eyed at the gray-riveted scenery surrounding him, unsure of where he was or how he got there.

He shook his head to clear it. He remembered accepting Amara's invitation to spend the night onboard the *Harbinger*. Still groggy, he checked his sports watch, fuming silently. It was four in the morning and odds were he wasn't going back to sleep.

Suddenly, he heard the call again. It was the same bass bellow that jolted him out of his slumber – a resonating cry, woeful in its tonality, reverberating like distant thunder through the ship's thick hull. The call was unfamiliar to the coastal town sheriff, who spent many nights as a teenager, laying in his bunk onboard the *Sayonara*, listening to the deep-throated songs of Florida's resident blue whales and humpbacks. It was lower in tone, longer in duration, and had an alien ring to it.

Spewing profanities, Jake leapt out of bed as if his sheets were on fire. He had his gun belt and boots on, and was making his way topside within seconds. As he negotiated the dimly lit corridors of the *Harbinger*, he overheard voices. He followed them to the ship's observation room, where he was surprised to find Amara, Willie, and Joe Calabrese huddled around an underlit desk.

"A bit late ta be wandering da halls, don't ya tink, mon?" Willie asked as he noticed their disheveled guest standing in the doorway.

Jake's reply was short-circuited by another rumbling cry. "That's the monster, isn't it?" he asked of Amara.

"It's *not* a monster," the cetaceanist pointed out. "But it *is* a creature that has to be dealt with, both for its protection, as well as the public's." She reached for a nearby coffee pot, pouring him a cup and gesturing for him to join them. "We have a plan."

"A plan?" Jake accepted the proffered mug. "I hope it involves baiting that thing to the surface and tossing the remainder of my dynamite down its gullet!"

"Not quite . . . I think we can capture it."

Jake spat hot coffee back into his cup. "What?" He stared incredulously at them. "Are you people out of your minds? Look doc, this isn't some porpoise or pilot whale we're talking about. That thing is *way* too dangerous to play around with."

Amara sighed. "It's just an animal. We can take it alive."

"We have to *kill* it! Willie, you were on the deck with us. Joe, you saw it too. You know what that thing is capable of."

"Yes, we do," Joe admitted. He folded his tattooed arms, looking grimly down at the table. "Look, I'm not arguing. The thing is beyond dangerous. Personally, I think we should go out and buy a bazooka, but Amara thinks the creature is worth more alive."

Jake felt his eyebrows reach his hairline. "Oh really, doc? And what makes your pliosaur so valuable? Wouldn't it be easier to study once it's on ice?"

"Actually, I'm thinking of it more as a display specimen than a lab one," she replied.

He sucked in a sharp breath, but before he could retort. Amara raised her hands in a soothing manner.

"Now hold on and think for just one minute, Jake Braddock. Barring federal aid, there's no way Paradise Cove can afford to reimburse the victims' families, let alone revive its demolished economy."

Jake bit his tongue. Since its expensive recovery from the last hurricane, the marina was just starting to turn a profit. The maintenance alone made it more trouble than it was worth. Dean Harcourt would be the only one sitting pretty when he collected on the cove's hefty insurance policy, leaving all its businesses to rot.

Amara continued. "The creature would draw tourists from all over the world. People would pay any price to see a living dinosaur."

"You mean 'marine reptile' . . ." Jake said sarcastically.

"Whatever, Jake." Amara rolled her eyes as she turned toward the drafting table behind her. She tilted her head to one side, gathering her long hair with both hands as she tied it back. "We've got a plan to capture it."

"Capture it how?"

She turned back with a wicked-looking, black and silver firearm in hand. It had a knobby contraption fixed to its barrel. "This is a Sea Wolf pneumatic speargun, loaded with a satellite transmitter. One hit and we can track the creature anywhere in the world."

Jake put his coffee mug down to take the weapon from her. He looked it over without enthusiasm and handed it back.

"Then what?"

"Then, we have to snare it." Amara flipped quickly through a pile of papers. She reached for her own coffee, pausing as she took a long draught. "To do that, we've hired the *Forsaken* and the *Nefarious*, a pair of trawlers out of Key West."

"And who's going to be in command of these trawlers?"

"Willie and I."

Jake rubbed one temple with his fingertips and shook his head. He could see where this was going.

"Look, even with you tracking it, there's no way a *fleet* of trawlers could catch that thing. It'll see them coming and either take off or rip them out from under you, depending on how foul its mood is."

"That's why, after we've tagged it, we're going to replace the transmitter dart with this." Amara held up a second projectile with a metallic cylinder situated directly beneath its barbed steel point. She grasped the four-inch-long aluminum tube in both hands and plucked it apart with a loud, sucking noise. One half contained a glass tube, filled with a viscous golden liquid.

Jake pursed his lips. "I guess it's too much to hope that's poison you're holding."

Amara scowled. "It's Cetaprol-50, a whale tranquilizer. We use it to sedate stranded cetaceans – especially the bigger ones. It makes it easier and safer for us to float them out to sea during rescue attempts."

"So you track it and hit it with some whale dope. Great . . . assuming it even works, then what?"

"Here's the kicker." Amara nodded to Joe Calabrese. "If you don't mind?"

"Sure thing, boss," the retired ironworker replied. He gestured at a series of rough schematics sketched out on the table's glass top. "These lines represent the seafloor in and around Paradise Cove. We've marked off the listed depths. And this rectangular shape here represents your old railway pier."

"Go on," Jake drawled.

"The pier's reinforced steel and concrete was the only thing able to withstand the pliosaur's attack. We'll use it as our main-stay. My contractor contacts can construct what we need with no problem."

"You're plan is to build a–"

"A wall," Joe finished for him.

"A wall?" Jake scoffed. "You mean like in 'King Kong?' Because, as I recall, *that* one worked great . . ."

Joe sighed. "Actually, it will be more of a fence: a mesh-like enclo-sure curving out and around from the end of the pier, until it blocks off that entire section of the cove."

"That's impossible. There's nothing to anchor it to."

"There will be," Joe emphasized. "The pier doesn't need strength-ening. But this curved section will require reinforced, steel-cored pilings driven deeply into the seafloor, every seventy-five feet or so. Once completed, we'll have an area of water measuring roughly five hundred feet square and a hundred feet deep. Compared to the whole ocean it's no playground, but it'll keep the lizard alive, at least until we effect construction of a more permanent enclosure."

"There's not a net in the world that can withstand that thing's teeth. It'll bite right through your fence," Jake said. "And escape."

"Not if it's made out of this." Joe tossed him a spool of silver-col-ored fishing line. "It's the latest in braided line technology. Synthetic super-fibers laced with pure titanium. It's already used in tuna farms here in the U.S.."

Jake pulled two feet of the flimsy-looking cord off the spool, wrapped it around his hand several times, and grunted as he tried to break it.

Joe looked on with satisfaction. "That stuff's only a millimeter thick, but it has a tensile strength of a thousand pounds. It's flexible enough that the creature's jaws can't tear it, and it's immune to the corrosive effects of seawater." He flipped open a notepad, scanning its pages. "In terms of a timeframe, I've got a rough construction time-table. We can–"

Jake wrapped the braided line back around its spool and tossed it back.

"Okay, I've heard enough."

Amara stared at him confusedly. "What?"

Jake shook his head. "Your plan is nothing more than a *Sea Crusade* pipe dream. Chasing down a creature that fast with trawlers it could run circles around, using drugs that probably won't even affect it, and penning it in an imaginary cage that it could jump right out of? Please . . . *none* of this will work, and even if it could, I'll be damned if I'm going to stand by and let you try."

"What are you saying?"

Jake folded his arms, his changing expression a violently shaken cocktail of anger and fierce determination. "That damned thing slaughtered people – *my* people! It's a public menace, and it's got to be destroyed. I'm making sure of it."

Amara's eyes peeled open wide. "You're going to try to stop us from capturing it?"

"Absolutely."

"But . . . I don't understand. I know we can pull this off. Why would you do that? We didn't even try!"

"Because it has to be done. You just can't see it."

"You have no right!"

Jake's nasal exhale was an ugly little chuckle. "You're wrong. I have *every* right. *I'm* the authority in these parts, and it's my duty to safeguard the public. From what I see, your 'plan' involves risk to everyone onboard this ship. I can't just stand by and let that happen."

"We're used to risks."

"You're not used to this, doc. Enough people have died. I'm not going to watch you and your crew be added to the list."

"I can take care of myself and my crew."

Jake shook his head. "I've heard that before."

Amara blinked, her expression softening. "Jake . . . I'm not going to die on you. Just trust me. I can *do* this."

"Forget it."

"I don't understand why you won't even give me a chance. I can make this right, and you can help. We can remove a danger to the public and do some good at the same time. Why is that so hard for you to accept?"

"Maybe because I don't spend my days sheltered on some ship. I live in the real world, doc." Jake's eyes hardened and his jaw tensed. "You should try it sometime."

"So, that's it, then?"

"Yep. That's it."

Amara's wounded expression disappeared and was replaced by a guarded and distasteful one. She interlaced her arms and stared at the floor, shaking her head. "My God, Jake. I can't believe you're doing it."

"Doing what? My job?"

"No, using your authority to hamstring our efforts, just so you can take revenge on an unsuspecting animal."

Jake's jaw dropped. "Are you kidding me? Have you forgotten everything that's happened over the last few days?"

Amara's lips quivered as they curled back from her teeth. She tensed, her body contracting like a compressed spring. She gave a calculating glance at Willie and Joe, then wheeled on Jake. Her eyes were ice-coated harpoons, poised to strike. "We've forgotten *nothing*. I'm just surprised, that's all."

"Surprised by what?"

She looked him coldly up and down. "By you. I didn't expect you to take advantage of an opportunity like this, just so you can be a hero again."

Jake felt the room's temperature drop and an uncomfortable feeling settled over him. He gave Amara a hard look. "And what exactly is *that* supposed to mean?"

"It means that you want to kill the pliosaur because you believe it will give some meaning to your pitiful existence."

He arched an eyebrow. "Oh, really? Is my existence so pitiful?"

Amara's eyes were snowy slits. "Absolutely. You curled up like a snail in its shell after your wife died, then slunk off to Paradise Cove to hide. You threw away your career, and unless I've missed my guess, you've been an alcoholic ever since."

Jake's features hardened. "I haven't had a drink in years."

"I *doubt* that. You probably lie awake every night, wallowing in regret. You hate yourself because you're not center stage anymore.

The limelight has passed you by, and all you do is hand out summonses all day. *Very* impressive."

"You've got a lot of nerve, coming down on me," Jake growled. His tone caused Willie and Joe to exchange nervous glances. "You want to try picking on *my* life? You've got no kids, no man, and from what I've seen, hardly any friends. At least I have people to care about. You've got *nothing*."

"I don't need a man, you vindictive bastard. I've got my work."

Jake sneered sarcastically. "Oh *yes*, of course, your work . . . how could I forget? Tell me something, doc – do those precious whales of yours keep you warm in bed? Do they wake you up every morning, cook you breakfast, and tell you how much they love you? Do they shower you with kisses every night? I don't *think* so."

Amara's face twisted up with untold fury. "You don't have that either, loser!"

"Loser, eh?" Jake shook his head and backed away, a sardonic grin on his face. "God help you, doc, if you ever end up with the loser I *could've* been."

He turned on his heel and strode out of the room, yanking the heavy metal door shut.

Behind him, the observation room shivered once more with the foghorn bellow of the distant super-predator.

———

Jake stormed along the corridor leading back to his quarters, his fists clenched and face on fire. As he rounded a corner, he collided hard with Christian Ho. The young intern uttered a grunt of pain and staggered three steps back from the impact. He opened his mouth to apologize, then took another step as he spotted Jake's infuriated expression. His apology came out as a strangled bleat of alarm, and he bolted for the nearest stairwell.

Ignoring him, Jake yanked open the door to his cabin and slammed it shut behind him. Exasperation and cold fury waged an agonizing tug of war through the center of his chest, the tightening feeling increasing until he wanted to scream. He couldn't believe how Amara had belittled and embarrassed him. He deeply regretted having opened up to her. He'd unwittingly given her a guided tour of all the chinks in his armor.

Jake squeezed his way inside his tiny washroom and stood in front of its painted metal sink. He flipped on the tap and hunched over, cupping his hands under the spigot and splashing handfuls of water over his face and throat in a futile attempt to cool off. He gasped. The ship's water was surprisingly cold and had a bitter, coppery aftertaste.

He rested his hands wearily on the edge of the sink, his arms locked straight, his head down. He stayed there, brooding. The sudden familiarity of the scene caused his mind to wander back. His head snapped up, and as he saw his reflection he shivered. It was two years ago, the night he–

It was 1 a.m. on a Friday night, in the middle of August. He was stumbling for the hundredth time out of the *Cove Hove*, bleary eyed and blind drunk. He had a buxom blonde clinging to him, her hip pressed so tightly to his that, from a distance, they could have been mistaken for Siamese twins.

Her name was Suzy. At least, he thought it was.

"So c'mon, sheriff," Suzy slurred. Her inviting eyes and shiny lips painted pagan promises. "You're in *no* shape to drive. How's about I give you a ride?"

Jake shook his head, as much to stop the surrounding wharf from spinning as to decline the invitation. The girl was well endowed and obviously horny, but he just wasn't interested. Still, drunk as he was, he was coherent enough to remember he didn't have a car – although fierce male pride kept him from admitting it.

"Okay, fine . . . but no funny business."

"Of *course* not . . ." The girl smiled sinfully. She took her index finger and made an exaggerated 'X' across the exposed portion of her honeydew-sized breasts. "Cross my heart."

Jake sighed and focused on putting one foot in front of the other, a daunting task as they wound their way toward the girl's silver Corolla with her belting out an adulterated version of "I Shot the Sheriff." He attempted to see her to her driver's side door, an act she found overtly comical. She started giggling, then stumbled and fell as one of her stiletto heels disappeared through a sewer grate beneath her. Jake's inebriated attempt at supporting her ended with both of them in a heap, the girl's previous chortling upgrading to hysterical laughter as he failed repeatedly to help her back to her feet.

A few minutes and a few Hail Marys later, Susie pulled up in front of Jake's rented bungalow. He dragged himself out and stood there, sucking in the moist night air in an attempt to clear his vision and his head.

"C'mon, big boy, I'll see you to your door," she chuckled, leaning heavily on him.

As Jake made his way toward the door the girl once again welded herself to his side, her body heat radiating through her skin-tight mini-skirt.

"Here, let me help you," Susie said as he dropped his keys.

She bent down, her long, golden hair a burnished cascade as she lowered her head. She looked coquettishly up at him as she grabbed his key ring, then accidentally rubbed her cheek against the crotch portion of his pants as she writhed her way to her feet.

"There you go, now *stick it in*," she breathed heavily into his ear, clamping both her thighs around his leg like the coils of a hungry python, as he fumbled with the key once more.

She was all over him the moment the door closed. Jake felt her fingernails digging painfully into his chest and back, her hot tongue probing its way into his startled mouth.

"Now . . . hold on a sec," he stammered, his head swimming from all the beer. His eyes went wide as the girl yanked off his loafers. Next thing he knew, she was clawing at the front of his khakis. He reached down, trying to wrestle her hands loose, and was surprised by how strong she was. "I told you earlier . . . I'm not looking for anything. I was recently wid–"

The girl uttered a throaty growl and released the top of his pants. She grabbed at his belt with both hands, heaving back on it with everything she had, as if to tear the leather and underlying fabric in one fell swoop. "Oh, please. I'm not buying that 'I'm in mourning' bullshit. You've gotta be itchin for a fuck, especially after a whole year of doing nothing but spanking it." Annoyed with Jake's continued attempts at fending her off, she sprang upright and grabbed the front of his shirt. She pulled hard, ripping the buttons off as she attempted to bully him toward the bedroom.

"Don't worry, baby. I'll be gentle!"

Jake sensed himself being manhandled. He felt annoyance force its way through the beer-induced fog obscuring his brain, stomping out the tiny flame of desire that yearned for a foothold. As gently as he could, he grabbed Suzy by the shoulders and held her at arm's length.

"Sue . . . I'm going to bed, and you're going home."

"What the fuck is wrong with you? What are you, some kind of faggot?"

Jake shook his head. "Just go home."

The girl's eyes went wide and her bird-like features contracted, giving her a cold, harpy-like appearance. She took a step forward and gave him a hard shove to the chest. "Like hell I am, asshole. I left a perfectly good scene to come here."

He turned his back on her. "Just get out."

Suzy's growl of frustration was more like a scream. She hauled back and punched him hard on the back of the head, then pounced on him like a cat, slapping and scratching and tearing away a large section of what remained of his shirt.

Jake staggered a step under the surprising assault, disbelief and anger welling up within him. He whirled back around, hands raised. "Jesus, lady! What the hell's your prob–"

The slap was an off-balance backhand that clipped the girl's face. Even so, the impact lifted her off her feet and sent her sprawling to the floor.

"Oh my God, you fucking bastard!" She cupped her hands to her mouth and nose. They came away bloody. "Look what you did!"

Jake's jaw dropped to his chest and his eyes grew to twice their normal size. He took a tentative step forward, his lips quivering as he tried to speak.

"Get away from me, you son of a bitch!"

More punch-drunk than intoxicated now, Jake swayed from side to side, his woozy eyes following the girl as she stumbled to her feet and bolted from the bungalow. Still cursing at him through the Corolla's open window, she roared off, her wheels burning rubber.

With effort, he walked to the open door, watching through blurred vision as the car disappeared. He sagged against the doorway, resting his clawed-up back against the cool wood. A shiver of horror ran through him. He saw his mother's face being slapped back and forth, battered, bruised and bleeding. He realized he'd done something he swore he never would.

He hit a woman.

A sickening sensation speared its way up his esophagus, like his guts were trying to escape his abdomen by spewing out of his mouth. He raced for the bathroom, bouncing off walls and barely making it. He spent the next fifteen minutes bear-hugging the toilet, the retching sounds he made as he vomited uncontrollably eventually fading into agonizing dry heaves.

He looped one arm over the sink, clinging to the cold porcelain like a long lost friend. He leaned heavily against it as he made it to his feet. He wrapped both hands around the sink's lip, his shaking fingers gripping it tightly as he hung his weary head. When he finally looked up and saw his vomit-stained face, his eyes bulged.

John Braddock stared back at him.

He could see his dad plainly: his heavy jaw, cruel lips, and dark, intimidating stare. He studied Jake, then leaned his big head back and laughed uproariously. The unspoken message was simple: *Like father like son . . .*

Jake's howl of denial sounded more like a mortally wounded beast's than a man's. He slammed his fist into the medicine cabinet's mirror, shattering it. A thousand fragments of his father continued mocking him, their voices resonating inside his head. He screamed and grabbed the cabinet itself, ripping it loose from the drywall in a shower of wood and plaster, slamming it violently against the sink. The ceramic held for two blows, then broke into large pieces.

Jake staggered back, his breath coming in sharp gasps as he fell out of the bathroom. He crashed into a nearby wall, knocking his wedding pictures down and stepping on them. The glass cracked beneath his bare feet, its splintered edges cutting into him. He grunted in pain, hobbling toward the living room. His foot slipped on a puddle of blood and he pitched forward, striking his head hard against the coffee table. The last sound he heard was John Braddock's sinister chuckling.

When Jake woke the next day, he wished he was dead. His head throbbed and his stomach felt like he'd swallowed broken glass mixed with acid. He had a deep puncture wound on his heel with the hunk of glass still buried inside, and there were dried bloodstains everywhere.

He sat up, leaning wearily against the broken coffee table. When his head finally cleared, he crawled on all fours into what remained of the bathroom. He sifted through the shattered medicine chest and found a dusty bottle of alcohol, tweezers, and some bandages. He spent the next fifteen minutes extracting the wedge-shaped shard and disinfecting the wound left behind. After he finished dressing it he grabbed a bottle of aspirin, choked down a handful, then put on a pair of rust-stained slippers.

Jake looked around the bungalow, his face systematically becoming an adamantine mask of determination. Moving as quickly as he was able, he limped through the house, searching out every single bottle of booze in the place. He gathered them by the armful, emptying them into the sink and tossing the spent bottles in the garbage. It took him the better part of an hour, but he finally found the last – a bottle of twenty-five-year-old scotch Sam's father gave him as a wedding present. He headed back to the kitchen, yanked the top off, and watched the fiery liquid vanish down the drain. When it was done, he walked to the trash can, popped it open, and held the empty bottle at arm's length, staring at it. His jaw tensed and his eyes grew hard. He opened his hand, listening to the clinking sound as the bottle shattered against its brethren.

Jake scrunched his eyes tightly closed.

"Go fuck yourself, Dad."

When he opened his eyes, he was back aboard the *Harbinger*. His heart was beating like a trip hammer, his hands still gripping the washroom sink. He exhaled slowly, savoring the sensation of the air leaving his lungs, then straightened up.

He studied himself in the mirror, his arms folded across his chest. He checked his injured side and shook his head. Amara was wrong. She had no idea what a loser was. His father was a loser.

And Jake was not his father.

Miles offshore, the pliosaur drifted across the darkened waters. The night sky swaddled it like a shimmering black cloak, its folds emblazoned with the glitter of a thousand stars. The pinpricks of celestial light shone down, reflecting back like fireflies in the creature's ruby eyes.

It appeared lifeless. Yet every so often it raised its muzzle out of the water and emitted the doleful summons of its kind. It might have been seeking a potential mate, or just the reassurance that there were still others of its kind and it was not alone. Its calls went unanswered.

With its appetite temporarily satiated, the predator was able to rest, conserving its strength for the endless hunts that plagued its existence. The jagged lacerations it sustained on its back, and the scorching burns on its muzzle, were healing at an astonishing rate. The prop wounds had already closed over, and new scales were forming where charred tissue had been. Even the dozen teeth it lost during its rampage were being systematically replaced. The tips of newly generated ones were already beginning to emerge from its wrinkled gums.

An anatomical miracle, and one of the gifts evolution bestowed upon the pliosaurs during their sixty-five million years of imprisonment, was that of accelerated regeneration. Amplified powers of healing were an absolute must for a race of isolated mega-predators that fed upon anything they could overcome, including the injured or infirm of their own kind. Only the strongest of the colossal reptiles – and the ones that recuperated the fastest – survived to grow to adulthood. Over time, the race's regenerative abilities, as well as their resistance to disease and bacteria, reached unheard of capabilities.

By morning it would be back at full strength. Then it would seek out viable sources of protein to fuel the rapacious furnace that burned within its belly. A high-speed metabolism was the price the scaly titan was forced to pay for its accelerated healing prowess.

Though content to wait until first light, the creature had already identified a potential food source passing along the periphery of its sensory field. It was a school of fast-moving mammals, similar to the rival predator it routed in the darkness of the abyss. There was a score of the swift creatures, cruising in the distance. It could hear their high-pitched whistles and squeals across the water. The mammals were a fraction of its size, many no larger than its immense head. They would make nutritious, blubber-enriched meals when the need arose.

Ignoring the school as it moved farther away, the marine reptile continued to float along, reflexively scanning the seas every now and then for potential threats. There were none. Even the annoying boats had all vanished.

Weary from its earlier exertions, and waiting for the rising sun to stimulate it into motion, the pliosaur closed its eyes and slept. As it slumbered, its savage brain dreamed, as it always did, of swimming and hunting. And killing.

TWENTY

Tense and tired, Jake made his way through the *Harbinger*'s narrow hallways, hoping to find the ship's galley and a much needed cup of coffee. He'd come to terms with the self righteous indignation that continued to tear at his pride. Although he was still aggravated by his confrontation with Amara, he was angrier at himself. He sorely regretted the argument. He knew he should not have allowed himself to be baited the way he had, and he should have been more disciplined than to retaliate in kind. *Stupid. I should've expected the girl to freak, once I made my intentions known. I knew she had a thing for protecting endangered animals.*

Of course, he mused, when it came to the pliosaur, odds were it'd be Amara who ended up endangered.

Jake uttered a low groan as he ducked down to pass through a narrow doorway. He was stiff and groggy, and the measly few hours of rest he'd managed were hardly sufficient to recover from his ordeal. His struggle to save the young swimmer had left his body patchworked with darkening bruises, and the laceration on his ribs ached non-stop.

He touched the dressing covering the injured area with nervous fingertips and winced. The butterfly bandages were holding it closed, but the thin red line seeping through his white undershirt would undoubtedly become visible through his uniform as well. The tenderness of the surrounding area indicated the wound was infected and would soon require medical treatment.

Unable to find whatever passed for a kitchen onboard the *Harbinger*, he made his way toward the main deck. It was 7 a.m., and after last night, he figured it would be another hour before Amara and her crew were up and about.

As he shielded his eyes against the early morning sun, the bleary-eyed sheriff was surprised to find the cetaceanist and her colleagues gathered against the ship's portside railing. They were distracted by something going on below, and caught completely off guard when their sleep deprived guest unexpectedly appeared beside them.

"Oh, Jake!" Amara jumped, her black mane whipping wildly and her hand clutching at her chest. "Jesus, try and make some noise when you move around, will you? You scared me half to death!"

Jake shrugged. "Sorry. Maybe next time you can find a bell for me to wear around my neck?"

"Good idea, mon!" Willie rested a big hand on Jake's shoulder. "Maybe Joe can rig someting up for ya in his workshop?"

Joe Calabrese smirked and raised an eyebrow.

"Sounds good," Jake replied amiably. He moved next to his three comrades and glanced down at the pier below. "So . . . what's up?"

Amara studied him, then nodded approvingly. "Well, for starters, you might want to know Rosalinda made it." She turned away, then leaned her forearms once more on the ship's railing and pursed her lips.

"Rosalinda?"

Joe spoke up. "The young girl you rescued. Amara called the hospital a little while ago and spoke to her mom."

Jake turned to her. "Why'd you do that?"

Amara's expression softened. "Well, with everything that's happened, I thought you could use some good news." She turned back to the railing and smiled, her eyes gleaming with ill-concealed mirth. "Besides, Mrs. Lopez was all over the news, trying to find out about her missing son and the name of the 'superhero' who saved her daughter. I think she's baking you a cake or something."

"Well, that's . . . very nice of her." Jake closed his eyes and swore silently; he'd forgotten to report what became of the boy.

"Yeah, *super hombre.*" Amara chuckled softly. She nodded toward the far end of the pier. "Right now, we're focusing on what's developing downstairs."

As if by magic, a police barricade had materialized at the pier's starting point. It was manned by a half-dozen state troopers, and was keeping a score of reporters at bay; all were chafing to make their way onto the *Harbinger* in the hope of following up on the region's sensational storyline.

Jake was hardly surprised by the presence of the media. Paradise Cove's woes had literally exploded onto the news. It was one of those impossible-but-true tales that transcends any and all barriers.

"So, Jake mon," Willie clapped him on the back. "Is it ya we have ta tank for dat lovely bunch of cops down dere?"

"Not at all," Jake said, as perplexed as the rest of them. "Not that I'm going to look a gift horse in the mouth."

"Really, mon? Dat's a surprise. We taught for certain it was ya."

"Sorry to disappoint you, Willie." His voice dropped and he turned to Amara. "So, doc, how are you holding up?"

She avoided eye contact by looking down at her shoes. Her lower lip disappeared and she cleared her throat noisily. "Listen . . . can I talk to you for a minute, in private?"

Jake cocked his head to one side. "Sure."

Amara excused herself and headed away from Joe and Willie. The early morning sun's golden beams illuminated her from the back, giving her exposed skin a radiant glow and causing her sleek legs to cast crane-like shadows across the *Harbinger's* decks. She gestured for Jake to follow, stopping only after she rounded a nearby corner and placed the ship's forecastle between them and her shipmates.

"Forgive the Bugs Bunny routine," Jake said as he caught up to her. "But . . . what's up, doc?"

Amara smiled nervously, but her eyes remained focused on melting a hole through the ship's deck plates. "Listen, about last night . . ."

Jake felt his lips part. "Oh. Yeah . . . don't even worry about it. Honestly. It's no big deal. I was probably out of–"

"Look, just let me get this off my chest, okay?"

Jake's expression went from awkwardness to pure befuddlement. "Okay, doc." He glanced back around the corner to make sure they were alone. "So, what's eating you?"

"An unfortunate, but hopefully not prophetic, choice of words," Amara replied. Her eyes elevated, locking onto his. "Look, over the last few days we've both seen and experienced the most horrifying things imaginable. I don't know about you, but I've been up all night. Actually . . ." She paused thoughtfully. "Make that the last *two* nights.

So, in the tact department, it's safe to assume I'm not exactly firing on all cylinders."

"Don't sweat it, doc." Jake folded his arms and leaned against a nearby bulkhead.

"I'm not finished."

"Oh, sorry."

Amara nibbled her upper lip. "I want to apologize to you for earlier."

"Listen, it's fine–"

"No, it's not. I shouldn't have . . . denigrated you like that." She shook her head and gave a sigh of regret. "I realized later why I lashed out at you, and that makes me feel even worse."

"I don't understand." Jake hoped he didn't look as confused as he felt.

"Occasionally, you remind me of my ex, so I treated you like an asshole, even though you're not."

"So, I remind you of an asshole? What kind of apology *is* this?"

Amara drew close to him. "A *real* one, mister. Look at me, and you'll see I'm not playing."

"Oh." As their gazes locked it was Jake's turn to lower his eyes. He found himself as engrossed with the ship's decks as she'd been a moment before. "Well, since we're being so blatantly honest and apologetic with each other, there's something I'd like to say, too."

Amara tucked her hair behind her ears and gave him an encouraging smile. "Okay, shoot."

"I think you were fairly accurate when you described how obsessively focused I am on hunting down and killing your pliosaur."

Amara's head angled slightly. "Really? But, I was sure you–"

"It's not for the reason *you* said," Jake interjected. He ground his molars and looked around the ship's sprawling deck. "You see, knowing your background, not to mention your borderline obsession on protecting and preserving marine life–"

Amara's eyebrows rose dramatically. "Borderline?"

Jake chuckled. "Exactly. Anyway, I figured you'd plan some quick-draw search and retrieval operation, hoping to take the damn thing alive."

"But you want to stop me because . . ."

Jake interlaced his fingers around the back of his neck and leaned back, pressing the back of his head against his makeshift headrest as he exhaled through bowed lips. "Because I knew, after that stunt you pulled yesterday, that you'd be reckless enough to do something like that again."

Amara wore a puzzled look. "Well, Jake, I certainly appreciate your concern, but I don't see why you feel like it's your job to protect me. You've got a whole town to look after."

His blue eyes latched onto hers. "I'm sorry, but I'm not going to just sit back and let something happen to you. The way I see it, if the creature's dead, then I don't have to worry."

"But why would you worry in the first place? This is what I do, remember? I protect whales from factory ships, sometimes risking life and limb in the process. Hell, I've had a harpoon grenade explode right over my–"

"That thing you're looking to play hide and seek with is no factory ship, doc." Jake remarked. He felt a cold wave of fear settle in the pit of his stomach and shook his head, blowing out hard to relieve tension. "It's an eating machine designed to hunt and kill *dinosaurs*. You said so yourself. And if I allow you to go after it, you're going to die. I can feel it in my bones, and I . . ."

"You what?"

"I don't want anything to happen to you. Not like . . ."

Amara's jaw dropped and goose bumps popped up on her exposed arms and legs. "But, I thought . . . Jake, what are you saying?"

"I'm really not sure. It's been so long since I–"

"Amara, ya better come back here, straight away!"

"Geez, Willie, can it *wait* a minute?" she yelled back.

"I don't tink so, mon."

Jake gave a gentle nod. "I guess we better go."

"Yeah . . ." Amara reluctantly agreed. She turned and started back toward Willie and Joe. "Can we continue this later?"

"Sure."

As they reached the *Harbinger*'s railing, Willie and Joe were both pointing at the far end of the pier.

"We been wondering where that barricade came from," Joe said. "I think the answer is headed this way."

Backlit by the sun, a group of vehicles approached in caravan formation. The front one was a dark colored SUV. After the lead truck was waved through, a big limousine and a second four-wheel drive came into view.

"Damn. It's Dean Harcourt," Jake said. Displeasure rough-edged his normally smooth voice.

"Dean Harcourt?" Amara looked confused. "The father of the kid that got eaten off his Jet Ski? What does he want?"

"Whatever it is, it can't be good," Jake said. He made his way to the *Harbinger*'s nearby gangplank. "He's brought a lot of backup with him."

Ignoring his throbbing ribs, Jake moved toward the surface of the pier, with Amara and her colleagues falling in behind him. He reached the gull-stained concrete of the dock right as the procession ground to a halt. He stood his ground, waiting for the unpleasantness to unfold as usual whenever Harcourt was around.

The senator hopped out of his limo with surprising vigor, his gaze intense and unblinking. Security operatives instantly surrounded him and his attorney. Jake recognized Darius Thayer, dressed in an impeccable Armani suit, as well as grim-faced bodyguards Stanton and Fields.

Oblivious to all, Harcourt stared contemplatively up at the *Harbinger*. He surveyed the ship for a full minute before turning his attention to her crew.

"Dr. Takagi, I presume?" he inquired. He moved toward Amara, a paw-like hand outstretched.

"Guilty as charged, senator," Amara said stiffly. She shook hands with him. "It's nice of you and your men to come down and see us off. That *is* why you're here, I assume?"

"Not exactly," Harcourt replied. He turned toward Jake as if noticing him for the first time. "Sheriff Braddock, it's good to see you again."

"Indeed," Jake snorted. "It's good to be seen at all, after yesterday."

Harcourt nodded. "As always, right to the point. You know, Jake, your single-minded directness was one of the reasons we hired you in the first place."

"Best buy you ever made," Jake said. "So, what can I do for you and your people?"

"Nothing." Harcourt looked up at the *Harbinger* once more. "I'm here to conduct business with Dr. Takagi."

"What kind of business?" Amara probed. She caught the ill-concealed smugness making its way across the faces of the senator's bodyguards.

"I need your ship, Dr. Takagi. I plan on leading an expedition to subdue the beast that wreaked havoc on my town, and your vessel is the best suited for the task. At least, within a five hundred mile radius."

"Excuse me?" Momentarily confused, Amara gaped at him for a split second before lashing out. "The *Harbinger* is not some oversized charter boat you can just hire. And, as for the animal you're referring to, my crew and I have already formulated a plan to deal with it. So, if you don't mind, I would appreciate you moving your vehicles away from my ship. Have a good day."

"Actually, it's *my* ship now," Harcourt said. His voice had a threatening edge to it. "In fact, if I desire it, you will end up working for me."

"Listen, you pompous creep," Amara snarled. Ignoring his bodyguards, she stepped right in his face, her icy eyes staring him down from less than six inches away. "The *Harbinger* belongs to me, and to the WCS, and it will be a cold day in hell when–"

"You know, considering the early hour, your breath is remarkably fresh, doctor. How nice. As for the Worldwide Cetacean Society . . . your partners were more than happy to sell me a controlling share of your ship, and at a tidy profit, I might add."

For the first time Jake could remember, Amara's face had an ugly look to it.

"That's bullshit!" she spat. "The society would never sell to someone like you!"

"Sure they would, Dr. Takagi. Not only did I pay them twice what this old bag of bolts is worth, I offered to cut them in once the beast is captured and put on display. I also absolved them from any and all liabilities, and even agreed to fund a portion of the cost of construction for the monster's future living quarters."

Amara was seething. "Let me see if I've got this straight, Harcourt. Your only son was one of the pliosaur's victims, yet you're in favor of taking it alive?"

"That's correct."

"I can't believe my partners bought that."

"You hit it right on the head," Harcourt said. He stepped to one side. "At least, about the *bought* part. This is my attorney, Darius Thayer."

The senator gestured toward a malevolent-looking suit. He watched with poorly disguised glee as his lawyer withdrew a set of papers from his inside vest pocket.

Smiling, Thayer stepped forward and handed them to Amara.

"Dr. Amara Takagi, this is formal notification of change of ownership. As of five o'clock this morning, controlling interest in the research vessel *Harbinger*, docked directly adjacent to us, now resides with Harcourt Enterprises. This includes any and all equipment onboard said vessel, as well as decision-making ability in regard to continued employment of all crew members, you included."

Amara snatched the documents from Thayer, scanning them with furtive eyes as Willie and Joe peered over her shoulder.

Unwilling to turn his full attention from Harcourt and his escorts, Jake watched Amara with his peripherals. Despite her cool exterior, he got the impression the tall cetaceanist was more than a little dismayed by what she was reading. Knowing Harcourt as he did, that could only make sense.

Amara folded the papers and put them in her pocket. She looked back at the senator, her expression one of cool resignation, coupled with defiance.

"All right, senator. It looks like you bought yourself a ship," she said, standing erect with her hands on her hips and shifting her weight from foot to foot. "A fat lot of good it's going to do you. You don't strike me as much of a sailor, let alone a one-man crew."

"Come now, Dr. Takagi," Harcourt said, grinning at a chortling Darius Thayer. "Surely you didn't think someone such as I would move on an endeavor like this without making appropriate preparations."

"What do you mean?"

As the question left Amara's lips, another group of vehicles approached. Barely slowing, they made their way past the heavily manned barricade. Like Harcourt's caravan, the newcomers had a large, black-colored SUV in the lead, but were followed by four larger trucks. Three of these were flatbed tractor-trailers that carried ratcheted-down loads of heavy equipment, concealed beneath oil-stained canvas tarps. The last was a refitted military truck, the kind used to transport troops.

Harcourt gloated. "I've taken the liberty of hiring my own team, Dr. Takagi. Although you may be permitted to stay on as an advisor, the rest of your crew will not be needed."

The lead truck pulled up with a harsh squeal of straining brakes and a small cloud of concrete dust. From its opened windows, the AC/DC song *"Highway to Hell"* blasted away at an unspeakable volume.

The music stopped.

"Listen, Harcourt," Amara glared first at the SUV, then at the troop transport. "I don't know what bunch of military yahoos you got your hands on, but I assure you it's going to take a team of seasoned professionals to track this creature down and capture it."

"Indeed it is, love," a distinctive voice called out from the SUV. "That's where I come in."

Jake watched with undisguised interest as the truck driver leapt nimbly down onto the surface of the pier.

To say his appearance was distinctive was an understatement. He was Jake's size, with a muscular build that stood out through his paramilitary-style clothing. His tattooed forearms were scarred from his knuckles past the sleeves of his black t-shirt, as if he'd been fighting in wharf front bars and back alleys all his life. Some of the healed-over wounds were highly irregular in shape, like large animal bites, and Jake couldn't begin to surmise their origins. A few, however, were identifiable, especially to someone in his line of work.

The driver made his way to Amara, smirked, and removed his mirrored sunglasses. Besides the assortment of scars, Jake noticed two other things about him. The first was that he had the most bizarre colored eyes Jake had ever seen. They looked like burnished bronze, if that was physically possible.

The second was much more interesting. Judging from the look of shock mixed with loathing that materialized on Amara's face, she knew the man.

"Karl, you son of a bitch," Amara snarled and took a step forward. "I should've known!"

"There, there, dear," the mustached newcomer chuckled as Willie and Joe moved forward to restrain their incensed commander. "Is that any way to say hello after all this time?"

"As you can see, Dr. Takagi," the senator said. "I've taken the liberty of hiring my own expert. And when it comes to tracking down big game, Mr. Von Freiling is tops in his field."

"Karl Von Freiling, at your service, chap." The black-haired big game hunter walked over and extended a gnarled hand to Jake. "And you are?"

"Sheriff Jake Braddock," Jake said.

"Impressive grip you got there, sheriff," Von Freiling smirked. "Oh, *wait* a minute . . . you're that master swordsman I've heard so much about. Fantastic! You know, it's a pleasure to meet someone who appreciates a fine blade as much as I do."

"Really," Jake remarked. "And *you* must be that jungle adventurer I saw on the news. You're the guy that captured that big anaconda a few years ago in Brazil, the one that made all the papers?"

"Give that man a gold star!" Von Freiling grinned even more broadly. "That's me, chap. You know, I made almost a million bucks off that bugger, if you can believe it. She was a thirty-six footer, making her the biggest snake ever recorded. Weighed almost twelve hundred pounds! And, the nasty bitch was delivered live, to boot."

"A million dollars, eh?" Still livid, Amara pulled herself away from her shipmates. "And how much is this creep paying you now, you jackass?"

"That's an interesting story, Mr. Von Freiling," Harcourt interrupted. "But it's not helping with current events any. From what I've seen, what you're hunting now makes that anaconda look like bait. Is your team ready?"

"Ready as they'll ever be," Von Freiling said. He shrugged, then whistled loudly through his fingers. "Gentlemen, front and center!"

As Jake and the *Harbinger's* crew watched, eight men hopped one by one out of the back of the troop transport and moved over to Karl Von Freiling's position.

Lined up, they were an evil-looking bunch, with every one appearing as hard and seasoned as their leader. Without exception, they were dressed in black fatigues.

Jake knew a gang of professional killers when he saw them.

There was no doubt about it.

"Mr. Stubbs," Von Freiling called out.

"Yes, sir!" a huge mercenary barked back.

"Have the men stow all our equipment and gear on board the ship, if you please. Just hand me that list first."

"Yes, sir." Stubbs handed his employer a digital clipboard and moved off. He was a massive, swarthy-looking individual who was missing all four fingertips on his right hand.

As the black-clad men headed back to their truck, Von Freiling scanned his clipboard.

"Senator Harcourt, with your permission?"

"Of course. Please proceed."

"Excellent." Von Freiling scrolled up and down his screen with an electronic pencil before glancing up again. "Now then, where was I . . . ah yes, the crew. Amara, if you've gotten past your initial hostility, I'd like to discuss the dispensation of your ship's complement."

"My crew?" Amara's pale eyes narrowed and she shouldered her way past Willie and Joe. "You've already got my ship. What exactly do you plan on doing with my crew?"

"For the most part, nothing," Von Freiling said absentmindedly. He glanced down, double-checking some records. "Most of your crew are useless for this type of expedition. They're interns . . . children, actually."

"It's a research vessel, Karl. And training interns is part of what we do. Anyway, I'm glad you find my crew so useless. The last thing I need is for any of those kids to be put at risk on one of your hair-brained adventures."

"I said *most* of your crew . . ." Von Freiling's eyes were hard and gleaming.

"Meaning?"

"Several of your ship's complement, including yourself – Brodsky, Helm and Daniels – seem to possess skills that might prove useful to us. They're under no obligation, of course. We're not pirates. Naturally, they will be well compensated, should they desire to participate."

"And the rest of my crew?"

"They stay here," Harcourt announced from a few yards away. "Safe and sound. Transportation and lodging will be provided, of course."

"So, how about it, love?" Von Freiling smirked. "Your guys in?"

"That's up to them." Amara glanced at her ship, then looked the scar-covered man up and down. "But I'll tell you right now, there's no way in hell you're taking the *Harbinger* on some adventure junkie's mission without *me*."

"I was counting on that," Von Freiling said, leering like a Cheshire cat before glancing at her second-in-command. "And you, Mr. Daniels?"

"Where Amara goes, I go," Willie stated matter-of-factly.

"Actually, I'll be going along as well," Harcourt added.

Jake noted with amusement the surprised looks on the faces of everyone present, the senator's gaping bodyguards included.

"What?" Stanton and Fields both sputtered at the same time.

Von Freiling hesitated. "But, uh . . . that wasn't what we talked about on the phone, senator."

"I agreed to fund this expedition in order to find the monster that killed my son, Mr. Von Freiling." The senator gave his hired gun an appraising look. "I don't recall saying I'd allow you to lead it, however."

"But, sir . . ."

"No arguments. This is *my* game," he warned from beneath plummeting eyebrows. He scratched at the jagged scar lining his jaw. "And just so you know, I checked you out after you called me. Your track record speaks for itself. But your methods are questionable, and you have an unprecedented history of violence. So, you'll forgive my lack of tact, but with everything that's riding on this, frankly, I'm not letting you out of my sight."

"Fair enough, senator. It's your money, you're the boss."

"Yes, I am."

Jake watched as Fields moved close to Harcourt. "Uh, Senator, if I might have a word with you in private?"

Behind them, Von Freiling's men struggled to push a large crate marked with red warning symbols up the *Harbinger's* straining gangplank, tearing ragged splinters from the thick wood as they went.

"Save your breath, Fields. I won't need you for this. You, Stanton and the rest of the team will remain here in Paradise Cove until my return."

"What?" Fields bristled. "Senator, that's completely unacceptable. It's out of the–"

"You disregarding my orders is what's out of the question." A thread of spittle bisected Harcourt's chin and he wiped it with the back of one hand. "You'd do well to mind your place, sonny. Or, you and your associate will end up spending the winter doing perimeter surveillance guarding a senile senator I know in Alaska!"

He appraised the grim expression on Fields' face, then turned toward a visibly amused Karl Von Freiling. "Now then . . . what about the subs?"

"We only have one," Amara interjected. "And it's badly damaged. I don't think you'll be able to use her for–"

"They'll do the job," Von Freiling said directly to his employer.

"Very well," Harcourt said, nodding. He stared up at the swaying *William*. "Have your men ditch their damaged craft, and load ours onboard."

"Excuse me?" Amara's aquamarine eyes flashed angrily back and forth between the two men. "What did you just say?"

"Sorry, love," Von Freiling said. "But I've brought a pair of submersibles specifically designed for this kind of thing. Your old fashioned clunker isn't needed."

Amara looked like she was ready to explode. "The *William* is a twelve million dollar piece of equipment! What the hell are you going to do with it?"

"Please calm down, Ms. Takagi," Harcourt said. Stanton and Fields moved next to him.

"Calm down?" To her credit, Amara held her ground, waving off Willie and Joe as they tried to rein her in. "So, tell me, what you are going to do, Karl? Dump our mini-sub in the harbor?"

"Not a bad idea," he said, sneering over the politician's shoulder. "But, as luck would have it, Senator Harcourt told me on the way over he approved the use of one of our flatbeds to transport your craft to whatever storage facility you deem acceptable."

"I'll stay behind and take care of the *William*," Joe Calabrese offered. He shot Von Freiling an unfriendly look before turning to Amara. "Don't worry, I'll make sure it's shipped carefully and in good shape by the time you get back."

"Thanks, Joe." She glowered at Von Freiling, exhaling through flared nostrils. "And for the record, if anything happens to my sub while it's being loaded or transported, I'm going to sue you. You *and* your benefactor."

"Whatever you say, love." Von Freiling winked as he reached for his radio.

"You know what? I've had it with this bullshit," Amara's lips quivered with pent-up rage as she whirled off, her shipmates in tow. She stopped a few paces from Jake and turned to her colleagues. "Willie, go back onboard and warn the crew about what's going on, please. I don't want a panic. And keep an eye on those soldiers, will you?"

"Ya got it." Willie turned and made his way back up the gangplank with quick strides.

Still watching from the pier's edge, Jake walked over to Amara as she conversed with Joe Calabrese. "So . . . I guess this little 'development' pretty much screws up your game plan, huh?"

Amara looked irritably at him. "Yeah, you could say that."

"So, what are you going to do?"

Jake followed her gaze upwards. High on the *Harbinger's* deck, two of Von Freiling's troops looked over the portside crane that supported the *William*. Despite being out of hearing range, it was obvious they were arguing over how to lower the damaged submersible onto the pier below.

Amara shook her head. She patted her pockets and snorted irritably. "Damn, my cell's in my quarters. I'm going to go find a landline and give my partners at the WCS a call. That's what I'm going to do, Jake." She spun toward Joe. "In the meantime, I'd like you to keep an eye on the *William* until I get back – starting with unloading her, before those yahoos damage her beyond repair."

"I'm on it," the retired ironworker responded. He galloped up the ship's congested gangplank, calling out to the two mercenaries.

Jake watched Joe vanish from view. "Would you like me to join you?"

"Sure, I could use the company." Amara turned on her heel, moving along the pier with purposeful strides. The sounds of people and equipment continued. She looked at Jake as the two made their way past the line of SUV's and trucks. "So, do you think the senator is serious about capturing the pliosaur?"

"I wouldn't count on it, doc." He cast a sideways glance at the heavyset politician and his lawyer as he and Amara moved out of earshot. "Don't get me wrong. When it comes to Dean Harcourt, anything is possible, especially if there's some political angle. But, given his well-earned reputation for ruthlessness, plus the loss he suffered, I wouldn't bet on it."

"I see." Her pace slowed as they approached the second flatbed truck. It was old and worn, its shocks weighed down by its tarp-covered load. Pausing while surveying the area, she positioned herself so she was obscured by the leading vehicle. She crept closer to the flatbed, an intense expression on her face.

"What are you doing?" Jake asked, following her.

"I want to see what they have under here." Amara glanced back over her shoulder. She grasped the edge of the thick tarp and grunted. It was practically welded to the vehicle's frame. "Ugh. If Karl's got some kind of new sub design like he says, I want to see it."

Despite Jake's whispered admonitions, Amara continued to pull and tug at the tarp. Cursing under her breath when the rough material resisted her efforts, she twisted her head sideways and struggled to peer under its rim.

"I see something yellow . . ."

She was straining for a better look when someone bellowed.

"What the *fuck* do you think you're doing?"

Caught off guard, Amara gave a frightened yelp. One of Von Freiling's men appeared from behind the truck. He was half-a-head shorter than Jake, though just as broad, and had a huge scar running down the right side of his unshaven face. Jake instinctively put himself between Amara and the scar-faced intruder. The merc had a large bone-handled machete slung from his belt. He reached for it as he drew closer, his already cold eyes growing wild and dangerous.

"I don't think so," Jake advised, resting his hand on the butt of his Beretta.

"Easy there, Markov!"

Half turning, Jake watched as Karl Von Freiling came jogging over. He had an amiable grin spread across his features. "What's going on here?" he asked.

"Your buddy Markov was about to attack us," Amara snapped as she stepped out from behind Jake.

"They were snooping around one of the subs," Markov replied matter-of-factly, not denying the charge.

"Is that so?" Von Freiling said. His amused smile seemed etched onto his face. "Don't worry yourself about my little toys, Amara. You'll have plenty of time to look them over at sea."

"Why wait until then? What's the big secret?"

"Now, now, love. There's no secret. And patience is a virtue." Von Freiling reached into his pocket for a pack of cigarettes. He turned to Jake. "Care for a smoke, sheriff?"

"No thanks. Not my thing."

"Suit yourself." Von Freiling nodded as he lit up. He puffed rapidly, running his free hand atop the edge of his craft. He drummed his fingertips contemplatively on the taut fabric, then turned to his waiting underling. "Markov, why don't you go back to the ship and get me a status report? I want to leave within the hour, and we still have to get these loaded and stowed."

"Yes, sir," Markov replied, casting Jake and Amara a dour look, before backing away and vanishing from view.

"You'll have to forgive my associate," Von Freiling offered. He took a long drag from his cigarette, funneling the smoke out his nostrils, then flicked the butt over the nearby railing. It struck a seagull sitting below, spraying embers and eliciting an irate squawk. "He's been with me a long time, and we often travel in parts of the world where people aren't as . . . *civilized* as we are here."

"No problem, Karl," Jake said. He began leading Amara away by the arm. "Now if you'll excuse us . . ."

"Of course," Von Freiling replied, grinning one last time. "Just be back within ten minutes of our claxon, Amara. That is, if you're still going."

Winking at Jake and the scowling cetaceanist, Von Freiling turned to go.

———

The pliosaur awakened. It surged to life, its eyes opening wide and its monstrous body submerging in a tremendous splash. Blinking repeatedly as it scanned the adjacent seas, the marine reptile uttered a resonating grumble. Its temporarily dormant appetite had returned, and it strained to lock onto the trail of the warm-blooded food it detected the previous evening. The pod was nowhere to be found.

Whipping its triangular-shaped head from side to side, it picked up on a school of fleet-moving fish. With a quick shift, it adjusted its course to intercept them, its paddle-shaped appendages switching to a simultaneous power stroke to close the distance.

With its toothy jaws already beginning to open in anticipation, it moved in for the kill.

———

Forty minutes after they left the dock, Jake watched Amara hang up her payphone in disgust. While he waited, he'd distracted himself by observing a pair of CH-47F Chinook military helicopters loading Von Freiling's mystery subs onboard. With their noisy task complete, the big copters faded into the distance. In their place, a group of gulls flew directly overhead. The abnormally silent birds arced slowly in the breeze, scanning the expanse of Harcourt Marina's damaged and deserted wharf for any possible meal.

"What did they say?" Jake called out as she moved within earshot.

"I don't want to talk about it," Amara steamed. Her lips were scrunched, her toned arms compressed tightly across her chest. "They're a bunch of hypocritical cowards. Either that or that damn senator of yours has a lot more power than I thought."

"Probably the latter," Jake said. He inclined his head in the direction of the pier. "They finished loading while you were on the phone. Looks like the remainder of your guys are headed this way."

Still fuming, Amara watched as Willie Daniels drew near, followed closely by Joe Calabrese and a disgruntled-looking Adam Spencer. The *Harbinger's* videographer was carrying a box piled high with data sheets, discs, and personal items, and his expression was every bit as outraged as his employer's had been when she first heard the news.

"Amara, what the hell is this?" Adam said. He stopped to adjust his thick glasses while balancing his burden against one hip.

"It's just like Willie told you. They've got the *Harbinger* and there's nothing we can do about it."

"Nothing?"

Amara shook her head. "Not for the time being."

Adam tugged nervously at his ear and looked down. "Look, boss, I don't want to seem like some rat deserting the ship, but there's no way I'm sticking around to work with those goons. You should see what they've done to my work station already."

Amara placed a hand reassuringly on his shoulder. "It's okay, things may get hairy on board anyway. I'd feel better if you stayed behind and waited for us to get back."

"*If* we get back, mon," Willie interjected, staring glumly at the nearby *Harbinger*.

"Hey, let's have none of that," Amara said. "I'm counting on you to look after me while we're out there."

"Don't I always?"

"Yes, you do. What about you, Jake? Are you coming with us?" Amara zoomed in on him with hopeful eyes. "We could continue our conversation from earlier . . ."

"Well, technically I can't say I was invited . . ." Jake said with a sardonic grin. "But being the law in these parts, I can pretty much assure you that as long as they're operating within the twelve mile limit, I'll be onboard and keeping an eye on things, whether Harcourt likes it or not."

Amara sighed with relief. "Thanks." She looked at Joe Calabrese. "What's the word on the *William*?"

"I lowered her onto their lead flatbed." The grizzled ironworker pointed back toward the pier. "Did it myself – and a good thing too. Those guys are pretty reckless. I tried to warn Karl about the problem we've been having with the starboard crane, but he was busy directing his helicopters and didn't want to hear it. After a few tries, I got their second submersible winched off the deck and locked in place. I just hope the hydraulics hold up."

"And the rest of our crew?"

"Already gone. They took cabs into town to whatever cheap-ass hotel Harcourt set up for them," Joe said bitterly. "All of em, even Lane and Mike. They wanted nothing to do with Von Freiling and his guys. Shit, can't say I blame them."

"I see. Well then, I guess it's just us," Amara announced, looking back and forth from Jake to Willie. She gave Adam and Joe each a tight hug. "Thanks guys. I'll call you when we get back."

Jake watched them exchange embraces, then turned toward the *Harbinger* as the ship's warning claxon sounded, its baritone bellow dispersing the birds overhead as it echoed across the marina.

"We better get going," he said.

"I guess you're right," Amara nodded. "Karl is asshole enough to leave us behind."

As Willie waved to Joe and Adam, Jake turned to Amara. "You know, it's not my style to pry into people's personal lives, doc. But, I've noticed a lot of hostility between you and that 'Doc Savage' reject. Is there some problem between you two that I should know about?"

"Hmm, let's see . . . Yeah, I guess you could say that."

"So, what is it?" Jake asked. He felt a twang of annoyance as Amara turned her back on him and started to walk away.

"He's my husband!" she yelled over her shoulder. Her stride increased, and she continued on without looking back.

"Your hus . . ." Jake stalled out. For reasons he couldn't fathom, he felt a sick feeling rolling around in the pit of his stomach. He stared slack-jawed at Willie. "Well, that . . . certainly explains it!"

Willie grinned reassuringly. "Now, don't go worrying about dis mon, Jake. Tings been over between dem for years."

"I see. Well, thanks for the heads-up," Jake said affably. His expression turned staid. "But I think we've got bigger problems."

As they reached the reporters and troopers encamped on opposing sides of the barricade, Willie edged close to Jake. "Who knows if we even got anyting ta fret about?" He glanced around, murmured under his breath. "Wit any luck, maybe we won't even find dat ting. Maybe da beast ain't even in da area anymore."

Before he could formulate his reply, Jake found himself distracted by a commotion on the nearby beach. He spotted a couple of early morning beachcombers – far fewer in number, due to the devastated docks – rushing excitedly down to the edge of the surf. They squatted down and started grabbing at several large objects, struggling to drag them from the water, up onto the sand.

Jake shielded his eyes and took a closer look. To his surprise, the gleeful tourists were wrestling with a small school of yellowfin tuna. For whatever reason, a dozen of the five-foot fish had ended up beaching themselves. As he watched the group of sun worshippers hauling the quivering tuna onto their towels, he wondered how a bunch of pelagic fish could end up getting stranded like that. He gazed past the surf, toward the foreboding waters of the harbor, and knew the answer.

"I think there's a good chance our pliosaur's still in the area." Jake turned from the beached fish with a grim smile and clapped Willie on the shoulder. "Trust me."

Up ahead, Amara waited for them.

Jake looked up at the *Harbinger* and hesitated. Her imposing form loomed over the edge of the old pier like some lurking monolith, poised to plunge any who boarded her into an impossible adventure. As he studied the ominous-looking whaler, the rays of the morning sun washed over her, altering her normal grayish coloration and giving her a more ruddy hue.

Jake shrugged and continued on, heading toward the converted murder machine they would all call home until their mission was complete.

TWENTY-ONE

Ten miles from shore, the *Harbinger* plowed through twelve-foot seas. Like a cast-iron juggernaut, the big vessel's reinforced steel foredeck rose and fell with the motion of the waves, while walls of white foam crashed thunderously against her bow.

Inside the ship's windowed bridge, a tall, black-clad mercenary manned the helm. Shifting position from time to time, he synchronized his movements with the approaching waves. Behind the pilot, Karl Von Freiling, Jake Braddock, and Amara Takagi stood watching, the latter with her arms akimbo as she scrutinized his every move.

"Well, your man seems to know what he's doing," Amara muttered. Despite appearing conciliatory, her words were laced with sarcasm.

"Who, old Barnes?" Von Freiling inquired over the roar of the big diesels. "Now, don't go worrying your pretty head about my man. He's piloted destroyers in the dark under full combat conditions. I think he can manage your little ship without difficulty . . . right Barnes?"

"No problem, sir," the soldier of fortune responded. "Wind's kicked up pretty fierce, but it'll die down soon." He glanced at Amara. "If you don't mind my saying, ma'am, your ship handles well. Considering her age and the heavy seas, that is. Diesels are in good shape, and she's seaworthy. My compliments to your maintenance team."

As he turned to look directly at her, Amara inhaled sharply. Barnes was missing an eye.

"Mortar fragment," Von Freiling said, chuckling in her ear before addressing Jake and Amara. "Perhaps it's time I show the two of you my new hardware. After all, you were both so eager to look over my little gadgets back on the dock. So . . . now's your chance."

"Lead the way," Jake replied.

Amara trailed behind, looking over the pile of crates and containers Von Freiling had stored in the old radar station behind the bridge. Most of the wooden and metal boxes were unmarked, leaving the beleaguered cetaceanist to worry just what her eccentric spouse had brought onboard her ship.

"So, Karl, where do you plan on starting your little safari?" Amara probed. Her gaze wandered to the largest crates, the two his men struggled to push up the loading ramp, earlier. "The creature was last seen by the marina, so why go so far offshore?"

"Not to worry, love," Von Freiling smirked back at her as he ducked through a narrow doorway. "We'll be stopping soon. As always, there's a method to my madness."

Methodically making their way through the *Harbinger's* cramped corridors, they emerged onto her sunlit aft deck. The two loading cranes stood waiting, their canvas-covered burdens gently swaying with the motion of the ship.

"Markov, it's time to reveal our two beauties," Von Freiling said to the guard stationed nearby. Amara gave a start; the sentry was the same machete-wielding thug that almost attacked them that morning.

"You got it, boss," Markov said, casting a malevolent look in Amara and Jake's direction. He drew his weapon and moved around the nearest mini-sub in a wide circle, deftly cutting the ropes that bound its coverings with quick and accurate strokes. From the look on Jake's face, Amara imagined the young swordsman recognized a formidable adversary when he saw one.

"Ah, Senator Harcourt . . ." Von Freiling spread a well-oiled smile for the approaching politician. "You're just in time for the unveiling."

"Good," Harcourt replied, slightly out of breath. "Let's see what you've got."

Amara's eyes widened. Looming behind the senator was an enormous albino mercenary, so huge, he towered nearly a foot over Jake's head.

"Indeed," Von Freiling said. His eyes shifted to Markov. "If you please?"

Nodding, the merc sheathed his bolo, then reached up and grabbed one end of the noisily flapping canvas. With a quick yank, the tarpaulin cascaded down into a fluid pile.

"Gentlemen, I give you . . . *Eurypterid I!*" Von Freiling exclaimed, gesturing at the bizarre craft hanging proudly in the breeze. Amara stepped forward for a closer look, her gaze intensifying. She could tell immediately, that compared to the *William, Eurypterid I* was an entirely different class of vessel.

Sleek and streamlined, as opposed to her blockier craft, Von Freiling's creation measured twenty-five feet in length. It was wedge-shaped in design, and had short wings like the fins of a colossal ray. Instead of the single rudder the *William* possessed, it sported a pair of matched dorsal and ventral fins to regulate pitch and yaw, like the tail section of an advanced fighter plane.

She also noticed its propulsion system, or rather, apparent lack of one. There was no visible prop, only a pair of sloped intake valves that ran from stem to stern.

There were some similarities between the two vessels. Like the *William, Eurypterid I* had an observation bubble and a pair of actuators. However, the yellow submersible's steel graspers were twice the size of her sub's and ended with powerful-looking pincers that appeared capable of wrenching a bank vault's door from its hinges. In terms of overall size, the ships were similar, but *Eurypterid I* was ferocious in appearance, designed more for undersea combat than exploration.

"Impressive looking vehicle," Harcourt announced, interrupting her thoughts. "Can it do the job?"

"Can *they* do the job," Von Freiling said, indicating the other craft hanging less than ten feet away. "And yes, they can."

Amara cleared her throat noisily. "Your design is very interesting, Karl." She moved to stand between him and Jake. "How long have you been working on this?"

"Since we parted ways, darling. Almost three years now."

"I see. So, basically, a few months before you moved that "Miss Bum-Bum" wannabe into our house."

"*My* house . . . and as I recall, *you* left *me*."

"Whatever."

"Exactly," Von Freiling sneered.

"Hmm . . . I don't see any sample baskets," Amara muttered, bending at the waist and knees to peer underneath the mini-sub. "And your manipulators are oversized, to say the least. It's safe to assume you designed your subs to–"

"To capture marine life," Von Freiling said. "The *Eurypterids* were initially intended to ensnare giant squid. I've got standing offers from some of the world's largest aquariums up to one point five million dollars for live specimens. I was in the midst of planning our first hunt for one when I heard about your little dinosaur problem. And you know me, always looking for a bigger trophy . . ."

Amara stiffened. "How deep can she dive? And what's your means of propulsion?"

"Crush depth has been calculated at five thousand feet, and the engines are a caterpillar impeller system. They're quiet, fuel efficient, and incredibly fast."

Amara glanced back at him. "How fast?"

"She'll go thirty-five knots submerged, faster on the surface," Von Freiling said. "Not quick enough to catch a big *Architeuthis* already on the move, but fast enough to put you in the strike zone if it's not."

"There's a big difference between chasing down a thousand-pound mollusk and grappling with a fifty-ton reptile."

Von Freiling's toothy smile turned suddenly serious, and he gestured to an array of features on the underside of his craft. "My subs come equipped with laminated, Kevlar-reinforced armor a full six inches thick. These flush-mounted ports expel four pairs of CO_2 powered harpoons that can punch through concrete at a range of fifty yards. The main port – located here – launches a larger, steel-cabled harpoon that's anchored to a hydraulic winch. When fired, the harpoon embeds itself in the target, discharging enough electricity to light up a city block."

"So, your plan is to electrocute it?" Harcourt looked the exotic mini-sub over with a critical eye. "Sounds brazen. I know a little bit about electricity. What happens if it gets too close to fire your weapon?"

"The mechanical arms are designed to immobilize a squid the size of a cabin cruiser," Von Freiling said. "They extend a full twelve feet and can hoist five tons each at nominal load. I'm sure they can keep our little dino at bay if it becomes necessary. Of course, if things get *really* ugly there's the stinger . . ."

"The what?" Jake moved over to stand next to the two men.

"The stinger," Von Freiling repeated with a grin. "After all, a *Eurypterid* is a prehistoric sea scorpion, Jake. And a scorpion's gotta have a stinger."

"So, are you going to show it to us or not?" Amara grated. She peered all over the exterior of the sub.

"You can't see the stinger from down here," Von Freiling said amusedly. He pointed upwards with a knobby thumb. "It's on the dorsal section."

"Enough games, Mr. Von Freiling." Annoyance laced Harcourt's voice. "Where is the stinger and what does it do?"

Von Freiling acquiesced. "It's a concealed device, senator – kind of a weapon of last resort. It springs up out of the back of the submersible, like an arm that bends at the elbow. It's activated by a lever contained within the pilot's right armrest and moves like this." He displayed a serpentine striking movement.

"And?"

"And, the tip is armed with what is basically an oversized bang stick, the kind divers use to fend off sharks. Except the shotgun shells we customized for this little girl are two feet long and six inches thick. They can punch a four-foot hole through a full-grown elephant. So . . . whatever the stinger comes into contact with, including your fifty-ton pliosaur, Amara, is going to have its guts exploded out the other side of its body. End of story."

He winked at her.

"That's barbaric! I should have expected that from you." Amara wore a disgusted look as she moved toward the bow of the sub. Shading her eyes with her hands, she pressed her face against the observation window's tinted surface.

Von Freiling turned toward Dean Harcourt. "Senator, do you disapprove of my use of military technology to even the odds against this thing we're hunting?"

Harcourt arched an eyebrow and gazed at the *Eurypterid*. He rubbed his eyes, reaching inside his jacket for a pair of dark sunglasses.

"*Canst thou draw out Leviathan with a hook? Or his tongue with a cord which thou lettest down? Canst thou put a hook into his nose, or bore his jaw through with a thorn?*" He looked at the faces surrounding him. "An excerpt from the Book of Job, people. And no, I believe your vessels were destined to be instruments of divine retribution before they left the drawing board."

"I see . . . well then, there you have it, people," Von Freiling announced, nodding. "If there's nothing else—"

"Actually, I have a question," Jake said.

At the sound of his voice, Amara glanced up from the mini-sub's observation port. She turned back, her eyes scrunching up. The *Eurypterid's* control panel had a familiar look . . .

Von Freiling followed Jake's line of sight. "It's layers of reinforced Lexan."

Jake shook his head. "I'm not talking about the sub's window. I'm curious how much these two ships cost."

"C'mon, Jake. That's not a topic for open discussion," Von Freiling said, smiling hawkishly as his wife's head turned in his direction. "Let's just say my investors have put a considerable amount of money into this particular project and leave it at that."

Jake stroked his chin as he looked the submersible up and down. "Humph. Well . . . I imagine you'll have to catch a hell of a lot of calamari before your backers start making any money back."

"You shouldn't concern yourself with such things," Von Freiling said amiably. He slapped his arm around the sheriff's broad shoulders with surprising force. "Where there's a will, there's a way. Besides, who knows? Maybe there are some military contracts out there, just waiting for my little toys."

"Karl, you son of a bitch!" Amara wheeled on him, her pale eyes flashing as she stepped angrily back from the *Eurypterid's* bow section. "You stole my design, you bastard!"

"Whatever do you mean?" Von Freiling wore an expression of mock fear on his leering face.

"My design for the *William's* manipulators." She started toward her estranged husband. "You thought I wouldn't recognize my own neural interface design through your little attack craft's tinted windows?"

"Actually, since we're still legally married, and worked on that project together, I have legitimate access to all our designs, Amara," Von Freiling replied, taking a step backward and ignoring the assorted looks he was getting. "In addition, you only filed for patent protection here in the US. My backers and manufacturers are foreign, so technically . . ."

"Technically, you found a loophole and felt free to steal my work," the infuriated cetaceanist said. "You know, just when I was starting to think there was no way you could stoop any lower, you surprise me yet again."

"Alright, that's enough," Harcourt said, stepping between them. "We don't have time to waste on nonsense."

"My point exactly," Von Freiling smiled. "In fact–"

He stopped in mid-sentence as one of his mercs rushed up from a nearby stairwell.

"What is it, Gibson?"

"Sorry to bother you, sir," the bearded merc said. "But we're approaching the coordinates you set."

"Thanks," Von Freiling turned to Jake and Amara. "We'll be anchoring shortly. I'm going downstairs to meet with my team. Feel free to come along."

"Oh, we're coming all right," Amara fumed.

Von Freiling started to head below deck. He paused at the doorway. "Senator Harcourt? Will you be attending?"

The burly politician ignored him.

Von Freiling opened his mouth to repeat his invitation, then had a change of heart, shrugged and walked away.

While the others disappeared below, Harcourt remained behind. His oversized escort waited soundlessly nearby, alert and attentive, his column-like arms resting atop his chest.

His eyes cool and calculating, the wealthy politician stared for long moments at the nearest *Eurypterid* before turning his gaze to the surrounding sea. He walked to the railing, grabbing onto the painted metal. Except for the faraway look in his eyes, his scarred face was impassive.

He gazed intently out at the windswept waters, the stiff breeze pushing his hair back. His expression hardened. Somewhere out there, within ten thousand square miles of uncharted ocean, his enemy roamed free. It was a creature that lived to kill, a mindless engine of primal fury whose insatiable lust for dominance exceeded even his own. If he had to track it to the blackest bowels of the abyss to have his vengeance, he would.

———

"Gentlemen, let's start our preparations," Von Freiling announced.

He moved to the middle of the room, his bronze eyes gleaming as he signaled for his men to gather round.

While the boisterous group of mercenaries eagerly surrounded their leader in the center of the *Harbinger's* high-tech command center, Jake and Amara took up position close by. Moments later, they were joined by Willie, who had been keeping watch at his sonar station with a wiry little mercenary nicknamed "Stitches."

The red-haired fellow with the goatee seemed friendly enough. But, given the nature of his peers and the moniker he went by, Jake was sure, when push came to shove, "Stitches" was just as dangerous and unpredictable as the rest of them.

Von Freiling held up a hand for silence. "Before we get started, Stubbs, if you wouldn't mind?" He signaled to his second-in-command.

The big, black-and-gray-bearded soldier with the missing phalanges nodded in response and vanished, returning moments later hauling an unwieldy polymer case four feet in length. The straining merc's arm muscles bulged like bridge cables as he lugged the heavy container to Von Freiling's position, depositing it on top of a sturdy metal table, where its oversized locks could be unsnapped.

"Okay, pass em out," Von Freiling said, heading to the case.

For a moment, Jake wasn't sure what was going on. Then, Von Freiling turned back and began fastening a military-style, ballistic nylon combat harness around his waist and shoulders. It came complete with a Glock semi-automatic pistol, extra magazines, a large, black-handled combat knife, and a pair of grenades.

"Whoa, what the hell is this?" Jake spoke up as the remaining soldiers armed themselves. His concerns were fueled further by the fearful expressions worn by both Amara and Willie. This was obviously something they hadn't anticipated.

"What's the problem, Jake?" With a suppressed grin, Von Freiling tossed several of his men Uzi submachine guns.

"The problem?" Jake shook his head. "Gee, I wonder what that could be . . ."

Deftly snatching the lethal firearms out of the air, the four recipients proceeded to check and clear them, before mechanically slinging them over their shoulders.

"Listen," Von Freiling said. "This is a potentially dangerous mission which may require us to defend ourselves with more than harsh words. However, if you're apprehensive about our weapons, rest assured my men and I are all seasoned professionals. And if it's legalities that are on your mind, we're in international waters now, so no laws are being broken."

"That may be the case," Jake looked intently around the room. "But, I don't think either Dr. Takagi or her first mate are comfortable with the idea of your men strutting around with all this firepower."

"In case you haven't noticed yet, you're not in charge here. Karl is," Stubbs said, checking the safety on both of his weapons and snapping them loudly into place.

Jake locked gazes with the massive mercenary, and felt a fight-or-flight adrenaline surge. Stubbs was undoubtedly dangerous; he had three inches and seventy pounds on him, and eyes that looked like they should be staring at you through the bars of a cage.

Jake's own eyes hardened, and his jaw became granite. "In charge of *you* Stubbs, not me."

The rapidly escalating tension dissipated as Harcourt and his escort made their way into the room.

"Senator Harcourt," Von Freiling greeted him with believable enthusiasm. "I'm glad you could make it. We'll be anchoring shortly. I was about to discuss our plan of action."

"Very well, Mr. Freiling," Harcourt said. He moved beside the tall adventurer and reached for one of his cigars. He was fumbling for his lighter when the nearest merc offered him a match. He looked up and carelessly surveyed the heavily armed group. With the scar on his jaw, he looked like a retired mercenary in a borrowed suit. Even Jake was impressed by how comfortable the wealthy politician appeared in his current surroundings, as well as the obvious deference he was shown by the gang of cutthroats, their smirking leader inclusive. Then again, their loyalties were assured by money. And if there was an earthly deity existing for blood money, the senator from Florida was it.

"Please proceed." Harcourt puffed a huge smoke ring that drifted across the poorly ventilated room.

"Excellent," Von Freiling said. He reached down with a rag and wiped away Amara's enclosure designs in a few quick swipes, then took a dry erase marker and proceeded to make a series of squeaking strokes.

"This jagged line represents Ophion's Deep." He gestured at his crude drawing, utilizing the marker as a pointer. "It's by far the deepest water in the region. Whereas the Blake Plateau in these parts drops to only about five hundred meters, Ophion has been sounded to over three thousand."

There was a sharp inhalation, followed by some low muttering. One of the mercs spoke up. "Whoa, we're not taking the *Eurypterids* down *there*, I hope?"

"No, Stitches, we'll be anchoring in this area, near the Cutlass," Von Freiling continued. "It's an underwater mountain peak that juts up into the shallower waters adjacent to the crevasse. It's as good a place as any to hold bottom."

Amara drew attention to herself by loudly clearing her throat. "Why have you chosen that area to start your hunt?" She edged closer, leaning her hands on the desk and bending at the waist as she glanced at the rough diagram. "Almost all the attacks we know of took place close to shore."

Jake felt a sting of annoyance as a high-pitched catcall came from one of the mercs standing directly behind them. It was either Stitches or the tall blonde guy next to him. He wasn't sure which.

"The attacks we *know* of," Von Freiling said from beneath raised eyebrows. He gave an irritated glance over Amara's shoulder at the men responsible, then continued. "This is a huge animal we're talking about. It's not going to survive snatching people off passing boats. It needs meat, and a lot of it."

The mercs behind Jake gave a low chuckle, with the blonde one speculating in hushed tones about just how much "meat" Amara needed. Von Freiling's eyes zoomed in on him like rifle sights.

Harcourt pointed at the chart with his smoldering Cuban. "And, you think it's going to go looking for it down in . . . what did you call it?"

Von Freiling held up a finger. "One second, senator."

Taking advantage of the two snickering men's distracted state, he made for them like a guided missile. Amara was directly in his path. Spotting his expression, the cetaceanist turned pale, nearly falling over herself getting out of his way. By the time the blonde-haired merc looked up, Von Freiling was right in his face.

"Do we have a problem, mister?" he asked quietly.

"Uh . . . what?" The merc wore a surprised look.

"You're quite the comedian, aren't you . . . Barker, isn't it?"

"Yeah . . ."

"You're our new sniper – Stubbs' friend, right?"

Barker grinned disarmingly, trying to make light of the situation. "Yeah, that's right. What . . . is there something wrong with two guys joking around?"

Von Freiling cricked his neck to one side and glanced up like he was reading an invisible computer screen. "You're the one they booted out of the Corps – tried to frag your sergeant, right?"

Barker's expression turned ugly. "That asshole tried one blanket party too many. And what the fuck does–"

"This is *my* team, mister!" Von Freiling snarled through his teeth. He stepped menacingly close. "And cherry or no, you will do things *my* way. I'm not losing any more men because of faulty Intel, or because a walking hard-on like you is too busy checking out a piece of ass to know how to do your fucking job."

"I'll do my job."

"You better, mister. Because if you *don't*, something very bad is going to happen to you."

"Oh yeah . . ." Barker's eyes were hard, but there was a hint of nervousness in them. "And what's that?"

Von Freiling moved a half-step back, his thumbs in his belt, his eyes never leaving Barker's. "Me."

He waited.

Barker's lips tightened and he hesitated, feeling the unwelcome weight of a roomful of watchful eyes. Finally, he looked down at the floor and nodded.

Von Freiling smiled. "Good."

As the merc's leader turned back to Dean Harcourt, Jake studied Vladimir Markov from across the room. During the confrontation between the two men, the squat merc with the machete paid rapt attention. He wore a blank expression, but his black eyes jogged back and forth between the two with undisguised interest. All the while, his hand tightly gripped his weapon's bone-covered handle, his thumb caressing its rounded pommel with what could only be described as abject fondness.

Jake's lip started to curl up in disgust, but he froze when Markov noticed his scrutiny. Their eyes met and a staring contest ensued, interrupted only by Von Freiling.

Jake felt the muscles running up the back of his neck tighten. He'd garnered a lot in the last minute or two. Markov was a true sadist, and Von Freiling was the leader of this pack of killers for good reason. It had nothing to do with money. He had earned his position. He was the most dangerous of them all.

And his wife was deathly afraid of him.

"I'm sorry for that interruption, senator," Von Freiling said, grinning broadly. "Boys will be boys. So, you were saying–"

Harcourt pointed impatiently back at the diagram. "I asked you the name of the place where you expect to find the creature."

"Ophion's Deep," Von Freiling said.

"What exactly is that?"

"It's a Cretaceous-era submarine canyon – a crack in the ocean floor – appropriately named after the god Ophion. It starts in the Straits of Florida, and carves its way some two hundred kilometers along Florida's continental rise, terminating in this vicinity."

"The god Ophion?"

Von Freiling smiled. "A mythical marine giant – and the original Lord of the Titans in Greek mythology. He was overthrown by his son, the Titan Kronos, who hurled him from the top of Mount Olympus, to crash into the waters Oceanus, far below. Ophion means 'the serpent,' ironically enough."

"I see. And this 'Ophion's Deep,' as you call it; you're confident the creature does its hunting down there?"

"Yes, I am. The entire region is nutrient rich, fed by the warm waters of the Florida Current, which run through the Straits of

Florida. The deep is home to a fairly dense population of giant squid, and it's frequented by the sperm whales that hunt them."

"But, if it's such a great hunting spot, why has the pliosaur been roaming the waters outside Paradise Cove?" Amara interjected.

As he watched her attempt at misdirection, Jake remembered Amara's tale from a few days prior . . . how the pliosaur had risen from the nearby abyss, frightening a pod of whales. Then there was the decomposing body of the bull sperm they found in the same area – the one attacked by the creature. Von Freiling was right about the pliosaur's localized hunting, and Amara knew it.

It was a wasted effort, Jake thought. When it came to hunting, her husband was obviously very good.

"It's a super-predator, darling, just like me." Von Freiling smirked. "It's undoubtedly got a huge hunting territory, one covering fifty square miles or more. But I'm betting that its home base – if you'd like to call it that – is right about . . . *here*." He smacked the marker's point down hard, directly on the Cutlass.

"Fair enough," Harcourt said. "I'll buy that. What's your attack strategy?"

"We bait it to the surface," Von Freiling said, speaking directly to his employer. "It's an air breather, so it shouldn't be hard."

"Bait it with what?"

Jake felt a sudden ping of nervousness vibrate down his spine.

"Let's just say we've brought something with us that should be to the creature's liking," Von Freiling replied. "Don't worry, senator. We'll get a rise out of your monster."

Amara leaned toward Jake and Willie. "You know," she whispered. "For a fat politician who's used to sitting behind a desk and hiding behind bodyguards, this guy certainly seems to have Karl and his wolf pack eating out of his proverbial claw."

"*Nature teaches beasts to know their friends,*" Willie murmured back. "Coriolanus."

Amara nodded. Her eyes met Jake's eyes and she gave him a pensive half-smile, then turned back to the discussion at hand.

"We can also use this," Stitches said, nodding at Willie. He pulled a recording disc out of his pocket. "It's a recording of sperm whales being attacked by orcas. Mr. Daniels was kind enough to give me a tour of the ship's collection of audio recordings. I dampened the orca calls, so all that's left are the sounds of the sperms and their young. If we broadcast it over the hydrophone array it'll add auditory appeal to our bait."

Von Freiling grinned as he accepted the disc. "Alright, we'll give it a go. It certainly can't hurt."

Jake glanced at Amara, clocking the cool look she was giving her second-in-command.

"How exactly do you plan on subduing the monster?" Harcourt breathed, his cigar clenched in his teeth. "Once you've got it in your sights, that is."

"If we're successful in drawing it to the surface, we'll deal with it using conventional means." Von Freiling looked meaningfully at his men. "It's by far the safest way to go. However, if we fail, or if we miss our mark and it sounds, we'll have to fight it in the water."

Amara cleared her throat. "You know, if you do get it to the surface, we have a spear gun onboard that's loaded with some serious whale tranquilizers."

Her impromptu announcement instantly garnered everyone's attention, especially Von Freiling's.

"Hey, I'm just trying to help," she offered. "I don't know if you've brought any sedatives with you, but a heavy dose of Cetaprol-50 might do the job."

Von Freiling glanced at Harcourt, then gave Amara an indecipherable stare. "Sure," he said. "I've used it before. It could slow it down a bit. Thanks for the offer. We'll take you up on it."

"I'm still curious about the intricacies of your plan." Harcourt stared at his hired gun. "If you do go into the water to fight the creature, how do you plan on doing it? I doubt you and your men have any experience at this sort of thing."

"I think it's safe to say no one in the *world*'s ever taken on a *Kronosaurus* before." Von Freiling chuckled. "They've been extinct for sixty-five million years, which makes it all the more exciting for us. However, our strategy will be the same as it would be, were we hunting any other creature of its type. Other than sheer size, it's still just a predator, and a predictably nasty and territorial one."

"You still haven't answered my question," Harcourt said. He dropped the remnants of his cigar on the floor and crushed it out with his heel.

"We're gonna do the old 'bait and switch' routine," Von Freiling stated, stroking his black mustache. "We'll use one of the *Eurypterids* as bait, make it wobble around a bit to feign an injury, and draw the beastie out in the open. Then, we'll use the second sub to blindside it."

"Just like that?"

"Yep, that's the plan," Von Freiling said amusedly. "I'm sure we . . ." The merc's leader paused as an interference-laden transmission screeched out of his radio. He held up a hand for silence and held the unit by his ear.

"This is Karl, I missed what you said, Barnes. Please repeat."

A harsh shriek of garbled sound hissed out of the radio.

"We've reached . . . initial coordinates, sir." Barnes's charged voice could barely be heard. "I'm . . . shift into . . . current and lower . . . anchors."

"Excellent. Let me know when we're good to go."

Jake detected a subtle change in the feeling of the ship as the *Harbinger* began to decelerate in the water. Soon, everyone in the room could feel the vibration of the ship's straining diesels, as her pilot maneuvered her nose-first into the fast-moving current adjacent to Ophion's Deep.

A moment later, the ship released its anchors. There was a series of lurching sensations as they caught hold, their chains creaking as they held the two-hundred foot vessel taut against the afternoon tide.

"Okay men, we'll be operational in a moment." Von Freiling turned to Harcourt. "I'm sorry senator, we're going to have to continue our conversation later. For now, you're going to have to trust me."

He folded his arms. "Gentlemen, I want this thing to go smooth and by the numbers. Your assignments are as follows: Stubbs, you and Markov put out the bait. Take Diaz and Barker with you. Let's see if we can convince our dinner guest to show up while there's still light out."

"Yes, sir," Stubbs said.

"Stitches." Von Freiling tossed him back the disc he handed him. "Get this playing on the ship's hydrophone. I want you manning the sonar station until we've launched. I don't want this critter sneaking up on us while we've got our asses half out of the water. Also, this ship's got some good underwater cameras, so let's take advantage of those. After Stubbs has got the bait out he'll relieve you, so you and Gibson can prep *Eurypterid II* for launch."

Stitches caught the disc. "What about you, sir?"

Von Freiling looked up as Barnes walked into the room, then turned back. "Barnes and I will be launching right after you on *Eurypterid I*," he said. "Oh, and before I forget, Stitches . . . you get to be the bait."

"Gee, thanks. That's wonderful, sir."

Jake watched him shake his head as he walked away. Stitches was obviously a little less enthusiastic than his colleagues.

Von Freiling focused on the pale-skinned giant standing a few feet away. "Johnson, you'll continue to keep our illustrious benefactor company." He gave a polite nod in Harcourt's direction. "You're to also keep an eye on things onboard while we're in the water."

Johnson said nothing, just dipped his huge head in what might have been a nod, then stood there like a seven-foot ivory statue. Jake was starting to wonder if the senator's polar bear bodyguard was mute as well as melanin deficient.

"What about us?" Amara indicated Willie and herself.

"Well, now, you'll be a darling if you go and fetch me that big spear gun you bragged about," Von Freiling said. "Other than that, I'd appreciate it if you two and our worrywart of a sheriff stay out of the way. I'd hate for something to go wrong once the action starts and one of you get hurt."

Jake exchanged glances with Amara.

"Alright people, you have your assignments," Von Freiling said. "We're anchored and good to go. Let's go make some money and go home!"

The observation room shuddered as the mercenaries raised their fists, cheering like barbarians before they bolted headlong out of the room. As he followed Willie and Amara out, Jake noticed Harcourt lagging behind. The stocky politician gestured for Von Freiling, leaned over and whispered in his ear. Though the angle prevented him from discerning what was being said, it was obvious the senator had his hired gun's undivided attention.

Jake hesitated. He was sorely tempted to lag behind and eavesdrop, but before he could make up his mind, Dean Harcourt's colossus of a bodyguard appeared in the doorway. Glaring malevolently down at him, Johnson slammed the heavy metal door shut in his face.

CRETACEOUS OCEAN
65 MILLION YEARS AGO

The big male was in a rage.

Moments prior, with the competition between himself and the one-eyed bull approaching its inevitable climax, an interloper unexpectedly interfered. The culprit, a fourteen-foot sea turtle known as *Archelon*, stumbled unwittingly into his path. Caught in the female pliosaur's route, the frightened creature tried desperately to flee. Unable to escape in time, it was bowled over by the giant cow.

Trapped in the vortex of her powerful wake, the chelonian whirled helplessly out of control, spinning beak over tail. By the time it righted itself and began struggling for the surface, the big bull pliosaur crashed into it with stunning force.

With his progress momentarily thwarted by the bone-jarring impact with the six-ton *Archelon*, the frustrated male pliosaur watched powerlessly as the third remaining jack, a powerful beast nearly his size with tiger-like stripes, flew right past him. Already foul-tempered from hormones brought on by the rut, the big bull brought his mighty jaws to bear on the hapless sea turtle.

Shearing through the *Archelon's* protective shell like it was an egg, the dominant male eviscerated the smaller reptile with a single bite. Disdainfully spitting out the source of his irritation, he shook his huge head back and forth, then snarled and charged after the other jacks with a vengeance, leaving the dying *Archelon* to sink slowly into the depths. Jagged pieces of turtle shell and flesh clung to his teeth and spun from his jaws as he raced forward.

The pliosaur queen spouted. Like the whales that would one day replace her kind, twin funnels of compressed water vapor exploded from her nostrils to a height of over twenty feet. With a quick inhalation, she closed her watertight nostril flaps and prepared to continue her mating chase.

Overhead, the sky was a virtual inferno, as a second sun, many times brighter and fierier, blazed across the heavens at inconceivable speed. Her scarlet eyes, with their pinprick black pupils, reflected the fireball's deadly descent. Sensing the powerful displacement wave of the approaching jacks, the bright distraction was quickly forgotten.

With a loud hiss, the female dove beneath the waves and sped on.

———

Topping out at over fifty miles an hour, the big bull quickly caught up to the remaining two males. He could see his rivals only a hundred yards ahead, the one-eyed male and the striped bull, violently jostling each other as they vied for position behind the queen. The big male was in a rage. His blood pounded in his brain and he saw the world through a ruby-red curtain. In that one critical moment, the normal rules of mating competition were completely forgotten.

With an extra burst of power from his giant flippers, he positioned himself directly behind the older male. His deadly jaws agape and razor sharp teeth poised, he prepared to attack his rival's exposed haunch, incapacitating the older bull and taking him out of the fight.

He moved to strike. Then he was blinded.

———

Five hundred miles away, the asteroid struck with indescribable force. The shock of the collision reverberated throughout the planet's core, starting earthquakes and tsunamis, and setting off volcanoes across the globe. On impact, the blast gouged out a gigantic crater measuring one hundred and ninety miles across, and emitted a blinding burst of light that blazed with the fury of a thousand suns. The entire asteroid was instantly vaporized, along with trillions of tons of water, earth and stone, and reformed into a continent-sized cloud of silicate metal vapor with a temperature that could melt copper.

Within moments, the white-hot cloud encompassed most of what would one day be North America, as well as large portions of South America and Eurasia, broiling to death every living creature it encountered. Reptiles, mammals, insects and plants perished on contact. Nothing was spared. On land, dinosaurs died screeching by the millions.

Accompanying this cloud, and devastating whatever areas the deadly vapors failed to permeate, was the shock wave brought about by the blast. In an instant, every creature in the air, from the smallest pterodactyl to the largest flying giant, was swatted from the skies. Helplessly they fell. Battered and broken, they crashed to the earth or plummeted into the sea. The shock wave shattered stone, started avalanches, and knocked down trees, bowling over and battering the largest of creatures.

Next came the inevitable inferno. Thousands of cubic miles of red-hot debris expelled from the impact zone mushroomed over forty miles straight up into the atmosphere. Carried by the prevailing winds, the glowing embers spread like lethal fireflies across the globe.

Gently drifting back to earth, the shimmering particles started forest fires wherever they landed. Within a matter of hours, most of the remaining planet was in flames.

Still reeling from the shockwave, the four pliosaurs milled aimlessly about on the surface. From over five hundred miles away they watched, mesmerized, as doomsday unfolded. The skies grew dark and foreboding, and the surface of the water was dotted with the bodies of flying reptiles and other smaller creatures.

The pliosaurs had survived the blast, though not unscathed. Several of them, including the big bull, suffered ruptured eardrums. Dark blood oozed from their tympanum canals as they lay, dizzy and disoriented. To their good fortune, the flash blindness was only temporary; the murky waters shielded them from the full strength of the burst.

Keeping close to the giant female, the three jacks drifted along, their conflict temporarily forgotten. The mating impulse was interrupted for the moment, though it was far from gone. Uncertain how to proceed, the great sea beasts watched as the awesome spectacle unfolded. A mushroom cloud of debris and vapor rose high into the sky, spreading rapidly.

All around them, panic-stricken sea creatures fled, heedlessly splashing over the bodies of the dead as they went. Among them were the three *Tylosaurus* the big male routed earlier and a forty-nine foot elasmosaur – two thirds of its length made up of a serpentine neck – that paddled right past the giant female's toothy muzzle. With the cow distracted by the devastation going on, the delicate fish eater sped by unmolested.

A short while later, glowing bits of debris began to fall around them, splashing into the water with a loud hiss. Some of the particles struck the pliosaurs, singeing their thick hides. The marine reptiles shook off the burning embers with low rumbles of irritation, submerging just below the surface when the fiery downpour became too great. Their huge size and strength had saved them from the shockwave. They would weather the falling fire as well. Lords of the oceans, there was nothing they could not withstand.

Then they saw the wave.

———

The tsunami had started over five hundred miles away, formed as the asteroid struck the coastline, displacing thousands of cubic miles of earth and ocean. Traveling at over eleven hundred miles an hour, it crossed the Abyssal plains with frightening speed. Its power only temporarily diffused and concealed by the water's depth, it began to grow geometrically as it reached the shallower waters of the continental shelf. In six thousand feet of water, the tidal wave measured only thirty feet in height. Now, in six hundred feet, it was three hundred feet tall. By the time it reached the coastline, it would measure three thousand feet or more.

With hurricane-force winds and a deafening roar heralding its approach, the wave loomed in the distance.

TWENTY-TWO

H is thoughts to himself, Jake accompanied Amara and Willie onto the *Harbinger*'s sunlit decks, leaving Karl Von Freiling and his men behind. As he donned his sunglasses, he cast a sideways glance at the marine biologist. Tension overshadowed her exotic features; her body language seemed off, and she was uncharacteristically quiet.

All of a sudden, Amara sucked in a huge breath through flared nostrils. She wheeled on Willie, her pale eyes shimmering. "What the hell were you thinking, giving them that disc?"

Impressed with her temper, Jake moved a discrete distance away, back to the *Harbinger*'s railing. Whistling softly to himself, he focused on the region's assorted cloud formations.

"Actually, dat recordin was marked already," Willie replied. He shook his head and cast a surreptitious glance toward the swaying mini-subs. "Anyone would've known what it was. I knew dey was goin to look over all our stuff anyway, so I pretended to be helpin, so I could keep dem from finding some ting else."

"What something?" Jake interjected.

The big Jamaican glanced over his shoulder to make sure no one was coming, then reached inside his undershirt and pulled out a disc.

"Dis!" he replied with a grin that showed off his strong, white teeth. "It's my recordin of da beast's audio profile and sonar signature. Wit out it, I doubt dey can distinguish it from any whale around here."

Amara's mouth opened, but only a tiny gasp came out. She stared dazedly at Willie. "Uh . . . Good thinking." Head lowered, she hugged him apologetically. "I'm so sorry I doubted you." She took the CD in her hand and stared at it, nibbling on her lower lip. "We should probably toss this overboard."

"I was goin to," Willie said. "But den, I figured if dis bunch of yahoos fail, den maybe we can get da boat back and use it to find dat ting ourselves."

"Okay, Willie," Amara agreed. She hesitated as she handed the disc back. "Just make sure they don't catch you with it. Karl will go berserk if he finds out."

Jake studied Amara through a cop's eyes. He cleared his throat and held out a hand. "Actually, it's probably safest if I hold onto that. I'm the last person our host would think to search." He stashed the disc within an inside shirt pocket, before gazing contemplatively at the blue and white waves that shifted the anchored vessel beneath their feet. He turned to Amara. "Speaking of our host, what's the story with you two? Karl doesn't exactly strike me as your type, if you'll forgive my prying."

Amara paused thoughtfully, her brow's smooth skin creasing up. "I was a young girl who was vulnerable and easily impressed." She shrugged her well-toned shoulders. "Karl can be quite impressive, and in case you haven't figured it out yet, he's definitely the adventurous type."

Jake nodded. "But you're no longer with him because . . ."

"Because he's a thief, a gambler, and a womanizer," Amara said. She cast a cautious glance at the battle-scarred adventurer, busy clambering over the chassis of his submersible. "And there's also the fact that the bastard tends to win arguments with his hands."

"Humph. Very nice." *Another Ben Stillman*, Jake thought. He waited until Amara's eyes turned back before asking the inevitable question. "So, if he's such an asshole, why don't you just divorce him? Sure sounds like you've got grounds."

"Because he refuses to sign the papers, that's why. And I don't have the time or the inkling to see him in court." Amara turned toward the horizon, her forearms resting on the cool metal railing as she stared wistfully at the beckoning sea. Her head drooped and she gave a long sigh. "I guess he finds it useful to be able to say he's married to an award-winning naturalist or something."

"Especially one with eyes like yours."

Amara's lips turned pouty and her cheeks reddened. "Very funny, Jake Braddock. You picking on me?"

"No, I'm serious. I've never seen that color before. Forgive me if this sounds ignorant, but how does a Japanese girl end up with eyes that look like they were carved from a glacier?"

"Oh, it's not so hard," Amara smirked. "All you have to do is have a shipload of Norwegian fishermen get drunk celebrating the end of World War Two, and have them run aground on the shores of Okinawa. Next thing you know, they become infatuated with the local girls and decide to stay." She winked at Jake, indicating herself with both hands. "A few generations later . . ."

Jake grinned, picturing the scene in his head "So, you're part Norwegian?"

Amara nodded. "On both sides."

"That also explains the height. You're pretty tall, for a Japanese girl."

Amara beamed at him. "Yeah? Well, you've got some nice height on you too, big guy. A cute smile too, when you use it."

Jake's grin vanished as he caught sight of some of Von Freiling's men struggling to push a large crate onto the windy aft deck. It was Stubbs and several of the others. Markov lurked in the background. An idea came to him, and he moved mechanically in their direction, leaving Amara and Willie where they were.

"Say, Stubbs, watcha got there?" he called out good-naturedly as he walked over to the straining group. "Looks like you guys could use a hand."

Stubbs grunted at his colleagues to hold on and rose to his full height. At six-foot-five, with arms like tree trunks, the out-of-breath mercenary was built like a 300-pound gorilla. He hesitated, giving Jake an appraising stare as the heavily muscled lawman approached.

"Sure thing, sheriff," he said, his previous hostility replaced with a sweat-soaked half-smile.

Jake gave a friendly nod and took up a position between Stubbs and Markov. He grabbed hold of the eight-foot wooden crate and heaved.

"Wow, this thing weighs a ton," he said, as the five of them wrestled the weighty burden toward a nearby railing. "What the hell do you guys have in here?"

"You'll see in a minute," Markov muttered, his demeanor as unpleasant as ever. A moment later, with the crate against the portside railing, the squat merc disappeared, returning a moment later with a pry bar. The crate's lid was quickly removed, and after a few creaky pries and some well placed smacks, the wooden box fell apart, displaying its contents.

Jake caught a glimpse of organs and intestines spewing blood and bodily fluids and fought down the urge to gag.

"Ugh, what the heck is that?" He gaped at the huge carcass lying on the deck.

"It's fresh beef, sheriff," Stubbs said, grinning at Jake's discomfiture. "C'mon man, surely you've gone fishing before? You know how it is – the bigger the bait, the bigger the fish!"

Jake stared down at the beheaded remains of what had to be a 1,500 pound steer. He was stunned. Von Freiling certainly came prepared. "And how do you intend to–"

"With this," Markov interrupted. He held up a heavy grappling hook affixed with a heavy locking pin assembly to one of the *Harbinger's* four-inch-thick nylon docking ropes. As the other three mercenaries disassembled the remainder of the crate and tossed the pieces overboard, Markov hauled back and slammed the razor-sharp grapnel ferociously against the carcass's chest cavity. Grunting loudly, he heaved back on it with all the strength of his powerful forearms, ripping away until he got two of the three curved points embedded between its ribs and was satisfied they'd stay there.

"Maybe you're right, Stubbs." Jake glanced at Markov and then nodded at Von Freiling's second-in-command. "Size *does* matter . . ."

Stubbs followed his gaze and grinned. "Exactly. Alright, Diaz, you and Markov give a quick grab over here. Barker, you and our candy striper can take hold of that end."

"Whenever you guys are ready," Jake remarked. He dropped down into a sumo-style crouch and dug his calloused fingers deep into the slaughtered steer's blood-flecked flanks.

"Okay, you fatherless sons of whores . . . on three," Stubbs said. "Up straight, then right over the side. One, two, and *heave!*"

Working as one, the five grappled the three-quarter-ton carcass up onto its bloodstained haunches and then, with a uniform roar of triumph, leveraged it up and over the *Harbinger's* sturdy metal railing. Disappearing over the side of the vessel, the double side of beef spiraled down some twenty feet before crashing into the swirling sea.

Jake peered over the gunnels, shielding his eyes and studying the carcass as it sank to a depth of thirty feet. It came to an abrupt halt there, suspended at the end of its tether in the thermocline, swaying enticingly back and forth. Experienced big game fisherman that he was, the young lawman had to admit the butchered bull's spurting remains certainly looked inviting enough.

"Nice work, gentlemen," Stubbs said, looking with satisfaction at the heavily breathing lot. He extended his hand to Jake. "Thanks for your help, sheriff."

"Anytime," Jake replied casually, shaking his hand and wiping his blood and grime-caked palms on his trousers. "I needed the exercise."

"You may get some more before this trip's over, cop." Markov mumbled, giving Jake an evil smirk before sauntering off.

Jake watched him go, then turned to Von Freiling's second-in-command. "Yo, Stubbs . . ." he moved closer to the big merc, his voice and eyebrows lowered. "Am I just imagining it, or does your man Markov have some sort of problem with me?"

"Yes, he does. And if you don't mind some advice, you stay away from him," Stubbs said solemnly. "Markov didn't take kindly to you getting ready to draw on him back at the dock. He's the kind that can't let something like that go. Develops a rage inside – eats away at him until he can't take it anymore. Then he just plain explodes."

"No problem. I've dealt with psychos like him before."

"With all due respect to your profession, sheriff, your town drunks and bullies ain't anything like Vladimir Markov," Stubbs advised. "Karl personally recruited him in Cambodia a few years back. He'd made quite a name for himself there. Cocaine, prostitution, political assassinations, gun running – you name it, he was doing it. You've seen that big bolo he carries, right?"

Jake nodded.

"If you look close, you'll see seventeen notches on the back of the blade." Stubbs kept a close watch on the nearby stairwell. "One for every man he's cut down in hand-to-hand combat. He keeps trophies, too: fingers, noses, that kind of stuff. Word is that the bone inlays on that thing's handle came from the skull of his first kill."

Jake mulled Stubbs' advice over. Despite everything the battle-hardened merc was telling him, it was the one thing he *wasn't* saying that told him to proceed with caution. As big and fierce as he was, Stubbs was afraid of Markov.

"Sounds like a likable sort." Jake commented. He studied the darkened doorway with calculating eyes before giving Stubbs a predatory smile. "Thanks for the info, brother. I appreciate the heads-up, but I can take care of myself."

Stubbs made a guttural sound deep in his chest that could have been a growl of approval. "You know, Braddock, you're not at all what I expected," he said, looking the big lawman up and down as if seeing him for the first time. "You're no donut-guzzling speed trap cop, that's for sure. In fact, you just might fit in with us. Something for you to think about, in case you ever want a career change."

"You know, I've been hearing that a lot lately," Jake said, chuckling. He clapped the black-clad merc on the shoulder before heading back to Amara and Willie.

As he made his way toward them, he caught sight of Harcourt and Johnson. They were standing by the portside railing, a few yards from where the ship's baited dock rope angled down into the sea. The two were engaged in conversation. Or rather, the senator was.

Jake noticed Johnson seemed quite interested in what the politician was saying, yet except for a few head bobs and changes in expression, he remained as silent as ever.

"What was that all about?" Amara demanded as Jake strode over to her and Willie.

"Just helping the guys put bait out, doc," Jake said. He felt a sharp spasm of pain in his side and pressed one hand against his injured ribs. He took a deep breath and cursed, realizing he'd reopened his wound. Across the deck, he watched Karl Von Freiling conferring with his pilot. Jake studied the big adventurer while slowly sucking in breaths. He took his hand away. It came away damp, but the blood was pinkish instead of red. He frowned. The wound was definitely infected, but at least the ribs underneath were intact.

"Not *that*," Amara remarked. She shot a quick glance at the rope draped over her vessel's reinforced railing. "I saw that, and it was downright disgusting. I'm talking about you getting all chummy with that scary looking guy with the missing fingertips."

"Just getting to know who I can, doc. You never know when networking can come in handy."

"I'll bet."

"Speaking of which, I think I'll go bond with your estranged husband," Jake said, leaning in close and giving her an amazingly accurate impersonation of one of Von Freiling's trademark smirks. He laughed at the look of surprise on her face, then turned and strutted off toward their host.

Jake's jaw muscles tightened. It was time to find out more about Amara's mysterious spouse, and to see if he was as dangerous and unstable as she believed.

He walked up to the merc's colorful leader, his voice loud enough that only Von Freiling and Barnes could hear. "So, Karl . . . Are you expecting any casualties during this mission?"

Von Freiling looked up, shooting him an unfriendly look. "Hopefully not. What's it to you?"

"I think it's something you might want to consider. Maybe have a triage station ready. I've seen that thing up close, and I know what it's capable of."

"Yeah, that's right," Von Freiling retorted. He glanced at Jake's injured side, then gave him a condescending look. "I saw the news footage, hero. Nice shots of you getting cozy with my wife. Tell me something. You tapping that ass?"

"Excuse me?"

"Don't bullshit me, Braddock. I see the way you look at Amara. It's obvious you've got a major chubby for her." He snickered, glancing over Jake's shoulder in the leggy cetaceanist's direction. "That is, if you're not slapping cock to that tight twat of hers, already."

Jake's eyes narrowed. He leaned in close and smiled, though there was nothing amiable about the look in his eye. "You know, Karl, all of that talk of yours about using bait to attract our sea monster reminded me of something. I met one of your Brazilian cameramen during a film shoot a few years back. I thought it was bull at the time, but he told me you used a child from one of the local villages as bait to catch that big anaconda of yours. Any truth in that?"

Von Freiling's omnipresent grin vanished. His raptor's eyes swept the deck, pinpointing Dean Harcourt's distant form before he responded.

"Now, now, Jake," he said, forcing a smile and stroking his mustache. "You, of all people, should know how it is when you're riding high. There's always someone trying to bring you down. Yes, there *was* an adolescent from one of the tribal villages involved in the capture of that snake. But, he was one of our hired guides, and was checking on a dead caiman we were using for bait. When the snake struck, it grabbed him by mistake."

Jake studied him intently. "Hmm . . . And this local guide – what happened to him?"

Von Freiling shrugged. "We did our best, but we were far away from doctors or hospitals, and his injuries were too severe. We couldn't save him."

"I see." Jake nodded and turned to walk away. He stopped in midstride, mentioning over one shoulder, "Well, I hope your friends in the mini-sub you're using as bait today fare better than your *last* volunteer did."

"You know, Braddock, if I didn't know better, I'd think you were challenging me," Von Freiling growled. He wiped the grease off his scarred hands with a rag and tossed it to the ground. His eyes turned to sniper scopes as he looked the lawman up and down. "Any truth in *that*?"

"None whatsoever," Jake replied. Out of the corner of his eye he could see Barnes tensing up. "But in case it's slipped your mind, just remember I'm responsible for the safety of at least two individuals onboard this ship. That being the case, I'm very interested in finding out what you're capable of."

"Time will tell."

As he walked away, Jake could feel Von Freiling's metallic eyes burning into his back.

Three miles from the *Harbinger,* the pliosaur hovered in the gloom. Its four flippers extended like the air brakes of a jumbo jet as it came to an abrupt stop. Its stereoscopic nostrils began to flare, feverishly pumping seawater back and forth through their scoop-shaped sensory passages as it worked to detect the source of the blood trail.

The creature twisted its gigantic body with quick flicks of its fins, angling its head to and fro as it combined its sound-imaging with its phenomenal sense of smell. Within seconds it detected the origin of the enticing scent. The smell was coming from high up in the water column ... near the surface ... from a nearby ship.

Enticed by the smell and taste, it rose up, passing a towering underwater spire along the way and tearing a path through a dense wall of kelp as it moved in the direction of the ship. When it was within a thousand yards, another stimulus began to call to the creature. It was the sound of prey bellowing in distress.

Echoing beneath the surface at four times the air speed of sound, the plaintive cries of sperm whale cows and their young permeated the pliosaur's tiny ear canals. It began to blink repeatedly, casting in every direction in an effort to pinpoint the location of the besieged whales, and whatever was attacking them.

It became perplexed. It was unable to detect a rival carnivore of any kind. In fact, there were no echoes in the vicinity that indicated the presence of *any* large life form. There was nothing, just loose strands of kelp and detritus, wafting in the current.

With a watery grumble, the gigantean beast continued to move forward. The stimulus was still there, waiting. Its scarred lips wrinkled back, revealing rows of sharp teeth. Its inability to sense the location of the other carnivore mattered not. *It* was the dominant predator.

And any creature that challenged it for a kill would simply become one.

Alone in the *Harbinger's* observation room, Stitches monitored the vessel's hi-tech sonar station. From the moment he sat down, he'd been dissatisfied with the machine's settings. He painstakingly realigned the entire system, adjusting the main screen's gain and recalibrating the sensitivity of the hydrophone. His goal was to eliminate the sonar emissions from the region's whales, as well as background noise caused by debris caught in the heavy Florida Current. It took him thirty minutes to finally get what he wanted; now, with his work complete, he sat back and smiled.

It always amused Stitches that organizations like the Worldwide Cetacean Society would purchase a dilapidated vessel like the *Harbinger*, refit her from bow to stern, and end up spending more money on the science equipment they crammed inside her rusty hull than the entire ship was worth. Perhaps, in their sheltered circles, it was possible their one-sided expenditures actually made sense.

Not this time, though. If Stitches was given the choice, he could name a dozen other ships he'd rather be hunting their rogue pliosaur on. And every one was bigger, better armed, and far faster than the forty-five-year-old whaler whose riveted belly he currently sat in.

God, the damn thing's hull plates aren't even welded . . .

He sighed and leaned back, puffing out his cheeks and rubbing his eyes against the harsh glare emanating from the main sonar screen. There was a bright green flash. He blinked spasmodically and did a double-take.

"What the hell?"

In an instant, Stitches was rigidly upright, giving the black-backed monitor his undivided attention. With all the interference, it was hard to tell if something organic was in the area or not. The vast kelp forests bordering Ophion's Deep were constantly shedding huge strands, many measuring a hundred feet or more in length. Swirling in the current, the giant sections of seaweed were a sonar operator's worst nightmare. They spiraled about, radiating false echoes, and duping even the most experienced technician into believing a sea serpent of epic proportions was bearing down on them.

After several minutes, Stitches lost interest. Whatever disturbance he thought he'd seen had vanished. Either that or it was concealed behind the vast swarm of debris that was clogging not only his sonar, but also his hull cameras. He leaned back again and considered sneaking a fat joint out of his pack of cigarettes.

Karl will never know . . .

Suddenly, he saw it again. This time, it was a definitive contact – and a damned big one. It was moving in their direction at high speed. Then, just as he reached for his radio, it disappeared again.

Frustrated, Stitches scratched at his goatee. He sucked in a deep breath, exhaling slowly through his teeth to relieve some of his pent-up frustration. He started to reach for the volume control of the *Harbinger*'s ultra-sensitive hydrophone system. An unpleasant possibility dawned on him and his eyes narrowed. He hesitated, tapping his fingers on the desk in front of him before he gave into his instincts and twisted the volume knob to max.

"Holy shit!"

With trembling fingers, Stitches fumbled for his radio. His astonished eyes were like ostrich eggs, locked onto the shimmering black and green sonar panel before him.

———

Up on the *Harbinger's* aft deck, Von Freiling and his co-pilot were finishing their final systems check of *Eurypterid I*. The big adventurer tapped a few keys and then cursed under his breath. He was aggravated by the local sheriff's meddling and pondering what he was going to do about it.

Perhaps that tiny Zodiac we're dragging – might be worth consideration. We don't need it. We could just throw Braddock's ass on it, give him a bottle of water and send him on his merry way. Maybe we'll give him a compass.

Von Freiling clamped his jaws together, his brow furrowing up like newly planted rows of corn.

We'd have to waste time draining most of the dinghy's gasoline first. Leave him with just enough to make it back to shore.

He thought it over and fought down an evil smirk.

Shit, if bleeding-heart Amara wasn't there, along with that pseudo-intellectual friend of hers, it'd be simpler to just toss him over the side and be done with him.

He chuckled to himself. Harcourt certainly wouldn't mind. He'd probably give them a nice, juicy bonus for doing it.

Von Freiling smiled, considering the idea for real.

Hell, his thrashing as he fights to stay afloat might even bring the pliosaur to our door . . .

"Karl! This is Stitches, come in!"

Von Freiling shook off his ponderings. He reached for his walkie-talkie. "Karl here, what's wrong?"

"We've got company, boss!"

"Are you sure? Do you have it on the screen?" Excitement laced the big-game hunter's deep voice.

"Not yet, but there's definitely something out there!"

"How do you know, Stitches?"

"Because something just scanned us with active sonar, that's how!"

"Are you fucking kidding me?"

"No, I'm not."

Von Freiling frowned. "Stitches, are you sure you know what the hell you're looking at?"

"Say *what*? I used to do this for a living, remember?" the irate sonar tech replied. "But if you don't believe me, listen to this!"

There was a moment's silence as Stitches held his radio next to the hydrophone's speaker.

A low grating sound emanated out of Von Freiling's walkie-talkie. A bemused expression on his face, the merc's leader exchanged glances with Barnes. He focused his sights on Amara and Willie, who were lollygagging by the portside railing.

"Okay Stitches, you've convinced me," Von Freiling growled. His alloyed eyes turned hard and calculating. "Keep watch for a definitive reading, and call me as soon as it shows up. I'll alert the men."

With his anvil-like jaw set, Von Freiling stalked straight towards Amara, the equally menacing form of Barnes shadowing him.

Five hundred yards away, the pliosaur surfaced for air. Filling its huge lungs, it submerged. It ran silently, leveling off at two hundred feet, and propelled itself forward in a wide, sweeping arc. Caught in its path, a school of squid scattered in shimmering terror.

Totally fixated on the bloody scent trail, it approached the anchored vessel from its port side. The excitement of the hunt started to build within it. Its jaws slowly opened and closed, and its monstrous heart beat faster and faster as it approached its target.

Just then, the creature spotted something suspended below the ship that its sensory field described from a thousand feet away as meat –fresh, bleeding meat – and in sufficient quantity to take the edge off its growing hunger.

Jake lounged against a nearby railing, enjoying a cool breeze as he listened in on Amara and Willie's discussion regarding Johnson, Dean Harcourt's hulking bodyguard.

"He has no tongue?" Amara stared with horrified eyes. "Are you sure, Willie?"

"Dat's what Stitches told me," the tall Jamaican said quietly. "He said da poor mon was taken prisoner during da war in Afghanistan. He was tortured and wouldn't talk, so dey cut out his tongue."

Jake cleared his throat. "That explains why he's so quiet."

"Dere's more." Willie's voice dropped to a whisper. "Before his unit found him, he lost it. He broke free and turned da tables on his captors. Killed dem all wit his bare hands."

"Impressive feat, for an albino." Jake appraised the towering merc, then turned to Amara. "Aren't they supposed to be weak?"

She gave a tight head shake. "He's not an albino."

Jake blinked. "He's not?"

"No, he's leucistic."

"Leucistic?"

"Yes, Jake. Haven't you seen his eyes? They're blue, not pink. He's not pigment deprived; he's a genetic mutation, like a white tiger. That means he's as strong as anyone else his size. Maybe stronger . . ."

"Interesting . . ." Jake said.

Willie glanced nervously around. "Wait, I didn't tell ya da best part. By da time da cavalry finally arrived, he'd gone totally Section 8. Dey found him playing some sick game of soccer wit dee insurgent's bodies . . ."

"How sick?"

"He was using dere heads as balls – kicking dem for goals."

"Imagine that . . ." Jake whistled softly. "Well, I must say, doc, your husband certainly surrounds himself with some interesting types." His head cocked to one side as he spotted Von Freiling and Barnes approaching. "Speaking of which . . ."

"A word with you," Von Freiling said, storming up to them.

Jake's muscles tensed involuntarily. There was trouble brewing. From Von Freiling's body posture and the timbre of his voice, the eccentric adventurer was on the verge of exploding. Strangely enough, his anger wasn't directed at Jake, or even Willie. He was after Amara.

"Yes, Karl?" she asked. She looked confused and scared.

"You know, you were *so* helpful earlier during our meeting downstairs," Von Freiling remarked snidely. "You know . . . offering to let us use your fancy spear gun and all. But I think you may have left a little something out, *darling*."

"I'm afraid I don't understand."

"Oh, I think you *do*. This pliosaur of yours . . . does it have echolocation?"

"Does it have . . . what?" Her mouth open and eyes wide, Amara stalled unconvincingly.

"I said, does it have *echolocation*?" Von Freiling bristled, his glittering eyes growing fierce as he moved closer. "You see, we've just been scanned by active sonar. So unless there's a military submarine following us around, I'd say this creature of yours is an accomplished echolocator!"

"And what makes ya tink we'd know dat, mon?" Willie asked.

"You know what, maybe you're right. Maybe I'm asking the wrong person," Von Freiling warned, his eyes locking onto Amara's first mate's. "After all, you're the sonar operator of this ship, aren't you, *mon*? So, if *anyone* should know the answer to my question, it would be *you* . . . right?"

Jake uncrossed his arms to draw attention to himself. "You know, Karl, I don't know much about sonar, but I don't see why you're getting so worked up. Even if someone onboard did know the answer to your question, what possible difference would it make?"

Von Freiling wheeled on him, his eyes as hard as the metal they resembled. "First off, Braddock, you should learn to mind your damn business. But since you asked, it makes a *big* fucking difference. You see, if this creature *does* use active sonar, then it also has a distinctive sonar signature we could use to track it. Something my beloved wife is apparently not in favor of us doing. And if it *is* a true echolocator, then it will have a significant advantage over us in the water. It'll see us coming from far off, and have time to react before we get anywhere near it. It could mean life or death!"

"I'm sorry Karl, but I don't know anything about this," Amara said. She swallowed hard. "This animal is almost as new to me as it is to you."

"We'll see." Von Freiling's thick finger was like a spear pointed at her nose. "I hope you're telling me the truth. Because if I find out you've been interfering with my operation, Amara, I–"

With a horrendous groan, the *Harbinger* lurched savagely to port. Caught off guard, everyone present was thrown hard to the deck and left scrambling for a handhold. All around them, loose tools and pieces of equipment shifted, slamming haphazardly into people and objects. Desperately clutching Willie and Amara to keep them from falling overboard, Jake caught a glimpse of Senator Harcourt and his escort clinging tightly to a section of railing adjacent to the bridge.

Jake watched through disbelieving eyes as the section of reinforced railing that held the mercenaries bloody bait in place began to buckle. The air was pierced by the sound of rupturing steel as the heavy metal barrier parted, the four-inch-thick cable shearing through it with a series of vibrations that shook the entire ship. Like a knife slicing through cheese, the nylon docking line continuing on, rail by rail, until it struck the solid metal decking of the ship. The powerful pull continued, with the portside dropping and the starboard rising, until several feet of the *Harbinger*'s belly was visible.

As he struggled to rise, Jake shook his head in disbelief. *It's impossible, nothing can be that strong!* Seeing the straining rope disappearing into the approaching waves quickly convinced him otherwise. It was simply a matter of time before the behemoth capsized the ship, turning them all into pliosaur puree. Lurching unsteadily to his feet, he half-staggered and half-crawled to where a gaping Karl Von Freiling fought to stand.

"It's the monster!" Jake bellowed at the bewildered adventurer, struggling to be heard over the cries of the astonished crew and the clattering sounds of falling machinery. "We've got to cut the cable! If we don't–"

His words were cut short as the rope parted. Snapping in two beneath the surface, the heavy docking line shot out of the water and slammed thunderously against a nearby bulkhead. Freed from the cable's pull, the *Harbinger* plummeted ponderously back toward starboard, throwing everyone and everything in that direction.

There was a moment of fear-filled indecision as the freed research vessel swayed sickeningly back and forth, before settling back into its previous position, its anchors holding tight against the current. The mercs collectively made their way to their feet, moaning and groaning as they went about making sure everyone was all right.

"Son of a bitch!" Von Freiling staggered like a drunkard, holding his palm heel against his injured forehead to staunch the flow of blood. "Okay men, it looks like our target has come to us, and a lot sooner than expected. No problem. It just made our job easier. You guys know the routine, so let's get moving!"

With a few grumblings, six of the seven mercenaries dusted themselves off and began to make preparations. Johnson alone remained where he was. He reached down, carefully helping Harcourt to his feet before surveying the surrounding seas. The senator had a wild look in his eye as he joined his bodyguard in searching for any sign of their enormous adversary.

It was Willie who spotted the creature first. "Dere he blows!" he cried out, pointing off the portside.

"Holy shit," Von Freiling sputtered. He moved next to Jake and Amara, staring wide-eyed at what glared up at them.

Brazenly surfacing amidst a blast of water vapor that reached the *Harbinger*'s gunnels, the pliosaur emerged from the ocean's depths. With its eyes blazing like garnet-colored footballs, the huge reptile circled the *Harbinger*, its five-meter-wide back breaking the surface.

"Holy shit is right," Jake said. He shook his head from side to side as he studied the primordial colossus.

Von Freiling's eyes never strayed from the creature. It spouted once more and hissed loudly, staring coldly up at him from less than twenty yards away. "Man, look at the girth on him! Amara, how much did you say this thing weighs?"

"I don't know – sixty or seventy tons?" Amara guessed. She leaned back, straightening her arms and gripping the railing before her, afraid she'd fall in.

"No fucking way, love." Von Freiling whistled aloud. "He's a lot more than that. I'd say a hundred is more accurate – maybe more."

"Who *cares* how heavy da damn ting is?" Willie's eyes spewed undisguised fright. "Da question is, what da hell do we do now, mon?"

Von Freiling looked amused. "What the hell do you think we do? We get to work. Now if you'll excuse me, I have a little surprise in store for our overgrown friend down there."

The big game hunter turned wordlessly away, moving past the deformed railing as he headed toward the bridge. He moved purposely, speaking in low tones into his radio.

Jake watched him disappear into the bridge. Wondering what kind of "surprise" the merc's leader had in mind for the marauding reptile that circled the *Harbinger* like a hungry shark, Jake signaled for Amara and Willie.

As Von Freiling passed her, Amara fell in behind him. Jake followed ten steps back, with Willie tagging along. As they passed Harcourt the two men hesitated, pausing to listen in on what the irate senator was saying to Johnson.

Ignorant that her escorts were no longer behind her, Amara continued blithely on, discretely trailing her husband all the way to the ship's helm.

Harcourt paced back and forth, waving his hands as if preaching to a non-existent congregation. *"The beast, which you saw, once was, now is not, and will come up out of the Abyss and go to his destruction."* He gobbled a noisome breath, gesturing at the boiling wake left behind as the creature looped around the *Harbinger*'s stern. He focused on Johnson. *"The inhabitants of the earth whose names have not been written in the book of life from the creation of the world will be astonished when they see the beast, because he once was, now is not, and yet will come."*

Jake stood ten feet away, watching as the hirsute politician continued his bizarre rhetoric. He leaned toward Willie, whispering in his ear. "What the hell is he talking about? Jesus, I think he's losing it. Look at him; he's practically foaming at the mouth!"

"Dat's a quote from da Book of Revelations, mon," Willie said. He cast a dire look at the senator. "And ya may be right. Dat entry is about da arrival of da Antichrist and da end of da world."

Jake grimaced, shaking his head. "As if we didn't have enough bullshit to worry about, now he's preaching doomsday? He was always unstable, but I've never seen him like this. Something must've really driven him over the edge if he's quoting Armageddon from the bible..."

"Da devil can cite scripture for his purpose," Willie said. He watched Harcourt continue ranting. "Dat's from da Merchant of Venice, in case ya wanted to know."

Jake smirked at him. He was beginning to see why Amara found her first mate and friend so entertaining. "I didn't, but thanks for telling me."

They turned away from Harcourt, moving toward the stern to resume observing the pliosaur. Distracted by the sight of the prowling titan, neither of them noticed that Amara was gone.

———

Dean Harcourt stood by the *Harbinger's* bridge, his rambling unabated. Having the source of his angst so close, he found himself unable to quell the rapid pounding of his heart. With Johnson steadfastly by his side, he continued spouting scriptures at length.

"Thou didst divide the sea by thy strength. Thou brakest the heads of the dragons in the waters. Thou brakest the heads of leviathan in pieces, and gavest him to be meat to the people inhabiting the wilderness!" he yelled, raising his fist to the heavens, and then glaring down at the marine reptile cruising by. It blinked as it studied him with undisguised interest.

As the huge creature once again vanished from view, Harcourt wiped a torrent of drool from his chin. He turned to his protector. "I know you can't speak, Johnson," he said, reaching up and taking hold of the giant mute's thick arms. "But I know you can hear me. The time for action is upon us. The time to strike draws near. Like Gabriel, who was sent by the Lord to punish the Leviathan once, it is you who must become God's emissary now!"

Johnson's blue eyes blinked repeatedly. He cocked his shaved head quizzically to one side, scratching the back of his neck as he stared down at his employer.

"Do you understand me?" Harcourt panted with exasperation. He turned toward the *Harbinger's* bow. Frustration and fury waged a tug-of-war across his face, the meaty scar on his jaw aching as it darkened and swelled with blood. He placed one hand flatly on the fore grip of the Uzi that hung by the merc's side.

'The sword of him that layeth at him cannot hold. The arrow cannot make him flee; he laugheth at the shaking of a spear."

When an even more confused expression emigrated across his escort's flattish face, the senator turned away in disgust. His shoulders tensed, and his sausage fingers tightly gripped the railing before him as he waited for his enemy's approach.

"All right, Johnson." Harcourt's balled fists shook like a prize-fighter battling Parkinson's. "It's obvious we're suffering from a communication barrier. So I'm going to spell it out for you in a language you'll understand." He looked to make sure no was within earshot. "I want you to kill the monster for me," he hissed through clenched teeth. "I don't want it alive, and I don't want to waste time loading submarines. Why risk missing the opportunity to destroy it now, while it swims at our feet? It's coming around now," he said, gesturing at the five-foot displacement wave heralding the creature. "For all we know, this may be its last pass. Kill it for me Johnson. Shoot it now, and I'll pay *you* what I offered Karl . . . five million dollars!"

Johnson's oversized head snapped up, and his eyes traveled furtively from the mercs still prepping the *Eurypterids* to the bridge where Von Freiling disappeared. He turned to the water, his lantern jaw set. With his hips pressed against the railing, he detached the nine-millimeter submachine gun from his side, cradling it in his ham-sized hands. Deftly removing and inspecting the weapon's box-shaped magazine, he reinserted it, slammed it home again, and pulled the Uzi's charger back in preparation for a full-auto burst. His eyes alert and determined, the giant merc waited.

Harcourt shifted his weight from foot to foot, unable to contain his gleeful exuberance as he pointed excitedly at the approaching pliosaur. The monstrous reptile was incredibly close to the ship. So close, one of its triangular-shaped pectoral fins scraped noisily along the *Harbinger's* hull as it passed directly underneath them.

It was staring hungrily up at them when Johnson emptied his machine gun into its face.

TWENTY-THREE

With her back to the sea and her hands on her hips, Amara Takagi straddled the doorway that led to the *Harbinger's* bridge. She gaped in disbelief at Karl Von Freiling, as her estranged spouse brandished the biggest rifle she'd ever seen: a black and gray-colored monstrosity he'd extracted from a polished aluminum case, resting on a nearby table.

"What the hell is that?" she sputtered.

"This little thing?" Von Freiling smirked as he made minute adjustments on the menacing weapon. "I guess you've never seen one this big before, hmm?" He hefted the gun, showing off its sheer mass. "Well then, allow me to introduce you. The thirty thousand dollars of unbridled excitement you're gawking at is the Barrett military-issue, XM109 anti-material rifle . . . in twenty-five millimeter."

He placed the weapon carefully back within its padded casing and reached for one of the oversized clips resting nearby. After inspecting the magazine's action, he popped open a box of armor-piercing rounds the size of bananas and began loading them into it with sharp, snapping sounds.

"Twenty-five millimeter?" Amara's jaw dropped and she glanced back over her shoulder. Her stomach tightened up as she realized Jake and Willie were no longer with her. She swallowed and took a hesitant step closer. "What are you going to do with that–"

"C'mon now, dearie," Von Freiling said. "If you're going to hunt dinosaurs for a living, you need a gun that's up to the job."

Amara's eyes popped. "Omigod . . . you're not here to capture the pliosaur. You came to kill it!"

"Not initially," he said. "But our overzealous and obviously unstable benefactor has informed me he'd much rather see the creature dead than captured. He believes it's some pre-ordained minion of Satan. Can you believe that? Anyway, ten million sounds much better than the five he initially offered."

"So, that's it?" Amara retorted. "You're just going for the money, and the hell with everything else? What about the thrill of taking it alive?"

"Well, I do have some reservations . . ." He cricked his neck to one side and then winked at her. "Mostly about building an extension onto my Daytona house big enough to contain a mount the size of that thing's head."

Amara's colorful response was drowned out by the sound of automatic gunfire erupting right outside the door.

"What the hell?" Von Freiling dropped the Barrett's half-loaded clip onto the table. He reached for his radio, changed his mind, and stalked off toward the door.

Alone in the ship's crate-strewn radar station, Amara stared at the empty doorway. She took a half-step, and then stared helplessly at the monstrous firearm resting beside her.

Jake's hand made an involuntary grab for his sidearm as he wheeled in the direction of the gunshots. He sprang for the *Harbinger's* port-side rails, just in time to see the pliosaur vanish beneath the waves.

Fifty feet away, Johnson stood by the railing, his smoking UZI still gripped in cadaver-like hands. He stared unblinkingly at the water, scanning for his wounded quarry. As Harcourt slapped him excitedly on the back, the oversized leucist removed his weapon's spent magazine, tossed it overboard, and inserted a fresh one. The joyous look on the senator's face as Johnson reloaded told Jake everything he needed to know.

Eyeing the water, the lawman started toward them, moving warily past the ravaged section of railing to his left. He could see the bearded form of Gibson as he emerged from below deck, shaking his leonine head back and forth as he bellowed furiously at Johnson.

Jake was thirty feet away when he noticed the ocean starting to bubble over like an unwatched cauldron. Eyes wide with alarm, he tried to warn them, but his words were drowned out by a thunderous noise.

Like an erupting geyser, the pliosaur's head and neck exploded up out of the water, its streaming maw spread wide. Rearing up and over the railing, it snapped its toothy jaws sideways with a deafening crunch. The *Harbinger* shuddered as a full fifteen feet of the remaining railing was torn away, annihilated by a bite force that exceeded fifty tons per square inch. The painful sound of wrenched-apart metal was punctuated by a pair of high-pitched screams as the creature fell back into the sea, spraying gouts of blood and particles of flesh all over the deck.

Von Freiling came staggering out of the bridge. "What the fuck was that?" Wild-eyed, he grabbed for the doorjamb to stop himself from slipping and falling. He took in the steaming charnel house that awaited him. "Jesus Christ!" He dropped down on one knee, reaching over and picking up a blood-soaked boot. He held it at arm's length, grimacing as he realized it contained a foot. He blanched, then turned toward Dean Harcourt.

"Senator?"

The stocky politician was sitting on the hard metal deck, his back against a nearby bulkhead. He was covered in blood and bits of bone, as was the surrounding deck, gunnels, and outer walls of the bridge.

Von Freiling crouched down in front of him, the oversized combat boot still in his hand. He held it in front of his employer's nose and shook it for emphasis. "Senator, what the hell happened?" Harcourt didn't appear to hear him. He just sat there with a dazed and drunken look in his eyes.

"I think your guy pissed it off," Jake remarked. He walked over, shaking his head.

A disgusted look on his face, Von Freiling rose to his feet and tossed the severed foot over the side. He gave Jake a baleful look, then exhaled resignedly.

"Johnson?" He pointed at the splattered bloodstains and chunks of flesh adhering to just about everything around them.

"And Gibson," Jake said. He wiped at the spattering of blood running down his cheek with the back of one hand and spat irritably over the side. "He was right next to him. It took them both in one bite. Almost got your trouble-making employer, too."

On cue, Harcourt uttered a cry of alarm and surged to life. Slipping and sliding on the gore that covered his hands and shoes, he staggered to his feet. He took one look at the grisly scene and bolted for the ship's bow.

"I wonder where he's going?" Jake asked, shaking his head.

"Doesn't matter," Von Freiling muttered through clenched teeth. He turned toward the bridge. "I'll be right back. If it's stupid enough to stick around, that overgrown lizard has about two minutes left to live."

———

Five hundred yards away, and five hundred feet below the surface, the pliosaur performed angry contortions in the water, its deadly jaws chomping open and closed. It pawed cat-like at its mouth with one of its enormous flippers, dislodging the three-foot piece of railing embedded in its thick, white gums. Freed of the annoying metal, it surfaced for a lungful of air, then arced back in the direction of the *Harbinger*. Further aggravated by burning saltwater, the stinging pain from its wounded face maddened it like a face full of red-hot needles.

The creature was seething. Despite its limited intellect, it now associated the hammer-like blows that struck its skull and muzzle with the noisy fire held by one of the tiny bipeds that crawled atop the big metal ship like flies on a beached carcass.

The injuries were hardly threatening, but the pain of the unexpected assault and the infuriation that followed it were enough to birth rage. Accelerating through the murky gloom to its maximum velocity, the creature quickly closed the distance. Its lips pulled back in a hideous snarl as it focused its attention on the source of its ire. An adrenaline-fueled rage made its way through its dense musculature, propelled through its bloodstream by contractions of its gigantic heart.

With its eyes ablaze and its crushing jaws spread wide, the pliosaur attacked the *Harbinger*.

———

Ten feet from Amara, Von Freiling remained frozen in place. He blinked confusedly, staring down at the thick-legged table that supported his Barrett's heavy metal case.

Eyes narrowing, he wheeled in Amara's direction. She stood with her hands in her pockets and her back to the largest of the wooden crates that cluttered a good portion of the room.

Von Freiling's tiercel's face darkened and his deep voice turned hard and dangerous. "Amara, where's my gun?"

Her eyes wide with undisguised fright, she tried to speak, then shook her head and said nothing.

"I don't like repeating myself, woman," he bristled, stepping threateningly close. "I just lost two of my men, and I need that weapon, so I'm asking you once more . . . where the *hell* is my gun?"

"I . . . threw it overboard," Amara managed through trembling lips. She tried to back away from him, feeling splinters prick her skin as her back pressed hard against the crate. She had nowhere to run.

"You *what*?" Von Freiling's bronze orbs went wide with fury. "Why you stupid . . . interfering . . . *bitch*!"

The slap came out of nowhere, a vicious, right-handed blow across the cheek that would have brought most men to their knees. Amara staggered back, hanging onto the crate for support. She barely had time to cry out before an even worse backhand caught her square across the jaw, splitting her lip and sending her sprawling to the ground.

Standing over her like a lion straddling its prey, a hateful look contorted Von Freiling's features. He reached down, seizing the front of her blouse with his left hand, and hauled her to her feet. He held her at arm's length, suspended like a sack of laundry. A toothy snarl spread across his face, and he drew his muscular right arm back to deal her another blow.

"I don't think so."

Von Freiling's punch was intercepted in mid-swing, his arm twisted powerfully backward until he had no choice but to release her. Battered and bleeding, Amara collapsed to the floor. She gazed up through blurred vision, unable to believe what she was seeing.

Ducking cat-like beneath Von Freiling's hastily-thrown left hook, Jake forced him back and off balance with a double palm heel strike to the chest. He glanced down at Amara as she lay prostrate on the floor and spotted the damage to her face. He shook his head, thanking God he'd gotten there quickly. He shifted position, placing himself directly between her and her attacker. His cobalt eyes were cool as he sized up his foe. A strange little thrill ran through him. Ever since Amara told him about her abusive husband, Jake had been itching to fight this man.

"You're not very smart, are you, Braddock?" Von Freiling was completely enraged, his ubiquitous grin a distant memory. "Do you really think you can just waltz in here and interfere in my business? Don't you know the penalty for that?"

"What do you say we skip the usual chit chat and move straight to the part where you show me what you're going to do about it?" Jake circled to the right, raising his fists as the infuriated soldier-of-fortune came charging.

Von Freiling cursed and threw himself at Jake, his teeth bared and intentions obvious. He hauled back and fired a barrage of powerful punches at the sheriff's head and ribs, attempting to overwhelm the younger man by the sheer ferocity of his assault.

Jake backpedaled and weathered the fusillade. He saw each attack coming and deflected each straight right and hook punch with quick movements of his forearms and elbows – but just barely. Von Freiling's speed and strength were astonishing, and he knew instantly the professional killer was by far the most dangerous opponent he'd ever faced. He started to wonder if he'd bitten off more than he could chew.

Jake grunted and covered up as a looping overhand left landed flush, causing him to see stars. Rolling with the punch, he staggered backwards and then leapt unexpectedly forward. The fake worked, and he caught Von Freiling off guard with a savage sidekick to the solar plexus, a strike which lifted him off his feet and sent him sailing backwards, bouncing him off a nearby stack of crates.

His eyes ablaze with unmitigated hatred, Von Freiling shrugged the blow off like it was nothing and uttered a bellow of pure rage. He charged Jake, pouncing like a hungry tiger as he sought to grapple him to the ground with the intention of beating him senseless.

The impact sent them crashing down on top of an empty crate with Jake finding himself in the unenviable position of having his opponent straddling him, powerful hands locked tightly around his neck.

Salivating at the prospect of victory, Von Freiling applied ever-increasing pressure to Jake's vulnerable throat region, while simultaneously using his legs to keep the lawman pinned against the creaking crate.

Jake felt a growing sense of panic. If he couldn't break free, it was just a matter of time before his brain shut down from oxygen deprivation. He felt a paralyzing wall of blackness beginning to loom in the distance and started flailing wildly about. Then he froze.

He'd been in this position before. Back when–

"You insolent little bastard!"

Jake's eyes went wide in astonishment. Von Freiling's face was gone and Jake's father's took its place. He was sixteen years old again and helplessly pinned beneath his father's crushing weight.

"You dare raise your hands to me, you little shit?"

Jake had come home from school just in time to see his mother collapse onto their family room's hardwood floor with blood spewing from her broken nose. John Braddock was standing triumphantly over his wife, his right fist raised, his left choking a bottle of tequila. He was going on and on, ranting and raving about how things were all her fault. He'd been laid off because of her; he was always in her shadow.

Jake's backpack dropped to the floor, sending his textbooks scattering. At first his mom didn't know he was there. Clinging to consciousness, she didn't hear his youthful screams as he sprang to her defense. It wasn't until he hoisted a nearby piano bench, slamming it against his father's broad back to put an end to the assault, that she realized he'd gotten involved.

Jake absorbed a blitz of humiliating smacks and slaps to the face before John Braddock pinned him to the bench and began systematically throttling him. He fought back hard, kicking and punching, but it was useless; his father was too big and strong. He could smell the booze on his breath as he raged on, each insult more vile and denigrating than the last. His voice was deafening, his spittle spraying. Jake shut his eyes tight, desperate to lessen the assault. He opened them as his dad poured the remainder of the bottle of tequila over his face, flooding his nose and mouth and searing his eyes. He watched through blurred vision as his father raised one huge fist overhead, preparing to bring it down on his adolescent son's face like a sledge-hammer. Jake saw the blow coming and knew he was helpless to avoid it. He braced himself, waiting for the sound of the strike and the inevitable darkness that accompanied it.

Whump!

Jake opened his eyes as a thunderous vibration shook the *Harbinger.* The room's contents shifted violently, as if they'd struck a submerged reef. His steely gaze collided with Von Freiling's, the latter's meat hooks still locked around the lawman's neck like eagle's talons. There was a moment's hesitation by the big game hunter. The look of hatred in his burnished eyes merged with confusion as he observed the myriad downshifts in Jake's rapidly-changing expressions.

Jake shrugged off the mental chains that bound him and resumed struggling to break free. Von Freiling gave a throaty growl of irritation and threw his full weight on top of him, struggling to maintain his position. There was a loud, groaning sound. The combined stress of the two men's weight and the sudden impact was too much; the overloaded crate collapsed.

Taking advantage of the split-second drop, Jake twisted free from Von Freiling's steely grip. He cracked him hard in the teeth with a short arm punch and then used the momentary distraction to worm his knees up past his opponent's guard, planting them against Von Freiling's midsection. With a Herculean effort, he heaved the surprised hunter up and over his head, depositing him headfirst onto the hard floor.

Incensed at the unexpected shift in fortune, Von Freiling was on his feet in the blink of an eye and instantly on the offensive again.

Jake absorbed a spitfire of knees and elbows, including an agonizing shot to his side that reopened his wound. He retaliated with a salvo of his own, snapping his adversary's head back with a stiff jab to the nose, then catching him in the left knee with a ligament-rupturing heel strike.

Grunting in pain, a feral-eyed Von Freiling resorted to grappling again. Springing on top of his opponent, he struggled to force Jake back against a nearby pile of boxes in order to regain the upper hand.

For a long moment the two men stood there, locked in mortal combat like male lions fighting for control of a pride, their hate-filled eyes glaring, their chests heaving, as each sought to overpower the other.

Frustrated at the stalemate, Von Freiling cursed and went for his knife. Reaching downward, he drew it free and, in one smooth motion, brought the black-bladed weapon down to plunge it into Jake's chest.

Jake spotted the knife at the last possible instant and melted to one side. There was a splintering sound as Von Freiling's blade missed its mark, punching through the thin hardwood of the crate behind him instead.

Jake's gleaming eyes and bared teeth bore testimony to the cold rage that swept over him. He retaliated, striking Von Freiling's exposed arm with his knuckles, nearly shattering it at the elbow. With a lightning fast follow-up, he knocked the offending limb away from the immobilized knife and pushed his opponent backwards and off balance.

Von Freiling uttered an inhuman growl, shaking his injured arm out before attacking again. As he sprang forward, Jake feinted back and then dropped straight downward, whirling in a circular motion so fast the eye could hardly follow. His sweep took Von Freiling off his feet and sent him crashing to the deck.

Before his opponent had a chance to recover, Jake lunged forward with an audible snarl, seizing Von Freiling by the windpipe with a pinch grip that could shatter a shot glass. Panting, he wrenched his defeated adversary onto his knees and held him by the throat, paralyzed and struggling to breathe.

It was over.

"That'll be enough, Jake. Let him go," a voice called out.

Jake's blood and sweat-streaked head whirled toward the speaker. A gore-covered Dean Harcourt entered the room through the starboard doorway. He had Diaz, Barker and Markov with him.

"You heard what the senator said," the latter said, an UZI held menacingly in his hands. "Let Karl go."

Jake watched as Amara made her way to her feet and leaned unsteadily against a nearby crate. Her left eye and cheekbone were already starting to swell, and a trickle of blood ran down her chin. He felt an overpowering adrenaline rush course through him, its intoxicating power whispering in his ear, urging him on, enticing him to do something awful. He could kill Von Freiling if he wanted to. He had the man's trachea pinioned between iron-hard fingers. All he had to do was squeeze and he knew it. Judging from the concern on their faces, the other mercs did too.

As if reading his thoughts, Harcourt said, "Now Jake, I don't know what the cause of all of this was . . ." he said soothingly, simultaneously placing a staying hand atop Markov's poised weapon. "But I insist that you obey me forthwith."

"Screw you, Harcourt," Jake said. His angry eyes locked onto Von Freiling's. "This asshole was beating up on the doc when I walked in."

"Perhaps with good reason. Regardless, I–"

WHUMP!

The *Harbinger* shuddered once more beneath a thunderous impact that knocked everyone present off balance.

Jake staggered a half step to one side, but managed to continue throttling his hateful adversary.

"Jesus, what the hell was that?" Barker asked, looking fearful.

"It's . . . the pliosaur," Amara managed, her right hand braced against the wall for support. "Johnson . . . wounded it . . . but not enough. It's . . . attacking the ship."

"What?" Markov's hatred-filled eyes zeroed Jake. "Son of a bitch! Senator, with all due respect, we don't have time for this negotiation shit."

"You're right," Harcourt said. He looked down and sighed. "Very well Jake, you leave me no choice. Either release my team leader so he can do his job or I will have Miss Takagi killed."

"What?" Amara's pale face filled with alarm. "You . . . wouldn't dare!"

"I'm afraid you underestimate me, *doctor*," Harcourt said with impressive coldness. "You see, unlike most men, I have the courage of my convictions."

Jake felt his adrenaline rush fade. He stalled, adjusting his grip on a wheezing Karl Von Freiling, his fierce gaze meeting Harcourt's. He studied the politician's face, trying hard to see if he was bluffing.

Harcourt signaled Markov. "Kill her. But do it quietly."

Markov leered at Jake. He stalked Amara, effortlessly swatting the hapless marine biologist's upraised hands aside as he seized her roughly by the hair. With horrific ease, he forced her up on her tiptoes, then reached down and drew forth his bone-handled bolo. Its notched blade made a low, rasping noise as it slid free from its sheath.

Jake yanked his nine-millimeter free from its holster and pointed it at Harcourt's face. "Let's see about those convictions now, senator," he said, cocking the Beretta's hammer back. "Because I guarantee you, I'll turn your head into a serving bowl, long before his blade touches her skin."

"Gentlemen," Harcourt gestured for the two mercs at his side. Barker and Diaz both moved a half step forward. They raised their Uzis as one, pulling the charger handles loudly back and pointing them directly at Jake.

"Kindly lower your weapon, sheriff," Harcourt said solemnly. "If you're lucky, you may kill me, but your lady friend will die at the same time, and my men will eliminate you a moment later. Of course, you can choose to shoot Markov instead . . . but then you'll still die, after which I promise I'll order my men to use the lovely doctor as bait to lure that thing back to the surface."

Jake's frustrated eyes met Amara's as she continued her useless struggles against Markov's powerful grip. He could feel the terror she was enduring as her horrified eyes were drawn to the machete in the sinister-looking merc's hand. He cursed himself as fear for her began to cloud his judgment.

WHUMP!

Once again, something plowed into the *Harbinger's* aged hull with unbelievable power.

Harcourt looked uneasy. "Well? What's it going to be?"

Jake's eyeballs ricocheted from Amara's frightened countenance to Markov's leering face to the pair of automatic weapons pointed at his chest. He felt all the fight drain out of him like water. With a heavy sigh of futility, he tossed his pistol to the floor and released his death grip on Von Freiling's windpipe.

The half-strangled adventurer collapsed like a house of cards, his inhalations guttural gasps. Long moments passed. Finally he clambered awkwardly to his feet and stood there, his hands on his thighs, his chest heaving. He wiped at the blood streaming from his nose with the back of one scarred hand, then felt his bruised throat with the other.

"Very impressive, sheriff," Von Freiling rasped. He cleared his throat several times and gave Jake what amounted to a nod of professional courtesy. His trademark grin started to return. He bent down and retrieved the lawman's discarded Beretta. "Of course, you got lucky. Regardless, we'll have to finish our 'conversation' at a later date."

"Anytime," Jake replied evenly.

"*Right* . . . in the meantime, tie him up, fellas."

On cue, Barker and Diaz lunged forward, pouncing on Jake, pinning his arms behind his back. Wordlessly they grabbed stout cord from one of the nearby crates and began wrapping it around his wrists and forearms.

"What about the doc?" Jake grunted as he was being bound, his gaze on Amara, still helpless within Markov's clutches.

"Not to worry," Von Freiling said. He nodded at his underling. "Release her, Markov."

"You're the boss," Markov replied, sheathing his weapon. He smiled coldly and yanked Amara uncomfortably close. "Too bad, I've never killed a Jap before."

"Guess today's not your lucky day, shit-breath," Amara muttered. She dropped down on her heels as her captor released his grip, catching her bearings and looking around the room. Her gaze lingered on her husband, and a wild look came over her. To everyone's astonishment, she turned sideways as if leaving, then whirled back and kneed her tormentor in the groin as hard as she could.

"You stupid, fucking whore!" Markov spat through clenched teeth, dropping to the floor and clutching his injured testicles. The other mercs exchanged stunned looks, their faces taut as they struggled to keep from laughing. "You're going to die for that!"

"Belay that shit!" Von Freiling said. His menacing tone caused Markov to freeze in mid-crouch, his weapon half drawn. "If anyone's going to kill my wife it'll be *me*, not you. Besides, we've got more important things to do."

With effort, Markov slowly straightened up. He nodded in frustrated acknowledgment of his employer's orders and remained where he was, immobile and unblinking. Jake could see his hate-filled eyes never left Amara. Not for a second.

Just then, Stubbs came running into the room with Willie hot on his heels. "We're taking on water!" the disfigured merc roared. He paused in mid-stride as he took in the scene. "Hey . . . what the hell's going on in here?"

"Just a simple disagreement," Von Freiling said, waving it off. "Now what were you saying?"

"We ran a check below decks. The creature's breached the hull in two places – by the bow, and amidships, below the waterline. We're taking on water."

"How bad is it?" Von Freiling asked Willie.

"Not bad yet, but da ship can't keep taking a pounding like dis, mon," the first mate replied. He stared at Jake with nervous eyes, then inhaled sharply as he took in the damage to Amara's face. "Da hull can't take it. If da ting's not stopped he'll sink us for sure."

"Well, then, *do* something!" Harcourt exploded, glaring irritably at Von Freiling.

"Alright men, let's get moving," Von Freiling ordered. "Mr. Daniels, if you don't mind, I'd like you to take this radio and keep an eye on the sonar for us. I'm short a man. I'd also like you to take my animal-rights-loving wife with you and keep her out of trouble." The merc's leader handed Willie a walkie-talkie, then turned to his remaining men. "Markov, take Johnson's place with the senator. And please, no more mistakes. The rest of you know what to do."

"What about this one?" Barker asked.

Jake's muscles tensed. The tight cord about his wrists dug in painfully as the two mercs continued to hold onto him.

"Take him to the bridge and tie him to the captain's wheel," Von Freiling replied, amusedly. "That ought to keep him from causing any more mischief."

Willie's face contorted. He took a step forward, fumbling in his pants pocket. "Why don't ya lock him in one of da storage rooms instead? It's faster, and I got da keys right here."

Von Freiling gave Jake a contemplative look. "Nah. He's gonna try to escape anyway . . . why make it easier for him?" He winked at Willie, then gestured for Markov. "Give them a hand."

"You got it, boss," Markov said, walking over and drawing his Glock from its holster.

Jake felt an agonizing blow to the back of his head and everything turned crimson. He sensed his body sag and the floor spring up to greet him. He could hear Amara and Willie's cries of protest and struggled valiantly, but was unable to rise. His head did a spin cycle and he rolled helplessly onto his back, his arms tied beneath him.

Von Freiling walked over and dropped down on one knee to whisper in his ear.

"By the way, boy scout, just for the record, you were right about me using that kid as bait. You see, that old anaconda had been feeding on the local villagers for decades, snatching them as they came down to the river for drinking water, and dragging them under. Guess the bitch liked how they tasted. And you know how it is when you're fishing; brother . . . you gotta match the hatch!"

The last thing Jake saw before he lost consciousness was Von Freiling's evilly smiling face.

———

A thousand yards away, the pliosaur completed a huge circle as it prepared to make another pass at the ship.

Still incensed by the pain of the machine gun rounds that tore up the skin on its face, the huge predator was further infuriated by the injuries it inflicted upon itself. Despite the *Harbinger's* rusty condition, colliding with its steel hull had gifted the creature with several loosened teeth and a pulsating headache. Large patches of torn skin now graced its armored head, beneath which dark bruises were starting to form.

Its inability to sink the invading vessel added to the pliosaur's growing rage. It roared out loud beneath the surface, opening and closing its jaws with thunderous snaps, venting its fury upon anything within range – even the surrounding water.

Spouting for a moment, it studied the upper portions of the ship. It could see several of the tiny mammals, scurrying across the topmost portions of the *Harbinger*.

The pliosaur's ruby eyes narrowed and its lips wrinkled back in a hideous snarl, revealing scores of ridged teeth. It emitted a hiss that could be heard for half a mile, then inhaled sharply and submerged. Its sound-imaging senses detected the slowly increasing list affecting its enormous adversary, along with the sounds of pressurized seawater rushing into its ruptured body.

The creature sounded to a depth of five hundred feet before arcing steeply upwards. With its eyes nearly closed, it aimed its snout directly at the damaged portion of the wallowing ship's hull, increasing its speed as it rose from the depths.

TWENTY-FOUR

Chaos ran rampant across the *Harbinger's* decks.

While his conservationist wife cowered within a nearby stairwell, Von Freiling watched his surviving mercenaries swarm like army ants, scrambling to launch their virgin craft.

Von Freiling stood between the suspended *Eurypterids,* his powerful legs braced far apart as he bellowed orders through a megaphone. With Barker manning one of the miniature construction cranes and Stubbs the other, the merc's leader prepared to order his two streamlined craft down into the white-capped swells.

"Diaz, I want you over by *Eurypterid II,* to help guide her until she's clear of the rails," Von Freiling said. "With Gibson gone, you have to ride shotgun with Stitches. Hold off on boarding until Barker's got her in position."

Diaz nodded, moving over to the fearsome-looking submersible as it creaked back and forth. He placed his stubby brown hands against her hull to steady her, then ducked down and moved underneath, checking the vessel's weapons pod one last time while waiting for Barker's signal to stand clear. As he did his inspection, Stitches clambered up the mini-sub's other side, popping open its heavy top hatch and climbing partially inside.

Visible from the waist up, Stitches rested his forearm against the hull and his other hand on one of the thick steel winch cables. He glanced down at the *Harbinger's* slanting deck, popped a stick of gum and started chewing nervously, staring at the nearby crane's booth as Barker, too, waited for further orders.

Von Freiling directed his megaphone at his second-in-command. "Stubbs, once Stitches and Diaz are in the water, I want you to wait a full three minutes before you drop us. That should give them enough time to get into position."

Stubbs gave his employer a miniature salute through the crane's open window, then reached down and turned over the diesel engine of the hydraulic powered winch, keeping it in low while he allowed the motor to warm up.

Von Freiling lowered his megaphone and reached for his radio. He glanced over at Dean Harcourt. The senator was accompanied by Markov and remained by the intact starboard railing, observing the activity with a critical eye.

"Willie, this is Karl, do you read me?" he said into the hand unit, his eyes still on Harcourt as the senator began gesturing for his bodyguard.

"Yeah, mon, I read ya," Willie radioed back.

"We're getting set to launch. Any sign of the guest of honor?"

There was a moment of silence.

"I don't see any ting on da screen since it last rammed us," Willie said. "But it's hard ta tell, wit all dat stuff floatin around in da water, mon. I can't say for sure da damn ting's not dere!"

Von Freiling wore an uncharacteristic frown. "I guess we'll just have to chance it. Keep looking."

"No problem, mon."

Replacing his radio, Von Freiling ran his fingertips absentmindedly across his bruised throat. He turned toward Barnes. The one-eyed pilot was standing beside *Eurypterid I,* waiting for the order to board. Von Freiling was still a few booted strides away when he spotted Harcourt moving purposefully in his direction. Behind their mutual benefactor, an annoyed-looking Markov scurried to catch up.

Von Freiling's nose crinkled up. With his expensive suit soaked with human blood and baking in the hot Floridian sun, the unstable politician was starting to look and smell like mid-July road kill. He raised an eyebrow. "Yes, senator?"

Harcourt looked down, staring distractedly at his rust-colored hands. They made a papyrus-like sound as he started rubbing them together, slowly at first, then faster and faster, in a pointless effort at sloughing off the dried blood. Exasperated, he gazed up at Von Freiling and then laid his stained fingers atop his hired gun's shoulder.

"Canst thou fill Leviathan's skin with barbed irons, or his head with fish spears? Shall not one be cast down even at the sight of him?"

Von Freiling prayed for patience. "Now what does *that* mean?"

Harcourt gripped him tight, his fingers digging into bruised shoulder muscles with surprising strength. "You are the instrument of God's vengeance, and my son's. The beast awaits you. Go and face it with pride. You have naught to fear."

Von Freiling tried hard not to snap. He stared at his employer, wondering how much of the senator's spiel was an act, and how much was actually worth worrying about. He decided he had no time to waste on such nonsense, and a humorless smile cranked up the corners of his mustache. "You know, senator; it was entertaining in the beginning, but I've had enough of your Bellevue bullshit."

"Oh, really?" Harcourt's dark eyes rounded in surprise.

"Yes, really," Von Freiling said. "I've lost good men, and there's a chance I may be killed in the next few minutes. That's fine, because it's how I live my life. But in case I do, I want you to know something, Mr. Harcourt." He stepped uncomfortably close to him. "I've worked with a lot of unstable people in my life, from demented dictators to the most murderous drug czars you could imagine. But, with all due respect, my good man, you are by far the *craziest* motherfucker I have *ever* done business with!"

Von Freiling whirled abruptly around, leaving the nonplussed politician standing there. He shook his head and walked over to Barnes. Raising one hand, he signaled for his chuckling pilot to climb aboard, then reached for the ladder himself. He just started up *Eurypterid I*'s bottom rungs when–

KA-BOOM!

The beleaguered *Harbinger* torqued hard to starboard, twisting violently against its anchorage.

"Jesus Christ!" Von Freiling lost his grip on the slippery rung and fell hard to the deck. His bellow was drowned out by the wail of buckling metal, as the wallowing research vessel struggled to right itself. He could do nothing but hold on as the mini-sub above him swayed dangerously on its thin, steel tether. A few yards away, his men were thrown across the hard, unforgiving deck, along with an assortment of loose pieces of equipment that crashed frighteningly close to several of them.

As Von Freiling watched in horror, the winch assembly that supported *Eurypterid II* succumbed to the strain. With a loud snap, the five-ton submersible dropped like a stone onto the *Harbinger's* deck. It landed on top of Diaz, who was clinging to the deck beneath it, waiting for the ship's swaying to subside. His high-pitched shriek was cut short by the sub's thunderous impact, followed by a wet crunch as it settled into place.

Von Freiling was on his feet in an instant. He took a step toward the metallic dust cloud rising up around the fallen *Eurypterid II,* then stopped. Rivulets of blood and urine flooded across the cracked flooring beneath his feet, telling him more than he cared to know.

He lunged toward the intact section of railing adjacent to his own sub. Pistol in hand, he gazed furiously outward, searching for their nemesis. Other than the swirling waves that marked the primeval titan's passage, there was nothing. The creature had submerged, vanishing back into the depths from whence it came, leaving death and destruction in its wake once more.

Angrily holstering his weapon, Von Freiling turned away from the frothing waters and stalked over to *Eurypterid II.* He stepped carefully over pieces of loose debris, taking care not to slip on body fluids that continued to stream out from under it. Out of the corner of one eye he spotted Markov, gingerly helping Harcourt back to his feet.

Stitches, caught half-hanging out of the submersible's opened hatch when it dropped, struggled to right himself. He clung to the edge of his craft's smooth hull with one hand, holding his aching head with the other.

"Barker, get her back in the air," Von Freiling bellowed through cupped hands, not bothering to look for his megaphone. "Let's launch before that damn thing comes back!"

Barker nodded through the window of the starboard crane, then turned over its diesel engine. The motor sputtered loudly for a few seconds, then flared to life.

"Stitches, you okay?" Von Freiling rested his hands against the armored hull of *Eurypterid II,* looking up at the dazed pilot. He glanced down at the submersible, noticing in passing that its winch connectors were still intact and in place.

"I'll live," the merc muttered. He rubbed his neck, shifted his head slowly from side to side. "Man, that fucking hurts. Where's Diaz?"

Von Freiling scowled. "Don't ask. Let's just say Barker will be going with you now."

Stitches shook his head skeptically. "Barker? But, he doesn't know the sub's interface system, boss . . ."

"Well, he's all I can fucking spare!" Von Freiling bellowed. "So he'll just have to do, okay?" Turning and stepping carefully away, he gave Barker the thumbs-up sign, then waited, readying himself for the sight of Diaz's crushed body.

Barker shifted the crane into reverse, watching for the weighty craft to make its way up off the debris-strewn deck. The steel cables tightened, slithering upward. The winch began to exert its power, its diesel engine revving into the red against the heavy load.

Barker blinked, squinting down at his gauge dials, then scratched his head in confusion. The mini-sub wasn't moving.

Quickly adjusting his equipment and tapping the unit's pressure gauges, the befuddled merc threw the winch into low gear and pulled back on the control lever once more. The groaning engine revved higher, screaming from the strain. White smoke began to spew from it, then black. Finally Barker shut it down. He shook his head. *Eurypterid II* refused to budge.

"What the hell's going on?" Von Freiling asked. "What's the holdup?"

"The hydraulics are shot, Karl," Barker surmised. He shook his head and swore, trying ineffectually to raise the sub one last time. "See? She won't move. There's a leak somewhere. I think that's what caused her to drop in the first place."

"Well, that's just fucking great!"

As he spotted his estranged wife still standing in the distant doorway, Von Freiling cursed himself. He remembered one of Amara's crewmembers, the stocky one with the Brooklyn accent, trying to warn him about the faulty hydraulics before they left port. Obsessed with his takeover of the *Harbinger*, he'd summarily dismissed the man. Now, he was paying for it – with lives.

Von Freiling lowered his voice. "All right, Barker, what are our options?"

"None that I can think of, boss," Barker said. He stepped out of the crane's cramped control booth and looked down at the tilted mini-sub. "These hoist booms only have about a 150 degree range of motion, and it's all extended over the same corresponding sides of the ship. We can't use the starboard crane to launch both, and the sub's way too heavy to be moved any other way. If we're gonna use both subs, we need another chopper."

Von Freiling clicked his canines together, pawing at one end of his mustache with his thumb and index finger as he mulled over his choices. The Chinooks were no longer an option. He'd called in every favor he could to get them on such short notice. He'd have to go through military channels now. And even with Harcourt's influence it would take days. He growled, slamming one fist into the opposing palm.

"Okay, we don't seem to have much choice," he said, turning back to Barker. He cupped his hands around his mouth once more. "Gentlemen, we're going to have to change our plans, so gather round!"

Stitches climbed carefully out of the *Eurypterid II*, skirting the bloody deck as he made his way over to Von Freiling. Barker, Barnes and Stubbs were already gathered around their leader. Only Markov remained where he was, watching from forty feet away, leaning against a bulkhead next to Harcourt.

"Well, guys, in case nobody's been keeping score, we've already lost three of our best men to this monster," Von Freiling said. He looked at what remained of his team, measuring their resolve. "And we've lost the ability to launch one of our subs. I think it's safe to say this mission is turning out to be a bit more dangerous than we thought."

"According to our contract, each of you was to be paid fifty thousand dollars for your part in this mission. Given our current losses, the gravity of our situation, and the added bonus our employer has decided to offer us, I've agreed to pay each of you five times that amount, if and when we kill this animal."

Von Freiling held up his hands. "There is a catch, however. One *Eurypterid* is not going to be able to take this thing down in a head-on fight. We don't have enough speed or firepower. We need to blindside it, like we originally planned."

"What exactly do you have in mind?" Stitches asked. He wore a pensive expression. "You just said the second sub was down."

"It is. We're going to use the sled as bait."

"Say what?" Stitches nearly choked. "Are you fucking kidding me? There's no way I'm going in the water on the sled with that thing swimming around. That's suicide. Forget it!"

"Look, I know the sled isn't as well protected as one of the subs, but–"

Stitches scoffed. "As well protected? Try not protected at all! It's wide open!"

Von Freiling tried to keep his expression supportive and understanding. Stitches was right, of course. The sled was not only wide open; it wasn't armed, let alone armored.

"The sled is faster and more maneuverable than either *Eurypterid*," he said. "And, we can give the guy in the backseat that big spear gun they've got on board. If the creature gets too close, it contains enough whale dope to knock it on its ass!"

"Sorry, but it's not happening, Karl." Stitches' eyes were as hard as agates. "If you want to serve someone up as an appetizer to that overgrown lizard it's fine, but it's not going to be me."

Von Freiling fought to keep his impatience from showing. He hated negotiating with underlings. "Stop worrying. I promise it'll never get near you guys. I'll nail it before it gets within fifty yards."

"Fuck you, Karl."

His bronze eyes compressing into slits, Von Freiling glared at his rebellious sonar operator.

"I'm giving you an order, mister," he said. His big hands twitched as they crept toward the arsenal of weapons hanging from his belt.

"This isn't the army," Stitches said, his right hand already resting on the butt of his pistol. "And I'm through taking orders from you, freak."

"Why you little . . ."

"Hold it guys." Stubbs stepped warily between the two arguing men. "There's no need to fight amongst ourselves. We've lost too many men today."

Von Freiling bristled, his whole body tensing up. "That's alright; I think we can afford to lose one more."

"No, we *can't*," Stubbs said, striving hard to keep his eyes on both of them simultaneously. "Anyway, we already have a pilot for the sled."

"Oh, really?" Von Freiling's fierce gaze remained fixated on Stitches. "And who might that be?"

"Me." A half-grin made its way across Stubbs' craggy features as he caught the look of surprise on both men's faces. "I'll go."

"You?"

"Yes, me, Karl. It's a suicide mission, but I'll be the bait to draw your little beastie out into the open."

Von Freiling smiled. "You know, Stubbs, that sounds like an excellent idea! Well then, it's settled. Let's get the scuba gear and sled up on deck and get prepped."

Stubbs held up a hand. "There is one condition, though."

Von Freiling's smile vanished. "Oh, and what's that?"

"This is my last mission," Stubbs announced. He peered contemplatively down at his disfigured hand, flexing it as he spoke. "Losing Johnson, Gibson and Diaz is enough for me. I'm tired of taking chances. I've made up my mind. I'm too old for this shit. I want out."

"And that's your condition?"

"No, a million dollars is my condition." Stubbs looked up with a sagacious grin. "It'll be enough for me to start over."

Von Freiling balked. "A million bucks? That's insane! Why the hell would I pay you that much?"

"Well for starters, because I overheard how much your fanatical pal over there is *really* paying you." Stubbs nodded his head in Harcourt's direction. "And, given our reduced roster, you seem to be a little short of volunteers lately. Or haven't you noticed?"

"And if I refuse?" Von Freiling's voice had an unpleasant edge to it.

"Then, I'll happily step out of the way and let you and Stitches resume killing each other." Stubbs grinned, looking back and forth between the two men. "Assuming you survive, you can relish the experience of taking that thing on all by yourself. You and Barnes, that is."

Immobile, Von Freiling intently studied his second-in-command. Inwardly, he was furious at himself. He'd always known Stubbs was craftier than people gave him credit for. He should've anticipated this.

"Alright, Stubbs . . . I agree to your terms."

"Hey, wait a minute." Barker took a step forward. He had a whiney look on his face. "If I'm going to be out there risking my ass along with Stubbs, I want more money too!"

"Fine, Barker, you can have Stitches' bonus," Von Freiling said. He turned away, smirking and giving the little red-haired merc a vindictive look. "That'll bring your pay up to a cool four hundred and fifty thousand."

"Done." His mood noticeably brighter, Barker spun off and headed for the bridge.

"Oh, and Stitches," Von Freiling paused, looking back at him. "Since you're too chicken-shit to go into the water, why don't you go keep an eye on Jake Braddock? He's tied up, so it shouldn't be so frightening. And make sure my wife doesn't get another rebellious idea in her head while we're gone."

Stitches glared petulantly back, but nodded his acceptance of the assignment and disappeared into the bridge.

Von Freiling was almost to his mini-sub when Stubbs extended a catcher's mitt-sized paw and caught him by the arm. Drawing him close, the hulking merc waited for Stitches and Barker to move out of earshot before he spoke.

"Oh, one more thing, Karl."

"What's that, Stubbs?"

"I know how you are when things get *hairy*." Stubbs said, holding up his scar-capped fingers and wiggling them. He was smiling, but his eyes and tone were menacing. "So don't get any bright ideas about hanging me out to dry down there. Because if you do – and that escapee from 'Skull Island' doesn't get me – it'll be you and I that have unfinished business. Not you and the young sheriff."

"You know, Stubbs, you're starting to hurt my feelings." Von Freiling grinned disarmingly. "I wouldn't dream of screwing you over. Now c'mon, old friend, we've got a sled to bring out."

———

Spotting Von Freiling's approach, Amara retreated below decks, anxious to put as much distance as possible between herself and her volatile spouse. She felt a wave of dizziness and held onto the stairwell's banister, touching the stinging mouse around her eye. Her body ached and her head was splitting from the beating she received. She gave an involuntary shudder. She was lucky. If Jake hadn't arrived when he did, her deranged husband would've crippled her.

Amara shook her head in disgust and her lips contorted as if she sought to spit out something distasteful. For the thousandth time she cursed herself for getting involved with Karl in the first place. She hated to admit it, but it was the money that enticed her. With her father and fiancé gone, she'd been desperate; buying into an available research vessel like the *Harbinger* seemed the sensible, even noble thing to do. It gave her the opportunity to set things right and the power to avenge her loved ones. Back then, she'd been willing to sell her soul to do so. In many ways, she had.

Karl didn't seem so bad in the beginning. A little scary around the edges, but his looks, physique and sheer fearlessness offset that, and then some. He was even romantic at times. It wasn't until their wedding night that the real Karl Von Freiling emerged. High on pain-killers and besotted with vodka, his usual love-making switched from being a tad rough to downright torturous, and when she complained he just laughed and hurt her more. Her life quickly spiraled down into a perverse form of learned helplessness. An ongoing series of beatings, coupled with occasions of horrifying sexual abuse. Karl was the type that didn't appreciate the word "no," and raping his wife to the point she bled was, in his eyes, just him taking what already belonged to him. Amara gritted her teeth as the suppressed memories flung themselves against the bars of the psychological cage she'd banished them to.

She let slip a nervous sigh. As her eyes adjusted to the dim lighting she moved nimbly downward. She could hear the sounds of her husband and his soldiers coming from somewhere up above, cursing and complaining as they dragged something heavy out of the old radar station. She descended into the ship's observation room and walked over to Willie. He was back at his sonar station, his back rigidly upright, and his eyes staring unblinkingly at his glowing monitor screen.

"Any sign of it?" she asked as she drew up a chair.

"I had it on da scope for a while, but den I lost it," Willie said. "Da tide is finally startin ta die down, so it'll be easier ta track soon."

Amara sighed, shaking her head as she watched the screen with him. Willie's stolid presence was reassuring, even in the God-awful circumstances they currently found themselves. He was like the old oak tree she used to scale when she was growing up – always there, and always dependable. "Good. Listen, I'm worried about Jake. That was some shot he took. Do you think he's okay?"

Willie shrugged. "I dunno. He's tough, dat one, and he's got a hard head too. I tink he'll be fine. I worry more about us right now."

"What do you mean?" Amara said. She touched her bruised cheek and winced, then looked around to make sure they were alone.

"I checked da ship's status . . ."

"And?"

Willie hesitated. "Well, let's just say dat *I have an alacrity in-*"

"In sinking?" Amara gasped as she recognized the all-too-familiar quote. "We're sinking? Are you serious?"

"Yep, dat last hit was too much." Willie looked grimly at her. "It's takin a while because I closed all da flooded compartments, but we be goin down by da head, bit by bit."

"God . . . how long do we have?"

"A coupla hours. Maybe tree or four, but dat's about it. Unless it hits us again, in which case . . ."

"Jesus." She grabbed onto her chair's armrests and sank slack-jawed into it, her overtaxed mind reeling from the news. She took a deep breath, holding it until she was forced to breathe. She felt light-headed and nauseous. Despite the traumatic takeover of her ship, it never dawned on her she might lose the *Harbinger* permanently. She figured that, no matter what the outcome of Dean Harcourt's manic quest for revenge, she would somehow end up getting the old whaler back. With the creature captured or dead, he'd have no use for it. The notion that her beloved vessel would soon be nothing but a reef for the region's resident fish population was something she just couldn't wrap her head around. It was preposterous. And yet, it was happening. She shifted awkwardly in her seat, the all-too-familiar reality of her aching hip helping her once more to focus. She turned back to Willie. "What should we do?"

"I been tinking about dat . . ." Willie glanced up at his screen, checking the room and doorway before he continued. "Da way tings is goin, I don't see dis bunch of killers helpin us. Fact is, dey probably don't want witnesses . . ."

Amara swallowed hard, nodded her agreement of his grim-but-accurate assessment of the situation. "Does Karl know how bad the damage is?"

"No, and I don't tink he will."

"Why not?"

"Because I turned off da damage control alarm system and dimmed da warning lights ta buy us time."

"Shit." Amara's pale eyes bulged wide. "Buy us time for what?"

Willie's voice became a whisper. "We gotta free Jake and get away, as soon as we can."

"How? They're everywhere."

"Nah, dere's not dat many of dem left," he said. "And when dey go into da water, dere will be four less. When dey go under and get busy wit dat damn critter, dat's when we make our move."

"On what? There's nothing to escape on but the *Sycophant*."

"Exactly. Dere will be only two of dem left, and dat crazy senator, mon. We'll take da Zodiac and run."

"Run from the *Kronosaurus*?" Amara shivered, her memory of the pliosaur's speed as fresh as ever. "You're crazy. It'll be all over us before we get half a mile!"

"No way." Willie's grin was huge. "It'll be too damn busy eatin your stupid husband and his hired tugs."

Not sharing his optimism, Amara focused on the sonar screen, watching for the reemergence of the horror that continued to stalk them like something out of an R-rated monster movie.

CRETACEOUS OCEAN
65 MILLION YEARS AGO

If the ensuing pandemonium of the lesser sea creatures fleeing the embers from the sky was great before, it was magnified tenfold by the sight of the great wave bearing down upon them. Turtles, mosasaurs, marine crocodiles, and plesiosaurs all swam for their lives, clawing and clambering over each other in their frenzied rush. Occasionally, two would collide, furiously tearing into one another and reddening the sea before sinking beneath the waves.

Of all the great reptiles, only the four pliosaurs appeared unfazed by the approaching wall of water. Spread out in a skirmish line, the giant predators floated serenely atop thirty-foot seas. Their ages ranged from thirty to over a hundred. All had survived numerous gales at sea, with waves that often measured a hundred feet in height. Even though the one sweeping toward them now was at least three times that size, they stoically prepared to face it.

With the wave literally looming over them, the female and the three males acted as one. Drawing huge breaths, they sounded, propelling themselves under the approaching avalanche with powerful strokes. Downward they plunged, diving deeper and deeper, with the current and water pressure escalating around them.

Suddenly, they gravitated back and started to rise. All realized that the vacuum power at the base of the mountainous wave was too much for even their might to overcome. With their huge flippers straining, they managed to reach the surface, spouting dense cones of vapor as they did. The bird's-eye view that greeted them was unmistakable. The four had breached the very top of the tsunami, with only fifty yards separating them from a four hundred-foot free-fall into its deadly trough.

The power of the wave was unstoppable, its current irresistible. The pliosaurs had one choice. Turning in the same direction as the wall of water, they began to backstroke. Stroking furiously, the huge female assumed the lead, a hundred feet from the crest of the rapidly growing monster. The males doggedly followed her, their tenacious mating instincts rekindled by the seeming chase.

Together, the pliosaurs prepared to ride out the tsunami.

Five miles to the south, the caldera waited for them, its craggy mouth gaping wide like the maw of some impossible beast. Rising up from the seabed until it reached a height of over two thousand feet above sea level, the semi-dormant volcano had remained silent for a million years.

Eons earlier, the mountain had erupted with a massive explosion that blew off its entire top and expelled over fifty cubic miles of magma into the surrounding seas and sky. With the majority of its magma reservoir depleted, the volcano's structural support slowly gave way, caving in on itself and leaving behind a bowl-shaped circular depression over eight miles wide and ten thousand feet deep.

A hot spring formed from tropical rains lay within the center of the caldera, its steaming waters superheated by the remaining magma reserves that lay barely twenty feet below the surface. The steam rose in billowing clouds, sending a white plume of smoke that spiraled up and out of the volcano's crater-shaped mouth a mile into the air.

As the tsunami approached the volcano, its already vast vertical height grew in direct proportion to the shallower water. Atop its crest, the pliosaurs found themselves riding atop a volatile mountain of seawater measuring a towering 2,500 feet in height and traveling at five hundred miles an hour. Worse, they were on a collision course with a jagged wall of solid stone.

With their point of impact in clear view, the four pliosaurs turned to flee. They were paddling with all their might when an unexpected newcomer burst through the surface of the wave. One of the giant mosasaurs had survived the tsunami's impact by traveling within the wave itself. Gasping for air, the fifty-eight foot long, twenty-ton sea lizard unwittingly rose up under the striped *Kronosaurus* bull, bowling the heavier predator over with the force of its rising.

Surprised and already on edge, the upended pliosaur reacted instantly, locking its giant jaws onto the scale-covered rib cage of the equally astonished *Tylosaurus*. With a frightful hiss, the mosasaur twisted its serpentine body around and fastened its own deadly jaws onto the neck of the writhing *Kronosaurus*. Locked in a deadly embrace, and bereft of any stabilization, the two struggling titans slipped inexorably forward with the current. Tumbling over the crest of the wave, they plunged two thousand feet to their deaths.

A second later, the tsunami smashed full-force into the side of the caldera. The impact defied imagination. Cubic mile after mile of seawater traveling at nearly the speed of sound exploded against the sides and over the top of the volcano with a concussive force that was heard a hundred miles away. So large was the wave at the moment of impact that it enveloped two-thirds of the caldera, swamping it completely before continuing on. Huge sections of the volcano's jagged walls, including giant boulders weighing a hundred tons, were smashed loose by the impact and washed away like grains of sand.

As the wall of water came crashing down over the lip of the caldera, the pliosaurs swam for their lives. The wave dumped billions of gallons of seawater over the top of the mountain, filling its enormous, bowl-shaped depression in seconds. Everything swept up by the wave: rocks, trees, fish, and marine dinosaurs were all deposited inside the caldera in a single, devastating moment. Anything still alive faced being dashed against the bottom of the mountain or crushed by the relentless avalanche of water and debris that hammered down from above.

The pliosaurs, swimming with every ounce of strength, managed to delay being swept over the top of the volcano by a precious second or so, saving them from being pulverized against bare rock. Their great bodies twisted as they fell, and the three came crashing down into water already three thousand feet deep and growing. Forced downward, they were held powerless beneath the surface and tossed like herring. Helpless, with their powerful lungs straining, the giant reptiles were battered and pounded on all sides by boulders and bodies alike.

Seconds later, the three were ripped violently apart from each other and vanished into the swirling blackness of the raging maelstrom.

of warm-blooded cetaceans. If the tiny mammals were foolish enough to leave the safety of their vessel and enter its watery domain, their fates were sealed.

With the seas rocketing past it boiling with the force of its passage, the pliosaur closed the distance between itself and the dying *Harbinger*.

Eurypterid I was ready to fight. Von Freiling and Barnes had taken up a defensive posture a hundred yards from the *Harbinger's* slowly rolling hull. Hovering in place with their weapons armed and ready, they waited and watched as Stubbs and Barker's attack sled entered the water with a loud splash.

Von Freiling sat back for a moment, lounging in the mini-sub's rear seat. He reached up, whistling heavy metal as he adjusted his helmet and visor. The sleek vessel's sonar screen and weapon's system were laid out before him like a high-tech chessboard. His position overlooked that of Barnes, who was seated directly in front and below him. His co-pilot was eager to get started, his chest leaning against his shock-absorbing sternum pad, his arms inserted into the pair of padded openings that controlled the *Eurypterid's* big steel manipulators.

Von Freiling gazed through his helmet's lighted visor at the sub's high resolution sonar screen and the three black and white monitor screens that served as windows for their port, starboard and aft. He scanned for any trace of their gargantuan adversary.

"How's the view down there?" he called to Barnes.

Up front, his copilot's face was pressed against the two foot-thick Lexan oval that made up their observation bubble. "Nothing to see yet," Barnes said as they glided along. His head swiveled back and forth as he scanned the blue void before him. "Thank God the tide's dying down. At least visibility's improving. I'd hate to be on the hunt for this thing with clouds of seaweed everywhere."

Von Freiling nodded, then clicked on his radio link. "Hey Stubbs, how's it going?"

"So far so good," his second-in-command replied, the gurgling sound of swirling air bubbles partially obscuring his deep voice.

"There's nothing to see so far. We're almost in position. You guys can get ready to pull your little disappearing act."

"Roger that," Von Freiling said. He took one last look at his screens before starting to maneuver *Eurypterid I*. Out of the corner of his eye he caught a glimpse of the tiny sled and its two riders, hovering far off in the gloom.

Von Freiling's calloused hands gripped the controls of his expensive craft, gradually increasing their speed. He felt the mercurial rush of water sweep unchecked over their swept-wing hull and reveled in the feel of his fast-moving submersible. The wedge-shaped craft sliced through the water like an F-35 does the air, and maneuvered with almost as much ease. It was the first time he'd been in a position to field test his older prototype outside their restrictive research and design environment, and the big adventurer found himself combating an overwhelming urge to take *Eurypterid I* on a high speed run, just to see what it could do.

He maintained twelve knots, heading directly toward the Cutlass. Its black, five-hundred meter spire spiked up out of the darkness like the neck of some vast sea serpent, its ragged head nearly piercing the surface.

"Hey Willie, this is Karl, can you read me?"

"Dis is Willie, I read ya."

"How's everything on board?" A drop of sweat poured into his eye and he blinked annoyingly before scanning his port and starboard monitors.

"Every ting's cool, mon," Willie radioed. "All tings considered. I got Senator Harcourt watchin."

"Good. Where's Stitches?"

"He's up on deck. Last I saw, he was checkin dat gear you guys left in da radar room."

"Guess that's about all he's good for. We're going to go slink off to our ambush point. Unless you spot something definitive on sonar, maintain radio silence. I don't want this thing knowing we're here."

"Dat's a ten four," Willie crackled back. "*Harbinger* out."

Von Freiling adjusted the squelch button on his headset, then called to Barnes. "Alright, I'm going to take her around. Be ready, in case we have an unexpected surprise waiting for us."

Barnes grunted and leaned close to the observation window, while readying his grip on the arm units that brought *Eurypterid I*'s powerful steel pincers to life.

Von Freiling decelerated, maneuvering the little sub at a forty-five degree angle. He made a cautious pass around a one hundred and fifty-foot thick section of the Cutlass. Despite the fact that the tide was starting to die down, the deepwater crevasse generated a frightful current, one that swirled up and around the jagged spire with enough force to move a submarine a hundred times the *Eurypterid's* size. It made the prospect of maintaining their position difficult.

"Okay, Barnes," Von Freiling breathed. "Give me partial on the reverse thrusters. I'm gonna keep her right here."

"You got it boss." He flipped a pair of switches. "She's all yours."

Glancing over at his monitors, the merc's leader pulled back on his control lever, adjusting their position until they were almost completely concealed behind the Cutlass. With a nail-biting effort, he managed to remain there, his iron hands gingerly shifting the streamlined craft's position as he compensated for the ongoing buffeting. He pushed a button, killing the external lights.

To an outside observer, the darkened submersible was practically invisible, peeking out from its concealing wall of rock like a cat lying in wait for a mouse. Three hundred yards away, and less than a hundred yards from the *Harbinger's* sheltering hull, the attack sled and its riders prepared to become bait for the trap. Neither they nor the operators of the mini-sub were aware of the monstrous shape that rose steadily up from the nearby abyss, unseen and undetected as it approached *Eurypterid I* from the rear.

Back onboard the *Harbinger*, Amara Takagi and Willie Daniels sat rigidly upright, their pensive eyes tracking every movement on their underwater monitoring equipment. Dean Harcourt and Vladimir Markov peered silently over their shoulders.

"Can you see them, Willie?" Amara leaned her elbows on the desk in front of her and stared at the monitors.

Unnoticed across the room, the ship's remote system station alarm continued to blink, its dusty orb flashing faster as the damaged vessel's forward compartments continued to fill with seawater.

"No," Willie replied, reaching across and checking the settings on Adam Spencer's complex video equipment. "Dey disappeared from sonar. I only see da sled."

A hundred yards off, the gleaming white sled cruised on, its cylindrical form swerving to and fro as Stubbs attempted to present it as wounded prey for the pliosaur. Though Amara dreaded it, there was a good chance Stubbs' antics, combined with the cetacean distress calls emanating from the *Harbinger's* underwater speaker system, would succeed in luring the colossal carnivore right to their door.

———

The pliosaur cruised just above the ocean floor, its huge flippers casting up great clouds of sand and silt as it moved. It scanned the waters ahead. The familiar sounds of whales in distress echoed once more through the water column, but it was no longer fooled. There were no whales in the vicinity.

It slowed its pace. Suddenly, waves of active sonar washed over its position. Alarmed, it ceased moving and sank quietly to the bottom. The pinging sound waves its body was absorbing were different than those manufactured by its kind. They were more regimented in nature, similar to those of the giant sperm whale it battled days before in the darkness of the nearby deepwater. Something was attempting to locate it.

Its primitive brain suspected the noises were related to the big metal vessel. It ceased using its own echolocation abilities and began to creep stealthily forward, hugging the sea floor to disguise its approach. It instinctively knew using its own sound sight would give away its position and decided to rely on its keen underwater vision and phenomenal sense of smell to stalk its prey.

Up ahead, it pinpointed two potential victims – one large and one small. The smaller one was hovering close to the anchored ship and was moving in a haphazard manner. It was obviously crippled and easy to obtain. The larger one, however, was attempting to conceal itself behind a huge stone outcropping that rose up from the seafloor. The bigger prey item was a rival predator; it was studying the injured creature and waiting for it to come within striking distance.

With cool, reptilian deliberation, the pliosaur made its decision. Focusing on the larger animal, it moved noiselessly behind its quarry, propelled forward by silent strokes of its paddle-shaped appendages.

The hunter was about to become the hunted.

———

Patience was not one of Dean Harcourt's strong suits. He continued to strain his eyes, attempting to keep watch on all the *Harbinger's* sonar screens and hull camera monitors simultaneously. In his mind's eye he visualized a thousand possible battle scenarios involving the *Eurypterid* and its highly-paid crew. In the end, all resulted in him reveling in his cold-blooded adversary's overdue demise. He gloated at the thought. It was going to be glorious – divine retribution of biblical proportions. His only regret was not going down in the mini-sub with Karl Von Freiling to contribute directly to the demon's destruction.

Harcourt stifled his recriminations. He felt a mountain of impatience landslide over him. His already heavy brow lines engraved themselves deeper into his forehead, and his thick hands fidgeted in his pockets as he irritably shifted his weight back and forth.

"Well, Mr. Daniels? Where *is* it?" he snapped.

"How da hell do I know? Maybe da damn ting's not comin?"

"This is the culmination of a long-awaited battle between good and evil," Harcourt replied. His eyes became intense and unwavering. "I doubt very much that that overgrown hell spawn is going to be absent."

Amara stifled a chuckle, then reached over and zoomed in with one of the hull cameras. "If you mean my husband, he's already there. A pliosaur is nothing more than a large reptile. Like a crocodile, only bigger."

Out of the corner of one eye, Harcourt noticed Markov shifting position, his cold eyes contracting. The psychotic bastard was looking for any possible reason to retaliate against the girl. He stayed the scar-faced killer with an upheld hand.

"If you believe that, Dr. Takagi, you're more foolish than I thought."

"I'm tired of sitting and waiting," Amara announced. "I'm going to go check on Jake and make sure he's alright."

"I'll go wit ya," Willie chimed in. He swiveled in his chair, gesturing at the assorted screens and monitors. "You guys can take over for a while."

"You two fucks aren't going anywhere," Markov hissed. He moved a half step closer, his hand resting on the handle of his machete. "I'm not familiar with this sonar shit, and neither is the senator." He gave them a diabolical smile. "If you'd like, *I'll* go check on your boyfriend."

"Oh, you'd like *that*, I'm sure . . ."

"I'd like what?"

"You know," Amara remarked. "Having another man tied up and helpless."

Markov's sinister smirk faded and his knuckles tightened on the machete's bone handle. "Excuse me?"

Willie shook with laughter. He grinned disarmingly at the nearby merc. "I tink she means ya be a batty boy – ya wants Jake for yourself!"

Markov turned on Willie, his expression as black as his eyes. "Listen, you–"

"That'll be enough," Harcourt interjected. He gave his bodyguard a stern look. "Markov, so far you've proven yourself a useful asset. In fact, I might even consider hiring you as my chief of security, once we return to port. But, you need to learn to remain silent until spoken to or summoned."

Still seething, Markov settled for shooting Amara and Willie a malicious look before stepping back.

"Omigod, what was that?" Amara blurted out. She pointed excitedly at the glimmering screen. "Did you see that?"

"See what?" Harcourt said.

"Over there by the drop-off, about a hundred yards behind the Cutlass. I thought I saw a really big signal. I . . . wait, there it is!"

Harcourt mouthed a curse. A huge sonar image popped up on the edge of the screen and then vanished, only to reappear in a different location a few seconds later and then disappear once more.

"Shit, mon! I tink ya right," Willie said, reaching for his headset. "Da damn ting's swimming so close ta da bottom we can't even see it!"

Amara's eyes peeled wide. "What're you doing? Karl said not to use the radio."

"Unless we had a contact," her sonar operator corrected, checking his frequency and flipping a pair of switches. He turned and looked briefly at Harcourt before he started transmitting. "Well Senator Harcourt, I tink ya about ta get dat battle ya been lookin for."

———

Suspended in near darkness, four hundred feet down, the *Eurypterid* held its position. Its weapons system was armed and ready, its external camera array and sonar equipment fixated on Stubbs' attack sled as the tiny craft continued its "dying baitfish" performance.

Inside the mini-sub, Von Freiling chafed. He was used to the interminable waiting that came with stalking big game, but sitting there in the dark listening to nothing but the groaning sounds of seawater exerting pressure on their hull was beginning to grate on his nerves.

"Anything, Barnes?" he finally asked.

"I don't see anything except water and a few fish," Barnes replied. His nose was pressed against the thick Lexan window. "Hmm . . . that's funny. Now, even the fish are gone."

A voice shrieked out of their overhead speaker system.

"Karl, it's Willie! Come in, mon!"

"What the fuck?" Furious, Von Freiling reached down and flipped a switch. "Willie, I told you not to–"

"Shuddup and listen! It's here!"

"What are you talking about?" Von Freiling's eyes scanned his sonar screen. "I don't see anything."

"It's behind ya, mon! Get out of dere! Right now!"

Shaking his head, Von Freiling twisted against the hold of his restraining belts. He glanced at the big monitor that served as their rear window. What he saw made his blood run cold. A mountain of teeth and muscle was headed straight for them at forty miles an hour. It was so close its spreading jaws filled the screen from top to bottom. Willie was right. The pliosaur had found *them* instead.

"Holy shit, hold on!" Von Freiling roared. He threw the ship's powerful impeller system forward at full power, twisting the controls savagely to starboard.

Nearing its full attack speed, the creature's lethal jaws closed with a snap that could be heard through their armored hull. Though it missed the weaving *Eurypterid*, its charge bowled the little sub completely over, sending it into a dizzying underwater roll.

"Son of a bitch!" Barnes cried out. He cursed and held on for dear life as his employer fought the controls, struggling to stabilize the off balance submersible.

"Damage report!" Von Freiling bellowed. His biceps bulged as he brought them back on plane, all the while scanning the nearby waters for their monstrous adversary.

"He just nicked us!" Barnes yelled back. His eye looked up from his screens. "He's heading for the sled now!"

"We'll see about that," Von Freiling growled. Gripping his controls tightly, he pushed *Eurypterid I* forward at full speed.

Already fifty yards from their position and accelerating, the creature closed on the sled. The tiny craft's exposed occupants spotted its approach and promptly started screaming into their leader's ear.

"Calm the fuck down, Stubbs!" Von Freiling snapped. He was holding his headset with one hand and steering with the other. "And stay off the radio, I don't need any distractions right now."

"Mother of God," Barnes said. "Look at the size of that thing! He's as big as a blue whale!"

"Good, because that religious nut of ours is paying us by the pound, brother," Von Freiling answered, then chuckled amusedly. He thumbed open the fire control switch cover on his joystick. "Hold on, Barnes!"

Von Freiling activated *Eurypterid I*'s harpoon cannons, then pushed a button and brought his visor's targeting screen system online. Closing one eye, he drew a quick bead on the surging behemoth. It was a hundred yards away and closing rapidly on Stubbs and Barker. He took a breath and tapped the trigger. Twice.

Too fast to follow, the first pair of titanium-steel harpoons missed their target completely. The second pair slammed into the pliosaur's exposed rear quarters with enough force to punch through granite. One hit at a steep angle and glanced off its armored back, tearing a deep groove in its thick dorsal scales. The other struck home, burying itself in the creature's right rear flipper.

The result was exactly what Von Freiling was hoping for.

The carnivore emitted a bellow that shook the mini-sub's occupants to their core, then turned its huge head and wheeled in their direction. Jaws agape and murder in its eyes, it came for them.

"Holy fucking shit, he's coming right at us!" Barnes's one good eye was the size of a saucer.

"Hold on tight and keep the actuators in repose," Von Freiling said. Beads of perspiration formed on his nose and brow. "We're gonna need all the maneuverability we can get."

"What are you going to do?" Barnes leaned involuntarily back in his chair as the *Kronosaurus* loomed closer.

"I'm gonna use the electric harpoon. His skin's too tough to take chances. I need to aim for a soft spot."

"You're not going to . . ."

"Oh, yes I *am*," Von Freiling said with a chuckle. "I'm gonna aim this thing right down that fucker's throat. So hold on, brother. We're about to play the world's most dangerous game of chicken!"

"Ah, shit!"

Accelerating to flank speed, Von Freiling annihilated the distance between them. The infuriated pliosaur headed straight for the mini-sub, its limousine-sized jaws spread wide enough to swallow a cow. Von Freiling kept one eye on the proximity meter in front of him, coolly gauging the distance between them. Fifty meters . . . then thirty . . . then ten. . .

Suddenly, the monster was so close all they could see was the inside of its mouth as it prepared to swallow them. With a scream of defiance, Von Freiling fired his weapon and flung his controls all the way to port, gunning his engines full out for additional power.

The pliosaur uttered a confused bellow as something jabbed it in the roof of the mouth.

"Got him!" Von Freiling exulted. "Harpoon's in. Hit the juice! I'm throwing her in reverse!"

His face a dire mask, Barnes reached back and flipped the red lever that activated the generators powering their primary weapon. Tethered to the mini-sub by its indestructible cable, the creature was jolted with enough amperage to light up a city block. Flailing to and fro, it thrashed in the water. Its fins trembled and its mighty jaws snapped repeatedly as it struggled to sink its teeth into the invisible foe attacking it.

Von Freiling eyed the voltage meter by his side. Based on its struggles, he calculated the creature would be dead in less than a minute – long before they were forced to cut the power. Everything was going according to plan. Their insulation was shielding them, and they had fifty feet of locked-up cable keeping them at a safe distance. It was simply a matter of time before he emerged victorious.

Von Freiling closed his eyes and smiled. He could visualize his grinning face plastered across the front page of every paper on the planet.

Unwilling to die, the *Kronosaurus* fought on, lashing its immense head to and fro. Out of nowhere, it clamped down on the insulated cable linking it to *Eurypterid I*. It felt the mini-sub's weight and the resistance of its engines and instantly yanked its head in the opposing direction, jerking the tiny submersible forward and off-balance – and within range of its mouth. As the brightly colored craft came within an arm's length of its baleful eye, the infuriated beast closed its jaws on *Eurypterid I* with a frightful crunch.

"Oh my God!" Barnes screamed as he was thrown about in his chair.

Von Freiling barely made a sound as he was struck hard on the head by a falling object. Struggling to stay conscious, the astonished adventurer could do nothing but hold on.

Outside, the berserk titan started shaking them like a bull terrier does a rat. There was a wrenching noise so high-pitched it was painful. Through a haze of pain Von Freiling recognized the sound. The pliosaur's ridged teeth were digging their way through the *Eurypterid's* reinforced armor. Sizzling blue arcs of electricity and showers of white sparks spewed forth from their control panels and indicator screens.

"What's happening?" Barnes yelled.

"His fangs are piercing our insulation!" Von Freiling cried out. Blood streamed down his face from his reopened scalp wound and his insides felt like a gallon of semi-gloss trapped in an out-of-control paint shaker. "The sub's not designed to be this close to the discharge area! He's burning out our electrical systems! You've got to cut the power!"

Still struggling to hold on, Barnes strained to reach the cutoff switch that killed the juice to their harpoon. He was almost there when the creature spat them out, causing the damaged *Eurypterid* to spiral off, end over end.

A second later, the insides of the embattled mini-sub went dark. Releasing his harness, Von Freiling staggered to one side as the floor shifted beneath his feet. He shook his aching head in an effort to clear it, leaning against what felt like a bulkhead as he tried to assess their situation.

"Barnes, can you hear me?" He could barely make out his co-pilot's shape in the near blackness.

"Yeah, I hear you," came the weak reply. "Shit, we're on emergency power!"

"Yeah, he got us good. Our circuits must be fried," Von Freiling said. Outside he could hear the roar of the retreating pliosaur as it moved away, gnashing its teeth. "At least the harpoon broke off."

"Well ain't that just great," Barnes replied. He unclipped his belt, cursing as he fell from his chair and crashed to the floor. "Fuck, we're upside down!"

There was a series of clicking sounds as the submersible's rose-colored emergency lights kicked in.

"We've got to replace the fuses," Von Freiling said, moving forward while holding his head. "Quick, before that damn thing realizes we're helpless and comes back to finish us off!"

"Let's do it." Barnes looked around the upside-down interior of their submersible, blinking at the dim, red lighting. "Where are the fuses?"

"They should be right about . . . here," Von Freiling said, moving unsteadily to a nearby section of their hull.

The spot was empty.

"Shit, the box must've been dislodged when he yo-yoed us. There's equipment all over the place!"

Just then a trickle of water fell on Von Freiling's head, mixing with his blood as it ran down his face. He stuck out his tongue and tasted it.

"Barnes, what's our depth?" he asked, looking nervously upward.

"Five hundred and ten . . . make that twenty . . . shit, we're dropping fast!"

"Damn it! The fucking lizard damaged our ballast systems," Von Freiling said. "The hull's been compromised!"

Overhead, the trickle of water increased to a series of heavy streams. Soon it was pouring down over them.

"Then, let's do something!" Barnes yelled. Soaked to the skin and shivering, he searched through the pile of equipment and debris that littered their inverted craft. "Shit . . . what does the fuse box look like?"

"It's a fiberglass box about fourteen inches square," Von Freiling said, tossing fallen cases and containers as he spoke. "It's red."

Barnes stared angrily at their emergency lights. "Everything's fucking red!"

"Just keep looking," Von Freiling said. He continued to feel in ankle-deep seawater. "I don't know what the seafloor depth below us is, but if we're over the crevasse and don't get our power back, we'll implode, whether he gets us or not!"

Pausing, as static shrieked from his headset, Von Freiling cupped one hand to his ear.

"This is Karl," he said into the mouthpiece. "Can you read me? I am unable to understand your message. Please repeat!"

The reply transmission came through as garbled noise, completely indecipherable.

"Fuck!"

"Hey Karl, I think I got it!" Barnes cried out triumphantly. He held up an open case containing four polymer cylinders with shiny metal end caps.

"That's it!" Von Freiling said, splashing through ice-cold water. "Quick, hand them to me one by one, once I open the panel."

Leaning against the nearest bulkhead, the bronze-eyed adventurer worked feverishly to remove the safety locks covering the submersible's insulated circuit panel. Throwing caution to the wind, he grabbed the three burnt fuses in his bare hands, wrenching the foot-long devices loose with soaked fingers and tossing them into the rising water. With Barnes holding onto his seat with one hand, and handing him the replacement fuses with the other, he fought to restore power to their dying vessel.

Suddenly, the floor beneath them groaned and began to shift. The increasing pressure continued to squeeze the rapidly descending

Eurypterid and shin-deep water started creeping toward the open circuit box.

"What's happening?" Barnes stared apprehensively at their depth reading, then at the rising water.

"The sub's shifting with the current," Von Freiling said. He removed his helmet. His face and mustache were soaked with perspiration. "Hurry and give me that last one. I've got to seal this panel before the water gets into it. Otherwise, we're dead!"

Deftly handing him the last, precious fuse, Barnes breathed a sigh of relief as his boss clicked it into place and slammed the panel's lid closed, sealing it just before the shifting pool of seawater reached it.

"That should do it," Von Freiling said. He fought down a shiver and waded toward his still-inverted station. "I'm gonna turn on the power and hit the exterior lights. Once we're back online, I need you to activate the emergency pumps and adjust our ballast so we can get this water out. Once we're dry and right side up we'll surface and decide on our next course of action."

"Yeah? Well, I hope it involves getting the fuck out of here and coming back with an Apache helicopter," Barnes remarked. He moved to *Eurypterid I*'s observation bubble, staring out into the blackness that surrounded them. "I'd feel much safer blowing that thing to bits with a Hellfire missile from a thousand feet up."

"C'mon, Barnes," Von Freiling snickered as he flipped the mini-sub's circuit breaker, causing the little craft's electric systems to light up like Times Square. "It's been how many years together, you and I? And how many adventures? Have I gotten you killed yet?"

Barnes grinned. As he opened his mouth to reply, *Eurypterid I*'s twin searchlights ignited, lancing out into the gloom and lighting up the darkness for fifty yards. His eye widened in terror, and he barely had time to gasp before the pliosaur's tooth-lined maw plowed into their submersible, crunching down with enough force to crush the entire prow, its observation window included.

Barnes' last thought as his world imploded into darkness was a single word.

Yes.

TWENTY-SIX

After nearly thirty years of surviving combat on the killing fields of four continents, retired Marine Corps Master Sergeant Stubbs Broder was re-learning the meaning of the word *terror*.

It was right behind him, its mouth gaping wide enough to inhale an ox. With its bass roar disrupting the surrounding water like a bomb blast, the pliosaur lunged ferociously forward, striving to bury its teeth in the occupants of the cigar-shaped sled that remained only a few, tantalizing yards ahead of its nose.

Stubbs glanced back and screamed into his scuba mask. This was *not* turning out to be one of his brightest ideas. As the creature lunged for them once more, he slammed the sled's controls ninety degrees sideways, sending them lurching hard to port. His extensive hours of training on the simulator once again saved both their lives; the pliosaur sailed past, its monstrous body dwarfing their craft. It was a close call, with the creature's jaws slamming shut like a giant bear trap less than three feet from Stubbs' exposed head.

Frantically gunning the sled's impeller engine back to flank, he torqued his motorized mount a hundred and eighty degrees and hurtled toward the *Harbinger*. She was five hundred yards away and obscured by a widening cloud of fuel and oil, but the sun silhouetting her battered hull against the surface made the listing ship easy to spot.

Stubbs glanced down at his dials, praying the sled would get them safely home. The fourteen-foot, toboggan-like vessel he manned was little more than a hastily modified prototype – a 500 horsepower undersea rocket Von Freiling's researchers concocted to use as one half of each *Eurypterid*'s drive trains.

Though he was bereft of sonar, and in the unenviable position of sitting in the open on what his comrades called a torpedo for two, there was no doubt in Stubbs' mind their illustrious leader was dead. He'd gaped from 150 yards out as the battle between the enraged reptile and his employer reached its climax. He watched the submersible sink from sight, spiraling down into the ocean's extreme depths. Like a hound at hunt, the pliosaur unerringly followed it. The subsequent flash and teeth-vibrating thump said it all. Despite *Eurypterid I's* hitech armament, the creature had breached its reinforced hull, imploding it and killing everyone on board. It was over for Von Freiling and Barnes.

"Barker, I'm gonna make another run for the ship!" Stubbs yelled into his transmitter. He glanced back though an obscuring cloud of air bubbles at his terrified comrade.

"Well hurry the fuck up!" Barker wailed, his eyes the size of teacups as he waited for the monster to reappear. "Why do you keep changing direction? Why don't you just surface and go straight in?"

"Because the thing's too damn fast, that's why! He'll catch us in a straight line run before we get there."

"So, what the fuck are we gonna do?"

"Hope Karl's widow was right about that whale tranquilizer of hers. Get that overgrown spear gun she gave us ready and hold on tight. If that son of a bitch comes at us again you shoot him right in the eye!"

As if hearing their conversation, the pliosaur materialized directly beneath them. Jaws snapping, it tried to seize the weaving sled. Stubbs accelerated to full speed, darting frantically from left to right, keeping them from death by inches.

"Shoot it, Barker!" he bellowed. He lost his voice for a moment as the sled's bottom was grazed by the creature's scarred snout. "I can't keep him off us much longer!"

Barker braced his legs, releasing his handhold on the bucking craft, and pulled the pneumatic firearm from its sheath. His position on the rear of the sled was awkward, and he twisted around in an attempt to get a clear shot. He craned his neck, looking behind them, then off to either side. He cursed and shook his head.

"Shit, Stubbs, where the hell is it?" he yelled over his shoulder, the heavy speargun held tight in his thick-gloved hands. "It was just here! Now, I don't see it any–"

The sled was hit hard from below, its twelve hundred pounds pushed thirty feet through a gurgling cloud of oil and bubbles.

"Holy shit!" Stubbs' powerful arms strained as he twisted the vehicle's handlebars, fighting to regain control. "Man that was close! I thought he had us! Did you get him?" He looked back and gasped. He was alone. "Barker!" He clutched his com-set as he changed course.

"Here!" his comrade's frightened voice radioed back. "I got knocked off, but I'm in one piece. I'm at your seven!"

Stubbs breathed a sigh of relief. He scanned the area for Barker, simultaneously keeping watch for their oversized adversary. A hundred yards ahead, he spotted him kicking gamely toward the surface. Deprived of fins and weighed down by gear and tanks, the encumbered merc was a sitting duck.

As he watched, the pliosaur circled back like a pale-bellied B-52. Jaws open, it closed on Barker.

Oh God . . . "Barker, he's coming right at you!" Stubbs screamed into his radio. "I can't get to you in time. You gotta shoot him!" The big merc knew what happened next would haunt him for the rest of his life. Despite Barker's screams of terror – audible even without a radio – he courageously twisted to face his attacker. From less than twenty feet away, he aimed his spear gun into the beast's wide-open mouth and pulled the trigger.

To his credit, his aim was dead on. To his misfortune, the sizzling projectile deflected off the pliosaur's arsenal of dentition, ricocheting away like it was made of rubber. Spiraling end over end, the barbed missile sank harmlessly into the depths. A half-second later, Barker was engulfed headfirst to mid-thigh in the creature's mouth. His agonized cries were silenced by a sickening sound as it severed his body right below the hip. Stubbs watched in helpless horror as his friend's amputated legs performed a grotesque Irish jig, kicking hard for the surface. A second later, he was shaken back to reality.

It was finished with Barker. Now it was coming for him.

Back in the *Harbinger's* observation room, Amara and the surviving members of the ship's complement remained ignorant of Stubbs' dilemma. They sat in stunned silence, the hull camera and sonar sound images of Karl Von Freiling's unexpected demise burned into their collective consciousness.

"Stubbs to *Harbinger!*" The panicked voice blared out of several radios, jolting everyone back to reality. "Do you read me?"

Markov cursed and snatched the Motorola from his belt clip. "This is Markov. I hear you!"

"No time for small talk. Karl and Barnes are dead, and the thing just got Barker! It's right on my ass! I need cover!"

"That's a copy," Markov said, already moving toward the exit door. "Head for the Zodiac's loading platform. We'll be waiting."

"On my . . . oh shit!" There was a split second pause before Stubbs radioed back. "Damn, that was fucking close! On my way!"

Markov sprang up the nearest stairwell and pressed his talk button once more. "Stitches, this is Markov. I hope you copied that transmission. Meet me at the railing overlooking the *Sycophant,* and bring the heaviest hardware we've got!"

"I'm already on it."

Amara watched as Markov vanished topside, then turned her bruised face toward Willie. "C'mon," she said, rising to her feet. "Let's see what's happening." Willie nodded and stood up.

Amara turned to Dean Harcourt. "Senator?" she prodded. "Are you coming?"

The politician continued to watch, immobile and unblinking as the drama continued to unfold on the monitors. If it wasn't for the rise and fall of his chest, or the occasional tightening of his lips, Amara would have thought he was an abandoned department store mannequin. She turned to Willie, shrugging her slim shoulders, then pounded up the nearest stairs.

Markov loped over to the section of railing overlooking the *Sycophant.* He focused hard on the grated stairs that led to the Zodiac's embarking platform. The wind was picking up, with white-caps lashing the steps. It would make dismounting from the sled more difficult than normal, assuming Stubbs was lucky enough to make it that far.

"Here!"

He turned to see Stitches running toward him. The little redhead tossed him an M-16 rifle identical to the one he carried. Markov snatched the weapon out of the air and checked it. "Shit, man. This is all we've got?"

Stitches' lips compressed. "That's it." He checked his own magazine and pulled the black weapon's charger back. "And only two clips each. They're steel-cored rounds though, so let's make em' count."

Markov stared down at the churning seas, willing Stubbs to appear. Something impacted against his boot heel. Annoyed, he shifted his foot out of the object's way, allowing the can of spray lubricant to continue rolling toward the bow until it deflected off a nearby pipe. He studied the sloping deck and exchanged glances with Stitches before turning to the situation at hand.

"There he is!" Markov pointed at a spot 75 yards out, as Stubbs and the battered sled surfaced in a watery explosion.

"And there *it* is!" Stitches cut in fiercely. He gestured with his rifle muzzle toward the mountainous form breaking the surface right behind Stubbs.

The big merc waved frantically at his two comrades. He was up on his heels, riding his craft like an oversized jet ski. He glanced back, then hunkered down and made straight for the platform, tossing his face mask over his shoulder as he went.

Markov could see the creature plainly. Its wedge-shaped skull broke the surface as it closed the distance between itself and the juicy tidbit bouncing before it. "Let him have it!" he snarled. He took aim and began firing full-automatic bursts.

With impressive accuracy, the two mercs emptied their forty-round clips directly into the pliosaur's exposed face. The creature roared like a hundred lions and reeled back, its sixteen-foot pectoral fins breaching the surface of the water as the high-speed rounds tore into it. It inhaled sharply, slamming its jaws down into the water, and submerged from sight.

Markov and Stitches ejected their spent mags and inserted new ones. Jaws set, they leaned over the railing, scanning the surface with their smoking rifles pointed at the spot where their gargantuan enemy had disappeared. Twenty feet below, Stubbs pulled alongside the wave-swept platform and struggled to disembark.

"Great work, guys!" he yelled up, giving them a thumbs-up sign. "You saved my ass for sure!"

Markov turned as Amara arrived with her Jamaican first mate. The two walked to the railing and stood there as Stubbs and his engine continued fighting the current. He sneered, giving them a contemptuous look. "What the fuck do you two want?"

"We don't want no ting," Willie said. "We just . . ."

"Omigod!" Amara pointed at the water. "Markov, tell him to forget the sled and jump for the landing!"

The merc targeted the cetaceanist with hateful eyes.

"Oh, for heaven's sake!" Amara ignored him and leaned over the railing, frantically waving her arms. The green and white water below her was frothing over an area fifty feet across. "Stubbs, forget the sled and jump! It's coming!"

The big merc hesitated. He gripped the handlebars of his bucking craft tight, staring confusedly up at Amara. Soon, the ocean around him was churning so violently he could barely hold on. His eyes bulged in realization and he sprang to his feet, preparing to dive for the rust-covered platform. Too late.

The pliosaur broke the surface with an explosive bellow, enveloping the entire sled within its jaws. Its bone crushing teeth met and it shook its huge head, spraying a vile mixture of gasoline, seawater and blood in every direction.

Markov cursed as he was forced back by the ferocity of the assault. He ducked behind the ship's railing, covering his face with his forearm as the creature spat the sled out. What was left sailed sixty feet into the air, arcing high over the ship's gunnels. A moment later, it crashed onto the *Harbinger's* decks with enough force to crack steel.

The sled settled noisily onto its side, its macerated hull a crushed tin can. Other than the diluted bloodstains that dyed its pearl-colored hull plates a grotesque pink, Stubbs was nowhere to be found.

"Son of a bitch!" Stitches spat. Eyes ablaze, the little merc spun from the carnage and swung his weapon toward the wind-whipped waters below. He took aim, his sweat-stained chest heaving as he howled in frustration. The creature had disappeared. Disgusted, he lowered his gun. "Damn."

"Well, so much for that," Markov said. He shrugged and slung his still-hot M-16 over one shoulder. "Too bad, I liked Stubbs."

"Me too," Stitches said. He looked at the frightful scene. "God, what a fucking mess! Now what do we do?"

As they conversed, Amara and Willie tiptoed away, moving around the pulverized sled, along the wreckage-strewn deck. As noiselessly as possible, they made their way past the *Harbinger's* abandoned cranes, slipping past the fallen *Eurypterid II* as they headed toward the bridge. They were almost there when Dean Harcourt lunged at them from the darkness of a nearby stairwell.

Suspended in the water with its fins extended like blades, the creature faced down the *Harbinger*. Its primitive brain pulsed as it studied its giant adversary. Enraged by the pain of its puncture wounds, it was beyond rudimentary thinking. A red haze clouded its thermal vision and its enormous heart pounded in its ears. Its wrinkled lips drew slowly back, revealing its entire arsenal of spiked teeth. It shook its huge head, trying to dislodge the indescribable fury that threatened to overwhelm it. Then it spread its cavernous jaws wide and gave forth a water-muffled roar of pure rage, flinging itself violently forward. Accelerating to full speed, it lowered its bullet-ridden skull into position like a gigantic battering ram and charged.

Jake Braddock regained consciousness. Stirred to life by the flashes of pain shooting through his bruised skull, the young lawman ratcheted his eyes open. He groaned, struggling hard to focus. His body felt like he'd been beaten with ball peen hammers and he was unable to move. He was lying on his side, bound hand and foot like a trussed steer, his wrists and ankles tied together around the stanchion that supported the *Harbinger's* oversized captain's wheel.

As he blinked to clear his vision, Jake fought the pulsating pain that detonated inside his head like mortar rounds. He sucked in air, struggling to remember what happened. He recalled the fight with

Karl Von Freiling, and surrendering his sidearm to save Amara from Harcourt. *But how the hell did he end up . . .*

Markov. He recalled the flash of movement from the scarred-faced merc. A cold rage seized him, transforming his ribcage into bands of ice, and he forcibly calmed himself to keep from hyperventilating. He focused hard, trying to ignore the throbbing that threatened to split his head in two. He gritted his teeth and twisted his wrists against each other with all his might.

"Son . . . of . . . a . . . bitch!" Jake stopped and caught his breath. It was a useless effort. There wasn't a man alive who could break the layers of expertly knotted, quarter-inch-thick nylon cords that held him. He caught his breath and lay where he was, refocusing his thoughts and looking around the bridge for any means to free himself.

———

Harcourt paced the near darkness of the *Harbinger's* observation room, his fingers interlaced across the top of his stomach. He wore a demonic look, an appearance exacerbated by the vessel's warning lights bathing his features in red as they continued their increasingly frantic warning

"I guess you didn't feel the need to tell us about this?" He pointed at the wall unit, then looked Amara and Willie disdainfully up and down. "Or, perhaps, after you muted the alarm and disabled its beacons, you thought I wouldn't have the brains to figure out that this ship's onboard computer system has been informing us for the last twenty minutes that her pumps can't handle the damage she's sustained?"

Amara cast a nervous glance at Markov and Stitches.

"That's alright." Harcourt said. He wore a humorless smile. "It doesn't matter, we're leaving anyway."

Amara gasped. "We are?"

"Yes. *We're* leaving, my dear doctor." He chuckled, reaching inside his bloodstained suit for one of his cigars. He lit it and puffed fiercely, pointing one end at Markov, Stitches and himself. "We're taking your Zodiac . . . or should I say, *my* Zodiac, and we're leaving what's left of this ship."

"And what about us, mon?" Willie said with surprising boldness. "What ya gonna do? Ya gonna just leave us here?"

"As a matter of fact, yes, I am." Harcourt held the Cuban close to his face, examining its smoldering tip. "As you may have ascertained, the last thing I need back home is any sensationalist storytelling on your part. But, just to show you there are no hard feelings, Doctor Takagi, I'm giving you back your beloved research vessel. Free of charge."

"Why, ya crazy muddah fuckah!" Willie exploded, lunging for Harcourt's throat with a viciousness that surprised them all. He slammed into the astonished politician with impressive force, wrapping his hands around the senator's thick neck.

Caught off guard by the unexpectedness of the assault, Markov and Stitches glanced at each other in astonishment. They cursed and sprang into action, hauling Willie off of Harcourt, with Markov restraining him with a half-nelson that made it impossible to move.

"You miserable, island-hopping lowlife!" Harcourt snarled. He clambered back to his feet, his eyes wild as he attempted to adjust his ruined suit.

"It's okay, Senator Harcourt," Markov said, tightening his hold on the senator's assailant. "I've got him."

"Let him go, you bastard!" Amara screamed, as fear for her long-time friend overwhelmed her shock at the sudden melee.

"I'm fine, Amara," Willie panted. He relaxed his shoulders, ceasing his useless struggles against Markov's powerful grip, then twisted hard against the immobilizing hold, shifting his body just enough to look Harcourt in the eye. "Ya know what ya problem is, rich mon? Ya fucking crazy! Ya one sick son of a bitch. Ya gotta lotta people killed today, and for what? Because ya tink ya da servant of God? No way, mon! Ya da devil. And I tell ya some ting. If ya leave us be, we'll die. But, ya gonna die too, mon. Sooner or later. And when ya *gets* ta hell, I'm gonna be dere waitin for ya. Just remember dat!"

"That's quite a speech, Mr. Daniels." Harcourt smirked, straightening what remained of his tie, then turned away. "Unfortunately, I have no more time to relish your virtuosity." He snapped his fingers. "Let him go. We're leaving."

Markov glanced over at Stitches, then released his grip on Willie. "Don't do anything stupid," he whispered in the big Jamaican's ear.

Her pale eyes wide, Amara rushed to her battered companion.

"I'm fine," Willie insisted, rubbing his shoulder.

Ignoring them, Harcourt instructed his remaining men. "Grab whatever you think we'll need. Weapons, water, fuel. We've got about twenty miles to cover." He paused beside a nearby table, noticing the partially used box of dynamite Jake brought onboard several days prior. He put his hand in his pants pocket and his eyes lit up. "Make sure you bring this."

Markov shook his head disapprovingly. "We don't need that stuff. We've got grenades."

"Just do as I say." Harcourt moved past him and headed toward the stairwell.

His fists and teeth clenched, Willie took a step in the heavyset politician's direction. "Ya know some ting? I tink it was better dat da beast got ya son, Mistah Harcourt."

Amara eyes widened and she threw herself in Willie's way, trying to hold him back.

"What the hell did you say?" Harcourt moved menacingly toward Willie.

"Are you crazy?" Amara whispered. "Stop it!"

Willie ignored her warnings, as well as the look on Harcourt's face. "I said dat I'm glad ya son got eaten by da pliosaur." He folded his arms defiantly across his chest. "Udder wise, he'd have ended up anudda spoiled, crazy mon, just like his fadduh!"

His face a latticework of unfettered fury, Harcourt uttered a bull-like bellow and rushed Willie, only to be restrained in mid-charge by Markov and Stitches.

"Cool down, senator," Stitches said. He stepped back, palms out, watching as Markov kept himself positioned between the senator and the focus of his fury. "It's not worth the effort. We're leaving, and they're staying. That's enough, don't you think?"

His breath coming in gasps, Harcourt stopped struggling and backed off. He looked around, then paused contemplatively. A serene look made its way across his rotund face.

"Perhaps you're right, Stitches," he said with a forced smile, looking genially at him and Markov. "After all, we've certainly got bigger fish to fry."

Harcourt turned to leave, then whirled unexpectedly back around, his hands clawing wildly at Markov's waist. Before the astonished mercenary realized what was happening, the politician yanked his forty-caliber Glock from its holster.

Amara's cry of alarm became a yelp as Willie spotted the gun and flung her bodily out of the way. She hit the deck shoulder first, stunned into immobility as Harcourt fired from less than ten feet away.

"Jesus fucking Christ!" Markov roared. Ignoring Amara's high-pitched shriek, he forced the senator's arm into the air and yanked the smoking gun from his grasp. "You stupid son of a bitch! You could have shot us both!"

Willie staggered backward and uttered a pain-filled gasp. He clutched at his stomach, staring confusedly at the layer of crimson that coated his hands, then dropped to his knees. A second later, he toppled over onto his side.

Amara sprang to her feet. "Omigod, you shot him, you fucking asshole!" she screamed. She rushed to Willie's side and grabbed at him, struggling to hoist him up into a seated position. "You're out of your mind!"

Harcourt snorted and turned around, raising one eyebrow as he gave his men an interrogative look. "Do we have a problem, gentlemen?"

"Not at all," Markov replied. An amused look crept across his face. "Aren't you going to shoot the woman, too? I'll be happy to do it if you'd like."

"No, that won't be necessary." Harcourt glanced at Amara sobbing as she cradled Willie's head in her lap. "We've got the Lord's work now."

"What about Braddock?" Markov asked pointedly.

"What about him?"

"Well, should we–"

Harcourt cut the conversation short with a wave of his hand. He made his way up onto the *Harbinger's* main deck with Markov and Stitches in tow. Behind him, the two mercs started gathering supplies and gear.

A moment later, a one hundred-ton torpedo slammed into the *Harbinger's* bow.

Jake was growing desperate. He realized if he was going to free himself and help Amara and Willie, he was going to have to do it on his own. He glanced up at the aged whaling harpoon, suspended far beyond his reach, and chuckled insanely at the gravity of his situation.

Suddenly, the sound of a high-powered pistol round echoed through the ship's helm. Alarmed by the proximity of the gunshot, Jake struggled against his bonds. His muscles bulged as he heaved against the nylon rope with all his might, pulling until he drew blood. His breathing became ragged from all the adrenaline and his mind raced with frightful possibilities.

Amara was in jeopardy. He could sense it. With Von Freiling in the water, she and Willie were alone with Harcourt and Markov.

Markov . . .

Stubbs was right. The scar-faced merc was a sadistic sociopath. Jake scrunched his eyes closed, trying to shut away the awful images running rampant through his mind. Markov was sick enough to rape a woman in front of her kids. And Jake was tied up when it mattered . . .

Screaming in fear and frustration, he heaved like a madman against his ropes once more, straining to loosen their constrictor's grip by alternately ripping his fists and feet back and forth against each other. He felt his skin tear, layer by layer, and the nylon loops around his wrists and ankles sliding back and forth from the lubrication of his blood. Salty sweat inundating the reddened patches of raw flesh, causing painful stinging sensations. His lungs became an over-stoked furnace but he ignored them, resolutely flailing away. Perspiration transformed his hair into a sopping wet sponge; merging with his sunblock, it streamed down his brow, burning his eyes and blurring his vision. He tried to blink it away, closing his eyelids tight as the fear and pain reached unbearable levels. He might lose Amara, just like . . .

When he willed himself to reopen his eyes he did a double-take. He was twenty-one again. It was the day of his mother's funeral – chilled, damp and blustery. Everyone was already gone, leaving him forlorn in the cemetery, his head lowered and the rain pressing his dark-colored suit tight against his athletic frame. The passing shower became a downpour, soaking him to the skin and obscuring his eyesight. He could smell the thickset odor of torn-up grass and soil, piled high around the freshly excavated grave, and heard the squishing noise of the tan-colored mud as it oozed up and over the top of his shoes.

He extracted the medal he'd won at the state fencing championships from his jacket pocket. Raindrops streamed across its shiny gold surface, a fitting substitute for the tears he could never bring himself to shed.

Suddenly, powerful fingers dug into his shoulder. Jake whirled around, wanton surprise stepping aside for cold anger as John Braddock materialized beside him. His father was dirty and unshaven but surprisingly sober. He'd kept a low profile for the last few days, avoiding public scrutiny by failing to attend his own wife's funeral.

John fumbled for words. "Listen, son," he began. "I, uh . . . know I probably wasn't always the best father . . ." He blanched as if the words left a bad taste in his mouth. "And, well, maybe my drinking was a little hard on you . . . but it was your mother's doing! She drove me to it! Even the accident . . . if she hadn't kept nagging me about my driving that day . . . I don't know."

A disgusted look appeared on Jake's face and he extended his palm outward in warning. His father persisted, waving his hands wildly and moving closer to him.

"Look . . . I can see it in your eyes. I know you blame yourself for your mom's death, probably Samantha's too . . ."

Jake gaped at him.

John's voice became louder and more authoritarian as he gained confidence. "Your mom's weakness was no more your fault than your wife's was. You have to stop beating yourself up about their deaths and be a man – like *I* am!" He slammed a hammer fist into his palm for emphasis. "You've got to be strong . . . especially now. It's you and me against the world. We're family and we've got to stick together . . . you know what I mean?"

The sheer ridiculousness of the words left Jake flabbergasted. He hadn't seen his father for months. Not a phone conversation with him in years, except to inquire about his mother. The man was a stranger, and now, a murderer. He wished his mother walked away from the accident instead of his father. The bile in his throat choked what would have been a chuckle of irony. He turned to leave, failing to mask his complete and utter loathing.

John ignored the obvious and persisted. His aging countenance was a montage of pent-up frustration and resentment, both at himself and the world. He latched onto Jake's shoulder once more, trying hard to spin him around, trying to use the remainder of his formidable strength to bully and intimidate his adult son.

Jake felt the familiar grip. His head snapped back as bad memories machine-gunned their way through his paper-thin patience. A relentless barrage of ill-submerged fear and anguish forced its way free. He saw his father's face, his expression warped, as always, by rage. For the first time he felt his own anger surge to the surface, a towering tsunami of bona fide hatred.

The punch was harder than he intended: a pile-driving right cross with all his weight and power behind it. His rock-hard fist connected with John Braddock's jaw, splintering teeth and bone and sending him sprawling across a nearby hillock of fieldstones and mud. He lay there, eyes closed and unmoving.

Jake stared contemptuously down at him, his heart pounding, his breathing harsh and ragged. He glanced around and straightened up, regaining his composure as he slowly opened his bloodied fist. He stared at the gold medal still within his grasp, its hard edges imprinted deeply into his palm. The rain intensified, washing it clean. He turned to the mouth of his mother's grave, stepping to the very edge. He took a deep breath. Then he tossed the medal inside and watched it fall, waiting for it to strike the bronze-colored casket.

Ka-boom!

Jake shuddered as an incredibly powerful blow rocked the *Harbinger*. The impact nearly capsized the ship, toppling a shower of antiquities from their resting places, including an ancient sextant. The heavy wood and metal tool came plummeting down, bruising his already-injured head, eliciting a plethora of curses.

Forced back to reality, the lawman strained to ascertain what was happening. The entire ship began to shiver, and a sudden drop caused his testicles to tighten up. From the angle of the bridge and the magnitude of the waves, he deduced the *Harbinger* was succumbing to the pliosaur's repeated assaults. Her armored prow began to dip sharply, inching its way toward the foam-flecked waves that lapped at her gunwales.

Jake's mind reeled at the sickening realization.

She was going under. And he was going with her.

"Hurry up, Stitches!" Markov bellowed from the *Sycophant*'s prow.

Nearby, Harcourt sat atop one of the runabout's rigid air chambers, his hands folded neatly across his stomach and his back to the waves. Above the tiny vessel, the *Harbinger* listed badly. Drawn down by sheer mass, her bow was almost completely submerged.

Markov shook his head. He gave the ship another fifteen minutes before she slipped beneath the waves. His loaded M-16 in hand, the mercenary scanned the turbulent water for signs of the monster. Minutes earlier, the creature rammed the *Harbinger*'s damaged bow with the force of a speeding commuter train, widening the gash in her foremost hull plates, sending thousands of gallons of seawater rushing into her flooded forward compartments. There was no saving her.

The pliosaur vanished after its last attack, a fact that gave Markov little comfort as he waited for Stitches to make his way down the creaking landing platform. "It's about fucking time," he muttered as his comrade placed the box of dynamite on the inflatable's rigid floor.

"Hey, I just follow orders." Stitches glanced nervously up at the groaning ship and swallowed.

"Yeah, right," Markov snickered. "You sure you took care of everything?"

"I staved in their lifeboats, destroyed the ship's transmitter and antenna, and tossed all the hand radios over the side."

"Okay then," Markov said. "Senator, I think we're about ready to shove off." He reached for the rope that bound them to the ill-fated research vessel.

"One moment."

"Sir?"

Harcourt stood up, his bloodshot eyes contemplating the thin docking line.

Markov scanned the surrounding waters once more. "Senator?"

"I hate to say it . . ." Harcourt folded his arms across his barrel-like chest. "But, it would cause irreparable harm to all present if anyone else survived the *Harbinger's* sinking."

"I see." Markov felt a sudden surge of sadistic excitement. "And you want to prevent this by . . . ?"

"Well, I'm certainly not endorsing executing anyone, if that's what you think."

"Go on . . ."

"Let's just say that I would sleep better if I knew the good doctor was as securely tied up as Jake Braddock. Just in case."

"Whatever you say, senator." Markov nodded and turned to his comrade. "Stitches, stay here and keep an eye out for the lizard. I'll go take care of our problem."

Waving off Stitches' complaining before it started, Markov stepped off the bobbing *Sycophant* and bounded up the straining stairwell to the *Harbinger's* main deck.

Unseen by those waiting below, he loosened his bolo as he went.

CRETACEOUS OCEAN
65 MILLION YEARS AGO

Seen from within, the caldera was a waterlogged charnel house. The onrushing wall of water had filled its bowl-shaped crater to within a thousand feet of its edges. The catastrophe had transformed the dormant volcano into a gigantic saltwater aquarium – one measuring over eight miles in width and nine thousand feet in depth.

It was an aquarium of the dead.

The water's surface was covered with sections of uprooted trees and the bodies of the wave's hapless victims. Broken pterosaurs, plesiosaurs, mosasaurs, crocodiles and turtles littered the landscape. Giant squid and ammonites bobbed alongside tens of thousands of fish of every size and shape, their bodies floating beneath ever-darkening skies.

Time passed. Suddenly, the big bull pliosaur surfaced amidst the widespread carnage with a loud exhale. The entire left side of his body was badly lacerated and one of his pelvic fins was broken, but he was alive. A few minutes later, two more spouts announced the arrival of the old one-eyed bull and the huge female. The two surfaced a hundred yards away, amidst a huge school of dead and dying salmonids.

The younger male pliosaur moved slowly toward the other two, stopping fifty feet away. The female was in surprisingly good shape. Many of her teeth were broken or missing, and from her shaky movements, it was likely she'd cracked ribs as well. But teeth grew back and ribs healed. She would live.

The one-eyed bull was not so fortunate. Already listing in the water with black blood oozing from his mouth and nostrils, the ancient male had sustained horrific internal injuries from the fall. Barely able to keep himself afloat, he paddled laboriously to the stony edges of their escarpment. There, in the shallows, he beached himself. His breathing was exhaustive and excruciating. Once a voracious predator at the top of the food chain, the nearly seventy-foot marine reptile was now just another victim of the catastrophe that enveloped his entire world. As the remaining pliosaurs watched, great shudders wracked his mottled body. His dark blood continued to spurt in great gouts, clouding the surrounding waters. In minutes, he was gone.

Alone in the caldera, the two survivors drew closer to each other. Although the female had ceased exuding estrus hormones, the male moved next to her with surprising boldness, nudging aside the body of a dead *Tylosaurus*. Cruising slowly along, the two giants surveyed their rock-lined prison. Around them, burning embers continued to fall, though with less frequency. The winds died down, but the sky continued to grow darker – an ominous indication, considering it was midday.

Suddenly, a small group of fish broke the surface of the water dead ahead. Then, off to one side, a dead plesiosaur twitched spasmodically. Next, a turtle began to bob up and down. It became apparent that the death toll was not complete. Vast schools of herring, salmonids, and even larger fish and squid had survived the maelstrom, just like the pliosaurs, and were coming to the surface to feed. The two giants had an available source of food lurking beneath the murky waters.

———

Outside the caldera, the skies grew dark and the air temperature became noticeably cooler. High up in the atmosphere, vast amounts of sulfur dioxide blasted into the sky blocked out the sun. An impact winter would soon engulf the once green and fertile world. Within a matter of days, all remaining life would struggle to survive in a pitch-black deep freeze that would last for months.

———

Snow was falling.

The surviving pliosaur pair had never seen snow before. Regardless, they knew one thing right away: They didn't like it. Their flanks shuddered as the tiny pieces of white fell upon them, and they blinked irritably whenever one of the icy particles touched their huge ruby eyes. They began to move, grumbling cantankerously in the growing shade. Though it was early afternoon, in their rocky prison it was twilight. Infinitely worse, the air temperature was dropping rapidly. Within days it would reach the freezing point and stay there. For reptiles of any kind, even ones their size, prolonged deprivation from the sun's warmth was a veritable death sentence.

The two pliosaurs cruised toward the center of the caldera in an effort to keep warm. The chilling precipitation continued to melt when it landed, and a strange mist rose off the surface of the water. Though the air temperature continued to plummet all around them, the waters of the caldera retained their temperature. Heated by permanent magma reservoirs lying directly beneath the surface of the dormant volcano, they would never freeze like those outside. Though nowhere near as balmy as the tropical paradise they were used to, the tepid climate of their new world would enable the two beasts to survive the night.

Side by side the pair remained, comforted by each other's presence. The snow continued to fall, and the darkness closed in. Outside the protective walls of their enclosure the rest of the world still burned, the ongoing fires lighting up the darkness. Soon, the entire planet would sleep – a deep, frozen sleep from which few would awaken. Ignorant of the incredibly fortunate hand dealt them, the pliosaur male and female waited patiently. They could not have known or even conceived that they would soon be the last of their kind.

A short while later, the world around them was black and blanketed in cold. The wildfires were gone, and even the embers extinguished. Motionless, the enigmatic reptiles remained where they were. Soon, nothing but the glow of their luminescent orbs was visible.

Alone, they shivered in the darkness.

Twenty-Seven

"Willie, hang in there!" Amara pleaded. She was propped against a bulkhead, sitting in a steadily widening pool of blood. She gritted her teeth and shifted position, cradling her wounded friend's head against her bloodstained bosom. "Please, don't give up! We'll get out of this somehow, I promise!"

At the sound of her voice, the tall sonar operator opened his eyes. Amara's throat tightened and she swallowed hard. Her tears flowed non-stop. She reached down, peeling up the edge of the shirt she held tightly against his gaping abdominal wound. It was heavy with blood. She peeked underneath and paled, averting her eyes.

"Dat's . . . what I taught," Willie said resignedly. He started to close his eyes.

Amara sensed him beginning to fade on her. The thought of losing her best friend caused an agonizing series of spasms within her chest, as if her heart was trying to punch its way through her sternum. She shook him gently by the shoulders. "Come on! You've got to fight!"

Willie sweat-soaked head lolled limp, the difficulty of hanging on showing more and more on his strained countenance. He opened his mouth to speak, but what came out was an airy whisper. *"All we see and seem . . . is nothing but a dream."*

"Is that Shakespeare?"

"No." He cracked a smile despite the pain. "Dat is Mistah Edgar Allen Poe. I . . . taught he was . . . more appropriate den . . . da usual stuff . . ."

Willie's eyes closed, and he collapsed into her arms. His face turned a horrible shade of gray and his breathing became raspy and erratic. A minute later, she realized he was dead.

Amara began to shake uncontrollably. She took in a deep breath to scream, but before she could vocalize her grief, a disturbingly familiar voice spoke in low, mocking tones.

"Well, well, well," Markov said as he strode into the room. "Isn't this touching?"

Amara's anger momentarily quelled her considerable fear of the sinister-looking mercenary, and she lashed out without thinking. "You murderous son of a bitch, did you come to gloat over your psycho boss's handiwork?"

"Nah, I came to do some of my own, actually," Markov said. He grinned evilly, drawing his bone-handled machete ever-so-slowly from its tattered sheath, and glared menacingly down at her.

Amara felt her heart descend into her bowels. Her mind raced desperately, and she tried to bluff her way out of it. "What the hell do you think you're doing?" she demanded as imperiously as possible. She became acutely aware of Willie's still-warm body weighing her down, and tried to shift as much off herself as she could. "Did that asshole put you up to this?"

"Oh, no, my dear." The huge scar that ran down Markov's face glowed blood red as he started to move toward her. "That fat fuck actually sent me to tie you up. You know, to make sure you go down with the ship. But my way is *much* more sure, and a *hell* of a lot more fun."

Markov leered at her. His narrowed eyes were full of amusement as he relished the pure terror oozing from Amara's pores. He raised his notched weapon high overhead, wiping at the stream of drool that ran down his chin. "Well, bitch? Any last requests?"

"Yeah, go fuck yourself!" she hissed through trembling lips. She knew she was about to die, but remained defiant to the end.

"Nah, but I think I'll fuck *you*." Markov's lips curled into a nasty little smile. "After you're dead!" Laughing maniacally, he reared back with his heavy-bladed chopper and swung it at Amara's head with all the strength he had.

———

"That'll be enough out of you, mister," Jake admonished. He tightened his grip and shifted his weight forward, using the iron head of the ancient whalers' harpoon to complete his parry of Markov's overzealous attack. He exhaled through his teeth and pulled up hard on the lance's heavy wooden handle, forcing the shorter man's weapon upwards and backwards with a powerful thrust. The two weapons rasped noisily against each other and the sudden loss of balance sent Markov staggering.

Stepping boldly between the astonished merc and his equally astounded victim, Jake drew himself to his full height. He chanced Amara and Willie a quick glance with his peripherals. The girl was bloodied, but alive.

Willie . . .

Jake cursed vehemently. He'd been on the scene of enough shootings to know a dead man when he saw one. His expression turned to ice and he leaned back on his heels, the harpoon held before him like a spear. "Okay, tough guy. Let's finish this."

Markov bared his teeth and flew at Jake like a demon, hacking at him from every possible angle as he ruthlessly tried to cut the taller man down.

Jake hopped nimbly backward, using the metal head of his weapon to parry the barrage amidst a shower of sparks, and keeping its sharp point constantly in his opponent's face.

Markov cursed and retreated a few steps as he sized up his foe. Faced with a weapon that increased Jake's already substantial reach, he changed tactics. He went on the attack again, but this time continuously altered direction, springing side to side and feinting repeatedly as he sought an opening. Frustration followed. Over and over he found himself in the same position: at bay, with thirty inches of cold-rolled iron thrusting at his nose.

Jake continued to backpedal, skillfully working the harpoon like a boxer's jab to keep the killer at a safe distance. It was dangerous work; Markov was surprisingly quick and completely unrelenting. Moreover, the 19th century harpoon Jake carried was designed for pinioning whales, not gladiatorial combat. It was weighty and its thick wood handle was slick – permanently infused with an oily patina of whales' blood, blubber, and the greasy hands of the men who killed them.

The minutes began to tick by, and the sheriff started to feel the effects of the room's sweltering heat. Sweat ran down his forearms and the back of his neck. His mind raced, searching for a shortcut to what was setting up to be a prolonged battle. He decided to go on the offensive. He made a series of thrusts at Markov's heavily muscled thighs, hoping to incapacitate him. It was a wasted effort that left Jake's hands aching from the shock of the harpoon being repeatedly swatted aside.

Markov sneered and came at him again. As he gave ground, Jake gritted his teeth. The reality of this battle was beginning to sink in. The man he faced was no Karl Von Freiling; he was a true psychopath. There would be no quarter asked or given. It was to the death. Jake realized if he and Amara were to live out the day, he would be forced to kill someone.

With a snarl, Markov dropped unexpectedly low. He extended his stubby arms and made a sudden thrust forward, worming his way past Jake's guard. Using his machete like a Hoplite's short sword, he sought to stab the big lawman through the groin.

Jake spotted the machete's point at the last moment and made a desperate hop backwards. There was a loud clacking noise as he blocked Markov's thrust with the center of the harpoon. The room shifted, and his back foot slid across a discarded toolbox. He stumbled, his ankle twisting out from under him. He came down hard and felt an agonizing pain shoot up from the floor, all the way to his hip. His eyes and nostrils flared wide and he gasped. For a split-second everything turned black and he tottered like an axed tree, trying and failing to put weight on his injured leg.

Markov spotted the sudden mishap and attacked. A gleeful grin spread across his hateful features as one of his strokes made it past Jake's compromised guard, opening up a nasty gash across the sheriff's left bicep.

"Gotcha!" Markov jeered. He sprang back, tap-dancing left and right before he resumed stalking his hobbled opponent. "What's the matter, big man, outta practice? Man, I'm gonna enjoy cutting you down to size!"

Fighting for his life now, and unable to stop everything coming his way with the harpoon's flanged tip, Jake hopped backward again. It was a desperation tactic. The landing was astonishingly painful. Barely blocking Markov's heavy blows, he gamely held his position and, through sheer arm strength, somehow managed to force his adversary back with a quick fusillade.

The bizarre duel continued, with the sound of crashing wood and steel echoing throughout the room. Perspiration streamed down Jake's chest and back and stung his eyes. He blinked repeatedly to clear his vision and glanced at his injured arm. He could feel blood trickling down his forearm and fingertips. His grip became even more slippery and his breath came in short gasps. He lurched frantically sideways to counter Markov's next move, trying to keep as much weight as possible on his lead leg. A growing sense of panic enveloped him, and he began doubting the outcome of the life or death struggle.

Things weren't going the way Jake expected as he'd fought to free himself. With the sound of gunshots resonating through his brain, he'd resorted to chewing through his bonds. It was an ordeal that left his teeth chipped and gums raw and bleeding; he could still taste the dirty nylon rope as he staggered to his feet and went charging to the rescue. He knew engaging Markov hand to hand was a dicey proposition. It was three years since he practiced with any weapon other than his sidearm. Only his overpowering instinct to protect Amara forced him to reach for the whale lance.

The moment the battle started, Jake sensed his debilitating rustiness. When he counter-parried, his reflexes were mired in quicksand, and when he shifted to compensate for his adversary's unorthodox fighting style, his sense of balance evaporated. The weapon he wielded was also a problem. The old harpoon was frightfully heavy, its prolonged usage tiring even his powerful wrists and forearms. Worst of all, he only had one leg to maneuver with.

Markov glanced in Jake's direction using his peripherals and smiled. The rabid psycho had detected the severity of the lawman's injury, as well as his rapidly burgeoning doubts. He was becoming increasingly bolder, and his deranged and highly vocalized attacks more and more protracted; his notched blade drew closer to Jake's sweat-soaked skin with each and every stroke.

Jake stumbled back, barely deflecting a savage downward blow meant to split his skull. There was a loud thump as the back of his cranium slammed against a low-hanging beam, and his head felt like it exploded. A wave of dizziness washed over him and he became incredibly tired. The harpoon was a ship's anchor in his arms, and he felt lightheaded and nauseous.

Markov snickered and attacked in a gleeful frenzy, relentlessly chopping and hacking. Fighting for air, Jake retreated a few steps under the assault, using the shaft of his weapon like a Bo staff to absorb the hammering blows. His sweat-soaked back struck the wall and he slid to one side. He heard Amara's cry as splinters of hardwood flew from the harpoon's hacked-up handle, ricocheting off his cheeks and hazarding his eyes like wood shrapnel.

Then, with a sound like the cracking of a whip, the harpoon came apart.

The blow was a double-handed horizontal slice that severed the weighty wooden shaft and continued across the front of Jake's shirt, incising a four-inch groove in the pectoral muscle underneath. The impact ripped Jake's already weakened guard apart, driving him to his knees. An agonizing spasm from his ankle added to his misery, and everything turned gray. Markov loomed over him, his victory smile more frightening than even the pliosaur's toothsome grimace.

It was over.

Barely conscious, Jake waited for the inevitable. It was Amara's high-pitched scream that yanked him back from the precipice. He opened his eyes and reflexively raised the two pieces of his harpoon in an X-style block, absorbing a downward chop that would have hacked through collarbone and chest. His bone-weary arms shook from the force of the parry, and he gaped at the realization he'd allowed himself to come within inches of being slaughtered. Followed by . . .

Amara. The thought of losing the fiery cetaceanist welled up within Jake, and a parade of images did cross-dissolves through his mind. He saw himself from first grade – when he clumsily picked up a foil for the first time and marveled at its weight – all the way through college, where he ended up atop a gilded podium, with the President of the United States awarding him a medal for wiping the floor with the best and brightest sabermen the country had to offer – men far more talented than the ravening butcher standing over him.

Jake felt a white-hot fury flood his veins like a thousand volts of electricity. His mind cleared and he locked onto the sensation, shaping it, molding it, making it his own. His pulse and breathing slowed until, with surprising ease, he disassociated himself from his injured ankle. He climbed to his feet, methodically blocking Markov's next blow with the bottom half of his harpoon. He took a mechanical step forward and then went on the offensive, using the two pieces of his weapon like oversized Kali sticks, clubbing and stabbing, forcing his panting opponent backwards. The sounds of wood and steel on steel rang on until Markov was nearly forced from the room.

Moving back a few paces, Jake glanced contemplatively down at the pieces of harpoon he held. His expression grew chilled and he flung away half his weapon. The ragged piece of wood clattered to the ship's floor and rolled away. He assumed a traditional *En Garde* position, saluting his opponent with the remaining piece of lance, then lowered it until its iron point nearly touched the floor. He stood stock still, taking in slow, steady breaths and reining in his adrenaline.

Confused by the unexpected turn of events, Markov struggled to catch his breath, his hairy chest heaving as he fought to channel the murderous lust within him. A wild look came into his eye, and he grabbed for the pistol at his belt. His black eyes met the sheriff's and he hesitated.

Jake wore a look Vlad Markov knew well. It was one he'd given many of his victims over the years, once he had them helpless and about to die at his hands.

Disdain.

Spewing forth a barrage of profanities, punctuated by an animalistic scream of rage, the enraged merc forgot his Glock and charged Jake. His well-used blade wove a lethal web of steel as he swung it in deadly arcs, intent on decapitating the lawman.

His face impassive, Jake waited motionless. At the last moment he moved, so quickly it was virtually impossible to see. He ducked under Markov's intended death stroke, sidestepping him and simultaneously lunging forward. It was a clothesline maneuver that caused the sheriff's right shoulder to smash into his adversary's torso with bone-jarring force. Jake continued hobbling on.

Behind him, Markov remained where he was, his mouth foaming and dark eyes bulging. Ignoring him, Jake knelt to check on Amara. She was propped against a nearby bulkhead, her legs pinned beneath Willie's bled-out corpse. A wet, gurgling sound drew his attention and he glanced back over one shoulder.

Markov stumbled drunkenly to one side, his silhouetted back turned. As he staggered sideways, Jake's eyes hardened. His harpoon was buried to the hilt in the merc's chest, its crimson-coated iron point protruding two feet out his back. Markov blinked in disbelief and crashed to his knees, his blood-filled mouth opening and closing like a beached fish's. A moment later, his hateful eyes glazed over and he collapsed onto his side and died.

Jake turned back to Amara and gave an involuntary start. Her head lay limp to one side, her eyes closed. Except for the split lip and purple mouse surrounding one eye, her skin was the color of milk. It looked like she wasn't breathing. At first, he thought she'd fainted, but as he leaned closer he gasped at all the blood. Her throat and forearms were practically airbrushed with it, her blouse soaked through like a hemorrhaging dishrag.

Jake felt a spike of panic. He reached over to check Amara's pulse and breathing, then cursed as his battered hands trembled so much he couldn't feel. His own heart pounded so hard he could hardly hear. A momentary vision of Samantha lying dead on the diving platform danced before his eyes: her cold, pale skin and lips, her lifeless expression. Desperate, he ran his hands over Amara's abdomen, checking her stomach and chest, feeling for wounds. He felt nauseous as his world started to spin.

"Um . . . Jake, what are you doing?" Amara moaned through half-opened eyes.

Jake stuttered as he realized he was cupping one of her breasts. "Oh God, I'm so sorry!" He yanked his hand back as if he'd touched a live wire. "I thought you were–"

"You thought . . . what?" Amara panted and tried to sit up. Her eyes rolled white for a split-second as her head lolled back. She groaned and tried to prop herself up, with him helping. Eyes open, she rested her head in her hands, peeking groggily between splayed fingers.

Jake's expression grew grim as he realized she was still pinned beneath Willie. He relaxed his grip on her shoulders and took careful hold of her friend's body, shifting his own weight to his uninjured leg to gain leverage. "Here . . . let me help you."

Amara didn't budge. Instead, she started shaking all over. She looked wildly around the room, her eyes huge and seemingly unable to focus. Finally, she looked down. She uttered a huge sob and grabbed onto Willie, clinging to him with desperate strength.

"It's okay . . ." Jake soothed. He cautiously caressed her blood-spattered cheek with the back of one hand. "I'm sorry, doc, but you have to let go."

A tremendous shudder shook Amara's already trembling frame. She sucked in a huge breath, then tentatively released her grip. Her jaw hung as he carefully lifted Willie off her. "Oh God . . ." She threw her arms around Jake's neck as he helped her to her feet. "I saw you stumble and heard your ankle go. I thought he was going to kill you, too! What happened?"

"I don't know . . ." Jake mused. The smell of blood and excrement permeated the room, and he glanced contemplatively at the body of the only man he'd ever killed during swordplay. "I guess I remembered who I was."

Still shaking, Amara wrapped her arms around him, holding on tight. Jake felt his face grow hot and he found himself staring at the floor. Her hot breath panted in his ear, and his blood pumped harder in response. He lifted his head and saw his own confused and elevated state reflected back at him. He realized suddenly that, despite the waking nightmare he found himself in, this woman was keeping him grounded. It had been a ferocious struggle, but he hadn't lost her like he had Sam. He'd protected her, and would continue to do so.

Smiling nervously, Amara slowly pulled away. She inhaled sharply as her eyes fell on Markov's remains. She shuddered, averting her gaze. Even sprawled lifeless in a pool of blood, the sadistic merc still looked dangerous.

Jake felt a slight pinch inside his tattered shirt pocket. He extracted the disc he'd concealed earlier. It was in two pieces, halved by one of Markov's ferocious blows. He opened his fingers, allowing the bloodstained fragments to clatter to the floor.

Amara watched the pieces settle. Hot tears streamed down her cheeks and she dropped to one knee. She caressed Willie's cheek with her fingertips.

Jake busied himself tearing away a strip of his shirt to make a dressing for his injured bicep. He shook his head regretfully. "I'm really sorry about Willie, doc. He was a great guy. I wish I'd gotten here sooner."

"Me too." Amara sniffled, wiping at her nose with the back of her index finger as she forced back fresh tears. "That's okay. I'm going to make sure Dean Harcourt pays for what he did. He won't be so arrogant when he's rotting on death row, waiting for his turn."

Suddenly the floor shuddered beneath their feet. The *Harbinger's* frame emitted an eerie groan that sent shivers up both their spines.

"Speaking of which, I think we better get the hell out of here." Jake shifted position, grimacing as the pain of his ankle made maintaining his balance on the sloping deck nearly impossible. "The *Harbinger* is sinking, isn't she?"

"Yes, she is."

Jake puffed out his cheeks. "Well, that's great. I'd say it's time for an SOS, don't you think?"

Amara shook her head. "That bastard, Stitches, destroyed all of our communications equipment – even our longboats."

"Figures. So, now what?"

Amara's opalescent eyes narrowed, then dilated. "Well, it's a long shot, but I may have something up my sleeve."

"Like what?"

"Give me a hand moving this stuff."

Amara gestured at a series of small crates, piled like children's blocks. Jake checked his injured bicep, then dabbed at the shallow slash that ran across his chest. His fingertips came away sticky. He frowned, then hobbled over and began helping as best he could. Within minutes, they were staring at some kind of antiquated, military-style footlocker.

Amara wrestled open the oversized trunk, extracting a trio of yard-long, gray and black metal devices with jagged spikes at one end. To Jake, except for the cable connector ports and heavy-duty batteries, they were jumbo-sized versions of the solar powered lights people line their driveways with.

"What the heck are those?"

"Old-style marker buoys."

"Markers for what?"

"Long story. Here, let me show you how to activate them . . ."

A few minutes later, as the two of them were carrying the devices out of the storage room's portside door, Stitches spotted them and opened fire.

Its face wracked with pain, the pliosaur circled, gnashing its teeth in silent fury. It realized that ramming the ship was causing it more harm than its enemy, and decided to hang back and play the waiting game. From the peculiar noises the *Harbinger* was giving off, coupled with its angle in the water, the oversized vessel was dying. Soon, it would capsize and plunge into the abyss. Once that happened, the surviving mammals would be thrown helpless into its domain. It could feed upon them at its leisure.

A moment later, the staccato noises that preceded its injuries repeated themselves. The sounds were unmistakable, even from two hundred yards away. Curious, the scaly titan cruised back to investigate.

"Son of a bitch!" Jake bellowed. He dropped the buoy he carried and yanked Amara back from the doorway. A second barrage of high-velocity rounds tore into the storage room's thick doorjamb and surrounding bulkheads. He cursed and pointed one thumb at the room's starboard entrance. "Toss them out there instead!"

Crawling over to Markov's lifeless body, Jake removed the dead merc's sidearm from its nylon holster. He crept back to the doorway, doing his best to ignore the throbbing pain of his assorted injuries. Using the heavy frame for cover, he took aim and fired three rapid-fire rounds from the dead man's gun in the direction of the retreating *Sycophant*.

"You're really out of your fucking mind, Harcourt! You better pray to God the *Kronosaurus* gets to you before I do!"

Seventy-five yards from the listing *Harbinger*, the Zodiac idled. Standing by the helm, Stitches shook his head and cursed. The last thing he needed was his ride home getting shot full of holes. He waited another minute to see what Braddock would do, then lowered his smoking rifle and resumed his preparations.

"Well, I'm assuming from what we just saw that Markov is either dead or incapacitated."

"He's dead," the burly senator responded with surprising casualness. He turned in his makeshift seat and directed his calculating gaze away from the dying ship, toward the windswept sea. "Trust me."

"Well, in that case, we better get going," Stitches said. He reached for the throttle of the big outboard. "It'll be dark soon, and considering what inhabits these waters, we don't want to be floating around out here."

"I wouldn't do that if I were you." Harcourt gestured at the motor.

"Why not?"

"Because, you're liable to draw his attention to us." He inclined his head toward a dark disturbance, some fifty yards off their portside bow.

Stitches' eagle eyes popped as he followed the senator's gaze. "Son of a bitch . . ." The pliosaur was cruising silently along beneath the surface, the top of its enormous head breaking the troughs of the overlying whitecaps as it circled the wounded *Harbinger*. As if it heard them, it altered its direction.

"Holy shit!" Stitches shrank back from the approaching monstrosity until the back of his legs collided with their vessel's rubberized transom. He looked around in alarm. There was nowhere to go.

"Actually, now might be a good time to start that engine, soldier," Harcourt remarked. He was on his feet, eyeing his enemy as it drew steadily closer.

"Screw that," Stitches snarled. He yanked one of the grenades off his belt and held it up. "I've seen how fast that thing can swim. I'm gonna frag his overgrown ass!"

Waiting until the giant reptile was within twenty yards of their position, Stitches pulled the pin on the ball-shaped grenade and lobbed it straight toward the creature's misshapen head.

———————

"Is it safe to come out?" Amara whispered in Jake's ear. She was on her tiptoes, peeking over his shoulder, as the lawman emerged warily from the dusty storage room, pistol in hand.

"Looks that way," Jake said. He slid the confiscated Glock into his vacant holster, checked the tightness of the makeshift pressure-bandage he'd applied to his arm, then tried some weight on his swollen ankle.

Definitely sprained or strained, but not broken. Thank God.

He took in the scene below him and gave a derisive snort. "Well. It appears they've got more pressing matters to attend to than dealing with us."

"What do you mean?" Amara moved to the railing next to him.

A muffled roar vibrated the ship's thick hull. *"That's* what I mean," Jake said with some satisfaction. He pointed first at the geyser erupting fifty feet from the idling Zodiac, then at the fast-moving shadow angling sharply away from the blast.

Amara watched in wonder as the pliosaur turned back and made another run at the *Sycophant*, parting the waves as it careened toward it at high speed, then wheeled away again as another detonation forced it to withdraw.

"They're using grenades," Jake said. He watched as Stitches hauled back once more and tossed something high overhead. "Or rather, they were . . ." he corrected himself, as Harcourt's sole-surviving mercenary bent down to light something.

"They've switched to dynamite," Amara concurred, gazing in fascination as the bizarre standoff continued. "God . . . being an echolocator, those explosions must be incredibly painful. Do you think they can stop it?"

"Doubtful." Jake shook his head. "The timing with dynamite is even harder to predict than it is with a grenade, and that thing's a fast learner."

"Should we do something?" Amara looked questioningly at him.

Jake blinked twice. "Are you kidding me? That asshole just tried to shoot us, and five minutes ago Dean Harcourt murdered Willie right in front of you!"

"You're right," Amara said icily. She moved close to him and rested her uninjured cheek against his chest. "God forgive me, but they deserve whatever happens."

Stitches couldn't believe the mess he was in. Their resident serial killer was gone, and the prehistoric monstrosity he and his comrades came looking for had systematically chowed down on everyone else. Barker, Diaz, Gibson, Johnson and Stubbs were all dead; even the seemingly indestructible Karl Von Freiling didn't make it. In the process, the monster had destroyed a state-of-the-art attack sub, and ripped the guts out of a steel-hulled ship five times its size.

And now it was after him.

The creature was proving itself both relentless and cunning. It wouldn't just sit there mindlessly and be blown up.

Stitches scanned the surface, trying to anticipate its next angle of attack. He felt himself start to shake and took a deep breath, fighting to steady himself. It was getting hard to hold it together. His hand trembled as he accepted another stick of dynamite from his employer. "Hurry up!"

"We're running low." Harcourt's dark eyes were cold and calculating as he held his lighter to the explosive's fuse. "There's only seven or eight sticks left."

"So, what do you want me to do?" Stitches shook his head as he hauled back, flinging the makeshift weapon almost a hundred feet. The dynamite landed with a splash directly in the monster's path. The pliosaur veered off before it hit the water. Its flippers stroked powerfully as it put as much distance as possible between itself and the sputtering explosive.

Whoomp!

"Damn it, he took off again!" Stitches removed his hands from his ears as the detonation faded. "I think he's on to us, senator!"

"You may be right, soldier," Harcourt said, studying the beast's powerful wake.

Stitches reached for the outboard's tiller. "We should make a run for it."

"Hmm, I've got a better idea." The politician held up a hand and rose to his feet. He reached inside his dilapidated suit jacket, fumbling about. "We need to lure him in close and keep him here. That way, if we use a shorter fuse, he won't be able to swim away in time."

"And how are we going to do that?" Stitches shielded his eyes from the sun's glare with one hand as he held a stick of dynamite in the other. He watched as the creature closed on them for the sixth time.

"By using bait."

"Bait?" Stitches wore a befuddled look as he turned around. "We're in the middle of nowhere. Where the hell are we going to get..."

He stopped talking when he saw the pistol. "What the fuck?"

"Call it a sacrificial lamb," Harcourt said. He stared with intensity. "Sorry, son, but the Lord's work needs to be done. Don't worry though. I'm sure you'll be rewarded in heaven."

"Are you fucking with me?" Stitches yelled. He could see his M-16 rifle out of the corner of one eye. It was resting against one of the *Sycophant's* cylindrical air chambers, only three feet away. He shifted his weight and tried to stall. "What, you expect me to jump over the side and start flailing around for you?"

"That would be perfect," Harcourt nodded. He pointed his weapon at Stitches' unprotected chest and smiled. "That is, if you don't mind, of course."

"Why you . . ." The little merc cursed and dropped low, lunging sideways for the gun. A microsecond later, he realized he'd underestimated Dean Harcourt's reflexes, as well as his aim. The first jacketed hollow point caught him mid-point in the left shoulder, tearing an inch-wide tunnel through flesh and bone, causing him to lose his grip on the heavy-barreled weapon. The second struck him square in the chest.

His hands still grasping, Stitches Anderson collapsed to the dinghy's floor, wheezing for air and spitting up blood, with the world turning topsy-turvy around him. As his blurred eyesight began to fade, the last thing he was able to contemplate was how truly fortunate he was that he was *almost* dead when his deranged employer tossed him over the side, wearing nothing but a rope tied about his ankles.

Jake exhaled through flared nostrils. He turned away from the murder scene, just in time to see Amara grimace and avert her eyes.

"Jesus . . ." She clutched at her stomach. "I can't believe it!"

"I can," Jake said.

"God, I can't look. What's he doing now?"

Shading his eyes with both hands, Jake studied the Zodiac's sole remaining occupant. "It looks like he's preparing more dynamite." A darkly malevolent but highly appealing thought came to him. "Hey, maybe he'll do us both a favor and blow himself up."

"And take the pliosaur with him?"

"Amen to that."

———

Onboard the *Sycophant,* Senator Dean Harcourt waited for his dinner guest, his lighter gripped tightly in one hand and a stick of dynamite in the other. He'd bitten clean through the explosive's fuse, shortening it to a length of less than half an inch to ensure it would detonate almost immediately. His already frenzied breathing grew more labored as he watched Stitches' bleeding body bobbing up and down like a topwater lure. The dead merc was kept afloat by a life preserver and tethered to the Zodiac by a twenty-foot length of rope.

Cautious, despite smelling fresh blood in the water, the creature zeroed the still-warm remains, but this time without its normal, aggressive approach. Instead, it floated up underneath the *Sycophant* – so slowly its mammoth body created no displacement wave at all – and opened wide from ten feet beneath the surface. Utilizing the powerful suction created, it inhaled its meal.

From his vantage point, Harcourt saw nothing but a sudden swirl. Then Stitches' corpse was yanked beneath the waves. There was a gentle tug, and a moment later, the chewed-up rope floated to the surface.

Harcourt stared blankly at the stretch of water where his bait had been. The wind died down, leaving the air hot and heavy with the cries of circling seabirds, and the sounds of waves slapping against the *Sycophant's* hull. He stumbled back, his eyes bulging so wide they threatened to pop from their sockets. Fury and frustration see-sawed across his face, and he dropped down onto the nearest gunwale, slack-jawed and indecisive.

Long moments passed, with Harcourt sitting there wallowing. Finally, a strange noise drew him back to reality. He twisted his head in the direction of the sound – and came face to face with his enemy.

Floating placidly on the surface, twenty feet away, was the gigantic creature he'd sacrificed so many people to. It was the biggest living thing he ever saw, as huge as the blue whale mount hanging in the

American Museum of Natural History. Its monstrous head, alone, was bigger than his stretch limo. Its jaws were lined with battery after battery of ivory-colored fangs, each as long as a machete blade and as thick as his forearm.

It was its glittering eyes that frightened him most. As big as footballs and the color of fresh blood, the creature's gleaming orbs and their abyssal black pupils were daunting. The senator peered spellbound into their depths. There was a primordial savagery mirrored there, a primitive brutality that stretched back over eons, to the dawn of time. He could sense an intellect of some kind staring back at him: a cold and calculating mind that glared menacingly into his power-mad eyes, boring through to his pitch-black soul. Then, as they drifted closer to each other, so close he could have reached out and touched the creature, he realized *he* was reflected in its eyes.

Screaming so loudly he spat up blood, Harcourt snatched Stitches' M-16 rifle up. He pointed it directly at the pliosaur, emptying it into its face and partially opened mouth at point blank range.

The beast reeled back as steel-cored slugs punched holes into its exposed tongue, roaring so deafeningly it sent the *Sycophant* bobbing a full five feet from the force of its bellow. A second later, it turned and plunged beneath the surface.

Harcourt dropped to his knees and started working feverishly on the remaining sticks of dynamite. His quivering hands moved so quickly they were a blur. He seized a small roll of tape from the box the dynamite came in and wrapped it around the remaining explosives, binding them tightly together. Then he clambered to his feet and raised the makeshift bomb to his lips. He bit down on the exposed wicks, chewing through the dynamite's foul-tasting fuses until there was almost nothing left. His weapon complete, he turned and made his way to the edge of the Zodiac, bracing his knees against its rigid hull. Smiling grimly, he reached into his pocket and removed his gold lighter.

Long moments passed. All of a sudden, he looked up at the sky and laughed uproariously. Coated from head to toe with the blood of dead men, his eyes were more like a cobra's than a man's. His mouth foamed uncontrollably as he shifted his weight from foot to foot, waiting for his own personal Armageddon to commence. It was divine providence, and he welcomed it.

The minutes ticked by and the senator remained where he was, unmoving except for the sweat that streamed in dirty little rivers down his bloated face and collected in steamy pools beneath his hairy armpits. As the tiny inflatable began to bob up and down, he smiled malevolently. He readied himself, flicking his lighter open and closed, watching its butane-fueled flame blaze away like a miniature blowtorch. The precious pieces of dynamite he clutched tightly to his breast, waiting for just the right moment.

It was coming up under him, just as it had when it killed Stubbs. He'd studied its approach from a nearby railing. It was heralded by the same displacement wave now surrounding the *Sycophant*. Predictable to the end, the creature would breach the surface of the water and seize him in its cavernous maw, just like the attack sled. But he had a surprise for it . . .

He grinned evilly at the thought. Although the beast would certainly kill him, it too, would die. He held enough explosive power in the palm of his hand to reduce a city bus to a pile of molten slag. Nothing on land or sea could survive a point blank blast like that. Not even the leviathan rising up beneath him. He lifted his eyes to the heavens and hoisted his weapons high. *"And in that day the LORD, with his sore and great and strong sword, shall punish the Leviathan."*

Other than Jake and Amara, Harcourt's audience consisted of a few birds and the vast ocean, its surface churning like river rapids across an area over a hundred feet across.

"The piercing serpent, even Leviathan that crooked serpent . . ." He bellowed louder, holding the blazing lighter and dynamite close to his chest. He leaned over the bucking *Sycophant's* edge with a delirious smile on his face, peering into the frothy depths in the hope of savoring his enemy's final approach.

"And he shall slay the dragon that is in the sea!" He screamed over the approaching maelstrom, his arms extended at chest level less than twelve inches apart, as he waited for the end.

A second later, the *Kronosaurus* erupted out of the water with enough force to punch a hole through the bottom of the *Harbinger's* hull. Like an ICBM, it soared one hundred feet into the bright blue sky, clearing the sea below it in its rage-induced desire to annihilate the insignificant mammal that dared to challenge it. Engulfed within its colossal jaws were the *Sycophant* and its pilot.

With a rumbling roar, the creature slammed its teeth together hard enough to bite through steel plate. Its devastating bite sheared through the Zodiac's fragile hull material, as the sixteen-foot inflatable and its screaming occupant vanished from sight.

Silently, the mammoth reptile plummeted back into the sea. The only thing remaining of Dean Harcourt was his hands, protruding like some grisly wall sculpture from the creature's wrinkled lips. Wedged tight between its conical teeth, they twitched spasmodically. His expensive gold lighter, its flame doused by seawater, was held tightly in one, the unlit dynamite in the other. They remained frozen as the creature crashed back into the raging vortex from which it came.

A second later, it vanished into the depths, taking Harcourt and his visions of biblical vengeance with it.

———

From the *Harbinger's* steeply sloping decks, Jake and Amara watched with satisfaction as Senator Dean Harcourt's political career was cut far shorter than his senatorial rivals could ever have envisioned.

"Nicely done," Jake said. His bruised and bloodied forearms were interlaced across his chest as he watched the enraged pliosaur vanish from view. "Too bad the creature didn't die too."

"Yeah . . ." Bending at the waist, Amara laid her forearms atop an intact portion of the research ship's portside railing, resting the uninjured side of her face on them. She sighed as a cool sea breeze pulled her hair away from her eyes, then looked up. "You win. This animal cannot be allowed to live."

A grim smile slid across Jake's rugged features. "You know, it's funny you should say that."

"Why's that?" Amara pushed herself upright and swiveled around, giving him a painful view of her swollen eye.

"Because, I have a feeling your little pet down there has reached the same conclusion about us!"

Less than a hundred feet away, the pliosaur's mammoth head and neck speared up from the water, rearing skyward until its toothy muzzle was extended thirty feet into the air. Keeping itself motionless with all four of its flippers, it remained there, gazing intently at the nearby *Harbinger* and the two remaining humans that stood atop her.

"Jesus . . ." Amara gasped aloud as she took in the sheer hugeness of the apex predator. "That's cetacean behavior; it's called spyhopping. He's studying us. The question is why."

"Probably trying to figure out how to get us off the ship," Jake said, his narrowed blue eyes every bit as intense as the creature's glittering crimson ones. "Or maybe, the easiest way to tear what's left of it out from under us."

"It doesn't matter. We're going down anyway." Amara gazed pensively at the ship's prow and shuddered. It was nearly awash, with oncoming waves continuing to crash over it. "All he has to do is wait and we'll come to him."

"Looks that way." Jake frowned. He noticed her shivering, and put a protective arm around her.

Amara turned and lowered her cheek onto his shoulder, pressing herself against him. She averted her eyes from the pliosaur's. "I always feel safe when I'm with you. I've . . . been meaning to ask you something, but I didn't want to pry. I guess now . . ."

"Ask me what?"

"I told you about my dad. But whatever happened to your father after your mom passed away?"

Jake stiffened. "He died screaming, nine months later, tied to a hospital bed."

"I'm sorry to hear that. From what?"

"Pancreatic cancer."

Amara continued talking into his shoulder. "That's awful. You have a lot of anger toward your father, and I don't blame you. There's nothing worse than loving someone who's hurting you. I can relate."

Jake kept one eye locked on the creature while gently caressing her back. "That's something you'll never have to live through again, doc. I promise you."

Amara's body shook in what he took to be an involuntary chuckle of irony. "I believe that. Can I ask you something else?"

"Anything," he said, and felt her smile.

"Did you and your father reconcile before he died?"

"No. I never even saw him in the hospital."

"Why not? He was an asshole, but he was still your father."

"Not to me. You remember I told you my mom was killed by a drunk driver?"

"Yes."

"That was my dad."

Amara gasped.

Jake's voice turned to granite. "I'm glad he's dead. If I could have stood the sight of him, I'd have watched him die."

Amara wrapped her arms around him and squeezed. "Your hardness is only on the surface." She drew close again, resting her chin on his chest and hugging him hard. She smiled as she looked up at him, her luminous eyes shining through the bruises. "You've got a good heart, Jake Braddock."

Jake looked away, willing his own eyes not to tear up. *No big deal. Just the pain of the injured ribs she's squeezing.* "Thanks, doc," he managed. Suddenly, his eyes widened in alarm. "Um, if you have any tricks up your sleeve to keep us ending up as dessert, you'd better unveil them."

"Why's that?"

"Because he's made up his mind . . ."

The pliosaur submerged. Powering its way beneath the waves, it moved purposely toward what was left of the *Harbinger's* bow.

"Shit!" Her pale eyes wide, Amara pulled away from Jake, stepping fearfully back from the railing. "Come on. We're getting the hell out of here!"

Jake instinctively reached for the pistol at his belt. He shook his head at the absurd notion, then turned and limped quickly after Amara.

"Um . . . exactly what do you have in mind, doc?"

Amara paused near the former whaler's starboard loading crane, surveying the frightful pile of wreckage scattered in front of her. She sucked in a deep breath. "We're leaving in this."

The pliosaur moved in for the kill. Though still wary of colliding with the ship's metal hull, the gigantean beast's territorial nature had fully reasserted itself. Its rage overrode its desire to simply feed upon the tender morsels clinging to the creaking vessel. For the first time it could remember, its relentless need for flesh was forgotten. It wanted the *Harbinger* gone from its territory, and every living thing on it destroyed.

As it cruised closer to the ship's reinforced bow, the creature exercised caution. Even though its utmost desire was to send the infuriating ship and the two bipeds infesting it straight to the bottom, it would no longer rush blindly in to attack.

Submerging and scanning the *Harbinger's* hull with its sonar, it probed once more for weaknesses. Again, it sensed the gaping wound in the ship's forward hull, as well as the water rushing into it, but it was incapable of comprehending what that meant. It needed something within the realm of its experience.

Then it saw the anchor chain. Its black and rust-colored length pierced the surface and extended all the way to the seafloor, its arcing span like the lashing tentacle of some monstrous squid. Surging forward and downward, the pliosaur crunched down on the thick iron links. Ignoring the cracking sounds as several of its teeth fractured from the strain, it twisted its huge head to and fro, pulling against the heavy fetters with all the power its one hundred plus-ton body possessed.

On the surface, the *Harbinger's* inundated bow reverberated with the sounds of shifting metal as the anchor chain was yanked to and fro. The ship's nose began to be hauled violently back and forth, succumbing to indescribable power. Then, with one final, monstrous tug, it was dragged completely under, unleashing a wall of water that came crashing up over the rails and went flying forward, immersing its telltale harpoon cannon and flooding any and all remaining compartments within seconds.

Moments later, the doomed vessel emitted its last call, a rumbling death knell that caused the water's surface to shiver for miles around. Then the entire two-hundred-and-twenty-foot, seven hundred-and-forty-ton vessel rolled sideways and sank beneath the waves. Pieces of equipment and debris flew from her decks like windblown chaff. Bubbles spewed from her holds and portholes as she plunged eerily downward, twisting and turning in a spiraling roll that carried her fifteen hundred feet, straight to the bottom.

TWENTY-EIGHT

With his gaze fixed on the horizon and his back to the *Oshima*'s stainless steel captain's wheel, Haruto Nakamura remained a stone study in discipline: posture perfect, feet braced to compensate for the slow roll of the ship. He peered through the helm's curved windshield, his watchful eyes crinkling up as the afternoon sun emerged from behind a nearby cloud bank, blazing its way through the twenty-foot wide portal like an acetylene blowtorch. His tense expression dissipated as their computer systems' chromatophores transmuted the glass to a dark brown tint, shutting out the painful glare.

He spoke over his shoulder. "Sonar, any update on target location?"

"No change, sir," the tech replied. "Location is steady, approximately twenty-four miles due east."

"Very well."

"Sir, I'm picking up more explosions."

"Caused by the same military ordnance?"

"No, sir. This is something different. Very loud. I'm embarrassed to admit it, but it's something outside the realm of my experience. Could be possible damage to that ship we've been tracking. Maybe her diesels have blown . . ."

"Very well, ensign. Keep on it and apprise me of any changes."

"Yes, sir."

Haruto's mind weighed possibilities. With the U.S. Navy and Coast Guard shutting down boat and aerial traffic over five hundred square miles, it was an easy matter for their advanced sonar and radar systems to pinpoint the location of the giant marine predator that damaged his ship, several days prior. The thunderous sounds it produced and its

472

unique sonar signature were unmistakable. Based on its current location, the brute posed no threat. It was laying siege to another vessel, a mile or so within U.S. territorial waters. The identity of the hapless ship was a mystery: probably an old freighter or an antiquated transport of some kind. Whatever manner of ship it was, it wasn't emanating a traditional transponder code to identify itself, and its crew ignored repeated hails from the *Oshima*. Even more bizarre: Its captain had failed to issue a distress call that might have brought aid. Only the explosions onboard kept Haruto from assuming it was a derelict wreck.

He shrugged, dismissing the matter. *Let the Coast Guard deal with the beast.* His only concern was getting his heavily-laden ship home safe, with its valuable cargo intact.

"Excuse me, captain?"

Haruto turned to see Watch Commander Iso Hayama standing awkwardly nearby, his eyes straight ahead and an electronic clipboard in hand.

"Yes, commander?"

"I came to get your signature, sir," Iso said. "And, if I may say, it's been a great honor serving with you. The *Oshima* has broken every record in the history of the company."

"Thank you, commander." Haruto reached over and scrawled his name using Iso's pen. Although he was pleased with their success, he wondered how much of it was really a byproduct of his oft-touted skill, as opposed to the pliosaur causing all sea life within a hundred miles to flee straight to their baited hooks.

"Um, captain?"

"Yes, commander?"

Iso hesitated, swallowing nervously. It was obvious he had yet to recover from the castigation Haruto gave him. "Will you be making an announcement to the crew, to notify them of our success prior to departure?"

Haruto nodded slowly. With their holds crammed to capacity, his exhausted ship's complement deserved to know their tireless efforts were so hugely successful, and that they'd all be receiving bonuses. He walked to the nearby communication station and grabbed a wired mike. He gestured to the technician, who nodded and flipped a switch.

Haruto cleared his throat. "Attention, *Oshima* crew. This is the cap–"

"What the hell?"

He released the mike's talk button immediately and wheeled on the startled sonar tech, his dark eyes fierce.

"I'm terribly sorry, captain-san," the tech stammered, his face turning pale. "It . . . it just popped up on the screen and I . . ."

"*What* popped up, ensign?"

"I'm not sure, sir. It's some kind of beacon, I think. It just . . . wait, there's more than one. Two or three, sir. It's strange. I've never seen a frequency like this before."

Haruto moved toward the sonar, bending at the waist, peering intently over his shoulder. The ensign was correct. There were three electronic beacons appearing on the screen adjacent to the other ship they were tracking. They were not standard radio emitters like the ones found on lifeboats and survival rafts. The signals were powerful and easy to trace, but intermittent. Their transmissions were repeatedly interrupted, like they were floating on the surface and submerging with the motion of the waves.

Haruto's brow lines deepened. With his sonar tech's limited experience, there was no way the youth could recognize the signals. But the *Oshima*'s captain was quite familiar with them. He'd used them during his tenure on the *Nagata*, back when the international community turned a myopic eye to Japan's illegal whaling activities. The beacons were used to mark the location of dead whales, enabling a ship's crew to chase down and slaughter entire pods without losing track of any carcasses. They were built like short, bottom-heavy spears, the bulbous end consisting of a float, a battery-powered transmitter, and an LED assembly. Their barbed points were driven deep into the blubber of dead or dying cetaceans. Once activated, they emitted a high-intensity radio signal and strobe light every time they breached the surface.

Haruto's expression intensified and he straightened up. "Ensign, I want you to email me the frequency codes of those beacons. At once."

The tech cocked his head to one side. "Um . . . email, sir?"

"Yes, email. Immediately." He turned to the con. "Helm, chart a course for home, but hold our current position until I give the order. I'll be in my quarters."

"Yes, sir." Both men answered as one.

His face unreadable, Haruto abandoned the bridge.

———

"Doc, are you sure about this?" Jake's expression was dubious as he adjusted the heavy-duty restraining harness holding him against *Eurypterid II*'s front seat. Around him, the enclosing thickness of the submersible's reinforced interior did little to create a feeling of security; it felt more like an armor-plated coffin. He glanced nervously back at Amara. "After crashing onto the deck so hard, maybe this thing won't even work."

"You got any better ideas?" Amara reached up and began flipping switches on the mini-sub's overhead control panel. "Besides, if I knew Karl at all, I'm sure he designed this thing to take a few knocks."

"Whoa!" Jake made a reflexive grab at his chair's padded armrests as the submersible shifted, shuddering noisily along the debris-strewn decks of the *Harbinger* as the dying ship's list dramatically increased.

"Just hang on," Amara said, trying to familiarize herself with *Eurypterid II*'s joystick steering controls. "I've adjusted our trim and ballast. Assuming my calculations are correct – which is far from guaranteed – we should just float off the *Harbinger*'s deck as she sinks out from under us."

"And if not?"

Amara paused thoughtfully, nibbling her lower lip as she adjusted a few more dials. Jake twisted in his seat, straining his neck in an effort to catch her eye. She held his gaze and frowned. "Well, in that case, this may be a very short trip."

"Wonderful." He turned and started peering through the oval-shaped observation bubble that made up most of the mini-sub's nose. He perused the confusing array of equipment and controls at his fingertips. "So, what's all this stuff?"

"Hang on a minute." Amara listened nervously as falling debris clanged like hailstones against the submersible's laminated hull. With a groan, the *Harbinger*'s death throes reached their climax. The ship's nose dropped sickeningly downward and a churning wall of seawater came surging toward them, slamming into *Eurypterid II* and enveloping them with a roar.

Jake held his breath, feeling his heart free-fall into his stomach. A few seconds later, the drowning research vessel rolled sideways and sank bow first beneath the waves, dragging them down with it.

"Damn!" Amara cursed, holding tight onto the controls as they were sucked under at a sharp angle. "Something's wrong, we're not coming loose!"

Jake felt his ears pop and gripped his armrests tightly, gazing apprehensively at the *Harbinger*'s bubble-spewing hull. Pieces of debris and drifting lifejackets flew from her holds, careening all around them. He gasped and jerked his head back as something big slammed into the observation bubble. He saw long fangs and a baleful eye, and realized to his astonishment that it was the bodiless head of the monstrous fish Amara had secreted in her freezer. Pinned in place by the current, the decapitated *Xiphactinus* glared hungrily at him through the thick Lexan, its eyes bulging, its bladed maw grinning evilly. A second later, it was whisked away.

"We're stuck!" Amara yelled out, stabbing buttons and heaving on her control stick as she gunned *Eurypterid II*'s powerful impellers to life. "Something's got us glued to the ship! Take a look and tell me what you see!"

Jake leaned all the way forward, pressing his chest against the thick pad in front of him. He squinted hard through the rapidly darkening depths. "It's pretty dark . . . I don't think . . . wait, there it is!"

"What is it?" Amara turned on the mini-sub's powerful searchlights, swiveling them to illuminate the area.

"There's a large section of railing looped over the portside wing," Jake said. He craned his neck, studying the entwining mass of twisted metal. "It must have happened when we slid forward, right before she sank."

Amara flipped on the exterior monitors and gazed intently at them. "I see it." She nodded. "Hang on tight, I'm going to try and shake us loose." Her jaw set, she pulled slowly back and forth on her steering controls, gunning the engines forward, and then throwing them into reverse. The sub didn't budge.

"Shit, this is bad!" Amara cried out, heaving back on the controls one last time.

"How bad?"

"We're at seven hundred feet." she said. "Max depth here is fifteen hundred, which is fine, pressure-wise. But if we can't get free before she hits bottom, she may continue rolling and land upside down."

Jake's eyes widened. "You mean, like . . . on *top* of us?"

"Exactly. Look, I know you've never done this before, but I need your help freeing us. I can't control the helm and cut us loose at the same time."

"No problem, just tell me what to do."

She suppressed a grin and pointed at his control console. "You have to use the actuators to cut the railing. They're controlled by those two interface portals in front of you."

"Okay . . ." Jake stared at the darkened openings.

"Put your hands inside the portals and feel your way to the end. You'll find glove-shaped compartments. Slip your hands into them and wait."

"No problem." Jake shoved his hands inside the padded openings and leaned forward against the chest pad. He extended his arms until he found what she described and slipped his hands inside. They were cold, metallic, and had a grainy texture to them. "I know why this thing is here now . . . ouch! Hey, what the hell was that?"

"Just hold still!" Amara studied a small monitor directly above her. "You're feeling the electrical tingle of the neural interface. It's linking to your nervous system. Try not to move, the discomfort will vanish in a moment."

"Discomfort?" Jake tensed and fought to remain immobile. The "tingle" she described felt like he'd shoved a dinner fork into a wall socket. "It feels like a bunch of fire ants are stinging me!"

"Don't be such a Mary!" Amara snapped. She checked her depth gauge again and exhaled slow. "Okay, you're linked. It's time to get to work."

"It finally stopped hurting, if that's what you mean," Jake griped. "Now, what do I do?"

"Just move your arms normally, but keep your hands on the grippers; otherwise you'll break the connection. The sub's arms will move like they're your own."

Jake inhaled sharply as the submersible's twelve-foot titanium-steel actuators swiveled out from beneath the sleek craft's prow and materialized in front of him. "Holy cow!" He felt like a child who'd just been given a giant toy robot. The oversized graspers mimicked his every move. The feeling of empowerment was intoxicating. "Wow, what can I do with these?"

"There's no time for lessons." Amara scanned another gauge and shook her head. "Just reach over and cut us loose, fast!"

"I'll try." Leaning as far forward as he could, Jake strained to seize the mesh-like mass of railing keeping them pinned to the rapidly-descending *Harbinger*. The metal tubing was just out of reach. Annoyed, he gritted his teeth and threw himself against the cushioned chest pad, willing his limbs to grow longer. By millimeters, he managed to close the portside pincer around the closest section and pulled it back in a single motion. There was a low vibration as the section of railing tore free. He felt the *Eurypterid II*'s hull shift, but it wasn't enough. They were still wedged tight.

Sweating from the strain, Jake continued to lunge and grab, tearing the remaining sections of steel railing like strands of spaghetti. Finally, they popped up off the *Harbinger*'s deck like a loosed buoy.

"I did it!" he shouted. The *Harbinger*'s foreboding bulk separated from them and continued hurtling into the depths, vanishing from view.

"And just in time too," Amara replied. There was a distant thump as her vessel impacted the seabed. "Hang on. I'm taking us back to the surface."

"Sounds good to me," Jake said, freeing his arms. He breathed a sigh of relief, taking a moment to carefully check the makeshift bandage on his wounded bicep. Outside, the darkness dissipated as they made their way back into the ocean's sunlit phototropic zone.

"What the hell?" Amara gazed wide-eyed at her sonar screen.

"What's wrong?"

"Hold on!" She threw the speeding sub hard to starboard.

With a thunderous roar, the pliosaur barreled past them, its gargantuan jaws slamming shut as it missed their portside wing by less than a yard.

"Son of a bitch!" Jake held on for dear life as *Eurypterid II* rocked back and forth.

"Bastard came at us from the rear," Amara fumed as she maneuvered away from the huge reptile. "He must've been hiding behind the *Harbinger* the entire time, waiting for us to abandon ship. He's learned since his battle with the other sub."

"Great. So, what's our plan?" Jake asked, apprehensively eyeing their attacker as it turned to follow them.

"Get back on the actuators and try to keep him at bay," Amara instructed, jabbing buttons faster than the eye could follow. There was an electric hum as she brought their weapons systems online. "If we're aggressive enough, maybe we can convince him we're too much trouble to be worth making a meal of."

Struggling to keep their nose pointed at the creature, Amara threw *Eurypterid II*'s engines in reverse, backpedaling as fast as she could. Jaws spread, the creature flung itself at the tiny submarine.

"Keep him off us!" she screamed, firing salvos from the sub's harpoon cannons. With impressive accuracy, she sprayed four pairs of the barbed projectiles directly into the pliosaur's wide-open mouth. At point blank range the compressed-air-powered missiles flew true, burying themselves in its white tongue and throat lining.

Simultaneously, Jake struck at it with the sub's twelve-foot pincers, nipping at its thick-scaled lips like an enormous crayfish. "Good lord!" Teeth clenched and face soaked with sweat, he jabbed away like a retreating prizefighter, repelling attack after attack as the creature tried to sink its teeth into *Eurypterid II*'s vulnerable prow section.

Discouraged by the sharp flashes of pain that stung its mouth's interior, the pliosaur uttered a rumbling snarl and broke off its attack. Gnashing its teeth together, it shook its monstrous head from side to side, trying to expel the sharp objects. Failing to dislodge them, it swam away, grumbling as it disappeared into the gloom.

"We did it!" Amara cheered. Her eyes were fixated on their sonar screen as they continued to race backwards.

Jake wiped his brow and breathed a sigh of relief. "Good, then let's put the hammer down and get the hell out of here!"

Suddenly, a powerful blow rocked *Eurypterid II*, sending them lurching violently against their seats, their bodies held in place by crisscrossed restraining belts.

"Holy shit, he got us!" Jake roared. He grimaced as his injured head hit his seat's headrest, causing him to see stars.

Amara yelled back. "It's not the pliosaur!" She looked up anxiously as several loud banging noises came from outside. Something heavy was impacting their hull. "He's three hundred yards to port!"

"Then what the hell was that? What happened?"

"It's the Cutlass!" Amara wore a disgusted look. She gritted her teeth as she pulled them a hundred yards forward. As they turned back, the soaring undersea spire appeared; erupting up out of the seafloor, it towered over them, looming over the edge of Ophion's Deep. "Damn, I backed us right into it!"

"Did we take any damage?" Jake asked, his eyes glued to the observation window.

"I don't think so." Amara studied readouts and gauges. "Hull integrity wasn't compromised, and the engines seem okay . . . uh oh!"

"Uh oh?" Jake echoed. He whipped his head around.

"Well, it uh . . . looks like we've lost our dorsal sonar array," Amara said. She held her breath for a moment, then exhaled heavily. "The falling rocks must've damaged one of the hull emitters."

"So, we're totally blind out here?"

"No . . . not totally. We can pick up movement on our level or below us. We should be alright, but just to be on the safe side we should stay near the surface."

"Then let's get there," Jake growled. He turned his attention back to the blue-gray seas beyond their window, his eyes jogging nervously left and right.

There was a sudden hum as Amara increased *Eurypterid II*'s impellers back to full power. She cruised toward the surface at a steep angle in the hope of preventing the creature from sneaking up on them again.

Beep.

"What was that?" Jake scanned the cockpit for the source of the sound.

Beep. Beep.

"Proximity alarm," Amara said. Her hair whipped around as she checked their monitoring screens. "Close range only. I turned it on to compensate for the sonar."

Beep. Beep. Beep.

"It's getting louder," Jake advised. He licked his lips and looked around anxiously. "Where is he?"

"Starboard bow, one hundred and twenty-five yards above us." Amara powered them toward the surface, blanketing the approaching reptile with active sonar pings. The pliosaur grew rapidly as its monstrous body picked up speed.

"Hold on. Here he comes!"

Jake clamped down on the stream of profanities begging to spew from his mouth. All he could do was hold on and pray Amara was a good enough pilot to keep them away from the wall of teeth and muscle closing in on them.

She wasn't.

An experienced hunter, the pliosaur adjusted its tactics to compensate for the mini-sub's superior maneuverability. Feinting side to side as it approached, it gauged Amara's reactions, forcing her to change course repeatedly. Then, with a sudden burst of speed, it closed the distance. Catching *Eurypterid II* off balance, it nearly pushed her out of the water from the force of its blow.

"Damn him to hell!" Amara raged as the creature's ridged teeth scraped nosily along their underbelly. They hit the surface and went airborne with it still tearing at them. As they crashed back down, she twisted the controls hard to port, sending the submersible into a dizzying spin in an effort to lessen the assault.

"Jesus Christ!" Jake closed his eyes as their hull was repeatedly grazed. It was simply a matter of time before the creature scored a direct hit: a strike that would enable it to gain enough purchase on their armored shell to bring the full power of its jaws to bear. Once that happened it would crush *Eurypterid II* like an empty beer can, just like it did the mini-sub's sister ship.

Just when Jake was certain they were finished, the pliosaur veered off. He opened his eyes and watched confusedly as it lay suspended in the water. A school of shiny silver baitfish appeared as if by magic, crowding it and exploring its vast bulk. A moment later, the creature's back arched and its body began convulsing. Before he could ask Amara's opinion, it opened its mouth and retched forth an enormous mouthful of orange-colored vomit that clouded the surrounding water.

Jake blanched. The big outboard motor the beast ingested minutes earlier emerged from the cloud of regurgitated bile. It spiraled slowly toward the bottom. Billowing above it like a tattered flag was the macerated hull of the *Sycophant*.

The pliosaur shook its head to clear the taste of gasoline from its mouth and prepared to charge again. Turning its back on *Eurypterid II*, it traveled a hundred yards before banking sharply around. It emitted a low roar of agitation before heading in their direction.

"It's unbelievable." Jake stared blankly at the approaching behemoth. "Even with a hangover he won't quit!" As the creature drew closer, it dawned on him *Eurypterid II* wasn't getting out of its path. "Um, doc, what's going on? Why aren't we moving?"

"I'm not sure!" Amara's eyes went wide as she frantically flipped switches. She tried steering again and got nothing. "I think its last assault damaged our power couplings. I've got energy readings for everywhere else, but I've lost power to the engines. It's like they've gone offline."

"*What?*" Jake exploded. "Are you shitting me?"

"No, I'm not shitting you!"

Instead of coming straight in, the pliosaur began circling the wounded mini-sub. From a distance of one hundred feet it eyed *Eurypterid II*, the black holes of its pupils constricting. From his position in the cockpit, Jake got the uncomfortable feeling it was looking directly at him. "Jesus, doc. Can't you get us moving?" he asked, unable to tear his gaze away. The creature moved closer to them with each successive pass, the water it displaced causing the mini-sub to wobble in the current.

"I'm trying!" Amara snapped. She craned her neck and peeked over Jake's shoulder. "What's taking him so long? Why hasn't he attacked yet?"

"I'm not sure," Jake offered. "Maybe he's waiting to see what we're going to do, or he's savoring his victory."

"I doubt that." Amara flipped a large console switch up and down several times and then frowned. "He's a reptile, Jake, not a person."

Jake shook his head. "You can say what you want, doc. But, I'm looking the damn thing dead in the eye, and I say you're wrong."

Amara fought with her harness and climbed out of her chair. Bracing her left hand against the hull, she moved to Jake's station and peered through *Eurypterid II*'s viewing portal. The pliosaur was less than fifty feet away, so close it caused the drifting submarine to sway dizzily back and forth. It glared menacingly into the cockpit, its toothsome jaws parting ever-so-slightly.

Amara met its cold reptilian gaze and recoiled. There *was* something behind those ruby-red orbs. The giant reptile was *enjoying* the effect it was having on them, like some monstrous cat reveling in the terror of a trapped mouse. And although her educated brain kept telling her it was preposterous, she could *swear* the damned thing was smiling at her. "Good lord." Her breath steamed up the Lexan in front of her. "I hate to say it, but you may be right."

"This is one time I'd rather be wrong."

"Hey . . . wait a sec!" Bracing her bad hip, Amara rushed to the rear of the mini-sub. She checked several gauges, then turned excitedly to Jake. "I figured out what's wrong! The impact shorted out our computers. The mainframe controls the engines to maximize effectiveness. All I need is five minutes to reboot and we'll be fine!"

"Five minutes is a long time, doc."

The pliosaur uttered a thunderous grunt and veered off. Two hundred yards away, it swung back toward *Eurypterid II*. They could see its jaws opening wide and its body swelling up as it gathered itself.

Jake's heart sank. It would be on them in seconds.

———

Haruto Nakamura's fingers were a buzz-saw blur as he hacked at his laptop's keyboard. He sat stiffly upright, ignoring his aching tailbone.

Since he entered his quarters, he'd worked at uncovering a confirmed link between the frequency codes of the mystery ship's beacons and the mechanical devices generating them. He was sure they were whaler buoys, but was having a frustrating time proving it. Most of the manufacturers of such things were now defunct companies. By sheer luck, he stumbled upon an outlaw site that sold archaic military equipment and outdoor gear. The devices were incorrectly posted as locator beacons, to avoid unwanted attention from the animal rights organizations that policed the web.

He opened another window and enlarged the mechanical culprits' design stats. They were Russian Mark-2800 whaler beacons that operated at 14,124-16.234 MHz. Transmit range was 120 nautical miles with an optimal battery life of 36 hours. Nasty things, with razor sharp, serrated tips. He'd used similar, superior Japanese versions on the *Nagata*, years prior.

Haruto smiled at his discovery. One great thing about whaler's beacons: if you had an onboard decoder or could access the whaling companies top secret sites, you could instantly link the frequency of any given buoy to its ship of origin. They were electronic fingerprints providing undeniable proof of possession. The unique radio frequencies were infinitely better than painted markings. They allowed a whale killer's crew to zoom in on their bounty from long distances, eliminating time wasted confirming ownership. Best of all, with the beacons bereft of any physical signage, there was no way to positively link one to a vessel if the authorities arrived and a carcass had to be temporarily abandoned.

Haruto closed his eyes for a moment and pursed his lips. The smell of Kona infiltrated his nostrils and he reached for his coffee, swallowing a gulp. He opened a pirate whaler's site, entering his old screen name and password. There was a low beep and he was in. He allowed himself a melancholy grin. His all-inclusive access rights still functioned, even though he'd quit whaling ages ago. Sometimes it came in handy being a living legend.

Haruto quickly uploaded the ID frequency codes of all three buoys. It took a few seconds for the system to spit out the results. The vessel that dumped the beacons was an antiquated Russian whale killer named the *Smirnov.*

He chuckled. *The fools must have chugged day and night to get to this locale, once they heard about the pliosaur. They must have figured they had a shot at killing it.*

Haruto shook his head and sat back in his seat. It was a bold move on the part of the whaler's captain. Unfortunately, the sonar and radar evidence the *Oshima* was gathering indicated he'd sorely miscalculated his gargantuan adversary. The *Smirnov* was dead in the water, with the beast punching holes in her hull left and right.

As he scanned the other ship's statistics and launch date, Haruto inhaled sharply. The ship was no longer an active member of the Russian whale killer fleet. It was decommissioned nearly seven years ago. Three years later, it was sold to an unlisted buyer.

Frowning, Haruto swung his mouse like a windshield wiper, opening sites linking him to the former Soviet Union's maritime records. His Russian was atrocious, and it took ten frustrating minutes for him to pinpoint and retrieve the *Smirnov*'s information. Finally, he pulled up the ship's complete history, including its shipyard of manufacture, launch date, command history, and date of decommission. He scrolled to her final sale date and decoded her purchaser. The buyer was top-rated: a well-funded, internationally acclaimed organization specializing in . . .

The Worldwide Cetacean Society–

The *Smirnov* had been refitted as a scientific research vessel and rechristened. She was the *Harbinger* now. It was his niece being besieged by the monstrous marine reptile that had already taken so many lives. *Knowing Amara, she must have foolishly elected to take it upon herself to protect the creature from harm. As if it needed her help . . .*

Haruto's expression hardened and he formed a tall steeple with his fingers, resting their rough tips against his chin. A landslide of turmoil inundated him and he closed his eyes against the unexpected avalanche of emotion. As his brother's sole child, Amara was the only surviving family the *Oshima*'s captain had. His own wife was gone nearly a decade. She'd left him childless, and he was away at sea too often to consider remarrying. His niece was in grave danger – assuming she was still alive. There were no other ships nearby, and she needed help.

Haruto inhaled deep, held it, then let it out slow. The always-calculating balance scales that comprised a good portion of his captain's mind swung hard, weighing his conscience down with everything he stood to lose if he took his ship on the fool's mission he was considering. The *Harbinger* was well within U.S. territorial waters. If caught he could be boarded, his vessel seized, and everyone onboard arrested. He would be risking everything: his career, his reputation, the *Oshima*, and its valuable cargo. He would be gambling with his crew's livelihood, not to mention their lives. And he would be betraying his sacred duty to his people, his company, and even his country.

Haruto's grim gaze lifted to the ancient katana and wakisahsi resting above him. He braced his palms against the edge of his desk and puffed a series of quick breaths, then shook his head decisively and jabbed the intercom button on his desk.

"Helm, this is the captain. Prepare to get under way . . ."

"Can't you shoot it?" Jake asked. He felt a sudden chill race through him, like ice sliding down his spine. The pliosaur was headed straight toward the incapacitated *Eurypterid II*, its flippers working in unison, its speed increasing with every stroke. Its angry roar resonated through the water around them, vibrating the underside of their seats and jostling their nerves.

Amara shook her head. "No. I used all our harpoons already except the big one, and we need the electricity from the engines to power it. It won't work. He's got us."

"Damn." Jake slumped back in his seat. He eyed the useless actuator controls. "I'd suggest abandoning ship, but I guess that wouldn't be prudent."

"No." Amara smiled sadly. "I'm really sorry."

Jake gazed deeply into her eyes. His softened and he rose wordlessly to his feet, wrapping his arms protectively around her and drawing her close.

The submersible shook violently from the creature's displacement wave. Jake saw its silhouette and his heart started beating so hard it hurt. He forgot about his own safety. The thought of Amara being eaten alive or ripped apart was more than he could bear. His mind raced, desperately searching for a means to protect her from that awful fate. A terrible notion came to him, and his hand crept toward the pistol at his belt. He took a deep breath . . .

"Oh my *God* . . . look!"

"What is it?" Jake yanked his hand back from his gun pommel and followed her gaze. "What the hell?"

The pliosaur was frozen in place, open-mouthed, right outside their window. It was so close all they could see was a wall of ivory fangs and the darkness of its gullet. They watched in fear-induced awe as the deadly jaws gradually closed. The creature remained motionless for a moment, then drifted back a few yards, cocking its head to one side like a dog straining at a whistle only it could hear. Ignoring the incapacitated submarine, it backpedaled another hundred feet. The muscles of its scaly neck and jaw began to throb, pulsating faster and faster, until the sounds of its low-pitched sonar emissions could be heard without a hydrophone.

"What's going on?" Jake asked confusedly. "Why did it stop?"

"I don't know," Amara mused. "It lost interest in us. Something else must have attracted its attention."

"Like what, a boat or something?"

Amara watched, fascinated, as the creature hovered in the water, fifty feet beneath the surface, suspended in place by synchronized movements of its flippers. "Hmm . . . I don't think it *is* a *Kronosaurus*," she said. "Leastwise, not a *queenslandicus*." Her eyes ricocheted like ping-pong balls as she studied it. "Besides the sheer size, you can tell from the cranial arches and the heaviness of the mandibles. Not to mention the teeth are ridged, not rounded. It must be a related sub-species, however . . ."

Beep.

Beep. Beep.

Beep. Beep. Beep.

"What the . . . ?"

Amara rushed back to her sonar screen as their proximity alarm sounded again. "I've got multiple inbound readings, Jake!" she exclaimed. Her eyes were padlocked to the monitor. "I have no idea what they are, but there are a lot of them!"

"What's that noise?" Jake tilted his head like the pliosaur, listening to a symphony of high-pitched sounds making their way through the sub's reinforced hull. "What's causing that?"

Amara switched on the mini-sub's external mike array. She adjusted the volume and sensitivity, then transferred the muffled noises to their craft's internal speaker system. Instantly, they were bombarded with high-pitched whistles, clicks and grunts blasting out of their speakers. It was so loud and painful, Jake was forced to clamp his hands over his ears.

"Holy cow, what a racket!" he yelled over the din. "Geez, kill that, will you? That's the worst sound I've ever heard!"

"Are you crazy?" Amara gave a huge smile as she lowered the volume and rushed to the observation portal. "Those are the sweetest sounds I've heard in my life!"

"I think it's you who's crazy," Jake grumbled. "And what the hell is making all that noise?"

"*They* are!" Amara proclaimed excitedly. She gestured with both hands as a squadron of sleek shapes cruised past.

"Holy crap!" His eyes wide, Jake released his harness and sprang from his chair. "Those are killer whales! What are they doing here?"

"Saving our lives," Amara replied, her palms pressed tightly against the Lexan window as she watched the circling cetaceans. "Look, there's more of them!"

Approaching from the south, eight more of the huge creatures came into view. Then, another half-dozen arrived from the north, followed by five more from the west that passed within twenty yards of *Eurypterid II.*

"There must be two dozen of them." Amara's head swiveled back and forth as she counted the fast-moving predators.

Just then, a scar-covered killer whale with a notched fin materialized in front of them. It paused directly opposite the viewing portal and stared inside, its jaws partially open. It was huge, at least twenty-five feet in length, and weighed over seven tons.

"Holy . . ." Amara squealed with excitement, rapping hard on the thick Lexan with her knuckles to attract the big orca's attention. "It's *her*, Jake. It's OB's mom!"

"What are you talking about, and why are you trying to get us killed?" Jake's eyes went wide with apprehension at the proximity of the big carnivore.

"That's OB's *mother*," Amara repeated, beaming at the old female. The orca gave her a contemplative look before cruising off to join her podmates. "OB is Omega Baby. He's one of the bulls we've been studying – one of those three monsters lurking over there." She pointed to a group of particularly huge orcas hovering in the water seventy-five yards portside. "Don't you get it? OB's mom is the matriarch and founder of the pods of transients we've been studying. She's their familial leader. She organized this!"

"Organized what?"

"What's about to happen." Amara seemed surprised he wasn't following her. "Killer whales dislike rival predators. That's why they attack great whites: to kill off potential rivals. They must have detected the pliosaur's presence in these waters and realized it poses a huge threat to them and their offspring."

Jake's jaw went slack. "You mean to tell me these whales . . .?"

"Came to finish what Karl died starting." Amara gave an involuntary shudder, her eyes fearful as she peered through the portal. "They've come to kill the pliosaur."

"No shit."

A few hundred feet away, the thing that destroyed the *Harbinger* drifted soundlessly beneath the surface, its only movement an occasional flutter of one of its flippers. If the huge creature was at all fazed by the growing number of killer whales circling it, it gave no indication.

"Do you think they can do it?" Jake asked, sizing up the combined strengths and weaponry of the two opposing forces. As he studied the immobile pliosaur he could hear Dean Harcourt's voice in the back of his mind, quoting a now all-too-familiar excerpt from the bible.

Upon earth is not his like, a creature without fear.

"I don't know." Amara's voice had a nervous edge to it. "Orcas are intelligent, organized, and highly skilled at orchestrating group attacks – including on whales as big as or bigger than our scaly friend there."

"Yeah, but that's no whale they're preparing to take on," Jake emphasized.

"No, it's not." Amara's chest moved rapidly up and down as she spoke. "But whatever the outcome, it looks like you and I are the only people on the planet sitting front and center for the greatest heavyweight fight of all time."

Jake stood silent, waiting for the battle's opening salvo to be fired. The killer whales did little to test his patience. Eight of the twenty-plus foot females – easily recognizable by their shorter, curved fins – suddenly sped off in a widening arc that took them so far back they vanished into the murkiness. Seconds later, they reemerged like black and white phantoms, right behind the pliosaur. Sensing their approach, the titanic reptile started moving forward. It began to build up speed, its movements carrying it directly toward the immobile *Eurypterid II*.

"Um, doc . . . maybe you can get the engines working now?" Jake asked, his eyes locked on the approaching behemoth.

"Not yet," Amara insisted. "The system will tell us when it's ready to reboot. Until then, I don't want to miss this."

"Okay . . ." Jake relaxed when the creature unexpectedly changed course. He ran his fingertips absentmindedly across the line of coagulated blood on his chest.

While the bulk of the killer whale's forces remained huddled together a hundred yards to *Eurypterid II*'s portside, the group of eight females closed on the pliosaur's haunches and launched their offensive, taking lightning-fast jabs at their adversary's exposed rear flippers and stubby tail. With their jaws spread and curved dentition bared, they lunged forward with impressive accuracy, sinking their teeth repeatedly into the creature's thick-scaled hide.

Strangely, it ignored them.

Resolutely pecking away, the oversized dolphins began to press their attacks, their excitement building as they struck and dropped swiftly back. It was a tactic they'd used for countless generations, designed to harass and hamper their much-larger opponent, to wear it down while simultaneously destroying its primary means of propulsion.

The pliosaur's huge body slowly spiraled, with the belligerent orcas slashing at anything they could gain purchase on. Finally, it retaliated. With an ominous grunt, it flared its flippers out from its sides like a jet plane's air brakes, incorporating a reverse power-stroke and coming to an abrupt halt in the water. Caught off guard and propelled forward by sheer inertia, the streamlined killers were unable to control their forward momentum. With their flukes flailing desperately, they sailed past their gargantuan adversary's hindquarters – and within reach of its jaws.

Scattering in panic, the orcas abandoned their hit and run strategy and dispersed in every possible direction. Their frightened clicks and squeals echoed through the water as they sought the shelter of the surrounding sea.

The aroused pliosaur – now fully focused on the school of pugnacious mammals – let out a roar. The tip of its wrinkled snout broke the water's jade-colored surface as it spouted and sucked in huge lungfuls of air. It submerged in a cloud of bubbles, propelling itself to a depth of one hundred feet. Jaws ready, it peered angrily around, its garnet-colored eyes scanning the surrounding water, probing for its challengers.

"Wow, that was quick," Jake remarked. His nose was pressed against the cold surface of *Eurypterid II*'s observation portal as the orcas vanished from sight. "Is that it? Did they give up already?"

"Not if I know my transients," Amara fretted. "That was what you'd call a feeling-out tactic. They're faced with something they've never seen before and have no idea what to do."

"They do now."

"I'm not so sure." Amara pointed to the far side of their viewing window. Another group of killer whales started moving in from the south. "Look, here they come again!"

"Are those the same ones from before?" Jake squinted in the dim lighting,

"No, they're not," Amara announced. "That last group was all females. The cows are faster and more maneuverable than the bulls. This group is all males. See their fins and how big they are? They're what we call the pod's heavy hitters. They deliver the coup de grace on large prey items like sperm whales. Apparently the orcas have decided to risk everything by taking the pliosaur on in a head-on assault."

Jake shook his head. "That's crazy!"

"Don't tell me, tell them!"

A hundred yards from *Eurypterid II* and a similar distance from their target, the six bull killer whales approached in a flying wing formation. Ranging from twenty-eight to thirty-two feet in length and weighing up to ten tons, Omega Baby and his fellow *Orcinus orca* were the dominant predators on the planet. Their kind had ruled the seven seas virtually unchallenged since the Pleistocene epoch.

Speeding toward them with its gaping maw spread wide, the pliosaur threw itself at the approaching whales, its beady eyes focused on the leader. Confident in its power, the giant predator never noticed the eight other whales hurtling toward its exposed flanks.

Jake's eyes peeled wide as the second group of orcas sprang their ambush. The cunning cows had used the more easily discerned bulls as bait. Attacking as one, they closed the horns of the trap on their misdirected adversary. Converging from every possible angle, they launched themselves at its vulnerable throat region, slamming into it and tearing away, while the impacts echoed throughout the water.

Jake gaped at the frightful vision. Over forty tons of enraged orca clung to the great reptile's wrinkled gullet, ripping away as the infuriated beast flailed wildly.

Amara remained frozen in place, unable to tear her eyes away. Squealing with excitement, the massed killer whale cows continued to pummel and punish their oversized opponent. Nearby, the agitated herd bulls circled back in preparation for their own assault. ""Oh my God . . ." she sputtered. "They're doing it!"

She was wrong. Used to brawling with others of its kind, and accustomed to feeding on schools of prey as large as the mammals that clung to it, the pliosaur was unfazed by the organized assault. Its mammoth neck was heavily armored by thick ridges of skin and layer upon layer of rock-hard muscles. Despite the cloud of dark scales and blood that began to obscure the ongoing melee, Jake could see the whales were finding it difficult to do any serious damage to their well-protected adversary. They didn't have enough size or sheer biting power to inflict a mortal wound.

Ferociously shaking its huge head back and forth, the pliosaur began to systematically dislodge the whales. One by one they were thrown off, until it twisted its entire forefront around in an explosive arc, flinging the last two orcas from its tattered throat. Exploiting its own inertia, it whipped its crocodile-shaped head back around and retaliated, crunching down on the nearest cow.

The high-pitched squeal the bitten orca gave off pierced *Eurypterid II*'s thick hull with a sound reminiscent of a giant's fingernails raking across the world's largest chalkboard.

"Oh God!" Amara slammed her palms against the glass before her. "He got her! He got the matriarch!"

As Jake and Amara stared, horrorstricken, the creature released a deep rumble of satisfaction and shifted its death grip on the big killer whale, plunging its ridged teeth deeper into the old cow's body. As her death cries diffused into the water with the last of her air, the orca's leader gave out a mournful final call and fell silent.

Watching in disbelief from fifty yards out, Omega Baby emitted an agonized squeal and started shaking. A moment later, the normally playful male went berserk. Though he knew his mother was already dead, he flung his 20,000 pounds directly at the pliosaur's scale-covered head. A split-second behind him, the remaining bulls scrambled to catch up.

With a sound reminiscent of thunderclaps, fifty tons of incensed orca plowed into the preoccupied marine reptile. For the pod bulls, all thoughts of personal safety were forgotten. Foregoing any semblance of strategy, they clamped their jaws onto the object of their enmity and tore into it, sinking their teeth into anything and everything they could and tearing away with all the strength they possessed. A second later, the equally vengeful cows joined the fray.

Bellowing like a herd of elephants, the pliosaur answered the orca's assault. It flung its giant jaws from side to side and retaliated, crushing, slashing and snapping at anything that moved. It was the ultimate battle of the ages; the prehistoric versus the present, in a no holds barred, kill-or-be-killed fight to the death.

Powerless, Jake and Amara watched in awe as the war for dominion of the world's oceans raged at their feet. Despite their proximity to the warring titans, they could see little. Within seconds of the killer whale's concerted attack, the water surrounding the combatants became obscured by blood, scales, and scraps of blubber and skin. Other than an occasional set of flukes flailing away through the murkiness, or the roars of pain and rage that buffeted their insignificant craft, they had no idea what was happening. Finally, several minutes after it began, the din of battle ceased.

With their noses pressed against their craft's reinforced portal, the two humans fought to peer through the gore-glutted waters. Then, as the current dissipated some of the obscurity, Jake spotted a hint of movement. Something big and dark emerged from the debris cloud, causing him and Amara to recoil.

It was Omega Baby. Badly injured from a bite to his dorsal section, the wounded bull struggled toward the surface. An unscathed cow sped up alongside him, supporting the significantly larger male, nudging him toward the much-needed air, some twenty feet above.

Watching as the two orcas vanished from view, Amara gave a hesitant smile. Two more bulls and a handful of cows limped away from the scene of the gruesome struggle. As the waters cleared more, her pride in her cetaceans vanished, and her increasingly grim expression reflected the toll the clash took on the killer whale pods. Three of the big male orcas were dead, and seven females. Drifting upside down as they floated toward the surface, their sundered bodies bore brutal testimony to the power of the primitive terror they'd pitted their collective strength against. The last of the surviving whales quit the field, emitting billowing trails of crimson as they went.

Out of the corner of his eye, Jake saw Amara's legs give out. He made a quick grab, catching her just before she collapsed to the submersible's hard floor. He lowered her gently into a seated position, cradling her until her head rested against the thick Lexan portal. She sat in a stupor, her breathing shallow and rapid, her eyes wide in disbelief.

"Are you okay?" Jake dropped to one knee and touched the side of her neck with his fingertips.

"Wha . . . what?" Amara stammered. "Oh, yes, I'm fine. Sorry, I'm just a little overwhelmed by what I saw."

"No one can blame you for that, doc . . . believe me."

She nodded slowly and covered her face with her hands. After a few deep inhales she exhaled through her teeth and rubbed her cheeks briskly in an attempt to clear her head. She blew out one final breath, then accepted Jake's help making it back to her feet. She dusted herself off, smiling weakly as he dropped back into his co-pilot's chair and started strapping himself in.

"So, can you get this thing going, or do I have to call the auto club?" Jake winked back at her.

"Aye, aye, captain." Amara grinned, making her way to a computer terminal built into one of the cockpit's interior walls. "Now that I know what the problem is it should be easy to fix."

"Best news I've heard all day," Jake said. He leaned back into his chair and closed his battle-weary eyes. *Thank God it's over.* A second later, he felt a faint vibration run through the soles of his feet. "What the hell?" His eyes popped and he sat rigidly upright, peering nervously around. "Doc, did you feel that?"

"Feel what?" Amara asked, her attention focused on the computer screen before her.

"*That,*" Jake said. The vibration repeated itself.

This time, Amara felt it too. Alarmed, she moved to her sonar screen. "I don't see anything. There's still too much gunk in the water."

Jake unsnapped his web harness and hobbled to the sub's viewing portal. He wiped away the cool condensation to peer through the gradually dissipating cloud that still marked the battlefield. He blinked repeatedly, trying to focus. He saw a hint of movement, but his brain had trouble registering what he was looking at.

Then something huge emerged from the center of the cloud.

Jake's concerned frown became a sagacious grin. What he'd spotted was nothing more than the pliosaur's drifting carcass. He could see its ravaged head and muzzle protruding from the cloud. He took a deep breath and started to relax again. He turned back toward his chair, laughing at himself for being so jumpy.

He stopped laughing when the "carcass" moved.

"Motherfucker!" Jake staggered backwards, his rear bumping painfully into a corner of his station's control panel.

Amara started. "What's wrong?"

"It's not dead! The whales didn't kill it! They must have cut their losses and made a break for it!"

"What are you talking about?" Amara's pale eyes struggled to pierce the remnants of the debris cloud.

"I said it's not dead!" Jake insisted. He could feel his voice growing noticeably shaky. "It's still alive. I'm telling you, I saw it move!"

"Jake, you just saw its body undulating in the current," Amara reassured. She continued scanning the nearly clear sea outside their oval-shaped window. All of a sudden, the current kicked up like a gust of wind and the cloud of gore vanished completely. To her bemusement, nothing occupied the space where the pliosaur had been. No body. No anything.

Amara frowned. She was about to check her sonar screen again when movement off the starboard side caught her eye. "Good God!" She rushed back to her computer keyboard and started furiously pecking away.

Jake felt a cold shiver crawl centipede-like up and down his spine. He sagged against his console, grabbing onto it for support as he stared in disbelief.

It was emerging from the blackness of the ocean's depths.

Invincible.

TWENTY-NINE

Jake shuddered as the pliosaur's monstrous form completely blocked his view of the surrounding sea. It was beyond belief. Not only had the colossal reptile survived its bloody struggle with the killer whales, it had emerged victorious. Its movements were unimpaired as it cruised past their portside, mandibles ajar. It was less than twenty yards away, and they were still dead in the water. He felt cold trickles of sweat run down his spine, causing him to shiver. For the first time since Samantha died, the lawman experienced fear in its rawest, most undiluted form. As it moved closer, Jake braced himself for the inevitable charge; closing his eyes tight, he held his breath and waited.

The moments passed in agonizing slow motion. He opened one eye, then the other. The creature wasn't coming for them. He moved cautiously to the mini-sub's observation bubble, squinting hard. He inhaled sharply as he realized it was missing an eye. The pliosaur's entire left eyeball was bitten out, wrenched from its socket, along with a substantial portion of the bony orbit. Jake whistled as he spotted the horrific wound. He took an involuntary step back, taking in all the punishment the marine reptile sustained during its battle with the frantic killer whales. Its enormous head was covered with oval-shaped bite marks and a five-foot section of its lip was ripped away, leaving behind bleeding gum tissue and exposing its ivory-colored teeth. Its throat was badly lacerated and both fore flippers were torn up, the right one in tatters, with large sections of carpal bone peeking through savaged tissue.

As he surveyed the creature's wounds, Jake noted with satisfaction that, although the pliosaur had won its greatest battle, the price for its victory was costly.

Suddenly, someone touched his shoulder. Jolted out of his head, the lawman whirled wide-eyed and found Amara standing next to him.

"Sorry . . . wow, he looks pretty beat up," she whispered.

"Yeah," Jake said quietly. "Like you and me." As their eyes met his grin vanished. He took a step forward, his hand palming her hip as he guided her behind him, instinctively placing his body between her and the creature. "He looks just as mean as ever. Maybe more so."

Amara nodded. "No surprise there. Wounded predators are always the most dangerous."

Jake cleared his throat. "I hate to say it, but I think he's looking for us."

"Us . . . or the whales."

"Shouldn't you be getting the engines working?" Jake asked. He moved carefully to his seat and eased into it as noiselessly as possible. "Sooner or later he's going to figure out we're here."

"The engines are already fixed." Amara's eyes locked onto the pliosaur's monstrous form. "Just so it doesn't come as a shock, as soon as I start them he's going to be all over us."

"Are you serious?"

Amara shrugged. "Hell, yes. All that noise?" She grinned half-heartedly, then cracked her knuckles by intertwined her fingers and extending her arms in front of her. "Get yourself situated. I'll need to do some fast maneuvering if we're to fight our way out of this one."

Jake winced as his restraining belts clicked loudly. "Can't we just wait for him to die?"

"He's not going to." Amara tiptoed to her station and seated herself. "Barring infection, none of those wounds are fatal. Even that missing eye will heal up. He won't get the eyeball back, of course, but his echolocation abilities will make up for it."

Jake stared. "So what are we going to do?"

Amara's bruised face became a steely mask of determination. "We have to finish him. Now, while he's hurt. If we don't, and there are others of his kind, and they start multiplying . . ."

"Good lord . . ." Jake shuddered.

"*Exactly*. I'm thinking of this from a species perspective now: us versus them. Last thing we need are a thousand of those things running amok."

"Okay," Jake slipped his arms inside *Eurypterid II's* padded actuator ports, ignoring the neural interface's bothersome sting. "Ready when you are. Let's do it."

"Just one second," Amara said. She flipped an overhead switch and grasped her control lever. She hesitated. "Jake?"

"Yes?"

She looked at him with big eyes. "In case we don't get out of this, thank you for saving my life. You're a real knight in shining armor."

"Anytime, doc." Jake twisted in his seat and grinned at her. "And for the record, you make an excellent damsel in distress."

Amara chuckled. "All-righty then. Hold onto your hat . . . because here we go!"

Jake sucked in a breath and prepared for the fight of his life. Just then, the chorus from REM's *"It's the End of the World As We Know It."* emanated out of the mini-sub's internal speakers.

"Oops, wrong button." Amara grinned sheepishly. "Okay, this should do it."

She hit the submersible's automatic engine start. Five hundred feet away, the wounded pliosaur's silhouette flickered as it swung its head from side to side, striving to locate the killer whales, the mini-sub, or *any* living thing to vent its wrath on. The instant *Eurypterid II's* engine's flared to life it whipped around, its gleaming eye zeroing the tiny sub with pinpoint accuracy. Its mangled jaws split apart, emitting a deep-throated challenge that echoed for miles. A second later, it charged.

"Holy shit!" Jake yelled. "He's coming straight for us!"

"And us at him," Amara announced. She threw them into high gear, heading straight for their nemesis. "Hang on, this could get dicey!"

At the last possible moment, Amara faked to port, then whipped them hard to starboard. She threw their starboard engine into reverse, gunning them into a steep climb.

With the pliosaur's maw beckoning, Jake's heart took an express elevator into his stomach. Miraculously, they made it past its deadly jaws and over its damaged flipper. Executing a seamless 180 degree turn, Amara started following the frustrated beast, keeping them on its blind side and away from its teeth. It was a tough proposition. Though less maneuverable than the mechanical marvel pursuing it, the wounded saurian was considerably faster. And, despite its impaired vision, it seemed to know *exactly* where its prey was hiding.

"Damn, he's pulling away from us!" Amara cried out. In the distance, the Cutlass loomed over them, a monstrous fin arcing toward the surface.

"Do something!" Jake bellowed. The frustration of having to sit there like some prepubescent wallflower was really grating on his nerves.

Amara made a grab for her console's targeting helmet. "I'm going to try the electrified harpoon. It's our only chance!"

Leveling off forty feet above the furiously paddling pliosaur, she flipped down her visor. A red and green virtual-reality sighting mechanism sprang up on the device's internal lens. She flipped the fire control cover open and aimed for the creature's broad back. Mouthing a prayer, she squeezed the rubberized trigger. A faint vibration shimmied their hull as *Eurypterid II*'s main armament launched with a hydraulic hiss.

Jake held his breath, watching the two-pronged harpoon sizzle through the seawater separating them. It slammed into the giant reptile's armored dorsal section, nearly burying itself.

"Bull's-eye!" he cheered.

"Okay, here goes!" Amara said. She flipped the switch on their main generator.

Bellowing in frustration as enough electricity to light up the Empire State Building once again streamed through its body, the pliosaur snapped its jaws in every direction. Its fins and stubby tail flailed like the water was fire, and its forward momentum ceased. Paralyzed by the high powered amperage, it writhed in the current. Arcs of electricity spouted from every part of its body, dissipating into the surrounding seawater. Even its teeth spewed bright blue sparks.

"You're doing it!" Jake cheered. His eyes gleamed from the pyrotechnics display.

The pliosaur's movements became more and more spasmodic. Finally, it gave one last shudder and turned belly-up.

"Yes, but we can't keep this up much longer!" Amara shouted. Her gaze fixed on a blinking gauge to her right.

"What do you mean?"

"We're going to short out!"

A high-pitched warning claxon began to sound, its wail filling the cabin.

"Our circuits are overloading from the backlash!" Amara cried. "If I don't shut down we'll lose power, just like Karl did!"

Jake watched in abject silence as Amara reached for the cut-off lever. Next to her, a dangerous shower of sparks hissed out of a control panel.

"Shit!"

A second later, the lever was thrown, and the cable's deadly voltage ceased.

"I'm sorry," Amara said. "If I didn't cut it we'd be done for."

Jake shrugged. "Hey, at least the lights are still on."

Fifty feet away, the pliosaur lay dead in the water, its eye half-closed, pupil fixed and dilated. For the briefest of moments they thought they'd done it. Then, one of its flippers twitched and its eye opened wide. It rolled right-side-up, its massive body displacing a wall of water as it started forward. It gazed furiously around.

"God, let's get out of here," Jake said.

"Good idea." Before Amara touched the controls, *Eurypterid II* gave a violent lurch. Jake's stomach heaved as they were hauled inexplicably forward. Their velocity increased, until soon they were careening helplessly along like a trolled marlin lure.

"What's happening?" Amara peered anxiously at her readouts.

"We're still attached!" Jake yelled. He cursed as he bit his tongue and removed his arms from the actuator ports. "The cable's still connected and I can't reach it with the actuators! You've got to release it!"

Amara scanned the maze of knobs, dials, and levers surrounding her. "I don't know where the cut-off controls are. I don't even know if there *are* any!"

The creature continued to build up speed. It was cruising purposefully, dragging them like an oversized dog on a leash.

"Hold on, I'm throwing us in reverse!" Amara cried out.

Pulling steadily back on *Eurypterid II*'s control lever, she exerted pressure on the high-tensile strength cable linking them. The sub's impeller engines whined loudly from the pull, and its reinforced hull started vibrating from the buffeting of the pliosaur's cavitations.

The creature continued to drag them inexorably downward. Below, the Cutlass loomed larger.

"I can't break free!" Amara shouted over the din. Her teeth bared as she yanked the controls side to side. "He's too powerful and the damn cable's too strong!"

"Well, you better think of something," Jake pointed at the blackness welling up beyond the Cutlass. "Because it looks like he's going deep!"

Amara's head snapped upright. "I've got an idea . . ."

"Good . . ." Jake said as they bounced violently up and down. "Because, this Nantucket sleigh ride is getting old!"

Jaw set, Amara floored it. She hit the switch releasing the winch cable's anti-backlash brakes, allowing the ten thousand pound test line to burn off its spool. The insulated cable formed a billowing arc, increasing in diameter as it was dragged through the current.

Jake saw the Cutlass clearly. The creature was headed for a one-hundred-foot thick section of the spire. Her face a mask of utter concentration, Amara fought to keep pace with it. As the behemoth veered to port, she released more cable and threw the mini-sub hard to starboard.

"What are you doing?" Jake asked, as they and the pliosaur went around the mountain in alternating directions.

"Just trust me," Amara said. Taking advantage of the cable's huge arc, she spun *Eurypterid II* one hundred and eighty degrees around. With their backs to the chasm, she locked the cable down and waited. Like a garrote, it tightened around the Cutlass's exterior, tearing along its craggy slopes and casting up clouds of sand and kelp. The moment it went completely taut, Amara slammed the engines into reverse and heaved back against the cable with everything *Eurypterid II* had.

Jake's jaw dropped. "Son of a bitch!"

Immediately, the submersible began to buck from the pull, its sturdy frame groaning. On the opposing side of the Cutlass the pliosaur, bewildered by the unexpected loss of freedom, began paddling wildly.

"Hold on!" Amara screamed. She braced her feet and pulled with all of her might. The wail of straining engines filled the cabin, increasing in pitch as pressure was exerted on the line.

Jake swore vehemently. Like a blowtorch, the braided steel cable began gouging a groove through the seaweed-coated stone and coral.

Eurypterid II listed to one side as it was pulled toward the Cutlass's jagged exterior.

"It's not going to work!" Jake bellowed over the complaining motors. "We're being dragged into the rocks!"

"Have faith!" Amara yelled back. Her forehead beaded with sweat as she continued to pull on her controls. "The cable shouldn't be able to . . ." Her sentence was cut short by what sounded like a gunshot. She slammed painfully against her restraining belts and groaned. Shaking her head to clear it, she fumbled to regain control of the spiraling ship.

Momentarily dazed, Jake glimpsed a burst of bubbles, followed by a flash of silver that sliced like a giant whip past the observation window. A split-second later, something smacked loudly against the hull.

"What the hell was that?" he blurted out.

"I'm not sure. It might be the cable." Amara looked over the interior, checked some gauges, then frowned. "I think it looped over us."

"Is that bad?"

Her eyes traveled from one shimmering screen to the next. "Not unless it gets in the way of our intake valves," she noted. "I don't see any obstructions on the readings or on our hull cameras, so I think we're good. We're lucky it didn't strike the observation bubble."

"Why, would it have broken?"

"It's Lexan, so I doubt it. But, then again . . . I'd hate to find out I was wrong."

"I'm glad we didn't." Jake breathed a sigh of relief. He reinserted his arms into the actuator's ports and resumed standing guard. Far to port, he spotted a school of Dorado flashing emerald, gold and sapphire as they fled. "Any sign of old faithful?"

"Nothing on sonar . . ." Amara powered them forward. Behind them, the Cutlass's daunting form faded from view. "By the way, you were right. We're directly over Ophion's Deep."

"I guess that gives our scaly pal plenty of places to hide, huh?"

"Unfortunately."

Jake peered into the abyss's blackened maw. He felt an uncomfortable tingle in the pit of his stomach – a prelude to nausea – and yanked his head back. He shuddered. The currents rocketing up from Ophion's Deep sent particles of plant matter and detritus soaring high into the thermocline, causing the mini-sub to pitch back and forth, and creating the optical illusion one was plummeting powerlessly into its depths.

"Yikes. So, how deep does this thing actually go?"

"Readings are seven thousand feet and plunging." Amara peeked at her sonar. "That's strange. The pliosaur's vanished. Hard to believe, given its size. I don't know whether to be worried or relieved."

"I prefer the latter." Jake studied the surrounding sea and saw nothing. "You still have the proximity alarm on?"

"Of course. But it only works on objects within 150 yards."

"So what do you want to do?" Jake twisted in his chair.

Amara scowled. "We're weaponless and our sonar is damaged . . . I say we head for home."

"And the pliosaur?"

"Still needs to be dealt with – but we're not going to be the ones to do it. We'd need a lot more firepower."

Although the thought of the creature escaping vexed him, Jake realized Amara was right. Short of throwing away their lives, they'd done everything they could. He exhaled and nodded. "You're the expert, doc. I guess it's time to get out of Dodge."

"It's time to alert the military."

———

Amara confirmed their location on *Eurypterid II*'s GPS and punched in a few coordinates. She realized the mini-sub was equipped with an autopilot feature, but opted not to activate it. Despite her fatigue, she preferred to grip the controls as they cruised for home, her weary eyes reflexively scanning sonar.

She tried to relax. She was bruised and battered and fantasizing about Ibuprofen, but happy to be alive. She gave Jake a surreptitious glance. He was rigidly erect and poised like an armed Phalanx anti-missile battery, jaw set and arms ready to bring *Eurypterid II*'s graspers into action. She smiled. The broad-shouldered lawman reminded her of a big guard dog, fiercely loyal and dependable. Even so, with all the bloodshed over the last twenty-four hours, it was a miracle either of them survived. She studied the rugged lines of Jake's face and nodded approvingly. He was like Omega Baby – a true alpha. Her eyes lit up and she found herself wondering if the future might be brighter than she thought.

Suddenly, her mind wandered to Willie, and she found herself fighting back tears. She controlled her breathing, forced herself to relax, and kept from falling apart by focusing on the fact that his murderer had already been punished. And that she and Jake would be back shortly to tell the tale.

She thought of being on dry land, away from all the horror, and closed her eyes. She envisioned herself getting home, taking a luxuriously hot bubble bath, and climbing into bed. She was going to turn off her phone, hide beneath the covers, and sleep for a week.

Before she realized it was happening, she nodded off.

A moment later, she realized the alarm clock rousing her out of bed was *Eurypterid II*'s proximal sensor.

—

"Where is it?" Jake pressed as he scanned the area. The sound of the submersible's proximity alarm had his blood pressure and adrenaline levels pulsing off the charts. "Do you have it on the scope?"

"No," Amara said. She blinked repeatedly, her aquamarine eyes glued to the sonar unit's screen. "He must be somewhere above us. Keep an eye out."

"Geez, I hate this shit," Jake grumbled. He kept his arms tight inside the actuator ports as he gazed toward the surface. "And, as if we didn't have enough to worry about, it's going to be dark soon."

Beep . . . Beep . . . Beep . . .

"He's got to be close!" Amara abandoned her useless sonar screen and scanned her side and rear wall monitors. "I'm going to reverse and head for the surface!"

"You're the pilot." Jake leaned forward, craning his neck to one side so he could glance straight up. His gasp of alarm filled the cockpit.

BeepBeepBeepBeepBeep . . .

"Holy shit, he's right on *top* of us!"

On pure instinct, Amara hauled back and threw *Eurypterid II* into reverse. She barely got their nose up before the pliosaur smashed into them with all its power.

"Mother of God!" The impact was heart-stopping, and Jake's biceps bulged like softballs as he fought the controls. Miraculously, he'd caught the pliosaur's mouth just as it closed. With its upper lip and jaw locked in his right pincer assembly and its lower jaw in his left, he battled to keep the behemoth from crunching down on the mini-sub's vulnerable prow.

Amara screamed in horror. "Don't let go! If he bites into the cockpit, he'll kill us both!"

Jake cursed and held on for dear life. His arms shook from the strain, and the submersible's actuator motors shrieked from being pitted against a crushing force exceeding fifty tons per square inch. His ears popped from the increase in pressure as the creature pushed down on them, plunging *Eurypterid II* deeper into Ophion's Deep. Outside his six-foot portal, all Jake could see was a wall of razor-sharp teeth, each as big as one of Amara's calves, and beyond them, the beckoning darkness of the pliosaur's gullet.

The darkness . . .

As the wave of nausea swept over him, Jake realized with surprising detachment that it was days since his last episode. Then, his breathing turned harsh and ragged and he felt himself slipping away. He tried to fight, but the cold queasiness quickly overpowered him, sweeping him away to a dark and distant place.

He was losing the battle. He saw Samantha's face staring back at him from the encroaching void. Strangely, she wasn't smiling and gesturing for him like she usually did. She was fearful, frantic. Then, fatigue hauled back and hit him hard, right between the eyes. His breath grew shallow and he slumped forward in his chair. His arms started to go limp. Behind him, Amara screamed in his ear.

There was a shudder as *Eurypterid II's* steel actuators began to power down.

"Jake, snap out of it!" Amara shrieked at him. "What's wrong with you?" Her eyes focused on opposing sets of sixteen-inch fangs drawing steadily closer. In moments they would contact the mini-sub's fragile viewing portal. A loud, metallic groan caused the distraught scientist to check her depth gauge. She gasped. They were three thousand feet down. If one of the pliosaur's teeth even *partially* penetrated their Lexan shield, *Eurypterid II* would implode instantaneously, pulverizing them.

Jake was dimly aware of Amara wrestling with her harness and climbing towards him. He sensed his body being shaken, and from the recesses of the collapsing house of cards that was his mind, heard her panicked cries. At first, he thought it was Sam. Still, the voice was hauntingly familiar.

His tightly closed eyes waged war against the screaming demons. The voice in his head grew louder. Despite the din, he realized he recognized it. It was someone he knew. Someone he . . .

Roaring like a lion, Jake raged back against the enveloping darkness. He could hear the voice clearly now, as it pleaded with him. He focused on it, using it like a beacon to guide him toward the light. His chest heaved and he sucked in a huge breath, opening his eyes just as the pliosaur's needle-sharp teeth moved within six inches of finishing them once and for all.

Jake's eyes turned to talons, and his lips peeled back from his own canines. A rage welled up within him as he plunged his arms fully inside the actuator ports, pressing back against the creature's jaws with the strength of a madman. With Amara hanging from the back of his chair in astonishment, he uttered a bellow that rivaled the pliosaur's and hurled himself against its rows of teeth. His joints cracked and his muscles began to tear, but he stopped the jaws from closing. Then, with the creature's frustrated rumblings shaking *Eurypterid II* to its core, Jake did the impossible: He forced its mouth back open.

"Oh . . . no . . . you . . . *don't!*" he spat. He felt a sense of awe as he realized he was holding two lives in the palm of his hand. "Doc, are you okay?" he shouted over his shoulder.

"I was just asking you that!" Amara gasped. She lowered herself back into her chair and fumbled with her harness. "What the hell just happened?"

"Something wonderful, I think." Jake smiled grimly. He gave a violent headshake to keep the sweat from his eyes. "We'll talk about it later!"

"Oh God, Jake – we're in big trouble!"

"Tell me about it!" he growled. Breathing hard, he leaned back into his David vs. Goliath stalemate against the creature.

"No, you don't understand!" Amara shuddered. "We're about to die!"

A throaty grumble of frustration escaped the pliosaur's disfigured mouth as it forced its enemy further down into the abyss. Still raging from the injuries it suffered from its previous battle, the marine reptile vented its fury upon the big yellow crustacean whose pincers were fastened onto it.

Like an underwater drill, the *Kronosaurus* bored its way relentlessly deeper. With the water it was pushing against leaving it unable to bring its jaws' full power to bear, it was opting for an alternate means to destroy its ammonite-like adversary. The incredible water pressure waiting thousands of feet down would squash its hard-shelled opponent beyond recognition.

Ophion beckoned.

With its lacerated jaws locked in place, the wrathful monstrosity continued its relentless descent, its damaged flippers powering ever deeper into the ice-cold blackness of the void.

Only death would stop it.

"What do you mean? Die from what?" Jake yelled.

Amara watched as the embattled lawman shook his head in exasperation, unable to look away from his protracted struggle.

"He's taking us too deep!" she shouted back. Her knuckles were white as she struggled in vain with *Eurypterid II's* steering controls. "Our engines are barely slowing him down"

"I don't understand!"

"Karl said this sub has a crush depth of five thousand feet, remember?" Her teeth clenched, Amara shifted her joystick back and forth in an attempt to dislodge their gargantuan opponent. From outside she heard a deep, coughing sound – almost a chuckle – as if the pliosaur was mocking her puny efforts. "We're approaching that now. If we don't get away soon we'll implode from the pressure, whether he gets us or not!"

"So *do* something!"

Amara snapped hysterically. "DO WHAT?"

"What about that . . . stinger thing Karl was talking about?" Jake was panting now. "He said it was a . . . weapon of last resort. Well, I'd say we're . . . down to our last resort!"

"Shit, you can say that again!"

Filled with an influx of hope, Amara fumbled with her right armrest. She found a small lever on one side and pulled it. There was a low hissing sound, and the smell of compressed air permeated the cockpit. The armrest's padded section flipped open, revealing a small console housing a series of switches and a steel lever similar to her steering controls, only smaller. It was ergonomic in design and had a button-styled trigger on its front, like the joystick for an old-fashioned video game.

"Let's see if I can make this work," she said, her eyes calculating as she tapped one button after another.

"Hurry up!" Jake bellowed. He grunted in pain as the pliosaur attempted another downward lunge. His arms were forced brutally back, the groaning actuators barely absorbing its power.

"Okay, I've got it," Amara said. With a low hum, a foot-wide monitor screen descended from the cockpit roof, positioning itself directly above her. There were glowing crosshairs on it, linked to an external lens centered directly above their prow. She could see every detail of the pliosaur's battle-lined skull, illuminated by the mini-sub's powerful searchlights. Its remaining eye blinked, narrowing malevolently as it continued its death struggle with the hydraulic-powered pincers holding it at bay. Amara took hold of the stinger's control lever, wrapping her fingers gingerly around its cold surface and pushing lightly to see what would happen.

It didn't budge.

Frowning, she pushed again, only harder this time. The lever moved a smidgen, then stopped. A loud warning sound emanated from her overhead screen, and a bright red text box replaced the system's targeting crosshairs.

DANGER - OBSTRUCTION - SYSTEM OFFLINE.

"What the hell?" Amara checked the controls and pushed hard.

"Oh, shit!" Jake sputtered. His cry of alarm yanked her attention back to the submersible's embattled bow. "Doc, look!"

The observation bubble was cracking.

With a sound like splintering ice, the first spider web fracture formed along its reinforced edge.

Amara managed a horrified gasp. She wanted to scream, but speech failed her. Outside, the pliosaur pressed its assault, its mandible muscles bunching like iron cords, straining the big steel manipulators to their absolute maximum. It could sense victory within its reach.

"How . . . deep are we?" Jake rasped. He was near exhaustion, his voice hoarse from grappling with the tenacious reptile.

"We're passing forty nine hundred feet!"

"If you're going to . . . do something, you'd better . . . do it now!" Jake roared as cracks in the thick Lexan increased in both size and number. "Because I . . . really don't want to . . . die down here!"

Amara pushed the lever again and got the same error message. She glanced at her portside camera monitor. There was a blurry object running across the screen, obscuring visibility. It was too close for the lens to focus on – something resting against their hull or wrapped around it . . .

The cable.

"God *damn* it!" Amara's adrenaline-fueled eyes flew open wide. She realized to her disgust that her impromptu means of breaking free from the mini-sub's line had also disabled their last line of defense. She'd bucked the odds, just like she always did. Only *this* time, her miscalculation was going to get them killed.

As their current predicament piled atop all the other horrors she'd endured, Amara Takagi's thought processes teetered on the brink of insanity. Over the last forty-eight hours she'd lost her crew, her ship, and had her livelihood taken from her. She'd been bullied, threatened, pushed around, beaten, and nearly murdered. She'd seen her best friend shot, and had him bleed out in her arms. And after all of that, the thing she'd been trying to save was about to annihilate her and Jake.

She could take no more.

Amara heaved against her restraining belts, fumbling with the release mechanism until she fought her way free. Teeth clenched, she lunged for the stinger's firing mechanism with both hands and yanked it to and fro with all her strength. Eight feet away, *Eurypterid*

II's window neared its breaking point, the sounds of its splintering layers matched by Jake's screams of rage and frustration.

"You slavering son of a bitch!" Amara slammed the frozen lever back and forth in a manic frenzy. "I am *sick* of this shit! Sick of being hunted, sick of being afraid, and sick of watching you *eat* people!"

The control lever came free, lurching backwards so suddenly the impact sprained her wrist. Dismissing the pain, she focused on her overhead screen. There was a loud pinging sound, and the glowing crosshairs reappeared. Accompanying them was an emblazoned box with yellow lettering that flashed across the bottom.

SYSTEM ARMED. SYSTEM ARMED. SYSTEM ARMED.

She grasped the firing mechanism and pushed it slowly forward. She heard an immediate thump, and the ceiling overhead vibrated as the stinger arm and its howitzer-sized shell curved up and out of the sub's dorsal section. Prepped and activated, it remained poised and waiting.

Amara was breathing so rapidly she nearly passed out. She maneuvered the joystick until the brightly colored sights were centered between the pliosaur's eyes. She took a deep breath and held it as she eased her finger onto the knurled trigger. As its tiny metal teeth bit into her skin, a thought flashed through her adrenaline-charged mind. She realized that, despite Jake's cries of fury, and the pliosaur's deep-throated rumblings, the loudest sound she could hear was her own red-hot blood, pulsating in her ears like a giant bass drum.

"Eat *this*, fucker!"

Arcing overhead like the scorpion's tail that inspired it, *Eurypterid II's* stinger lanced forward, its explosive tip slamming into the pliosaur's head and detonating.

To Amara's credit, she didn't collapse until after the explosion.

———

She was alive.

She almost wished she wasn't. The softly coaxing sound of Jake's voice felt like ice picks buried in her ears. Amara mouthed a curse and opened her eyes. She looked up at him and tried to ask what happened, but all she heard were croaking sounds. Her voice was gravel from all the screaming, and her headache increased exponentially when she tried to sit up.

"You did it." Jake nodded, somehow understanding her. He wore a proud look as he dabbed a moistened towelette to her bruised forehead and eye. "You hit your head pretty hard. You should rest for a while."

Amara nibbled her lip, embarrassed by him tending to her with those oversized paws of his. Her pride kept needling her to wave him off, but she didn't. She took a slow breath. "No . . . I'm fine. So . . . where are we?"

"Cruising toward the surface." Jake indicated the depth gauge to his left, then pointed out the dim lighting now visible through what remained of their viewing portal. "I don't know jack about driving this thing, and I didn't want to go fast in case that window wasn't going to hold. I just pointed us up and left her slow and steady."

Amara tapped her lips with a fingertip and nodded. They'd been lucky. Jake's concern about *Eurypterid II*'s compromised portal not only got them out of the danger zone, it also saved them from a serious case of decompression sickness. She placed one hand on the floor and tried to put some weight on it. *God, I hurt in places I didn't know I had.*

Jake offered her a hand.

"Thanks." Drawing on his strength, Amara made it unsteadily to her feet. She paused a moment to get her bearings, then eased herself down into her pilot's chair. She closed her eyes and pressed the back of one hand to her aching forehead, hoping the cockpit would stop spinning. "What happened to the pliosaur?"

"Dead as a doornail," Jake said. His sapphire eyes were filled with admiration. "I don't know how you got that stinger thing working, but you blew the entire top of its head off. I watched it sink like the Bismarck."

"Are you sure?"

"I'm sure." He nodded solemnly. "It's dead as Dillinger. Trust me."

Amara shook her head. "Wow, thank God it's finally over. What a day!"

"Yeah, I'll say." Favoring his injured ankle, Jake moved along *Eurypterid II*'s gently sloping floor and took his seat up front.

Amara groaned, leaning back and closing her eyes. "How's our depth?"

"Less than four hundred." Jake leaned back, interlacing his fingers behind his head as if he were watching a football game. "It's a little after seven. With any luck, we'll be home in time for supper."

"Good, because I'm hungry enough to eat a pliosaur." Amara chuckled despite her headache. Her gaze suddenly hardened, and she stared intently at the lawman. "By the way, what was that damn business down there with you freezing up on me? You suffer from chronic hypoglycemia or something?"

Jake sucked a breath and looked down, his hand rubbing at the two-day scruff on his chin. He sighed. "I don't know if you've figured it out, but for several years now I've had a . . . burden I've carried around with me. Or used to, anyway."

"Used to?" Amara didn't bother hiding the doubt in her voice.

"Yeah." Jake glanced upward, a strangely serene expression on his face. "Funny as it may sound, I think I left it down there in the abyss, along with our scaly friend."

Amara nodded approvingly.

Jake smiled sadly. "Hey, loss comes with life. But, like you said before, you shouldn't let it stop you from *living*." He peered out their fractured window as the surface's glow drew steadily nearer. In the distance, a large manta ray sped up to avoid them, its wings flapping as it veered off. "So, do you think this thing can get us home?"

"Sure." Bracing her hip, Amara made her way to a flush-mounted keyboard. She logged onto the web, scanning her homepage. An email caught her eye, and she snickered. "The winds have died down and seas are calm. I think we'll be okay."

"What's so funny?"

"Not funny . . . more like ironic."

"Do share. I could use some irony right now."

Amara hesitated. "Okay, but I hope you won't get mad at me."

"I promise." Jake grinned.

"Well . . . I, uh, just got an email from the Department of the Interior, AKA the Endangered Species Act."

"Go on . . ."

She cleared her throat. "It says . . . *Dear Dr. Takagi: Your request for probationary admittance of the species you submitted has been approved, based on the materials and evidence provided. Pending further investigation, as of 0600 hours today, the species you awarded the scientific name* Kronosaurus imperator *has been granted official protection under the United States Endangered Species Act. Any harm to or harassment of said species, adult or juvenile, is henceforth a violation of federal law, and is punishable by up to five years in a federal penitentiary and a fine of up to two hundred and fifty thousand dollars."*

Jake sniggered sarcastically. "Guess it's good nobody saw us kill the damn thing."

"Yeah," Amara said. She closed her email and peered into space. "So, Jake . . . now that you've helped save the world, what will you do next?" She looked intently at him.

"Besides going to Disney?" Jake winked at her. "I'm thinking about getting back into competition." He had an excited, almost predatory gleam in his eye, one Amara had never seen before. "I'm a little rusty, of course, but after a few months of training I think I might have a comeback or two left in me."

"That's wonderful!" she beamed. "I'm happy for you." Without realizing it, she found herself looking him up and down.

Jake caught her stare. He hesitated for a moment, his brow furrowing up. Then his expression changed and he rose and limped toward her.

"So *tell* me something, doc," he said with a sheepish grin. "Has any of this excitement served to help you work up an . . . appetite?"

Amara felt her heart flutter. *Omigod, I don't believe it; he's going to make a move!* Recovering quickly, she tossed her hair back and incorporated her best southern belle accent. "Why, Sheriff Jake Braddock. Are you asking lil' ol' me out to dinner?"

"Oh, I guess you could say that." Jake's grin widened as he drew closer.

"Hey, whoa there, stud." Amara tittered at his amorous expression, extending one hand to keep him at arm's length. "Dinner will be fine. Dessert you're going to have to work for."

"But, didn't I save your life twice already?" Jake unabashedly studied her curves, following her every move as he helped her reseat herself by holding her hips.

"You're unbelievable, Jake Braddock. We both look like losers in a no-holds-barred cage fight and you're thinking about sex?"

Jake stared dejectedly at the floor. "Well, it *has* been three years . . ."

"Oh, really . . ." Amara moistened her lips with the tip of her tongue and exhaled slowly. "Gosh, that sounds like a long time." She reached coyly down, guiding his calloused hands up and running them smoothly along her ribs. She winked, then lifted them up off her tattered blouse, depositing them perfectly on the waiting halves of her restraining harness. She studied his befuddled expression and smiled coquettishly. "The buckle has been giving me problems. Would you mind inserting it for me?"

Jake swallowed nervously and wiped his brow with the back of one hand. "Uh, sure. No problem, doc."

Amara watched his crestfallen expression as he knelt and began fumbling with the heavy harness. His expression was so intense she had to fight to keep from cracking up. "Are you having a problem? Maybe you need some lubricant?"

Jake made a face, grunting as he finally snapped the metal buckle closed. "No, but I think it got damaged during that last battle. Damn prototypes . . ." He exhaled hard and gave both sides of the harness's webbing a hard yank. "There. That should hold."

"Thanks." Amara reached out and grabbed him by what remained of his shirt. Jake's yelp of alarm as he fell on top of her was quickly silenced when their lips met and her tongue found its way inside his mouth.

As their mouths weaved their magic upon each other, Amara quickly realized she had more than she bargained for. Their pent-up carnal impulses cascaded down, escalating from a hot and heavy downpour into a scalding monsoon of purest passion.

Her shocked inhalation as Jake pressed his hardness against her was a throaty gasp of delight. His lips and tongue peppered her mouth and throat and the sensitive spots behind her ears with hot, wet kisses. Hissing when she found herself restrained by her harness, she raked her nails repeatedly across the muscles of his upper back and pulled him tight against her, arching her back to press herself more strongly against his heaving chest. His teeth bit gently into the muscles at the base of her neck and she gyrated in her chair, grinding herself insistently against him. She felt his hands fumbling with her harness as he tried and failed to release it.

As Jake's hands started caressing her breasts, Amara felt a moment of panic. Her innate modesty and reserved nature doused her like a pail of ice water. She moaned aloud as the awful battle between desire and caution began. Common sense pleaded with her to push him away, but her hormones laughed at the sheer absurdity; it was like putting out a fire by tossing kerosene on it. She threw her arms around him in a huge hug and melded herself to him, burying her chin alongside his neck and trying desperately to ignore the insanely pleasurable sensations his fingertips created as they skillfully exerted pressure on her aching nipples.

She sucked in air, gasping like an exhausted swimmer who barely makes it to the surface. Finally, caution won out and she seized hold of Jake's hands, trapping them against her chest and squeezing with all her strength. She forced him gently back, her suddenly dry mouth unable to speak while his hotly aroused lips continued smothering hers with undisguised desire.

"Oh, God . . ." she moaned, straightening her arms to hold him at bay. "Please . . . We . . . we've got to stop."

To his credit, Jake nodded, despite his ragged breathing sounding like he just completed a decathlon. He swallowed hard and noisily cleared his throat. "Yeah, you're right, doc. Sorry about that. I, uh . . . ahem, don't know what came over me."

Amara's eyes narrowed wickedly, then widened as she looked down. She gave him a knowing smirk. "Oh, I think I know . . ."

Jake followed her gaze and flushed. He looked away, his eyes momentarily unable to focus. He seemed totally forlorn; a lost waif, so boyishly cute Amara couldn't help herself. She reached out and cradled his strong face in her hands, studying his bruised mouth and feeling his sandpaper stubble on her palms as she drew his lips unerringly back to hers. He came willingly but nervously, his half-opened mouth cautiously meeting hers, as if he was afraid of what might happen next.

She kissed him softly but deeply, then drew back just enough to see his face and smiled. "Now you *definitely* owe me dinner, mister." She made an exaggerated pouting face and winked at him. "Because you already *had* dessert!"

Jake grinned broadly and cupped his hands protectively over hers. Their eyes met and his shone. He lowered his chin to his chest, his warrior's equivalent of a bow. "It would be my honor, doc." His face was suddenly silhouetted and he glanced back over his shoulder, basking in the golden rays of sunlight that pierced the water and began to fill *Eurypterid II*'s cockpit. "We're almost to the surface. Guess I better get strapped in."

As he rose and made his way toward his co-pilot's chair, Amara took a moment to shamelessly admire him from the rear. He turned and caught her in the act, grinning and wagging his finger at her. She blushed, grinning mischievously, then grabbed her joystick and gunned *Eurypterid II* forward, causing the surprised lawman to stumble and nearly lose his footing.

Amara's adolescent giggles were drowned out by a deafening shriek that filled the mini-sub's cabin. She heard Jake's surprised cough as a wrist-thick jet of seawater punched him in the chest like an out-of-control fire hose. He made a desperate grab for the back of his seat, missed, slipped and crashed headlong to the floor. Her shocked eyes flew open wide and she tried to gurgle a scream as she, too, was inundated.

Eurypterid II's portal had ruptured.

THIRTY

"We're sinking!" Jake bellowed. Behind him, he heard Amara scream something, but her words were drowned by the sounds of rushing water and collapsing Lexan. He clawed at the slippery metal of his station, fighting for a handhold to pull himself erect. A foot of cold, churning brine already swirled around inside *Eurypterid II*, with more lasering its way through their compromised viewing bubble by the second.

Jake was nearly to his feet when his sprained ankle gave out, causing him to hobble to one side. He went down, striking his forehead against the edge of his chair. He saw a flash of white and a burst of scarlet. Ignoring the blood streaming from his temple, he braced himself on one knee. A fresh water jet plowed into him and he cursed as he was dropped again. He uttered a bellow of pain and frustration; he was being punished by a giant pressure washer. Yet another blast caught him, pummeling the side of his neck and face. He twisted onto his side to save his eyes, then raised his head above the rising water and glanced at what remained of their portal. Three palm-sized holes had been punched through the thick Lexan, with the remainder ready to go at any moment. Heart hammering, he placed his palms on the floor and straightened his arms, ignoring the beating his injured ribs took. He shook his head, thankful they were already at the surface. If they weren't, the mini-sub would have imploded already. His eyes met Amara's and he read her terrified thoughts.

We have to get out of here!

Still in her pilot's chair, Amara twisted at the waist to lessen the painful hosing and sputtered seawater. She gripped her joystick and jerked it side to side repeatedly, failing to move them. "I can't control us!" she screamed. "I've lost helm. We're a dead stick!"

Jake sprang to his feet and splashed toward her. "We have to abandon ship!" He placed himself between her and the punishing spray.

Soaked and shivering, Amara nodded. She tapped a button on her overhead console, turned a large dial, and shook her head. "Damn it. Not even manual override." Suddenly, there was a deep, groaning noise and *Eurypterid II* began to nose downward. The floor tilted sharply and the bright bits of sky still visible near the top of the viewing portal vanished. The cockpit grew noticeably dimmer. Amara grabbed at the buckle of her safety harness and pointed to the overhead hatch they used when boarding. "You've got to pull the release lever and pop the hatch. It's our only chance!"

Jake followed her gaze, then nodded, waiting for her.

"Don't wait for me," she snapped, fumbling with her buckle. "Hit the hatch now, before we submerge completely!"

Jake managed two steps through knee-high water, then stumbled to one side as the sub lurched down again. There was another painful groan, and a shoebox-sized section of their six-foot bubble shot inward, propelled by a torrent of ocean. The cold seawater he stood in rose dramatically, scaling his thighs, soaking his hips and chilling his groin. Despite the blinding spray, he managed to keep from falling and grabbed the bottom rung of their debarking ladder. He turned to Amara, extending his hand. The look of pure terror on her face froze him in his tracks.

"I'm stuck!" she cried out, yanking repeatedly at her safety harness. "It's jammed. I can't get out!"

Jake was instantly at her side, grabbing the discus-sized buckle. He jammed his calloused thumbs repeatedly into the release buttons but the mechanism failed to catch. A sickening thought occurred to him. He'd damaged the buckle, moments before. And now, she was trapped in it. His stunned eyes traveled up to meet Amara's panic-filled ones.

"What are we going to do?" she asked, tugging once more at her harness and staring at the rising water.

"We get you out," Jake announced. Teeth bared, he seized the heavy webbing with his hands and ripped. When it failed to give, he grabbed the metal buckle with both hands, tugging with all his might, trying to tear it apart or wrench the heavy belts from their anchorages. Nothing. Frustrated, he raised one soaked pant leg out of the water and braced his booted foot against Amara's armrest, throwing his entire body back and pulling with everything he had. He hesitated as reality sank in.

Oh, Jesus . . . I can't break it!

"Jake?" The trembling in Amara's voice echoed the fear he felt. "Can't you do it?"

His reply was an infuriated snarl. He took hold of the harness once more and heaved on it with desperate strength, raging as he pitted tendon and sinew against the unyielding material. His body screamed from the effort, his muscles bulging to the point his pressure bandage burst and blood spritzed from his bicep wound like spray from an aerosol can. He stopped, his mind reeling in disbelief at how well-built the harness was.

The shifting floor dislodged Jake from his stupor. The dying *Eurypterid II* was pointing nose-down at a forty-five degree slope. Relief swept through the lawman as the increased angle drained water away from Amara. The mini-sub's viewing portal uttered a final crackling sound and failed completely. The remnants collapsed inward like a shattered igloo, leaving a gaping five-foot wide hole that allowed the sea in unchecked.

"Oh God - Jake, help me!" Amara screamed. The water swamped the cockpit, reaching her chin in a second, and forcing her to tilt her head back in order to breathe.

Desperate and unable to keep from panicking, Jake scanned the cockpit, then frantically checked his pockets. His heavy jackknife was gone – undoubtedly removed by Markov while he was unconscious. His eyes lit up when he realized he still carried the maniac's sidearm, and he ripped the waterlogged .40 caliber from its holster. He scanned Amara's harness, searching for an effective spot. "Turn away!" he yelled. "I'm going to shoot through the webbing!"

Barely able to move, Amara swallowed hard and angled her chin to the right. She started making awful gagging sounds and Jake realized to his horror the seawater was reaching her lips and nostrils. He seized a portion of her shoulder belt and twisted it as far from her body as possible, placing the muzzle of the high-powered pistol against it. His lips tightened up and he wedged his forearm between Amara and the barrel. He said a quick prayer and pulled the trigger.

Nothing happened.

Jake pulled the trigger three more times. He lifted the gun out of the water and checked it. He chambered another round and tried again, cursing as he realized saltwater had fouled the firing mechanism. Howling in dismay, he flung the useless weapon away.

"Jake!" Amara spouted a mouthful of brine and sucked in a panicky breath. "Help me, please!"

"I'm trying!" Jake yelled. Her cries of terror were a spear rammed through his heart. He reached under her, hoisting her higher in her seat to give her a few more precious seconds. Her head raised an inch or two and he held her there as she sucked in terrified breaths.

"The sub's position created an air pocket," Amara gasped. "That's why the cockpit's not completely filled, but it won't last." She was shaking uncontrollably, a combination of fear and hypothermia. She closed her eyes and started taking tiny, rapid breaths. Her breathing slowed and she opened her eyes. "J-Jake, I want you to look at me."

He leaned closer, keeping one hand under her bottom while cradling the back of her head. Cold fear swept over him and his voice shook more than Amara's. "Yeah, d-doc? What can I do? Tell me what to d-do."

Their eyes met and he felt her reading him, sensing the terror overwhelming him. He felt an awful shame, something he'd never felt before, and swallowed hard. He tried to look away, but he couldn't.

Amara's eyes bored into his. "You have to g-go. P-please . . . this is it for me. There's n-no need for you to die too."

Jake shook his head so hard the room spun. He drew in a huge breath and ducked underwater. Feeling his way along, he grabbed a piece of her harness and bit down on it. The waterlogged material was tough and hard and tasted like a dirty car tire. His jaw ached and his gums bled, but he kept at it. Finally, when he reached the point where he was about to drown himself, he thrust his head above water and sucked in a huge lungful. Ignoring Amara's frightened cries, he plunged back under, returning to the same section of webbing to gauge his progress. The piece he found was the wrong one. It was smooth and unblemished. Horror filled his aching lungs as he felt along its length. Whatever military-based materials Von Freiling's manufacturers had chosen for their little attack craft, they'd spared no expense. He had the right piece. It was simply undamaged.

Jake surfaced once more and uttered an agonizing scream of denial. He seized the harness in his free hand and yanked uselessly against it, then lowered his lips to Amara's ear, his chin partially submerged, and began sobbing hysterically. "I . . . can't do it . . ." he moaned. "I can't . . . get you free. I'm so sorry . . . I *tried!*"

"It's okay," Amara comforted, her eyes welling with tears as she thrust her jaw out to breathe. She reached underwater for him, putting her arms around him as best she could. She stroked his shuddering back muscles, trying to comfort him. "I know you tried. Believe me. If you can't save me, no one can."

Jake lifted his chin up out of the water, rubbing his cheek softly against hers. Their eyes met, and through the veil of tears that shrouded his vision, he saw something that gave him pause.

"I love you, Jake," Amara confirmed. "I know it's c-crazy, and I picked a hell of a time to tell you, but I want you to know."

"Oh, Jesus, no . . ." Jake moaned, shaking his head in denial of what was to come. "I can't lose you. Please, not like this . . . I can't . . ."

"Shut up and kiss me, you big Mary," Amara insisted.

Shivering in waves, Jake cradled her face in his palms and pressed his lips lightly to hers. He felt a jolt of electricity run through him, traveling from the tips of his toes to the hair on his head. Her lips were warm and vibrant, not cold and . . .

There was a low rumble, and the min-sub began to wobble in the current. Amara touched Jake's cheek with pruned-up fingertips and looked him in the eye. She stroked his face gently. "You are *here* for me, Jake. You were *there* when it mattered and you tried your best. Do you understand?"

Jake stared at her, unable to reply.

She grabbed him by the chin and shook him gently. *"Do you understand?"*

Too drained to argue, Jake nodded and looked down.

Amara made a face and spat out a mouthful. "I know this is going to be hard, but I want you to go. Do you hear me?"

Jake's eyes became angry and he shook his head.

"I want you to go," she repeated. "It'll be easier if I know you've made it. Just pop the hatch and g-go."

"No. If I do your air bubble will vanish and you'll drown."

Amara twisted hard in her seat, pressing up with her toes to raise herself a tiny bit farther from the water that was slowly killing her. "I'm already drowning, Jake. It'll just b-be quicker."

Jake shook his head again.

"Okay, *fine*," she snarled. "Then take a deep breath and go through the portal. We're near the surface, and I've s-seen you swim. I know you can m-make it."

Jake glanced at the section of water leading to the submerged observation bubble. Another shiver ran through him and he leaned closer, kissing her tenderly. "I'm not g-going anywhere," he announced.

"What do you mean?"

"I'm staying with you," he said resignedly.

"What the f-fuck are you *talking* about? You'll die too, you b-big idiot!"

Jake smiled sadly. "I died three years ago, doc. I'm not going back without you. Sorry."

Amara flailed angrily against her bonds. "Why you stupid, p-p-pig-headed . . . what the hell's wrong with you? Do I have to kick your ass to save your life?"

Jake leaned over her, palming her chin and cheeks so their gazes locked. "I wish you could. And by the way, that just may be the nicest thing you've ever said to me."

Amara opened her mouth to scream at him but he kissed her again. He kept his lips pressed to hers, waiting until the angry quivering faded and he knew her ire was past. He pulled back a few inches and caressed her lips with a wet fingertip. "Oh, and for the record, I love you too."

She started sobbing. "This is crazy! How can you do this?"

"How can I do what? Die with the woman I love?" Jake shook his head ruefully. "How can I *not*?"

"But, Jake . . . I . . . please . . ."

"Shhh . . ." He cuddled up against her, hoisting her up and keeping his quavering body pressed against hers as best he could. "I'm staying to the end."

Jake held onto her as the moments ticked by, stroking her cheeks with his fingertips and whispering comforting things when her fear got the better of her. He kept a close watch on the rising water, dreading the moment when *Eurypterid II* filled completely, but also feeling surprisingly at ease.

A sudden vibration began to assail the dying mini-sub, causing it to wobble sickeningly back and forth. Amara gave a gurgling cry as the shifting water completely covered her face, causing Jake to use his hands to clear her mouth and nose as best he could. He took a series of deep inhalations, preparing to breathe air from his own lungs into hers. The sub continued to shift from side to side and a huge form took shape above them. Jake gave a start, his surprised inhalation pure dread. A powerful pressure wave was pushing them around.

Oh, Lord, please don't tell me that thing had a mate, after all!

A sudden clanging sound startled him. It was followed by an elongated grating noise, as if a giant cat was sharpening its claws along *Eurypterid II*'s flanks. Their position in the water shifted abruptly, and he was forced to grab onto Amara's chair as they began to be hauled inexplicably upward.

"Jake, what's happening?" Amara gasped. She shook her head to clear her ears, astonished that the water levels around her face and throat were plummeting, exposing first her shoulders, then chest and waist as they drained out the mini-sub's open nose in a powerful rush.

"I have no idea," he replied, holding on to her armrests.

There was a loud thump as their momentum abruptly ceased. Still trapped in her station, Amara was unaffected, but she made a desperate grab, latching onto Jake's soaked sleeve and holding on tight to keep him from falling. The water around them continued to drain away; it was already below waist height. The two exchanged nervous glances and gazed apprehensively around the cockpit. There was a painful scraping noise as their damaged prow dragged against something metallic, followed by another high-decibel clanging noise and the same scratching sound. A moment later, *Eurypterid II*'s nose was hoisted upward. The remaining water inside the submersible began to flow like quicksilver to the rear of the cockpit, collecting in a four-foot deep pool and leaving Jake and Amara exposed and shivering. They held on to each other, still unsure of what was happening.

"Jake, look!" Amara exclaimed. She pointed to the jagged opening that was their Lexan viewing portal. They had breached the surface and were being dragged relentlessly up along the steel hull of a much larger vessel. Jake heard muffled voices shouting in an unfamiliar language and braced his feet to compensate for *Eurypterid II*'s wild swaying. Soon, they were pointing up at a steep angle, their prow ten feet above the sea spray. Their noisy progress was accompanied by a low humming sound that intensified as they traveled further up. The other ship's gunwhales became visible at the very top of their missing portal, and then its sturdy railing. With a violent shudder, their progress slowed to a crawl, leaving their bow level with their rescuer's deck.

Jake spotted a group of seamen moving rapidly around. They were Japanese. An officer was barking orders to those nearest him. To his right and dead center stood a person of obvious import, most likely the vessel's captain and commander, based on his immaculate white jacket and the obvious deference he was shown by the other crewmen. Jake focused hard. Despite the contrasting glare and the dim lighting inside their mini-sub, he could see the man's face. He had silver hair and dark, fathomless eyes.

"Holy shit," Amara whispered from behind him. "I don't believe it!"

Jake followed her stunned gaze. Her eyes were locked onto those of the ship's commander. Another shudder passed through *Eurypterid II*'s sturdy hull as they came to a complete halt. Though pointing up at an odd angle, they were locked in place, tightly affixed to the other ship's hull. The vessel's commander gestured to a nearby sailor, who saluted and rotated a lever atop the section of railing directly adjacent to the mini-sub's bow. The railing swung in and back, opening like a six-foot wide gate. A pair of crewmen stepped boldly through, ducking their heads and holding onto jagged pieces of Lexan still edging the missing observation portal, as they made their way into the submersible's cockpit. They carried blankets and a large medical kit. The first one looked up, his eyes meeting Jake's. He had an apprehensive expression and bowed quickly, muttering something in broken English. The second focused his attention on Amara. When he realized she was stuck he reached into his pocket, producing a curved folding knife with serrated edges. Jake tensed and held up a hand. The man bowed and wordlessly handed the weapon to him. Even with the knife's razor-sharp edge it took the lawman nearly thirty seconds of frustrated sawing before he was through her restraining belts. When he finally finished, he closed the knife and handed it back, then leaned down to help Amara stand. Drained from her ordeal, she smiled weakly as she accepted his hand and tried to rise. With one hand clutching her aching head, she swayed like a sapling in high wind. To her credit, she managed to make it to her feet before she doubled over to vomit. His face wracked with concern, Jake took one of the blankets from the crewmen and draped it gently over her shoulders, stroking her back and whispering comforting words until she finished regurgitating seawater. When she recovered sufficiently, he wrapped one arm around her and helped her back to her feet.

"God, that was awful . . ." Amara blanched, hugging herself with the blanket while still shivering. She glanced at the two rescue personnel waiting awkwardly nearby. "Thanks, Jake. As much as I hate it, we've got to go thank the bastard responsible for saving us."

"The bastard?" Jake echoed. He cocked his head to one side, holding her hand and bracing his free palm on the cockpit's ceiling to steady their trip toward the bow. "I don't understand."

"You will in a minute," Amara announced. Her chin up and shoulders pulled back, she marched up to the opening in the railing and the stern-faced man waiting beyond it.

———

"Nicely done, commander," Haruto Nakamura said. He stood ramrod straight, one hand behind him, the other resting on the nearby railing. "Your man did an amazing job. I can see the incident with the whale shark was no fluke."

"Thank you, captain." Watch Commander Iso Hayama's nod of acknowledgment was more a bow. He swiveled his head to the two hoist crews. "Keep her tight, and lock those gears down, men!"

Haruto glanced at the two winches flanking their position. The hoist crews had their oversized hooks and cables locked onto Amara's mini-sub like grappling hooks. With their combined pulling power, the opposing winches had hauled *Eurypterid II* completely out of the water, dragging it up the *Oshima's* thick steel flanks and pinning it tightly against her hull. Without hitting the releases, the fancy submersible wasn't going anywhere.

Haruto nodded his approval and braced himself for what was to come. He watched his emergency personnel make their way out of the mini-sub's ruptured bow. Its two passengers trailed the *Oshima's* crewmen as they made their way toward their captain. As expected, Amara was in the lead. She was accompanied by the man he'd seen on that online news video. He was bedraggled and limping badly, but there was no mistaking him. Judging from their body language and the big American's obvious attentiveness toward Amara, the two seemed much closer now.

Haruto frowned and stepped forward to meet them. "Amara, it is good to see you again." He bowed formally, then straightened and extended his hand. "I am sorry we were unable to aid you in your battle, but I am relieved we arrived in time to render assistance."

"Thank you," she replied, her internal conflict brewing in plain sight. "You saved both of our lives." She hesitated, but bowed in turn.

"It was an honor," Haruto said with an appraising look. His niece's blouse was stained with blood, and one of her eyes was bruised and swollen. He turned to the equally bloody man standing by her side, sizing up the tall lawman.

"Please forgive me," Amara cut in hastily. She put an arm around her companion's waist and drew him closer. "Uncle Haruto, this is Jake Braddock, former U.S. national fencing champion, and the sheriff of Paradise Cove. Jake, this is my uncle Haruto Nakamura, commander of the shark-finning ship *Oshima.*"

"It is an honor, Sheriff Braddock," Haruto said. He took Jake's hand and shook it firmly. Despite being wounded and near exhaustion, the young man had a penetrating stare and a formidable grip. Haruto liked him immediately.

"The honor is mine," Jake replied. "Thank you for what you did."

Haruto noticed Iso draw near, then turned back to his guests. "Please excuse me for a moment."

Accompanied by the watch commander, Haruto moved out of earshot. He accepted Iso's binoculars and scanned the approaching ships with the electronic range finders. "Are they the same two we've been tracking?"

"Yes, captain," Iso said, nodding. "They kept their distance until we crossed the line, then came at us full-bore. They're running silent."

Haruto zoomed in on the two vessels and stifled a curse. They were U.S. Coast Guard cutters, the newest of the Island Class, the

Rampart and the *Freedom*. The sleek warships were approaching at high speed, converging simultaneously on the *Oshima* from northwest and southeast. He did a quick calculation, scanning his memory banks. Island Class Cutters were small and fast: 110 feet long, crew of 16, maximum speed of 29.5 knots. They were also heavily armed. With the weight of a full belly and Amara's mini-sub to boot, there was no way the *Oshima* could top their speed. The Japanese ship was trapped between the Coast Guard and the coastline.

Haruto shook his head. He had nowhere to go. He couldn't dodge them and he couldn't outrun them.

Iso touched his earpiece. "Captain, we're being hailed." He hesitated, his youthful face paling. "It's the U.S. Coast Guard, sir. They're demanding we hold position and prepare to be boarded."

Haruto's jaw clenched so tightly his teeth ached. His head started thumping and he combed his fingers through his hair. He had gambled and lost. The risk was clear the moment he'd made his decision to intervene. "Very well, commander. Please be so kind as to inform the crew."

"But sir, shouldn't we try to make a run for it?"

Haruto shook his head and spat over the side in an uncharacteristically coarse gesture. "No commander."

"But cap–"

"I said no!"

Leaving Iso to ramble into his radio, Haruto returned to Amara and Jake. An alarm soon rang out, and panicking crewmen began running around, many abandoning their stations. The two cutters drew closer. They were moving in from both port and starboard, sandwiching their target, their heavy 25 mm machine guns trained on the *Oshima*'s bridge. They were obviously expecting Haruto to make a break for it.

He grabbed Iso, catching him by the shoulder as he hurried past, and whispered into his ear. The man looked shocked, but bowed and took off running.

"Please accept my apologies," Haruto said to Jake and Amara. "I wish we had more time," he indicated the two ships less than five hundred yards away. "Unfortunately, we do not."

Amara scrutinized the approaching warships. Her lower lip disappeared and her eyebrows scrunched tightly down. "Although I'm relieved to see that you and your crew will no longer be able to strip-mine the oceans of life, I am sorry you will suffer for aiding me."

"I am not," Haruto said. He sighed heavily and straightened up. "Truth be told, I am not without regret. But I would do it again if I had to."

Amara's eyes narrowed contemplatively. "Tell me something. Did you come because of what you did to Robert? Did you think this would make things right between us?"

Haruto noticed Jake politely averting his gaze and focused on his niece. "We never spoke of your fiancé," he admitted. "Then again, in many years we haven't spoken at all. I wish we had."

Haruto folded his arms across his chest and studied the waves. He watched as the *Freedom* executed a tight turn, preparing to pull directly alongside the *Oshima*. He sighed.

"It is not my place to assign blame. But I will not let you leave believing anything other than the truth."

"No riddles, uncle."

"As you wish." His expression turned stony and he held Amara's gaze. "It was Karl Von Freiling who seized control of the *Nagata*'s wheel that day," he said. "He surprised me. I tried to stop him, but failed."

"What?"

Haruto nodded. "Yes. Your husband made the *Nagata*'s bow spin out of control and caused the crash that took all those lives."

Amara's lips drew back over her teeth. "Do you actually expect me to believe that?"

"I have no control over what you choose to believe. I simply wish for you to know the truth."

"Prove it."

Haruto pursed his lips. "I have no recording of the incident, none except the one in my mind. I will replay it for you if you so desire."

"Go on. I'm all ears."

His expression turned contemplative. "After Von Freiling grabbed the captain's wheel and caused the crash, it took seven of us to restrain him. He injured two of my crew during the struggle; at one point he seized me by the throat and hurled me across the bridge, bellowing something about how I had 'dared to interfere in his plans,' and that I was about to discover the 'penalty for doing so.'"

Jake shook his head ruefully. "Hate to say it, doc, but . . . that sounds kind of familiar."

Amara's eyes were unable to focus and her breathing became uneven. "Why didn't you tell me? Why didn't–"

"I tried to warn you, once word came to me of your pending nuptials," he said. "Did you not get my letter?"

Amara's mind raced as she tried to recall a letter. She stiffened suddenly. "I . . . burned it."

Haruto glanced up as Iso came running, carrying a long, cloth-wrapped bundle. "I wasn't trying to clear myself of any wrongdoing. I simply desired to warn you about the person you'd involved yourself with. I am sorry I didn't try again. I felt you wanted me out of your life."

Amara shook her head. "I don't blame you."

"I was in command of the *Nagata*. Ultimately, anything that went on that day was my fault. I hope one day you will forgive me."

Amara hesitated. Then, to his astonishment, she walked over and wrapped her arms around him. She hugged him delicately, conscious of the uniform that served as a barrier between them. She waited until he hugged her back, then pulled slowly back beside Jake.

Haruto reached for the bundle Iso carried and weighed it in his hands. His words were interrupted by a blaring megaphone.

"This is the U.S.C.G. Freedom. You are in violation of U.S. territorial waters. Heave to and prepare to be boarded!"

Haruto shrugged. "We are out of time. Amara, I would like you to have this." He offered the bundle to her, watching attentively as his niece opened one end and gasped in astonishment. "I present to you the ancestral katana and wakisahsi of the Nakamura clan, worn by our ancestors on the field of battle for nearly one thousand years. They have taken many lives." He relished the astonished look on her face. "I do not want them to fall into strange hands, and I know you will appreciate them."

"I . . . don't know what to say," Amara stammered. She held the swords at arm's length as if she was grasping a dead snake.

"You do not have to say anything."

Amara's eyes wandered to Jake, taking in the hypnotic expression he wore as he studied the ancient blades, then shifted back to her uncle. "Listen, I'm not into weapons."

"What?" Haruto nearly choked. "You can't be serious. They've been passed down from generation to generation for centuries!"

"I'm sorry," Amara said. She shook her head vehemently. "I just don't want them."

"But, if you don't take them, they will end up lost or in some military footlocker somewhere!"

Jake chimed in. "I could take them off your hands," he offered. "At least temporarily . . ."

Haruto shook his head. "Absolutely not. The only way I would hand over the family's battle swords to an outsider is if they married into our family."

"That's no problem." Jake looked up, grinning from ear to ear as he reached for Amara's hand. "For *those*, I'll marry her in a heartbeat!"

"Oh, *will* you now?" Amara replied. She pulled her hand away, folding her arms irritably across her chest.

Jake's face drooped and his cheeks reddened. "Oh, c'mon, I was just kidding, doc. I mean–"

"Put a lid on it, mister."

Haruto's expression turned contemplative as he studied Jake.

The discomfited lawman gave a hesitant smile. "Okay . . . how about if I just hold onto them until you can take them back? Unless, of course, Amara and I marry, in which case I get to keep them?"

"Humph. Very well . . . in that case, I accept."

Jake's eyes lit up and he rocked back on his heels. "Are you serious?"

Haruto groaned. "Yes."

Jake smiled. "Excellent." He added, "And know that I will treat them with the utmost respect and regard for your family."

Haruto took the swords from Amara and formally handed them to Jake. "See that you do."

Amara glanced at Jake, catching him shamelessly admiring the newfound additions to his collection. "Thank you, uncle," she said. "From *both* of us."

Haruto's next words were overpowered by the roar of the *Freedom*'s straining diesels and the clanging of its metal boarding ramps as they slammed onto the railings of his ship. A group of men came storming aboard, pistols drawn and shouting angrily.

The seizure of the *Oshima* had begun.

To Jake, the score of armed Guardsmen storming the *Oshima*'s decks were reminiscent of a horde of African driver ants. Within minutes of boarding the high-tech fishing vessel, her crew was lined up and kneeling against her gunnels, fingers interlaced behind their heads.

As he and Amara watched from the shelter of a secluded doorway, Jake noticed that the shark hunters of the *Oshima* appeared completely unruffled by the ordeal; they faced their pending arrest and incarceration with stoic calmness.

Keeping Amara behind him, Jake stepped out of the darkened doorway and reached out to a young seaman jogging by. "Hey, kid, who's in charge here?"

"Right now, I am," a gravelly voice rang out. "Who the hell are you?"

Jake turned to see a senior officer stomping toward him. He was flanked by two ensigns under the age of twenty. He was big, raw-boned, and covered with freckles, his blue eyes bright and brimming with animosity.

The officer pointed a thick finger at Jake's badge. "I'll ask again. Who *are* you and what are you doing here?"

"Take it easy," Jake began, ignoring the obvious hostility. He took a step forward, extending his hand. "I'm–"

"Hey, you guys missed a crewmember!" the officer barked as he spotted Amara. Ignoring Jake, the Coastie's hand moved to the holster flap of his .40 caliber Sig Sauer. His expression turned nasty. "Line her up with the rest."

One of the ensigns reached for his sidearm and started forward. He froze as Jake placed himself in front of Amara. "Touch her, and I'll shove that pistol up your ass," he warned.

"What the fuck do you think you're doing?" the officer snapped.

Jake tensed, shifting his weight to his good leg and cursing under his breath. He realized the situation was about to get very complicated.

"She's with me, and she's not a member of this vessel's crew," he said. "Her name is–"

"Dr. Amara Takagi," someone finished for him. "Sheriff Braddock, it's a relief and a pleasure to see you again."

Jake turned toward the speaker. "Captain Dobbs," he acknowledged. He grinned, extending a hand as the *Freedom*'s captain drew near. "Your timing is impeccable, as always."

"Indeed. Well, we do try," Dobbs chuckled. The weathered-faced captain turned to his subordinates. "At ease, men. Lieutenant O'Malley, these are the people we were hoping we'd find. Sheriff Braddock is a long-time acquaintance, and the law and order back in Paradise Cove." He drew close to Amara, his expression apprehensive as he spotted her bruised face. He shook her hand gently. "And Dr. Takagi is a respected American scientist, and the commander of the research vessel *Harbinger*. She's been doing cetacean studies in this area for years."

Dobbs turned to O'Malley. "Take your men and find me this ship's commanding officer. He's my height, with silver hair – very distinguished looking."

"Aye, sir."

"Jesus, Braddock, you guys look like hell," Dobbs muttered. He leaned closer, peering over his glasses and inspecting Jake's ill-bandaged wounds. "You're definitely gonna need some stitches on those gashes. Holy crap . . . are those knife wounds?"

"Stitches sound a little strange right about now," Jake replied, dismissing the mental image of the dead merc. He put a protective arm around Amara. "Can your guys check out her eye first?"

"Jake, I'm fine," Amara muttered. "All I need is some ice and a few aspirin."

Dobbs cleared his throat. "I'll get my medical officer on it right away."

"Thanks," Jake said. "I appreciate it."

"No problem. Oh, by the way, Braddock, do you think you can you do me a favor?"

"Sure, if I can."

"Can you put a call in to your prepubescent deputy, please?"

"My deputy?"

"Yeah." Dobbs grinned and shook his head. "The kid's gone all mother hen on us. He's been calling my superiors every fifteen minutes – from his *hospital bed*, mind you – trying to make sure you guys are okay, and demanding that we check up on you. He's a real pain in the ass!"

Jake snickered as he exchanged amused glances with Amara. "Sure, I'll, uh, see what I can do."

"Thanks." Dobbs glanced toward the *Oshima*'s bridge, watching as O'Malley and his men hit the landing and stormed inside, weapons drawn. "So, which one of you dumped those old whaler beacons?"

"That was the doc's idea," Jake said.

"Stroke of genius," Dobbs chortled. "Ordinarily, we might have missed them. But, since we were scanning nonstop for the creature, we happened to spot your signal buoys and decided to investigate. We didn't even know what the damned things were, until we fished them out of the water a few miles from here."

"Is that how you found the *Oshima*?" Amara asked.

Dobbs shook his head. His eyes swiveled back to the *Freedom,* and the crew manning her heavy machine gun. He tensed. "No . . . hold on one second." He reached for his hand radio. "Starkey, this is Dobbs. Tell the men on Ethel to stay alert. That damned thing may still be in the area. I don't want to miss an opportunity if it surfaces nearby."

"Roger, captain."

Dobbs turned back to Jake and Amara. "Sorry, guys. With your beastie still on the loose, Dr. Takagi, we've been going at it non-stop for the last few days. I guess my guys are getting tired."

"It's not on the loose anymore," Amara stated.

"What do you mean?"

"It's dead," Jake announced. He cricked his neck to one side. "We killed it a little over an hour ago."

Dobbs' jaw dropped. "Are you serious?"

"Actually, the doc killed it," Jake said, grinning proudly. He put his arm around Amara's shoulders and gave her a gentle squeeze.

"Oh, stop. You helped plenty, silly," Amara said, flushing at the praise. "And don't think I'm paying that fine by myself!"

"That's amazing," Dobbs said.

Amara shook her head. "Amazing wouldn't begin to cover it, but at least it's over. By the way, you didn't answer my question, captain."

Dobbs folded his arms across his chest. He glanced up and spotted O'Malley and his men marching a disheveled Haruto Nakamura out of the ship's bridge. "Actually, we've been after that bastard for years, but he's so slippery he's always managed to evade us."

"How so?" Jake asked. He shifted the weight of the cloth-wrapped swords and watched as the *Oshima*'s captain was led down the bridge's steps, heading in their direction.

"He's a tactical genius," Dobbs admitted. "He knows the sea lanes and currents better than anyone, where to hide, and how to use other ships to cover his trail." He indicated the vessel they stood upon. "And whatever ship he commands is the best the Japanese have: stealthy and incredibly fast. He also tends to stay well outside the twelve mile limit, loitering just inside our Economic Exclusive Zone, so he's got plenty of room to maneuver if he has to make a break for it."

"Sounds like a worthy adversary," Jake commented.

Dobbs snorted. "A pirate nonetheless." He pointed past them to a series of turret-like stations. "You see those big winches? He designed them. He's able to ditch his lines, so we've never been able to catch him in the act until now, thanks to you."

Amara cocked a brow. "To us?"

"Yes. Once our LRIT satellites started zooming in on your buoys, we focused them on this entire area. With no boating traffic to conceal them, once she crossed into U.S. territorial waters, the *Oshima* stood out like a sore thumb." Dobbs smirked as Haruto came within earshot. "I choked on my coffee when we confirmed it was her. Even though we missed nailing the monster, we ended up with one helluva consolation prize."

Jake watched as Amara's uncle was brought before them. His hands were bound behind him, his eyes focused straight ahead. The lawman recalled all the dirtbag criminals he'd seen on the news: murderers and rapists, covering their heads in shame with their t-shirts to hide their faces from the public. Though his hair was mussed and his jacket torn, Haruto walked with perfect posture and his head held high.

Dobbs regarded his prisoner with cool deliberation, obviously expecting a reaction. When he got none, he glanced at O'Malley. The freckled Coastguardsman was carrying a large clipboard, jam-packed with papers. "Alright, what've we got, lieutenant?"

O'Malley gave his superior a crocodile smile, before handing over his evidence. "We arrived just as he was preparing to delete all the files from the ship's mainframe, sir. I grabbed all their logs. I even managed to print up their coded catch list."

Dobbs removed his glasses, squinting as he flipped through the first few pages. His eyes widened. "Captain Nakamura, you and your entire crew are under arrest for violation of the Economic Exclusion Zone of the United States of America, as well as international bans on harvesting shark fins." He held the heavy clipboard up for emphasis. "Both your ship and its cargo are seized as evidence. And I hope they put you away for a long time. You're a bigger threat to our oceans than a hundred pliosaurs."

Dobbs waited for a rebuttal. When none was forthcoming, he waved Haruto off with a dismissive hand. "Confine him to his quarters, men. And post a guard inside."

Jake studied Amara's expression as her uncle was led wordlessly away. She caught him staring.

"What?" she asked. "Don't look at me like that. Dobbs is right. It is what it is."

Jake pursed his lips. Yeah . . . I know." He turned to the captain. "So, what happens now?"

Dobbs handed the clipboard to a nearby warrant officer. "I'm taking command of the *Oshima*. We'll sail her back to base, where she'll be impounded as evidence. This situation is a political mess. A lot of people are going to have egg on their faces."

"You mean shark fin soup . . ." Jake corrected, causing Amara to roll her eyes.

Dobbs straightened up, uttering a groan as he stretched his lean arms high overhead. "I'm going to take a quick tour of the ship. In the meantime, I'll have my medical officer sent over to check you two out. I'm sure they have a better sick bay here than on my cutter. Afterwards, if you'd like, I'll be happy to offer you two the hospitality of my quarters onboard the *Freedom* until we make port. It's the least I can do."

Jake exchanged tactful glances with Amara, then struggled to clear his surprisingly dry throat. "Sure, that would be great. Thanks."

"Excellent. It'll just be a few minutes."

"We'll be here," Jake said after him.

Amara waited until Dobbs disappeared. "*That would be great,* eh?"

"What? No, I mean, I figured we could use a few minutes to relax after our ordeal."

"Oh, really?" She studied him long and hard through her lashes. "You sure this has nothing to do with your 'it's been three years' routine? I mean, that's a *long* time . . ."

Despite his best efforts, Jake found himself grinning. Unable to hold her gaze, he looked sheepishly away, his downcast eyes trying to drill a hole through the ship's painted decks. He shook his head vigorously. "Positive, doc."

"Okay, then." Amara smirked and poked him in the chest with her index finger. "And let's get something straight, mister. Just because you were willing to die with me doesn't mean you'll have it easy, understand?" Ignoring Jake's stunned protestations, she turned and began working her way along the ship's railing, past the guards and kneeling prisoners, until she reached the opening leading to *Eurypterid II*. The mini-sub was still bound securely in place, and gave no signs of budging as the *Oshima* wallowed with the afternoon tide.

Jake excused himself as he limped past a nearby sentry. He drew close and stared over Amara's shoulder. "So what will you do now, doc? I mean, you lost everything when the *Harbinger* sank, didn't you?"

"No way." Amara grinned. "That ship was fully insured. Don't worry; I'll get my thirty percent back, and then some. Besides, I'm staring at a veritable goldmine right now!"

"You mean the *Eurypterid*?"

She laughed. "Yes, my dear swordsman. Remember, Karl and I were still married. What's mine was his, as he so happily boasted. And vice versa."

"I see." Jake smirked approvingly. "So, what are you going to do with it?"

"Who knows?" Amara pondered. "It would certainly make a great prototype to develop a new line of undersea exploration vehicles. Or, maybe I'll consider acquiring some military contracts . . ."

"Good for you." Jake smiled and rested his forearms on the ship's railing. For the first time since the creature appeared, he was able to close his eyes and relax. He listened to the sounds of whitecaps slapping willy-nilly against the *Oshima*'s hull, and reveled in the refreshing feel of sea spray racing down his face and forearms. He opened his eyes and ended up locking gazes with the setting sun, its glowing ruby orb glaring down at him.

Jake held the sun's stare for a moment, then ran his tongue contemplatively over his teeth. "Say, doc. You don't think there are any more pliosaurs running around out there, do you?"

"Maybe." Amara nodded. "Although, I certainly hope not."

"Well, if there are more, I'll tell you now." Jake shook his head emphatically. "They better find someone *else* to go after them, because my days of hunting sea monsters are officially over!"

"Mine too. Oh, and one other thing, mister," Amara said, smiling.

"Yes, doc?"

"I'm sick and tired of all this 'doc' shit. I told you the day we met, my name is *Amara*. It's not 'doc', or even *doctor*, for that matter."

"I know, doc, I *know* . . ." Jake winked at her. *"You're not into titles."*

"Exactly." Amara laughed aloud and grabbed onto the railing with her hands. Leaning back, she rested her upper back against his chest.

A gust of wind blew her long hair into Jake's face like a silk cloak. He sucked in an involuntary breath and angled his head, rubbing the edge of his jaw softly against the crown of her head, inhaling deeply. He sighed contentedly. Even after everything they'd been through, she still smelled fantastic. He wrapped his arms around her, feeling her cheeks contract against his forearm as she smiled. A moment later, she whirled unexpectedly around and threw her arms around his neck. As their lips became one, Jake felt the nagging pain of his collective injuries vanish. Even the nightmare he'd just lived through was momentarily forgotten. He hugged Amara tightly, feeling her warmth pressed against him. His senses soared, and he rested his cheek against that of the woman he loved. He smiled. For the first time in three very long years, all was right in his world.

High above, the evening sun continued to shine down on the *Oshima* and those populating its decks, its unfettered brilliance creating a shimmering sea of scarlet as far as the human eye could see.

EPILOGUE

It was late summer on the tiny island, and the midday sun's rays warmed the seagull's body as it soared high above a virgin stretch of sand. The bird cried out as it flew, flapping its brown-tipped wings against the stiff breeze, circling in its endless quest for food.

Hovering a hundred feet above a lone palm frond, the seagull scanned the low-lying dunes below it, its eyes alert for signs of movement or danger. The gull was waiting for something – something its engrained memories and collective experiences assured it would soon take place.

It was waiting for the baby sea turtles, nestled within their buried nests, to claw their way through their flexible eggshells to the surface as they always did this time of year. At any moment, the surfaces of the sand dunes would erupt, releasing thousands of defenseless hatchlings from the seclusion of their pitch-black nurseries into the searing daylight. Freed from the confines of their sandy wombs, the tiny newborns would begin their arduous struggle toward the beckoning surf.

The seagull's jagged beak whipped to one side. It spotted a hint of movement on the sand far below. Circling around for a second look, it strained its bright yellow eyes to make sure. The brownie was old and wanted to be the first to line up at the feeding trough, giving itself the chance to stuff itself without the risk of injury from competing with younger birds.

Adjusting its wings once more, the seabird focused hard on the shifting sand.

The mass exodus of the turtle hatchlings had begun.

With its beady eyes transfixed on the first glistening form bursting through to the surface, the gull spread its beak wide and uttered its shrill predatory cry. Tucking its slender wings against its body, the grizzled bird plunged directly toward its victim.

Far below, the oblivious turtle struggled to make its way toward the water, using its four, paddle-shaped flippers to move it forward.

The ravenous bird straightened the vertebrae of its neck like a tiny battering ram. Accelerating, it pointed its bony beak directly at its target. As it careened toward the immobile turtle, the old bird's instincts whispered that something wasn't right. Its target was much closer than it appeared . . .

. . . or much larger.

Its eyes widening in alarm, the gull flared its wings out on both sides, spreading its maneuvering feathers wide in a desperate attempt to break its downward momentum.

Lunging upward, the newborn *Kronosaurus imperator* snatched its astonished victim out of the air. Its jaws closed hard, sinking inch-long teeth deep into the screeching bird's body, ending its hysterical flapping in a single bite.

The five-foot marine reptile held the dead gull high in the air, shifting it until it could be swallowed headfirst. It tossed its head back to ingest its prey, but was frustrated by the sheer size of the meal.

Aggravated, the hatchling shook its head from side to side. Opening and closing its jaws repeatedly, it used its interlocking teeth like a pair of scissors. With sharp snaps, it sheared off the obstructive wings of its victim. They fluttered down like palm fronds, spiraling onto the blood-spattered sands below. Raising its head once more, it swallowed the seagull in a few quick gulps.

Now satiated, the carnivore licked its scaly snout with its thick tongue. It lowered its head onto a nearby dune, rubbing the edges of its mouth on the dry sand in an effort to remove the feathers that clung to its bloody lips. Its repast complete, the miniature monster sat boldly upright, its body elevated off the sand by its sturdy flippers.

The male pliosaur remained still, his ruby eyes blinking repeatedly. Gender notwithstanding, he was a miniature duplicate of his gigantic mother, the lone female that crawled ashore several months prior, to lay her eggs beneath the sand as her ancestors had for millions of years.

Looking warily around, the ocean's future king watched as dozens of his brethren emerged from the nest. Their scaly little muzzles straining, they pushed their way past the clinging white sand, greedily sucking in their first lungfuls of fresh air. They were all similar in size to the young male, their inherent sexual dimorphism not evident as yet.

Uncomfortable sitting in the open with the oppressive heat radiating off the white sand below, the baby *Kronosaurus* made his way down toward the pounding surf. Waddling along with his body low to the ground and his wedge-shaped head held high, the fledgling superpredator plunged into an oncoming wave, disappearing from view.

Behind him came his brothers and sisters – nearly eighty in all. Circling high above, a handful of gulls remained wisely out of reach. Oblivious to the frightened birds, the pliosaur hatchlings continued their mass migration. Already formidable predators, with no natural enemies once they reached adulthood, they spread out into the surrounding sea, reveling in the water that encompassed them.

A single hatchling remained at the water's edge. She was similar in build to the others, but darker in hue and noticeably larger. Peering enigmatically about the beach, she studied the tiny island and the nondescript patch of sand she came from before turning toward the welcoming swells. Her instincts were derived from her ancestor's eons-long confinement within the caldera, and would serve her and the other newborns well. Inherently fearful of the cannibalistic adults of their kind, she and her brood-mates would remain within the sheltering shallows that surrounded the island, concealing themselves within submerged coral reefs and kelp beds until they were large enough to fend for themselves.

When that time came, they would multiply and spread to all the oceans of the world. Without equal, their power and ferocity would make them the greatest predators the planet had ever seen, and all the creatures of the sea would be their prey. Eventually, they would reclaim that which their forebears relinquished sixty five million years ago: undisputed dominance of three-quarters of the planet.

Gazing one last time at the remote shore that was her birthplace, the last of the pliosaur hatchlings shook her head and snorted before turning toward the beckoning surf. Filling her lungs with air, she plunged headfirst through the trough of a cresting wave. Propelled forward by powerful thrusts, she cruised past the pounding breakers, out toward the deeper waters of a nearby reef.

Spread out below her like some vast azure carpet, the unsuspecting sea waited.

THE END

GLOSSARY OF NAUTICAL/ MARINE TERMS

Abyssal Plains: vast underwater plains at the bottom of the ocean, with water depths typically ranging from 3,000-6,000 meters. Largely unexplored, they represent more than 50% of the Earth's surface.

Acoustics: the science and study of mechanical *waves* in liquids, solids, and gases. This includes vibrations, as well as sound, ultrasound, and infrasound waves.

Aft: Naval terminology, used to indicate the stern or rear of a ship. "Aft *section*" indicates the rear portion of a ship.

Beam: A ship's width at its widest point.

Berth: A designated location where a boat or ship is *moored* (attached), usually for purposes of loading and unloading passengers or cargo.

Bow: The foremost point of the hull of a boat or ship.

Bridge: The room or point on a boat or ship from which it is commanded.

Bulkhead: A wall within the hull of a boat or ship.

Cachalot: Archaic term for the Sperm whale, from the French word *cachalot*, meaning "tooth."

Caldera: A bowl-like geological formation, usually formed by the partial collapse of a volcano, following an eruption.

Center Console: A single-decked, open hull boat with all the controls (console) located in the center of the vessel.

Cephalopod: Marine animals such as the octopus, squid, and cuttlefish, wherein limbs or tentacles extend from a prominent head. Cephalopods are also *mollusks*.

Cetacean: Marine mammals, including whales, dolphins and porpoises.

Chelonian: Turtles and tortoises.

Circle Hook: A fishing hook with a point that curves sharply inward. Circle hooks are designed to catch a fish in the corner of the jaw and are rarely swallowed.

Claxon: A low-frequency horn used by ships to signal one another.

Cleat: A nautical term for a narrow, anvil-shaped device used to secure a rope or line. Cleats are often used to tie boats to docks.

Conning Tower: An elevated platform on a ship or submarine, from which an officer can command ("*con*") the vessel.

Continental Shelf: The extended (and submerged border) of any given continent and its associated *coastal plain*.

Crustacean: Crustaceans are members of a large group of *arthropods* and include such creatures as lobsters, crabs, and shrimp.

Detritus: Referred to as *marine snow*, detritus is non-living particles of organic material suspended in water.

Dinghy: A small boat, often towed behind a larger vessel for use as a ship-to-ship or ship-to-shore boat.

Dorsal: The upper side of an animal that swims in a horizontal position. The dorsal *region* refers to that general area on the animal. Dorsal *fin* refers to one or more fins that protrude from that region, i.e. a shark's distinctive, curved fin.

Draft (or Draught): The measurement from a vessel's waterline to the bottom of its hull. Draft determines the minimum water depth a ship or boat requires in order to navigate safely.

Economic Exclusive Zone: An *EEZ* is a sea zone over which a country has specific rights relating to the exploration and exploitation of its natural resources. It stretches from the end of said country's territorial waters (the *12 mile limit*) an additional 200 nautical miles.

Ensign: Naval rank, equivalent to a second lieutenant in the U.S. Army.

Flats Boat: A small draft boat designed to safely run and operate in extremely shallow bodies of water, such as the Florida Keys.

Flying Gaff: A specialized gaff designed to land very large fish. The hook portion of the gaff detaches when embedded in a fish and remains secured to the boat by a strong cable or rope.

Fore: The front or *bow* of a ship or boat.

Foredeck: The bow portion of a ship's deck.

Forecastle: The foremost portion of a ship's upper deck. In medieval ships it served as a defensive stronghold where archers could rain fire down upon opposing vessels.

Galley: The kitchen or a ship or boat.

Gangplank: A moveable construct, often formed of strong planks, which bridges the distance between a ship and its mooring station. It enables the loading and offloading of goods and personnel.

Gimbal: The receiving point (socket) of a big-game fishing fighting belt or chair. The butt of the fishing rod inserts into this point and can swivel up and down to exert pressure on fish.

Gin Pole: A strong, vertical pole or tower, equipped with an extending arm and pulley system. Gin poles are used on fishing vessels to hoist very large fish onboard.

Gunnels/Gunwhales: The uppermost/top edges of a ship or boat's hull.

Harbormaster: The official that enforces the regulations of a particular port or harbor.

Helm: A ship's wheel or other steering mechanism (tiller, steering wheel, etc.).

Helmsman: The individual that steers a ship or boat.

Hydrophone: An underwater microphone.

Hydrostatic Pressure: The pressure exerted by water due to the effects of gravity.

Idling: When a boat sits *idle* with its engine running (in neutral). Idle boats tend to drift as a result of wind and tide.

Knot: A nautical unit of speed equivalent to one *nautical* mile per hour, or about 1.151 mph.

Kraken: A mythological marine monster said to feed on whales and drag ships to their destruction. The Kraken is believed to be based on early sailors' encounters with the *giant squid*.

Landing: A designated docking location for vessels at a marina.

Lanyard: A length or cord used to carry something and worn around the neck or wrist. Safety lanyards on boats and Jet Skis function as kill switches and shut down the vessel's engine in the event the pilot falls overboard.

LRIT: Long Range Intelligence and Tracking. An international system of tracking ships using shipborne satellite communication equipment.

Manifest: A document listing the passengers, crew, and cargo of a vessel for official purposes.

Marguerite Formation: A defensive formation utilized by sperm whales and other cetaceans to defend their young. The adults encircle the vulnerable calves, typically with either their flukes or jaws pointed outward, in an attempt to ward off attackers.

Mollusk: A large phylum of invertebrate animals, including gastropods (snails and slugs) and cephalopods (octopus and squid).

Mooring: A permanent structure where a boat or ship may be *moored* (attached) such as a dock or jetty.

Mooring Line: Line of rope used to tie off or affix a boat or ship.

Mooring Station: An assigned location for a boat or ship to be attached or tied off.

Outboard: A non-integral and removable propulsion system for boats. Outboard motors attach directly to the transom. Multiple motors can be used for larger boats, with horsepower typically ranging from single digits all the way to three hundred or more.

Pectoral Fin(s): Paired fins in fish that provide dynamic lifting force, enabling some fish to maintain depth.

Phototropic Zone: The upper portion of a body of water where sunlight is the primary stimulus for growth and nourishment.

Plankton: Tiny organisms that live in the water column. Plankton are incapable of swimming against either tide or current. They are an important food source for many marine organisms.

Pod: A group of whales. Unlike a school of fish, pod members are often related individuals.

Port: Direction-wise, turning a boat or ship to the left. *Portside* = the left side of a boat or ship.

Porthole: A round window on a boat or ship.

Prop: A boat or ship's propeller.

Prow: The foremost portion of a ship's bow. The prow cuts through the water and is the portion of the bow above the waterline.

Runabout: A small boat, often used in the service of a larger vessel.

Schooner: A sailing vessel characterized by fore and aft sails on two or more masts.

Shoal: A group of fish that stay together for social reasons.

Slip: A reserved docking space for a boat, similar to a rented parking spot.

Sloop: A sailboat with a fore and aft rig and a single mast.

Sound: Also known as a seaway, a sound is a large inlet between two bodies of land.

Starboard: Direction-wise, turning a boar or ship to the right. Also, a term for the right side of a boat or ship.

Stern: The rear portion of a boat or ship.

Sub-Aqueous: Beneath the surface of the water.

Swells: Ocean surface waves moving in long-wave formation.

Thermocline: A distinctive layer in a body of water where temperature changes more rapidly than in the layers above and below it. Thermoclines can be either permanent or transitory, depending on prevailing climate conditions. They separate surface water from the calmer, often colder, deep water below.

Transom: The flat, back panel that comprised the stern of a boat or ship. Outboard motors are affixed directly to the transom.

Watch Commander: Nautical term for a shift supervisor on a marine vessel.

Water Column: A theoretical column of water, ranging from the ocean's surface, all the way to the seafloor. The water column consists of thermal or chemically stratified layers, the mixing of which is brought on by wind and current.

Waterfront: A group of manmade structures designed to handle boats and ships.

Whale Killer: Also known as a *Whale Catcher*, a high-speed surface ship designed to hunt and kill whales, then hand the carcasses over to a larger *Factory Ship* for processing. Whale killers typically use grenade-tipped harpoon cannons to disable and kill their prey.

Wharf: A structure built along the shore of a harbor where boats and ships may dock while loading or unloading passengers or cargo.

Zodiac: A rubber inflatable boat, equipped with an outboard motor. Used as a dinghy or runabout.

ABOUT THE AUTHOR

Max Hawthorne grew up in Philadelphia, graduating with a BA from Central High School and a BFA from the University of the Arts. He is a world record-holding angler whose writing has appeared in a multitude of outdoor magazines and periodicals. He is an avid sportsman and conservationist. His hobbies include hunting, fishing and the collection of fossils and antiquities. He lives with his family in the Greater Northeast.

Made in the USA
San Bernardino, CA
07 June 2014